"Fast-paced, remarkable adventure with a significant depth of layers in By Arrow, Blade, and Claw.

"In By Arrow, Blade, and Claw: Book One, Jeff J. Jarvis takes creativity with Werewolf lore; adds a command of language for descriptions that project the reader into the book; mixes in characters who are rich in the most admirable of values; sprinkles in love, family, and respect; stirs in military strategy and covert operations; folds in treasured traditions passed through generations; and animates the story with characters from more diverse backgrounds who add their own twists as they all become a tightly formed unit dedicated to saving lives and eliminating threats.

"Main character Cody Dugway was involved in an accident at a young age that left him with a health challenge but also gave him a most special gift, one that proves to be of matchless value in the efforts to stop the planned raids of the coordinated Werewolf groups. He grows from a high school student to a young man in college and also in service to his country to eradicate these attacks using his unique talents. His life is filled with many questions as he ponders relationships with girls and more. But his many experiences and the people who are and who become a part of his life influence his priorities and goals.

"Not all animals are as vicious as the Werewolves, as the cast of characters builds to include some much unanticipated members. The brutal Werewolf attacks, heartwarming gentleness between friends and family, respect for selves and others, and generous punches of humor are wrapped throughout this fantastic story.

"I tip my hat to Jeff J. Jarvis on the creation of By Arrow, Blade, and Claw, clearly the product of an interesting mind. I have opened book two and 'read on' for the continuation of the story, with book three ready to go."

—J4USA

I0562686

BY ARROW, BLADE, AND CLAW—BOOK ONE

COMES
DREADFUL
DEATH

JEFF J. JARVIS

CLAY BRIDGES
PRESS

Comes Dreadful Death

By Arrow, Blade, and Claw: Book One

Copyright © 2020 by Jeff J. Jarvis

Published by Clay Bridges in Houston, TX
www.ClayBridgesPress.com

ISBN: 978-1-953300-11-9
eISBN: 978-1-953300-12-6

Special Sales: Clay Bridges titles are available in wholesale quantity. Please visit www.claybridgesbulk.com to order 10 or more copies at a retail discount. Custom imprinting or excerpting can also be done to fit special needs. Contact Clay Bridges at Info@ClayBridgesPress.com.

This first in a three-book series of Lycan tales is dedicated to my extraordinary wife, my burgeoning family, my lifelong friends, and our many uniformed brothers and sisters who daily choose personal sacrifice, selfless service, and unflinching commitment to those who stand in harm's way both here and abroad.

Thank you all for the blessings of life.

TABLE OF CONTENTS

Author's Note	ix
Preface	xi
Lycan's Lament	xiii
Episode One	1
Episode Two	53
Episode Three	95
Episode Four	163
Episode Five	231
Episode Six	327
Episode Seven	405
Epilogue	479
Acknowledgments	481

AUTHOR'S NOTE

The stories in this series, By Arrow, Blade, and Claw, did not start out as fantasy fiction. They started out as actual military memoirs that I later learned I couldn't openly share. But I wanted my children to understand some of the unique experiences I encountered in Southeast Asia and elsewhere during and after the Vietnam War. My unit in Southeast Asia was attached to the Military Assistance Command, Vietnam—Special Operations Group (MACV-SOG). It was headquartered in the city of Saigon, now Ho Chi Minh City. The incredibly beautiful countryside and jungles of Southeast Asia along with the great Mekong River that sliced through a three-country area of keen military interest to us could be dangerous adversaries, much like our human enemies already were.

We were tasked with missions for which some security caveats have not yet been lifted even now years later. However, very few of our missions involved active fighting. The majority did not include deliberate firefights as our objective. They were more like obligatory considerations. Our primary purpose was to gather intelligence through covert operations. Our motto was simple: *We were never here.*

Cody Dugway, the mythical hero of these books, uses four extraordinary weapons in his fight to subdue or kill the Werewolves that roam the United States. He has an exceptional skill with bow and arrows close up or at a distance. He supplements that skill with a gifted Japanese short sword for close combat. His weapons of choice are complemented by the claws and jaws of a Hungarian wolverine and the talons of an Arctic gyrfalcon. His fourth weapon is perhaps his greatest of all, the result of a boyhood, life-changing accident. It is the limited ability to communicate with most animals.

By Arrow, Blade, and Claw, books one, two, and three, present the saga of Cody Dugway, his metamorphosis from military protagonist to an eventual Clan Leader and apologist for the Werewolves and the deadly animal aberrations he encounters on his many adventures.

The author understands that possible additional records of Cody Dugway were recently unearthed by accident at an archaeologist's dig in the giant Palo Duro Canyon in the Texas Panhandle. Like many others, the author eagerly awaits the verification and translation of those records. There is some speculation they may be extensive enough to fill the volumes of at least one or more books.

PREFACE

It's not every day our country calls on us for help in its hour of need, but when it happens, our country expects a prompt and willing response. These stories are taken from the journals of a young man whose unique talents set him on a course of adventure he could never have imagined. His name is Cody Dugway. In these stories, you will learn about some of his military experiences in an undeclared, secret war of extermination between humans and Werewolves, a war that eventually morphs into a dreadful quest for peace at great cost. Cody also learns that love can blossom unexpectedly and endure both time and distance. When all is said and done, Cody learns that love is the only real victory worth fighting for.

Cody, Casey, Sunstar, Dusty, and all the characters in the first of three books in this series actually exist. They just live in our world by different names. They were all my friends along the way. Here and there, I may have been a bit generous in describing their talents, but exaggeration is not a felony. As to the Werewolves, well, although I've never found irrefutable proof of Weres, I have stumbled across some surprising evidence that leaves me open-minded about them and a lot of other things.

(And some of those "other things" can kill you graveyard dead in a New York minute!)

—Jeff J. Jarvis
Bountiful, Utah

LYCAN'S LAMENT

Book One

The Were Clans first, and then came Man when Werewolves held the upper hand
> Until Eve's offspring did by birth crowd out the Were Clans' place on earth.

And then came war between each race as Were Clans fought to hold their place,
> But by their number, mien, and might, Man cast aside the Were Clans' right

And driven from their sunny lands, reduced to small and smaller bands, the Were Clans
> sought Man's pledge of peace for lesser lands in shadow's crease.

But of his promise Man made sport and cast out yet once more Weres' sort
> And once again by deed and will, Man taught his children how to kill.

By arrow, blade, and claw they fall, the Were Clans, male and female all.
> Enraged they now hunt Adam's child in city streets or tangled Wild.

The debt is Man's and must be paid. Too long hath Man his honor laid
> Beside the biers of history as he embraced perfidy.

Now from each lost and lonely den that houses what was Man's first kin
> Comes dreadful death by Weres forlorn, Man's nemesis in shaggy form.

Book Two

Of colors four the Were Clans were, those Elders with their brandished fur,

    The Grays, the Reds, the Pales, and Browns, their pride displayed on shaggy crowns

While lowly Man with skin born bare adorned himself with measly hair,

    Beneath Were kind, this naked race, to those whose fur was proof of grace.

And when the hairless ape displayed a thirst for glory, Weres dismayed,

    They sought to break this malcontent who would not to their rule assent

And soon took back from Man the chance to grow from truth Weres first advanced.

    Kept from Man the Were Clans' bribes of patience, cunning, strength of tribes.

Then left alone Man grew apart from Were Clans' law and Were Clans' heart

    And roiled by rude temerity, Man sought a different destiny

That one day at some future date to rise above his Were-set fate.

    But grew among the Weres a seed of jealousy they failed to heed.

And from the colors four there rose dissention as to which of those

    is greatest of the Elder race, for each Clan claimed the sovereign place.

Then came great wars between each Clan as Weres ignored the spread of Man.

    And slain were Grays and left for dead a great majority of Reds.

Then rose the Pales with iron hand and killed the Browns from off the land.

    And to this day Pales reign supreme of all the Weres in fact or dream,

But wander yet in silent dread of Man someday allied with Reds.

Book Three

Now down the corridors of time where memories lie in silent mime
    Are found displayed in caverns deep earth's sagas bound in troubled sleep.
One Age above all others stands to stay the creep of Time's cruel sands
    And brings to fore from hidden lore the lost intent of Weres and Man.
As brothers, once designed to be each race's greatest complement
    T'were doomed by envy's foul intent to blessings lost though heaven sent.
Upon the mounds of prejudice that blinded Weres to Fate's demand
    There grew a hate between the Weres that warped the love and growth of Man.
And then appeared in dream and script a prophecy of sacred writ,
    A formula for what should be, an excerpt from the gods' decree
That children of the furry nape and children of the naked ape
    Should one day find among their kind a cur that dared to cross the line,
To bring to pass in one the blood of both that love might stem the flood
    Of vengeance each race sought to take within the bounds of mutual hate.
An Archer struck by no disease would fall and by his Change unleash
    A new race that with purposed charm would quell Weres' appetite for harm.
For from his loins would come one day a blended child to show the way
    To Were and Man of those who would, a pathway back to brotherhood.

—Jeff J. Jarvis
9/17/2012
Bountiful, Utah

EPISODE
ONE

DAY ONE 7:30 P.M.

My name is Cody Dugway. I can talk to animals when I'm not killing Werewolves. Well, technically, I can actually talk to them when I'm killing Weres, but those conversations are far too short to really count as conversations. I also drive a wheelchair part-time when I can't walk or hobble. I am six feet two inches when standing. I can bench-press better than 285 pounds deadweight. I can't do squats. My reflexes are generally quick enough to stop a striking snake before he gets his fangs in me, provided I see him first.

I generally try to mind my own business. I don't bother with anything dead if I can help it—unless they're Werewolves, of course, those you have to bother with. They stink when they're dead. But then again, they also stink when they're alive. I learned that early this morning. It's not something generally covered in school classrooms or in dinner-table conversations at home, at least not in my experience.

I never thought I'd see a Werewolf much less kill one. It made me sick, throw-up sick. It's the kind of sickness that gets inside your head and makes you a little crazy. But I was lucky to come out alive because I've since learned that Werewolves are skilled killers. Most humans are not. Humans usually die when encountering a Were because (1) they're momentarily paralyzed from fright, or (2) a previously unimaginable creature just brought slaughter to their doorstep in a way they don't really understand and in a manner for which they have no natural edge.

Werewolves view death as the natural extension of their existence. They don't fear it. A Were expects to die violently just as humans expect to live peacefully. Since a Were certainly doesn't expect to be let alone if a human is anywhere around, there's no lost reaction time and no attitude adjustment for a Were when a human confrontation occurs. Werewolves automatically go into attack mode with humans. The result, of course, is that Werewolves generally view humans as mobile fast-food in the Weres' long food chain, sort of like a blue plate special. But humans also die because Werewolves are uncommonly quick. A Were may come head-on only to turn at the last second and strike from an unexpected angle or blind side. Their teeth are adapted to slashing and tearing, but they can and will chomp your head up. Their teeth are larger than the incisors of their four-footed cousins, the North American great gray wolves. Besides its split-second reaction time, a Werewolf also has two other potent weapons: its breath and its reach.

A Were's breath is fetid, poisonous, and neither sweet nor salty. It is fueled by rotten bits of debris that cling to the Werewolf's long fangs. That includes oily scraps of dead flesh and poorly ground bone bits. A Werewolf's breath sickens a victim. It disorients its victim when the Were is right there in their face.

Werewolves also have size. Adult Weres usually top out at seven feet tall or more when standing erect. They tower over most humans. Even when running on all fours, a Werewolf will still come up to the average man's throat. The problem is, they come up way too often and usually leave with the throat. By any measure, then, a Werewolf is classic Trouble with a capital T. So if you're a human, it helps to know when they're out and what they're doing. For this, of course, humans need all the help they can get, such as from other animals. They need the eyes, ears, and sometimes the teeth, claws, and talons of both four-footed and winged friends, to say the least.

Now, I'm very serious when I say I talk to animals. I really can, although few people know it. I've learned that it's better that way. There are very few species I can't understand, excluding fish and insects, of course, but who'd want a conversation with them? I picked up my talent some years ago. It was a gift I'd rather have refused at the time, but I had no say in the matter. Accidents happen. Most animals that eventually learn I can talk to them know I sometimes understand more than they say. But they also learn that I don't pass on idle gossip, so I'm tolerated.

Eavesdropping on another species can either be a real trip or just a dead-end hustle. I've found that truly listening to others can help keep the peace whether the others are furred, finned, or feathered. I've also found that a fellow can make a friend or two along the way when he keeps what he's heard to himself. A little discretion with those who don't look, think, act, or even smell like you lends itself to peaceful coexistence. It's a good rule for any creature in life. Sadly, I've found most humans generally ignore it.

I practice what I preach because I've discovered that when I do, no creature seems to go out of their way to make nasty deposits on my car. Nor do any stop by my house to chew through my electrical systems or yank out any telephone or other electrical wires that would leave my lights, appliances, and me sitting idle in the dark. To be sure, some animal species are just boring, especially some of the more ordinary North American birds. Common everyday backyard garden birds are hardly the most imaginative conversationalists in the world. There are, after all, only so many ways to describe a worm or chew out a prowling cat no matter how the message is styled or delivered. Those conversations just don't do it for me.

But if birds are really your thing, then give me an owl or even a pelican over the average blue jay or robin. Owls and pelicans get around, you see. They are among the real behind-the-scenes movers and shakers in the bird kingdom. There's very little backyard worm nonsense with those guys because owls are real meat eaters. Like any meat eater, they have to be good or they starve. Besides, owls occasionally see things you might want to know about, secret things that move at night when everyone else is asleep, things like Werewolves.

And pelicans are somewhat like owls, more of the same only with sand and surf, not forest and turf. But heck, even a hummingbird will occasionally come out with something worth listening to, just not very often. Hummingbirds are really nothing but flying appetites. They rarely make noise about anything but the next flower or prevailing wind speeds or maybe, just maybe, how wretched squirrels are, a bias apparently typical of all small American garden birds.

My experience over time is that almost any animal is more interesting than a backyard bird, especially animals as diverse as mice or warthogs. That's probably because mice seem to know about everything that's going on behind a neighborhood's closed doors, and warthogs, well, warthogs just have a unique sense of the weird. Mice can be droll and tedious, but warthogs can really be funny. They are definitely worth listening to. It could be their accent.

But I'm getting ahead of myself.

For starters, it's important that you know I am also the current state archery champ. That's because archery is a handicap-friendly, not handicap-resistant, sport. And while shooting from a wheelchair isn't especially a great advantage, neither is it necessarily a major disadvantage as with some other things in life. For example, with a compound, weighted competition bow, I can generally put two out of three arrows into an eight-inch bull's-eye at 50 yards in less than 30 seconds. My third arrow will probably cut the center ring curve at high right. But with a short recurve bow, my favorite kind of hunting bow, I get real serious. I'll put all three arrows into a four-inch bull's-eye at 30 yards and can do that in less than 15 seconds from first release to last.

There are some things, like archery, at which I am very, very good. Some would say I'm even dangerous. I'm not bragging when I tell you this because there are a few dead Werewolves this morning to prove it, and the day's not over yet. Not nearly. I've got still more places to be after my home settles down. Tonight probably won't be much of a night for sleep. I've a strong feeling that Death will walk our streets before tomorrow's dawn. I hope to be the reason he comes out to party as my guest.

SOME YEARS AGO (PART I)

I don't know exactly when I started talking to animals, probably around my 10th birthday. It was sometime after I regained consciousness from the accident. I was in a coma for three weeks in July, put there by a joyriding high school sophomore. She didn't fully understand the mechanics of driving a 4,000-pound car down a city street while trying to tune her favorite song on the dashboard radio and still sing harmony with three Yell Squad friends who were shoulder dancing and belting out the song beside and behind her.

I was crossing the street with Casey Allegro. Casey was my best friend and soul mate. At 10 years old it's important to be connected. We were. Casey lived next door to me. She shared my passion for soccer. She was a better kicker than I was, but I was quicker. I could steal the ball from anyone, even her. Few people ever got past me when the coach placed me at fullback.

Casey and I also shared a common desire to be astronauts. We would sit by her backyard garden swing or lie on the grass behind our houses for hours on a summer evening just gazing up at the stars. We were trying to figure out if a kid on another planet at that very same moment was looking down at us and wondering if anyone (like us) was gazing back up at him or her.

I remember that the car hit me at a lighted intersection. It was an intersection with a full electric stoplight, not just a red octagonal stop sign. Casey and I had started across the street when the light first turned green. I always figured that if we, as children, could read the lights and follow directions, then so could all those licensed drivers around us. I figured wrong. Following directions only works if you first see and then choose to obey the light. The young driver of the car that hit me hadn't even bothered to look up when she came barreling through the intersection. When her car finally came to a stop, I think she was afraid to look at anything. I was unconscious by then and could not have cared less.

I saw the car out of the corner of my eye at the last instant. It was coming fast. I also remember immediately pushing Casey away from me, back toward the curb we'd just left. I didn't even think about it. I just swung around and pushed her. My reaction time saved us both.

I pushed her so hard that she twisted her ankle and skinned her knee pretty badly as she stumbled onto the curb. She still carries a small scar from that incident. It was a sudden and brutal thing to do, but it saved her life and mine.

Pushing Casey made me twist around so the car hit me on my hip and legs and not my back or head. It was my head hitting the ground that made me unconscious. The car apparently jammed the nerve sheath in my backbone at impact. It didn't break anything, but I was numb afterward for months from my sternum to my knees. I still have tingly feelings in my thighs. Each year there's a greater tingling that goes on in my legs, so I keep hoping and stumbling on. My dad described my gait then as a barely controlled but determined lurch.

I believed I would eventually get back full use of my legs. My doctor still thinks I'm a dreamer. I'm never sure if that's because of my positive attitude or because I tell him I can listen and talk to animals. "Whatever!" he laughs. He concurs that I will walk normally again before I grow too old. Heck, he says, I may even run. That's why I say I *drive* a wheelchair, not I'm *confined* to a wheelchair. After a while, no matter what the vehicle may be or how long the road, a *driver* will eventually get out and walk.

So I'm a driver, not a prisoner. My friends know how I feel about the difference. Some call it hope. Some think I'm just stubborn or crazy. Me, I call it faith. I believe what can happen will happen with a little faith and a lot of effort. I truly believe I will run again someday, maybe even fast.

SOME YEARS AGO (PART II)

I didn't really understand what had happened to me when I first came out of my coma. It was enough of a challenge just to try to stay awake each day. I was continually groggy from all the pain medication I was getting. I felt like every part of me hurt. Just thinking about turning over in bed could bring tears to my eyes. Actually, turning over made me cry out loud.

All I wanted was blissful quiet, but hearing all the chatter outside my window each day after I regained consciousness really did wonders for me. It helped me keep my mind off how badly I really felt, especially since I didn't know what had happened to me in the first place. I really had to concentrate, and not just on my physical condition. I was hearing something I'd never heard before.

It sounded strange but strangely familiar, too, like hearing pig latin for the first time. Somebody or something was speaking, but the meaning and words seemed to be just beyond my reach, somewhere out past the edge of consciousness. It was the animals talking, of course, but I didn't know it then.

It helps to understand my talent if you first understand that animals don't use sentences or punctuation like we do. They don't use our breathing patterns or have facile tongues. Listening to them is kind of like learning English while sitting under a waterfall. Enough coherent sound comes through to get the meaning, but the details get fuzzy or occasionally lost because the words, grammar, or speech patterns are so very, very different than anything we employ. I call it pictographic language. Certain sounds convey specific mental pictures that are more like video impressions. You hear and see to understand. It all happens at the same time.

What surprised me most when I first listened to two sparrows argue was that I never knew there were so many kinds of worms. The birds were arguing about taste. One sparrow was vehement that different species of worms all tasted the same. (They don't.) Nor did I know that some birds just have no sense of humor, while others, like crows, can be hilarious.

Ravens, on the other hand, are generally more reserved. Ravens are bigger, sleeker, and cleverer than crows. Ravens also discriminate. Ravens consider themselves the elite of yard birds, the swans of the city as it were. I consider them just an inevitable nuisance, occasionally useful in the eternal scheme of things.

I had been lying in my hospital bed several days listening to the drone of chatter made by my parents, nurses, doctors, janitors, aides, and whomever when it occurred to me that I was still listening to chatter when everyone finally left my room. That puzzled me. I knew my room had no radio and that my folks hadn't paid the TV deposit. They wanted me to rest and sleep, not get involved in some TV cartoon or game show that could send my blood pressure through the roof. But the puzzling chatter when they were present wasn't coming from my room. It came from just outside my room. It came in through a window that one of the nurses left open during the day. That let the sunlight and a breeze filter in through the trees. It kept the room smelling fresh.

I took me awhile to finally understand that the muted noises I was hearing were actually conversations between birds. A small finch flew onto my window sill one day. He asked if it would be all right to fly around inside for a while. He wanted to see what the inside of the great building looked like, but he needed an open window to enter and exit, especially exit. I didn't answer him with my mouth. I remember looking right at him. I was groggy but concentrating as hard as I could. I thought I was in no shape to get up. I could not close the window myself, and he could do as he liked, but I desperately needed my rest at the moment. I was determined to go back to sleep. I felt this was certainly one of the weirdest dreams I'd ever had. I even wondered if maybe I was already asleep. The finch twittered a "thank you" and promptly flew into my hospital room. He caused no end of excitement, as I later learned from my parents and the nurses who attended me. They called that day the Battle of the Bird. Everyone tried to shoo him out. I learned that the finch finally exited through my window. I missed the whole thing because I was asleep, exhausted by the lingering pain from my injuries.

It was a small mouse that came each night that really helped me develop my new talent. She worked with me every evening after dark. Eventually, I could carry on a decent conversation with her. She taught me that different animals had unique thinking and speech patterns. For instance, I learned that animals that eat meat or protein are usually much smarter than animals that eat only grain and fodder. I guess they have to be cleverer and more cunning in order to survive. But they are also generally good companions once they know you are not trying to eat them.

Animals recognize humans as the most dangerous predator of all. They know humans can kill whatever they set out to kill and have a hundred ways to do it. They also know that there are an awful lot of humans around. They know, too, that humans are careless and often kill by accident as well as by intention. That makes most animals frightened of people, but not so much of children. Animals know that children are children everywhere in any species. Yet animals don't quite know what to make of our teenagers. Most animals don't have teenage years. Once they get their claws, horns, teeth, and so on, they are generally considered adults. They must leave their home, lair, burrow, or nest to get by on their own.

So animals are very wary around teenagers. Animals know that teenagers can bite but wait to see if teenagers will bite. Most won't, of course. Most teenagers or preteens just want to be friends with an animal. Many animals feel the same way. Cats and dogs have made a living off this. Larger predators such as lions, bears, and tigers have never mastered those get-along skills. Few big predators have ever learned to put loyalty ahead of hunger. Spiders also flunk the cuddle test.

I learned day by day to listen and learn the thought-speak of animals. There was little else for me to do that summer or little else I could do. As it happened, the accident was one of my greatest gifts. It actually strengthened me in several unexpected ways. I learned that humans are not the only creatures who believe in a Creator. Nor are they the only creatures who can recognize His handiwork. And I learned that people, at times, are just a different kind of animal.

Casey came by the hospital almost every day. She shared her day with me. She could never really listen to animals as I could, but she sparkled in a way I did not. Few animals were ever frightened of her. Sometimes she would sing to me as I lay exhausted in my bed. Her words and songs comforted me, but they did something more. They comforted animals as well. If I just tried to concentrate on Casey, things usually worked out well.

The girl who ran into me came by once with her parents. She apologized for what happened. She was in tears the whole time. So was I. It ended well, though. She left knowing how close she had come to taking a life. I hoped she would remember the incident forever and hopefully never drive so stupidly again. I also told her in confidence about the gift I had received from the accident, being able to listen to animals and all. That seemed to make her cry all the harder. She left thinking that I may be alive but had truly been knocked senseless in the accident. She thought my chances for a full mental recovery were nil.

SOME YEARS AGO (PART III)

By the age of 12, I was pretty accomplished as an urban wildlife listener. By 15, I could hold my own with most species, especially after spending summers working odd jobs at the city zoo. By 16, I had learned that animals really aren't very much different from any of my friends when it comes to conversation. Most folks want what's said to be received in privacy and courtesy. No one—haired, furred, plated, scaled, or otherwise—likes a blabbermouth or a flaming idiot. Sometimes listening was all that was necessary, particularly if someone was coming to you for advice or sympathy. In fact, in most instances, animals and humans preferred someone who could really listen over someone who preferred to talk.

My reputation got around. Very few animals had ever heard of a human who could communicate with them, who could really listen to and understand what they were saying. Our yard was constantly besieged by well-meaning but curious animals of all sorts. Some flew in, waddled by, or crept past just trying to get a look at the fellow who could talk with animals. Not many believed it at first. In fact, some neighbors complained about the number and noise of animals that somehow passed through our neighborhood. I never explained to my folks what had happened to me until sometime much later. Some things you experience are best kept private until you better understand the experience.

Neither Casey nor her folks ever complained about the animals. Her folks saved their attention for Casey. They believed I had saved Casey's life the day I almost lost mine. There was little they wouldn't do for me. They even bought me a racing wheelchair that was faster, lighter, more maneuverable, and smaller than the standard hospital-issued one I initially received to come home in. Over the years as I grew, I kept exchanging it for racing chairs more appropriate to my size and strength. Racing that wheelchair around gave me the shoulders, chest, and arms I have today. Archery helped, of course, since drawing and holding aim with a recurve hunting bow takes exceptional strength, most of which I gained the hard way.

One day I wheeled by our high school wrestling room to visit with one of my friends there. The coach was temporarily away on an errand. I asked my friend if I could try a round with some of them. I pinned the second- and fourth-best varsity players and did so much damage to the first player that he missed a mid-season tournament with a strained back. When the coach arrived, he was appalled. He made it clear that the district rules wouldn't let me participate as a team member. He asked me to go away and not come back anymore. He wasn't very polite. Frankly, he was more than furious. He was also loud.

I understood where he was coming from. We parted, but each of us had made a point. Since archery was one sport I could do and do well, I stayed where I was welcome. In time, I made a name for myself. I became state champion after a lot of hard work and constant encouragement. My family really supported me. It was a good feeling to finally be the best at something. It gave me confidence in everything else I tried.

Casey had also developed as an athlete. By the age of 16, she was playing on elite teams and at 18 was leading them. Colleges were talking to her about future choices and scholarships. We no longer played soccer together regularly, of course. As strong and fast as I was, I could not move that racing wheelchair like she could move her feet. She could blow by me every time, even in her sleep. One day I got so frustrated trying to wheel and block one of her deadly, long, curving shots that I grabbed my bow. I pulled and put an arrow through the ball while it was still on the fly toward the goal. I pinned it to the goal's wooden frame.

I'm not sure who was more astonished. The ball was suddenly planted against the front edge of the wooden bar that framed the goal. It was deflated and draped over the still-quivering arrow shaft I used to pierce it. I had pulled and fired faster than the ball could travel from her foot to the goal. It was a sobering experience for both of us. She had been in contest mode. Apparently I had unconsciously gone beyond that into hunting mode. I had learned more from my animal friends than I realized. Adult animals rarely play any kind of games, otters excepted, of course. Animals live in a life-or-death world. Much of their life is devoted to activities that let you live or die.

With that shot, I had become a hunter in my mind, not a gatherer. Nor did I see a way back anytime soon. I think Casey sensed that. We were still best friends after that incident and still soul mates insofar as I could tell, but she looked at me and treated me a little differently. That incident put some distance between us. It scared her just a little bit. It scared me, too.

I really didn't think too much about it at the time. I was more concerned about getting my arrow out of the goalpost. It had gone in almost half the length of the arrowhead. It took me half an hour with a penknife to finally get it out. Casey just stood and watched me curiously for a long time. She then quietly turned and went back to her house without saying a word.

I think that was also the day I felt I began to fall in love with her, even though it was sometime later before I told her. I really didn't have to. She knew even before I did. Maybe that's why she put a little space between us that day. I learned that hunting emboldens the spirit.

Even the animals knew something changed that day. I was no longer just a human curiosity. I became a hunter. Big time. They knew and talked about what my shot meant. I could bring down a bird on the wing or hooves or pads on the plain, so to speak. They didn't necessarily fear me, but they learned immediately to be much more cautious around me. They learned I could now kill. What had once been a possibility was now a certainty in their minds. A hunter I would be to them from then on, no matter how well I could or would empathize with them. Something else changed that day, although it was some time before I figured out just what it was.

I realized I had begun to define who I was. I had acted impetuously, but it was my action. I realized I couldn't off-load its consequences on anyone else. The *me* I was becoming would have to straddle two different worlds—the world of humans and the world of animals. Sometimes it was an uncomfortable stretch and would probably get worse. Still, for better or worse, it was my stretch. I saw myself in third person as a kind of gatekeeper. I had a growing influence between two sacred trusts, between two very different worlds that shared many of the same values.

I just hoped that when those moments came to let me help one world take a peek at the other I would know what to do and how to do it. It was more responsibility than I wanted. Nevertheless, I was stuck with it. And all you can do when you're stuck with something is do your best. I hoped that would be good enough when the time came. Sometimes it isn't.

I got my chance to find out the day the Werewolves came.

DAY ONE 6:00 A.M.

I was awakened in the predawn hours by the long, rasping screech of an outraged cat. He was letting everyone in earshot know that something truly horrible was out and about in the neighborhood. That *something* dealt in death. The cat's squeal quickly became a frantic scream for help. It was the kind of call an animal gives out rarely, usually only once in their lifetime, unless they survive. The modulation, frequency, and volume of that cry alone would have had the hairs on my neck prickling, but it was the message torn from the dying cat's throat that really set my senses on edge.

The cat was screaming something about a man beast tearing at him. I'd never before heard any animal described by another with reference to a human being. It was a scream the cat never got to finish. At some point through that awful wail, there was an abrupt, guttural choking sound followed immediately by a profound silence. I was instantly awake and clambering for room to move as I fought my bed covers. I finally managed to untangle myself before sliding onto the seat of my racing chair. I was out of my room and rolling silently down the hall toward our den and its patio door before I was fully awake. A scream in the night is a great people-mover.

Then, realizing I had no real idea what was happening, I told myself to take a deep breath and slow down. Just. Slow. Way. Down. I knew that no matter what I did from this point on, I couldn't help the cat. It had been a death cry. He had attempted to warn anyone who would listen that he was being disemboweled by a creature he didn't have words for and desperately needed somebody's help right then, thank you very much. But it was too late now. He never finished his scream.

I stopped rolling my chair down the hall and came to a complete stop just past the entryway into our den. I deliberately held back in the deeper shadows of the room. I was away from the patio windows and the slowly shifting pool of light from a distant street lamp that collected on the far edge of the rug. It was a good time to listen while I worked out what to do next. I sure didn't want whatever was outside to see or hear me until I was ready.

For that matter, I didn't want my family to see or hear me either. I didn't want them worried, but there was no reason to suppose they had paid any attention to the cat's scream. An alley cat wailing in the night would mean nothing to them. Even if they had heard it, they would likely not have heard me rolling softly by their closed bedroom door. I keep my chair like I keep all the equipment I depend on—well oiled, at hand, and fully loaded.

After about five minutes of silent waiting, I quietly wheeled my racing chair over to the far den wall where my motorized chair was plugged in. I shifted myself onto its higher seat. Unplugging the motor chair from its receptacle, I turned on the small control switch for a quick scan of the instrument panel. I had a full battery charge. It was good for about two hours of sustained use or four hours of intermittent use.

My electric motor chair will comfortably do about 15 miles per hour. Getting about on sidewalks and streets is something I can easily do in all kinds of weather thanks to its balanced design. I could go faster on my manually operated racing wheelchair, but doing so takes both hands and arms pumping hard. My racing chair leaves me little or no opportunity to use my bow while I'm on the move. That's why the electric wheelchair was my clear platform of choice for what I was about to do. I was going out to see what had come into my neighborhood. I was going out armed. I was prepared to shoot and kill something that killed cats and might even attack people like me.

I deliberately dropped a quiver full of broadhead hunting arrows into the hammered metal sheath that my father had fashioned for me on the side of the motor chair. A quiver normally holds about 12–15 arrows, 15 if they are metal-tipped target arrows, 12 if they are razor-edged hunting broadheads. My father once joked that fixing that clamp to my motorized chair made the chair look like a Tuscan war chariot. I just wished he'd have fashioned a clamp for the javelins that also used to adorn those chariots. Tonight I wanted lots of things around me that would cause harm to whatever was out there. Unfortunately, javelins were just not on the ticket.

I picked up and strung my small recurve hunting bow instead. I took immediate comfort from its sturdy shape as it lay nestled in my hands. It was a 34-inch Black Widow bow with a 70-pound pull. It threw an arrow on a very flat, very quick trajectory. It was incredibly accurate. It was almost as fast and certainly as lethal at short ranges as a handgun, anything from 40 yards in. It was and would usually be my weapon of choice in a bad situation. A hard-driven arrow is the embodiment of original stealth technology.

Bow at the ready, I rolled over to the sliding patio door. I eased the latch back until the door traveled freely on its castors. Then I pushed the door back slowly and deliberately. I quietly rolled out onto our backyard deck. I refastened the door, still in partial shadow from the roof's overhang. I made my way over to and then down the ramp from the porch to the backyard proper. I didn't believe I had made much noise, but I was about to find out, possibly the hard way.

13

DAY ONE 6:15 A.M.

My home has a large backyard. The yard borders a narrow alleyway that runs through our block from side street to side street. The alley is usually dark, partially hidden by trees that grow at the rear of most of the yards on our block and partially obscured by the absence of any reliable street lamps at either end of the alley. There are two ways into the alley from our yard. One way is through a small gate near our western neighbor's property line. The other is through a door set in the back of our detached garage at the yard's eastern edge. I was betting the alleyway was the scene of the cat's death. That was the direction from which its cry had come. I'd seen nothing in the yard when I'd carefully reconnoitered it while waiting in the shadows of our den.

I figured whatever had been back there in the alley might still be back there. I didn't want to be at an immediate disadvantage when I came rolling out to make its acquaintance, so I chose to go out through the small garage door. It was a good decision. That door opened on a slant. I could see along the length of our back fence while looking through its glass windows. I couldn't see any part of the alleyway in the other direction, and I couldn't see everything along the way the door faced. Nevertheless, that door did shorten the odds against a nasty surprise, so I took it.

As I wheeled into the garage, I nocked an arrow and held it against the bow in my left hand. I used an overlapping finger. It would take but seconds to aim and release the broadhead arrow. I was comforted as I remembered that a hunting arrow had more penetrating power than a .306-caliber rifle bullet, so long as you hit what you aim at. The silence of the night seemed to deepen as I rolled out. I grasped the garage door's handle and slowly eased it around to me until the door lay almost flat against the garage wall. I rolled to the edge of the doorway. Darkness still covered me. I savored the night. I tried to catch any scent or sound that would give me some clue about the adversary I expected to confront. I really wasn't sure what to expect.

I had barely started to lean outward, moving my head forward to the plane of the door, when suddenly I was aware of a small, distant rodent scurrying down the alley toward me. He was two houses down and across the alley. He was moving quickly toward me like a jittery shadow. He made little to no effort at concealment. As he hopped and skittered closer to me, I could faintly hear him muttering to himself. His thoughts were jumbled, but the sense I got was fear, predator, and pursuit. Whatever had spooked him had spooked him badly. He was determined to put distance between himself and something moving up the alley behind him.

I was far enough away that I couldn't hear what the rodent could hear, but his sense of panic was clearly growing as each second passed. Just as he came into the stretch bordered by our yard, I saw a large black shadow detach itself from a darker patch of fence two yards down. The shadow moved quickly after the rodent. I squinted to focus my eyes in the predawn's false light. Suddenly, what I could see slammed my eyes open. Chills ran up my back as my mouth got too dry to scream. What I first thought to be a large man wasn't. A huge, barrel-chested, wolflike creature emerged from the gloom. It leaped forward on all fours and then stood partially erect, claws exposed on each paw, as it nosed the wind for a scent of its prey. It had clearly set its sights on the rodent. It appeared to be trying to either herd him or flank him, I wasn't sure which. So startled by its appearance was I that I felt as if I were frozen to my spot of concealment. The creature had an elongated face with both jaws slanting inward to a narrow muzzle. The muzzle resembled a rough triangle with a flared nose. I could not make out the actual shape of its mouth, but its teeth caught the dim light about us. Its shaped ears were much longer than a human's ears. They were canted forward. Its eyes were also larger than a human's but not so dissimilar as to appear completely alien. Its arms and legs, however, were grotesque parodies of a human body. They were hairy and twisted. They resembled the musculature of a wolf. The legs were particularly offsetting. They bent slightly backward as if a human knee had been broken and reversed.

The effect on me was an immediate shudder and revulsion. The effect on the creature was an ungainly gait, jerky, not smooth. The creature moved swiftly in a crouched shuffle, bobbing and weaving as it closed on the now frantic field mouse. Watching it come closer made my stomach turn. I fought to control my own sense of panic and raised my bow to a shooting position. I quickly drew back my arrow and then held it in place as I waited for the moment to resolve itself.

The mouse unexpectedly broke across the alley and ran for my door. He squealed in open fear as the creature drew close to him. The rodent spotted me. Several things happened at once. The rodent shot underneath my motorized chair and ran to hide deep within the confines of the garage. He screamed for protection as he passed by. The large creature, seeing my image take shape from the alley's otherwise gloomy atmosphere, stopped mid-stride. It reared up on its hind legs, spitting and growling. Its powerful jaws gnashed in anger and frustration. At the same time it emitted a grating, ugly cry while leaving a considerable space in its mouth for whatever it chose to bite. Like me.

I didn't hesitate. I loosed my arrow even as I was reaching for a second. The arrow took the creature through the mouth. It pierced the cranial cavity and came to rest halfway through its skull. The second arrow was through the creature's throat. I did that in less than five seconds. The sounds of its growls were unnerving to me. They were having an uncanny effect. I knew real fear. I also knew that if I had not shot it again at that moment, I would likely have succumbed to its forbidding mien. My fear had grown to flagrant proportions. I was mere steps away from oblivion. It was not my first time facing imminent death, but this time, there was a possibility of dismemberment. The creature was dead before its body hit the ground.

DAY ONE 6:30 A.M.

I slid off the motor chair and stood up. I slowly hobbled to the fence and threw up everything that had passed through my stomach during the previous three years. I could hardly bring myself to stare at much less examine the creature, but it had to be done. The smell of death suddenly hung heavy over the alleyway. Finally, I composed myself enough to hobble over to the body. I used my bow as a lever and turned it over. The creature's fall against the alley floor had snapped the arrow that had penetrated its skull. I was relieved that the arrow through its throat appeared to be intact. On impulse, I reached down and pulled it free of the creature. It was coated in bloody tissue.

From its genitalia, I could see that the creature was male. From its size, I could only guess it was a mature adult. At least I hoped so. If this thing I'd killed was a teenager, then my town was in serious trouble. The creature was at least a foot taller than me, possibly more. I'd gauged its height as it came for me. I'd aimed upward for its mouth and throat.

Its hands and feet were oddly shaped. They resembled something between a paw and a man's foot. It had clawlike nails. Its torso appeared to be covered in sparse, thickly curled dark hair. I saw no vestige of a tail. I estimated its weight to be 280 to 300 pounds. The body exuded a musky stink, more of a sewer smell than a field or farm smell.

I no sooner reached down to yank out the first arrow that had pierced the creature's maw when I was startled by the sound of a metal garbage can being slammed into a fence well behind me. The sound came from the alley in the other direction than where the creature had appeared.

I nocked another arrow as I brought my bow up and spun about, only to encounter as frightening a sight as I could have wished for. A larger creature was literally leaping its way toward me. Its eyes were blazing. It uttered the same unnerving, guttural cries as had the first. It covered ground at an astounding rate. The sense of its cries hit me even as I pulled and released the arrow just before the creature could swarm over me.

As with the first arrow, this one went through its mouth. The force of the arrow snapped the creature's head back as the shaft burst through its skull. His body had been in full flight when the arrow hit him. He flopped forward and died instantly. His body landed in a disorderly heap almost at my feet. I stood there shaking. It had been as close a call as I'd had with the car accident years before. I could not stop trembling until I turned away.

Feeling suddenly weak and still nauseous, I hobbled back to my motor chair and nocked a third arrow. I then turned back to examine the second and larger creature that now lay in the alley. As with the first creature, it was a large male but with considerably more graying. Its color was almost pale. It had come at me with a more pronounced intent than I'd experienced with the first attack. I presumed the second creature was somehow related to the first, perhaps its father. Even as that thought occurred to me, so did another. A family or families of these things meant our town was in *very* serious trouble.

Assuming the two creatures were traveling or hunting as a pack, there would probably be more such creatures, likely a female or two. What I had sensed from the second creature's cries was kinship, anger, revenge, and evil. I also had the impression of mission, as if the presence of these creatures was purposed. I felt that the creatures' very presence in Chagrin Falls was not by accident so much as by design, although whose I could not possibly tell.

Unwilling to discard my bow even long enough to pull the two bodies to the side of the alley, I remounted my motor chair as I tried to watch in all directions at once. It's a wonder I didn't fall off the seat. I wheeled back into the garage and carefully closed the door behind me. I then sought out the mouse who had first alerted me to the creature's presence. I had more questions than I could readily form and wanted to start with him. Someone, somewhere knew about these creatures, especially what they wanted and possibly how to get them to go away. I was going to question every animal I knew of or could find until I got some answers.

Unfortunately, the mouse was nowhere to be found. He'd probably scurried off when the second creature arrived. He was probably still putting distance between him and my garage.

Not finding him, I rolled back to my house. I replaced and resettled everything and then returned to my room. My family was hopefully none the wiser regarding my temporary absence and the events in the alley. I saw that the sun would soon be up. Only a sliver of darkness remained to cloak the dawn. Once in my bedroom, I pulled the covers over my head. Closing my eyes, I soon fell asleep.

As my eyes closed, my thoughts were of my family and Casey. I felt I had to warn them and Casey's family, but especially Casey. Then I had to find a way to explain these creatures and, if need be, protect us all. I knew I couldn't do it on my own. But I thought my talents might make a difference, and there were bound to be some animals that could help protect us. I needed a plan, but before that, I also needed sleep. I thought creatures such as I had killed would probably not make themselves visible during the day. Consequently, spent by what had already transpired and tired of what was likely to come, I stopped shaking and dropped off to sleep.

DAY ONE 8:15 A.M.

It was my mother's screams that woke me.

The sun was barely up, and a glance at the clock told me I'd been asleep less than an hour. The sound of her screaming was coming from the garage I'd just left. I

17

heard my father yelling her name as he slammed open the patio door and ran outside. By the time I arrived, he'd calmed Mom down considerably, but both were staring out the garage's back door, slack-jawed in silent disbelief at the remains of the two creatures I'd killed. I had to admit that they were worth screaming about. Their lifeless forms spurred the worst kind of revulsion. They seemed completely at odds with the order of the universe as we humans know it. But there they were in plain, awful sight, as real as the alley floor on which their horrific forms were sprawled.

My dad immediately recognized the broken arrow shaft still protruding from the larger male's skull. He gave me a penetrating stare as I joined their vigil. I nodded slightly "not yet" and remained silent in the garage as he escorted Mother back to our house. The questions and concern on his face were obvious when he came back alone. I explained what had happened as clearly and succinctly as possible. To his credit, he listened carefully. He made no judgments but walked over to me. Holding me gently by my arms, he asked if I had been hurt in any way.

When he was assured I was okay, we discussed the problem of disposing of the two creatures. The larger problem of who or what they were and how the heck they got to our town was simply beyond us at the moment. Besides, they were starting to smell even worse than I remembered. Their body fluids had already stained the alley floor. Death is a messy business no matter where it occurs, so we ignored the question of motive and origin and set about wrapping the remains. We also sluiced down the entire alleyway surrounding the bodies. We hoped to eliminate any direct evidence of their death. Didn't work.

We had a problem. We couldn't just haul their bodies to the dump and ignore the problem they posed. We certainly couldn't stuff them into the large, plastic waste management canisters the city had provided for once-a-week curbside pickup. Dogs would likely smell and have the bodies for food or sport. Any kids seeing the carcasses would have nightmares and emotional damage for the next 40 years. Left with few options, we decided after a short conference to take the bodies to our small City Hall and leave them with the Police Chief and Mayor. We figured these creatures were really their problem, not ours. Once the bodies were removed, we thought there'd be no more night visitors.

Optimism is a wonderful salve.

Unfortunately, we were wrong. Some problems just won't go away by themselves.

DAY ONE 9:20 A.M.

By the time we arrived at City Hall, the growing smell of the two carcasses had settled any questions we might have had about a later breakfast. Stink just isn't word enough to describe the smell coming from the back of my father's truck. I was grateful he tended to have a lead foot. I was especially glad I wasn't in any following vehicle and that Dad's truck made few stops en route to our destination. Once there, he was the first out as I struggled with my crutches. His truck bed was too small to haul the carcasses and my wheelchair without one touching the other. I surely didn't want anything of mine even in the vicinity of those remains, so it was canes or walking sticks for me this morning. I'd chosen the latter.

Too bad we didn't get quite the reception at City Hall we'd hoped for.

The Mayor was away, but the City Manager was in. He came outside to the truck and promptly threw up all over the truck's tailgate when Dad turned back the tarp that covered the bodies. Choking and gagging, he scrambled back into the city building screaming for the Police Chief as he disappeared through the main doors. His panic and yells brought several city employees and some of our braver citizens rushing outside. They congregated nearby but away from us. They, in turn, were followed by a trotting Police Chief. Two deputies were trying to keep up with him. Apparently, the deputies weren't used to moving much faster than a power swagger.

Huffing and puffing, they stopped short of the truck as they peered into the bed. I watched as they first saw the two carcasses. All three paled, and one of the deputies turned away taking deep breaths. The Chief had the courage to walk up to the truck and prod the bodies with his nightstick. He turned to us in anger, asking just what in blue blazes we thought we were doing. He thought the two carcasses had to be the worst prank he'd seen in his 14 years on the force.

My dad's quiet response and dead-level gaze were more forceful than any answering shout. Dad explained the circumstances in which he'd found the bodies and my experience in killing them. The Chief listened, wide-eyed, turning to me several times to ask if my father was telling the truth. I answered in the affirmative and pointed out the very visible arrow shaft holes through the back of each head and the throat. Things got very quiet after that. The small crowd who had gathered nearby began sliding back toward City Hall. After a few steps, they broke into a stumbling, shoving rush to get back inside the building.

The Chief had the smarts to send one of his deputies after them to corral them and keep them in an isolated group. He put them in one of City Hall's conference rooms until a plan of action could be formed. The Chief knew mass panic would quickly ensue if any of those people began spreading the word to family and friends. He knew, too, that rumor is a powerful weapon able to cause more civic death and destruction than any two such creatures could ever do by themselves, dead or alive.

His quick thinking probably saved our city from a mass riot.

Someone called for an ambulance, which took the carcasses to the small city morgue. The city medical examiner would perform an autopsy on them there. The looks and reactions of the EMTs and driver who transferred the bodies to the ambulance explained why they left in such a hurry. Or maybe it was the sobs and gasps from the EMTs who had to ride inside with the rapidly decaying bodies.

I spent an hour or so of tedious repetition as I explained and reexplained when, where, and how I encountered and killed the two creatures. I was finally released by the Chief, and my dad and I headed home. I was certain the Chief was aware of the danger posed to our town. I also believed he had no plan whatsoever to find, control, or combat this emerging menace. I wasn't really surprised. How do you train to fight what you've been told for your entire lifetime is merely a supernatural myth?

It's simple. You don't. You can't, at least not at first brush, and I'd certainly had mine early this morning.

I surmised that some myths are told to us to hide a frightening reality. What I shot earlier that morning was just that, a kind of reality far too up close and personal for any sane person's taste. Certainly it was for mine. But I also thought that fate had given me a talent that few, if any, others had, a talent by which we might find a way to fight these creatures, assuming there were more.

It was one of my better assumptions.

DAY ONE 11:00 A.M.

Immediately upon arriving home, Dad left me to go find Mom and tend to her. He was worried she might be in shock or frantic about his long absence while we were at City Hall. I made my way to my room and promptly phoned Casey next door. She was home for the day but was preparing to leave for an impromptu soccer match with some of her teammates. I asked her to cancel and meet me outside my garage ASAP. What I had to tell her was about to shatter her world. I didn't care. I needed some help. Casey always had good advice. Besides, I wasn't sure I could face this threat alone.

To her credit, Casey met me within minutes after I rolled outside. She had called and told her team cocaptain that something unexpected had come up. She wouldn't make the game. Moreover, she'd be out of touch for a while. She came outside wearing one of those what-in-the-world-is-wrong-with-you looks that border somewhere between irritation and curiosity. I ignored her stare and blurted out my thanks that she'd come to meet me.

It took me 10 minutes to bring her up to speed. It took me twice that long to calm her down as I showed her where the shootings had occurred and then walked her through them. I got a hug I didn't expect. I didn't know I wanted one so much before she suddenly threw her arms around me and held me close for a bit. Then I realized hers was a nurturing hug rather than a congratulatory great-hunter-reward sort of hug. I quickly calmed myself down. Nevertheless, it was still a great hug. Heck, *any* hug from Casey is a great hug.

I thought to myself, *Nurture?* Yeah, nurture is good; indeed, nurture is fine!

Casey and I then talked a bit about the possibility of other creatures that might be active in the area. I wondered where any might have gone if my daylight hiding hypothesis was correct. Since she'd heard no sirens while my dad and I were downtown and since none had sounded after our return home, we concluded that if there were other creatures, they were probably in hiding. I figured they would likely remain so during the rest of the day.

We then thought there were only three likely places from which these creatures could have emerged. Our first choice was an area in the forest west of town. We high school kids called it the Dead Zone. It was an area of several hundred acres of mostly old growth trees and bitterly tangled underbrush spread out on some steep hills. Few people ever visited there. Fewer wild animals were ever seen there. It was graveyard-quiet most of the time. Even most birds seemed to avoid it. We'd grown up hearing stories of an old lumber mill that had been back there in the early 1900s. Supposedly, the mill was abandoned when a puzzling series of accidents drove away the original workforce. The owner finally moved to Dayton. The smell that still permeated the nearby hills was attributed to the rotting lumber and sawdust piles left behind. We also thought the apparent absence of many birds was due to the foul vapors occasionally carried aloft by fickle winds. Sometimes those winds crept into Chagrin Falls.

The second possible site was a natural cave down by the rock quarry. The quarry was four miles southeast of town. It was still occasionally used by the state to collect gravel and other scattered aggregate. The cave beside it had been the supposed death site of two boys and a girl who'd gone in exploring during the 1930s. They went in with candles and a lantern but never emerged. One candle and the lantern had been found about 100 yards into the cave at the edge of two good-sized sinkholes. The search team concluded that the children had fallen in and died there. One of the sinkholes was more than 100 feet deep as measured by a rescuer's rope. The other sinkhole was more than twice as deep.

The search team's crude equipment at the time and the probable high body-retrieval risk led the team to evacuate the cave and seal its entrance. Metal cyclone fencing had been stapled to the rock that framed the cave's opening and a commemorative marker had been placed there. Over the years, weather and curious teenagers had dislodged one side of the original fencing so even an adult could squeeze through into the cave.

Still, very few tried it, especially after a few daredevils over the years came back with stories of weird cries, snapping sounds, and what some believed were guttural, huffing grunts occasionally heard upon entering the cave. It made for great campfire tales that would curl hair. We thought of it as merely a rite of passage for kids, teenagers, and gullible visitors. After all, wind can make strange sounds.

The third and most likely site was an abandoned barn containing a deep well that purportedly ran dry in the late 1950s. The well had been badly damaged during

National Guard training during World War II. An overeager soldier driving a water truck had backed up to it and then gone through the rocks that formed the aboveground rim of the well. The broken truck had to be towed away. The well was damaged to a depth of about 10 feet since a third of the retaining wall was knocked loose and fell to the bottom of the well.

The well was originally a spring emerging from soft sandstone. The owners had enlarged, formed, and deepened the well over the years. It was apparent that the well was a human-made extension of a natural cave formation that no one had really ever explored. Local supposition was that the well cave probably tied into the Quarry Cave a few miles away. No one knew for sure. No real exploration had ever been done, at least not by anyone I ever knew or had heard of. A barn was built over the well in the late 1950s.

The field where the barn was located bordered a well-traveled road to a nearby small lake. Families used the lake in the summer as a children's retreat and play area. The water basin that formed the lake was very shallow and therefore warm. The barn well's original owners had long since stopped farming the barn property. The property was currently in contested receivership by some of the original owners' immediate descendants. *No Trespassing* signs were plastered all over the property's various fence lines. The signs were generally obeyed. The field was full of rocks, stickers, and other bothersome plant life anyway.

I tried to make our conclusions available to the City Manager and Police Chief by phone. I got repeated busy signals each time we called. I soon quit trying. I imagined those City Hall officials probably had their hands full trying to contain some of what our more panicky population might be spreading about. They would have had little time for my call.

I should have stuffed my imagination and kept trying.

DAY ONE 11:27 A.M.

Unloading my story and accompanying emotions on Casey left me feeling a lot calmer, more in charge of myself. I began thinking about what my next step would be. The first, obviously, was to check out my hypothesis that one of the three sites we'd just discussed harbored these recent menaces. Casey forcefully reminded me that it was *our* hypothesis, not mine alone. She was going to have a role in this with or without me. Arguing with Casey once her mind is made up is futile at best. I'm neither slow nor stupid. I simply sat there and waited for the next shoe to fall.

After considerable discussion (I had another word for it), Casey and I decided to split up and reconnoiter the sites separately in the interest of time. Casey and one or two of her soccer teammates would check out the barn by the swimming hole road. It was in plain sight of a well-traveled county road and only a few miles from the city's edge. It was easy to get to and easy to approach from several vantage points. I, on the other hand, would check out the Quarry Cave. I wasn't going alone. I planned to seek help from some of the animals in the area. Failing that, I would try to get some information that I might otherwise miss from any people nosing about the quarry. We agreed to report back to my garage by 3:00 p.m. sharp.

As we split up, I kind of hoped for a goodbye-be-careful hug. Casey apparently had other things on her mind. She just smiled, turned, and ran for her kitchen door. She left me standing there with a lopsided hopeful grin on my face. I wondered how I was going to borrow my dad's truck. More importantly, what was I going to do if I really did find something at the quarry?

I solved my first problem by simply borrowing Dad. The truck came with him. After I explained what Casey and I concluded and were planning, he enthusiastically put himself right in the middle of the equation. He volunteered himself as sidekick, transporter, and fellow investigator. I was more than happy my father wanted to back me up. It wasn't our job to hunt down and deal with these creatures. Still, fate had placed me squarely in the midst of this mess. Dad always taught me the best defense against any problem was a good offense.

I grabbed my bow, a full quiver of broadhead arrows, my hunting knife, and a pair of leg braces. I used the braces in my weekly rehabilitation workouts at the hospital. With them on, I could walk fairly decently, especially over uneven ground such as we would find at the quarry. Still, the steel ribs of the braces slightly pinched both legs' calves and ankles when I wore them. They were not comfortable. But this was no time for mistakes. Wheelchairs, crutches, or any other automated contraption would be so much meaningless ballast if we actually entered the Quarry Cave.

I gathered a few other things together, including a water bottle, two flashlights with a spare set of batteries for each, and my first aid kit. I put everything into a day pack. My father prepared himself in similar fashion. The difference was a .357 magnum pistol he chose for himself rather than a bow and arrow. It was the gun he always carried while hunting. Along with it were 20 rounds of hollow-point ammunition as backup. He also carried a short-barreled, side-by-side, 12-gauge shotgun he'd used in the Korean conflict. Some called it a street sweeper. I just referred to it as Sir and left it alone.

The shotgun was deadly at any distance up to 25 feet. After that, the shot separated too much for immediate killing. However, there was enough pellet concentration from 25–35 feet to maim, rip apart, or tear up almost anything in the way. I always felt I would have a better chance of facing a charging lion than that short-barreled shotgun carried in my dad's able hands.

I said a short "Goodbye! Keep the doors closed and the TV on" parting to Mom as I headed for the garage and Dad's truck. He came along behind. I heard the first growl just as I entered the dark garage from the sunny driveway apron. Temporarily blinded by the light contrast, I screamed and dropped to my stomach. I frantically rolled under the bed of Dad's truck. I sensed rather than saw something large, dark, and shaggy come at me from my left side. It was moving faster than I had imagined anything that big could. I felt my quiver ripped from my hands. I frantically tried to squeeze back against the truck's rear axle to avoid whatever it was that was scrambling to get to me. Everything was happening so fast. The screaming, growling, and grunts seemed so loud that I didn't even have the presence of mind to pull my knife out and defend myself. I later found out that most of the screaming came from me.

Fortunately, my father acted quickly. He pulled his .357 as the beast came into the sunlight. As the creature came after me, it slid sideways past the end of the truck while its claws fought to gain a purchase on the sealed concrete floor. I had ducked and rolled backward, pressing myself flat against the concrete. I frantically tried to avoid the creature's reach. That gave Dad time to put at least three slugs into the beast's back. It quickly ignored me and turned swiftly toward my father. It snarled and growled as it came to its full height. It gathered itself for its leap at Dad, but it never left the ground,

It suddenly collapsed in front of my father. Its back was a bloody froth. One clawed paw came to rest on Dad's shoe. My father backed away immediately and leveled the short-barreled shotgun at the creature. His finger tightened on the trigger as the Werewolf turned his way. Both stared at the other. The beast drooled blood and mucus from its muzzle as it started to push itself erect. We could not understand how it was still alive.

My father backed up even faster and caught his heel on the raised edge of one of the driveway's concrete panels. He tumbled over backward. His fall made the shotgun barrels point skyward. Then he managed to discharge both barrels as its butt and his head slammed into the ground. Groggy, he sat up with both hands on the ground behind him. He tried to clear his head as he looked to see where the shotgun had fallen. The beast had gained some footing by this time. It crawled relentlessly toward Dad. Its arm was extended, and its eyes were wild with bloodlust. I was already rolling out from under the truck bed when my father tripped and fell. I had no time to string my bow and loose an arrow. I grabbed the hunting knife from my side and launched myself at the beast's back. I swung my knife at its neck as I flew through the air. I missed its head and shoulders entirely. I fell about two feet short.

The knife swing intended for the back of the creature's neck sliced its right leg's hamstring instead. It also severed muscle as it buried itself in the Werewolf's hindquarter. Enraged and now partially crippled, the creature swung clumsily about and dove for me. I'm not sure who was yelling the loudest at that point, me from fright or the creature from the victory it sensed it had in its paws. It seized my right leg and, opening its maw, bit down with every bit of strength it had, trying to sever my leg from my body. The slam of its teeth against the steel ribs of my leg brace and the crackling snap of its teeth being broken off were nothing compared to the screams and growls of rage and pain it registered in utter frustration. The Werewolf's painful attempt to dismember me had utterly failed.

The matter was finally settled when Dad slammed one of my mother's large, decorative, ceramic garden pots against the back of the Werewolf's head. He watched both break into pieces, the potsherds falling to one side of the downed creature and several pieces of the Werewolf's bloody bone and jagged skin slices falling on the other. Quickly reloading his side-by-side shotgun, my father fired both barrels into the creature's head. The shot separated the creature's head from its body and shredded most of the head's remaining flesh and bone.

Breathing hard, Dad and I just sat on the ground on either side of the creature. We both gasped for breath. We were stunned at the suddenness and sheer ferocity of the beast's attack. All the while, we wondered how we managed to somehow survive its charge, much less kill it. We both felt sick to our stomachs.

After a few minutes, Mom, Casey, and Casey's folks all crept quietly onto the garage apron. They all stared at the abomination we had managed to kill. Mom and Casey's mother began to cry. Each turned to their husbands and held them tightly, horrified at what had transpired. They were terrified at the creature's appearance. Casey looked at me with eyes that seemed as big and round as silver dollars. She did not easily accept but could not deny what she had just seen. She now knew the creatures I had described to her just moments earlier were as real as the driveway beneath her feet. Trembling and shocked, she came softly to me. She nestled against me as my arms enveloped her. She turned her face into my chest trying to avoid the sight and smell of the beast at our feet. She held me tightly and sobbed quietly.

The beast was a buckskin-colored female.

My dad eventually took control of the situation. He marched everyone into our den. Any explanations, recriminations, and expectations were all tossed about until all agreed on the menace. We also agreed on a plan of action. The one change in our marching orders was that Casey's dad would accompany her instead of her friends. Casey's mom also accepted her husband's request that she would stay with my mother in our locked house until we all returned.

We figured the female had tracked the scent of the male and young male I had killed that morning. She was probably exploring the garage's shadowed interior looking for her companions when I unexpectedly walked in. We surmised that the female had assumed her companions were dead. She likely wanted to return the favor and hence the attack on me. Her attack would have succeeded had my father not followed me outside when he did.

Our grandfather clock struck 12:00 noon as we all stood up to follow our plan. Three Werewolves were down, and the day was only half-over. I did not want any more encounters. All I wanted was to make a report to the authorities and stay in my room or with Casey until our town officials successfully dealt with the situation.

But then, as I've learned over time, we don't always get what we want.

DAY ONE 1:30 P.M.

The first clue that something was radically wrong in our neighborhood was the absence of animals anywhere near our property. Usually there were creatures of all sorts rummaging about, my Baker Street Irregulars, according to Sherlock Holmes. We suffered everything from mice to owls whose thoughts usually gave me a *Reader's Digest* condensed version of what was happening in an eight-block area. Today, those reporters were silent. Not a bird, mouse, nor snake could be seen or was within reach of my thoughts. Not a dog nor cat was out and about sniffing or sunning itself or on the hunt, as it were. Had I heeded the stillness earlier when my dad and I first returned from City Hall, I might not have been so surprised by the Werewolf's abrupt attack in our garage.

Of course, just holding Casey would make walking over stickers seem wonderful. She usually banished most of the lucid thoughts from my mind. So I forgave myself for my initial lack of vigilance and found myself concentrating on not concentrating on her. The appearance of three Werewolves in one morning was a major prompt for me to shift my focus elsewhere.

The female Werewolf's presence had apparently scared away any early warning line the neighborhood animals represented. I felt frustrated that I couldn't bring my gatekeeper talents to bear just when they seemed to be needed most. Nevertheless, assuring ourselves that the ladies were safely locked away in our house, Dad and I and Casey and her father bid our goodbyes. We left in different directions, they for the Barn Well and Dad and I for the Quarry Cave. We still planned to keep the 3:00 p.m. rendezvous. We realized we'd have to hustle to keep that deadline. Fortunately, my father liked to speed. That turned out to be a good thing.

By 12:30 p.m., we had parked Dad's truck at a spot near one of the main quarry entrances. A five-minute hike brought us to the screened mouth of the Quarry Cave itself. We had our first real look at the barrier fencing that had been torn away at one side. To our mutual surprise, it wasn't simply separated from the cave lip from age and weather (even aided by teenagers) as we had imagined. The screen looked as if it had been torn from the rock on two sides and then folded back on itself. Only the top and left sides of the screen were still actually attached to the rock face. Instead of squeezing in under the fencing as we had supposed we would have to do, we could stroll right in, upright. Alarms were going off in both our heads at this discovery. I strung my bow and nocked an arrow before we entered. Dad cocked both barrels of his street sweeper and stepped into the lead position. I motioned Dad to wait a moment as I cast my eyes and thoughts all around us. I hoped to pick up a sighting or sensing of some animal in the immediate area. I wanted one that could tell us something, anything, about who or what had been using this portal. I got nothing. That alone was a bit scary. Forewarned, we stepped into the cave's mouth. We headed down a gradual slope into darkness. Dad used his left hand to hold his flashlight. I simply turned on my headlamp. It was familiar equipment that I'd used for several years whenever I went camping.

Our beams cut bright swaths through the cave's darkness, sometimes crossing paths and sometimes illuminating opposite sides of the cave as we carefully made our way into its bowels. We moved slowly as we listened for any noise other than our own breathing or footsteps. It was almost tomb silent for the first 80 or 90 yards as we wound around several corners. We finally came to the first drop-off. Dad suggested we sit for a minute and turn off our lamps so we could just listen. It was a sensible albeit scary suggestion.

Almost a minute passed before we heard the first sound that neither of us was making. It was a faint rustling, like cloth passing over a bush. It was hard to make out a clear rhythm as the sound seemed to come and go. And then it seemed as if the sound doubled, not in volume so much as in magnitude. I sensed that the author of the first sound had been joined by a second or even third entity. My father's hand clamped around my arm as the sounds appeared to grow closer. I could feel Dad's breath as he leaned close to my ear. He told me to turn on my light and look to the noise as he counted to three. His whisper wasn't what scared me. What scared me was that I realized the sound was coming from behind us, from the now hidden entrance to the cave. When he said "three," we both yelled, and two lights lit up the passageway behind us. They were like searchlights frantically looking for enemy aircraft in the Battle of Britain. Three sets of eyes immediately popped out at us. I was already drawing back my arrow when I realized the eyes belonged to a family of raccoons hopping over the rocks. They'd been following the scent trail we'd left on our way in.

Both my father and I made the mistake of looking at each other with sheepish grins when I realized my headlamp had temporarily blinded him. Fortunately, his flashlight was still pointing in the direction of the raccoons, which, when I looked back, were desperately scrambling back along the passageway to the cave's entrance. I started to laugh until I listened to what they were telling each other.

"Hairy man creatures that tears! Hairy man creatures is near!" they squealed at each other as they scrambled ineloquently away from us. My first thought was one of offense. We didn't tear animals. We weren't savage. And then it hit me almost too late. We weren't the "hairy man creatures that tears" they were frightened of. They were the Werewolves, and more than one must be near.

I had barely enough time to shout a warning to my dad. As I did so, two large shapes seemed to materialize from the deep shadows that draped the passageway walls in front of us. Momentarily blinded by the light from our lamps, the shapes paused. They sniffed in our direction, trying to shield their eyes. Having located us, both crouched abruptly to spring at us. My dad fired both barrels of his sawed-off street sweeper as they moved.

The Werewolf closest to my dad separated. Just separated. Its top half tore away and smeared against the passageway wall. Its bottom half collapsed to the floor. Blood, body fluids, and whatever else comprises a Were spurted and flowed freely. The second Werewolf wasn't so lucky. Its left arm, shoulder, and left side of its head peeled back, partially shredded. Its arm fell limply to its side as the echoes of that double blast assaulted our ears for what seemed like minutes.

The second Were was growling and screaming an awful wailing sound as it turned its shoulder and head trying to look at its damaged left side. Snapping its head back around, it staggered, erect. It prepared once again to leap at my dad. It never made it out of its crouch. My first arrow took it through the right shoulder and my second through its sternum. In poor lighting and especially if a target moves after sustaining a serious wound, always aim for an animal's largest body part that you can still see.

Immobilized, choking on its own blood, the beast lay crumpled against the wall where it fell. One baleful eye was rooted on us. We watched its legs and shoulder occasionally twitch as it rapidly bled out. My dad was the first to get to it. Dad knelt down just outside the reach of the shredded stub of the Werewolf's left arm. He then peered closely into the Were's undamaged eye. The Were's mouth and sharp nose bubbled and ran with fluids as it tried to snarl something. The sound was unintelligible. However, its thoughts were manifestly clear to me as I approached and knelt close to it in the few moments left before it died. "This cave is unsafe. Polluted by humans. Not like the other cave. I must tell the Pack!" Then its mind blanked out as its breathing stopped. Its stench began to encompass us within seconds. My head hurt.

DAY ONE 12:55 P.M.

I managed to get Dad moving back to the entrance as our heads and thoughts cleared. He was stunned by his experience just as I had been early that morning with my first kills. Reality seemed far away from him for a while, yet he was coherent and moving on his own terms by the time we exited the cave. I told him of my impressions of the second Were's thoughts just before it died. We reached the same conclusion at almost the same time, each turning to the other and shouting, "The barn well!" We were running for his truck before we finished each other's sentence. Well, Dad was running. I'm not sure what you'd have called my style. I was somewhere between hitching, flopping, and a controlled lurch. But I made good time.

We were afraid the two Weres we'd killed must have discovered a link between the Barn Well Cave and the Quarry Cave. Apparently, our kills were scouts sent out to reconnoiter and report back. The main pack, whatever was left of it, was most likely nesting at the barn cave. But who knew how many Werewolves comprised a pack? All we could think of was Casey and her father climbing into the barn's interior and being shredded and eaten alive by Werewolves.

We hit Dad's truck at a dead run. Dad leaped for the inside, ground the starter, and slammed the gears as I clambered over the tailgate and flopped into the back. In seconds, we were nothing but a quarry cave's fading memory. We left with four wheels churning and the truck fishtailing all over the gravel road until we hit highway pavement. Dad did not spare the horses as he flew through town. His speedometer jumped around like a monkey after a jalapeño enema. My father drove as if he were possessed by a NASCAR ghost. We don't have many traffic lights in our town, but he ran most of them. He also ran off a number of cars that thought driving in an orderly fashion in one's own lane was a guarantee of safety. Me? I hung on to the truck bed rail as tightly as I could, trying to look through the cab's window or occasionally trying to gain my feet and look over the truck cab.

Our speed and the force of the wind in my face brought tears to my eyes every time I stuck my head up. Soon, I gave up trying to see where we were going. I contented myself with a huddle against the truck's back sideboard as I desperately prayed for deliverance. When I thought God had had an earful and it was time for some new material in my personal prayer-a-thon, I would sneak a quick look through the cab window once again to see if we were anywhere close to those Pearly Gates, the ones I'd so often heard about in Sunday school. It was just our luck that not one cop saw us or much less gave chase as Dad rocketed down the highway. And here, all along, I'd never thought of our town so big that a grand prix driving effort wouldn't automatically bring out every officer on city and county payrolls.

I soon realized we had cleared the town limits. We were rapidly approaching the field where the barn stood out in stark relief well ahead of us. My dad didn't pause to look for a fence gate much less stop to open one as our truck raced ahead. We hit the fence's barbed wire strands at full speed. We must have been going somewhere between 80 and 90 miles per hour. Heck, maybe it was 140 miles per hour. I couldn't tell. I was fully occupied hanging on to the truck bed railing as tightly as I could squeeze my fingers, yelling in terror as loud as I could.

I hoped Dad would hear my cries and slow down before we smashed into a field depression or were bounced to smithereens. As our truck plowed through, it chopped off the fence post in front of us at its base. The strands of wire holding it to the other posts acted like a giant rubber band. They stretched with the truck as post after post was uprooted from the ground by the force of our mad dash. The wire strands finally snapped. The barbed wire was jerked back, its flaying strands forming almost invisible scythes. They cut through everything in their path until their tension-fueled thrashing finally halted. The flailing fence wires had effectively cleared a wide swath through the overgrown field behind us.

Dad had been blaring the horn since we hit the field but had stopped as the truck came to a bouncing, skidding, slamming stop against the side of the old barn. I watched in shocked silence as the structure's entire side quivered and then quieted down. Only a few boards popped loose. Some siding peeled off.

When the rocking stopped, I was out of the truck bed like liquid smoke. I lurched for the barn's old door. I had nocked an arrow before the truck stopped hissing and vibrating. I was so glad to be alive. I wanted to kiss someone and just hold on tight. I was hoping I'd find Casey just beyond the old barn's closed door, but I was so happy to be on solid ground again that I'd have settled for a halfway decent Werewolf kiss if the occasion presented.

But she wasn't, and it didn't.

What I did hear once inside, however, was her voice calling my name. It seemed so far away. I practically launched myself into the old well in the barn's interior. Her voice seemed to get fainter then, and I started throwing rocks over my head, behind me, and in any direction I could. I desperately sought a clear way down into the well's cave-like opening. I knew it must be somewhere below me. Calling her name over and over, I moved several hundred pounds of stone before her voice came clearly down to me. "Cody, stop! Stop! Cody, stop! Please stop!"

Down to me? Down to me! The realization that her voice was coming down to me finally sunk in. I whirled and looked up. Standing there were my father, Casey, and Casey's dad. They all looked at me with something of an astonished grin on their faces. Suddenly, the stone in my hand seemed awfully heavy, and I practically dropped it on my foot as it slipped through my tired fingers. I was stunned. Where had they come from? Why were they up on the floor of the barn while I was down in the well searching for the entrance to the Weres' lair? Where had they been trapped?

So many questions, but the answers suddenly didn't seem so important anymore. Casey was up there with our fathers. She was safe and sound. My world came crashing back into focus. I climbed slowly out of the well. Casey met me with a hug, and this time it wasn't that nurture nonsense. The old gloomy barn above us notwithstanding, it was an all-things-bright-and-beautiful moment.

Okay. Moments.

Once outside, we leaned against Casey's dad's car and heard the rest of the story. Upon our departure from home while Dad and I were speeding to the Quarry Cave,

Casey's dad had calmly driven to a hardware store. He wanted to pick up a couple of flashlights and some vials of sulfuric acid. He had no weapon and thought that acid would work on any creature that got too close to them. Wanting to buy time to run away if need be, he gave one vial to Casey and put the second into his own pocket. As they pulled away to drive to the barn well property, he decided he might want to keep an even greater distance between them and any foul creature should they encounter any Werewolves. They returned to the store to purchase a long-handled pitchfork. It was one Casey's dad could carry in one hand while using the other to hold his new flashlight. They were only a quarter mile away from the field when my dad, intent only on reaching the field and barn, oblivious to all traffic around him, blew by them as if they were in reverse.

Astonished, they followed at a safe distance and watched him plow through the barbed wire fence and eventually collide with the barn. By following Dad's twin furrows onto the property, they were clear of the slicing wire that had snapped backward and now lay tangled in the brush around them. They then saw me leap from the bed of the truck and stagger around the corner of the barn as they pulled up to Dad's truck. Reuniting with him, they ran into the barn to cover me, expecting that there would be Werewolves inside. Casey was continually shouting my name. We shared our experiences and fears and received affirming handshakes and hugs once again from each of them.

As we sat and talked, each watching over another's shoulder lest we become too complacent and be surprised by the pack, I glimpsed a red-breasted nuthatch perched on the edge of its nest. It was high up in the bole of a stand-alone ash tree shading the south side of the barn. I walked over to the tree's base to study and listen to the nuthatch's whistling and chirping. At the same time, a pair of barn swallows came flitting back over the field to the west of the barn and, ducking under the sagging roof, slipped one after the other into the cavernous structure. I knew then we were on a false trail. Nothing I felt or sensed from the birds was out of the ordinary except a rather scathing critique of my dad's pell-mell driving from the disturbed nuthatch.

The Werewolves were not here. Our hypothesis had been wrong. The other entrance to the Quarry Cave was not here. That left only one other possibility in a 20-square-mile area—the Dead Zone. It was the worst of all possible places for us because of its remoteness and the tangled terrain that surrounded it. If the creatures were there, all I could see ahead was a dangerous and nasty encounter with a species as stubborn and deadly as ours. But we would have to take the fight to them on their terrain anyway. We were in a conundrum. We were seeking an enemy we couldn't really talk about and an encounter we didn't want on ground we didn't know.

Where was Superman when you needed him or, for that matter, the 101st Airborne Division and the 7th Cavalry combined? The job of eliminating the Weres had suddenly outgrown our small group. We needed more help than we could marshal. We needed it sooner than we'd hoped, like yesterday. But how do you ask for guns, bombs, and bullets to fight a nightmare? That was the trick. We just didn't have an answer. Not yet, anyway, but I assumed eventually we would. And we did.

DAY ONE 2:45 P.M.

We drove back to our house. There we changed vehicles and picked up our mothers. Then we waited outside the Police Chief's office for a break in the confusion that spilled into the hallways of our small City Hall. My mom overheard the first dispatch report of a mauling on Benton Road Terrace. A squad car was on the scene of a crashed car with a dead man sprawled across the front seat. A presumed passenger was missing. In the words of the officer on site, the driver "looked like he'd been pulled through a cheese grater." As Mom relayed to our small group what she'd heard, several reporters and city council members who had been standing just outside the Chief's office turned to listen. They immediately began peppering her with questions.

Mom simply shrugged and pointed to the dispatch desk that was several desks away in an adjoining room. The mini-crowd fought each other for access as they hurried through the door into the room. That left our group momentarily alone for a moment. As we pondered what Mom had said, Dad suddenly looked up and asked where Benton Road Terrace was. Casey responded that it was on the town's far west side, a side road off the Chagrin River Road reaching up into the steep hills dotted by high-end houses. She remembered that she'd once driven through the area in her driver's education class. She had gone slowly to admire the houses and the beautiful lawns and gardens that framed them.

When Casey said "west side," my dad, Casey, and I all looked at each other. The Dead Zone was only a few miles from there. That only underscored the inference that the abandoned lumber mill was the probable home base for the Werewolves. Eventually we got in to see the Police Chief. He was decidedly unhappy we were there. I think he saw us as the source of his growing troubles, which seemed a highly unreasonable supposition to me.

Nevertheless, we told him of our respective excursions and what we had and hadn't found. He dispatched an ambulance and squad car to the Quarry Cave to pick up the two bodies. He gave repeated instructions to the EMTs and accompanying officer not to say or show anything to any interested bystanders. He made his point with some of the most interesting and colorful language I'd heard up to that moment in my life. My dad promptly made me promise never to repeat the Chief's words on pain of having my skin peeled back by a deranged witch doctor while standing in boiling water up to my waist.

I told Dad he'd made his point and then some. Truth was, Casey, our moms, Casey's dad, and I were all blushing when the Chief ended his mini-tirade. The Chief was once a naval petty officer with plenty of sea service. I surmised there probably wasn't much to do on a long sea voyage but practice one's vocabulary. Apparently, the Chief took that to heart. He had certainly mastered a command of unusual phrases and then some!

By the time we left the Chief's office, we were all in agreement. He and his local police force, the county sheriff, his deputies, and a small contingent of state troopers would assemble early the next morning for a search and sweep of the old lumber yard and adjacent mill. All would be armed and expecting a keen resistance. Black bears are not uncommon in Ohio, and reports of a rabid bear would be the public excuse for going in armed. Casey and I, along with our parents, were asked not to be anywhere near the Dead Zone for this operation. The Chief promised he would call us when the small army of peace officers returned. Presumably, we'd hear something by early afternoon that same day. With that and a promise he'd send an ambulance over for the Were carcass by our garage, he showed us out. We drove home in silence.

Our parents chatted on the driveway a minute before turning to their respective homes. Casey and I stood alone, rehashing what had happened to us since I'd shot the first Werewolf. It was hard to get the turn of events out of our minds. As a teenager, it's hard to get your mind around anything that doesn't taste like ice cream or look fabulous in a pair of jeans.

That said, I pointed out to Casey that without some sense of what lay in wait at the old lumber yard, the Chief and all his troops would likely be ambushed, perhaps badly hurt or killed. I knew firsthand just how quick and dangerous these creatures really were. I had experienced the immediate fear that seized a person the first time their eyes truly beheld one of these monsters.

Tangled wood or clearing, either one, it made no difference. Anyone expecting a black bear who suddenly confronts a Werewolf instead will lose life or limb if not both when the creature unleashes havoc in a matter of seconds. I decided then that I would do a reconnaissance tonight when everyone had gone to bed. Casey immediately objected in a rising voice. I quickly pulled her to me and quietly whispered in her ear that I wouldn't go in there myself. I had feathered and furred friends who could and might if I asked nicely. If not, and only if not, I would go in partway. She seemed mollified by that. She immediately shut up. What she didn't do was break my embrace, at least not for a long minute or two. I got the message. Loosening my hold, I gently let go and stepped back. I told her I would not risk something that would permanently take me out of her life. She looked at me quizzically for a moment. Then, with a flash smile and a quick peck on my nose, she disappeared into her house.

I was relieved. Uncrossing the fingers on my right hand, I turned and went into my house.

DAY ONE 10:00 P.M.

It had been dark for almost three hours when I pinned a note to my pillow and slipped out of the house through the den. The ambulance that had come for the carcass was long gone. I could hear Dad's distant snores through the walls when I left. I knew that Mom would be asleep beside him, open book on her chest with her reading glasses askew on her nose.

I'd worn my leg braces for most of the day. As much as they hurt and pinched, I put them back on for my excursion. No way was I going into any hills and underbrush without them. Pushing my dad's truck out into the street, I quietly jumped in and started it up. I drove to the end of our block before I stopped at the corner and turned on the headlights. As soon as I did, I was almost startled out of my skin by a hammering on top of the cab. Looking quickly behind me through the rearview mirror was one of my more courageous moves. My jaw dropped when I saw Casey's grin and her shaking finger wagging no-no. She'd been waiting for me the whole time in the bushes at the front of her house. She had climbed into the back bed of the truck when I climbed into the cab. She knew I could neither hear nor see her there.

She was not all that happy with me but climbed into the cab anyway and slid over next to me. I sat there like an idiot, mentally kicking myself for again underestimating this wonderful young woman. She reminded me once again that it was *our* problem, not mine. That said, she promptly laid out the course of action she thought we should take for tonight's expedition. It wasn't a bad plan, but it wasn't the best we could do together.

Her plan didn't allow for reconnaissance at a distance. Her plan had us going to the old lumber yard and mill in person, by ourselves. My plan had animal friends making that trek while I waited on the nearest road for their return. My plan won.

All we had to do now was drive to a spot not too far away, find some furry friends, and convince them to be our eyes and ears. We would then sit tight and await their triumphant return and report. Easier said than done, as we found out. We did finally find an owl. I convinced him to be our reconnoitering surrogate. It wasn't all that hard. He saw the meat-eating Werewolves as competitors. The Weres ate whatever they came across, including prey in the owl's food chain. The Weres then scared everything else away.

What was hard was getting the owl to help us find some wood mice who could go into places the owl couldn't. The owl finally understood what we wanted and why we were asking this of him. He agreed to help. He demanded a concession in return. I mean, who knew owls were so filled with avarice? C'mon now, a raw steak in place of a few measly mice? But the bargain was made nonetheless.

At once, the mice gave us directions. They would take us to the nearest mice den. The owl flew off into the night, an absolutely silent shadow with natural night vision and more dangerous in his own way than a black-clad ninja. We would see him again after an hour or so as he flew in and around the old lumber mill. He would be watching and smelling for traces of the creatures. An owl makes no noise when flying. It is a miracle of their feathers. Any prey in their way gets no warning of a strike. Their talons are fiercely sharp and incredibly strong for any small animal. An owl is truly an angel of death, just the sort of folk we needed at the moment.

Getting the field mice to agree to put themselves in harm's way was far more difficult, but they eventually agreed as well. They had recently birthed a small litter and were loath to leave it. Ground snakes and the occasional fox were around, so I agreed that Casey and I would babysit the nest until their return.

They waited to leave until I returned from my dad's truck with my bow, arrows, and backpack. They then quietly set off to the old mill. They knew that something lurked there from the disappearance of relatives and other mice who'd tried to nest at or by the mill. They didn't know just what manner of creature lived there except that the mill smelled horrible, as if a pack of dogs who slept and washed in sewers had taken up residence there. I told Casey what the mice had said. I noticed that she quietly sidled over closer to me as we waited.

DAY ONE 11:50 P.M.

Casey and I were dozing back-to-back when we both heard the owl's first screech. It sounded like sharp fingernails on a blackboard and simply tore the night's silence apart. I was up on one knee in seconds, bow raised with arrow fully cocked. My head was turning frantically this way and that trying to see through the blanketing night gloom for a kill shot when the owl's second screech rattled our ears. His first call was a danger call. It was a call to alert all living creatures within range that a killing animal was chasing him.

His second, later screech was of a different tone and timbre. It was a taunting cry that mocked whatever had tried to catch and kill him. The owl trumpeted his own superiority and the glory of flight as he soared up into the night and into the realm he controlled. I immediately loosened my pull but held the arrow against the bow's bridge with my left index finger while I stood up to ease the tension in my body. I could feel Casey behind me doing the same thing. She stood and stretched. Getting the owl's report should prove interesting, I thought. I didn't know what Casey thought. She rarely volunteered information.

Minutes later, without a sound except a muted swoosh, the owl landed at our feet. We had a chance to finally learn something that might be helpful for tomorrow morning's expedition. The debriefing was quick. There were at least seven adults and three young Werewolves spotted, feeding by the side of one of the mill's old sawdust and shavings piles. The owl had seen no other movements or indication of any other such creatures in the hour he had circled the immediate area or perched nearby.

He'd flown to the sawdust pile to see if there were any meal leavings after he thought the last Werewolf had disappeared into the mill. He'd been surprised by one of the youngsters who had been chasing a small mouse that burrowed into the sawdust pile before the Werewolf could capture him. Seeing the owl, the creature lunged instinctively at him. The owl was quicker, and having gained flight decided to taunt the whelp Were and then return to us and report it. Besides, the Were's flesh smelled too much like human flesh. That was something no self-respecting owl would ever eat unless he was starving. With that, the owl leaped up and circled into the darkness. He reminded me of my steak promise as he disappeared back into the gloomy night.

Casey took her place again by the mice nests. She looked up at me with a questioning look in her eye. It was getting late. We'd gained some valuable information. Staying there much longer would probably push our luck.

"Let's give it fifteen minutes," I said. I was sure the mice would return momentarily, and we had promised, after all, to guard their little ones until the parents came back. Casey muttered something like "Great!" and then hunched over her knees and closed her eyes. I was tempted to join her. It had been one long day, and tomorrow's dawn would be with us all too soon.

Despite my best efforts, I was starting to nod off when I heard the soft rustling of quick little feet and soft fur climbing over rocks and logs. Quickly, I nudged Casey, bringing her to immediate attention. With four eyes straining to see what would emerge from the darkness, we waited at the ready. Both of us gave an audible sigh of relief when we saw the mice highlighted in the moon's rays and scurrying up to us. Their report was short and complete. They had the same count of Werewolves as the owl had observed with the same breakout, seven adults and three youngsters. One difference, however. The sleeping nests inside the mill appeared to hold many more. Thanking the mice, we picked up our things and started back toward the truck. We were conscious of how tired we were and how good it would feel to crawl into our respective beds.

But it was a feeling we would have to postpone. I heard a muffled thump in the general direction and location of the truck. It could have been anything, but the sound shouldn't have been there at all. With Werewolves about, Casey and I both froze in place. After a short moment and hearing nothing, I motioned for Casey to sink down ever so slowly in order to reduce her silhouette. I handed her my dad's truck keys.

I began stepping quietly away from her. I was trying to put as much distance between us as the undergrowth allowed. My strategy was simple. If it was a Were we had heard, I wanted it to come after me. I wanted to be well clear of Casey if it did. I wanted no distractions if it came to a fight. Should there be mayhem, it was important that one of us get back to City Hall with information to rescue the other or better protect the law enforcement officers scheduled for the coming morning's raid. Casey knew what to do.

I got my wish. I had moved about 30 yards away from Casey before I deliberately stumbled over a small log. I gave a yell and then screamed for Casey to count to 30 and then run to the truck. I figured Werewolves didn't speak English and all they would hear was a man screaming. I was wrong, but this time it didn't matter. I stopped screaming and listened again. Nothing moved. So I started hobbling back toward the mill. Then I heard two things that sent chills down my spine. I heard the sound of bushes being pushed aside and small sticks breaking. Something was coming at me from the direction of my truck. I also heard guttural growls and the beginnings of a howl from the direction of the mill.

It was trouble in stereo. I did the first and only thing that came to mind. I climbed a nearby tree. I didn't stop until I was at least 30 feet off the ground, primarily pulling myself up from limb to limb with my arms. I wished I could go up a couple hundred feet more. I had placed my bow over my neck and shoulder when I started the climb. Both the bow and the quiver snagged on a couple of branches on the way up. I spilled out several arrows but made it to a relatively safe place. I finally settled down in a tree fork two-thirds of the way to the top. Once seated, I tried to catch my breath and quiet my trembling hands.

Two good things happened when I finally regained control of myself and could start breathing deeply again. First, I found my weapons were still with me. Second, I saw the taillights of my dad's truck disappearing down the gravel road we'd come in. Casey had made it back to the truck. She was going for help. Great! All I had to do now was hang on for an hour or so and wait for the cavalry. I didn't count on Casey getting turned around on the back-county logging roads in the dark and losing her way for a bit. I should have. They could fool anyone.

It turned out to be a much longer wait than I'd anticipated. Things happen when you wait too long. Bad things.

DAY TWO 1:20 A.M.

I checked my wristwatch for the umpteenth time. I'd been up in the tree for more than an hour, and two adult Werewolves were standing silently at the base of the tree looking up at me. They made no noise; they just stared at me. They'd been down there for almost the entire time I'd been up in the tree. They silently watched me. Feeling cocky and somewhat safe, I'd taunted them when they first showed up. I showered a few branches down on them, but there had been no reaction other than their silent, sentinel stares. It was as if they were carved in stone. I was starting to worry.

Their presence was becoming unnerving. I couldn't seem to get comfortable squirming around in the tree fork. I didn't have a lot of room to maneuver. I kept asking myself where Casey and the rescue efforts were. I didn't get any answers.

By 2:20 a.m., I'd had it. Werewolves or no, I had to move and get out of that fork. My tailbone was so sore that I was constantly shifting. My taunts had degenerated eventually to grunts and finally whimpers. The two Werewolves hadn't moved in the more than two hours I'd been in the tree. They were still there, looking up at me without so much as a twitch or a lick of their lips—just a focused stare of implacable hatred. It was becoming unnerving. After all the excitement, I found myself with an increasing amount of discomfort from my bladder as well. "What next?" I thought and then realized I should never ask that question.

Apparently, with Werewolves there's always a "next," and it's never pleasant.

Coming from the direction of the mill was a series of soft grunts interspersed by the sound of something heavy being dropped or falling in almost rhythmic fashion, sounds that kept increasing in amplitude. It wasn't hard to figure that whatever was responsible for the sound was drawing nearer. Sure enough, it was much nearer, so close that from my relatively high vantage point I could make out what appeared to be the form of a very large Werewolf. I saw it was awkwardly holding something long and semi-pliable. As I looked more closely, the Were finally pulled up and dropped its bundle at the edge of the small clearing underneath my tree. I recoiled in sheer horror when I clearly saw the bundle. I turned my head away and vomited the meager contents of my stomach.

If the very appearance of a Werewolf inspired revulsion, then this semi-pliable bundle inspired more. It was a human. He was missing some body parts. I stared, fascinated but sick at what tried to stand on wavering legs below me. I was dumbfounded that the human could still even move. His left arm was missing from the elbow down, and the stump was wrapped in bloody rags. One eye socket appeared to be empty. Part of his cheek, neck, and left foot and shoe had been ripped apart. Blood stained his clothing. His left leg bowed inward. He whimpered softly and made mewling noises like a frightened, beaten cat. He stared about himself with a blank look of total incomprehension. His face muscles twitched, and he occasionally jerked his head to the side. He had once been a man but now was one in form only and pitiful at that. Whatever feelings of empathy I might have formerly harbored for these Werewolves had congealed into pure loathing.

The big Werewolf that had brought the man to the clearing below my tree then stepped forward. It bit into and tore off the man's right arm with its teeth, ignoring the man's screams as he fell to the ground, writhing and kicking until he bled to death. With the man's torn arm in its mouth, the big Werewolf stood with the others, merely looking up at me. It said nothing, only growling in muffled, steady rumbles. An echoing sound emanated from its nearby companions.

I carefully brought my bow forward, nocked an arrow, and leaning out, aimed for the large Werewolf's forehead. He was noisily gulping down the dead man's arm. Letting my breath out slowly, I lifted my fingers, released the arrow, and sat there in astonishment as the arrow cleanly missed its target. It buried itself in the creature's left eye socket instead. The Werewolf grunted, its jaws suddenly slack. Then it toppled snout forward onto the ground. It was stunned. By piercing the eye socket in a downward trajectory, the arrow had missed the creature's brain and merely blinded him in his left eye. But the pain was apparently immense if measured only by the sheer volume of the shrieking cries the creature let forth as it scrambled to and fro at the tree's base trying to claw the arrow out.

All it did was break off the part of the arrow's shaft protruding from its face. While it was still struggling, I put a second arrow through the back of its neck. This one pinned the creature to the ground. The big Werewolf's two companions simply stood straight, looking up at me. For whatever reason, they had not managed to put cause and effect together. I thought they looked at my bow and accompanying arrows as merely simple curiosities, not as devices able to bring a rain of death down on them. Happily, I proceeded to do just that.

Three arrows later, there were two more dead Werewolves sprawled out on the clearing. I dropped down from tree branch to tree branch as if each tree limb were on fire. At last I dropped to the ground. There I promptly collapsed, my legs numb from sitting so long in the narrow tree fork. My braces pinched tightly. They were a distraction I didn't need at that moment.

DAY TWO 3:00 A.M.

As I staggered back to my feet, I readied my bow and arrow once again. To my chagrin, I discovered I had only three arrows left in my quiver. Using my knife, I managed to pry out two of my arrows from the three Weres I killed. I wiped them on the grass and plunged them back into my quiver. Now I had five serviceable arrows. Better than three to be sure, but I still couldn't afford to miss.

A glance at my wristwatch told me it would be dawn in two or three hours and that I'd best clear the area if Casey had made it to police headquarters and the force was on the way. Those guys would come in wary. They would be packing all sorts of firepower, and I didn't want to end my life as swiss cheese because some officer shot first and identified his target afterward. It happens all too often in shootouts.

I started for the road when the owl unexpectedly returned and flew down beside me. He asked if I wanted any more information on the pack. After calming my nerves, I said yes. I felt my jaw drop when he told me that upon leaving Casey and me, he had flown back by the mill. There he'd come upon a second group of Weres numbering 20 to 22. They arrived at the mill from different directions. Four of them were young adults. The remainder appeared to be fully grown adults, males and females, about equally divided. The owl was up and off before I could ask any questions.

The owl's news was grim indeed. If the police force ever did make it here, there was going to be one big fight. The odds possibly but barely might be in our favor thanks mostly to the guns our side carried. But my objective was to get away from this area as soon as possible, hopefully unseen. I turned back toward the road and walked stiffly at first, then with increasing fluidity as my muscles warmed up. I made my way out of there as hastily as I could. I reached the road with no apparent alarm being raised. I started a fast walk away (well, fast for me). I initially followed the ruts Casey had made when departing in my dad's truck.

I had gone about half a mile when I heard distant howls behind me. Some were way off to my left side. The Werewolves had apparently discovered the kill site at the tree I'd climbed. They were voicing their anger. I knew it would be only a matter of time before they found me. I immediately started looking for a place to fort up or escape them.

The stretch of road I was on had plenty of tall trees on both sides, but all were separated by new growth. None of the nearby tree trunks were more than 9 to 10 feet high. Not high enough. Climbing a tree again wasn't my first or any choice then. What did look promising, though, was a sluiceway about 100 yards ahead that ran above and across the road I was on. It then ran down a hill to some unknown destination. It was built for the original loggers. Apparently no one had seen fit to remove it when the mill shut down so many years ago.

I didn't have the luxury to wonder why it was still standing or whether it would hold me. I only knew a pack of highly perturbed and disgruntled Werewolves would soon be after me. They would have every intention to use my chewed and splintered bones as satisfying toothpicks after a hearty meal of me. I hustled toward the sluiceway as fast as I could hobble. I glanced nervously over my shoulder again and again as I stumbled toward my objective. When I finally reached the sluiceway scaffolding, I threw my bow around my arm and neck. I grabbed a cross brace and began pulling myself up to the actual watercourse V on top. I was about eight feet off the ground when the first Werewolf burst from the surrounding forest cover and spotted me. It let out an outrageous howl as it dropped back to all fours and galloped toward me.

I climbed as I had never climbed before, tumbling over the sluiceway's top edge just as the Werewolf and two of its following friends came sliding to a halt beneath the cross brace I had used for my initial leverage. Shuddering so badly that I could hardly lift myself up and look over the edge, I nevertheless forced myself to do it. I had to know if the Werewolves could climb a human-made structure. I knew they couldn't climb a tree, but I wasn't trapped in a tree.

It took only seconds to realize they couldn't climb up to me. It took only a few seconds more to realize they could do worse. They could tear apart the foundations of the sluiceway with brute strength, and it and I would come tumbling down to them like manna from heaven. They had come to the same realization because they immediately set to tugging, pushing, and kicking at the old timbers. They were shaking the structure with their great strength. They tossed me about like a pebble in a tin can tied to an old truck as it bounced down a country road.

I found my perch indefensible. My capture seemed inevitable unless I changed jurisdictions in a hurry. So I did. Crawling, stumbling, staggering, and rolling with the swaying platform, I made my way down the slope of the sluice box as fast as I could possibly move. The wide V of the sluiceway's top and its 14-foot height kept me out of the Weres' immediate sight. I made good progress for 50 yards or so until the treetops and branches of the forest's old growth were thick enough to further shield me from their sight. I could then stand partly erect. I made better time.

In fact, I thought I was making a grand escape until the sound of crashing and a great shudder of the sluiceway told me the Werewolves had toppled the timber at the road where I'd first climbed onto the sluiceway. I knew Werewolves couldn't climb trees, but I also knew they could easily run up the collapsed lumber into the sluiceway's top and be after me within seconds.

Looking around frantically, I spotted a great tree with an outstretched limb capable of holding my weight. It was just a few yards farther down the sluiceway's slope. The false dawn's light was barely enough to give me a perspective and allow me to judge some distance, but it was all I had. Securing my pack and weapons, I hobbled as fast as I could and leaped from the sluiceway's lip to the branch, arms outstretched and desperate. I managed to grab the intended limb with my right hand and, flailing with my left, secure a purchase on a slightly higher adjoining limb before my body swung to a halt. Throwing my right leg over the lower branch, I got a sufficient platform to release the first branch. I then swung my right arm over the second, higher branch, bringing my legs up and clinging to it like a giant sloth until I could finally gain footing from adjacent limbs to clamber over and mount the higher branch. Then I just inched my way along it until I could duck under some foliage. I eventually reached the tree's broad trunk. I turned myself around to sit with my back to it. My legs were astraddle the branch that had been my temporary highway to safety.

I was breathing heavily, partly from the exertion, partly from fright. It was fear well founded. Within a few minutes, I could hear growls and scratching noises from the sluiceway as several of the Weres crept precariously down the sluiceway in pursuit of me. They were moving slowly in the early gloom but more surely than I had because of their night vision ability. The first Were had passed by unseen to me when suddenly there was a half cry, half howl from below me.

Several Werewolves were apparently on the forest floor keeping pace with the sluiceway creatures above them. One had stopped below my tree. I hoped it was by chance. I immediately held my breath and tried to imitate a tree vine. Several minutes passed (or was it hours) as grunts, whines, and growls were exchanged, and then both parties moved on. Slowly, carefully, I let my breath out and quietly gulped in as much air as my poor mouth would allow. I repeated this process several times until my breathing once again stabilized.

I'd made up my mind that I was going to stay right where I was until full daylight or until the police arrived. I knew where I didn't want to be was on the forest floor with angry Werewolves looking for me under every rock and in every crevice. I also knew that my close calls and exertions had made me sweat. That meant my spoor would be drifting all through the forest around me unless I could do something about it.

Having no shower or change of clothes in the tree with me, I did the next best thing. I broke off several small boughs, crushed the leaves, and smeared myself with the leaves and juices as much as possible. It wouldn't actually hide my scent, but the wood scent would mingle with mine and possibly confuse whatever was sniffing around for me. In life or death situations, misdirection is often as good if not better than outright deception.

DAY TWO 5:00 A.M.

It was déjà vu all over again.

Once again, I found myself perched high in a tree with Werewolves standing at the base looking up at me or at least in my general direction.

It had taken them some time to realize I was no longer on the sluiceway. Only one Werewolf had crept back along the way that several had gone down an hour or so earlier. A number more had stopped ranging the forest floor about a quarter mile away. They began casting about, sniffing the air, running to and fro trying to pick up my scent. I could occasionally glimpse them from my new, higher perch. My attempt to disguise my scent had thrown them off for a while, but as I continued to perspire, eventually tracking me down was a foregone conclusion. Still, the experience had bought me time, and the coming dawn was bringing daylight. Hopefully, some well-armed officers with a penchant for shooting first and asking questions later would show up soon. I fooled myself into believing that things were starting to look up.

In the interim, the Werewolves began gathering at the base of my tree one by one until seven were present. They were as silent as sentinels on a combat night watch. They were all standing upright trying to see me with muzzles turned skyward. Their nostrils were twitching. Seven creatures waited patiently to tear me apart, and I had only five arrows to dissuade them. That was bad math and a stupid stratagem. I certainly couldn't shoot my way to freedom. I then did the only outrageous thing I could do. I marked my territory.

That is to say I stood up, balanced on the two branches that comprised my new perch, unzipped my pants, and peed as long and forcefully as I could. I hit one and splattered two others before they all jumped back. It intensified the growling. Why shouldn't it? A canine peeing on another canine is the height of insult. It says to the victim, "I own you!" That was the message the Werewolves received. They couldn't have been more surprised than if I'd dropped a bomb in their midst. They certainly couldn't have been angrier.

One of the splattered ones seemed especially upset. It tried to climb the tree. Had I not been so scared, I would have laughed aloud at its attempts. When it finally gave up, both the Were and the tree were the worse for wear. The creature was growling and biting at its companions. Its anger had made the whole bunch uneasy. They all started milling around, gnashing at me and at one another. It was building up to a regular donnybrook when I heard the crunch of gravel above me as cars drove up to the downed sluiceway and stopped, brakes squealing. I heard the distant sound of car doors opening and looked down only to see the seven Werewolves disappearing one by one up the slope of the hill.

I had no whistle, and I was too far away for my shouting to be clearly heard. I had no visible way to warn the person or persons who had stepped out of the vehicles that the predators were in two places, not one, starting with the bunch that had surrounded my tree. Then I had an inspiration, the kind that never seems to come normally but occasionally shows up when all hope seems lost. I would use one of the creatures as my mouthpiece. In a matter of seconds, I leaned out from my shaky perch and drew a bead on the last Werewolf as it was about to turn and start back up to the sluiceway. My arrow took it through its lower right side just about where a kidney or liver ought to be if their physiology even remotely resembles ours. It must have. It went down immediately, arching its back and grasping for the arrow shaft.

It then let out a bloodcurdling howl of pain so loud that two of the Werewolves that immediately preceded him up the hill stopped in their tracks and turned back, probably as astonished as I was at the volume and hurt of the injured Werewolf's cry. Immediately, I heard faint shouting and then gunfire, lots of gunfire. I also heard sirens that came and stopped and always the sound of heavy rifle and handgun fire moving slowly up the road toward the old mill grounds. When the slight breeze died down, I heard another exercise of gunfire in the far distance. So the police had come to the abandoned mill on at least two sides, I thought. *Maybe they're not so inept as some folks believe*, I said to myself, and then lit up like a Christmas tree.

Hey! I thought. My part in this cabbage patch war is likely over. Things are starting to work out. I'd given the police the warning they didn't know they needed. I'd separated the Werewolf pack, dividing their strength just before an armed raid on them by true authorities (albeit by accident, not by plan). I'd killed my share of Werewolves and then some, and best of all, I'd saved my girlfriend from a horrible fate.

Even better, the screaming Werewolf with the pierced kidney at the bottom of my tree had finally stopped twisting, grunting, and squealing and had done the right thing. He died.

I was counting kisses, hugs, and accolades coming my way as I swung down through the tree branches when I suddenly arrested myself about 15 feet from the ground. *What am I doing?* I said to myself. The day is young yet and I have no idea whatsoever if the good guys are even holding their own in their rescue fight with the Weres. All I knew about the fight unfolding on the hill above me and at the mill was that a whole lot of lead was being expended. I had no idea of any Werewolf casualties. I didn't even know if these police officers could shoot straight enough to hit a barn. *Time for a reality check,* I mumbled to myself as I wearily started pulling myself back up into the tree. I was headed back to the perch I'd just abandoned.

It was good I had stopped my drop to freedom. I had gained only a few branches upward when the two Werewolves that had turned at their pack member's cry silently stepped out from concealment into the slight clearing at the tree's base. I tried to draw backward, closer to the tree's trunk, while balancing on two limbs so I could better see these adversaries. With no warning, they each sprang for the tree's base. The larger of the two Weres quickly knelt atop the tree's roots and held the trunk. The second Were scrambled up its back and, gathering itself, leaped upward toward me. It waved its upper arms in a windmill fashion hoping to hit and grab me or stick on a branch somewhere near me.

It was a wonderful performance and a grand leap of faith. It was one to be applauded and talked about for years to come whenever or wherever Werewolves congregate. However, I could not render the Were its just due at that moment. My hands were otherwise occupied. Holding my bow with an arrow fully pulled back, I loosed it at the peak of the Were's leap. The arrow took it through the left breast within inches of its sternum. My second arrow took it through the throat. It was dead before it cracked the first tree branch on its way down.

Its body fell onto its companion. Both went down together in a tangled heap. The larger creature finally managed to wrench itself away from its companion. Struggling to stand, it was too tempting a target. But it was also tough. I put it down with my last two arrows, one through its hip to cripple it and one through its neck when it turned to roar at me. It was fully enraged.

It was suddenly quiet all around me. It was one of those moments when you just know something momentous is about to happen or has already happened. All I could do was look at that last Werewolf and try to remember some ditty we children used to sing. I was also completely out of arrows. That wasn't so bad since I was also out of

Werewolves, but it was always better to be prepared. I climbed down to the ground, took out my knife, and managed to dig out two of my arrows.

Well, two's a start, I thought to myself. Having no reason to stay where I was, I popped them into my quiver and started climbing slowly up the hillside toward the old dirt road and the now-collapsed sluiceway. I was listening and watching for anything out of place along the way.

DAY TWO 6:15 A.M.

When I finally lurched onto the road, I found one scared deputy. He was holding a shotgun, guarding a number of empty cars and small vans. He was also standing over the body of one fully aerated Werewolf. The sluiceway had been torn down (almost torn apart). Its wreckage pretty much blocked the road so all the vehicles were on one side, the side opposite where I'd appeared. I called out to the deputy and made sure he knew I wasn't a Werewolf before I approached him. I sat down exhausted near him. I was grateful for the canteen of water he offered me. I'm afraid I drank most of it. Stress, strenuous physical activity, combat, and peeing on Werewolves will drain your body of moisture faster than most things I can think of. I was so dry I could hardly speak or move.

I used the time to rest for a moment and get my bearings, as well as to catch up on what had happened since the police contingent's arrival earlier that morning. In a word, plenty.

All the officers involved in the morning's operation had been sequestered at City Hall at about 4:00 a.m. and fully briefed on what was really happening, not the cover story of a rabid bear. They were told why they were gathered together and then given detailed instructions on how the morning's raid would go. Everything appeared to be going well in the raid's initial stages although the police had suffered several casualties among those in the raid's first wave. At least 12 to 14 dead Werewolves were already accounted for. The rest were presumed to be on the defensive or on the run.

It was the on-the-run presumption that worried me. The only time I'd ever seen or imagined Werewolves running was toward something they could eat or dismember. As to where they were running, the deputy had no idea. He only knew that if they came his way, he was to shoot as much of his ammunition as he could and then barricade himself in one of the police cars. He was to be prepared to fight from there as a last resort. He would not have to worry about blowing out the windows. The Werewolves would most assuredly take care of that small problem on their own as they tried to reach him and eat him.

I gave the deputy the total body count that our late-night reconnaissance had turned up. The original group was 10 and the latter group was 22, a part of which had chased me. I asked him to radio that to all the other members of the force who came out that morning to do battle. He did as I asked. I also explained that there were three of the latter group of Werewolves down by the tree I had used as my safety platform. It would be an easy spot to find. His relief only had to follow the sluiceway downhill and turn right at the base of the big tree with bodies lying around it. That would be the spot.

I also asked him if Casey, her dad, or my father had come along. He said the fathers had not but the Chief had asked the girl to come along. She was to show them the way she'd come out with her truck and where I had last been seen. The deputy believed she was still up the road with the Chief at the mill area from where all the firing was still coming from.

I perked up immediately. Casey anywhere near the Werewolves this morning was two states too close. The troopers might be brave and well equipped, but a Werewolf was big, mean, and treacherous. And fast. No telling what could happen if I wasn't there to guard her. The troopers would be worried more about themselves and not especially about Casey once they actually saw a Were. I had to get up there and find her, and I had to be there 20 minutes ago.

I knew it would take me some time in my current state to hobble back up the road I'd so hastily traveled the night before. I was tired and hungry and felt weak. But I just had to get up there. A feeling of dread had come over me when the deputy told me Casey was at the mill. The feeling was like an anchor around my neck. It weighed more and more each passing minute.

Looking at the remains of the sluiceway blocking the road, I began to see how a police car might just get through the roadblock. If the deputy and I could move only one or two main pieces of timber, he pushing by hand and me pushing with a car's bumper, we might make it. I quickly apprised him of my idea. He pondered a minute, walked around the debris pile for a short bit, and then returned to me with a positive nod. "Let's do it," he said. He gave me his keys.

A few minutes later, the car I was driving was gouged down one side. An outside mirror was ripped off on the other side. I'd taken the car through the debris' obstacle course. Once free, I accelerated toward the road's end by the mill. The firing sounded louder as I neared the spot where Casey and I had parked my dad's truck the night before. I slowed to a stop close to the tree I'd climbed for refuge. I needed arrows. I remembered that I'd dropped some in my hasty climb when the Werewolves were first closing in on me. I'd ignored them in the dark when I left, but they'd be visible now. I wanted them back.

I found them after a few minutes of poking around the grass and limbs that littered the area at the tree's base. Four of them were in good condition—four to add to the two I'd recovered from my last stand at the base of the second tree. With an arrow nocked,

I made for the mill where the firing was heaviest. I moved as fast as I could hobble. One advantage I had was that an archer doesn't look like a Werewolf. But I was new to this fight, and the police still wouldn't know me from Adam.

DAY TWO 8:15 A.M.

As I neared the mill, I began calling out Casey's name over and over again. I could see the police had formed a kind of skirmish line to the south side of the mill. They had trapped what appeared to be a bit more than several of the Werewolves in a small copse of trees. They were firing sporadically instead of continuously. They were not wasting bullets but killing each creature that made a break for the cover of the mill or tried to run over cleared ground to the nearby forest. The mangled bodies of two state troopers lay at the edge of the copse. They were mute testimony as to what happens to brave men who believe they can take on a Werewolf in regular hand-to-hand combat.

I was sure Casey had warned them all against just that sort of fighting when she briefed the Chief before this morning's raid. Nevertheless, some folks just learn by doing or, in this case, by not doing. Either way, I could not see Casey among those forming the skirmish line. I approached one of the officers while he was reloading. I asked where Casey might be. He gave me a grunting reply as he cocked his rifle. She was last seen with the Chief when he and two officers entered the mill. That had been a little while ago, and would I please move out of his way now, thank you, because he had some creatures to send back along the Hallelujah Trail.

With that, he turned to the trees and began a searching fire while I turned and scrambled back to the mill. It was a building of some size with not a lot of noise going on inside. In fact, there was almost none. I didn't know what that meant, but a chill ran down my spine. I knew firsthand that Werewolves don't howl when they eat and that guns don't fire when they're out of ammunition. And when guns are out of ammunition, Werewolves dine with vengeance.

"Casey!" I called out as I finally limped around the building's far end and approached the entrance. "Casey, are you in there?" I called again. And finally, "It's me, Casey. It's Cody!" I screamed it out as loud as I could while trying to catch my breath at the entrance doorway. Gulping some air and flattening myself against the outside open door, I peered into the dim, dusty interior. I listened for any reply. "Cody, we're in the back," came her faint response. That was before she was interrupted by a crash of guns in what sounded like a short but furious firefight. It was punctuated by screams, howls, and yells.

Once I heard Casey's voice, Genghis Khan and all the hordes of Asia could have been in that mill on the side of the Werewolves for all I cared. She was alive, and that was all that mattered. That she was in serious trouble was secondary. That is why I was there. I set about trying to fix the situation posthaste. I didn't go racing in through the entrance silhouetted against a bright sun so all could see me. I wasn't that stupid. Instead, I went in on a forward roll like I'd seen GIs do on TV shows. It was disorienting to be sure, but it made me a difficult target. It was also absolutely unnecessary when I remembered the Werewolves weren't firing guns.

As I rolled back onto my feet in a crouch, I saw five Werewolves loosely surrounding the entrance to a small office in the building's far corner. The firing was coming from inside the office. The shots had dropped off to almost nothing. The creatures must have sensed that the Chief's group was low on ammunition. They began grunting and growling as if communicating. They steadily advanced on the office door until all were tightly grouped to one side or the other. None stood directly in front of it. An occasional shot came through the splintered door. From the amount of light streaming through it, a number of shots had already passed that way.

One Were started howling in a pitch that raked across all my human sensibilities. It was like dragging broken glass shards down the side of your skull and then jamming them into your ear canal. It was a predecessor sound to what would later be called heavy metal rock. It must have been an action cry of some sort. The remainder of the Weres joined in. They all began simultaneously hammering at and kicking in the walls of the corner office. If it was pandemonium outside, it must have been sheer bedlam inside from the noise and impact tremors assaulting the office walls.

Feeling myself focus, I knelt down, grabbed my arrows from my quiver, and laid them out on the stone floor before me. All were within close reach. Six arrows, five Werewolves, I thought. Pretty even odds. Then I picked up the first arrow and began the slaughter.

My father had taught me that when attacking a column of any kind with bullets or arrows, always begin at the edges and work in. Soldiers or combatants always tend to lean toward or turn toward the middle of a column for psychological and physical strength. They are aware of what happens in the middle but don't pay all that much attention to what's happening at the ends of the column. So I started by putting my first arrow through the lower back of the Werewolf on the right end. It arched backward and tried to reach the protruding shaft before it pitched forward and fell against the outside of the corner office wall with an audible groan.

My second arrow was on the way before the first Werewolf had collapsed. This time, I aimed for the Were on the door's far left side. It went into its right hip and turned it around. Confused, it stood on shaky paws as it turned its muzzle down and tried to comprehend the shaft sticking out of its hide, unwittingly presenting a full torso view to me. I took advantage of its pose with my third arrow. It went into its neck center on, ripping through its spinal column on its way out. It dropped the Were in its tracks like a sack of wet cement. No sound passed its jaws as it folded.

I shot again at the remaining creature on the left side of the door. I drove an arrow through its right thigh, causing it to tumble sideways as it screamed and thrashed about. We could all see it was growing weaker by the minute from blood loss. I must have torn an artery. The remaining two Werewolves on my right turned toward me and immediately separated. They ran quickly around me until they were on opposite sides of me. There was nothing between me and the office door but inviting floor. They began to warily approach me. Each was erect and growling, paws and claws extended. I knew I could pick off either one but in doing so would probably fall to the other, so I made my choice.

Yelling "Open the door!" as loudly as I could, I jammed my arrows back into my quiver and ran toward the office door as fast as my hobble would let me. Both Werewolves broke at the same instant. Dropping to all fours, they leaped forward to the spot just in front of the perforated door where they wheeled to intercept me. I wasn't there.

In their frantic haste to cut me off, they failed to anticipate that I had stopped at the side of the crippled Werewolf. Grabbing the shaft of the arrow through its thigh, I jerked it out with all my strength. Then I rammed the broadhead arrow point home into the creature's throat to quiet and kill it. I then wheeled and put my fifth arrow through the eye socket of the first Were now leaping at me.

The Were's momentum knocked me over, and I lost my last arrow. It spilled out when I crashed to the floor. It slid well beyond any quick grasp. I quickly pushed the Were's body from me and started to stand when I looked up and discovered the eyes and maw of the last Werewolf now suddenly looming over me. Its claws were extended and eyes burning with demonic delight. I stopped moving. I remained in a kneeling position before the creature. I slowly grasped my bow in two hands as I lowered my head in a subservient bow. I could feel the hot breath of the Werewolf against my forehead, and the smell of its body scent was gagging me, but I remained immobile. I awaited his next move.

I was jerked back into awareness by Casey's scream as she flung open the splintered office door and saw me beneath the jaws of the creature that only minutes before had been trying to reach out and kill her and her companions. The Were's deep growls stopped the Chief and one other man as they piled into Casey in their haste to escape the office room. They saw and instantly comprehended the tableau unfolding before them. Their two guns were raised, and both men began firing at the creature as fast as they could pull their triggers. All that was heard was the rapid and repeated *click click click* of firing pins falling on empty chambers.

The Were cocked its head sideways at this and looked steadily at them from the corner of its great eye. With a grunt, it slowly opened its jaws as it prepared to turn and tear off my head. Casey screamed again and fainted, falling to the floor before the Chief and the other officer could grab and steady her. That was the distraction I'd been waiting for. I knew Casey would find some way to distract the Were. That split second of distraction as the creature momentarily paused and turned its eye back to Casey was my lifeline.

With all my strength, I stood up and drove the pointed end of my recurve bow through the soft under jaw of the Werewolf. Up it went through the cartilage, muscles, and tissue comprising its throat and then well into its cranial cavity. The bow tip was embedded well into the creature's foul brain. The Werewolf stiffened, arched upward, as it bent itself backward into an almost impossible angle and then choked as various brain and body fluids streamed back through its now slack mouth. With little more ceremony, it simply keeled over and died.

I put my foot against its neck and jerked my bow out of its distended jaw. I wiped it on the Werewolf's matted pelt and quickly hobbled over to Casey. Kneeling and gently picking her up in my arms, I cradled her head against mine. "Casey, Casey," I called out softly. "Casey, come awake now. It's all right. I'm here with you now." The look in her eyes as she slowly opened them and comprehended what had happened was a look I will take with me to my grave. She realized it was really me holding and whispering to her. She flung her arms around my neck and turned her face into my chest, crying and laughing at the same time. She hugged me tightly. We stayed that way seemingly for some minutes until the Chief cleared his throat. Putting a hand on my shoulder, he suggested that perhaps it was time to leave because the fight wasn't over yet. I reluctantly helped Casey stand up. I was smiling inside because those weren't nurture hugs I'd just received.

Pausing only a few minutes, I was able to reclaim two of the arrows I'd fired and the one that had rolled loose across the floor. Three arrows now. Better than two for sure. With that, we all walked as quickly as we could to the mill's entrance. I kept one of the three arrows nocked and held against my bow. The police might be out of ammunition, but I wasn't. Nor did I ever want to be with these creatures around. Not with Casey back with me.

DAY TWO 9:40 A.M.

The firefight I'd left when I rolled into the mill was still going on. The police had now formed a close half circle around the copse of trees. They were in a much better position to kill any of the last Werewolves that tried to flee across cleared ground to the surrounding forest. They were also able to better see into the copse for any of the creatures there trying to hide within its depths. It was turning out to be a good day for the humans after all.

The Chief asked how I'd managed to come on the scene and where I had been during the early stages of the firefight. I put him off for the moment before I answered. I did mention, however, that I'd driven one of their police cars to the tree where I'd been held up during the night. That immediately got the Chief's attention. He took my keys from me and sent an officer on the run back to the car. The trunk contained a whole host of alternate firearms as well as a good deal of ammunition for the service revolvers and shotguns the police already carried.

The Chief wanted those available to his men right now. Right now is what he got. Within 20 minutes, his officers were fully rearmed, and the Chief coordinated a walk-in attack on the copse of trees. He first stationed outlying officers on a clear line-of-sight perimeter outside the copse to pick off any of the Werewolves that would rather flee than fight.

I had explained to him my dad's experience in the Quarry Cave. I strongly recommended shotguns as the preferred attack weapon. There was a better chance that an errant shot from them wouldn't slaughter an officer and a real good chance that they would do just that against the Werewolves where the shots would be directed. He agreed. He picked up one for himself and gave the signal for his men to search and destroy, a tactic then being tried overseas in Vietnam. A group of eight officers then started into the copse with 12-gauge, pump-action shotguns. They fired in a narrow field of overlapping fire at anything that so much as quivered. The screams and howls were horrific. Several Werewolves tried to escape the rain of pellets and bolted for the nearby forest. The perimeter sharpshooters cut them down as they ran. One appeared to fall at the border of the forest, although no one was absolutely sure in the noise, smoke, and confusion.

It was over in 20 minutes. The smell of death, or rather dead Werewolves, was everywhere. I was grateful I had no role to play in the cleanup. Whoever was unlucky enough to be assigned that detail would have nightmares for weeks. They probably wouldn't eat meat for a longer time. As for Casey and me, we were given an escort home in the squad car I'd commandeered at the sluiceway. We were asked to be back at City Hall later that day for a full debriefing. We were also allowed to tell our families about our experience, but they had to swear to secrecy before we did. The Chief threatened us all with arrest if any word of what really happened got out.

We never did find out where the Werewolves had originally come from or why they had picked our city at that time for an appearance. The officers who had been killed were given honors and burials attended by the Governor and other dignitaries. Those who survived the melee were given medals of valor. Most were subsequently promoted and transferred to other Ohio metropolitan police forces. The Chief stayed behind to make sure we kept a tight lid on events. The story of cleaning out a den of rabid bears got quite a play in state as well as national papers.

A group of self-proclaimed tree huggers blamed the State and National Parks services for wildlife mismanagement. They managed to get a small publicity play from that. Some townsfolk even tried to get investors to put up money for a Beware the Bear theme park to be located on the old lumber mill grounds, but the effort died almost as soon as they raised the possibility. The Sanitation Department condemned the grounds as polluted and applied for a Super Fund clean-up grant (not given).

What bothered me most, however, was the lack of a final, firm Were body count.

The Dead Zone pretty much went back to what it was before, a place almost everything living avoided. It was still an occasional source of olfactory nuisance that pushed its obnoxious odors as far as Chagrin Falls. About a month after everything had quieted down, Casey and I borrowed my dad's truck. We drove back up to the mill site in the late afternoon. I didn't expect trouble but carried my hunting bow and a full quiver of arrows just in case. Dad let me carry along his short-barreled, side-by-side shotgun as a backup. It was stored beneath the bench seat, loaded. We finally stopped near the tree I'd climbed the night Casey had gone for help. We got out just to sit in the back of the pickup and reflect on all that had happened. My arm somehow found its way around Casey's shoulders. She snuggled up against me. She closed her eyes as we sat in the rapidly gathering shadows.

I was content, but I wasn't tired. I was waiting for a visitor that I thought would give us a little notice. He didn't. One minute we were quietly snuggling, and in the next, a beautiful short-coupled gray owl landed at our feet with barely a swoosh to be heard. I could read his thoughts as clearly as I could a book. I laughed at what he called me. Leaning forward to the truck bed's tailgate, I unwrapped a beautiful, 16-inch, raw porterhouse steak. I then sat back. The owl stepped around it with astonished open eyes.

He could barely lift it and couldn't begin to take off while carrying it, so I cut it into five pieces. He could then ferry it back in pieces to his tree nest, wherever that was. While he was doing that, I grabbed a bag of seeds and a rind of cheese. I wandered over to where the field mice nests had been. The nests were messed up. They looked as if they had been long abandoned, but I knew that mice were creatures of habit. One or more of the parents would be back this way sooner or later. I left the bag and cheese as a goodbye thank-you.

In my world, you never know when you'll need an ally. They could come in all shapes and sizes and usually did. So I always paid my debts. Good friends do that. That's one way they become good friends, and Gatekeepers can always use a friend. Well, most of the time anyway.

In our ease, neither Casey nor I saw the angry eyes that watched us eventually drive away from the ragged edge of the forest.

THE END OF EPISODE ONE, BOOK ONE

EPISODE
TWO

DAY ONE 4:30 P.M.

It had been three weeks and a few days since I had been back to the Dead Zone with Casey Allegro, my neighbor, friend, and soul mate. While there, we'd paid off an owl and left a small tribute to some wood mice that had helped bring an apparent end to an invasion of Werewolves that had quietly come to our town. I happened to be out in our backyard preparing to soak up what was left of a rapidly waning summer sun. Casey was with me when a curious thing happened.

A small hawk, apparently seeking a meal of unwary finches, stopped for a quick rest in one of our backyard trees. He was planning how to acquire his next meal. As a Gatekeeper, I could understand most of what was going through his small head. Much of it wasn't complimentary to finches or to cardinals. That I ignored, but I suddenly perked up when the hawk began complaining out loud to himself about not being able to hunt west of town because a gathering or parliament of owls was driving away all other predator birds in the area. It was as if the owls had posted and were enforcing a no fly zone. They were keeping their own counsel as to why, however.

The hawk's impression was that the owls were in a payback or revenge mood following the death of a small northern saw-whet owl. The owl had recently flown into the area to hunt near the old abandoned lumber mill and its adjacent woods. The Dead Zone was my first thought as I quickly came fully awake at this news. I scrambled to my feet and walked closer to the tree where the hawk was roosting. "What's that you say?" I inquired of the hawk, who almost fell off his perch when he realized a human was speaking to him. "What's that about the mill and the owls?"

The hawk was angry about being driven away from the hills west of Chagrin Falls. He probably could have ignored one, two, or maybe three owls trying to make a fight of it, but he couldn't ignore a whole parliament of them, and that's what he had encountered. "Why?" I asked, but got only a sense of anger as the hawk flew up and away, dismissing me and leaving me in confusion as he circled back to his hunt.

I was confused in part because a hawk, like a falcon, will attack almost anything. The size of the target isn't in these raptors' vocabulary, and although owls have razor-sharp talons and an overdeveloped attitude of superiority, I found it difficult to imagine an adult hawk being put off by owls. If nothing else, most owls will not tolerate a hawk's daylight hunting hours because of the owl's enormous, light-sensitive eyes. Owls are generally creatures of the night. There's no direct competition although neither the owls nor the hawks I've known will concede this point. They are both very stubborn species.

Anyway, hawks generally have a bad attitude about everything, especially owls. They view owls as up-start competitors and inferior at that. But the fact was that a parliament had gathered. While not that rare, a parliament was generally such an uncommon occurrence that that alone invited a trip back to the old mill for a personal on-site investigation and look-see.

It also didn't escape me that I was probably going to have to go back to the Dead Zone alone. Casey had little free time now because of her soccer club commitments. She guarded her sun time jealously. My dad was back on a business project that lately took his days, evenings, and most weekends. As for my mom, well, I've always thought Mom and hardship, risk, or danger go together like fish heads and belt buckles—which is to say they don't.

When I returned to Casey, I told her of my impressions and that I'd probably better cut short our joint tanning opportunity. I felt I needed to go on out to the old mill before the afternoon got too far along. She protested weakly and asked if I needed her to go along, but I can spot a charity gesture a mile away. To her obvious relief, I assured her that she could probably better spend her time acting as a cheerful host for the traveling sunbeams that seemed to be blanketing our backyard. With a quick nod of her head, she smiled and lay back down on her towel while putting a pair of clay goggles over her eyes. She was falling asleep even before I finished rolling up my towel and picking up my water bottle to go inside.

So much for my charisma and a shared sense of adventure, I thought to myself.

Once inside, I changed into an old pair of jeans and a T-shirt. I decided to buckle on my leg braces as well. They were a little uncomfortable and I needed to eventually replace them, but they'd proved their worth in my previous go-round with some Werewolves. I got nothing but uneasy feelings when I thought about going anywhere near the Dead Zone, much less into it, but the braces did help me with uneven terrain. The Dead Zone had plenty of that.

But I did decide not to take my hunting bow and arrows. I just didn't see the need, not after the police and I had made short work of the Weres the last time we'd encountered them. All of us acknowledged, however, that we'd been incredibly lucky to escape. What I did carry with me was a used javelin my dad had recently given me. It would eventually fit into a special holder he was going to weld onto my motor chair or, as I liked to imagine it, my Tuscan war chariot. I liked the javelin's heft. With my strength, I could throw it fairly far from a sitting or standing position. At short range, I could also throw it through most anything in my way. Equally cool, I thought, it was pointed on both ends.

Little did I know then how important that javelin would be to me before the day was over.

DAY ONE 5:00 P.M.

I made a quick call to my father, asking if I might borrow his truck. I got a short but preoccupied yes. It didn't take me long after that to find my way back to the logging road and the smashed overhead water-logging trough that had once straddled it. Before the police left the area the last time, they'd cleaned up enough of the Weres' debris so a car, truck, or van could now easily slip by the demolished site and travel up the hilly road to a cleared area immediately adjacent to the old mill itself.

A tall tree near the mill had saved my life only weeks before. I parked in its shade such as there was. Out of curiosity, I walked over to where a den of field mice had once been. I found that the cheese I'd left weeks earlier was now gone as if it'd never been there. I just smiled to myself. I'd have been shocked if I'd found anything there. Nevertheless, a fellow likes to make sure his gifts are received and his debts paid. Mine apparently were.

I then walked to a spot between the tree where I'd parked Dad's truck and the mill building. I found a bit of shade and sat down with my javelin across my knees. My back was against a young tree as I waited. Sooner or later, an owl would be by to greet me. While it was likely I might never see him, I'd probably hear some of his cries as he passed by. I was hoping for a clue as to the owls' recent assembly and hostile actions.

I waited longer than I thought I would. If there was a parliament of owls in the area, they must have been in recess, for I saw, felt, heard, and experienced nothing, just that peculiar silence that seemed to blanket this whole area. Silence in a large outdoor area is never a sign that all is well, no matter what hermits may say. What bothered me most, however, was the absence of wind. There just wasn't any up by the mill, yet I could see the tops of the trees on the slopes below me gently swaying to and fro. I'd been puzzling over this for some time when I heard the loud snap of wood breaking. In the quiet of the moment, the sound rolled across the top of the hill like a gunshot.

It had come from far behind me and to my left. It seemed somewhat far away. Knowing the trunk of the tree was partially between me and the sound, I quietly slid a bit to my right. I judged a point to stop so the whole tree trunk was between me and the sound. At that point, I slowly stood up and rotated the javelin to vertical so that it, like me, might be hidden. Breathing slowly, I checked my watch and softly closed my eyes so I might listen better. After five minutes elapsed and after a number of peeks at my watch, I slowly turned into the tree's trunk. I moved slowly and stuck my head out until my right eye was clear of the trunk. I could now see the area from where the sound had come.

It took all my self-discipline to freeze in place and not hobble, screaming for my dad's truck. What I saw was worse than my greatest fear, a nightmare come to life. Standing almost 30 yards away was a creature of even more fearsome appearance than the Werewolves I'd fought two months earlier. It was a man or what had once been a man. He was horribly disfigured. His limbs were contorted and bent. His clothes, what

57

there were of them, hung from his frame in tatters. His ears had elongated and were pitched forward. His face, or muzzle, still partly resembled a human. One of his arms was distended and hairy like a Were, while the other one still had a hand rather than a paw. It was much smaller.

I gripped the javelin more tightly and prepared to bolt for the truck when the creature called out to me. His voice was rough, like coarse sandpaper. His accent could have come from the other side of the moon for all I knew or cared, but he was intelligible. That alone terrified me. My mind just went from horrible to horror. I could barely face him, but I did. I was plastered to the side of the tree as if I'd grown there. That's when I heard the soft grunts behind me over by my dad's truck. Without turning my head, I immediately knew I was boxed in on two sides. I had no apparent escape. It was one of those moments when you just wish the ground would swallow you up.

"Do not run," was the garbled cry of the creature who had appeared to me. "Do not run. Please listen to me," was his grunting cry. "Just listen. We will not hurt you. Just listen!"

The voice was more of an invitation than a command. I obeyed anyway. My thought was that as long as we're talking, we're not fighting. Besides, with a javelin rather than my bow, any fighting would be a lot closer and more personal than I would have wanted on my best day. So I stepped out an arm's length from the tree trunk. I glanced quickly upward to see where and how I could climb up if need be. I then turned to face the creature addressing me. I held the javelin in front of me, my arms hanging down, each end of the javelin pointing to each side of me. It was about as nonthreatening as I could get. I was still ready to swing it in any direction to defend myself.

Then began one of the most disturbing conversations I was ever to have. The creature first claimed to know me. "You were the Archer," he said. He knew what I had accomplished. He knew my capabilities with a bow and arrows. He professed to be the latest in a group of people who had become infected by a lupine virus that caused disfigurement, bodily change, and eventually an emotional and mental change. The change took him from his human status to that of an animal. Most of these humans assumed the rough form of a wolf. Some humans changed into other forms resembling a bear or mountain lion.

Apparently, the virus had been around for centuries. There was no known cure. He knew his form was upsetting to humankind, both as he was now and as he would be. He growled that he was about midway through his change. As his change progressed, he would soon lose the ability to form sounds. He wouldn't be able talk as humans do with one another. That was why he had been chosen by his pack to act as their spokesperson. He claimed they wanted nothing but peace. The Weres wanted the privilege of stealing away to some other place without interference from any gun or bow-bearing humans. "Peace," he claimed. "That's all they want. Peace."

DAY ONE 5:45 P.M.

Initially I was mesmerized by his manner of speech. The content of his talk was appealing. But I noticed that he was stealthily but steadily crabbing his way closer to me as he talked. He shuffled from side to side. He gained inches and even feet doing this as he spoke with me. Abruptly, somewhat alarmed, I called out to him to stay back. He laughed and asked what my worry was. In his state of change, could I not see that he represented no threat to me? Nevertheless, he did stop, but the 30 yards was now more like 20 yards. That was about 10 miles too close for my taste.

What I did *not* see was a large Were creeping silently up behind me. It moved as stealthily as a predator can when all its energies are in hunt and kill mode. Just before it lunged for me, arms outstretched and jaws distended, the creature in front of me tilted his head slightly to my left as if to look behind me. It was that movement that saved my life, for I tightened my grip and swung the javelin from its position across and parallel to my chest to a position where the point was forward.

The javelin then pointed directly at the creature who had engaged me in conversation. This, of course, meant the pointed rear end of the javelin was now aimed directly behind me. I then unexpectedly impaled the creeping Were behind me as he lunged forward. His roar of pain in my ear almost caused me heart failure. I was taken completely by surprise.

The Were's arms dropped to the javelin shaft as its bulk crashed into me and sent me sprawling forward onto my face and chest. The impact raised a small dust cloud of leaves and pine needles and other droppings that momentarily obscured my vision. The javelin's nether point had taken the Werewolf through its chest, and it was bleeding out. It coughed terribly as it experienced oxygen deprivation. The javelin had apparently pierced and collapsed the Were's left lung. It had also broken a rib or two as it tore a hole into its chest. Its body lay across the back of my legs, pinning me as securely as if I had been nailed to the ground.

The creature who had been speaking to me immediately started forward. He cackled like a banshee as he raised his voice in a half howl, half cry. Pinned to the ground, immobilized, facedown with that awful weight on my legs, I knew I was out of options. I had no idea what the half creature scrambling my way could do to me. I did know it would neither be pretty nor painless.

Without clear thought, I screamed out vocally and mentally for help. I was as terrified as I had ever been twice over. I knew my next struggle would be for my life. Squirm and tug as I could, I could not move the big Were dying across my legs. The demented and drooling half creature who now knelt in front of me about to extend himself to me began a throat-rattling howl as he threw his head-muzzle back and laughed. That was his second mistake. His first was stopping to kneel in front of me.

Unbeknownst to either of us, he went from being a moving target to a momentarily stationary target. That move was his doom.

Two great horned owls hit him almost at the same time. One came from behind and sunk his razor-sharp talons into the creature's ear, eye, and scalp. The second hit on his human side, sinking his talons into the creature's outstretched arm. The second owl practically tore it off. Frantically beating their wings and using their beaks like knives, they smashed against the creature again and again as he screamed and twisted beneath them. The owls raked and pecked at the transforming Were until a good part of him was covered in a bloody sheen. There were sharp rents in his skull and upper body.

Only when the creature's ineffective flailing stopped and his gasps and grunts were no more did the owls cease their attack. Then they hopped to the ground beside the carcass and faced me. Feathers askew, both smeared with blood, they appeared as delivering angels. I poured out my thanks. They preened a bit and strutted and were appreciative of my kind words. They also indicated that they had been at watch the whole time. They were prepared for the perfidy of the Werewolves since my arrival earlier that afternoon.

A parliament had been called to deal with the Weres following the killing of the small saw-whet owl. It was a senseless killing that the owls would not abide no matter who or what the killer might be. To be killed in fair battle with a prey was one thing. To be killed by another predator for the sake of killing was an insult to the honor of birds of prey. It was an insult that would not be ignored. The woods surrounding the mill were silent because of the owls. All small game had gone to the ground because of the Werewolves. All other mammals and flying animals were warned away from the killing ground by the owls as they sat in silent sentinel duty 'round the clock. They would not leave until justice was visited on the Weres.

The owls were exceedingly curious about me. They had never encountered a human who could converse with them. They had heard from the mice that a human had that capability. It was a human who had wrought a great battle trauma on the Weres on these very grounds weeks earlier. They did not know who that human might be. Meeting me, they said, was their honor.

The owls felt fortunate to have gleaned that bit of information because the mice feared the owls would eat them if the mice remained overly long in their presence. Nervous, the mice had spoken quickly and sparingly before scampering away to their den.

I gave them my story and explained what I believed my role as Gatekeeper was. Part of that role was to rid these woods of the Werewolves or any of their kind that could be found. I also explained that most humans discounted both Werewolves and my ability to talk with animals. I therefore had only limited help. I told them I deeply appreciated their assistance this day when it appeared my life was in jeopardy. With that, I asked them to try to help pull the Were off my legs so I might free myself. After much tugging and flapping, they did.

I took back my javelin as I gained my feet. Curious, I asked the owls how it was that the Werewolves could be so quiet as they moved. Their answer was something between a kind of laughter and a resigned if not exasperated explanation. Could humans really think they moved quietly? Could their ears really not hear as the owls did, that the slip of a mouse's foot off a log in a forest was like a hawk's cry or that the soft brush of a fox's coat against a bush was like the croak of a pond frog? Were we really so incapacitated?

I explained that the ears of a human were so used to the loud clamor of their machines that they were unable to hear the quiet when they encountered it. I also said that days in the woods such as the owls were wont to spend actually sharpened their human senses. Quiet country allowed humans to regain a once-held capability. The owls looked at each other and exchanged the same thought: "Poor humans!" They then turned to me and asked if I needed their help.

I was puzzled for a moment and wondered what they meant. I pointed out that the two Werewolves were both dead now. That had been generous help indeed. What else exactly did they have in mind? Again, the owls looked briefly at each other. The older of the two stepped forward and peered into my eyes as if to see that I was paying attention. He then said, "Why, the colony, of course! Do you want some help clearing out the colony?"

My knees almost failed me as I suddenly sagged and then pushed myself upright with the javelin.

"What colony?" I asked.

"Why, the colony of Werewolves that live in the caves," the owls replied.

"What caves?" I frantically asked.

"Why, the caves in the hills just a short fly away from here," they responded, clearly puzzled at my ignorance, "where the Werewolf colonies are found."

"How many are there?" I asked.

"No more than three, possibly four," the older owl answered.

"Oh," I said, suddenly relieved. "I was afraid there would be many more."

"No." said the younger owl. "We've flown all through these woods for miles to each side. There are only three real caves and one opening that might be a cave, although no one has seen anything going in or out of it."

"Caves?" I practically shouted. "Caves! I'm not speaking about caves," I cried out. "I'm speaking about Werewolves! How many Werewolves are out there?"

"Oh, that," said the older owl. "Well, maybe as many as a full parliament three times over, but a good number are youngsters, maybe a fourth of them. So do you need some help?" they both asked again. I sat down immediately. From their description, there could be 100 to 120 Werewolves quartered in a series of caves nearby. The battle we had fought weeks ago was, in fact, nothing more than an opening skirmish. Nobody knew about this current threat other than a few owls and me, the Gatekeeper, or, as the

Werewolves called me, the Archer. This was far, far bigger than I had ever dreamed. It could be our small city's destruction. An organized pack of Werewolves could wreak untold havoc on the citizens of Chagrin Falls if left unchecked. They apparently were already operating in an intelligent fashion.

Clearly, there were bad times coming, and I had no plan at all, just an overwhelming need to tell the authorities or someone who could handle this budding crisis. Maybe that was the plan.

But I was to learn that local authorities generally manage crisis by foisting responsibility on others under the guise of expediency. They keep a hand in it, as it were, to appear responsible but often impede any clear action by their sometimes not so well-meaning bureaucratic bungling. And as it turned out, I had a bigger part than I would have imagined in the struggle to come.

The evening was wearing on. I didn't want to be anywhere near these woods in darkness. I again thanked the owls. I told them I would be back within a day or two with a plan. We would surely need their help. I reminded them that any violence with a Werewolf meant somebody would die. I asked them to be careful. I then thanked them yet again and hobbled back to the truck. I drove off in a hurry. I was a little fearful of what might be out there watching me. I was glad when I once more entered the familiar city streets of Chagrin Falls.

My mind was filled with the exchange I'd had with the creature. Humans turned into animals because of a virus that had reigned unchecked for centuries? My mind reeled with that possibility. What was the virus? How was it spread? Who was susceptible? Was anyone immune? How fast did the change occur? When did one's will give over to that of an intelligent animal? What was the life span of a Were? What exactly were their full powers? With whom had the creature been in contact with so a trap was laid for me?

So many questions! But one fact kept coming to the fore. Werewolves could not communicate with me as animals could at a distance. Perhaps that was because most started as humans, and humans had long since lost that mental capability (if they ever had it in the first place). That meant neither a Werewolf nor I could read the thoughts of the other unless we were almost nose-to-nose. But could a Were discern the intent of other Weres through thought or some other esoteric means of communication? That— and a whole lot more—we would have to know if we were ever to be successful against this furred calamity. What we needed was a spy in their camp. Failing that, we needed a prisoner with whom we could talk. We needed someone from the Weres' camp that was undergoing the change but not so far along as to render it incapable of communication using human vocal chords and any remaining wit. How to secure one was now the overriding question. How indeed?

The answer, of course, was simple. Just go get one.

DAY ONE 8:30 P.M.

My mom reminded me when I finally walked into our kitchen that I was late for dinner.

She said I would find some leftovers in the fridge. She told me that Casey had called when I wasn't back by dinner. She seemed a little worried that I wasn't home yet. Was there something wrong she should know about? I gave my mom a quick squeeze, a quick kiss on her cheek, and told her everything was okay. I said I wasn't hungry just yet. I probably would be after Casey and I chatted. I then ran upstairs to my room as Mom turned away muttering, "That boy. I just don't understand the men in this family."

Casey answered my call on the third ring. I felt a kind of peace for the first time since I'd left for the Dead Zone earlier that afternoon. Casey does that to me. She brings peace to my heart and mind. Even the turmoil that follows when I think about her has an edge of peace to it. Casey's smile would make an angry alligator change his bite to a grin and a snake twist itself into loops. That was pretty much how my stomach acted whenever I held her close. She might be my best friend and childhood companion, but I felt I was also in love with her. I had never really told her how I felt. In fact, I was usually just goofy around her, probably because I was frightened by the feelings she stirred in me.

Nevertheless, I had much to tell her this night. I recounted my trip and the things that had happened to me in great detail. It was after 10:00 p.m. when we finally finished our call. I acted immediately on the advice she gave me. "Tell your dad now!" she'd said. "Now, Cody. Tonight! Then call me back, please!" I promised I would and did just that. Only I didn't call Casey back that night. My bad. It was after 1:00 a.m. when Dad and I finished our conversation. I was so tired that I went straight to my room and collapsed on the bed.

Dad and I had come up with a plan between us. I had much to do, but one worry was now off the table. My dad was there for me—my mom, too, in her own way. But my dad would have my back and trusted me to have his. A fellow can't get a better gift than that. As tired as I was, I fell asleep with a grin. What's a war with Werewolves when a fellow has a family like mine and a friend like Casey? My dreams that night were not sweet. In fact, they were awful.

At breakfast the next morning, I was a bit sullen. Sleep had not come as easily as I had hoped. My dreams had left me in a state of restlessness. My mom said I was cranky, but she cheerfully prepared my breakfast. She completely ignored my reticence to speak louder than a mumble. She was soon off on some of her own errands for the morning. She reminded me that last night's leftovers would be my lunch. Kissing me on the cheek, she sailed out the door. My dad had left for his office much earlier. Nobody home but grouchy me. That only lasted about five minutes until Casey barged in. She wanted to know just why I had not called her back the previous evening. What was going on?

I started to protest, but she pushed me back into my chair. She plopped down beside me. She poured herself a glass of orange juice. She told me to eat my eggs before they got cold. But before I could start, she told me to first spill everything my dad and I had discussed. I told her I couldn't do both at the same time. She reminded me that she couldn't protect me if she was kept in the dark. Casey is normally a handful, a whirlwind when riled up. This was one of those whirlwind times. I sighed and bid my eggs a silent goodbye. I then told her everything I could remember about my talk with my dad the previous evening. It was a two-glasses-of-orange-juice conversation. She drank all the orange juice before I finished my spiel. My eggs were cold by then, so I just dumped them in the trash. I covered them with a napkin. I chowed down instead on a couple of Pop-Tarts I rescued from our toaster before they became extra crispy. That's when I really missed that orange juice.

DAY TWO 8:30 A.M.

Casey was out the door in a flash, hollering over her shoulder that I was to get dressed. I was to meet her at her back door when I had showered and changed. I was to bring along my javelin and bow and arrows. We were going hunting today but not for Werewolves. Oh, I was to bring along about 100 feet of climbing rope as well. What for she didn't say, but that was like Casey. She never told me a lot and was used to giving directions. She was captain of her soccer club, like an on-field general. She was good at it. She was a natural leader. Besides, she could argue longer than I could, and a rope and unknown destination just weren't worth the effort to oppose her, not this early in the morning.

By 9:00 a.m., I was waiting by her back door. I carried my bow, arrows, rope, and javelin. I'd also brought along a light canvas jacket and my lace-up camping boots. They weren't nearly as good as my leg braces for uneven terrain, but they were so much better than sneakers. Anyway, my legs still hurt a bit from wearing the braces all yesterday afternoon and evening.

When Casey came out, I noticed she was dressed similarly but had traded her sneakers for her camp shoes. "In case we step on a snake," she said.

"Indeed," I replied.

"And just what sort of snakes are we finding today?" I asked. "Two-legged or slicks?"

"Maybe both," she answered with a grin. With that we were off in her slightly cratered Volkswagen.

Our first stop was the city library. Casey's idea was to research Werewolves first so we could build a profile of their strengths and weaknesses. That seemed like a good idea to me. We spent the next five hours combing the shelves for any and all references to

Were anythings, especially wolves. Just before we broke for a late lunch, we sat down. In conspiratorial whispers, we made a list, trying to separate fact from fiction. The fact that I had killed a Werewolf yesterday, even accidentally, made me want to refile most of the reference works we'd used under history and not new age fiction or parapsychology. I was sure the librarian would be upset, though, if I tried. After all, hers was an orderly and sane world. Her stylized world was totally unlike the reality we faced.

Over fast-food hamburgers, we reviewed our list. We'd learned that Werewolf legends had been around for several thousand years. We learned that almost every civilization had its own folk stories about them. While size differed, all such creatures had a dog-bear-lion-wolf-like shape. Some types ran on four legs. Some were able to attack on two. We learned they had great strength, did not speak words as we did, preferred dark ambushes, occasionally had an infectious bite, were cruel and intelligent, and had great stamina. Their eyesight was better than a human's. Their appetite was voracious, and they loved meat, preferably torn from their victim's body. And we learned one thing more. Werewolves are not your friends. They lie and bite with big teeth. Armed with our pooled profile, I stood up and asked Casey just where in heck were we off to. She bounced up beside me, gave me another of her winning smiles, and just said, "Follow me!" I did, all the way to her car. We climbed in and were off on another great adventure, which really turned out pretty well. She took me to a different sort of shooting range than I'd ever heard of. It was based on the FBI's (and other federal agencies') model. It allowed a person to rent time to walk, run, or crawl through a course of pop-up dummies. Some of the dummies were bad-guy targets. Some weren't.

It was a reaction course owned by an ex-Army Commando. It was favored by a number of county police department officers in their off-duty time. Casey and her father had been through it several times. Her dad had taught her how to use a 9-millimeter Glock, the G17 STR with its 17-bullet magazine capacity, and the Ruger LCP .380 for concealed carry. She preferred the latter because of the small size of her hands and the ease of concealing that weapon. Casey was going to follow me through the course as backup. I would use my bow and arrows. She wanted to see if we could work together, if teaming an archer and a shooter was even possible.

The owner was just as curious and asked us to wait for a bit while he reconfigured several of the pop-ups and changed some of their timing. Some were set to pop up as we broke a hidden beam in traversing the course. Others were set on a timer, and still others were activated by the course master himself as he watched our progress from a bullet-proof, glass-enclosed tower.

With ear plugs and safety goggles in place, I led the way when the owner gave us the all clear. Casey was two paces behind and to my left. She would stay there throughout the entire course so each of us would know just where the other one was as we ran the targets. She would be free to fire if I missed a target or ran out of arrows. In the latter case, she would assume the lead, and I would be her shadow throughout the remainder of the course.

We had 16 targets that were bad guys, seven that were good guys. The course master told us not to worry, that many of the good guys get killed on each person's first try several times through. That was the point. The course was there to teach the individual how to wait and judge and not shoot when all the adrenaline was flowing and nerves were on edge because of competition or whatever.

My quiver carried a max load of 15 metal-tipped arrows. The course master told me to double the load because otherwise I'd run out halfway through the course. I politely declined. I intended to use all 15 of my arrows in the quiver and walked in carrying one nocked, held against the bow by my index finger. That gave me a total of 16 arrows for 16 bad guys, and Casey still had her five shots in her small Ruger. The ex-Ranger just shook his head, laughed, and said, "It's your money. Go have at it."

And did we ever!

It took 21 minutes to run the course. The average time for a repeat user was 25 minutes with three good guys dead and 12 bad guys hit with a death wound. Our score the first time through was no good guys dead, one wounded good guy, and 15 bad guys with an arrow through a fatal spot—neck, head, or heart. One was dead by bullet. We walked back through the course with the owner as I gathered my arrows. He said little. He just shook his head quietly at each kill. He finally told me I could come back for free anytime as long as I called first so he could bring a few of his buddies out to watch. I don't think he really understood that bow hunters must focus and concentrate before losing an arrow, while firearm users invite a more general recognition before acting on their impulse to fire. Consequently, lesser trained gun enthusiasts will likely kill more innocents than a bow hunter of comparable training.

I thanked him, and Casey and I left, grinning. I told Casey that it had been one of the best things we'd ever done together. I'd missed the 16th bad guy target, but Casey's immediate follow-up shot took him through the jaw. Technically, all bad guy targets were dead. The good guy target wouldn't have been wounded, either, if Casey hadn't startled me and caused me to miss before her bullet blasted by my ear.

I'd known she would fire, and she did so safely. Nevertheless, a guy from a bow and arrow background is never really comfortable with firearms. My yelp caused her to pull her weapon back to vertical when she heard me yell. That instant's reaction had spoiled her follow-on aim, and she let me know about it plenty when it happened. Partners have to work together. The incident was a valuable team learning experience for both of us.

Secretly, I couldn't have been more pleased. A head shot is among the most difficult shots to pull off, and Casey had done it like an expert. There are a lot of people in life you can mess with and some you just don't. Casey was a just don't.

The afternoon was getting on. I still didn't know what Casey wanted the rope for, but it wasn't long until I found out. She drove us to a rocky escarpment on a small cliff face about 40–50 feet high just northwest of town. She wanted to practice rappelling. She wanted me to coach and, if need be, to catch her. My pleasure, I thought, but she was all business. For the next 50 minutes or so, we both got a workout.

When we were done and headed home, I asked her why the rappel practice. "Simple," she explained. "Werewolves in changed form apparently live in caves. Caves have drop-offs and steep descents. If we want a prisoner, we'll have to be able to work our way through a cave and get out again." She wasn't volunteering for that mission. She just wanted to make sure in her own mind (and mine) that she could handle the job if need be. I sat in the front seat looking out the window, not replying. I didn't dare.

As we pulled into her driveway, she stopped and asked me to step out of the car with my javelin. I did. She pointed to a clump of gray-green moss attached to a sapling in her backyard. It was immediately next to her garage, a good 30–35 yards away. "See if you can hit the moss," she said as she slipped back into her car. I weighed the javelin carefully, flexed my arm several times, and studied the nearby trees to get some idea of wind velocity and direction. Then, running down the driveway with a grunt and yell, I let it fly.

Afterward, Casey admitted she never thought I'd even come close to the tree and certainly not the moss patch on the tree. But I did. It broke the javelin's tip and shattered the tree (which she later blamed on a lightning storm). I made a believer out of both of us as to a javelin's value. I appreciated her congratulations. I didn't have the heart to tell her that the moss patch I'd been aiming at was not the one I'd hit. Close, to be sure, but not what I had aimed for.

A long day. I was glad to be home to turn in, but we had a strategy session looming. We needed to create a plan for a creature capture. I grabbed a Dr Pepper and headed for our kitchen. That's where all good plots originated anyway. In this case, we had an even better reason to assemble there. It happened to be where my mom and dad were.

DAY TWO 9:30 P.M.

Mom, Dad, Casey, and I were sitting in our living room. We had just finished dinner. Dad had run through his proposal for attacking the colony a third time. None of us were completely sold on his approach. The questions and answers came thick and fast between us. Most had to do with the practicality of taking on this chore with volunteer labor and the risks involved. The answers were easier than the questions. We answered with "not very practical" and "high risk."

Dad finally suggested that this time we let the police take on the primary responsibility of dealing with the Weres. Our role was to be strictly limited to initial alert and follow-on support or reporting (i.e., no fighting). In short, stay out of the field of fire. I didn't like it, but I wasn't going to dispute him, either. I knew all too well what an angry Were could do. I wanted no part of that equation unless forced into it.

Casey thought my dad's approach was interesting. She asked how the police would capture a Were in its change mode or understand how their defenses were organized without the support of a Gatekeeper. Couldn't animals easily do what humans could not do in ferreting out information on the Weres without a major risk of human life and limb? Since I was the only Gatekeeper around that she knew of, my role had to be paramount and protected. That meant the police had to coordinate with us. That meant we had to run the operation, not the police. That also meant, of course, that we had the primary responsibility for handling the Weres.

Wait! I thought. *What happened to the military principle of economy of action or thought here?* I quietly interjected myself into Casey and Dad's rapidly escalating discussion. I pointed out that we were merely a resource of four against a force of 100 to 120 entities. We also had limited weaponry at our disposal. In no way were we a match unless someone had managed to obtain a 2,000-pound bomb somewhere. Even at that, the only delivery system would be Dad's truck, which, if employed, was ideal only if the driver planned to be a sacrificial martyr.

And so the argument went on back and forth for a long time until we were interrupted by a terrific crash against the living room window. It scared us all. It caused my mother to shriek before she tried to reach out and pull Dad to the floor. Dad's reaction was to leap to his feet shouting and reaching for Mom. Casey dove for the protection of the floor against the large sofa between her seat and the window. She grabbed a nearby footstool as a weapon as she rolled.

I was already on my feet and about halfway to the window empty-handed before I realized what had happened and pulled up short. We all froze. No other sound immediately followed the sound of the crash. As I turned and looked back, several thoughts came to me at once. One I shared with the others in the common silence that followed.

I asked everyone to note what each person's specific reaction had been. Mom was a mother. She had been momentarily overwhelmed at the interruption but reached for Dad, her first concern. Dad's first concern was Mom, not the threat. Casey, sitting farthest away, preserved herself but gathered a weapon in order to be ready for any follow-up attack. I, the closest to the window, had leaped at the threat, not away from it and not toward anyone else.

I had traveled practically halfway across the room. My reaction had been uncannily quick. That was simply the way I was. But I had been the only one in true attack mode in a threatening situation.

So Casey's instincts could be right. In a high-risk physical situation, Casey and I were the only ones there who reacted offensively to the stimulus. Ours was an eye toward *confronting* the perceived threat. Mom and Dad had reacted defensively by first trying to reach and protect each other from the threat. The police motto, "Protect and Serve," was essentially a *defensive* motto.

Casey's notion that the police would be inclined to contain the threat of the Werewolves rather than exterminate them meant that their plans would likely focus on avoiding rather than taking risk. Those plans rarely allowed for the extraction of a target such as a Werewolf in change mode. Nor would they have the will to kill every last one of the creatures before the whole surrounding area was secured. That demanded time. Once this started, we would likely not have much of it.

Stir up a nest of Werewolves, and you have a fire ant syndrome. Everything but the queen, her immediate attendants, and the larvae would come boiling up out of the nest trying to bite and kill every living thing touching the ground surrounding the nest, anything that didn't chemically smell like a fire ant.

In the case of the Werewolves, no human in change mode would come out fighting. They would remain in the caves under strict guard until the fighting outside was over. They would be spirited away if the outside fighting went against them. The fact that we even knew about humans in change mode was entirely unexpected. It was a valuable piece of intelligence for us. It was one they apparently had not intended humans to have since I was set up for an ambush and not a parlay at my last confrontation.

A sporadic knocking against the front window interrupted us. We all turned to stare at this new interruption. Springing to the side of the large picture window, I yanked back the curtain cord. I pulled open the drapes in a flurry of movement. There, grasping the outer window sill, was a disheveled great horned owl.

He was blinking furiously at the light from the living room that spilled out onto him. He was calling for me. Concussed owls sound drunk. I had to laugh as I excused myself. I ran outside to take him in my arms. That he was dazed was an understatement. Given how hard he'd flown into the window and that he was alive seemed a miracle. But there he was, evidently with a message he'd come to deliver. And deliver he did, once he'd had a sip of water and collected his wits.

It was the senior owl from my earlier confrontation. His news was urgent. The Werewolves had discovered the two dead Weres. All the local Weres were assembling for action. Runners had gone out in three directions. What should the owls do?

DAY THREE 7:30 A.M.

Daybreak at last! My back was starting to hurt in my cramped position. Worse, I needed a potty break. Rubbing the drowsiness from my eyes, I thought about what had happened since the owl's message was delivered last night.

Essentially, I'd gotten little to no sleep. I was presently up in a tree about 50 yards from the mill's south side. I'd been there since 4:00 a.m. I'd made my way to the tree with the owl's guidance.

My bow and a quiver of broadhead arrows were with me. I also had the broken-tipped javelin. I had gone to considerable trouble to haul it up into the tree with me. I'd laid it across two branches in highly cramped quarters so I could half sit, half lean against it. After three and a half hours, it was putting a crease in my backside and a frown on my face. My legs were killing me, too.

In my right front pocket was a Smith & Wesson Extreme Ops FR2S folding pocket knife. It was one of the most affordable and toughest knives around. It had a four-inch partially serrated tanto blade. I rarely carried a knife. Nevertheless, from hand-to-hand fighting to other extraordinary conditions, it was among the best pocket knives a person could wield. My dad had given it to me at the last minute. He put it into my pocket as he put his arm around me and told me to come back in one piece, breathing. My mom just gave me a hug and a kiss. She whispered into my ear that she loved me and that I'd better bring that knife back. It was hers. She was the one who'd loaned it to Dad.

Wow! I mean, who really knows about their parents? I made a quick mental note not to shortchange Mom again. Then I made a second mental note. *Try real hard, Cody, not to make her mad. Like ever.* As it would turn out, that knife would salvage my life from a desperate situation before 24 hours had passed.

A movement near the corner of the mill suddenly jerked me out of my reverie. Two Weres, one very large and one of shorter, stockier build, came trotting around the corner of the building. They stopped and spun about as they nestled against the corner of the building. They looked back the way they had come. It looked like an ambush, but I couldn't imagine who else would be out here to ambush them. I didn't have long to wait before I would know.

With gruesome howls, a large black bear came lumbering around the corner behind the Weres. It looked for all its worth as if it were in a panic. It looked ragged, like it had been running for a while. It was trying to gulp down great draughts of air. The two Weres waiting in ambush hit the bear as it turned the corner. They rolled it over as their bodies clashed.

With a roar, the bear was up on its haunches, claws extended and swinging its arms like two scythes through a wheat field as a pursuing group of Werewolves joined the two. One of the Weres was caught chest high as the bear's claws literally ripped four horizontal tears across its chest. The bear then clamped its jaws down on the other Were's neck when the first wounded Were tried to leap aside. With a loud snap, the bear broke the Were's neck and threw its body to the ground. But by that time, at least three other Weres were on the bear, and then more. They were all tearing at the bear with their teeth and claws. They flung chunks of shredded bear in an outward spray as they pursued their grisly feast. Within a matter of minutes, the bear was no longer recognizable as anything other than a loose pile of torn fur, meat, broken bones, and blood—lots of it.

I was filled with revulsion at the scene before me. I was also astonished at the speed and ferocity of the Werewolves in dismantling the bear. I had never imagined how efficient a pack of Weres could be in dealing death. I trembled a bit as I thought how easily that could have been me. I didn't move from my perch for almost 30 minutes after the last of the Werewolves had wandered away. I then dropped down to the ground and began to follow their rather obvious trail. I kept an arrow nocked and my javelin hung across my shoulder.

I had been designated as the scout last night. My job was to verify just where the Werewolves secluded themselves. Several owls would act as my outliers or contacts. They would help me track the Weres as well as help me should I be discovered. The mill seemed to be a main gathering place. That was where I started, and hence my presence in the tree this morning. Unlike my first encounter a couple of months before, I was better prepared this time to communicate. I carried with me a RadioShack walkie-talkie with a three-mile range. It was plenty for this terrain. I was to use it only in an emergency or when I was sure I was free of the Weres and their extraordinary hearing.

At 9:00 this morning, my dad, Casey, the Chief of Police, and several of his deputies were to roll up to the mill. They would either meet me or wait for my contact. The police would direct the operation from there, much to Casey's dismay and silent objections. But my dad had settled that issue before we all went our separate ways last night. It simply wasn't a voting matter any longer. A family decision had been made.

My concern was what they would think when they discovered a dead Were and a shredded bear. I hoped they wouldn't worry about me. They had enough on their own plate to worry about, for themselves and for Chagrin Falls. At least they'd have proof that Werewolves were still about.

The trail of the pack ran in irregular pathways for almost a mile. It always followed the path of least resistance insofar as impeding rocks, bushes, or trees were concerned. It wasn't that the Weres were lazy—far from it, in fact. They were just efficient hunters. They wasted little energy in covering ground. They saved it for fighting instead.

Finally, at the top of a fairly steep hill, the trail dropped down quickly on the far side. A series of steep switchbacks led to a small glen. Boulders, heavy brush, and some trees crowned the hill. They afforded plenty of cover, of which I took full advantage. From a concealed ledge, I chose my vantage point. I could see down the steep trail into a deep ravine formed as the hills abutted one another.

Two fairly large cave mouths were evident. From where I was positioned, I could not see the third cave spoken of by the senior owl, nor could I see the small mouth of what the owls had assumed was a fourth cave, even though it was supposedly nearby.

What I could see was far more evidence than I needed to assure anyone that this was the spot for the colony. Sentry Werewolves were on guard in the glen. They could also be seen on the hills above the cave mouths. A number of wolves of all sizes and both sexes were passing to and fro between the two caves where I could see and to an apparent site I could not see.

DAY THREE 8:45 A.M.

After 20 minutes of watching the scene below, I glanced at my watch. I realized I had little time to make it back to the rendezvous. I'd overstayed my welcome. I was fascinated at the sight of so many of these creatures going and coming with such regularity doing the business of the colony. It was hard to break away. Clearly, they were communicating. But how? I thought Werewolves were mad creatures of bloodlust, seeking only someone else's death and destruction. What I witnessed didn't change that thought but added to it.

These creatures were dangerous. No dispute there. And intelligent? You bet, and that made them *incredibly* dangerous. The act of changing into a beast did not rob them of the ability and disposition to act in an ordered fashion against a common objective. These were not wild, drooling beasts that acted on impulse and killed wantonly. No, these were wild, drooling beasts that acted by plan. They killed deliberately. They were assassins without a shred of soul.

My respect for these hairy predators rose correspondingly with my desire now to get back to the mill unseen and in one piece if at all possible.

I did, but it took much longer than I'd hoped in order to avoid a hunting party of five Weres in wild pursuit of several deer. The last quarter mile back to the mill I covered at a ground-eating hobble, my leg braces now thoroughly uncomfortable and a blister apparently forming on the outside of my right knee. Oh, how I longed for the ability to run again!

Once back to the mill, I found a grateful dad, a perplexed Police Chief, and a very angry Casey waiting for me. Dressing me down for not contacting them on the walkie-talkie, Casey was furious that I'd missed the rendezvous and caused them so much worry. My father cut her short before her tirade ended. He said there wasn't time for a lover's quarrel. He demanded I tell them quickly what I had learned. It didn't take long to give them my summary.

We left the area in the Chief's patrol car. Even if he didn't turn the siren on, it was a neat experience, almost as neat as seeing the look on Casey's face when my dad used the term *lover's quarrel.* The way her eyebrows rose when he said that was one of my life's highlights to that point. I selfishly played that again and again in my memory as we drove back to town.

My greatest disappointment of the day was that the ride wasn't longer. By 10:00 a.m., we were all back in the City Hall conference room in a meeting called by the Police Chief. The Mayor and his assistant, the city planning manager, the county surveyor, the chief architect, the fire chief, and the city engineer were all there. Also joining the meeting were the state trooper area supervisor and a full colonel in charge of the military armory just outside the Chagrin Falls city limits.

All these and a few others had been called to this meeting very early this morning after my dad, the Mayor, and the Police Chief had all conferred on a telephone conference call late last night. All were here to assess the current situation. They were to make a recommendation to the Mayor that he could forward to the Governor if need be.

The Mayor began his address after swearing everyone to secrecy and silence outside the conference room walls. Each politico and professional was given a chance to introduce themselves, make a statement, and explain their capabilities or potential contributions to the matter at hand. The meeting began to drag as several of the folks decided to use the occasion to prune their own feathers or plead for departmental funding. It was getting out of control when the Chief suddenly interrupted the colonel in charge of the armory. He rather curtly and forcibly reminded the group that this meeting was to deal with a real problem *at hand*. His chill cut away much of the posturing. Things began to move along quickly after that.

The county surveyor was asked to spread out his most detailed maps. We all spent some time examining the terrain where I thought the caves were located. The maps gave no indication whatsoever of what I was coming to believe was a geologic anomaly. No one had really surveyed that area for 50 years, before the lumber mill had been established. It was not unusual because it was private land. We had to rely on my best guess as to which of the hills actually contained the three hidden caves. Two of them I had seen with my own eyes, and the third I had surmised based on what I had seen and what the owls reported.

Only the Mayor, my dad, the county medical examiner, the Chief of Police, and a deputy guarding the door showed no hesitation believing that Werewolves were the challenge. The others believed it could be wolves but that the menace was more likely wild dogs. That somehow didn't seem to warrant this exaggerated response. With that proffered, the county medical examiner leaped to his feet. With a fairly interesting vocabulary, he told everyone there in no uncertain terms that he had examined the bodies of several of these creatures my dad and I had killed. By all that was holy and some things that were not, these creatures were *not* wild dogs or North American wolves.

The Chief asked me to describe some of my experiences. He described what he had experienced in the encounter almost two months before. After about half an hour of that with interrupting questions, everyone got deadly serious. As I feared, the general plan emerging was one of containment. Specifically, everyone was for blowing up the

Were caves and sealing in whatever survivors were left. That would happen after first assaulting the Weres and trying to drive the mass of them into the caves. Speed was of the essence. The assault was planned for dusk at 6:00 p.m.

The Chief liked the idea of capturing a creature in change mode. He asked my dad, me, and two of his deputies to take charge of that part of the operation. Do whatever we had to do, he said, but get out of the cave complex area by 6:45 p.m. when the planned set charges would blow. "No! Be out by 6:30 p.m.," echoed the colonel. The charges he would use would do a landscape renovation the likes of which eastern Ohio had not seen since the New Madrid earthquake in the winter of 1811. When those charges went off, the whole county would tremble.

Dad, the two deputies, and I left to go to a smaller office and plan an extraction. One deputy was about Casey's size, the other about one-and-a-half of me. After two hours, we finally agreed on an approach that we took to the Chief for his tentative blessing. The plan called for the smaller deputy and me to enter the fourth cave opening, the one the owls reported but the one we had yet to find. We would discover if it connected to one of the major caves. Then, if possible, we would capture a Were in change mode and haul it out the way we'd come in.

If the opening couldn't be found or didn't connect, we'd go into the third cave and force the issue there. Dad and the big deputy were to provide cover and fire support for the opening we chose. They would come in and help us as needed to fight our way out. It was a high-risk opportunity. The payoff made it worthwhile if we could pull it off.

We had little time to prepare but enough time to eat, arm ourselves, copy the county surveyor's pertinent maps, and leave for the forest. Our objective was to be in and out before the bombs were placed to blow the big caves. We understood the police assault to drive the Weres into the caves would begin 45 minutes before the charges were set to go off. The Chief issued us some SWAT clothing and shoes. To everyone's chagrin, I modified them by spraying irregular patches of green, blue, pink, and white all over to mark them.

When I finished, any human seeing us would immediately think some clowns were loose in what were rather garish coveralls. I was betting that the Werewolves, however, would simply ignore us. Weres are believed to be able to see the same colors we can, perhaps fainter. But they generally show no interest in any colors other than yellow, red, and orange, the colors of urine, blood, and some of the fecal material of their traditional prey. But Werewolves don't have guns like humans do. That's why I wanted to be human proof as we came out into an area that would likely be under fire.

On the way back to the mill area, I had the SUV stop at Pete's Pet Emporium on Maple Street off Salon Road for a surprise package. I had a hunch it would come in handy. I asked the group to wait in the car. I spent about 20 minutes inside before everything was arranged to my satisfaction. I came out carrying a small box under my arm. Everyone in the car tried to see what I had brought out. I sat silent and smiling to myself as we rolled out to our destination. No specific sound but an occasional shuffling noise came from the box.

DAY THREE 3:15 P.M.

Casey was our designated driver. She was assigned to watch our car when we arrived at the forest. We were using another old logging road that severely taxed whatever four-wheel drive capabilities the SUV we'd commandeered might possess. We stopped about a mile away from the suspected cave complex so we wouldn't be heard. From that point, we would walk in. Uneasy about leaving one person alone, Dad asked the smaller deputy to remain behind with Casey. The three of us would go in for the possible extraction.

I nixed that and suggested the larger deputy remain behind with Casey for two reasons. One, I had seen Weres travel in groups of two or more but never just one by itself. It might take two or more humans to kill them. Two, we were trying to enter and negotiate a cave opening that the Werewolves themselves didn't use. That suggested it was small, not big like an adult Were. I was the biggest of my Dad, the smaller deputy, and me.

We would likely need wiggle room getting in and getting out. I wanted us to have every advantage we could. Although my reasoning convinced the others, Casey was thoroughly miffed. She was definitely not wallflower or stay-behind material. She let us know that. I frankly would have preferred Casey to the untested deputy, but it wasn't my show. I had to remind Casey of that several times before we finally left to find the cave opening.

As I had hoped, we hadn't gone more than 50 yards when, with a near-silent swoosh, the younger of the two great horned owls landed at my feet. He peered at me closely and then hopped away about 10 yards into a small clearing. I followed him, and we quietly conversed for a moment. I told him our plan. I asked that he and any others available make a display of flying over the heads of any Weres they spotted, particularly those that might be acting as lookouts or could raise an alarm.

I then shielded the box under my arm from the deputy and my dad behind us. I lifted the lid, tilted it, and showed its contents to the owl. With a quick screech, he jumped backward and started to flap his wings before I could quiet him. He gave me the benefit of the doubt, folded his wings, and again peered up at me. I then explained what I had in mind. I asked him to pass a word to the other owls. The package I was carrying in the box was *not* anyone's prospective dinner. Its contents were not to be attacked or hindered.

The owl peered at me as if he were judging my sanity. "What owl in his right mind would even think of trying to kill and eat your passenger?" he asked. Then, shaking his head from side to side, he was up and off immediately. He would give instructions to the parliament scattered throughout the forest by the screeching cries of a hunting owl. Swiftly, he disappeared up and through the overhead tree cover.

The deputy wanted to know how I'd managed to train an owl to stand near me without fear, a wild owl at that. "And what was in that box?" he asked. I told him I'd used an old birdwatcher trick with some pieces of meat to get the owl to stand near me. The box was simply a distraction so he'd not fly away. That said, the deputy stifled his curiosity and turned back to the route we were following to approach the cave complex. He started to dogtrot in his haste to get to the cave complex.

Unfortunately, in less than 25 yards, the deputy inadvertently stepped through a rotting log across our ill-defined trail. From a distance, it appeared solid to all of us. Falling forward and flailing his arms wildly, he twisted as he fell and broke his ankle with a loud pop. Muffling his screams by turning his face into his jacket, he quickly became disoriented and pale. He went into shock. There was nothing to do but lug him back to the car and regroup, which we did.

The big deputy ran to us to take his companion as we got close to the car. He asked what had happened and suggested the plan need now be called off. Both my dad and I objected almost simultaneously. We said we still had three people with Casey. We believed she was as accomplished as any of the two deputies for this operation. With that, we simply turned and walked away. Casey and Dad walked with a ground-eating casual stride. I hobbled after with an excruciating limp as my brace rubbed my outside knee blister.

The deputy had been too startled to answer. He just stood there watching as the three of us disappeared into the nearby woods. His calls to wait until he could report to the Chief went unanswered. In a few minutes, we couldn't hear him. We moved more carefully as we got farther into the woods. The box was still under my arm. I talked to it quietly and constantly. Occasionally, I got an answer: "Whoof." We had walked a mile or so by my reckoning when the unnatural quiet was split by the screech of an owl we'd not heard before. We stopped immediately. We slowly crouched down and then froze in place. Our eyes rapidly searched the woods and sky around us. My dad was the first to see the owl circling tightly about 300 yards away to our right. My thought was that a sentry Were was beneath him. We'd asked the owls to spot and paint such creatures. Almost immediately, another screech split the air. We saw a second, smaller owl about 400 yards away, again way off to our right. Another sentry, I thought. We waited for yet a few more minutes and then heard a third screech repeating itself, only this time the call was much closer to us.

As we crept forward to the edge of a tree line, before us in the direction of the last call we could see that the ground sloped steeply down to a junction with the opposite hill. A small opening was visible at the side of a ravine where the two hills abutted each other. From our vantage point, it looked like the large rabbit hole from *Alice in Wonderland*. The third owl slowly circled downward in a tighter and tighter spiral directly above the opening.

All of us watched this with not a word spoken. We nodded at each other as if to say we were here. What we didn't know was how close the opening was to the third cave. Seeing no movement or activity in the general area after 10 minutes of silent observation, we concluded that the third cave must be at least 150 yards away and around the bend of the hill's slope, out of our direct line of sight.

Chatting quietly among ourselves, we rehearsed the opening's entry and exit plan. We assured ourselves that everyone was carrying a loaded firearm or arms of their choice. Taking responsibility for the lead, I stowed my box in a small ammunition pack I'd taken from the SWAT room. I draped it over my neck and shoulder then started crabbing my way down the hill. I tried to take advantage of every bush and shrub that offered cover along the way.

When I was halfway down, Casey started. She used my path and cover as her own while my dad watched. When we were both down, Dad started down as well. He followed closely in our path until he was able to come beside us. We were behind some casually strewn boulders that shielded us from the end of the hill and supposedly the third cave. I carefully placed the small ammunition pack with its box intact at the passageway's outside entrance. Then Dad handed me the rope he'd carried from the SUV. I tied it around my waist, surveyed the situation, and then plunged into the small opening we'd named the Rabbit Hole.

DAY THREE 4:00 P.M.

With my bow, quiver of arrows, and javelin tied and trailing behind me, I managed to crawl forward about two or three of my body lengths as the passageway narrowed until my shoulders were touching each side. My small flashlight illuminated a short way ahead where the crawlspace bent sideways at a sharp angle. I could see no farther. Although somewhat claustrophobic, I nevertheless reasoned that the way ahead was not a dead end because of the air blowing against my face. So I pushed on, struggling to bend with the passageway with my arms severely encumbered in the close quarters. As I emerged from the bend, pushing my flashlight ahead of me, the tunnel suddenly dropped away, and I felt utter darkness closing in on me as my light slipped from my hand. Its illumination bounced down the cavity now in front of me. In not more than three to five seconds, I heard it hit something solid. The light coming up the shaft was steady, although very dim.

I wasn't sure I could back out feet first because of the difficulty I'd had getting through the bend headfirst. However, knowing that the cavity ahead had a floor, I gathered my courage and pulled myself over the edge. The cavity was wide enough to let me hang on to the rim as my body fell over the edge. By twisting quickly I hung from the rim with my feet hanging down. Looking down, I gauged the distance to be no more than four to five feet. I let go. I landed on the chamber's floor with a solid thump. I jarred my knees and tumbled forward in a heap. I was down.

I recovered my flashlight and surveyed the area immediately around me. I found myself in a fairly wide area about the size of a two-car garage. The ceiling through which I had fallen was about four feet off the floor. It slanted up to a height of 12 to 14 feet at the chamber's other end. A fairly large passageway twisted through the rock at what could be called the far corner of the chamber. A phosphorescent glow could be seen at irregular intervals down its undulating pathway. I listened for several minutes and heard nothing except the soft rush of air back up the hole through which I'd come. I untied my dad's rope from around my waist. I secured it around a boulder nearby and gave three hard tugs. That was the signal for Casey to follow me.

Her passage through the Rabbit Hole was uneventful. She had an easier time than me. She easily pulled herself along by the rope. She used it to lower herself into my chamber by climbing down hand over hand. My dad's trip was not as successful. He was all right until the rim of the cavity. When he pulled himself over the edge, his hand slipped. He tumbled sideways and then bounced his way down until he crashed onto the floor near us. I was able to break part of his fall, but he came down on his left elbow. Casey and I watched as the weight of his body forced his forearm into an unnatural bend. With a cry, he grabbed his arm and bit into his coat to stifle his scream. I quickly raised him up and cradled him against me. I felt helpless as he groaned. His eyes filled with tears from the pain he suffered.

Casey, as usual, did the right thing without thinking. She grabbed his hand. She placed her hand on his forearm to steady it, pulled sharply, and twisted his arm back to its natural inclination. Dad almost fainted at the pain. He simply sunk back into my arms, semiconscious. Casey had seen a medical aide do that in a soccer match when an opponent had crashed into the side of a goal. The impact had bent her arm unnaturally, dislocating her elbow.

We had no time to waste. We were in a bad spot. Dad's arm was virtually useless for now. It was clear we would not easily get him out the way we'd come in. The clock was ticking toward 6:00 p.m. I told Casey our mission now changed. It was to simply get out safely and get clear of the caves. If we could capture a Were in change mode, great. Otherwise, we'd simply make for the nearest exit. As my dad recovered, I bent to pick up my bow and arrows only to find that Dad's ill-fated landing had been on my bow. It was broken. My arrows were intact but were now effectively useless. I left them there, taking up my javelin instead.

When my dad could stand, I handed Casey his side-by-side, sawed-off shotgun and a handful of his cartridges. I then gave Dad the Smith & Wesson .357 revolver the police had given Casey to carry. Dad's good arm could fire that. We tied his left arm in a sling. With all of us now fully aware of how vulnerable we were, we made for the corner passageway and whatever was ahead. I led the way. Dad was in the middle. Casey brought up the rear. Dad kept his light off, and Casey kept hers on its lowest setting. We did not want to telegraph our presence any more than necessary in the event this passageway led into any of the three known caves.

We walked carefully but as quickly as we could. We were hampered by my hobbled gait and Dad's injured arm. After five to eight minutes in the labyrinth, we were somewhat befuddled by the twists, turns, and undulations we'd walked through. I heard noises ahead. They were guttural sounds made from deep within one's chest. They were delivered in a sort of barking cadence. Snarls and growls accompanied the grunts. They sounded as if several creatures were delivering the sounds. Suddenly it came to me. The Werewolves could communicate. They did so by audible sounds generated by each Were. There were apparently a full range of sounds to describe and direct their many activities.

Beckoning Dad and Casey to remain behind, I stole forward to see if I could glimpse the reason for the noise ahead. I discovered a kind of window between our passageway and a fairly large area adjacent to it. The window was narrow and elongated. It stretched from waist high to a little over my head. It was about 16–18 inches across. It canted at an angle so I could look in at the adjacent chamber unimpaired. The occupants there would have difficulty seeing my portal much less me because of the way the shadows fell across us.

We had found the third cave. There was both light and activity in it. Glancing at my watch, I saw the time was now almost 4:45 p.m. We had a little more than an hour before the assault would begin.

DAY THREE 4:55 P.M.

I crept back to Casey and Dad and reported what I'd seen. I was certain we were in a branch of the third cave. Gunfire would erupt in a little more than an hour at 6:45 p.m. as the police and probably military forces outside would start driving the Weres into the three caves slated for blast destruction. Dad suggested that we sit tight for another 15 minutes. If nothing changed, we would try to break out. Casey suggested that we not sit tight but retreat the way we'd come. We could use the full time to get my dad up and out of the Rabbit Hole. I liked her plan better but pointed out that we could wait a few minutes before leaving. I wanted to hide by the portal and learn what I could about the Werewolves. I won.

Casey went back to prepare for an exit. Dad stayed where he was while I crept back to the portal. I'd allowed myself 15 minutes max before I'd grab Dad and head for the Rabbit Hole's entrance. When I once again peered out into the adjoining chamber, I was not prepared for what I saw.

With a great deal of noise and snarls, the Werewolves dragged the two deputies we thought were safe in the SUV into the adjoining chamber. Dozens of Weres crowded in behind them, some snapping their teeth and others raking their claws across the deputies' arms and legs. The deputies were covered in smears of their own blood.

The two men were in deep shock. The large deputy had been manhandled and tossed to the floor. He lay quivering in front of a Werewolf with wizened features and an almost solid pale golden coat. The Were looked to be the senior Were at the assemblage. The smaller deputy with the broken ankle had been dragged in by his arm and leg. His clothes were practically ripped from his body, hanging about him in tatters. His whimpers and mewling cries were pitiful to hear. He was badly battered and bleeding from dozens of cuts. He was lame but alive.

The grey Were raised its arms. Immediately a hush fell over the Lycan crowd. The Were tossed its head back and gave a long, warbling howl that reverberated against the cave walls and made shivers run up and down my spine. It seemed to be a blend of rage, loneliness, and frustration. It ended in a series of yips and snarls that silenced and terrified the two deputies. At the pale Were's barking command, the big deputy was brought forth. As he was held, he bowed his head before the old Were.

With great ceremony, the hay-colored Werewolf slowly stomped over to the deputy. Raising his shaggy head, it suddenly bit into the deputy's exposed shoulder several times. It left large puncture wounds bathed in saliva. The escort Werewolves immediately released the deputy who fell to the ground writhing and twisting in apparent pain. An immediate transformation began as the deputy's back and neck muscles started to distend. His face and chest pulled in separate directions. The deputy rolled over and over in his throes and began a series of unending cries as his body continued to twist and contort while he flopped about on the cave floor.

We later learned it was a process that would go on sporadically for seven to 10 days. Each minute brought him closer to being a full Werewolf as his body stretched and his bones reformed to his new identity. As for the small deputy, hampered as he was by a broken ankle, the gray Werewolf yanked him to his feet, opened its jaws, and bit off the deputy's lower arm. Then it tossed the screaming deputy into the mass of Weres.

Howling and yelling, the pack ripped, tore apart, and devoured the deputy in a matter of minutes. It was all I could do to hold my mouth and not throw up. The pale Were then apparently instructed two black-furred Weres to guard the previously bitten deputy as it led the mob of Weres back out through the passageway where the two deputies had been brought in as prisoners. There were howls and snarls as the mob made its exodus and retreated. The cavern's chambers suddenly seemed overly quiet and somewhat ominous.

The thought occurred to me that now was *the* perfect time to attempt an extraction. If we could kill or cripple the two guard Weres, we could kidnap the change creature, the former deputy. We could then make a run for Chagrin Falls and its safe havens. I scrambled back to my dad who was a good deal more lucid and energized than he'd seemed after first falling on his arm. I proposed my plan to capture the deputy for our side. He listened closely. He asked some pertinent questions and then gave his okay. I would need Casey to pull this off. My dad crept back to talk with her as I turned back to the portal to keep our prize under observation.

DAY THREE 5:30 P.M.

We were in a quandary. Casey had been beside me for several minutes looking at the two Weres and their captive. The deputy's throes had settled down somewhat, and he lay on the ground moaning and crying at the discomfort and outright pain his body was experiencing. The two Were guards simply ignored him for the most part. Neither of us had yet come up with an entirely foolproof scheme that would guarantee we could snatch the Were-to-be without alerting and fighting the two Weres. That was something we wanted to avoid in case the pack was alerted and came rushing back in. If that happened, we had nothing but death or enslavement as Werewolves to look forward to. That we clearly did not want. I did think of a plan, albeit a bit of a desperate one.

We would wait until the firing started outside. The noise and distraction of that would likely pull the two Were guards into the cave's front environs, if only temporarily. That would leave the change creature on his own. At that time, we could infiltrate the larger cave chamber through the portal and drag, push, or stuff the deputy back through the opening. We would eventually take him out through the Rabbit Hole. Casey had nothing to add but agreed to go back and brief my dad. She would update him while I kept watch.

To my surprise, Casey was back by my side in minutes. She told me that without my strength and heft, my dad wasn't going anywhere. She would have to stay as a lookout while I managed the logistics of getting my dad up and out of the Rabbit Hole. As much as I hated leaving Casey relatively exposed, I knew she was right. I gave her a quick, unexpected kiss, smiled at her confusion, and ran back up the twisting passageway to my father. He could use one arm to pull himself along but could not get up the 10-foot chute by himself. I first thought I had no way to pull him up unless I went outside on my own and pulled from there. But the steep bend in the tunnel would likely add too much friction. It would rob me of any easy leverage.

Instead, I asked my dad to stand on my shoulders. Perhaps that would give him the height he needed to get his upper body over the chute's rim. Then he could pull himself along using his right arm. He knelt down and, ducking his head, stood up in the chute. I tucked in beside him and then knelt on one knee as he stepped up on one of my shoulders and balanced himself against the chute's side until he could place his remaining foot on my other shoulder.

With some effort, I was able to stand. He managed to get at least his chest over the ledge. It was not enough. We both struggled this way for several minutes until he said to quit and let him down. We needed more height. Since I was long past my big adolescent growth spurt, things were looking pretty bleak. I suddenly thought of moving the tie-down boulder to the hole and standing on that. That would give me plenty of height if it could be managed. Dad and I dropped down. I began to push and shove the big rock, trying to move it where we wanted it.

It was an embedded boulder. It was apparently quite comfortable staying just where it was, thank you. Although I pushed, snorted, strained, and shoved, it didn't move. Then I again experienced one of those rare epiphany moments of lucid thought. I grabbed my broken bow and handed my javelin to my dad. We now had two levers. I reminded Dad that Archimedes said he could move the world with a lever. All we had to do was move a rock. We immediately bent to the task.

Straining and groaning, we were finally able to make the rock first wobble and then roll over out of its bed onto the cavern floor. Once I got the rock moving, I was able to guide it to the chute entrance. I positioned it slightly to the side. I left enough room for Dad and me to enter and stand alongside one another. Dad ducked into the chute and climbed on the rock. I ducked in beside him, leaned into the wall, and let Dad walk up my back to my shoulders. With both of us precariously balanced, I slowly climbed onto the rock and stood up. Eureka! Dad's waist was well over the ledge. He immediately pulled himself up and over to the sharp turn where he began edging himself around the corner. I stayed in contact until he said he was through the hard part. I then dropped down and ran back for Casey.

DAY THREE 6:02 P.M.

Casey and I had been sitting opposite one another underneath the portal for just a minute or so while I tried to get my breath back. I had run back to her as quickly as I could. Helping my dad had taken more effort than I'd counted on. I was laboring to breathe without gasping so the two Were guards wouldn't hear me and come over to investigate. When the firing started outside, it was so loud I could have stood and yelled and it would have gone unnoticed.

The bends and turns in the main cavern distorted and muffled some of the sounds outside. The grenade explosions, the rapid fire punch of several .50-caliber machine guns, and the sporadic sound of small arms and semi-automatic weapons fire still managed to make their way through to us in a cacophony of sound. It sounded like war was breaking out. And that was exactly what was happening. With a quick glance at their change ward, the two guard Werewolves immediately broke and ran for the cave's entrance. They left the still writhing deputy on the floor by himself.

Casey and I were over and through the portal lip in seconds. We ran to the deputy. Tugging and pulling, we managed to get him back to the portal lip where we struggled to push him through. We soon rolled him over into the passageway leading back to the Rabbit Hole. Casey was the first one over the lip and grabbed one of the deputy's arms. She began tugging at him, slowly inching him along until a space had cleared so I could clamber over and drop down to the passageway behind him. It was an awkward fit and effort until Casey said, "Drop your javelin and lift him up!" Between us, we managed to get him standing with our support. At that point, Casey said to put his arm around my neck and walk him up the passageway. "We don't have time to lug this nut all the way back," she whispered. "Those guards will be back in a minute, and they won't be happy that we've gone for a walk. Now get moving!"

I did, all the way back to the chamber and the chute. I was tired from carrying the deputy for the most part, but we were at the brink of success. I dumped the insensate creature at the bottom of the boulder we'd placed at the chute's entrance and straightened, holding my back with one hand and my small flashlight with the other and then turned to Casey. No Casey.

Frantically, I looked around and reconfirmed for myself that an empty room without Casey was, indeed, an empty room without Casey. "Casey," I called softly. "Casey!" I yelled. Then I left the change creature where I'd dropped him and ran down the passageway to the portal. Halfway there, I heard the sounds of struggle and the snarls and coughing grunt of a fully enraged Werewolf. As I ran up, it was spitting and snarling at Casey who was holding it at bay in the portal.

The Were had most of its chest and one arm through the portal. It was swinging its long arm and claws at Casey. She was trying to ward off its blows with my javelin. Without thinking, I grabbed her at the waist from behind. I literally picked her up and swung her around to face back up the passageway toward the chamber and the Rabbit Hole. She shrieked in surprise. That just seemed to madden the enraged Were even more.

I quickly grabbed the javelin from her. I yelled at her to run for the Rabbit Hole as I turned back to the Werewolf. Forcing him through the portal was the second Were who'd been selected for guard duty on the change creature. If the second Were kept pushing, it would force the first Were's chest all the way through and over into the passageway where I stood. If that happened, it was a matter of minutes before the Were would pull himself and fully emerge into the passageway. Broken tip or not, my javelin was about to get intimately acquainted with a Werewolf.

DAY THREE 6:25 P.M.

I straightened up. I gripped the javelin with both hands. I drove it all the way through the first Werewolf's chest from side to side. I jammed the broken point into the rock face framing the portal's far side. I then leveraged the shaft and wedged the near end into a bit of rock forming the portal's near frame. The first Were, now dying and frothing, was caught fast. He could neither go in nor out of the portal but was caught squarely in its gate no matter how frantically his companion tried to push or pull him.

Seeing that he was secure for the moment, I turned and made my (hopefully) last run back to the chamber and chute where we'd first dropped down the Rabbit Hole. I was wearing out fast. I tried to think as I ran how to get the change creature out. I could think of no other solution than to do as I'd first thought of doing to my dad. Loop the rope around him and pull him up and out with brute force. To do that, Casey, Dad, and I would all have to be outside the cave's entrance pulling from there. I explained this to Casey as I gently but firmly pushed her to the chute. I told her how I'd lifted my dad out and that she would have to stand on my shoulders as he did.

She was cooperative until we got into the close confines of the chute. Then, putting her arms around my neck preparatory to climbing onto my shoulders, she held my gaze for a moment and leaned in and up and kissed me. It was a moment of peace in the middle of insanity. Then she was up and onto my shoulders while I was still recovering from her kiss.

"Turnabout is fair play," I heard her laugh as she pulled herself over the ledge and around the sharp bend. I ducked back under the lower chute's opening and untied the rope from around the boulder. I retied it around the chest of the trembling, semiconscious deputy. Then, standing on the boulder, I grabbed the rope and pulled myself to the upper lip of the chute. I began my own fight to lever myself over the chute's upper lip. Wrapping my right leg around and under the rope gave me a place of friction to stand when I placed my other foot on top of the rope against my lower foot. I began to make real headway in negotiating the tight curve by shuffling myself forward inches at a time like a caterpillar. I continued this way for a few minutes until I finally emerged into the sunlight where Dad and Casey grabbed and hugged me.

I quickly turned and told them to help me haul up the deputy. We pulled and strained for several minutes as the sounds of bedlam and weapons rolled up the ravine like a flash flood. As we kept the rope taut and tried to pull in unison, the rope suddenly jerked backward, and I was pulled partially back to the Rabbit Hole's opening. I called out to Dad and Casey to pull harder from their end, that the Werewolves had apparently broken through the portal and found the chamber. More importantly, either the Weres or the deputy was fighting back. We were about to lose our prisoner. We then pulled hard together. We watched the rope come our way for a foot or two before we stopped to catch our breath and start a second pull.

Immediately, the rope was snatched from our hands as whatever was on the other end exerted greater force. It practically ripped the rope back down the passage to the Rabbit Hole. "Let go!" I shouted to my dad and Casey, forgetting the rope was still wound around my leg. The pull from the other end then jerked me off my feet and back into the narrow passage before the steep bend. I started sliding toward the back of the Rabbit Hole. Casey and Dad grabbed the rope and tried to pull back, but the effect of that was to tighten the rope around my leg until it cut off all circulation. It began to cause me incredible pain.

DAY THREE 6:40 P.M.

"Let go! Let go!" I shouted to my dad and Casey. "You're killing me! Let go!"

They finally got the message and let go. That immediately relieved the pressure. It also gave me a moment to unwind my leg from the rope. Too late. The Werewolves below began pulling even harder. My left leg was jammed against the lip of the sharp turn, preventing me from being pulled through and back into and down the Rabbit Hole. The rope began to burn my leg as its rough surface tightened more around my skin. If the pain earlier had been excruciating, this was unbearable. Then the situation added insult to injury as the upper end of the rope outside came loose from its rocky anchor. It began to disappear down the passageway through and around me as the Werewolves continued their relentless pressure and pull.

The rope snarled as it reached my leg. Instead of spinning around my leg and falling down the shaft, it was caught and held down by the pressure of my leg. With all that downward pressure, I could not pull it free. Again, I was being dragged inexorably into the Rabbit Hole.

The screams and snarls of the Werewolves below notwithstanding, I could hardly think in the confusion of the moment. I had little shoulder room to move and could barely leverage myself against the pull. Nor could the strength of my left leg continue much longer to wedge me against the lip of the sharp passageway bend. That was all that was saving me right now. My dad and Casey had nothing to snare me and pull me back to freedom. I was about to surrender myself to a fate I would not wish on my worst enemy. Then I remembered my mom's hug and whisper. The knife!

Quickly, I tried to reach for my pocket and the knife I'd placed there only hours before. I could not feel it at first. I started to panic. Without it, I was doomed. At last I found it. Flat on my back with my left leg jammed against the sharp bend's lip, I was able to snake the knife out of my pocket and open it with my thumb. Once free of the haft, I placed the blade against the rope and began frantically sawing back and forth, anything to cut and release the rope. The blade was exceedingly sharp. With two or three cuts, the rope suddenly snapped and jerked down the Rabbit Hole. I was free!

Casey crawled partway into the cave entrance. She grabbed my extended hands as my dad grabbed her ankles. With all of us pulling, kicking, and inching backward as best we could, I was soon free of the small cave. Dirty, tired, and disheveled, we knew we had to leave the area before the saturation charges went off. We did, but not before Casey crawled partway back into the Rabbit Hole to retrieve and hand me my mom's knife. We had minutes at best by my watch. Casey kept Dad's side-by-side scattergun, and Dad kept her .357 Magnum pistol as we prepared to run up the ravine.

I had one task left. Turning to the ammunition pouch I'd placed earlier beside the Rabbit Hole's entryway, I opened it, took out the box, and flipped up the lid. Then I watched as the occupant casually stretched himself as if he had been snoozing. With stately grace in the face of confusion and calamitous noise, the large black-and-white skunk I'd purchased at Pete's Pet Emporium stepped from the box to the ravine floor. He looked up at me questioningly.

I told him it was safe here but that a few large, angry Werewolves, maybe even a lot of them, might be coming this way soon. Maybe even some men like me with slightly different colored uniforms. "Just sit tight and walk out into the sun to greet them," I said, laughing. They will run away from you faster than they ran toward you. You will soon have this area to hunt all to yourself. Since skunks are food-driven, my words were encouraging to him. He settled down by one of the rocks near the Rabbit Hole's entrance, partly in the shade.

"Rear guard!" I shouted to Casey and Dad as I turned and lunged up the ravine. Shocked, they looked at each other and then grinned and ran after me. They easily overtook my hobble. They disappeared into the growth at the top of the ravine. Panting hard, I caught up with them a minute or so later. We were all laughing at what the reaction would be to whatever was following us. In good spirits, we managed to keep up a good pace as we pushed ourselves farther and farther away from the Rabbit Hole.

Without warning, the ground beneath me suddenly lurched upward and sent me literally flying through the air. I crashed into the lower boughs of a large evergreen tree. I scraped my face and hands on its needles. No sooner had I landed than I heard a nearby crash and then a second crash as both Casey and then my dad also landed in or at the base of a similar fir. Loud explosions followed immediately. Our ears rang for several minutes afterward. The charges at the caves had evidentially exploded. I wondered which of the Werewolves, if any, were left and if the three caves had really been successfully sealed off.

DAY THREE 7:00 P.M.

Curious, we all stood. We brushed ourselves off and checked for any injuries. Fortunately, there were none. We started back to the brush line we'd entered to see what we could see. Clouds of dust rolled up the ravine and, from our distant vantage point, it seemed to pile higher and higher, spreading over the former cave entrances until the sun was measurably dimmed. The dust cloud that eventually enveloped us made sight beyond 20 yards or so difficult. We could no longer see the Rabbit Hole.

We started to turn away and find a trail or pathway that would lead us back to the police units near the cave entrances. We all heard a sudden exclamation from the direction of the Rabbit Hole. It was a howl and cough that together sounded like a grunt on steroids. That was followed by a deep, resonating squeal and an angry series of snarls and barking noises from the skunk.

The look of horror on our faces as we turned to each other was universal. Somehow, someway, one of the Werewolves had come up the Rabbit Hole and was at the entrance. If one was there, more would follow. With only two weapons among us and me without my bow and arrows, we were in a very precarious spot. It would only get worse with time.

The only nearby help we knew of were the police forces near the far cave entrances. We had a small advantage in the dust cloud since it provided some cover, but the winds were already starting to clear away that advantage. We'd certainly not have it for long. What we also had were reasonably sound legs. My dad was quick to push each of us, Casey and me, to the front of him facing a higher ridge that separated us from the two main cave entrances.

"Run!" he said. "Run for your lives!" And we did, Dad passing me almost immediately as he and Casey disappeared into the haze. I hobbled along as best I could. While I set no records, I did manage to break a personal best over the first 50 yards. It was then that the local winds picked up and the deep haze lifted around the hills we were on. The haze dispersed in rather dramatic fashion. One minute it was there and our vision was limited. The next minute, the haze was gone, and visibility was blocked only by trees and hilltops.

I heard shouting ahead over the crest of the second hill I was climbing. It sounded like Casey and Dad had hooked up with some of the police or military units that had destroyed the cave entrances. As for me, I stopped to catch a labored breath. I heard branches breaking and the sudden shrill howl of a Werewolf somewhat behind me. I spun about and was shocked to see not one but three Werewolves coming on the run after me over the crest of the first hill. They weren't much bigger than I was, so I assumed they were females or adolescents, but that wasn't my interest. Their teeth were a *lot* bigger than mine, and they could move. Fast. And they were running. They were coming presumably to kill and eat me. I turned and yelled as loud as I could and then plunged up the second hill as fast as I could awkwardly go. I pulled myself along by grabbing handfuls of brush or tree branches or anything that would get me closer to the top of the hill that separated me from my dad and Casey. Behind me, the troika of Weres was fast closing in, plunging through bushes that had forced me to go around them and leaping over rocks that forced me to clamber over them. I could almost feel their breath on my exposed neck as I strained for the crest of the hill. I started to imagine what it would be like to have a leg or arm ripped off in my maddeningly slow flight. I was startled out of my desperate reverie when a loud voice cried out, "Get down! Get down flat, Cody!" I am usually compliant where persons of authority are concerned. I immediately stopped my mad climb uphill and obligingly dove behind a small rocky outcropping. I buried my face in the mud and sparse grass. I flattened my body as much as I could. I brought my hands up to cover my ears and protect the back of my neck.

Within seconds, the air above was split time and again by the zip and whine of bullets fired from the police sharpshooters. They were taking positions along the crest of the hill ahead of me. One of the Weres screamed out an anguished howl that fell off halfway through. Its cry was so close I was tempted to see if it was lying beside me. Whatever had hit him had apparently killed him. Then the shuddering grunts of another Were coughed behind me as it went through its death throes. I heard no sounds after that. I had the good sense to stay exactly where I was until one of the sharpshooters on the hill crest above called out, "Cease fire! Cease fire! All clear!" The firing ceased, but I kept my head down for another 20 seconds or so in case 10 percent didn't get the word. When all seemed quiet, I slowly raised my head and saw Casey and my dad standing on the crest of the hill. They were with five men in military uniforms and one sniper in a SWAT uniform. All were holding their weapons at waist level looking down the hill behind me. As I turned around to see what they saw, a yelp involuntarily escaped me. I backed up against the small escarpment now behind me. Not 10 feet away was a perforated Werewolf, muzzle ploughed into the turf and front legs and claws stretched out toward me.

I had been incredibly close to being Were-ke-bobbed or becoming a not-so-fast-food snack for one of the Werewolves. I silently thanked God for Casey's strong soccer legs. She'd been in the lead and the first over the hill to contact the police. Had events unfolded more slowly, I would only be a chewed-up and digested memory. That was far too close for me. I sat down and then promptly collapsed against the hillside behind me. I felt as weak as a newborn kitten.

DAY THREE 7:30 P.M.

After a few minutes break and a couple of deep drinks from a soldier's kindly proffered canteen, I felt enough of myself to get back on my feet and hug Casey and Dad again. Dad pointed out that with the appearance of those three Werewolves chasing us, we had to assume that a number had escaped the firefight and cave explosions and had found a way out. At least three had, and others would soon be trailing behind. We had to go back to the Rabbit Hole as fast as possible and "put a cork in it," as Dad said.

Four of the soldiers, one carrying satchel charges, started running for the Rabbit Hole. Casey went with them to guide them. Dad and I followed at as rapid a clip as my legs could endure. We had an escort of the soldier and the remaining police officer. My pace was somewhere between a fast lunge and a controlled lurch. Thanks to downhill, we covered ground much more quickly than I thought we would. Dad's sling was still hanging around his neck and still working, and his legs were fine. His legs were just a bit tired from the sudden hill climbing. I felt he was glad I set the pace, not him.

As we crested the smaller first hill, we heard sporadic firing below us and near the mouth of the Rabbit Hole. Descending quickly, we broke out from the underbrush and tree cover. We could see that the soldiers were spread out, firing into the Rabbit Hole. Four dead Werewolves were sprawled immediately outside the Hole's entrance, and another one was about 20 yards away, almost at the feet of the lead soldier. Casey was kneeling behind the third soldier, the one with the satchel charges. The first soldier called a cease fire as we drew close and turned to come toward us, as did the other three. For a quick moment, no one was watching the mouth of the Rabbit Hole.

I spotted movement as we walked up and yelled to the soldiers that had kept their position but turned in our direction. Too late. With fearsome howls, three very large Werewolves broke from the small cave's entrance, each taking a soldier as its objective. Two reached their goal before the soldiers had fully turned to engage them. The first soldier died with his head peeled from his body, his rifle firing indiscriminately before his missing brain could send a message to his fingers that he was dead. Several of his random shots apparently tore into the attacking Were that screamed in pain and collapsed, coughing and grunting up blood before it expired.

The second soldier died when his attacking Werewolf crashed into him. It ripped his weapon from his hands, knocking the soldier flat to the ground. It was hard to say which was faster next, the soldier who drew his knife from his leg sheath and pushed himself off the ground or the Were that leaped at him, fangs extended. They each met in air, the Were fastening its teeth on the soldier's neck as the soldier rose to meet the

Werewolf and the soldier's knife plunging into the Were's chest as the Were crashed down on it. Both gave a spasmodic jerk, and both died.

The third Werewolf sped for the soldier guarding Casey. The Were piled into him at a dead run, knocking him into the air and down on top of Casey. Spinning in an instant, the Were leaped for the tangled pile of Casey and the soldier, jaws extended. I heard a giant sob as the Were landed and the crunch of teeth tore into bone. Then all three bodies were instantly entangled in frantic movement while each sought to escape or attack the others. Without thinking, I grabbed for the Smith & Wesson Extreme Ops knife in my pocket and cleared the blade as I ran (that's right, ran) to the mess of heaving limbs and biting teeth.

I clearly saw the Were's head as I approached. I literally dove for it, grasping the head with one arm around its neck and holding it firmly, pulling back with all my might as I slit its throat. Blood poured out on all of us. I pushed this way and that trying to get us all untangled to tend to Casey. I found her dazed but relatively unscathed except for a covering of Were blood. She was just stunned. The soldier had not been so lucky. His leg was partially severed. His artery had almost bled out before we could find and stop the bleeding.

He died minutes later but not before I wept and thanked him for saving Casey's life. Casey knelt beside me. She gently kissed his cheek before he closed his eyes. He quietly stopped breathing. With that, Casey turned and simply clung to me. In our own excitement, we hadn't noticed that our escort had resumed firing directly into the mouth of the Rabbit Hole. Apparently, the charges that had closed the other cave entrances had dramatically altered the ground strata where we were. They had opened a large passageway into and through the Rabbit Hole. Adult Weres were now trying to escape. The soldiers were running low on ammunition so their weapons were no longer on automatic fire. It was single shot directed fire with only an occasional burst.

One of our escorts hollered that we had to place the satchel charges next to the cave entrance, preferably in it so we could close off this last escape route. Moreover, we needed to do that *now*! I stood and hobbled back to the spot where the soldier had been hit by the Were. I picked up the satchel. I started to turn to the cave when Casey snatched it from my hands. With as steely and determined a look as I had ever seen cross her face, she told me I'd get everyone killed with my hobbling around. She was going to do this.

I had the good sense to stand aside as she turned and dashed back toward the entrance. She ignored the firing from the remaining soldiers and SWAT team member. They had the good sense not to hit her or I'd have swapped sides and joined the Were contingent before she hit the ground.

A large Were, seeing her coming, tried to reach out with its arm and claw her to the ground. She unflinchingly stopped and flung the satchel charge into the Were's face with all her might. She knocked it back into the Rabbit Hole's entrance chamber as it clawed at and caught it.

Almost without a pause, Casey turned to the side of the entrance and ran parallel to the hill. She raced up the ravine, scampering upward as fast as she could while the soldiers switched their weapons to automatic fire and poured the last of their ammunition back into the entrance. Nothing could live through that, I thought, until one of the soldiers who'd escorted us yelled, "Fire in the Hole!" We all dropped to the ground as he electronically detonated the satchel's charges. The resulting explosion lifted all of us off our feet or bellies. It threw me eight to 10 feet away from where I'd first dropped to the ground at the soldier's warning.

Clouds of dust and debris swirled around us. I was deafened by the blast, my head simply ringing and ringing. I was totally disoriented. I had to wait on my hands and knees until some of my senses returned and I began to hear again. Gradually my senses came back to me. Finding that I could stand up, I did so. I staggered off in the direction Casey had gone.

I found her crumpled against the hillside about 30 yards up the ravine. She was unconscious. She had no other body injuries as far as I could see. I took her into my arms and cradled her against me. I quietly rocked her. I said whatever soothing and soft things came into my mind. I didn't know I was weeping at the time.

Dad found me there. He simply sat down beside me. His eyes held a question about Casey. I just shook my head and shrugged. I was interrupted in my rocking by a tap on my left shoulder. It was the SWAT team member. He gently took Casey out of my arms. He checked her neck pulse and broke open an inhalant that he waved under her nose. Casey came awake in seconds. She struggled to sit up. She was coughing and choking and trying to swat the policeman's hand away.

"She'll be fine," he said, and clapped me on the shoulder. "That's quite a brave young lady you have there." He smiled. "If I was twenty years younger, I'd fight you for her." He then stood up and walked back to join the remaining soldiers and survey the damage.

DAY THREE 8:00 P.M.

Casey, Dad, and I sat back against the hillside. We said nothing, each of us once again going through the series of events we'd just experienced. We knew that in a matter of hours the police would be debriefing us downtown. After that, we could go home, take a shower, and sleep. Maybe they'd let us go home tonight and debrief us tomorrow, I thought. But I was frankly too tired to worry about it. I was considerably relieved a little while later when the Chief and a couple dozen or so well-armed officers showed up to bring things to a close.

In fact, the Chief let the three of us go home with our promise to be back in his office by 9:00 a.m. the next morning for a formal debriefing. We caught a ride back to an escort car with a police officer on an all-terrain vehicle. It was a bumpy ride but a sweet one nonetheless. He asked us about the two deputies who had been assigned to us. We simply told him they had been killed by the Werewolves, that they died defending us. He grew almost bitter for a moment and said that was how a lot of good people died, defending helpless civilians.

As we rode along, we were all silent until Casey spoke up. She thanked the driver for his service. She expressed our sadness that good people had died that night, some on our behalf and some because they believed they were defending a population much greater than the three of us. She looked at me as she talked to the back of the driver's head. I added a few comments, essentially praising the officer and his fellow officers for their bravery and contributions in the face of a horror few would ever encounter.

That exchange seemed to please the driver. Nothing more was said until we arrived at a place where a number of vehicles were parked. A different officer then drove us home. By 10:00 p.m., bathed, fed, and hugged a number of times by my mom, I hit my bed and collapsed on top of the covers.

DAY FOUR 7:30 A.M.

I'd been up for an hour. I was shaved and fully dressed before Mom called me down to breakfast. I was halfway through a fairly heaping plate of eggs and bacon when Dad wandered in. He, too, was shaved and almost dressed. He was scratching his elbow and arm that had been in a sling the day before. "I still need it," he said when I looked up questioningly. "The sling. But Mom's washing it so I don't look like a panhandler when we go to the police department." I just grinned. We all knew Mom's penchant for making everything look right, even (or especially) in the face of disaster.

He picked up the newspaper. He read the same headlines and article I'd read earlier about the natural gas leak and series of explosions that had rocked the hills west of Chagrin Falls last night. We understood the police had cordoned off a very large area. Crews were in there even as we sat at breakfast. They were looking for further leaks in the lines that ran through that area. The paper warned that there could be more explosions. Everyone was warned to stay clear.

Several radio stations entertained call-ins all morning. We were told they were evenly divided. Some listeners thought a UFO had crashed and that the cordon was just another cover-up while the alien survivors, if any, were captured and spirited off to a top secret base in Nevada. Other callers were assured that in light of President Johnson's new tax initiatives, police had surprised a large bootlegger gang making moonshine. The explosions were nothing more than the feds blowing up the stills after a considerable gunfight, of course.

Still others had seen trucks going that way from the armory. They figured the Reserves were simply getting some night training in combat situations. There were other theories as well. All were given attention by the hometown press for several days until the next US crisis captured the headlines.

Our debriefing went on for several hours until the Chief called Casey, Dad, and me into his office and shut the door. "If I had a medal, I'd pin one on all of you," he said. "But I don't. And even if I did, I might have second thoughts because I don't want the average Joe or Jolene out there getting the idea that he or she can be as effective as my police force in confronting danger. But you folks are clearly the exception. I don't know how you get into these messes, but you sure have a way of fixing them once you pull us into them. I'm sad that Chagrin Falls will never know what you've done, but they won't. You're still under a gag order. You will stay under one as long as I'm Chief. The public simply isn't ready to know what you know. I couldn't stand the panic and deaths that would result if what you know and have seen were made public. So, thanks again. Now go home and try to be quiet citizens. And Cody," he said as he reached behind his desk, "here's a new Black Widow bow to replace the one your dad broke. Use it well. We want to keep our state champion right here in Chagrin Falls."

He then pulled me aside and whispered in my ear before he escorted us to the door.

It wasn't until we were back home that Casey asked me what the Chief had said. Dad chimed in and said he was curious as well. Was it about the mop-up going on right now, or was the city going to replace the arrows I'd lost in the chamber beneath the Rabbit Hole as well? I told him it was just a good luck wish for the archery championships, nothing much else. Dad laughed and turned back to his office.

Casey just looked at me, grabbed me by the arm, and marched me outside where we were alone. "Now tell me the truth," she said. "I know you, Cody, and I know when you're not coming clean." I had to laugh at her determined look, and then I remembered this was the gal who had carried death and destruction right into the Weres' teeth, literally, so I got serious in a hurry.

The Chief said they had recovered the deputy when they went into the rubble at the Rabbit Hole after we left. They placed him in a containment facility early this morning, and he was being watched and monitored 24/7. He was communicating to some extent, and some rather dramatic physiological changes had already occurred. It was ugly, but they were getting some hard intelligence from him. They would be better prepared for the next onslaught because there would be one. The deputy had been adamant about that. Adamant. Absolutely adamant!

Casey looked at me, thanked me, and then softly put her arms around me and hugged me for a while. And it wasn't one of those nurture hugs, either. I wondered as I stood there if I should try that kiss again and then remembered the look on her face when she'd taken the satchel charges from me. Okay, I thought. Hugging is good. Hugging is really good. But as I wrapped my arms around her even tighter, I couldn't help but think just once more. What if it's only a *little* kiss?

THE END OF EPISODE TWO, BOOK ONE

EPISODE
THREE

DAY ONE 5:30 P.M.

I'd been sitting in my room alone for several hours trying to understand the female mind, specifically Casey's. I wasn't having any luck. No matter what amount of reason I could bring to bear on the subject, I couldn't seem to fathom even a particle of her mental or emotional workings. *Why can't girls think logically like guys do?* I kept asking myself. Can't they read minds? I mean they always seem to know what's going on and are usually two or three steps ahead of us guys, but sometimes I just don't get them.

Casey Allegro, my next-door neighbor and soul mate, the girl I'd had my most secret crush on for years, the light of my wretched and deprived life, had accepted Brad Thorney's invitation to our high school's annual Thanksgiving dinner and dance. Moreover, she practically told me I had no one to blame but myself. But really, how *could* she? After all, everyone knew I was going to ask her. I *always* asked her. No one else was right for me but Casey, and she should have known that. But did she say no to that weasel-brained football braggart Brad Thorney? Oh no! She said yes right there in the lunchroom before hundreds of kids. So now she couldn't back out if she wanted to, and I wanted her to even if she didn't.

Where is the fairness? I raged as I pulled my pillow over my face and tried to suffocate myself by wrapping my arms tightly about it, choking when I managed to temporarily cut off my air supply. Tossing the pillow aside as a bad idea, I cried out instead, "Where's the justice?" I moaned and then pulled my pillow back over my face and howled, "There is *no* justice! There *is no* justice, I tell you!" I yelled again and then let all the jealousy and frustrated longings of a young man wash over me as I lay there in a blue funk until my mom called me down to dinner.

"It's your own fault. You know that, and I don't want to hear another word, another sigh, another cry, another *anything*. Do you hear me?" Mom said. "I mean it, Cody. You could have asked her anytime in the last three weeks, but you kept putting it off, and I, for one, am glad Brad Thorney asked her. She's too special a girl to have to wait around for anything or anyone. You had your chance and blew it. So just sit quietly and eat, or go to your room. I don't particularly care which. I don't have the energy for this nonsense anymore."

"But," I started to say when my dad interrupted me.

"You heard your mother, Cody. You don't want to hear from me, too," he said with a warning in his voice.

Now, I may be a bit dramatic from time to time. What fellow isn't? But I'm not stupid. I'd heard that tone in my dad's voice a number of times before. I'd learned the hard way that my dad doesn't bluff and doesn't waste words. So I shut up and asked Mom to please pass the mashed potatoes. Then I got real serious about the meal she'd put in front of us. Mom is an excellent cook and a great mom. She knows when and how to give a guy a little leeway as he bumbles his way through late adolescence. Most important, I know my parents love me even when I'm not so lovable, like now at the dinner table. But it still hurt inside that Casey had accepted a date for *the* fall dance with that lummox Brad Thorney, of all people.

After dinner, I stayed to help Mom clear the table. We talked a bit while she washed and I dried the dishes. I felt I could talk to my mom about anything. After dinner at the sink was probably the best time in our respective schedules. I told her about my confusion with Casey, that my feelings were all over the place. I liked her as a friend. I loved her as my soul mate. I even felt I might be in love with her, but at 18 years old, what did I know about love anyway?

Point was, I'd come to see Casey almost as an extension of myself. I knew that both of us had talked a great deal about when we'd be at different colleges about a year from now, she on a soccer scholarship to North Carolina and I somewhere here in Ohio or maybe at Texas A&M where I could explore engineering and veterinary medicine. That certainly didn't bode well for a long love life for either of us. I knew Casey was what I wanted in life, just not right away.

Somehow, just talking with Mom with her soft, occasional questions or pats on the shoulder made it seem okay, even if neither of us didn't always have the answers for the questions I posed. As I learned from her, it's always good to suffer with someone, just never in silence.

When we were finished, I went up to my room and hit the bed early. This was just one of those days when I was the bug, not the windshield. But boy, did it hurt! In fact, I was feeling so sorry for and wrapped up in myself that I pictured Brad Thorney as my personal javelin target as I drifted off to sleep. He was pretty shifty, but I had a stack of javelins and lots of dream time. Unfortunately, I never heard the squirrel tapping and scratching on my window trying to get my attention. It was the next morning before I learned that something other than Brad Thorney was not right with my world— something *much* more important than Brad.

DAY TWO 7:00 A.M.

I slept restlessly all night. I tossed and turned, continually trying to adjust my pillow with an underlying fear that it might attack me during the night. Maybe it just seemed that Brad Thorney, star halfback on our football team, always dodged my well-thrown dream javelins. He always ran into the arms of Casey no matter how many times I threw one at him. Whatever, it was a rough night. I awoke cranky and ready to focus on anything that didn't wear a skirt.

As I sat there swamped in my covers, I could hear an irritating tapping as though someone was hitting glass with a stick, a sharp stick. It was a regular cadence. The sound wasn't loud. It was just insistent and irritatingly endless. Rubbing my eyes, I looked toward its source. I was surprised to see a northern flying squirrel peering at me through my window and knocking on it with his paw. When I looked at him, he reacted immediately by turning this way and that as if to find a way in. I slid out of bed and hobbled over to the window. I raised it slightly to let the little fellow in. I then quickly closed the window behind him to shut out the chill that followed him in.

He immediately hop-jumped to my bed and threw himself onto the pile of bed covers. He nestled in with a satisfied smirk on his face and then burrowed even deeper as if he were swimming underwater. I started laughing. I couldn't help myself. He was a welcome break from my morose nighttime thoughts. I was anxious to know what he'd been doing on my window ledge. When I finally uncovered him and confronted him, he told me he'd been sent by a big gray owl with a message for the man who talked with animals. He asked if I were that man. I dryly answered yes. Just with whom did he think he was speaking?

Squirrels are not nature's academicians. They speak like their minds and muscles work. That's at 80 miles per hour with gusts up to 120, detours expected. Nevertheless, once I had his attention, I asked what the message was. He spent a lot longer telling me than he needed to. Werewolves had been sighted once again in the Dead Zone. Not many, but all adults and somehow different. They were moving in small groups. Each night two or three would leave the Dead Zone for our town, Chagrin Falls. When I asked what they were doing in Chagrin Falls, the squirrel answered, "Nothing. All they do is watch." He said they went into our town at night and came back just before dawn. In fact, one of them always came to the alley behind my house or the house next door.

Every alarm in my mind went off at that statement. The Weres were not only back, they knew just where Casey and I lived. Apparently, we'd been under their observation for some time. My first instinct was to bolt from the room and tell Dad and Mom, but after a second or two, I realized the Weres were only doing night surveillance. They would be back in the Dead Zone by now at early daylight. Still, chills were running up and down my spine. These were not pretend bad dreams that would go away with the daylight. These were evil incarnate creatures that were targeting my family and Casey's family, perhaps others as well.

The owls were worried because now more Werewolves were going out at night into the town, sometimes as many as five or six. At times, they came back with small animals such as dogs, cats, or even squirrels. I was worried because they'd be bringing home humans soon if someone out for an early morning jog or late evening walk happened to cross their path.

The owls were apparently maintaining their surveillance on their own. It had been literally weeks since our last encounter with the Werewolves. The police and military authorities in that raid thought the Weres had been contained when we blew up their main caves. Not so, obviously. But how many had survived and where they were coming from were my burning questions. We needed answers and needed them sooner rather than later. I didn't have them. But I knew who would, so I dressed in a hurry to catch my dad before he was off to work.

I was pounding down the stairs as he was putting on his coat by the door. I startled him. With his lazy grin, he told me to slow down unless we were on fire, and if we were, to keep right on running to the phone in the kitchen and call the fire department. He was off to work. He'd see me again at about 6:00 p.m. I grabbed his arm and told him I needed to talk with him now, that it was about the Dead Zone and the Weres. That got his immediate attention. He pulled me into the living room. Both of us plopped down on the couch. "Tell me everything," he said.

I did.

DAY TWO 9:20 A.M.

We were waiting in the small reception area at City Hall outside the Police Chief's office. We'd been waiting about 10 minutes. The Chief was finishing up his morning management meeting with his lieutenants and staff. His secretary left us alone for a few minutes. She came back with some small milk cartons and a selection of 12 donuts. She offered the tray to us. My dad politely declined. I politely accepted and took the tray from her hands. I sat down and began a wonderful morning feast. My dad and the secretary watched me, dumbfounded, as I finished up the last crumb and sat back with a smile on my face. I had cleared the plate.

Werewolves or not, a chance to eat plenty of donuts was rarer than hen's teeth. In my defense, I felt a man had to keep his priorities straight. The secretary just looked at Dad as one parent to another. He rolled his eyes, and both turned their attention back to me. I was sure they were wondering what was coming next. Nevertheless, I was glad I'd chowed down in a hurry. The Chief's door opened. When he stepped out and saw us, his face started to brighten and then immediately fell. He saw the empty donut plate as well. With a weary tone in his voice, he asked us to come in. It carried that been-there-done-that, got-the-T-shirt finality. He simply nodded and stepped aside so we could enter. Closing the door, he did not walk back to his desk with a light step. We spoke for almost 30 minutes. Several times, he told his secretary to take a message, that he was busy, that he could neither speak with nor meet with whoever was vying for his time.

After giving us his full attention and listening to my message, he asked my dad to take a half day off work. He also asked if I might be excused from school that morning. He wanted to meet with both of us at what he called the containment facility. It was the same place they'd taken the deputy who was in change mode when the police recovered him at the Rabbit Hole cave. The Chief had some things to tell us that could not be discussed in his office. Dad said yes and made the requisite calls, and then we left with the Chief. The Chief put us under oath not to reveal the location of the containment facility and drove us to an unmarked cement slab between the polo fields northwest of town and the Chagrin River.

A slanted, bomb-shelter-like entrance was the only distinguishing thing about the great slab. As we approached, the slanted door opened. Two large men in sanitation department uniforms emerged and walked toward us. Greeting us, they started to inquire about our business when they recognized the Chief. They then stood aside, letting us all walk to the entrance from which they'd emerged. We stepped down into a steel-sided room approximately 12' x 12' in dimension. A battered desk, some old folding chairs, and some old magazines on the floor were the only things in the room. A large metal door with a bar and lock on it adorned one cement wall. One of the sanitation workers closed and locked the slanted door above us. When he was done, the other worker opened the large metal door in front of us. We walked into as modern an office facility as I had ever seen. There were a number of people, some in lab coats and others in suits and ties. They were working in what appeared to be a span of offices. The large, hangar-like room measured about 30 yards by 100 yards. A series of steel cages were erected against the far end of the complex. Muted sounds of deep growls and occasional howls emanated from there.

The Chief welcomed us to the containment facility. It was initially built during the last stages of World War II as a possible armory. It was later abandoned. Then it was refurbished and outfitted as it now appeared by a government division concerned with chemical warfare research. Since chemical weapons were outlawed, the facility became an unconventional weapons development lab for a clandestine government agency. It had recently been turned over to a small group in the Defense Intelligence Agency (DIA) engaged in classified biomedical research. That's why Weres were brought there, for study and testing.

DAY TWO 11:00 A.M.

When the Chief's former deputy had been captured at the Rabbit Hole in change mode, the colonel in charge of the armory had alerted DIA authorities. The deputy was brought to the containment facility by DIA security personnel in covert status. The facility's workers all lived within a 35-mile radius of Chagrin Falls. They were encouraged to move into outlying communities in order to minimize the chances of the facility's purpose being discovered. All the employees were members of or ostensibly worked at the Polo Club. They carpooled to minimize the number of cars seen at the Club each day. Personnel entered the actual facility through two separate, secure, secret entrances at the Club. One was in the main clubhouse itself; the other was in the stables. Almost all the Polo Club staff were military or government civilians assigned to the secret lab. Very few were third-party private contractors.

All this and a number of other things were explained to us in the course of an hour's briefing in the facility's conference room. The Chief then introduced us, explained our role in the matter, and opened the floor up for questions. A number of the scientists questioned us at length about our respective observations and experiences. So many questions came so fast that the Chief finally called a halt to the open interview. He promised to bring us back another day soon. That seemed to mollify everyone until I explained that the Weres were still around. Moreover, they were conducting directed reconnaissance against me and possibly others. They had changed their assembly and movement tactics because of our last raid.

I explained that our watchers were concerned that some event was imminent. My dad and I shared that concern. I was asked what I meant by "watchers." I responded that just as they had secrets to which I was not privy, so did I have some I could not share. They weren't happy with that answer but had no comeback. They were, however, keenly interested in the fact that there were still Werewolves out and about in purposeful clandestine activities.

We were finally taken to the big cages at the facility's far end. There we saw the creature we had first known as the deputy. Its change had long since become complete. We stood several feet away from the cage. A painted yellow caution line on the floor was the barrier between life and death. We looked at a full-grown adult Werewolf that was not a happy camper. It prowled restlessly back and forth, stealing sidelong glances at us from time to time.

Suddenly, pivoting its head to look directly at me, it sprang forward with an alarming force that bent the metal cage bars it crashed against. It roared its disapproval. It tried time and again to reach through the bars to rip and ensnare me. It gnashed at the bars as if to bite through them. Finally, wearying, it rested its head against the bars and glared silently at me. Hate poured from its fathomless coal-black eyes. If it blinked, I didn't see it.

The creature's posture had an immediate effect on both of us. Nearly nose-to-nose, I found I could suddenly read this Were. Its snarls, murmurs, and thoughts opened up to me as if we were two individuals having a street-side conversation. I said nothing to the men and women around us. I stared at the Were intently as it stared back at me. Each of us was locked in a silent, furious confrontation in an apparent test of wills.

Overriding everything else in its mind was a total and absolute hatred of humans. It knew it had once been one. It knew it was now in a condition from which it could never return. It considered its circumstances so unfair that its consuming desire was to attack and kill or change every human it encountered. It was aware of technology but could use it only on a limited basis. In many cases, it and its newfound kind could not use it at all. With paws and claws instead of hands and fingers, its grasp was severely limited. It could communicate with other Weres by audible sounds, but it could not communicate with them by thought or other expression as it was doing with me.

The Were knew I was a dangerous threat to all Weres as long as I drew breath. It didn't know why. It was aware that I had been targeted by a very senior Were council to be captured or killed, preferably killed. It knew little of the council except that it existed. The council considered it too coincidental that I had played a major role in two disasters that befell them. They did not want me around for their latest forthcoming operation.

The Were was aware that his group of Weres was only a small group compared to several much larger groups operating throughout the United States. Other small groups lived mostly near small cities in places that offered great concealment. Two of the main nerve center groups were in North Carolina and New Mexico. Other lesser regional groups were in Texas, Kentucky, Wisconsin, Wyoming, and Oregon. The Were had no idea of the specific locales. It did know that the Chagrin Falls Weres would soon launch a model community attack coincident with the holiday we called Thanksgiving. Werewolves from some of the other areas were here to observe or participate. The Chagrin Falls attack was to be the forerunner of others yet to be scheduled for launch elsewhere in other states.

I asked our Were how it could know all this since it was captured shortly after it started its change. It had no real opportunity to communicate with any of the Weres in the third cave or even at the Rabbit Hole. It said it didn't know how. It just did. The knowledge was there immediately after the deputy was bitten and the change started. There seemed to be more it was willing to share, but I had a headache that had almost reached migraine proportions.

I pulled back from the yellow line four or five steps and knelt down, holding my head. I pressed my hands into my temples. The headache hurt. I felt as if a vise were squeezing my very brain. It was some minutes before I felt fully recovered enough to stand back up and answer the questions my dad and the Chief were throwing at me. They couldn't understand why I'd been in a staring contest with the Werewolf. They feared he had managed to hypnotize me or something.

I said no, that I probably had a headache from trying to concentrate and stare him down. At that, the scientists and personnel around us just looked at each other and shrugged. They began to wander off, heading back to their respective offices, desks, and duties. When they were gone, I asked the Chief to find us a small room where we could talk in confidence. I had much to tell him. He'd want to take notes.

Once there, I admitted to both men that I could read the Werewolf's mind to some degree. I told them what I had learned. The Chief was an immediate nonbeliever. He said people couldn't do that. I agreed but said I could, nonetheless. I said if he thought that was really impossible, just walk back out to the Were's cage and tell me if the creature in it is real or a figment of his active imagination, because everyone *knows* Werewolves aren't real. The Chief sat down immediately. He just looked at me. He was flabbergasted. He then took out his small binder and started taking notes as I gave him information. We were there for almost an hour. He checked and rechecked what I'd told him. He then left for a few minutes to return with the facility's Director. We spent another hour with the Director. We then spent yet another hour with several scientists and specialists the Chief called in to review everything one more time.

It was 4:30 p.m. before we finished. I had a real headache by then. I'd had nothing to eat but those donuts and had long since suffered a sugar low. At that point, the Chief broke up the conference and signaled that we were to leave. Before I stood up, the Director stopped him and made it clear we were now in a national interest mode. The Director felt he couldn't afford to let me just go off as if nothing had happened. I was his only asset besides the Werewolf.

He asked, "What if you were hit by a car or, worse, captured by the Werewolves?" No, he was not willing to risk that given what I had revealed. I was effectively the government's property now. At that point, my dad spoke up. He made it clear that we had come as volunteers, not as subjects to anyone's whim. Nor had martial or military law been declared by a duly constituted authority, and that authority was way above the Director's pay grade anyway. My dad told the Director that we were still in the United States the last time he'd been outside. Unless the Director felt he had to hold us at gunpoint, we were leaving.

Dad also added a by-the-way statement. He noted that if anyone should pull a gun on us, they could kiss any covert cooperation goodbye forever. And he also noted that his wife and our neighbors would raise such a bad stink that the Director's job, this facility, and the DIA would ultimately be compromised with details of the Werewolves smeared all over every free press paper they could speak with. Then the panic would start. The Director would be lucky if he wasn't busted back to a GS-1 level before being shot by the government or a panicked populace for not telling them about the danger to their families that this facility and its mission represented.

You could have heard a pin drop. I was stunned. My dad's face was about four inches from the Director's before Dad pulled back and put his arm around me. At that point, the Chief quietly cleared his throat. He said we'd be in touch. He softly pulled my dad and me away from the stunned group. We exited the facility with the help of the two sanitation workers. It was a long drive back. About halfway back, the Chief started chuckling. Soon Dad and I were laughing with him. We all knew we had work to do and would do it gladly with the Director, but we would do it as citizens and not conscripts. We would work together as equals.

I'd relearned something about my dad that buoyed me up and gave me great confidence about my future. He didn't waste words, and he didn't bluff, even when it looked like the other guy held all the cards. It was an example I would use many times in the years ahead. A time would come, although I didn't know it then, when that tactic would save my life.

DAY TWO 7:00 P.M.

We were scheduled for a late dinner that Mom had prepared for our arrival home. Dad had called Mom from City Hall when the Chief dropped us off where we'd left Dad's car that morning. It had been a long and tiring day. I wanted to share it with someone other than Mom. When we walked into the house, Mom told me to wait before I cleaned up, that someone was waiting for me in my room. I immediately thought of Casey and dropped my coat. I lurched up the stairs two at a time before Mom could say anything more, bursting into my room prepared to sweep Casey up in my arms when she told me she'd turned down Brad Thorney.

What I got wasn't the embrace I'd been hoping for. I got a flying squirrel splayed out on my bed covers flat on its back, deep in sleep. And snoring. Apparently, he'd been in my room all day since morning. In my haste, I'd forgotten to let him out before heading downstairs to catch my dad. My mom appeared in the doorway. She let me know that he was a welcome guest *only* if he stayed in my room. She'd been in several times to do some cleaning. She found him hopping from my bed to my desk to the top of the bookcase, then launching himself on a short glide to my tangled bed covers. Over and over and over again. After watching his unvaried routine for four or five minutes, she simply closed the door and let him leap to his heart's content. She left me to deal with the consequences when I returned. "Good luck!" she said as she turned and walked back downstairs. "Don't take too long. Dinner's ready, and your dad is hungry."

Picking up a fully contented, sleeping, flying squirrel was like lifting a freshly washed and fluff-dried dishcloth. It is the definition of limp. No matter which end I picked up, the other end just flopped and lay flat. I finally bent low and whispered explosively into the squirrel's ear. "Hawk!" He came awake like a spring recoiling. He immediately dove deep into the tousled bed covers. He moved so fast that I almost missed him. I was able to plunge my hand into the covers and gently extract him. He was wiggling frantically all the while.

I apologized for scaring him before he could bite me. My mere apology didn't work well with his disposition. He was one unhappy squirrel. Nevertheless, I thanked him once again, slipped him some shelled walnuts that were loose in my desk drawer, and carried him to the window. There I placed him on the outside ledge and bid him adieu. As I closed the window, I told him to keep a close watch.

About 20 seconds later, I was pulling my chair up to the dinner table. Mom, as usual, had cooked another culinary feast. I was determined to do it justice. Suddenly, my appetite was lost as I looked out the window in the rapidly fading twilight. I remembered what the squirrel told me earlier. One or more Werewolves would likely be watching my house tonight. Nothing puts a chill on a festive gathering like the thought of a dedicated killer lurking nearby and looking for action.

I ate everything my mom put in front of me, but that was all I ate. I cautioned Mom and Dad to stay inside, if possible. I walked back up to my room to just lie on my bed and think. I knew Dad would fill Mom in on all the pertinent details of the day. Sometime that night I fell asleep, but I don't remember just when. I think it was late because I still felt a little sleepy the next morning. It had been a deep and dreamless sleep, what there was of it.

Oddly, I awoke full of energy. I was clearly in a better frame of mind than the day before. I was even starting to be grateful that Brad Thorney had asked Casey to the fall dance. If the (former deputy) Werewolf was right, a big fight was coming. I felt I'd better concentrate on that than worry about corsages, deodorant, and aftershave. If it came down to a choice between a dance and a fight, I would take the fight every time. Unless, that is, I had a date with Casey.

But I didn't. I started worrying that if students were targeted by the Weres, would Brad be able to take care of Casey? Then it hit me. I started to laugh. I should be worrying if she could take care of him! Brad only played with footballs. Casey played with satchel charges.

DAY THREE 9:00 A.M.

Third-period algebra and calculus was an honors course for the very few students who had demonstrated an aptitude for the subject. It was also the first class of the day that I shared with Casey. We had two other honors classes together, English and organic chemistry. We were both at the top of each class. We often studied together two or three nights per week. That's probably why we were high achievers. Neither of us wanted to lose to the other on quizzes, papers, or projects.

Casey came over to my desk when she walked in. She immediately asked where I had been yesterday. Had I been pouting because she had accepted Brad's invitation? I told her no, that was nonsense. I said I was happy she had chosen Brad. I felt they should have a wonderful time, that she'd be the belle of the ball. I'd been absent because Dad and I had been with the Police Chief all day. I promised to fill her in after we got home.

I then opened my book and pretended to be reading my notes while she just stood there. She looked at me with that skeptical gaze of hers as she tried to divine the truth. Finally, she shrugged slightly and walked to her chair. I thought she dropped her books with a little more emphasis than needed before she sat down. I noticed from the corner of my eye that she kept giving me long looks during class. I couldn't have been happier.

Several times that day, she stood close to me and tried to strike up a conversation or two in the hallways or lunchroom. I made sure I was always with someone else or busy with my notes or books so she never really had a chance to follow up that morning conversation with me. I don't know when I smiled more or displayed such a keen interest in other kids and things. By the end of school, I made sure I took a different route home than I normally did. I even stopped by a 7-Eleven convenience store for an ice cream bar and Twinkie before I finally headed home.

Casey was sitting on her driveway step waiting for me when I walked up. She was more than a little mad, if the look in her eyes was any indication. Her steely-set jaw was back. I'll have to handle this carefully, I mused, but I was thrilled at her discomfort. I thought my chest would burst.

"Why have you been ignoring me all day?" she demanded before I even had a chance to say hi as I walked up to her.

"Well, hello," I said. "What in the world are you talking about?"

"Cody Dugway, you know exactly what I mean. You have been nothing but a snot to me since I agreed to go to the fall dance with Brad. That's not how good friends treat each other. That's not fair, Cody. It's not fair!"

I looked at her for a moment. Her mouth was slightly turned down, and her eyes were on the verge of watering. I felt like an idiot and a numbskull. She was right. She was my best friend. I should want nothing but the best for her, even if it meant I couldn't get what I wanted. "I'm sorry," I said, and quickly picked her up in my arms and just held her tightly against me in the air for a minute. I then set her gently down. I told her she was very important to me, the most important person in my life outside of my mom and dad. I said I wanted nothing but happiness for her and even for Brad Thorney if he was what made her happy. After all, who was I to stand in her way?

"Oh, you idiot!" she said, and stood there defiantly. "You idiot!" she exclaimed once again, and then hit me on my shoulder harder than I've been hit in quite a while. Then she turned and stomped back to her side door. She slammed it shut behind her. It bounced open again. Her mother poked her head out, saw me, winked, and then gently closed the door.

"What?" I exclaimed. "What is wrong with you, Casey? What did I do?" It fell on dead air. After standing there like a fool for several minutes, I picked up my backpack and walked around to my back door. I hadn't even started to tell her about yesterday.

Now I wasn't at all sure I'd even get the chance. I still felt it was important. In frustration, I threw up my hands, grabbed my hunting bow and a quiver of arrows, and went in the back to practice. *Girls!* I thought. *Who can possibly understand them?* "And who'd want to?" I turned and yelled at Casey's house. But not a shutter or shade moved. I knew I was all alone. With a bite in my jaw, I yanked an arrow from my quiver, drew my bow while I was turning, and put an arrow through the bull's-eye of my target 30 feet away. I then put a second beside it less than five seconds later. My rush of emotions having cooled off a bit, I then got deadly serious about practice.

There would likely be a Werewolf in my alley tonight. I would be waiting for it. I wanted to be ready to kill it. I no longer cared about school dances. I only cared that I would be in a calm mood when the time came, but to anyone who's seen Weres in action, that's a wish that rarely comes true. The old football adage came to mind: you play like you practice. I put so many arrows in bull's-eyes during the next 30 minutes that I broke or shredded more than a quiver of arrows. It was worth it.

Game on! I thought to myself as I headed inside to dinner.

DAY THREE 11:30 P.M.

I'd been up on our garage roof for the past hour or so waiting quietly with my bow and arrows beside me. I was sprawled flat on the roof where the shade of a tree cast a shadow over the rear portion of the roofline when the sun was up. That had been several hours ago. I was watching and listening, waiting for any sign that a Were was near or had come for the nighttime surveillance of our home, of which the squirrel had spoken. I was prepared to stay there the whole night. I draped a dark blue blanket over me to help conceal my shape. I laid my head at the roof's far edge. By turning slowly, I could see both up and down our alley. Everything was quiet. Even the insects seemed to be taking some time off. Then again, in an Ohio winter, there never really are many insects out at night.

Two things happened next that raised the hackles on my neck. They made me wish I'd not had that pseudo fight with Casey. A large, dark shape appeared to materialize about three houses down from where we lived. I carefully moved my eyes along the alley. Our alleyway had no streetlights except at each end, at the intersections. Our neighborhood kept the alley reasonably clear of debris and obstructions. That posed a challenge to me. Anything moving through our alley at night could do so silently without much effort.

As the shape neared, I could see it was the form of a Were. Unexpectedly and immediately behind and to the side of it, a second shape began to emerge from the dark. Not one but two sentries, I thought. Well, bring it on was all I could think from my rooftop perch. I was in an extremely safe place with no wind. My scent would not tip off the Weres to my presence before my first arrow hit one of them.

Softly, slowly, I slid back the blanket and picked up my bow and the arrow I'd previously nocked. Slowly, ever so slowly, I turned, bringing my left leg out so I could roll up on my right knee in a firing position. The Werewolves crept forward to our back fence. They stopped there. Carefully, they peered over the fence at the back side of our house. Lights in the kitchen and in my parents' bedroom still glowed dimly through the pulled curtains.

DAY FOUR 12:30 A.M.

I've got you, I thought to myself as I began to draw my bow. The silence of the night suddenly exploded as Casey entered my yard holding her coat shut and calling out my name. "Cody," she whispered at a noise level closer to a holler. "Cody! Where are you? Cody, I know you're out here somewhere, but I can't see you. Where are you?" she called again, only this time even louder as she turned her head back and forth trying to peer into the shadows.

I made the mistake of taking my eyes off the Weres for just a moment as I turned to see just what in blue blazes was happening. I then heard the unmistakable growl and snarl of a hunting Werewolf. Frantically, I turned my head back to the fence only to see that the closer of the two Weres had leaped the fence. It was making its way to Casey in a furious rush, jaws fully extended and accelerating with each stride. *One shot*, I thought to myself. *One shot is all you've got or Casey is nothing more than a memory.* I spun to my left, spotted the Were, and let my arrow fly.

It caught the Were high up on its neck, pushing its head to the side so it fell to the far side of Casey rather than on her. It kicked and made awful choking sounds while desperately trying to bat the arrow away. It was frantic to ease the pain, but all it did was break off the shaft. Weakened, it tried to turn toward Casey. It could not raise its head from the ground. It started to pull itself closer to Casey's legs when my second arrow drove through its neck close to the first shaft. My second shot pinned it to the ground, killing it.

I'd had no time to warn Casey. So occupied was I with the first Were's attack that I completely ignored the second Werewolf. However, it did not ignore me. When I turned to find it, I found myself looking straight into its eyes as it scrambled its way onto the roof of the garage. It had cleared the alley fence in one bound and leaped for the garage roof on its second. It hit the gutter waist high. Throwing its chest down on the tiles to give it a purchase, it tried to secure itself by digging its claws into the roof tiles. I quickly reached for another arrow but slipped on the blanket. I yelped in fright as I watched my foot slide out from under me. I fell backward. Slowly I began to slide down the roof into the Werewolf's extended jaws, the blanket starting to slip with me.

I tried to jab the Were off the roof with the end of my bow as I closed in on it. But it wouldn't have it. It grabbed my bow from me, literally snatching it from my arms. The Were threw it down behind it and almost took me with it as I tried to grab it back. Its strength was incredible. It kept trying to swing a leg up and over onto the roof so it could pull its whole body up to better attack me. All the while, we were having a tug-of-war with the bow. Fortunately, it was having no success.

In its gyrations, it seemed to be on the verge of losing its balance entirely when its leg and foot pad finally caught in the gutter. It glanced to its right to assure its victory, and then within seconds, it rolled over onto the roof. Turning quickly, it threw itself at me or where I'd been only moments before. When I saw its leg and foot gain purchase in the gutter, I threw myself off the roof behind it and into the tree that bordered the alleyway.

It plowed into the spot where I'd just been. It broke several of the roof tiles with its muzzle as it hit, jaws opened. Shaking its head, roaring with anger and hellish intent, it spun about to find me desperately grabbing limbs to pull myself farther up into the tree. "Run, Casey! Run!" I screamed, and then dropped down several branches to draw the Were's attention to me as (I hoped) she made her escape. The Werewolf glanced to its left at the sound of a door slamming and then launched itself at me, swinging its arms trying to grasp on to any tree limb that would hold him. It broke the branch I was standing on with its chest as it hit the tree limbs and then fell to the ground, breaking off other smaller limbs and bouncing off bigger ones on its way down.

As the Were crumpled to the ground, the lights in my house and Casey's house came on. My dad came running out into the yard holding his street sweeper in front of him. Spotting the Werewolf at the base of the tree, he ran forward, bringing his shotgun up to fire when the Were howled and leaped over the fence. It hobbled rapidly down the alley into the darkness. Dad came up to the dead Were pinned to the ground and kicked it, making sure it was dead. Casey's dad also came running out with his pitchfork, the one he had purchased to investigate Werewolves at the barn well two months earlier. Casey's mom came running out behind him. All walked over to me as I fitfully climbed down and dropped from the tree. I was scratched up and bleeding from several spots where tree branches had stuck me, but I was otherwise okay.

DAY FOUR 1:30 A.M.

"Inside! Now! Everyone! We've got some sorting out to do," Dad said, "and I, for one, want to know what you were doing out here in a tree, Cody, being chased by a Werewolf. And just how and why is this one stuck here with your arrows through its neck? But come inside now, all of you, in case there are more of these creatures out here." Dad warily looked around our yard. "This is insane!" I heard him mutter to himself as he closed our patio door once all of us were inside. "Cody," he thundered, "you've got some explaining to do. Now's a pretty good time to start."

I have to say it was an interesting next hour, and it wasn't my best. With explanations given and everyone in the two families finally brought up to speed, I got a chewing out by my dad that I fully deserved, but he finished it by saying, "Never, do you hear me? Never go up against a Werewolf without someone having your back. Never!" he shouted. Then, feeling a little foolish, he walked over and hugged me and told me with tears in his eyes that to lose me would be a crushing blow to him and Mom, one he wasn't sure he could stand. Mom joined him. I felt all of six inches tall for the risk I'd taken. Casey's parents echoed my dad's sentiment with respect to her. I said almost the same thing to her directly, which earned me a hug from her I won't forget for a few years, if ever.

Dad and I walked Casey and her parents outside and back to their side door and then turned and walked back to our yard. Dad stopped by the dead Werewolf to get another look. I ambled on over to the tree to recover my bow that had finally come to rest at its base. As I knelt down, I caught the whiff of rotting debris. I started to warn my dad that the Weres were back again when, with a snarl and a howl, a Were bounded over the fence to a spot directly behind where I'd been.

But this time, on hearing its growl, I immediately rolled to my right, bow in hand. I kept rolling trying to make it to the wall of the garage, which I could use as a backstop when I faced the Were.

My dad hesitated all of a second or two. When he saw I was clear, he pulled both triggers of his street sweeper. He literally blew off one of the Were's arms and shredded its leg. The Were fell to its left, howling miserably. It began flopping around before it finally fell silent. Blood was pouring out of the stub that had been its arm. My father then ejected the shells from his shotgun, running to the downed Were even as he reloaded. He recocked his weapon as he slid to a stop. He kicked the Werewolf as he arrived at its body and got an incoherent response. The Were was still alive. But as he raised his shotgun to kill it, I yelled for him to wait. Maybe we could capture this one and learn from it. He nodded his head without taking his eyes off the Were.

"Then get over here, Cody. See if you can put a tourniquet on this arm," he yelled. "The Were's bleeding out fast. You don't have much time." I was moving even as he spoke. Whipping off my belt, I tied it around the Were's bleeding stump as tightly as I could. The blood flow stopped almost immediately.

"Watch him, Dad. I'll call the police." I ran for the house. I called two numbers, the Chief's and the coroner's office. The latter had an ambulance that had been used to pick up the first dead Werewolf at City Hall. Any civilian service would go nuts at their first glance of a Were. They'd tell everyone. I then ran out to Dad, and we just waited.

If we had needed any confirmation that Werewolves were serious about killing Casey or me, the evidence on our back lawn was staring us in the face. It lay there in the forms of one dead and one unconscious Werewolf, or maybe two dead Werewolves if the ambulance couldn't get there any faster. But it came in time. It arrived with the Chief who, once the creature was strapped in and settled, sped away to the containment facility.

The Chief asked us to report to his office by 8:00 a.m. for a debriefing. He asked if I could still make it to school by 9:00 without suffering any penalties or missing any tests. I replied that I could. He said he'd see us then. We might have some interested observers there as well. With that, he was off. Dad and I trudged back to the house. I noticed that Casey's porch light was on. I saw her watching all the commotion as I glanced her way. I gave her a brief wave and followed my dad into our den.

I already knew that Casey would corral me at lunch hour today. She would go over again in detail whatever the Chief would explain to us in the upcoming meeting. That meant I would talk, and she would listen and eat.

DAY FOUR 11:15 A.M.

I entered the lunchroom looking around for Casey. We spotted each other at the same time. She started walking toward me. Brad Thorney suddenly appeared and fell in beside her. He kept trying to ask her something I couldn't hear or make out. I saw her give a quick negative shake of her head and then heard her say she'd see him later. But he looked up and saw she was heading for me, so he stayed right by her side. He came up to me first and said, "Hey, hobblehead! Look who's standing up all by himself!"

"What's your problem, Brad?" I asked. I started to turn to Casey when his hand shot out and grabbed my arm. He pulled me back to face him. "Look, Brad," I said. "I don't know what you're obviously mad about, but this is neither the time nor the place to start anything. I've been waiting to speak with Casey all morning. Just give us a few minutes, will you?" I jerked my arm free and turned to Casey.

Freeing myself like that apparently made him feel like I'd challenged his manhood in front of possible witnesses. He was quick to reach out and grab my arm again. Once more, he tried to spin me back around toward him. It was a game I wasn't playing. I don't like being bullied. So I let him spin me toward him and brought my left elbow up as I helped spin myself. It connected solidly with his jaw. He went down as if he'd been gassed. I fell with him and landed on him, quickly kneeling and putting my arms around his shoulders as I tried to lift him up. He was groggy. He couldn't clear his vision.

"What's going on here?" yelled Mr. Blanton, the vice principal, as he rushed over. He reached down to haul both of us back to our feet. "Nothing, sir," I quickly replied. "We three were talking, and I think Brad wanted to tell me something. He grabbed my arm for attention, but I guess he's stronger than he thought because he spun me. As you know, my legs have never been solid since my accident years ago. I tripped and fell, and it happened to be on him. I hope he isn't hurt." I reached for Brad and dusted him off.

"No, no," said Mr. Blanton. "He appears to be okay."

With that he walked off, helping Brad stand erect. He chided him for using his strength on someone who needed a wheelchair part-time. "Some of these kids are fragile, you know," were the last words I heard Mr. Blanton say as he walked away helping Brad clear his head.

I turned to Casey and got as withering a stare as I have ever received. She stood, arms folded, like a granite slab with about as much warmth. "Really, Cody? Really?" she coolly questioned me. "What is it about testosterone and you guys? Did you *have* to slug him?"

"Well, yes," I replied. "But it was for his own good because otherwise he'd have pushed me. I would have fallen. I would have screamed to make sure everyone saw it. They would have called him a bully, and the vice principal would have had to come over and take him away, putting him in detention, which means he'd have to forfeit one football game and our team would have lost their chance to win the district championship. Then hundreds of school children and possibly thousands of townsfolk would have had their hopes dashed, and gloom would have settled on this city, leading me to believe several people would have started kicking their dogs in frustration. But I happen to love dogs, so I stopped him."

Her jaw dropped, and she just looked at me in amazement. Then she burst out laughing and hit my shoulder again, only this time it was different. She grabbed my arm and marshaled me out of the lunchroom to a space in the hallway nearby where we could talk without being overheard. She couldn't keep the grin off her face. In no uncertain terms and tone, she asked me to tell her what was going on with the Chief and where I had really been all day yesterday.

"It's complicated," I said, "and I've been sworn to secrecy on some things. But there's a lot I can tell you and not much is good. We're in for a real fight with the Werewolves. It's coming soon, and we don't know where or how, only that's it's soon. And Casey, that's not the worst. There's a national network of these things. We seem to be the testing ground in their war on humans. Hooray for Chagrin Falls!"

I was interrupted by the bell. Before we broke apart and went to our separate classes, I promised I'd tell her more when we got home after school. Several people stopped by my locker as I changed my books. They all said something quietly like "Good job, Dugway" or "Way to go, man!" It told me two things: I'm not as good an actor as I imagined, and Brad Thorney's fan club wasn't as big as he might have hoped it was. Either way, neither my acting ability nor Brad Thorney was my real problem right now. I wanted a crack at that second Werewolf if he'd survived the trip to the containment facility. I had questions, and he likely had the answers I needed. Maybe I could talk the Chief into letting Casey come along as well.

DAY FOUR 3:30 P.M.

School was out, and I was well on the way home when a car pulled up to the curb and kept pace with me as I walked. Brad was in the front shotgun seat. One of his pals was driving, and there were two in the back seat. Brad started beating on the car door with his arm and calling my name. "Hey, Dugout! Where you going, man? We have some unfinished business, or are you too chicken to face me this time when I'm looking?" I kept walking and ignored him. I hoped he'd grow tired of his tirade and that he and his friends would drive away. Didn't happen.

It wasn't Brad so much as his friends who kept egging him on, demanding that he recover whatever face he'd thought he'd lost in the lunchroom altercation. Brad, for all his on-the-field elusiveness and football fame, wasn't strong enough to push back. I could see this was building up to a confrontation. It was one I didn't want and really didn't have time for, so I stopped, turned, and challenged him to a duel.

"A duel? What the heck is a duel?" he asked. "You mean with guns or something?"

"Yeah," I said. "Only you get to choose the weapon." Well, that stopped them. This had escalated way beyond a push and shove or simple beating. I had just gone nuclear. They all realized I was dead serious. Brad's friend stopped the car. They all got out and walked over to me. They formed a kind of semicircle around me as if to cut off any escape I might attempt.

"If you're really feeling like you've no choice but to fight me, Brad, then let's get beyond the sophomore stuff. Let's fight. I don't play around. If you choose to hit me, I will use every advantage, every weapon, every dirty trick I know, and I will seriously harm, maim, or kill you. I'm just telling you right now that I don't fight for fun. When I do fight, someone will wind up crippled, dead, or dying. So you choose. Now!" I was as serious as polio, and they knew it.

They all started to back away then, kind of a slow shuffle back toward the car. I invited them to give me a lift home so I could show them something. By this time, they were starting to get confused. I promised them no funny stuff, just come with me for a few minutes and let me share something. My earnest appeal seemed to take some of the sting out of the moment. They reluctantly agreed. I climbed into the front seat next to Brad. We rode quietly without speaking for the several blocks to my home. They pulled up in my driveway and piled out. Casey had heard us approach. She had arrived home earlier since she had the last period free. She stepped out onto the driveway, saw us all, and did a double take. She asked what was going on.

I explained I wanted to put on a small demonstration for the guys since they put on a demonstration for all of the school each Friday night. I led everyone to the backyard. I brought out my competition bow. I put on a 20-minute demonstration of my archery skills for the fellows. Casey just sat in the grass by Brad and smiled without saying a word. I think I missed the bull's-eye once.

The guys were fairly impressed. They were laughing and talking with each other when I picked up my hunting bow, put on my quiver, and asked Casey to kick a few soccer balls toward the side of our garage. I invited the guys to see if they could catch and stop them. They all jumped up at that. I quietly promised Casey I'd pay for the balls I destroyed.

She ran to her house, brought back four balls, and lined them up about 20 yards from the garage. Taking her stance as if she were doing a penalty kick, she sized up the line of four guys and kicked the first ball as hard as she could. It went whistling between two of them much faster than they'd anticipated. Casey was a champion in her own right. She could literally kick like a mule. Her scholarship was riding on that ability.

Calling each other a few names, the guys lined up again. Casey kicked the second ball. This time she added spin, and the ball whirled around Brad who was directly in its path. He was set to kill it dead. No chance. Once again, Casey lined up. This time she kicked a grounder that almost literally cut a path through the grass as it sped beneath and between the legs of the two young men at the end of their line. One ball left. The football players were now getting angry. They were rocking back and forth, arms and hands extended, digging in their sports shoes as their expressions made clear that this time was a do-or-die moment.

Casey approached the ball and suddenly stopped. Two of the guys leaped high, and two threw themselves forward low. All fell and skidded on the grass while Casey casually lifted the ball with her foot and daintily lobbed it over their sprawled bodies. Four kicks. Four goals. It was a humbling experience, but neither she nor I was finished.

I asked the guys to step back to the sidewalk while I did it my way. Curious, they all moved back. When Casey had realigned the balls, I asked her to kick at leisure using whatever tricks she had. Four kicks later, there were four deflated soccer balls pinned to my back fence. The players were goggle-eyed. I asked one more favor after I'd retrieved the deflated balls.

I asked Brad to please throw them behind me in any random pattern. I would attempt to turn, draw, and shoot four balls in less than 15 seconds. The guys guffawed at that. One bet me I couldn't even come close. "Let's make it loser buys a milkshake for everyone," I offered. I got four quick takers. I asked Casey and Brad to time me with Casey giving me the go. She did. It was all over in 14 seconds. Every deflated ball had a new arrow through it.

With that, I turned back to the guys and asked if they had any questions. They just looked at me agog. Casey broke the silence by saying, "Okay, guys. Let's go get those milkshakes. She sat in front with Brad, and I happily sat in back between his two friends. We had a great time. It was an hour or so later when they dropped us off. We exchanged friendly goodbyes. I told Brad that Casey liked small violets if he was going to buy her a corsage. He looked surprised and then grinned and thanked me. He shook my hand before he and his friends drove off. They left Casey and me standing on our common driveway.

Once they were out of sight, she turned to me, crossed her arms, and said, "Really, Cody? Really?" She grinned, pulled my head down, and gave me one of the sweetest and softest kisses I'd ever gotten. Then she grinned at me again, took my hand, and led me back to my yard where she sat me down. She got her serious look back again, plopped down in front of me, and simply said, "Now, tell me *everything*." It was back to business, and I obeyed. As I once opined, Casey is a don't-mess-with one-of-a-kind. I'd learned the hard way over the years with her that obedience is better than sacrifice.

DAY FOUR 5:25 P.M.

I started by telling Casey about the meeting that morning with the Chief, a man called the Director, several scientists, and another man who attended and sat behind everyone else but was never introduced. Three police sergeants were also there. Two I recognized from the bombing attack on the three Were caves. My dad and I were the guests of honor as it were. Dad let me do most of the talking about last night's ambush and aftermath. We learned that both the dead and wounded Werewolves had been taken to the containment facility. The wounded Were was still hanging on, but barely. At that point, one of the officers expressed a desire to see Dad's shotgun. He wondered how a regulation shotgun could do so much damage. The Chief merely waved him off. The rest of the discussion centered on how they would preserve the wounded Were so I could question it. Thankfully, they didn't ask me how I could do that.

At that point, I asked for permission to bring Casey in on this with me. I explained who she was, that she'd been part of this since the beginning. Several of the men objected at once. They said a woman had no part in this sort of violence. That lasted about five seconds until one of the officers who'd been at the Rabbit Hole—the SWAT officer, in fact—stood up and silenced everyone. He said he'd take Casey as part of his squad today if she'd volunteer. He then described what she'd done. When he was finished, he looked around the room. Everyone was now a go. The Director bowed to the pressure. He told me to bring Casey with me to our next meeting. He then added that he had security and nondisclosure forms for all three of us to sign—my dad, Casey and me.

A meeting was set up for the next evening. That would allow three additional representatives time to fly in and attend. They were coming in from North Carolina, New Mexico, and Oregon. Werewolf activity was apparently starting to build at each locale but had yet to break out into the public eye. The three were on separate fact-finding missions, but all were part of the same military group. With that, our meeting was closed. I was taken to school by the SWAT officer.

He told me he'd been very impressed with both of us. He told me as well that if I should ever consider law enforcement to call him. I was excited when I exited his car. I got some strange looks from the kids who saw me before I entered the high school. It had been a good start to the week until Brad's lunchroom fiasco. Fortunately, that had eventually ended well, too.

Casey was pleased with what I'd said. Taking my hand, she asked me if I was really upset about her going to the fall dance with Brad. I said yes, and no, but my feelings were all messed up now that I'd had a chance to start to get to know him personally. She laughed at that. She told me she'd been friends with Brad for a long time. She thought he had a crush on her, but she did not have a crush on him.

Nevertheless, she was really delighted he'd asked her to the dance. It solved a ticklish problem. "Why," I asked, "if he's just a friend?"

"Because," she said, "the whole women's soccer team has been practicing several of the new dances for weeks now at our at-home get-togethers. Each girl wants to have a chance to demonstrate her routine at the fall dance." Then she looked at me with those deep eyes and said, "Face it, Dugway. *You* can't dance a lick. This is my last chance in our senior year to kick up my heels because I'm not going to the prom with anyone else but you."

I just sat there with my mouth hanging open, surprised and feeling like my heart would pound itself right out of my chest. I then let out a big "Whoooop!" and pulled her to me. Like the hug the night before, that was a kiss I'll long remember. It was a good thing my mom drove up then or I might still be in a trance. Casey jumped up laughing and ran to help my mom with her groceries. I just sat there floating on air for a few moments with all the brain activity of a contented cow. Casey can do that to me.

DAY FOUR 7:30 P.M.

This was a study night. I had some equations to memorize for an organic chemistry test coming up in a day or two. I was busy at my desk when I once again heard a persistent tapping on my window. It was the squirrel who'd been there before. I raised the window and let him in. He immediately sprang for my desk. He hopped to the top of my bookcase and then launched himself onto my bed covers. I stopped him as he scampered to my desktop for a second try. Gently holding him before me, I asked him why he was here. He said with his staccato delivery that he was here to see the man who could speak with animals. I shook my head in resigned frustration. I sighed and told him that would be me. I asked him again why he was here in my room. He said he had a message from the owls. The Werewolves in the Dead Zone were very concerned because two Weres had not returned from a reconnaissance mission the day before. They had targeted this house. Since this morning, no Werewolves had been seen for the entire day. The owls were afraid something bad was going on. They wanted to know if I had any directions or suggestions.

I thanked him and left him alone for a few minutes. He started to practice his aerial gymnastics while I went down to the kitchen. I found some nuts, returned, and fed him. I put him back outside my window with instructions to tell the owls that I would be driving out the day after tomorrow ("in two suns"). I'd talk to them then in person.

That break was a lot more fun than my chemistry equations, but I knew Casey would be studying even harder. So I put everything out of my mind but chemistry. By midnight, I was confident of my progress. I headed for bed thinking morning always comes too early after sessions like the one I'd just finished.

Just before I drifted off, I had several thoughts. If we were successful in interrogating the wounded Were and my talents were recognized, I just might be able to turn that into a scholarship opportunity. I'd try first for North Carolina at one of the colleges there. Maybe North Carolina State would be my best choice. I'd learned that North Carolina was an acknowledged center for Were activity. Surely some success in Chagrin Falls could very easily boost my stock to help in North Carolina's eradication problem. It was an opportunity worth thinking about anyway. I tucked it away for future reference and promptly fell asleep.

It was another difficult night. I was awakened several times by the howling wind outside. At least I thought it was the wind. Whatever, I wasn't in a cheerful mood when I awoke the next morning. Missing sleep does that. Worrying about Werewolves does it, too. But so does a major organic chemistry test. That was the next threat I was facing. It was ridiculous, I knew, but I felt a small twinge of regret that Brad Thorney wasn't taking organic chemistry that semester.

DAY FIVE 11:30 P.M.

The morning passed uneventfully. I'd seen Casey earlier. We made a date for lunch together at school. I wanted to fill her in on the latest regarding our response to the Were threat. I'd managed to secure two seats across a table from each other so we could talk. I stood and signaled to her as she walked in. She was halfway across the room when it was déjà vu all over again. Brad Thorney walked in from another entrance at that same time. He saw her and started for her immediately. He arrived at our table just as she did. He asked her if he could join us. I was rolling my eyes and silently mouthing "no." Either Casey didn't see me or just ignored me so we wouldn't have a repeat of yesterday.

"Of course," she said and took the seat across from me. Brad took the seat next to her. Turning to me, he said hello and smiled. He told me how neat yesterday had turned out. He asked, "What's up with you two today?" and then settled back in his chair. I muttered that Casey and I had been working on a project with the police and Sanitation Department. The site was west of town in the area we all knew as the Dead Zone. We'd been asked to attend a meeting this evening at 7:00 p.m. at City Hall, specifically the Police Chief's office.

His ears immediately perked up, but his eyes narrowed as he asked, "Why?" Before Casey could respond, I told him our organic chemistry class project involved the study of certain gasses and their combustibility when mixed at certain ratios. Several of those gases had been found to be present in the explosions in the Dead Zone a month or so ago when the area had been partitioned off. Our teacher suggested we prepare a joint paper on what some of the causes might be. We were working with city officials to do just that but needed escort supervision whenever we went there to collect samples and debris from the explosion pits. It wasn't all that dangerous, I proffered, but it could be if we inadvertently set off a spark in a pocket of methane or some other gas.

Mostly it was just getting dirty and trying not to twist an ankle when walking over the explosion sites. I started to ask him if he'd like to join us. I noticed he was looking around rather than at me.

I think we lost Brad at combustibility. His eyes were glazed over. He quickly excused himself to go sit with his football buddies who'd just come in. "Good luck, you guys" was his parting shot. Two people were immediately glad at his departure.

"Well done, Cody" was Casey's response as he left. Her eyes twinkled. "Well done, indeed! You are now in his "okay egghead" file. He shouldn't see you anymore as his potential rival. Life in the next week or so ought to be a lot easier for all of us."

"It ain't Brad Thorney who's going to make the next little while easier," I said dryly.

"Isn't," said Casey. "Isn't." She opened her lunch bag and began to eat. My grammar may have been incorrect, but my logic and conclusion were spot on.

DAY FIVE 7:00 P.M.

We'd been sitting in the City Hall conference room for about 15 minutes when the Chief and the Director walked in together. They apologized for keeping us waiting and took their seats. The Director, not the Chief, opened the meeting. We'd come to the Chief's office at 6:30 p.m. per his request to sign several security and nondisclosure forms. Apparently, the Director and DIA required them. The government promised several severe penalties should we tell anyone about this project. That included the people involved or the threat itself. Signing those papers immediately sobered us up. It removed any hint of levity should there have been any there to begin with. We were in our seats and mute as we waited for the Director to open the meeting.

Once again there were several faces new to us. A round of introductions took care of that with one exception. The unintroduced man who'd been at the back of our last meeting at the confinement facility was again in the room. He was sitting away from the conference table in a chair at the rear of the room. He was observing everything and all of us.

I noticed that his eyes kept resting on Casey and me, but I simply shrugged it off. Casey and I were the youngest ones there by far. She was also a darn sight prettier to look at than any of the other women at the table, so I could hardly blame the fellow. In fact, I soon forgot all about him. I learned sometime later that he was a personal aide to the general who headed the DIA.

He personally briefed the President of the United States on projects of exceptional nature and security such as ours. I believed it. His eyes missed nothing, and his attention never wandered from his focus. I liked him. Even without meeting him, I thought him capable and dangerous. Casey had the same reaction.

The agenda was simple. How was this group of various agencies and individuals going to prepare for a Werewolf onslaught that we felt was coming? We didn't know when, where, how many, how equipped, or what mobility or communications they had. We just knew an attack was in the offing. Moreover, any defense had to be mounted in secret or at least shielded from the general public.

The Director then opened the floor for discussion and set a time limit of 90 minutes for the meeting. He said if this group couldn't figure out an answer by then that he had the wrong group. Reassignments would begin in the morning. That got everyone's attention. Everyone started talking at once. The Director interrupted, thanked people for their initial response, said he was glad they were awake, and then suggested that everyone take 10 minutes and write down their ideas. We would then go around the table. Each person's idea could be delivered quickly and accurately without wasting time.

For 10 minutes, most pencils and pens scribbled furiously. Casey was writing as fast as the best of them. I chose to merely make talking points and came up with eight. By the time the Director got around to me, he'd heard from all but three of us: Casey, the Chief, who had taken the end seat at the table, and me. The Director then called my name. He asked me to stand and deliver my thoughts in a clear voice. Several people had been cut off at the 10-minute mark. Several more had spoken less than three minutes.

I thought there had been some great thoughts advanced, but it was clear these folks were mostly administrators, not field-qualified. Their ideas didn't start from a position of personal accountability. They didn't push out their ideas as if they personally had to take charge and implement them.

I cleared my throat and said I'd do eight things starting now:

- Appoint a battle commander, choose key subordinates, designate a headquarters
- Have the military and police armories increase their weapons by 300 percent and their ammunition supplies by 1,000 percent starting tonight
- Put the town under an ever-escalating rabies quarantine beginning tomorrow
- Start restricting movement within city limits tomorrow
- Put out a press release that packs of feral, rabid dogs have gathered in the Dead Zone and been seen in the vicinity, and that military and state police officials are being called in to help eliminate the packs
- Interrogate the two Weres in hand to discover the new Were gathering site, the Weres' likely force strength, and any support capabilities (weapons, communications, additional fighting bodies, etc.)
- Form an extra intelligence support unit (the watchers) to operate under me with direct communication access to the defense leader
- Send in an armed test team tomorrow to learn firsthand the Dead Zone terrain and then develop countermeasure and assault tactics

I sat down to silence. Casey stood up and tore up her notes. She let them fall to the tabletop. Her comments were simple and straightforward. "Cody and I have fought these creatures nose to nose. We know what they're capable of. I back all his suggestions and suggest you all do likewise. Start tonight." She then sat down abruptly.

The Chief wasted no time standing up as the last speaker. "I second the motion," he said. "You all pick the head honcho. I'll be second in command because it's my town and my people. Pick somebody who knows how to fight dirty." He then sat down.

There was silence in the room. They had not been prepared for such direct suggestions or blunt talk. Heads were turning back and forth and looking at the Director. He made as if to rise when a voice in the back of the room spoke up. It was the unnamed observer. He stood and came to the head of the table. He stood beside the Director.

He did not introduce himself by name but said to all, "I am here as the personal representative of the commanding general of the DIA and the President of the United States. Thank you for all your suggestions. The time for talk has passed. Mr. Director, you will continue as Director of the containment facility and its personnel. Starting tonight, you will now report to Lt. Col. Arthur Spikes who is currently assigned to one of our Special Operations groups. He is providing force augmentation and support in South and Central America. Anticipating this meeting, I contacted him yesterday. He will be here by 1000 hours tomorrow morning. He will bring three officers with him. They will take command of the combined resources here. They may request other personnel or materials as they deem necessary. Those three are Major Matt Ludlow, communications; Major Sara Sanchez, intelligence; and Captain Koko Yamata, operations. Please be here seated at 9:30 a.m. tomorrow to meet and reorganize yourselves according to their wishes. We will waste no further time. Thank you all. You are dismissed."

He then turned to Casey, the Chief, and me and asked us to stay for a minute. He waited until the others had cleared the room. He sat down in the Director's chair and said, "You all are the only people who have actually been in fights with these creatures. You lived through them. We have lost more than 50 people so far at various US locations trying to get some sort of handle on this problem. I've read the reports on the two offensives you've taken against these creatures. I am amazed at what you've gone through. I'm even more amazed that you're still willing to hop back into the thick of it. Thank you. Now, we've got one hour. Tell me all you think I should know about what we should do and why. I like your list, Cody. That's going to be the genesis of our battle plan. Art Spikes is anxious to meet with you two. Sara Sanchez is practically drooling to meet with you, Cody, if you can do what the Chief says you can."

So he briefed us for almost a full hour. We answered as many of his questions as we could and just as truthfully as we could. When we were finally done, he asked if we had any questions. I said I did. I asked him about the two other officers he said were coming with Lt. Col. Spikes. He smiled and said Matt Ludlow was a whiz at setting up communications, from hand signals to the most advanced computer networks. He said he had served with Ludlow before. I then asked him about Captain Yamata and what "operations" meant. He smiled even more. He said operations is the actual warfare. And Captain Yamata? Well, Koko Yamata is the best "dirty fighter" he'd ever seen. With that, he stood up, bid us good night, and left the room.

I watched the Chief watch him leave the room. The Chief had a smile about three miles wide on his face. He was almost licking his chops. I took that as a good omen.

It proved to be.

DAY SIX 7:30 A.M.

I'd been up since 7:00 a.m., fed, dressed, and ready to go. I was anxious about the meeting this morning and missing more school. I didn't want my absentees to count against me in any way in this my senior year. I didn't want to miss a pop quiz or any assignment that would reflect on my grades. My mom and dad were doing all right, but we were not rich by any stretch of the imagination. I knew I would have to have a scholarship of some sort to go to a good school.

Casey was a bit more privileged. As an only grandchild, she had a family trust set up for her by her now-deceased grandparents. She could draw directly on those funds for college.

She had loved her grandparents and always worried about using their trust money correctly. I kept telling her the trust looked at it as her money now. She just didn't see it that way.

At 8:30 a.m., our house phone rang. Mom answered, listened for a few minutes, and then said, "Thank you. I'll tell him myself after this call." She then hung up and turned to me with a most peculiar look on her face. "Cody," she puzzled, "I'm not quite sure how to say this. That was your principal. He received a call from the Mayor and the head of the school board just a few minutes ago. You are being given a special leave from school indefinitely so you can work with the Chief of Police on a special project. He said you would know all about it. You are to come to the meeting this morning dressed to go out to the Dead Zone. Oh, and you are to bring your bow and arrows."

I thanked her and went back upstairs to change and strap on my leg braces. Mom gave me a ride to City Hall when I was ready. Casey had already left with her dad. I wondered if she'd received the same call. When we talked later, it turned out she had not.

I saw few people in the general reception area of the building as I walked in. I chalked that up to the early hour. When I walked into the conference room, it was a different story altogether. Everyone from the night before was there. Most were sitting at the same spot they'd been in last night. I placed my bow and quiver of arrows against the wall behind my chair. Three chairs were lined up against the back wall. They were by the chair the unnamed man had sat on last night.

There was very little chatter. People kept looking apprehensively at the door. We were all waiting for Lt. Col. Spikes and his crew. I'm not sure what anyone else expected, but I expected a tall, ramrod-straight, spit-and-polish, starched camouflage group. What walked in was anything but. I think my expectations dropped further than my jaw as in walked a somewhat tall but rather thin man. He was smoking a battered pipe. He wore a wrinkled camouflage uniform of a design I'd not seen before.

Behind him came the unnamed man in unmarked US Army fatigues. He had a .45-caliber automatic pistol strapped to his side. Following him came a stocky Anglo-Saxon man and a Hispanic woman with the blackest hair I'd ever seen and a smile that wouldn't quit. A rather small Japanese gentleman who seemed to glide rather than stride over the floor brought up the rear. All three were wearing camouflage uniforms just as wrinkled and of the same design as the first man's. They showed no rank. Introductions were made as the unnamed man presented Lt. Col. Spikes and his team. There was no applause, just silence.

They looked almost shabby. There was a day or two's worth of facial hair on the two Anglos as if they had not bothered to shave. If their overall appearance was to impress and comfort us, they had failed miserably. But I learned that appearances truly can be and often are deceiving, especially with the motley-looking bunch that had just walked into our lives.

As we were also to learn, each one of them was as finely honed as a knife's razor edge. They had different specialties and different capabilities, but they all had one thing in common. They were fully mission-oriented. They were like falcons. They were like raptors in every sense. They just did not worry about size or obstacles. Once pointed at a target, nothing was allowed to deter them in accomplishing their objective. They were not killers, but each had killed, as we were to find out. Nor were they unfeeling automatons willing to needlessly risk lives and resources to accomplish their objective.

But they were deadly. They were probably individually more deadly than any three Werewolves hunting together. As I came to learn, they actually enjoyed their jobs. They had fun and expected others with them to stay positive as well. They inspired trust, obedience, and confidence. They were the right medicine for our ailments. They were exactly what the doctor ordered, although we did not know that upon seeing them for the first time.

Most surprising to those of us who came to know them, each person had at least one advanced degree. Yamata had two. His doctorate was in theoretical physics.

DAY SIX 10:45 A.M.

Lt. Col. Spikes stepped forward. In a soft voice, he introduced himself and his three companions. His eyes were constantly moving. They took in each one of us and all of us seemingly at the same time. He explained that if our intelligence was correct, we had little time before the Werewolves would launch their attack, whatever that might be. He said the best defense was a good offense. His plan was to find them, hit them, and hurt them before they hurt us. He told us that two companies of US Army Advanced Infantry would be joining us by midafternoon. They would be under the command of Captain Yamata.

Major Ludlow was already arranging for communications among the various command elements. Major Sanchez would be the go-to person for all information relating to the Werewolves. He stopped at this point and looked at me. He asked if I would leave the meeting now with Major Sanchez while he continued to organize our efforts. I stood up, grabbed my bow and arrows, and walked out following Major Sanchez. Before I could leave the room, Captain Yamata stepped over to me. He glanced at my bow and asked in a low voice if it was true I knew how to use that thing. I said I knew how and stopped there. He looked up at me coolly and asked me to meet with him back here in two hours. "Bring your bow," he told me.

Once outside the conference room, as Lt. Col. Spikes continued his briefing, Major Sanchez turned, reached out her hand to shake mine, and, with a grin I couldn't resist, took me into a nearby office. She sat me down, pulled up a second chair for herself, and looked me right in the eyes. She said, "For now, our only job from here on out is to find and fight Werewolves. You're the man to help me do it. Welcome aboard, Cody. You now report to me. Not your parents, not your girlfriend, not your friends or teachers. Not even the police. Just me. Are we clear on that?"

"Yes, ma'am," I said, and I was. I matched her grin. That was the last real grin of uninformed enthusiasm I had for a good time after.

I spent almost two solid hours answering her questions about everything. If there was a pertinent thought or bit of knowledge in my brain about Werewolves and my experiences, she found it, pounced on it, chewed it up, and went digging for more. She taught me more about focus in two hours than I'd learned in more than 18 years. When we finished, I felt tired, irritable, elated, and angry all at once. But we were in sync.

We realized very quickly that we could work together. I trusted her. I think after our session she began to trust me. If I knew an answer, I told her. If I didn't, I didn't. I had no ego fight in this game. I neither lied nor expanded the truth. Nor did I guess. And just when I thought I could break free and go get something to eat, she reminded me I had a meeting with Captain Yamata. I was bordering on being late. She lowered her voice and told me confidentially that no one wants to be late to a meeting with Captain Yamata.

With that, I scrambled to get my bow and my quiver. I dashed out the door to the nearby conference room. It was empty save for Captain Yamata. He was sitting on the conference room table when I entered. He was holding the eight-point plan I'd briefed to the Director the day before. His first question surprised me. "Is this yours? Are these your original thoughts, or did you copy or collaborate with anyone else?"

"No sir," I replied. "Those are my thoughts." Then I just stood silently looking at him. We stayed that way for literally two or three minutes before he broke the silence and asked me if I was intimidated. I told him no, that once you've faced and fought a Werewolf firsthand, very few things in life intimidate you anymore.

He grinned, hopped down off the table, and walked over and shook my hand. "I was told you were exceptional," he said, "and I can see that for myself. Welcome aboard. If Sanchez looks the other way and you want a piece of the action, come see me."

He then walked me outside to a government SUV parked out front. He reached in and pulled out a Japanese bow with a quiver that looked handmade. It was unlike any I'd seen before. "Let's go have a shoot." He smiled. "A beer to a milkshake I can beat you." I told him he was on. We spent 20 minutes setting up a series of makeshift targets from items in a nearby gardener's shed. We had nine targets, and we'd worked out shooting lines before each target. He wanted to run the course so he could see how I shot when I was tired at the course's end. I pointed out that with my legs, it would be a task just to try to walk the course quickly. I pulled up my pants legs so he could see my leg braces. He stared at them for a minute and looked up at me. "And you did all the things in those reports with those legs?" I answered that that was correct. He just stood there and looked at me for a long time in silence, weighing this apparently new information.

"We'll walk the course at your quickest pace. You shoot first. Go when you're ready." I took a deep breath. As I walked up to the starting line, I noticed Major Sanchez and the unnamed man watching us from the porch steps of City Hall. They were some distance away. I couldn't hear what was being said between them, but I did see them shake hands and turn and give us their full attention as they walked closer.

I nocked an arrow, took a half pull, and stood on the starting line. Then, letting my breath out, I snapped up the bow and loosed my first arrow as I took my first quick step. I finished in 13 minutes. Nine targets. Nine bull's-eyes. Tired, with braces that pinched, I sat on the grass and stretched out my legs as I prepared to watch the Captain. As I had done, he took a deep breath, let it out, snapped his bow up, and took his first shot as he stepped off at a walking pace similar to mine. Nine targets. Six bull's-eyes. Two more targets hit just outside center point, and one target missed.

"Nice shooting," I said as he walked up and flopped down beside me, "but I'm going to hold you to that milkshake." He just grinned at me and asked if he could handle my bow. I passed it to him, and he held it.

"It's been years since I hunted with one of these." he said. "Mind if I try it on that first target?" I said no bother and handed him an arrow as well. He took it. He walked to the starting line, took a deep breath, let it out, focused on the target, snapped the bow up, and let his shot off as he took his first fast stride. The arrow went whizzing into the dirt about five feet in front of the target. We both started laughing at the same time. He graciously retrieved my arrow and brought it back to me with my bow. He sat down beside me again.

He started to say something when the unnamed man and Major Sanchez walked up. Major Sanchez was handing the unnamed man a bill of some denomination. Both were smiling. "Major Sanchez," I teased her. "You didn't bet against me, did you?" Before she could answer, the unnamed man spoke up.

"She bet on loyalty and experience. I bet on a sure thing." My chest puffed up enough at that comment that I was afraid I'd float away. The unnamed man then reminded us that we had our first Dead Zone reconnaissance that afternoon. Both of us were needed for that. Major Sanchez asked me to join her for a quick sandwich in the City Hall break room, after which we were going to spend some more time with the Werewolves. That sobered me up. I silently followed her back to City Hall.

DAY SIX 2:25 P.M.

The sandwich I'd had in the break room was horrible, but I remembered that the government always accepted the cheapest bid. I pushed aside thoughts of a deliberate food conspiracy against the Mayor's people. I thought that Chagrin Falls' public employees were evidently the most frugal in the state. If ever there was an advertisement for private industry versus public employment, the contents of that break room were prima facie evidence that private industry held the upper hand. My stomach was a little rumbly as Major Sanchez and I drove to the containment facility. Once there, we were escorted in by the same sanitation workers I'd seen previously. We walked back to the far wall cages together. The Director and the unnamed man were already there. They greeted us as we walked up.

The Director looked at me. He said it was important we have another go at this. He knew it would be taxing on me. He told me everyone appreciated my sacrifice. That said, he asked if I would again attempt a mind link or whatever it was I did and see what more information I could get from the former deputy or the wounded Were in the cage next to him. I told him yes. I stepped up to the yellow line. Once again, the Werewolf recognized me and threw itself repeatedly at the bars with howls of rage. Its frenzy lasted four or five minutes until, as before, it bowed its head against the cage bars, exhausted. Then we began our contest of wills.

I spent 10 to 15 minutes exchanging thoughts with the former deputy before I had to back away and just cradle my head. My headache passed quickly, rather like an ice cream brain freeze. Once it was over, I asked to be let into the cage with the wounded Werewolf that had been firmly strapped down.

The unnamed man entered with me and stood to one side between the Were and me as I sought the Were's mind. The Were's thoughts were weak but just as hostile as the former deputy's thoughts about humans. Its thoughts were full of unrelenting hatred and anger. From the Were, I learned that the strike would be on Thanksgiving Day when almost all families would be home. Likewise, the streets would be void of traffic. The Weres would strike in groups of five.

They would carry with them a bag, vial, or something similar that could hold liquid. The liquid was even now being prepared. It was almost like an acid, the same type the old Werewolf had injected into the deputy when it bit the deputy and transformed him.

Since only a few Werewolves had the power to produce the change virus, distributing the vials to every attacker would ensure that many bite victims would make the change. They would not just die from the bites and rips a Werewolf gave them. Its only limitation was that there had to be a wound for the liquid to enter the body. It could be swallowed, of course, and that would certainly work, but just throwing it on a person would not effect change. It had to get into any one of the body's circulatory systems.

Those included air passageways, blood veins or arteries, and the lymph system. It had a short in-air life cycle. The virus died quickly when exposed to air. After 25 seconds or so in the air, it became just ordinary goo.

From these and other comments made to me, it became clear that the Werewolves' mission was to incapacitate and infect, not necessarily to wantonly kill. They saw this coming raid as a way to build up their ranks. If the tactic worked here, it would be replicated at other Were camps across the nation.

Again, my head was splitting, and I backed away from the strapped-down Were so I could clear it. Major Sanchez was quick to put an arm to my shoulder and steady me. She guided me to a nearby chair so I could sit for a while. When I returned to my normal self, she brought in a transcriber, and we went to work. Lt. Col. Spikes had also shown up while I was interrogating the Weres. He walked up and shook my hand when the moment offered itself. He thanked me for being willing to use my talents even at the risk of great pain to myself.

I felt grateful I'd been able to contribute something. I was wondering what was next when Captain Yamata showed up, reported to Lt. Col. Spikes, and softly said, "We're ready." Spikes acknowledged his report. Half turning to us, he invited us to go along. Yamata told Sanchez I was to stick with her. The two of us were joined outside the facility by a squad of four infantry. They would be assigned to us for the duration of the operation. They were spit and polish with the Major but were uncomfortable with me.

Major Sanchez told them to address me by my name, Cody. They were to protect me with their lives. She said I was more important than she was or any of the other three leaders. She'd explain more later, but right now, we were heading for the Dead Zone and the first terrain sweep planned by Captain Yamata. "This ought to be fun, boys," she said as she settled into her seat in the Suburban vehicle assigned to her. "Just make sure you aim the pointy end of those rifles at the enemy." Then we were off.

DAY SIX 5:15 P.M.

The grid search was conducted by the two infantry companies working together. Three soldiers walking together in groups 30 yards apart were stationed at the east side of the grid that Captain Yamata had laid out. The grid included the Dead Zone and extended about half a mile on either side. The objective was to walk straight through the terrain within a three-hour period comparing actual ground observations to the piecemeal area maps available to us. Helicopter support was also being given. Aerial mapping would also be conducted from there. A debriefing would be done later in the evening when all information was collected and tallied. Major

Sanchez said I would likely be excused from this formation. She explained that several other people would join us separately. We all would be busy on another project.

Forces dispersed and communication checks completed, Lt. Col. Spikes gave the order to advance. The soldiers soon disappeared into the bushes and trees. Major Sanchez asked me if I would share with her who the watchers were. She swore to secrecy. I told her of my history and abilities. I then asked her to walk with me along the edge of the woods as I gave her a demonstration. She was skeptical but agreed. We set off. We had walked no more than 200 yards when the scream of an Eastern screech owl floated down from above us. The owl drifted silently down to land near us by the bole of a tree. I asked the Major to remain where she was but to stay in my sight.

I then walked forward to greet the owl. I stopped several yards away. We conversed for a moment. I complimented him on his eyesight and his help in the parliament watch. He asked if the human with me could also speak with owls. I said no, that she, like the rest, was handicapped. I did indicate she was essential if we were to fight and destroy the Werewolves. I explained what was happening with the soldiers. I asked the owl to pass that along to the others. I then asked for his specific help to show the human with me that the owls were more valuable than any other creature if we were to win this fight. He puffed and strutted at this and then asked what he could do to help.

I asked him to first fly north along the line of trees and then turn south and fly back down the same track in the opposite direction. When he passed over the car with four soldiers and the human with me, he was to look for a symbol the woman made on the ground. He was to look at it, fly back, and tell me what that symbol was. Within seconds, he lifted off and was winging his way north along the tree line, screeching out his message to the other owls. Answering screeches came from all over the woods at various volumes as he disappeared to the north.

Meanwhile, I walked back to the Major. I asked her to run back to the SUV and make some symbol on the ground for the owl to see. I explained that he would return to me and draw the symbol on the ground with his talons. I would return and report to her what he had seen.

She looked at me like I was nuts but still turned and jogged back to our four guards. I saw her kneeling in the dirt in the distance after she arrived back in their presence. We both waited for the owl. The afternoon light was fading. I was worried it would soon be too dark for the owl to see anything from any real height. I worried in vain. Within 10 minutes, he was back over us, circling at a height of several hundred feet. He broke his glide abruptly. Turning on his wing, he came racing down out of the sky like a cannonball until he suddenly pulled up before me with wings flared. He virtually stopped in the air before gently settling to the ground.

He quickly scratched a symbol in the ground and then told me to move back to the other group because two of the night watch Werewolves were coming my way on the run. He guessed they were only minutes away. With that, he was up aloft and gone into the twilight before I could respond. Then the import of what he said hit me. I nocked an arrow and started stumbling back to the Major's group as fast as I could. I shouted for help and saw the soldiers look up at me. They grabbed their weapons and started running toward me, but 200 yards to a human in a combat outfit seems a lot less distance for a running Werewolf. The four guards, for all their good intentions, might just get to me as the last Werewolf polished off any leftover scraps of what I once was.

DAY SIX 6:15 P.M.

I hobbled, ran, and lurched for another 10 or 20 yards and then stopped, wheeled about, and prepared to meet the Weres as they emerged from the woods. And emerge they did, running at an unnatural speed and raising a hunting howl. They abruptly turned my way when they spotted me in the open. I had an arrow nocked. I put a second between my teeth as they drew near. The soldiers couldn't fire for fear of hitting me, at least not from the direction from which they were coming. However, they were hollering and screaming as they ran. They were trying desperately to distract or intimidate the Weres as they came closer to me. The Weres weren't fooled one bit. They just redoubled their efforts and speed.

I heard Major Sanchez screaming my name as she pulled out her sidearm. She actually kept ahead of one of the soldiers as all five of them leaped and dodged the brush and dips that lay between me and them. As the Weres came within 30 yards of me, I knew I was the only one who could save me. Facing them, I turned away at a 45-degree angle, drew my bow, and launched my first arrow. I mistimed the leading Werewolf's rise and fall as it ran. The arrow just missed its head and back and flew into the shoulder of the Were behind it. That second Were did a spectacular summersault as its right shoulder and then leg crumpled under it. It rolled for several yards before sprawling to rest on its wounded shoulder. It immediately began tearing at the shaft with its jaws and paws, choking and snarling in fitful gasps. Its newly damaged leg could not support it as it tried several times to rise up.

Snatching the arrow from between my teeth, I stood straight and, as the leading Werewolf leaped for me, jaws agape, I released my arrow almost straight down its throat just before it hit me. I was completely bowled over. My bow was knocked out of my hands. I was dazed as my head hit the hard earth. I felt like I'd skidded 10 yards with the Were's body on top of me.

Its stench almost overpowered my senses before I could force its weight off me to crawl and hobble away. The Werewolf had other ideas as it regained its senses. It snapped its body around even as it was choking on my arrow. It was losing blood fast.

In desperation, it slashed out at me. Its claws hooked my quiver and literally flipped me over. Its strength was unbelievable.

I started scrambling to get away from it even as I hit the ground spinning. Its eyes had a crazed look in them. In a final attempt to kill me, the Were managed to twist itself into the air, claws extended. The sudden thwap of a bullet sounded as a round from one of the infantry rifles literally exploded the Were's head. Fragments, blood, and tissue splattered everywhere. As the group came pounding up, one of the soldiers stopped and dispatched the other Werewolf with a quick flurry of shots.

The Major reached down and yanked me to my feet. She checked me for tears, slash marks, and puncture wounds. Finding none, she sat me down and checked my eyes and vital signs. I managed to tell her I was all right as my head cleared, but she just sat there shaking her head. I could hear her talking to herself in quiet disbelief. How could any creature that big move that fast? And why hadn't I fallen before it? And what was going on with the owl and the sign? All these questions and more she was muttering to herself. When my eyes suddenly came back into focus, she stopped murmuring. I picked up my bow.

The soldiers had maintained a respectful silence as they tried to regain their breath. I could see they were looking with some fear at the remains of the creature before them. There was some confusion as well. One of them spoke to the Major in a kind of kidding tone with an edge to it. With the courage it took to stand firm in the face of the Were's charge, he wondered if the Major was sure he shouldn't be protecting her and me. The others kind of laughed at that since I'd made an instant reputation with some of the toughest and most capable soldiers America depended on. I was both humbled and assured by their good-natured kidding.

I was no longer just some civilian, know-nothing kid. I was a warrior like them. They let me know it. I then turned to Major Sanchez and drew a symbol on the ground. It matched the one she'd drawn. It finally dawned on her that I had a priceless gift. She was more confused and yet excited than I thought was proper. She clapped an arm over my shoulders and led the way as we walked back to the SUV. She asked the soldiers to bag the bodies and follow us back. She wanted a few moments alone with me. She interrogated me at length by the SUV until the soldiers came up dragging the remains of the two Weres behind them.

She had suspected I had some hidden talent but would never have guessed I could actually communicate with animals. She was still wrestling with the enormous implications of that when we arrived back at City Hall.

She sent me home with an escort instead of returning me to the upcoming meeting. My instructions were to be ready for pickup at my house at 7:00 a.m. She pulled her hand through her hair and shook her head several times before telling me that it was going to be a long night for all the brass, just based on her input alone. With that, she turned away from me and slowly climbed the steps to City Hall to prepare for Lt. Col. Spikes's debriefing later that evening.

I was hungry and dirty and wanted nothing but a shower and some food when I got home. I saw Casey and my parents waiting for me in the den when I walked in. I knew then it would be a long night for me as well. Their first question was about packs of rabid, feral dogs in the area west of town as reported in the newspaper and evening news. They were curious as to how this would impact our safety while we were hunting Werewolves.

DAY SEVEN 6:30 A.M.

My alarm went off at 6:00 a.m. I lay in bed for about 15 minutes reviewing Friday's events. It had been an eventful day. I had been anxious to get back to the Major and see what the morrow (today) would bring. I remembered last night's meeting with my folks and Casey. I recalled how perturbed she'd been that she'd not received a call asking for her services in Lt. Col. Spikes's task force. I had suggested that it might be because everyone knew she was going to the fall dance and it's hard to fight a Were in heels. I was smiling as I said it. She turned, grinned, and poked my arm really hard.

I grabbed her hand before she could poke me again. I told her I wasn't going to be a combatant either, just an observer assigned to Major Sanchez. I said I'd ask if she, Casey, could join us as well. That seemed to temporarily mollify her. With Casey settled down, I was able to bring Mom and Dad up to speed and answer all their questions until Mom finally put a stop to it. She reminded everyone that I had to eat and still get up early tomorrow, and the clock was ticking.

I eventually bid everyone good night and trudged upstairs. I was frankly too tired to get that bath. I promised myself I would first thing in the morning. All I remembered after that was my head hitting the pillow and a stale odor. Mom was going to turn up her nose at these sheets.

The SUV from Major Sanchez carrying two of my escort infantry was right on time, if not a few minutes early. I climbed in with my bow and quiver of arrows. The driver wasted no time pulling away as we headed back to City Hall. Not much was said, although one of the soldiers asked me how long I'd been using a bow and arrow. He also asked whether I had ever won any contests with it. I laughed. I said I was state champion, and yes, I had won some contests here and there along the way.

He asked me if I could use a handgun. Again, I said yes but that I preferred a bow and arrows for anything up to 40 yards. He liked handguns, too. We chatted quietly about different makes and calibers until we reached City Hall. My escort walked with me to the large conference room and then turned away and stood just outside the doors.

Major Sanchez came in a few minutes later. She saw me sitting on one of the side chairs that ringed the main table. She beckoned me to join her. I slid quietly into the seat on her left during the lull before Lt. Col. Spikes showed up. Everyone was shuffling papers or taking a last sip of coffee. I asked the Major if Casey was going to have a role in this and if she could join us. She was about to give her answer when Lt. Col. Spikes walked in with the unnamed man and a woman I'd not seen before.

Lt. Col. Spikes called the meeting to order. He introduced the woman, Dr. Dana Abernathy, a geneticist and department head at Ohio State, who would be working as the Director's civilian counterpart. She nodded and promptly took her seat to the Director's left across the table from me. She had on a rough shirt, trousers, and what looked like well-used field boots. Her hair was pulled back in a bun. I estimated her age at about 50 years old from the few gray streaks running through her blonde hair. She was just about the same size as Casey. She had a rather severe face that lit up when she smiled. She seemed altogether a competent sort. We were to find out later that among her other attainments, she was a fearless and good shot. The room quieted considerably after she was seated as Lt. Col. Spikes turned, closed the door, and locked it.

Lt. Col. Spikes looked a bit disheveled, more so than at his first appearance yesterday. His eyes were tired and his body looked wilted, but his voice was as strong and confident as I had ever heard. He spoke for almost a solid hour with few breaks and few hesitations. His news was not good. We left the conference room in silence when he dismissed us. He'd given us plenty to think about and more to do. Major Sanchez and I went immediately to her temporary office to talk. She closed the door. Our four soldiers remained close by outside.

Lt. Col. Spikes had told us the soldiers' survey sweep conducted the day before had been scheduled to last three hours. They'd finally closed it down at 5:00 a.m. this morning when the last of the 10 missing soldiers had been found, or at least enough to identify him. Much of yesterday evening had been spent updating information on the area's topography as each team reported. By midnight, two teams on the line's more northern side were deemed to be missing. A four-man squad was dispatched to find them when no radio contact could be established. After another two hours of silence, they were deemed to be missing as well.

Two squads of 10 men each went in after them. They found the remains of the soldiers badly torn apart at a junction of two hills. The junction was breached by a low angular cave that did not appear on any of the maps available to Lt. Col. Spikes. The soldiers had been surprised and slaughtered. That was something almost no advanced infantry group had ever suffered. But they were really surprised that no rifles had been fired and only one handgun had been drawn. They only found the handgun because it was clutched in the hand of a severed arm. The ambushes had been unbelievably quick and enormously brutal. The enemy had taken the soldiers' measure first.

We discussed this setback at length. Several major ramifications came from our conference. There was no longer an element of surprise to our forces. Potentially worse than that, we did not fully understand Werewolf battle tactics or their command and control infrastructure. We didn't even positively know where their base was. We could reasonably suppose it was a cave or caves or maybe an entire system that ran for miles. Last night's experience, if nothing else, convinced us we were ignorant of all the Weres' true ingress and egress portals.

The loss of the soldiers also told us the Weres were entirely capable of launching stealth ambushes. That meant we needed good communications, a knowledge of tactics and planning, and the use of overwhelming force appropriate for the occasion. We then surmised that perhaps we were trying to fight with the wrong equipment (i.e., rifles and handguns).

But what was equally clear was that if left to hand knives, axes, or bayonets, essentially cutting and stabbing weapons, then Werewolf bulk, stealth, claws, teeth, and speed were absolutely far more than a match for us. I reminded the Major of the shotguns my dad and the Chief had used once before in our earlier confrontations. "Not enough, Cody," she said as she shook her head side to side. But as she mulled this over, she suddenly raised her head, looked at me, grinned, and shouted, "I've got it!"

Quickly she stepped past me to the door and ran the few steps to the conference room to Lt. Col. Spikes. She yelled back at our escort to stay by her office and keep an eye on me. In a few minutes, she came walking back and sat down again by me. She tried but could not contain her excitement. "Flamethrowers and shotguns! We'll get 'em with both," she exclaimed. "As quick as they are, no creature can outrun a moving wall of flame or lead pellets. We'll use our rifles and handguns on the stragglers or wounded."

Captain Yamata loved it. It was the insight that proved to be our salvation.

DAY SEVEN 2:30 P.M.

Lt. Col. Spikes, his three deputies, the Police Chief, the State Highway Patrol liaison, and the County Sheriff had been meeting since lunch. When they finally emerged from their planning session, things started to move quickly. Three separate demonstrations were planned for our side: a troop and police force inspection of our captive Werewolf, the former deputy; a demonstration of a flamethrower; and a demonstration of the tactics the soldiers would use to attack the Weres. The demonstrations would be held in the open at the Polo Grounds at the invitation of the Police Chief, primarily because there was ample space there away from the immediate eyes of the townspeople and any transient population. The demonstrations were scheduled for 3:30 p.m. Immediately, troops and officers began to load up and move out in respective convoys as directions were given and all prepared for the afternoon's formation.

I took the opportunity to ask Major Sanchez once more if Casey could be with us. I knew she should be, but the Major wanted to "keep things manageable." She declined my request. I replied that Casey and I were partners and that she knew more about the Weres than anyone but me. If I were hurt or incapacitated, someone like Casey would have to step in, and she had already proved herself. The Major finally relented. She sent me with an escort to pick her up with instructions to make it back by the 3:30 p.m. demonstrations with or without her.

We made it just fine. Casey's confidence in me was higher than mine. When we rolled up to her door, she was already dressed in her exploration clothes. She had overnight essentials in a small backpack she carried over her shoulder and was also carrying her .357 Magnum revolver. She'd been dressed and ready since 8:00 a.m., just in case. Her very presence gave me greater confidence. I believed the soldiers would do their best for me. But now I absolutely knew someone had my back just as she knew I had hers. On the way over, I told Casey generally what to expect in the three demonstrations. As we discovered to our dismay, neither of us, nor anyone for that matter, was truly prepared for what happened when they brought the Werewolf out.

By the time we arrived at the Polo Club, the large majority of the troops and police forces involved had already assembled. They were on the broad concrete expanse that sat atop the containment facility. Few to none actually knew of any facility's existence below their feet. Those who did question why the concrete was out here were simply told it was the county's parking facility for various water filtration and pumping station repair equipment when not in use.

We made our way to one of the ringside tables occupied by Major Sanchez. We took our seats. I noticed a caged enclosure covered by a larger canvas drape located across the concrete from us. When I asked about it, the Major replied that it housed the Werewolf we'd known as the deputy. It was the Director's and Lt. Col. Spikes's belief that every soldier or police officer should see him up close. That should help dispel some of the super-creature myths that had begun to spring up as a result of the Werewolves' successful forest ambush the night before.

DAY SEVEN 3:30 P.M.

At 3:30 p.m. sharp, Lt. Col. Spikes walked out onto the concrete slab with a jerry-rigged portable broadcast system fashioned by Major Ludlow. He asked for silence. He explained the objectives of the assembly and the activities that would occur there for the next hour or so. With that, he introduced the Director, who was to initiate the first activity. When Lt. Col. Spikes had taken his place at a table near ours, the Director told the assembly that his group had captured and was holding a live Werewolf for study. He explained that through means available to him, the Director and his staff had been able to ascertain some of the Werewolves' objectives and capabilities, which he wished to demonstrate. He gestured for the tarp to be taken off the cage.

To everyone's uneasy shock and Lt. Col. Spikes's evident surprise, he had the cage opened. The Werewolf was brought out with ropes held by four burly men. There was stunned silence as every man or woman at the assembly actually saw, many for the first time, one of the creatures up close and personal. It had grown to be huge. The Werewolf seemed to simply take everything in stride, standing erect but still, calmly gazing out over the crowd.

Two ropes were connected to the Were by loops around its neck. Two more loops were around its waist. Very slowly and without obvious intent, the Were let its claws casually drop to the ropes about its waist, closing around them in plain sight of those few who might have noticed. Lt. Col. Spikes and I both did and were rising to our feet to warn the Director when literally everything broke loose.

The Were suddenly crouched down and then immediately stood back up to gain leverage. With a roar, it simultaneously yanked inward on the two ropes that encircled its waist. The two men holding the ends were taken completely by surprise and thrown off their feet. One man dropped his rope, and the other held on until he crashed into the concrete and smashed his elbow. That caused him to cry out and let go of the rope with his injured arm. Without stopping, the Were grabbed the two ropes about its neck and, holding one, turned its head, bit though the other, and turned back and bit through the first. It was essentially freed but for the ropes around its body. The Were then leaped for the Director and opened him up from collarbone to waist with one great swipe of its claws. The astonished Director, too shocked to respond, sank down like a deflating balloon as he bled out on the concrete. His eyes were open as he lay gasping for breath. They closed as he rolled over, his intestines slipping out around him.

Surrounded by yelling soldiers and police who dared not fire lest they miss and kill one of the surrounding crowd, the Were sensed its advantage. It leaped to the side of one of the men who had been holding one of the waist ropes. It stooped down, grabbed the man by his shoulder and his crotch, and lifted him high above its head. With a growl, the Were hurtled the man down onto the concrete. The impact force smashed the man's head and chest.

Several soldiers from the audience closest to the Werewolf jumped forward to grab one of the ropes still encircling the Were's waist. One apparently succeeded only to find the Were's fury directed entirely at him. He suffered multiple slashes from the creature's fearsome claws as the Were fought to free itself.

In the confusion and shouting, I found myself clambering over the table to get at the Werewolf. I was hauled back by both the Major and Casey. Each one was shouting at me to get back and let it be. Others would take care of him. I resisted their efforts and pulled myself free only to be flattened as two of my Ranger escorts tackled me and bore me to the pavement. But I wasn't the only one besides the ringside soldiers who was moving. Seemingly out of nowhere, Dr. Abernathy ran up behind the Werewolf as it was otherwise occupied, placed a small pistol close to its spinal cord, and pulled the trigger three times.

The Werewolf dropped like a sack of cement, its legs paralyzed. The sound of its screams and grunts was awful, full of shock and despair as it weakly tried to pull itself erect without success. The ambush was over. Dr. Abernathy showed great leadership in how she bade everyone return to their places while she had several volunteers return the wounded Werewolf to its cage and start to treat it. Our dead and injured were loaded into appropriate vehicles and driven away in silent haste.

Lt. Col. Spikes then apologized to all. He said the decision to allow the Werewolf to come out of its cage was a surprise. It needlessly resulted in lives lost, but the Director's rash act may not have been in vain. He asked to also correct the Director's brief speech by introducing me and, to everyone's surprise, Casey. He explained our roles and histories. He cautioned everyone to remember how quickly the Were had moved, almost with lightning speed, how he had acted with utter ferocity inflicting death and injury. He then praised Dr. Abernathy's actions. Finally, he asked me and Casey to step over to him. We did. He placed his hand on my shoulder and then turned us both around so everyone could see us.

DAY SEVEN 6:30 P.M.

Lt. Col. Spikes remarked to everyone there how hard it was to kill a Werewolf and what the risks were to life and limb. He then announced that I was a man who had killed more than 10 of these adult creatures with a bow and arrow, not a gun. That brought gasps of astonishment from the crowd. He reached down and pulled up one of my pant legs, exposing my leg brace. "And he did it wearing braces because he can't run, walks badly, and often uses a wheelchair," he concluded.

There was absolute silence and then spontaneous applause that grew and grew. Lt. Col. Spikes had made his point. He continued to say that as fearsome as these creatures were, a young man without military training or weaponry, hobbled by physical challenges and with little mobility had used his head (and more than his share of luck) to put away a significant amount of these felons from hell. Two of my escorts grabbed me and lifted me aloft as a large number of soldiers sought to close in to touch me or shake my hand. I was grateful to see when I could turn around that the other two soldiers were quietly spiriting Casey and the Major away.

Lt. Col. Spikes finally got things settled down. The other two scheduled demonstrations and a concluding general briefing went on for almost an hour and a half more. The bloody death of the Director had underscored just how serious and important this mission was. This was no practice. From that point on, laughter or general banter was as scarce as gold nuggets. Lt. Col. Spikes then announced that our search and destroy operation would begin shortly, within three days max and probably much sooner.

Given that, every man or woman needed to be ready at a moment's notice to launch the planned offensive. Because of the timing, he called it Operation Turkeytrot, which elicited an immediate groan from every human in hearing distance. "I don't name 'em, boys and girls," he said. "I just paint 'em the way the Pentagon tells me, and Turkeytrot it is. Any questions? No? I thought not. Now let's get ready to go do what we're paid for."

Lt. Col. Spikes then called for a quick supper break for everyone on his staff with a closed staff meeting starting at 9:30 p.m. in the City Hall main conference room. He then surprised us all. He addressed me by name, asking that Casey and I attend as well if at all possible. I assured him we would be there. Major Sanchez gave us a ride over to the City Hall complex after she sent one of our soldiers for some fast-food hamburgers, fries, and shakes. "Can't get those in South America." She winked as we all fastened our seat belts and were driven away.

On the way back to the City Hall complex, Major Sanchez announced she had a detour we needed to make. She'd had one of her sergeants make some calls earlier in the day. She wanted us to see what she thought might be a tipping point in our favor, provided I agreed and was prepared to carry out her wishes. Casey and I were riding in the back seat of the SUV.

When Major Sanchez said that, she turned around and gave me that million-dollar smile she had, the one that oozed confidence and multiplied a man's testosterone level by a factor of 10. I nodded my head and grinned back until Casey quietly elbowed me in the ribs. My grin stayed, but it was pretty sickly. The Major just smiled even more. She winked at us as she turned back to look ahead.

We stopped at a small dog kennel I'd occasionally driven by but never paid much attention to. The Major took the lead. One of her sergeants was waiting when we entered the small building. He led us to a small courtyard behind the building. Waiting there, under tether, were four bull terriers. Three were white, and one was black and white. All had the egg-shaped head and triangular eyes of the breed. All stood watching us with quizzical expressions on their mugs.

Major Sanchez took me aside. Speaking in a low tone, she asked me to stay with them for a while as she took the rest of the party on to City Hall. I was to quiz them.

I was to determine for myself if they would work with us to find and flush out the Werewolves from their caves or underground dens or wherever they gathered. With that, the Major herded everyone else back through the building and into her SUV. I figured I had about an hour or so to interrogate the dogs.

DAY SEVEN 9:00 P.M.

The same SUV that took the Major, Casey, and the others away came back for me. It dropped me off at City Hall shortly after 9:00 p.m. With me were five dogs—the four bull terriers who had all volunteered for a good fight (and a steak for each when it was done), and a pugnacious rottweiler named Honey. She didn't get the name for her manners or disposition but for her penchant for sweets, especially honey. Honey had been a last-minute addition at the strong recommendation of Mr. Chance, the black-and-white bull terrier. In fact, he was insistent that Honey join us once I had spelled out the proposed mission, the danger, and the operation.

The other dogs gave Mr. Chance his name because, like most bull terriers, he usually wasn't the one who started fights. He was the one who finished them. He was a tough and able fighter no matter the size, weight, or number of teeth. Few were more stubborn or refused to quit once an attack started. With him, you always took your chances, and hence his name.

I figured if Mr. Chance recommended some dog as a fighter, then that recommendation was good enough for me. It took a little sweet talking to be sure, but Honey agreed to join us for the specific purpose of keeping an eye on Casey. I told Honey that she was the alpha female Casey wanted to be if she had a chance to grow up. Unfortunately, when people went after Werewolves, not a lot of them ever got that chance. Who knew Honey had a maternal streak?

None of the canines had ever heard of a Werewolf. They chuckled at my attempt to describe one. But they turned mean when I told them they were angry, sick, former humans who had tried unsuccessfully to become wolf dogs and couldn't. In their anger and upon their failure, they believed in mistreating and killing pups. I said they smelled like death and that death followed them, that they hunted in packs because they were too cowardly to fight one-on-one, and that they were much bigger and faster than humans or any other dog species, including Russian wolfhounds.

The more I tried to discourage these terriers, the more they wanted in on the fight and the more I fell in love with them. Bruno, Killfish, and Lockjaw were the names their masters had given the three white bull terriers. They all were telling me their stories when the sergeant came for us at the small kennel. Like most soldiers, they were willing volunteers and afraid of nothing.

The interview experience taught me something more about Major Sanchez. She was one smart cookie. Of all the dog breeds that could be successful in helping us go after the Weres, she had probably picked the best. Bull terriers were nimble, stubborn, highly intelligent, and imaginative. They were also prey dogs. Blood didn't frighten them, and size didn't intimidate them. And if we had to go into caves to hunt Weres, the white-coated terriers would have an advantage. It was the color the Werewolves weren't. That made it easier not to shoot them by mistake.

I noticed that Mr. Chance, the black-and-white bull terrier, gave an uncomfortable shake at this latest bit of information but then seemed to dismiss it as he looked at Honey and realized she was 95 percent black and hadn't even blinked. My respect for Honey just kept climbing.

At any rate, I wanted to take the dogs inside with me so the leaders could see them and agree with Major Sanchez's plan. I knelt, gathered them about me, and told them where we were about to go. I told them a number of people would be curious about them. Some might even try to touch them.

I asked them to not bite, to be patient, and to take care of their necessities before we entered the building. The four bull terriers immediately scattered, each looking for the nearest tree or bush. Honey, in as demure and modest a dog trot as possible for her, discreetly vanished around the corner of the building.

When everyone was present again, I led them in. I'd asked them to walk proud, and they did, heads erect, eyes missing nothing. We entered the conference room moments before Lt. Col. Spikes stood up to start speaking. We took a place at a cleared space in the conference room. Lt. Col. Spikes looked at me curiously, cleared his throat, and smiled. He asked if I'd like to start the meeting by introducing my new friends. He surprised me. I started to stumble over my words until the Major stood up, grinned, and announced to all that the Dugway Irregulars had now joined us. They would be the primary scouts when we went into the Werewolves' caves. That brought a smile and agreeable nod from almost everyone as they craned to see the dogs.

As I anticipated, one of the secretaries there started to pat Killfish's head when he suddenly turned to face her. He snapped his magnificent jaws. He growled in a rumble that made everyone automatically back up, eyes wide open. The secretary seemed frozen in shock. Tears formed in her eyes. I quickly spoke up. I reminded everyone that these dogs were volunteers like the soldiers and were just as deadly. I then reminded them that we don't pat the soldiers either.

That brought a cautious laugh. The temperature and attitude in the room returned to normal. Casey had been sitting across from me along the other wall and just smiled. As I sat down, I leaned over and pointed Casey out to Honey. Honey looked up with a quick lift of her head, winked at me, and then trotted around to first push her head against Casey's leg before plopping down directly in front of her. Honey's sleek back was nestled against Casey's lower legs. Lt. Col. Spikes watched all this, and when Honey had settled, he looked up at all of us with a sly smile. He asked if everyone else was comfortable. Seeing the answering nods, he invited us to get to it.

DAY EIGHT 8:15 A.M.

I woke up to Bruno's grunting and twitching. He must have been having a bad dream. He was bumping his head against my arm in his sleep. As I sat up stretching, I woke him. He tumbled to the floor, quickly catching himself and trotting around the room seeing where everything was. I noted that Mr. Chance was also awake and looking out my window. Killfish and Lockjaw were each posed silently at the side of my room, just watching me.

The briefings and follow-up meetings had lasted until midnight. The Major had sent Casey and me home in the SUV with the five dogs. She kept our four-man Ranger escort with her for some follow-up items. She figured any Werewolf stupid enough to take on a carload of proven fighters was too stupid to do much damage. She also said the SUV would be back for us at 10:00 a.m. We were to get some real rest and eat as much as we could for breakfast because we were going into the caves at 4:00 p.m. on Sunday afternoon. That was to be confidential, although we could tell our parents if they were sworn to secrecy.

Dad let me in. When I explained about the dogs, he opened the door all the way so we could make our way upstairs and to bed. Honey went with Casey. "Can't wait until tomorrow morning," Dad mumbled. "Your Mom's going to make breakfast for all of us." Then he disappeared back into his bedroom and quietly closed the door.

"Good morning, guys," I greeted the dogs when the sun was up the next morning. "Stay here while I get ready, and then we'll all head downstairs where you'll be fed." They did, and I did. By 8:45 a.m., we were all standing in the kitchen as I explained the situation to my mom. She was nonplussed about a lot of things, but this was the first time I'd seen her totally not impressed.

I gathered that my dad had given her a heads-up. Like all moms, she was ready for almost anything. She'd been up since 6:00 a.m. thawing out some of our steaks and sausages for the dogs. My spirits picked up until she served me oatmeal and told me the milk was in the fridge. Always good to know where you stand was the thought that came to me. I let the dogs out, took their meat out to them, asked them to stay close by, and went back inside. I briefed Mom and Dad about Turkeytrot.

We were all standing in the driveway at 10:00 a.m. when the SUV drove up. Dad shook my hand, put an arm around me, and gave me a quick hug. Mom just gave me a hug. Then she hugged me again, over and over. Casey's dad came over and quietly asked me if there would really be any danger. I told him I didn't know, but I didn't think so. We were part of the rear guard. We wouldn't be going into the caves.

Much relieved, he smiled. He asked me to take care of Casey. He then lowered his voice and asked where that rottweiler had come from. She'd gotten into their cabinet and cleaned out their jar of honey. She growled and showed her teeth when he tried to shoo her away. He told me how glad he was when Casey came down because that rottweiler was starting to make goo-goo eyes at his stash of maple syrup. He asked me what rottweilers actually ate. I told him outside of small children, I just didn't know.

I think Mr. Allegro was glad to see us off, at least Honey and me.

DAY EIGHT 12:00 P.M.

At noon we left City Hall for Turkeytrot's initial staging point near the Dead Zone. A small contingent of troops had been sent to survey and secure the Barn Well property. The powers that be believed the cave entrance might somehow be connected with the ones in the Dead Zone. A second group had been sent to the Quarry Cave. We had definitely seen Werewolves there. Bruno went with the troops headed for the Barn Well property. Killfish went with the troops sent to the Quarry Cave.

Mr. Chance and Lockjaw would go into the recently discovered cave with the main body of troops split between Captain Yamata and Major Ludlow. Captain Yamata's group would take point. They would be the first troops into the cave. Major Sanchez, her people, our four-person guard squad, and Casey and I would stay at the staging point unless needed elsewhere. Any redeployment from there would be at Major Sanchez's explicit direction. Lt. Col. Spikes and his immediate entourage would stay with Major Sanchez until and unless circumstances deemed they'd best be somewhere else. Everyone was armed. Major Sanchez carried a shotgun slung over her shoulder. Casey had her .357 handgun. I had my bow and arrows. This time, Mom had kept her knife. I suppose with all the soldiers around, she didn't really think I needed it.

DAY EIGHT 3:45 P.M.

A number of flamethrowers had been obtained, enough for one per every 10 troops. Lt. Col. Spikes sent no flamethrowers to the Barn Well or Quarry Cave sites. Every second soldier carried a 12-gauge pump-action shotgun. Two over-the-shoulder cartridge bandoliers went with each shotgun. Lt. Col. Spikes wanted overwhelming, not just sufficient, firepower. We'd estimated there would be

130 Werewolves max based on the owl's estimate. Spikes said to plan bigger, so we settled at 400 Weres. We armed ourselves accordingly.

I gave last-minute instructions to each of the bull terriers. Yamata and Ludlow stood by along with the squad leaders of the small forces going to the Barn Well and Quarry Caves. Honey was going to stay with us, more particularly with Casey. I watched as those two actually seemed to be communicating with one another, although I knew it wasn't the same as my talent. Nevertheless, they seemed to be connecting in a way I didn't understand. Got to be a girl thing, I thought, and then promptly dismissed it from my mind. The bull terriers communicated by barking. One bark meant one Were sighted, two barks meant two, and three meant hold on to your hats 'cause there's a parade a-comin'. The dogs would all follow the same simple code. They were to growl if they were on a recent trail or sensed Weres close by.

The state police and city officers were deployed along all the affected streets and roads that ringed our target sites. They had been briefed on what to expect. They were to reinforce the story that a pack of rabid dogs was in the area, that steps were being taken to eradicate them. "In the meantime," Spikes said, "please pardon the inconvenience and turn around and go home. Now. It's for your own safety. Oh, and thank you!" The soldiers were prepared to stay in the cave(s) for four days if necessary. The police were prepared to shut down the town for just as long, especially the schools.

Captain Yamata led his troops into the recently found cave at precisely 4:00 p.m. local time. Mr. Chance was actually the first one in. Yamata was hot on his tail. By 4:20 p.m., all communication with Yamata's group ceased. Lt. Col. Spikes said not to worry, that they would most likely be too deep for the radio waves to penetrate the rock. That was expected. At 5:00 p.m., Major Ludlow's group started squirming in. They were led by Lockjaw. Ludlow's group trailed, so communications continued as his group followed Yamata's marked path. Forty minutes into the cave, Ludlow's group came under heavy attack. He reported wave after wave of Werewolves coming at them in narrow passageways both in front and behind their line of march. Steady, heavy firing could be heard for almost 30 minutes until it dropped off to sporadic fire.

Ludlow reported that he had taken moderate casualties as the shotguns, not the rifles, had stopped the initial onslaught. But it was the flamethrowers, he said, that eventually turned the tide. An adrenaline-filled, hopped-up angry Werewolf could apparently take several bullets and still be dangerous. But nothing could stand effectively against the flesh-shredding, pump-action shotguns and still qualify as any kind of a threat save perhaps as a gooey slippery spot on the cave floor. When the Weres came in waves, the shotguns gave way to the flamethrowers, and the Were attack halted.

Ludlow said it was like fighting in a barbecue pit except the burnt smell of oil mixed with Were flesh made everyone who smelled it sick. Nevertheless, Ludlow said, his soldiers just kept on fighting. It was pull the trigger twice, puke once, and repeat, over and over and over ad nauseam. Ludlow also said if there was anything exceptional to report, it was the bull terriers. Lockjaw had prevented the Weres from any effective surprise time and time again by warning the troops in his simple barking code. He was slashed twice; he was not crippled, only bloody. He had personally killed one Were and damaged several others. His ferocity gave the soldiers following him the courage to confront the Weres face-to-face. If we could find more dogs like Lockjaw, we were to send them in to Ludlow with the highest priority.

An hour later, a small squad sent back by Yamata reported over Ludlow's communication line. They, too, had survived several severe attacks and ambushes. Like Ludlow's experience, it was the flamethrowers that made the final difference. The Weres were everywhere. When backed into pockets or seemingly trapped in numbers, they went insane and charged anything. It was a battle of eradication. There would be no prisoners, which was not the soldiers' choice in the matter. Oh, and it was evidently not good to make Mr. Chance angry.

So it went on into the evening and through the night. Casey and I slept fitfully on our cots when we could sleep. Our blankets were pulled tight over our outer clothes. We were ready to go into the cave(s), if requested. It seemed we waited for an interminable time between reports sent back to give us some sense of what was happening underground. Each soldier carried a compass. Each report gave a directional indication of the way the various groups were headed as well as some indication of how far they'd traveled underground. However, we learned nothing is precise in the heat of battle.

At 5:00 a.m. Monday morning, Lt. Col. Spikes set up an armed relay between his headquarters and the main cave entrance. The relay was to evacuate the dead and wounded when possible. More than 30 men walked, stumbled, or were carried out in the next several hours. Twelve bodies were also carried out. Of an initial attack force of 200 men, more than 20 percent of the casualties were incurred in the first 12 hours of fighting. This was serious stuff. I listened in as Lt. Col. Spikes got confirmation that 200 more soldiers and some Special Forces demons were on their way from Ft. Benning, Georgia. They were expected to arrive before midnight on Monday.

DAY NINE 6:45 A.M.

The Barn Well property remained as quiet as a tomb. Since no activity report had come in from the Quarry Cave in more than five hours, the small group of soldiers sent there were also assumed to be okay.

But when Lt. Col. Spikes heard that report, he almost came unglued. Each of the two remote sites was to report on the half hour, every hour, with no deviations. None. Nyet. Nada. To have missed five reports meant something bad was going on at the

Quarry Cave site. Major Sanchez was alerted and dispatched immediately. "Let's go!" she hollered at Casey and me. "Get the lead out and get into the SUV now!" We ran for the SUV. I practically threw Casey in while Honey barreled in after her. I piled in right behind them. The Major told two of our soldiers to stay behind with her immediate staff and two to come with us.

The driver was moving before the last door was slammed shut. The SUV threw gravel everywhere as we made our exit. Casey, Honey, and I bounced around until we could find and fashion our seat belts. The ride gradually became bearable as we finally hit Chagrin Falls city streets. I was leaning through the back seat divider shouting directions to the driver. Major Sanchez kept trying to raise the Quarry Cave soldiers on her radio. It was futile.

As we sped up to the Quarry Cave's parking lot, the only thing to be seen was an abandoned Armored Personnel Carrier (APC). We piled out and started for the cave entrance on the bounce. Honey ran ahead. Halfway there, she began a series of combined barks and growls that was unlike any signal we'd discussed with the dogs. It was just out-and-out hatred. What she smelled and what we all saw together as we pounded (hobbled, in my case) up to the cave entrance turned my stomach. Several gutted soldiers had literally been thrown about the cave entrance. It looked as if several more bodies were just inside the cave's opening lip.

Major Sanchez stopped us all just outside the entrance. She pointedly cocked her shotgun. One of the Ranger escorts with us fired up his flamethrower. At the Major's signal, he swept the entranceway. Oily flame and smoke bellowed out for a few seconds followed by a series of barks and yowls. Whatever was in there waiting for us was suddenly burned to a crisp. Yelling at us to stay put, the Major and the two soldiers leapfrogged their way into the entrance. They immediately disappeared into the blackness. Within seconds, we saw the flamethrower light up the cave again as the Ranger pulled the nozzle back and forth in sweeping gestures. Outlined against a wall about 20 yards into the cave was a pile of Weres. They were lying on top of the legs of two squad members. The squad members were dead, but the Weres had obviously paid a steep price for their temporary victory.

Sanchez hollered back at us to radio Spikes and get reinforcements there ASAP. She could hear movements and a lot of growling and barking deeper in the cave. The sounds seemed to be rapidly coming closer. Casey did the radio honors as I strung my bow. I threw my quiver over my shoulder as I lurched into the opening. I stopped short of Major Sanchez and the two soldiers. They were kneeling in a firing position. I stood immediately behind them. I had a full quiver of broadheads, all 12. I couldn't think of a better time to use them than right now. Honey came running back to us. She stopped beside me. She let me know more than three times that our adversaries were creeping closer. Her eyesight was invaluable. I told her to growl when they were within 20 yards and then back away toward the cave entrance. Her signal meant we would light up the flamethrower.

A dog's vision in darkness is almost as good as a cat's. A dog's night vision is also about five times keener than a human's. Honey could both see and count bodies. All we humans could do was fidget in the darkness. A few moments' pause and then Honey growled with a ferocity as great as that of the yelling Weres. The Ranger lit his flame as planned. The oily flame shot out. It blinded the line of Weres advancing on us. It also set them on fire. They were roasted as they stumbled to and fro. Already blinded by the loss of their sight, their eyeballs literally fried. Their outer skin and furred pelts crackled in the intense heat. Major Sanchez held back from using her shotgun in concert with the flamethrower. I assumed it was to preserve ammunition. When the cave was still again, she ordered the second Ranger to open fire, a single shot, and put down any Weres still moving. He stood and did just that. The echoes of his shots seemed to bounce back along the cave walls for minutes.

When silence came again, Major Sanchez ordered Casey and me to remain at the entrance with the radio. She and the two soldiers moved forward another 20 or 30 yards to try to find and block the cave tunnel from which the Weres had emerged. In seconds, they were again enveloped in darkness as they passed around one of the bends in the passage. Twice more we saw light as the flamethrower lit up the passageway ahead of them. Still, we heard no shots or cries. As a precaution, I asked Honey to walk forward to the first bend and become our advance sentinel there. I asked Casey to try the radio once more and see if someone at headquarters could tell us when reinforcements were coming.

DAY NINE 8:15 A.M.

Our solitude was suddenly interrupted by muted gunfire and the distant reflected glow of the flamethrower. The fight seemed to go on for some time, and then it stopped abruptly. Silence reigned for several more minutes. Then Honey suddenly came alert and barked at me. Something was coming back down the cave corridor. Its smell was like burned oil, and it was panting hard. It seemed to be dragging something heavy with it. "Is it a Were?" I asked. The dog said no but couldn't identify the source of the sound.

I told Casey to break for the SUV with the radio. I hobbled as quickly as I could to Honey's side, bow strung and arrow halfway drawn. When I finally heard footsteps and rocks being kicked aside, I pulled the arrow back. I was about to kill whatever came around the cave bend until I heard the sob of someone making a determined but faltering effort. "Who's there?" I called out. And the answer came immediately in the form of a question. "Cody, is that you? Quick! Help me, please!"

I walked to the corner and peered around it. The Major was there with her jacket and shirt almost torn away and gashes in her left arm and shoulder. She held her shotgun in her left hand by only its trigger. Her right arm was around the shoulder of the Ranger with the flamethrower. He was missing a big piece of his leg, and blood was seeping out of his jacket. Someone had put a belt tourniquet above his knee to stop the bleeding. It was clear he was already in shock. The Major was filthy. She was gasping from the effort she'd made to bring the soldier to safety. Despite her instructions, I placed my bow and its unfired arrow against the wall before I picked her up and hobbled back to the entrance.

Casey saw me from the SUV. She came running to our aid. Honey bounded out to meet Casey. I hobbled back to the flamethrower, unstrapped, and slipped it into the rig. Only when it was secure did I pick up the inert soldier and drag him to the Major. I dropped him by her side.

"Show me how to work this," I told the Major. She shook her head to stay focused. She was barely coherent as Casey arrived. "Put her in the SUV and then come and get this fellow," I told Casey. "Honey and I will stand guard. And Casey, please hurry faster than you've ever hurried," I pleaded. With the Major leaning on her shoulder, Casey started for the car just as Honey turned around. Once more, Honey began barking and growling in a frenzy. "Flame on!" I cried and lit the nozzle. This time, instead of just standing my ground and sweeping the flame from side to side, I started forward, driving the advancing Weres back amid snarls, growls, and yells as they were burned and stymied in their attack. The cave stunk from the smell of burning flesh. Breathable air was becoming hard to find. I gradually had to give back hard-won ground. Grudgingly, I was forced back toward the entrance.

I made the mistake of turning too far and stumbled just as I approached the entrance. I was hit from the back almost immediately by a Were who had managed to conceal itself against the wall as it stalked me. It bit into the tank on my back, shattered several of its teeth, and immediately howled in pain. The bite penetrated the flamethrower's fuel tank, and it began to leak. I could feel liquid dripping off my back and pooling at my side as the weight of the Were kept me facedown. I thought I was dead when a great weight was abruptly lifted off me. Honey had come from the side and plowed into the Were. She took its forearm in her mouth and bit down hard. I could hear the Were's bones shatter from the terrific crunch of her jaws. A hyena couldn't have done better.

The Were screamed as it was knocked from its perch above me. It scrambled up on its haunches, bringing Honey with it. The Were snarled fiercely as Honey dangled from the Were's now useless arm. Honey's bite was like a steel trap. The Were ineffectively swiped at Honey with its other limb. Honey moved faster. She let go of the Were's broken arm and jumped for its throat. She fastened herself beneath the Were's jaw with her own jaws clamped shut. She dragged the Were down to the cave floor using her weight. The Were died seconds later, jerking as I placed an arrow against its ear and jammed it into its brain. Honey returned to my side wild-eyed. Stirred by her up-close-and-personal encounter, she was looking for an excuse to kill again. I couldn't remember when I had ever such a peaceful feeling as having that dog by my side at that moment.

We heard the deliberate movement of many creatures grunting and growling. They were coming down the dark corridor. Again, I lit the nozzle and spewed death into their ranks. This lasted a minute or two until the flame faltered badly before regaining its pyrotechnic ferocity. It seemed as if the flamethrower had hiccupped. Yet again, the Weres were driven back when abruptly the flame simply quit. No more fuel.

DAY NINE 8:45 A.M.

I quickly disengaged from the flamethrower rig. I grabbed the Major's discarded shotgun and a bandolier of cartridges. I crammed in load after load until the 10-shot magazine was full. Pumping it once to load the first cartridge, I backed to the lighted entrance and waited. Once again, Honey was at my side. This time the charge was almost linear. Some Werewolves came in tandem rather than in a spread. It was a new tactic and would have worked fine with the flamethrower.

With that instrument, one would have gotten past me and could have brought me down from the rear while I was still trying to stave off those in front of me. But with the shotgun, it was a different story altogether. I could kill two abreast as fast as they could come at me, and that's exactly what they did. Eight shots into the magazine, and I had 13 shredded Weres on the cave floor. But I also couldn't hear a thing since the cave walls amplified each blast. My ears were constantly ringing. They certainly weren't listening.

I'm sure that's probably why I almost fainted when I felt a tap on my shoulder as Lt. Col. Spikes brushed past me. He was followed by 20 or 30 soldiers. They all carried shotguns and flamethrowers. A corporal stood in front of me. He motioned for me to lower the shotgun. When I did so, he took it from me. Then he carefully took my arm. He walked me out of the cave into the sunshine. I screwed my eyes shut against the glare. I opened them slowly as they gradually accommodated the late afternoon light. Although I could tell the soldier was speaking to me, I could hear nothing. My ears were still ringing. His message became clear when Casey walked up. She took my arm, gesturing a thanks to the corporal. She started walking me back to the Major's SUV. My part in this fight was apparently over.

But not Casey's. As I walked in a daze, she suddenly pushed me to the ground and spun around. She pulled and emptied her .357 Magnum into a creature that was obviously hidden when Lt. Col. Spikes's men went by. It had just ambushed and killed the corporal. Now it was running for me. Honey's barking growl had alerted Casey none too soon. She and her reflexes and courage had done the rest. I crawled back onto my feet, stunned at what had just happened. Casey looked over at me only when she had reloaded her pistol and calmly holstered it. Once again, she took my arm as she steered me to the SUV. It was almost as if we were out for a Sunday stroll. I saw that both of us were shaking. Honey joined us. We all managed to climb into the SUV. We simply sat for a while in silence until I could start to hear again.

The first thing I did when my hearing returned was hop out of the SUV and go pick up the discarded shotgun and bandolier by the dead corporal. As far as I was concerned, nothing was safe for the time being. I reloaded the weapon as we again sat in the car per Spikes's orders to Casey. We sat for some time in a now familiar silence. Casey absentmindedly stroked Honey's back and behind her ears. Me? I absentmindedly stroked the reloaded shotgun. I was trying to remember just what had happened and the order in which it had happened. I knew Major Sanchez would debrief me in detail. I wanted to be ready. With that, I suddenly sat up and cried out, "Major Sanchez! Casey, where is she? Is she all right? Where is she?"

Casey grabbed my arm and motioned for me to calm down. She told me the Major was safe, that she and the tourniquet soldier had been taken away by Lt. Col. Spikes's people when they arrived.

Apparently, Yamata and Ludlow had joined their two groups while pursuing the Werewolves through the deeper limestone caves beneath Chagrin Falls. From the presumed direction and distances reported back to headquarters, Lt. Col. Spikes ascertained that the Werewolves were running for the Quarry Cave, a suspicion that had become a working reality when Spikes found out that communication had been lost with the quarry contingent. Sending the Major and us had been an emergency stopgap only. It wasn't intended to deter the Werewolves but merely to have someone on-site who could observe and track them. He must have forgotten how gutsy Major Sanchez really was.

Lt. Col. Spikes planned to bring the firepower and reinforcements with him, which he had done. He simply hadn't counted on the personal bravery of the Major and the two soldiers in the interim. Nor had it occurred to him, despite his comments at the demonstration the day before, that Casey and I could make a startling difference in this assault. He saw himself as the plug in the bottle to cut off the Weres that were fleeing Ludlow's and Yamata's men. Lt. Col. Spikes planned to hold this entrance while Yamata and Ludlow and their combined forces slaughtered the Weres from the rear, pushing them inevitably into Spikes.

DAY NINE 2:00 P.M.

We had waited at the SUV for almost 30 minutes when Lt. Col. Spikes's second convoy of local reinforcements arrived. One of Major Sanchez's sergeants who had ridden over with the convoy found us. He informed us that the Major needed us back at headquarters—now. She had been treated, was okay, and was asking for us on the jump. With that, the sergeant climbed into the

SUV and drove us back. He answered practically no questions en route. We were tired, disoriented, and slightly nauseous when we arrived at the base camp. There, one of our two escort soldiers told us that was normal immediately after a period of intense fighting.

We were taken from the SUV to the Major. She was acting as commander while Spikes was engaged with the enemy in the Quarry Cave. She was heavily bandaged with her left arm strapped across her chest. Otherwise, she seemed no worse for the wear. She rose to her feet as she saw us enter the tent. She stepped forward, smiling, and hugged us both. Then, with a twinkle in her eye, she asked if we'd had fun with her play toys, the flamethrower and pump-action shotgun. She assured us from the reports that had come back to her that the Weres had not enjoyed us. It seemed we were both pretty dangerous characters with or without a bow and arrow.

I don't know if Casey blushed, but I think I did. At least my face suddenly seemed awfully warm. It was that darned hug. I didn't know where to put my arms, so they just hung there like I was an idiot. I think the Major was tickled, but Casey saw my awkwardness and was beaming.

The Major's face then changed. She said she had some bad news to relay. Both Mr. Chance and Killfish were dead. They didn't die alone. Lockjaw was pretty beaten up but was being brought back out of the cave for treatment. A local animal hospital had been put on notice. They were standing by to receive and treat him. He would likely lose his right rear leg. Bruno was okay, having seen no action at the Barn Well site.

She looked down and remarked that Honey seemed fine as well. She then looked up and thanked me for convincing the terriers and Honey to fight with the soldiers. It would have been much, much worse without them. She then added that each of the two dogs who had perished would be given full military honors. They would be interred in a special K-9 graveyard soon to be dedicated at Ft. Huachuca, Arizona.

With that, she said she had to get back to directing the logistics support necessary to keep the soldiers fully supplied at combat strength. She suggested we grab a quick bite to eat. We were to report back to her in one hour. We would be going out again on a mop-up operation later in the afternoon. We would take Bruno and Honey with us. Bruno was being brought over by car even as the Major was speaking to us. She then turned back to her field desk. She was immediately pulled in by the staff waiting patiently to speak with her and receive her direction.

"Sounds like good advice," said Casey as she turned to walk toward the canteen tent. I followed, unexpectedly saddened by the news of Mr. Chance and Killfish but hopeful about Lockjaw. The thought came to me that maybe my career path was destined to be in veterinary medicine after all because of my peculiar ability. My thoughts drifted to Casey and her college choice in North Carolina. I wondered if that state had good veterinary schools.

We didn't speak very much at lunch, such as it was. I did manage to put down most of a roast beef sandwich. Casey was able to find a healthy plate of scraps and some water for Honey. We made sure Bruno was also fed and watered when he arrived. Neither of the dogs took the news of Mr. Chance's and Killfish's deaths very well at all. Honey took some time to communicate to Bruno her impressions and experiences with the Weres. I watched as both dogs became more and more incensed. I would like to be a lot of things in life, I thought, but not the next Werewolf that crosses the path of either Bruno or Honey. That beast would have a *really* rotten day.

We were back with the Major in less than an hour and received our new orders. We were going back into the cave system at the entrance that Yamata and Ludlow had used. We would be tracing their route, looking for Were stragglers, wounded, or any that might have hidden away from the initial assault. We would go as far in as the current fighting. We would then return and report our findings to Major Sanchez or her superior if she was otherwise incapacitated. Honey and Bruno would go in ahead of us. They were to be our eyes and ears. If both became unable to continue, we were to turn around and come back immediately. A heavily armed escort would take us in. We were to follow their orders on the march or in a firefight, but they were to obey our warnings. We were to be scouts, not primary combatants. The Major took some pains to emphasize that. We said we got it, and she finally moved on to something else.

As we stood up to go, she introduced us to a tall lieutenant with the last name Cosic. He had a shy smile and great handshake. He was deliberate in his speech. He also used ma'am and sir a lot, even to us. Honey and Bruno walked over and sniffed him out and then trotted back to stand beside Casey. They both gave me the he's-okay sign. He was to be the squad leader for the group going in with us. He'd never been in actual combat and had never seen a live Werewolf, and neither had most of his men. He said he thought they'd do just fine. He was anxious to get on with the mission. "Saddle up," he said to the troops behind him as they put on the ammunition bandoliers and flamethrower packs. "Time to go to work, men."

As I turned to leave, one of the Major's sergeants stopped me. He handed me my bow and quiver of arrows. "She said you might need these. She had them brought over from the Quarry Cave while you all were grabbing a bite to eat. Good luck, and be careful," he said, and then turned and walked back to the Major's table.

DAY NINE 4:00 P.M.

Bruno led the way into the low cave with me right behind. Honey came in next. Casey walked in just behind her. Lt. Cosic was right on her heels, too much so, I thought, a little too close. I charged it off to his first-time combat experience.

I figured he was just a bit over-zealous. After he stepped on her heels the second time, she warned him off in no uncertain terms. Honey let out a low growl, and Lt. Cosic got the message. He put his corporal up as point man as he moved back to the middle of the column. It was where he should have been in the first place. We had no problems after that. Bruno and Honey took us through our paces for the next two hours. We found several stragglers and squeezed through more than one false trail. We became familiar with dead ends, but we kept moving. Lt. Cosic would occasionally rotate his troops so everyone eventually got the privilege of acting as point. It was not an honor one normally sought, but it was valuable experience. I silently saluted the Lieutenant for thinking of his men's readiness progress in a relatively dangerous environment.

Early in the third hour, we began to hear sounds of fighting ahead. The roars and howls of the Weres echoed off the cavern walls. They were accompanied by the yells and cries of our soldiers and the explosions that marked the terror of the shotguns. Sounds in a cavern can travel a long way. It was some minutes before we encountered several wounded soldiers getting first aid treatment while the fighting raged ahead. Our orders were to turn back at this point after we'd made contact with Major Ludlow or Captain Yamata. We were to get their report and a list of support and supply needs we would be expected to fill.

Lt. Cosic sent a runner ahead to meet with Ludlow as we all found places to squat and wait on the cave floor. The fighting finally seemed to have quieted down a bit. Suddenly, we heard a small explosion followed by a massive explosion. Pieces of the walls and roof above us cracked. A lot of debris came down. Debris was everywhere. "What on earth was that?" asked Casey as she choked on the dust swirling about us. We found out minutes later when one of Ludlow's sergeants came running back asking for the Lieutenant. "You're in charge, sir!" he yelled. "Ludlow's been killed; Yamata is missing. What do you want us to do?"

It was one of the questions most dreaded by any officer in combat. Cosic, bless his heart, rose to the occasion. He announced to all that he now had command. He directed his first sergeant to take control of his squad, ordered Ludlow's sergeant to take him immediately to Ludlow's body, and asked Casey and me to follow. "Bring those dogs!" he said. We did.

The way ahead was terrible. The closed-in channel we were in opened abruptly into a very large area almost the size of a basketball court with a ceiling height that ranged from 20 to more than 100 feet, or at least that was the way it now appeared. Dust and debris were everywhere. The faint groans and crying of wounded men and Weres could be heard ahead of us beneath what appeared to be tons of crushed rock. Lt. Cosic played his handheld light all around, as we did ours. We could see parts of both Ranger and Werewolf bodies buried beneath the fallen rock. It was a dusty cauldron of death. At the far end of the chamber, what had once been an opening was completely closed off by a massive rock fall. Dust swirled everywhere. We stood silently as that chamber of horrors gradually quieted. The groans and cries quickly ceased. Then the sound of silence was almost overpowering.

DAY NINE 6:15 P.M.

I was stunned. I knelt and asked both Honey and Bruno to walk out onto the debris pile and see if anything lived—Honey to the right, Bruno to the left. They circled, climbed, and jumped from ledge to ledge for almost a half hour, crossing and recrossing each other's route, checking to see if anything had lived through that rock fall. They both returned with the same verdict. They could neither smell nor hear anything alive. Whatever or whoever had been under that ceiling when it collapsed was no longer living. I reported that to the Lieutenant. He somberly turned away and asked Ludlow's first sergeant how many soldiers had been in the chamber before it collapsed. The sergeant had already done a count of the combined squad members remaining. He extrapolated saying seven men had been on the floor when the explosion happened, Ludlow fighting with them.

The Weres had been fighting a strategic retreat. They were trying to get back to the relatively narrow tunnel from which they had first emerged. They had passed the area we referred to as the coliseum. Yamata and his group had just entered a narrow channel on the far side of the coliseum. He and his men were hard on the heels of the main body of the retreating group of Weres. Ludlow's element was starting to cross the coliseum floor area when a group of 20 or so Weres ambushed Ludlow's group from the side. The Weres spilled out of what must have been a hidden cross-chamber. Ludlow's group was initially overrun. He somehow managed to seize a flamethrower from one of his men who'd been gutted in the Weres' first sweep through the soldiers' ranks. Ludlow aimed it at anything higher than four feet tall. He shouted to his men to drop and cover before he turned on the flame.

He'd burned the bulk of the Weres when the first explosion went off on the far wall. It was followed shortly by the second and larger explosion above it. Then heaven and earth moved, and the entire coliseum ceiling came down. The result was the enormous rubble pile now before them. The second explosion sealed off the chamber into which Yamata had disappeared.

The shock of the massive blast and the thought of Ludlow and his squad dying left all of us in a pall. Lt. Cosic quickly sought to remove it by activity. He ordered everyone to police the area (clean it up and leave no trace) and then form up. We were going back to base the way we'd come in. He moved Casey and Honey to the front of our newly combined and somewhat bedraggled column. Bruno and I were moved to the rear. He wanted no Werewolf ambushes.

The flamethrowers were to be turned off. Every person with a shotgun was to load live rounds and intersperse themselves between other segments of the column carrying a flamethrower or just a rifle and handgun. When everyone had formed up and were counted, Lt. Cosic gave the order to move out at a fast walk. He took his proper position at mid-column.

The Lieutenant then asked what had caused the explosion. He wasn't aware that any heavy ordinance capable of that kind of blast had been authorized for Turkeytrot. The sergeant explained it wasn't an ordinance that had caused the explosion. It was a gas pocket that the flamethrowers had ignited. They had experienced small fizzles and gas pocket explosions for the last half mile or so as they penetrated deeper into the cave system, sweeping the Weres before them. This was one no one had expected, especially in such strength or concentration. The sergeant had ordered those with backpack units to stand down immediately after the first explosion as a matter of safety. Then the secondary explosion hit, and the world came tumbling down.

The column walked in silence for the next two and a half hours until we neared the cave portal though which all of us had entered. Seeing fading light ahead was a wonderful morale builder. Our steps picked up slightly until we all emerged from the cavern into the cool Ohio evening air. The Lieutenant ordered a route march on the way back to base camp. He sent a runner ahead to make sure he could report to the commanding officer as soon as our group arrived in camp. Major Sanchez was there to receive his report. She asked Casey and me to sit in while he gave it. She had it taped and started a transcription process immediately. She then dismissed the Lieutenant with her compliments and congratulations on his new command. He had now officially replaced Major Ludlow for the remainder of Operation Turkeytrot.

When he was gone, she asked that we telephone our parents and inform them we were safe and sound and that we would be home later tonight, probably very late. She then asked that we grab a drink and a bite to eat and report back to her in 30 minutes. She wanted our take on what happened. She promised to fill us in on what had taken place on the other end. Lt. Col. Spikes and Captain Yamata and their men were concluding a mop-up operation at the Quarry Cave even as she spoke.

Casualties had been heavy, but 100 percent replacements would be coming in before midnight. She had much to do to assemble all the information they would need to know. We needed to be out from under her feet for a bit. She then shook hands with both of us and thanked us again for being part of this. As terrible as the human toll was, without Turkeytrot, it would have meant the lives of hundreds had the Weres been able to amass and launch their attack.

We did as she asked. We each grabbed a sandwich and a couple of small milk cartons. We settled down gratefully behind her tent out of the way of the couriers who seemed to come and go with mercurial speed into and out of her temporary headquarters.

DAY NINE 10:15 P.M.

The last debriefing was over. Casey and I were finally free to go home. Lt. Col. Spikes had asked that Bruno be allowed to stay with him. I was to give him roaming instructions. He was free to roam the area, but when the new deployment arrived, it would be best to have him stay close to Spikes so as not to get trampled or lost. Bruno understood me. He agreed to Spikes's wishes. He knew he was there on standby, just in case soldiers had to go back into the caves that same night. Honey would go home with us, or rather with Casey. Those two ladies had been through a lot of strain today. They were fast becoming inseparable.

Lt. Col. Spikes summarized the fighting in which he had been involved since we'd left the Quarry earlier that day. Basically, he'd done exactly what he said he would do. He had originally thought of his group as a plug in a bottle until it became apparent that the Werewolves were being driven inexorably forward against him by some force that he logically assumed would be the Yamata-Ludlow group. As the Weres increased the fervor of their fight, Spikes's troops responded in kind until Spikes understood that he was really the anvil against which Yamata-Ludlow was hammering.

Understanding the Weres' increasing desperation to break out through the Quarry Cave meant a change in tactics on Spikes's end. He therefore ordered more flamethrowers for his narrow front and started advancing rather than just forming a defensive center. The Werewolves were in a pincher movement and grew wild in their desperation to escape the flames. Finding none, they had turned on themselves, tearing into anything that moved between the two walls of constant flame until they had literally destroyed each other.

At this point, no one knew if any Werewolves had survived or escaped through some alternate cave channel missed in the course of the fighting, but Spikes had great confidence that their back had been broken in Chagrin Falls, especially because of the dogs. Neither Honey nor Bruno had come across any sign of an escape route or hidden Werewolf survivors in their trek back with Lt. Cosic's group. Similarly, Yamata's escape from the coliseum ceiling fall meant no escape for the group of Weres pinched between Yamata and Spikes, a group that had ultimately destroyed themselves.

There would be a lot of mop-up and wrap-up for the police and military, but our part was essentially over. Lt. Col. Spikes thanked us again. Major Sanchez gave Casey a quick hug and me a big cheek kiss and hug that colored me to my roots. It left me tongue-tied with a grin so big that it hurt the corners of my mouth. Casey was steaming. She gave the Major a look that would have turned her into a Crispy Critter had it been from a flamethrower, but the Major never even looked her way. Lt. Col. Spikes gently coughed and, clearing his throat, suggested we move along. There would be school for us tomorrow and a final debriefing he would want to have with us and our parents before he and his team left the area.

Sleep never looked so good.

DAY TEN 9:15 P.M.

I was late to school, and Mom gave me a note just in case. But apparently, the principal remembered his call from the school board, and I was still technically off-limits. I explained that I was temporarily back but would have to miss a little more school when the project I was working on was ready for presentation. That should be in a couple of days. No one seemed to have missed me, and everyone was still talking about last Friday night's football game in which Brad Thorney had run wild, scoring two touchdowns and making a crucial interception to save the victory.

We live in different worlds, I thought. These kids have no idea what's happening in the real world. I was sorry I couldn't tell them. Then I thought, *What if I could?* All that would happen is panic, so maybe a little knowledge *is* a dangerous thing. Then I shrugged and kind of mentally kicked myself for being so negative. I went on to my organic chemistry class and the test I'd been dreading. To my surprise, I managed to do rather well. I was really curious to see what sort of grade Casey got. We might be a lot of things to one another, but we were still competitive and enjoyed learning.

Casey and I talked briefly between classes about how our most recent experience seemed so far away, well out of the old reality that school offered. Both of us felt a little bit lost. I asked how Honey was doing. I laughed as Casey described Honey's most recent shenanigans. The Allegro house was quickly being turned upside down by two strong females. I had no hope for Mr. Allegro's attempts to regain control of his home.

I went home after school and had a long talk with Mom and Dad about this recent adventure. Mom paled visibly a couple of times as I described certain scenes and actions, but both of them were still very much supportive of me and the choices I was making. My mom told me that Lt. Col. Spikes asked that we attend a meeting with him tomorrow at lunch in the City Hall conference room. It would be a working lunch; we would eat while he talked. The meeting was scheduled to last a little over an hour. I was asked to stick around for a few minutes alone with him before he left town. Mom had given her okay. She already alerted my principal of my forthcoming absence.

After our talk, I changed clothes. I was in the backyard shooting arrows when Brad Thorney came walking up the driveway. He was on his way to see Casey, but seeing me first, he walked over and said hello. He asked why I hadn't been around for a few days. I told him Casey and I had been finishing up that chemistry project. I told him she had talked a great deal about how excited she was to go to the dance with him. His chest kind of puffed up, and he admitted that being a star athlete had its advantages. I ignored that and pointed out that his reputation on the gridiron was less interesting to her than his prowess as a dancer because Casey *really* loved to dance, and Brad was, well, probably the best around.

He was really riding high when I told him that. He had a swagger in his step when he turned to walk over to Casey's door. "But Brad," I called out. "There's really something you should know about Casey."

"What's that?" he asked as he turned again and faced me. He was a little challenging in his manner and posture. I think he thought I might know something special about the girl that he, Brad Thorney, had decided to sweep off her feet.

"Well, it may be nothing," I said, "but I thought you ought to know. Casey dated a fellow last year who was really sweet until he tried to make a move on her on a second or third date. He ended up in the hospital. I think she likes you all right, but I'd go mighty slow if I were you. She may seem like just another defenseless girl, but bad things happen when she gets too excited."

"What are you saying, Cody? You're making that up because you really are jealous that she decided to go with me. I think you're just full of yourself. You can't stand that I'm the better man."

"Okay." I shrugged. "It's not my problem, but I like you and respect you. I just think you ought to know the truth. Casey and I have grown up together. She has no secrets from me or me from her. When Casey was 13 years old, she got a rash from a trip to Mexico that the doctors still don't understand. She picked up an oral virus from drinking water out of a gourd in some out-of-the-way marketplace. The virus causes someone to break out inside their mouth and in their armpits in small open sores. It's like jock rash only worse because it spreads by contact. I made the mistake of trying to kiss Casey in the ninth grade on a dare. It took me a year of doctors' appointments to get rid of the virus. I ate a bland diet with no sodas, no sugar, no popcorn, no nothing. I would scream when my mom rubbed in the salve each night. It burned and had an aftertaste like dog poo. Now, Casey's a great dancer, yes, and great fun, but she literally has the kiss of death. Cuddle up all you want, but just remember that a kiss will be the last kiss you'll get for months. Your armpits and mouth will likely never forgive you."

I turned away before he could see my eyes start to water from holding back my grin. I was grateful my bow was handy, and I started slamming arrow after arrow into the target while he stood there and watched me, eventually turning back and walking over to Casey's house. She met him at the door, and they sat on her steps for a while just chatting. I finished with my last arrow, gathered the bunch up, and walked back to my house, waving at them before they were blocked off by the corner of my house. I almost fell over with laughter when I entered our den and closed the door. I then ran to a side window and peeked out at them.

It wasn't long before Brad stood to go. Casey jumped to her feet, gave him a quick hug, and then stood as if to receive a quick kiss. At the last minute, I saw him turn his head slightly and back off. He held her hands as he gave a nervous nod and walked away. I saw her standing there watching him for a minute. She turned and looked at my upper window for a few minutes. She was clearly puzzled about something. At last she shrugged and went back inside her house.

"Yes, yes, yes!" I screamed as I rolled around on the carpet. "Yes, yes, yes, you sorry so-and-so! Mess with Casey, and you mess with me, the Archer, slayer of Werewolves and leveler of football players who believe their own press clippings!" I rolled around for a few more minutes, stifled my grin, and then went on up to my room to study. I was in a great mood.

Several minutes later, there was a knock on the front door. I came downstairs to open it, and there stood Brad. He asked if he could come in and talk with me. I thought, *Oh no! I'm dead meat. He found out that I lied.* But it wasn't so. He said he and Casey had sat on her step and talked about a number of things and that she didn't seem timid or frightened about things other girls he'd dated were. She also said she'd recently acquired a rottweiler named Honey. "No one gets a rottweiler, Cody, unless they're crazy. Rottweilers eat people. They're dangerous. Is she really telling me the truth?"

I nodded my head sadly and said it was true, that I'd made her mad by a remark about her not being able to eat ice cream with me, and she had sicced Honey on me. I'd barely escaped and still had a tear in my old blue jeans from Honey's attempt to bite me. Brad's eyes widened. I could tell he was starting to have second thoughts about their forthcoming date. I told him to just forget what I'd said. Casey and I were always fighting. In fact, I was sure she'd probably already forgotten she'd been mad at me. "Just be a perfect gentleman," I told Brad. "Have a great time with a great dancer. But don't tick her off," I reminded him, "or she'll likely go wacko on you." That would mess with his reputation as a ladies' man for months.

I stood up, helped him to his feet, and walked him to the door. He thanked me for being so candid. I said, "Sure. What are friends for except to run interference for each other where girls are concerned?" As he started walking, I asked him if she'd shared her love for firearms. "She's a dead shot with a .357 Magnum, you know, and often carries a concealed 9-millimeter, not to school, however. Says she doesn't want to scare the sissies, whoever they are."

I quietly closed the door as he stood there with his mouth hanging open.

DAY TEN 10:15 P.M.

Casey called me just as I was getting ready for bed. She asked if I had a moment to talk since we'd not seen much of one another all day. I said sure. I asked how her chat with Brad had gone. I told her Brad and I had talked a bit about archery and stuff, his outstanding performance at last Friday night's game, and actually how excited he was to have a date with her to the fall dance. I told him to wear his dancing shoes and be prepared to rock it out with the prettiest girl in our class.

She paused and hesitantly said that was kind of what she wanted to talk about. She'd had a nice conversation with him while I was out target practicing. She had seen him with me before he walked over to her. Had he said anything to me about her or had I said anything that might make him act differently? I replied not that I knew of except that he had asked me if she might get mad if he tried to kiss her. I told him I knew nothing about that and wasn't going there. I did offer the opinion that if I had a date with Casey, you'd better believe I'd want more than a polite handshake on her doorstep when I brought her home.

I told Brad that everyone knew he was quite the catch. And he did have a reputation as a superior kisser. I was sure she was well aware of that when she accepted his request. The tone of the conversation seemed to change, and Casey immediately lightened up. She asked if I'd heard from Lt. Col. Spikes yet. I said yes, my mom had taken a message. We were meeting with him tomorrow at City Hall for lunch. I told her to check with her mom, that she'd probably taken the same message for her.

Then I bid Casey good night and hung up the phone. I yelled as I threw myself on the bed. I congratulated myself over and over for being so clever. When it comes to Casey, all gloves are off. I hadn't been pining away for my soul mate for nothing.

DAY ELEVEN 12:00 P.M.

Mom and Dad and I rolled up to City Hall a little before noon. We were standing outside the conference room exactly at 12:00 p.m. The Police Chief and Lt. Col. Spikes walked out of the Chief's office about that time. Casey and her folks showed up as well. The Chief looked pleased that everyone was there. He invited us into the conference room. A nice buffet had been laid out on a sideboard. Some dishes looked more than inviting. Best of all, Major Sanchez was sitting at the end of the table in a pretty civilian dress. A fresh set of bandages covered her arm and shoulder. That great grin of hers was sparkling.

We all filled our plates and took our seats. Lt. Col. Spikes closed the door. He addressed us. He thanked us again for our crucial part in Operation Turkeytrot. Quite simply, he told us that they would not have succeeded without Casey and me. He wished we were of recruitment age because he'd love to have us under his command in unconventional warfare, but we weren't, and we had school to complete. He spent an hour filling us in on the aftermath of the Operation, what had happened to some of the troops we knew. He then spoke to our parents about some of the specific acts of heroism all had witnessed during our time with them. He did not speak openly about the confinement facility or my talents but reminded us that we had signed a nondisclosure document. We had given our oaths that what had been told us was to be treated as classified material. What we experienced must continue to remain classified until we were notified otherwise. That likely would not be in our lifetime.

He closed by stepping outside the conference room for a moment. He reentered with the Mayor and the unnamed man who had briefed the President. That man asked Casey and me to come forward. He presented us with a letter of personal thanks for our part in a Defense Department exercise of significant value to the United States, citing that without our personal and heroic efforts, it could not have been successful. The letter was signed by the President of the United States, one letter for each of us. He then handed each of us a small case with a bright orange cloth inside, along with a small bronze pin in the shape of the United States and a bronze-covered medal. He explained that this was a coveted but rarely awarded Medal of Personal Freedom. It was given for extraordinary acts of heroism to civilians affiliated with the Department of Defense. Both Casey and I were entitled to wear and display it whenever and wherever we chose, but he asked that we do so in a manner to render honor to ourselves and our country.

He shook our hands, smiled, leaned close to me, and said to enjoy this last semester of high school while I could. He had a hunch we'd be seeing more of one another in the not too distant future. He then straightened up, smiled again, thanked our parents, and left the room. Everyone gave congratulations and hugs all around, and then the Chief spoke up.

He echoed the unnamed man's sentiments and presented to me five Police Academy K-9 citations for bravery, two awarded posthumously. I was asked to communicate the feelings of a grateful city and the soldiers to each of the surviving bull terriers and Honey. We were then told that Lockjaw and Bruno would have a home at the future Chagrin Falls K-9 Academy for the rest of their days.

We said our goodbyes after that. Lt. Col. Spikes and the Major asked if I could speak with them privately for just a few minutes before I left with my parents. My mom and dad said sure. They closed the conference room door on their way out. The three of us were alone in the room.

Lt. Col. Spikes asked what plans I had after my graduation. I told him I wanted to go to college but the money would be tight and I'd probably have to go somewhere in Ohio. He asked about Casey. I said she had a soccer scholarship to play at North Carolina, that she was that good. He asked me if I'd ever thought about going out of state, say perhaps to North Carolina. There were other good schools there such as Duke and North Carolina State.

I sat back in my chair and grinned at both of them. "Here's the deal," I said. "I've already had this conversation with myself, and this is what I want. Full tuition for both undergraduate and eventually veterinary school in North Carolina with some sort of monthly allowance since I'd be working for the US government as my schedule permitted."

Both the Lt. Col. and the Major blinked their eyes, pulled back a moment, and then burst out laughing. The Major turned to Spikes and reminded him that Yamata had said I was exceptional. "He's way ahead of us," she laughed. She looked at me and turned back to Spikes to get his reaction.

He just smiled and said in that soft voice that I would get a brevet commission as a Second Lieutenant for up to four years in college. I would then be commissioned as a Second Lieutenant upon graduation. I would get a monthly salary of two-thirds the pay of a Second Lieutenant while I held the brevet rank. When awarded my veterinary license, I would be assigned to the K-9 division of Special Operations. I would serve four years of commissioned service before I was eligible for separation from the service.

In the meantime, I would be on call during breaks and summers to give aid to the classified anti-Werewolf operation soon to be established as Growler I. Time spent in any phase of Growler I operations would merit monthly combat pay on top of any other allowances. All travel and purchases for training or equipment necessary for my specialty would be paid for by the US government. This offer, by the way, was limited to this afternoon only.

"Wow!" I said. "Where do I sign?" The Major slyly slid a pen and paper to me. "On the dotted line." She smiled. "And hurry up, Cody. We need you in North Carolina yesterday."

I walked out of the room with a smile as big as Texas. I felt sorry for myself that it would probably be some time before I ever got down Texas way. But then, I thought, Texas is a wide-open place and isn't going anywhere. After all, those Weres down there might just be the biggest targets yet. I was smiling all the way home. There would be challenges ahead for sure, but there were rewards, too, rewards for hard work and dedication. I wanted to have a life of meaning. Suddenly it was possible. I never, ever wanted to look back and say, "What if?"

DAY TWELVE 12:30 A.M.

My telephone rang, waking me from a not-so-sound sleep. In fact, I hadn't meant to fall asleep at all. I had planned to be awake, peeking through my window blinds as Brad brought Casey home from the big dance. I hadn't gone, of course, but I really wanted to know if he had the guts to kiss her good night. Well, I'd missed the moment and would probably never know. But the phone had awakened me. I grabbed it and mumbled an answer. "Hello," I said.

It was Casey. She asked if I would come outside and sit with her on her doorstep at the side of her house. "What?" I said.

"Come sit with me, Cody, right now. I need to speak with you." Said like that, there was no comeback other than to put on my robe and slippers and walk on over. She was sitting on her doorstep in her best prom-type dress. She looked like $10 million with her hair and makeup. I saw that her eyes were glistening. I thought, *Oh no, I've been found out! Here comes Armageddon.* But I was wrong.

She stood up and looked down at me. She asked what was wrong with her. Wrong with her? I told her absolutely *nothing* was wrong with her. I asked her just what she was thinking or maybe *not* thinking to even think that. Well, she told me that she'd had a wonderful time with Brad, he'd been a perfect gentleman, not at all like his reputation, and here she was home on time all dressed up, and he hadn't even tried to kiss her good night. He'd just held her hands again and bolted for his car. I stood up and gently enfolded her in my arms. I'm not Brad, I told her, but I know a treasure when I see one, and I, for one, am not a shifty-hipped idiot. I would never let an opportunity to kiss her pass by. And I didn't. In fact, that night we lost count of how many times I didn't.

THE END OF EPISODE THREE, BOOK ONE

EPISODE
FOUR

DAY ONE 10:00 A.M.

It wasn't until they started playing "Taps" that my tears started, and then they came quickly. Up until then, tears had been just a nagging suggestion, one I'd been straining to ignore for the past two days ever since the Chief of Police had called to let me know that Bruno and Lockjaw had died trying to defend themselves against larger, stronger, and quicker adversaries. Lockjaw had been a fighter all his short life. Everyone agreed that he had fought this last battle as valiantly as he had all his others, but it was impossible to win this one given the damage he'd received trying to defend himself during the Werewolves' brief raid.

On three legs, Lockjaw had discovered the hard way that he just could not outrun or outfight the three Weres that came for him that early Wednesday morning. He'd been near the tree line bordering the large training field for the Police Academy's K-9 Corps when the Werewolves rushed from cover for him. Bruno and Honey were a good distance apart, half a field away, when they heard his bark of alarm. Both turned and ran straight for the Weres as Lockjaw was pinned. Lockjaw managed to hold his own for his first few bites. He broke the forearm of one Were and ripped open the hind leg of another with his powerful jaws before the remaining two Weres clawed him open, throwing his remains to the ground like a discarded offal.

The Weres then wheeled about to face the two dogs coming at them in a rage. The dogs arrived at full tilt, Bruno in the lead. Two Weres tackled Bruno as he launched himself at the lone Were that had pinned Lockjaw. Bruno's momentum pulled his two attackers to the ground. Everyone crashed together in a tangle of claws, teeth, and maniacal grunts. The resulting donnybrook was bitter, desperate, and fast. Honey had rolled in behind Bruno like a dark cloud carrying nothing but bad news and torrents of hard rain. She slashed right and left with her teeth, using her bulk to smash into the Weres as she tried to distract or do them serious harm.

Meanwhile, Bruno managed to fasten himself to the throat of the larger Were that had first slashed Lockjaw when he was pinned to the ground. Lockjaw's bite had almost torn the Were's throat open. Despite the Were's desperate gyrations, Bruno had somehow held on while the larger Were successfully disemboweled him. It made no difference. Even on the threshold of his own death, Bruno's choke hold killed the frantic Were. The remaining two Weres then concentrated on Honey. They managed to critically wound her but not before one Were lost the better part of an arm to Honey's bone-shattering bite. With Honey felled, both remaining Weres struggled to exit the killing ground in all haste. They dragged their dead companion after them. The body plowed a shallow furrow through the forest floor detritus. The blood trail the two Weres left behind wasn't all from the corpse they so unceremoniously tugged along behind them.

Several of the Academy students had heard the ruckus. They rushed to the murder scene from their classrooms only to glimpse the Weres as they disappeared into the bordering forest. As students, they carried no weapons. The Weres thus made good their escape without any immediate human retaliation. In the early morning light and from such a distance, the students couldn't see who or what had killed the dogs. And they had been deliberately kept in the dark about the existence and local presence of Werewolves. The authorities had treated them no differently than they had the surrounding Chagrin Falls civilian population.

All the curious students could see as they arrived at the battle site were two dead dogs. Two canines had obviously had been ripped apart. A third dog, Honey, almost died until they were able to staunch the blood flowing from her wounds.

With no clear visuals, the students assumed vagrants had slaughtered the two dogs while trying to slip onto Academy grounds, probably in the hope of stealing something. But when the Chief and county medical examiner arrived at the scene of the killings, there was no question in their minds what had really happened. Privately, the two men compared notes. Werewolves were rumored to have long memories. If the attackers had been Weres, they would have remembered the significant role the bull terriers had played in the successful raid on the hidden cave, especially the climax of the fighting at the Quarry Cave's entrance only a few months earlier. But we all questioned what had brought the Werewolves all the way out to the K-9 Academy in the first place. The arrival of the Chief at the murder site meant transportation was at hand. Honey was driven immediately to the K-9 kennel infirmary on the Academy grounds. She went through a long and grueling operation to save her life. Casey and I were told Honey would be several months recovering. The remains of Bruno and Lockjaw were sent to the Ft. Huachuca burial ground. They were interred with honors beside Mr. Chance and Killfish. Today was the formal memorial service for all four of the terriers. Casey, my parents, and I were reluctant attendees. When you fight beside someone who is willing to die for you, as the terriers had been, their death truly turns your world upside down. At least that's how Casey and I felt all the way through the service.

As nice as the service was, it was still a sobering reminder that although we had likely broken the back of the Werewolf population in Chagrin Falls late last year, they were like cockroaches. No matter how much poison you spread out or how many nests you destroy, some always survived. It seemed to be a law of nature, one a number of us wanted to break.

When the service was over, none of us said much. The ride home in Dad's car was very quiet. Casey sat beside me in the rear seat. My folks sat up front. Casey Allegro proved once again she was my best friend and true soul mate as she suffered with me on the inside. She sniffled from time to time using my one Sunday handkerchief she'd plucked from my suit coat chest pocket. Occasionally, she reached for my hand or I reached for hers. Neither one of us really had to say anything; each of us thought we knew what the other was thinking. She was worried that Honey wouldn't make it back from her wounds. I was worried that Honey wouldn't make it back in time to help me find and kill the creatures that had wreaked havoc on the bull terriers.

Why now? I kept asking myself. It had been almost 12 weeks since the Quarry Cave fight when the three Weres attacked the terriers on the Academy grounds. I truly thought we had killed all the local Werewolf population. We'd also sealed up their recently found cave. We had painstakingly gone over all the geologic records of our county trying to see if there were any other cave entrances we could find and close down. It was an exercise in vanity. I'd even gone out periodically to the Dead Zone. There I asked the few owls that remained if they had seen or heard any Werewolf activity in the area, but nothing. So we all assumed the problem was solved. I was therefore finally looking forward to my last summer at home before packing up and heading out to North Carolina for college. Veterinary school would come in its own time.

My work with the terriers at the Quarry Cave slaughter had earned me a brevet rank of Second Lieutenant. It also paid me a modest monthly stipend. It was enough to pay tuition and room and board so I could attend college in North Carolina between assignments with Lt. Col. Spikes's Special Operations group. I would be working on the Werewolf eradication operation known as Growler I. The State of North Carolina was a reputed hotbed of Were activity. My skills as Gatekeeper were needed there. It didn't hurt that Casey would be attending the University of North Carolina on a soccer scholarship. She would be half a state away from where I would attend pre-veterinary school at Lees-McRae College near Boone, but at least she would be within same-day driving distance. My hope was that we would be able to see one another from time to time.

The AP, or honors, classes I'd taken my last two years of high school allowed me to graduate with not only a high school diploma but an associate's degree as well. It was a trial program sponsored by the US Department of Education and a limited coalition of accredited universities and colleges mostly in the South and Southeast. Although I would be 19 years old when I started college, I would enter Lees-McCrae as a junior. If I studied hard and passed my courses, I would graduate in two years with a bachelor's degree. I would then be awarded a full commission as a Second Lieutenant and be ready for vet schooling.

Casey had taken much the same route but would not be a junior until she completed her first semester in college. On a full four-year soccer scholarship, she would likely stay on and work on her master's degree before her four years of playing eligibility were up. One way or another, it seemed that North Carolina was going to be pretty important to our respective families for the next four years. But all that was in the future. My concerns at present were how many Weres were still alive, where they were, and when we could go kill them. Or if *we* was not an option, then when could *I* go after them?

As I would learn, some concerns are never addressed in our own time frame. They just fester for a while until the stars line up, and even then, apparently the constellations also have to be in sync. Truth is, I was frustrated, angry, and impatient. I wanted a bloody revenge right now. Every day that passed made it hurt more. Patience is a hard attribute to acquire when you're young and sure of yourself.

DAY ONE 1:00 P.M.

We'd been back from the dogs' memorial service about an hour when I decided I couldn't stand it anymore. I needed something to take my mind off the recent tragedy. I determined I would do some reconnoitering back at the Academy grounds where the Werewolf attack had taken place. There might be some animal in the woods nearby who remembered the attack and could give me a clue as to where the Weres had gone. It was a long shot since most animal memories are not always accurate and often short, but it was the only shot I had. My mom had already fed us, and I had gone to my room to lie down, but that only made me more fidgety. Out-of-the-house action was the cure for my impatience, of that I was sure, and hence my determination to go back to the Academy.

A big part of my interim assignment from Lt. Col. Spikes was to take advantage of the biomedical research group hidden away in the containment facility beneath the city's Polo Grounds. The group had formerly been headed by the Director. Subsequent to his death, it had been placed under the authority of Dr. Dana Abernathy, a geneticist from Ohio State University. Dr. Abernathy and a small group of doctors and technicians at the containment facility had taken over my case with real interest. They were very interested in how to restimulate nerves that had long lay dormant since the car collision I experienced at the age of 10.

I was put on a program of exercise, diet, and electric stimulation both by active current and through a form of pulsed acupuncture. Something was working because I could now walk up to one mile without using my wheelchair, a walker, or a cane. I was leery about trying to trot or jog yet, but the basic mechanisms were there. I still looked forward to the day I could run once again. In the meantime, the new braces

I wore gave me not only support but confidence. I was just sorry they didn't give me speed or flexibility, but beggars can't be choosers. Uneven rocky terrain in the woods was still dangerous for me. Before I left, I made a long-distance call to Major Sanchez in North Carolina, apprising her of what happened. She listened carefully, asking me all the requisite questions and ending the call by not only expressing her condolences but by telling me she had another brainstorm. With Honey out of action for a while, she was even more convinced that she was a borderline genius because of what she was arranging. It was all about timing, she said. I didn't ask much but would have agreed with her even if she hadn't had a plan. Her last plan involving flamethrowers had saved our city and countless lives, including our own. She was right up there at the top of my heroes list. I couldn't see how that would ever change.

With that call behind me, I suited up and borrowed my dad's truck. I took along my bow, a full quiver of arrows, and my new javelin. I also wore my new set of leg braces. The old one's had pinched ever since I had a real growth spurt almost a year ago. While I could move about with greater ease with the new braces, there were actually times now that I didn't have to use them.

Casey intercepted me as I was backing out of our common driveway. She asked where I was going. When I told her my plans, she asked me to hold on one moment while she grabbed her backpack. She told her folks she was going with me. I was glad to have company, especially Casey's company. She thought logically. She paid attention to her environment. She always seemed to know just where she was in relation to the sphere of activity in which she was engaged. I was a far more intuitive thinker. We often reached the same conclusions but got there by different paths. We acted as a sort of check and balance on each other. When we did it right, we had confidence in our joint decisions.

It didn't take all that long to make the trip to the Academy. The hard part was finding a spot close by the exercise field to park so I wouldn't have to walk so far. We eventually did, and it turned out for the best. I encountered several birds and one very troubled squirrel on the way to the spot we thought the Weres had first emerged and then later reentered the woods. The birds only remembered there had been a disturbance among the little dogs and the very big dog-like things with claws. The little dogs were left lying on the ground after their fight.

The squirrel, however, was a virtual gold mine of information. He remembered the Weres' passage out because of their smell and the fact that they left a blood trail right through his territory. He hid behind a tree trunk as they passed and followed them for a short way to see if they were leaving his area. They frightened him big time, and he was still upset. I asked him to lead us along their path for just a bit, if he would. I told him we were trying to find the creatures and make sure they never returned. He was all for that. He guided us a short way through the woods to a gully that led gradually away from the woods and in the direction of Chagrin Falls as the gully disappeared into a field. The squirrel quickly scampered up and away through the trees, leaving us alone, but we had what we wanted. We had a starting point.

With a lot of daylight left, Casey suggested we follow the gully for a ways, keeping alert for any sign of the Weres or their passing. We agreed we'd walk no more than an hour before we turned back and headed home again. Casey, having shifted her pack to a comfortable position on her back, set off in the lead. I walked carefully behind her. I used my javelin as a kind of walking staff for balance and hung my bow over my shoulders. The gully gradually deepened as we walked along until our heads were below the field level on either side of us. Occasionally, we saw troughs in the sandy bottom. The depressions looked like something large had been dragged for a spell, but the soft sand yielded no specific prints.

About 20 minutes into our walk, the gully split with a deeper channel bearing away on the right and the shallower channel breaking sharply to the left. I felt uncomfortable separating, but Casey felt strongly that we would be safe if we each walked a different channel for no more than five minutes. We would then come back to the divide so we could compare notes. We would decide which gully we would pursue, if any. I reluctantly agreed. I offered her my javelin for general protection. She laughed and pulled her .357 revolver and side holster from her pack, fastened it on her belt, stuck her tongue out at me, and started down the left gully after checking her watch. I saw her disappear around the corner, and then I turned and started down the deeper gully after also checking my watch. I figured I'd give it four and a half minutes just in case Casey might find herself in an awkward situation. What I didn't know was that Casey was having the same thoughts about me, only she'd planned to turn around after three minutes. It meant the difference between life and death. Mine.

DAY ONE 2:30 P.M.

I was gone no more than a minute down the twisting gully when the soft sandy bottom gave way to a harder, slightly wet sand. *We must be at the water table*, I thought. I suddenly felt rather than heard a muffled thump behind me. I paused midstride and then turned to see what might have caused the pressure wave that had passed beneath my feet. I looked squarely into the red-rimmed eyes of a very big, beige Werewolf crouching about 12 feet behind me.

Everything in my body signaled alarm. The short life of 18 plus years I'd enjoyed flashed before me in less time than it took to turn around. I deliberately brought the javelin around in front of me, holding it with both hands at a 45-degree angle. I was prepared to ram it through the Were if it charged me. There was no way I could get the bow off my chest and shoulder, nock an arrow, and pull and release it before the Were's teeth and claws ripped away some crucial part of my anatomy—like my head.

I froze in that position for at least three eternities before the Were shifted slightly, cocked its head, and just studied me. Its eyes seemed to take in every detail of my being. No sound escaped its maw until I felt two jarring impacts behind me. My heart felt as if it had sunk into my shoes. I was terrified. I knew I was, well, truly trapped. Those two impacts could only mean two Weres were now behind me, but I could not risk a quick look lest I invited the beige Were to attack. It growled in a very low, throaty manner, changing the inflection twice, but it still didn't move toward me. It did straighten up until it towered over me, again just studying me.

I could see no easy way out of this trap. I would have to fight, but maybe I could do it on my terms to start and upset whatever ambush they'd planned, even if only a little. That would give Casey a chance to get away. I decided to try. I began to whistle George Cohan's "Over There" as loudly as I could. I hoped Casey would hear and recognize the song and remember its lyrics. A piercing whistle will often carry where a voice call will not. I was hoping this was one of those times. Actually, I was also hoping my mouth wouldn't be so dry from fear that I couldn't whistle at all. Then, thinking of Casey at the mercy of these beasts, I got mad.

Captain Yamata of the Special Operations Group (SOG) had told me to channel any anger I felt. Anger was the flip side of fear and just as dangerous. One had to avoid irrational action. I was to use my anger to reinforce what deliberate steps I chose to take. All of that flashed through my mind as I decided to turn and attack the two Weres behind me. I was betting they weren't old enough to produce the virus venom that forced a transformation. If so, while I might be bitten or clawed, I would still retain my humanity until I killed them or died. Yamata also drilled into me that with thought comes action. The two must not be separate, especially with Werewolves who move at lightning speed.

All of that passed through my mind in seconds. With the commitment to attack, I whirled and did. The Weres were less than 10 feet behind me. They were standing rather than crouching where they had landed after jumping down into the gully from the field above. I took two steps toward the Were on my right and then feinted with the javelin as if to spear the Were on the left. It jumped back as the javelin tip came at it, while the Were on the right just stood there and watched its companion's reaction. I was already turning back toward the Were on my right as its head turned to watch the javelin. I thrust the spear up into its right eye with all the strength I could muster. The javelin penetrated its brain as screams of pain died in its throat.

Yanking the javelin back, I stepped to my right. I spun in front of the Were and reversed my arms so the javelin's tip rotated 180 degrees. It now pointed at the second Were's chest and upper belly. But I was now in a position to pull the spear rather than push it with my stronger right arm, and pull I did. I jammed the javelin through the Were's sternum until my right hand hit its breastbone. The weight of the sagging Werewolf immediately pulled me down. It tried to maul me as it rapidly lost its strength from the death wound.

The fall put me in immediate danger. The angle of entry stopped me from jerking the javelin out of the Were's chest and pulled me down with it. I was aware that my back and right side were completely unprotected. I could hear the howl and the scrabble of claws on the earth as the beige Were launched itself at me. I simply closed my eyes as I held the javelin in the second Were's chest. I sank. I knew the beige Were would not let such an open opportunity to kill me pass. The thought crossed my mind that I'd like to see a rerun of my life again. In my fear of the beige Werewolf, I'd cut it short the first time. Then, without warning, the air seemed to explode around me. It was as if the sound of rolling thunder briefly overtook me, a series of rapid explosions from above amid the screams of the second dying Were and the angry howls of the beige Were as it charged me. Within seconds, there was nothing but silence. The second Were lay crumpled behind me. The beige Were lay prone beside me. I couldn't seem to focus for a moment. Faintly, I heard a voice calling my name.

"Cody! Cody! Are you all right? Cody, talk to me!"

It was Casey. She was on the cut bank above me looking down. In her hand was that most wonderful smoking .357 Magnum pistol her dad had taught her to shoot. She had emptied the revolver into the beige Werewolf with her typical steady aim. She saved my life and whatever pieces of my anatomy on which the Were had designs. I rolled onto my knees and took several deep breaths. I then shook my head and stood up on wobbly legs. As I had learned time and time again over my years with Casey, some people you can mess with, and some you just don't. Casey Allegro had just given a graphic lesson on why she was a "just don't." She reloaded as I climbed slowly to my feet.

"I like your timing," I gushed, "but I like your aim even more. Don't ever let me talk you into carrying a bow instead of a pistol. And if I try, remind me that you're smarter than I am, and I will always be well served to give you free rein."

With that, she scrambled down into the gully. She took my arm, suggesting we leave now and report all this to the Chief as soon as we got home. I agreed but asked her if that pack of hers still contained her camping knife. She silently unshouldered the bag, dug in, and handed me her blade. She asked why I wanted it. I told her I wasn't sure but felt it might be useful to take back a sample of the beige Werewolf for the folks at the containment lab. I remembered that these odd-colored pale Weres, usually older, seemed to carry the virus while the younger Weres did not. I thought maybe the scientists could study a piece of the beige Were and compare it to the carcass of the deputy, which they still had. With that in mind, I severed the beige Were's forearm from its body. I tied it to my belt, and we started back.

We said little to one another until we finally got back to the car. Casey carried my javelin in her left hand and her pistol in her right as I walked slightly behind her. This time, I walked with my bow drawn halfway and my arrow nocked. I would not be caught at such a disadvantage again.

DAY ONE 4:00 P.M.

On the drive back, Casey told me how it came to be that she'd shown up in time. The left-hand shallow gully simply ran up and out. She had planned to turn back at three minutes, but finding herself standing on the field above, she cut across to where she thought I might be. She heard my whistling and then the snarls of the beige Were. Seeing no other Weres in the field, she figured from the song that I was in trouble. She started running for the sound with her hand on her weapon in the holster. She pulled it out at the rim of the gully and then slid to a stop. She drew and fired almost immediately, catching the beige Were as it sprang for me. She wasn't sure how many bullets a Were could take, so she simply kept firing until the revolver's chambers were empty.

As I sat listening to her, I marveled at my good fortune of having Casey in my life. She was smart, clever, beautiful, outgoing, athletic, well spoken, and ambitious, and she had a killer instinct when it came to sports or competition. Moreover, she was loyal to a fault and fearless when it came to protecting her family and friends. Best of all, she was a darn good shot! With friends like Casey, a fellow would have little to fear from life and very little to fear from Werewolves. It was no wonder I'd had a secret crush on her for years. I'd be surprised if anyone didn't. I was comforted by the fact that while secret crushes may not last, friendships do. With college and a career looming ahead, I could at least count on that. I had a feeling that down the road, our friendship would be more important to both of us than we now realized.

We stopped at City Hall on the drive home in the event the Chief might be in for the day. He wasn't. We left a message with the corporal on duty that we needed to speak with him when he could. We then drove to the Polo Grounds. I parked at the same barn where I parked when I went to my twice-weekly medical appointments. I showed Casey how to use the tunnel entrance through the old tack room. I had her demonstrate the combination to the door lock several times to make sure she remembered it. We then walked down to the main facility where the Weres were housed. I left the beige Were's arm with the scientist on duty. I also left instructions to pass it along to Dr. Abernathy. I then showed Casey the room where I had my treatments. With no further ado, we turned and walked back out the same way we'd come in.

It was almost suppertime when we returned home. Casey went to her place, and I parked Dad's truck and took my gear with me to my place. I washed up and sat down with Mom and Dad and told them of our experience. They were alarmed at first, as I knew they would be. I didn't dwell too much on the sequence of events. I told them we'd had a fight and that both of us, armed, managed to kill three Weres. I also mentioned our detour to City Hall and the confinement facility. Dad took the time to call the Chief personally when I was done. The Chief arranged for the medical examiner's personnel to go and retrieve the three Weres' bodies that same evening lest they be found by someone else.

About two hours later, Dad got a call from the Chief. The medical examiner's people had gone out to the field as we had described it. They found a gully that seemed to be the one we described. What they didn't find were any bodies. Four men were on the retrieval team. They looked around for almost 20 minutes with no success. They called the Chief. They complained that maybe my dad and I had better get our facts straight before they called again. They went back to the morgue, gassed up the ambulance, and went home since their shift was over. They let it be known they were not happy about a useless trip.

When Dad relayed the message, I sat up in a hurry. Dead Weres don't just get up and walk away. I was sure the retrievers must have gotten turned around. I could feel apprehension start to take hold of me. My dad must have felt the same because he suggested that the two of us go back immediately and find the spot. We would then meet whatever team was on duty at the Academy and lead them there personally. In virtually minutes, we were back in the truck and about to go on our way. I decided not to bother Casey, but Dad stopped his truck at her door as she came out of her house and climbed into the cab. He'd called her while I went to my room to get dressed and grab my gear. She was miffed that I'd tried to leave her, but Dad explained that with both of us together, he could be absolutely sure we would find the site.

Dad figured we would have about an hour or less of twilight to find the place. His timing was right on. We took him through the woods and to the mouth of the large gully. We then walked along to a place I felt was the spot I had been trapped. Nothing was on the ground save a few furrows and some soft sand scattered around. I was dumfounded. Almost frantic, I walked back and forth between the gully walls looking for a clue or sign of our experience. Nothing. I even walked up and down the gully for about 40 yards in either direction. Nothing. Dad stood silently, watching me all the time as I prowled around for signs. I could sense his impatience and the start of his doubt until Casey hollered at both of us.

She had climbed out of the gully at what I thought was the original spot. She started looking for signs in the field above where she had run to my aid. She saw nothing until at the very lip of the gully's wall she spotted a small print of the tread from the toe of her left shoe. Casey was right-handed and always fired by placing her left foot forward and leaning into her leg to absorb the recoil of her weapon. That forward pressure would have pushed her shoe down at the toe, and the impression would have been the result.

My dad and I climbed up to examine her find. I felt a wave of relief wash over me. Then I felt a wave of fear. The absence of the carcasses was mute evidence that there were yet more Weres around, that they were acting deliberately to hide their presence. But even worse, we still didn't really have a clue where they were or how many there were. Casey and my dad seemed to come to the same conclusion about the same time as we all jerked our heads up and looked quickly around us. I wasn't so worried about the moment as I was about the future because between my bow and arrows, Dad's Korean War Street Sweeper shotgun, and Casey's .357 revolver, I didn't think anything short of a reenactment of the Battle of Bull Run would stop us from making it back to Dad's truck. But the missing bodies meant there were at least four more Werewolves out there somewhere, two critically wounded and two more healthy enough to haul three bodies away and clean up the site of their deaths. That was way too many under any conditions.

However many there were, it seemed they wanted to keep their presence secret. That was scary enough on its own. That meant they were either regrouping for another attack or trying to melt away and go somewhere else. While I hoped it was the latter, none of us wanted our mess to be somebody else's problem, especially not with Werewolves. Weres were nothing but harbingers of death, almost always unpleasant, a legacy no good person would willingly leave for another.

Dad jolted us out of our reverie by grabbing our arms. He practically shoved us back toward the woods. "Move!" he said sharply. "Night is coming and we will not fight them in the dark if we can help it." He took the lead, put Casey in the middle, and told me to bring up the rear. He set a hard pace. By the time we finally reached his truck, I was grateful for the weeks of biomed conditioning I'd had.

DAY ONE 7:00 P.M.

A quick drive home, a rather long phone call to the Chief, and tomorrow morning's agenda was set. The three of us and a team of 10 heavily armed police officers familiar with Werewolves would assemble at the K-9 Academy early tomorrow morning. We would start a detailed search of the gully and the surrounding field at 7:30 a.m. We would be joined by an additional 10 deputies from the Sherriff's office at 10:00 a.m., either to expand the search area or fight whatever turned up. Cadets from the K-9 Academy would assist by keeping traffic away from the surrounding fields or rerouting traffic that might otherwise have to come close to the fields' boundaries. Outlying residents and the owners of the fields would be contacted early and evacuated from the area under the supposition that bullets would be flying before the morning was up.

I didn't fall asleep right away that night. Neither, I suspected, did anyone else who was assigned to the Chief's show of force. No one with any experience whatever wanted a rematch with the Weres, at least no one in their right mind. But troubled or not, sleep comes inevitably. Shortly after midnight, when I'd just settled down into a heavy doze, I was startled awake by what seemed to be a bomb going off in our downstairs den.

The crash of glass bursting and the roar of Werewolves lusting and crying for blood combined to jerk me awake. I heard screaming. I was fully disoriented. I rolled off the bed, tangled in the bed covers. I tried to gain my feet as my ears were assaulted with the crashing sound of objects being thrown about, the splintering of furniture, and glass bursting against walls and tables. It was bedlam downstairs. I could hear Dad's angry yelling and my mother's screams echoing through the upstairs hallway outside my door.

Werewolves were loose in our home! We had been targeted once more, and this time, they weren't playing a waiting game. The Weres were rampaging through our downstairs, obviously looking for me or my dad. We were known to them. Only months before, my dad and I had killed two that had come to watch our home. Sentinels, we called them. Shortly after learning of them, we had set a trap and killed them. After that came the slaughter at the Quarry Cave and what we had hoped was the end of the Werewolves at Chagrin Falls. Obviously, that hope was dashed with the mayhem going on downstairs. We would be slaughtered, too, if they managed to gain the upstairs. *Where are Honey and the terriers now?* I thought to myself. *Right when we need them most.* Dumping the covers from my legs, I grabbed my bow, slung my quiver over my shoulder, pulled and nocked an arrow, and reached to open my bedroom door just as a very large and dangerous Were kicked it in. Part of the splintered door hit my left knee as it went flying by. It spun me to my left, breaking my arrow against the floor as I tumbled. I lost my grip on my bow. In a near panic, I scrambled to my knees. I threw the nearest object I could reach at the Were that was now forcing itself through my door. It was my advanced algebra textbook, 206 pages of dense equations and formulaic math, that hit it in the neck. I could see it stagger slightly as it choked off a snarl and reached for its throat.

That was all the delay I needed.

I grabbed my bow and slid another arrow from my quiver. Steadying my aim, I drilled the shaft through the paw that was holding its throat. The Were collapsed immediately, choking, gasping, and clawing at the arrow with its free paw while I nocked a third arrow. I put that one through its eye and into its brain. It died in seconds. Its body filled the doorway. I could hear its companions pounding on my parents' door down the hall. Tossing my bow over the first Were and into the hallway, I frantically tried to pull or push the dead creature out of my way. When I couldn't, I managed to clamber over him. I had a clear glimpse of the havoc. Not one but two Werewolves were at my parents' door.

The two Weres were not as big as the one that had kicked in my door. Fortunately, each one somewhat impeded the other as they tried to beat down my folks' door. I fell to the hallway floor when I finally managed to pull myself over the big Were that had attacked me. The sound of my landing prompted one Were to turn its head and see me sprawled out helplessly beside its now dead companion. With a roar, it literally spun, ran, and sprang for me with open maw and claws outstretched. I grabbed the uprights on the balcony railing beside me for leverage and then kicked with all my strength as the Were rocketed into me. My feet met it while it was still in midair. My knees bent back and absorbed its momentum as I let myself roll backward. I then extended my legs as much as I could. The Were was really heavy, but all I had to do was slightly alter its trajectory. It flew right over the top of me, splintering the balcony railing as it went through it, flailing wildly before crashing into the downstairs wall. With a bellowing roar, it staggered up. Determined, it bound for the stairs again.

Now I had time. Grabbing my bow and an arrow, I nailed him to the wall through his neck. I then spun to see what was happening at my parents' door, only to see that it hung crookedly by one hinge, and the doorway was empty. Nocking an arrow as I stumbled down the hall, I pulled up at the doorway with bow fully drawn to see an awful scene. My father had been flung against his far bedroom wall, and his left arm looked as if it had been clawed from shoulder to wrist. Blood ran down his arm in bright rivulets, and he appeared to be groggy, dizzy, and losing consciousness.

The last Were had backed my mom into a corner and was slowly stalking her. It taunted her with promises of a horrible death as it prepared to rip her apart. Just as it hunched its shoulders and raised its arms to rend her, I put an arrow through the middle of its back. It reared up on its toe pads, arching itself backward as if it were a gymnast, and then its legs failed it completely. Feebly, it tried to reach over its slumping shoulders and grab the quivering shaft that had partially severed its spinal column and was protruding from its chest.

But as it fell backward, snapping the arrow shaft against the floor, I saw that my arrow point wasn't the only thing protruding from its chest. Surrounded by a deep red stream of blood coursing slowly down its chest was Mom's knife, her S&W Extreme Ops FR2S knife with its tanto blade still quivering. My mom was never anyone's patsy.

Mom and I both shouted simultaneously to each other to call 9-1-1 even as we scrambled to get to Dad. She managed to slide to his side before I could, so I ripped off

177

one of their bed sheets. Rapidly tearing it into long strips, I began to wrap Dad's arm as tightly as I could, hoping to staunch the blood flow. Mom grabbed several of the strips and shooed me aside. She was a better wrapper anyway, a veteran of many Christmas packages. She kept saying soothing words to Dad who looked now to be unconscious. I threw myself over their bed. I grabbed the phone, called 9-1-1, and then, with still trembling fingers, dialed the Chief's home number.

An hour later, what was left of our home returned to some normalcy. Mom went to the hospital in an ambulance with Dad. The Chief followed them. I was bedded down in the Allegros' spare basement bedroom. Several police officers were keeping watch and running a crime scene at our home. I presumed the neighbors were back in their homes after the ambulance took Dad away. The last of the several squad cars that came with sirens blasting had also departed.

The Chief's public affairs representative put out the word that a black bear had gained entry through our unlocked back door after smelling some of my mom's berries that she was getting ready for canning. The bear had become frightened, they said, when Dad tried to shoo him away. The bear literally ransacked our house, wounding Dad in the process. To seal the story, the police carried out one of the Weres, strategically covered with a draped sheet, so the neighbors could get a glimpse of what they thought was a very large, shaggy bear.

The second and third Weres were removed quietly at 4:00 a.m. in a garbage truck. The truck also hauled away some of the debris that had once been our furniture. All in all, the encounter was nicely managed and the public kept unaware of what really happened. The last thing the Chief said to me was this: "Be there on time, Cody. We're going to finish this tomorrow with or without you."

I fell asleep at 4:30 a.m. I was still trembling from the shock of seeing my dad so badly wounded. I'd always thought of him as indestructible. But now, the only thoughts that cluttered my mind and impeded my sleep were thoughts of revenge. I'd been on an adrenaline high for several hours. When it finally wore off, I dropped immediately into a deep and dreamless sleep, despite myself.

I was rudely awakened at 6:15 a.m. by Mr. Allegro. He was shaking my shoulder and calling my name. He wouldn't leave the room until I was up on my feet and headed for the guest bathroom. Breakfast was upstairs a few minutes later before he drove Casey and me to the Academy. We were to be there by 7:00 a.m. sharp. Mr. Allegro had advised me to stay home for the day and sleep or maybe go see my dad, but I didn't hesitate one minute to ignore him.

I dressed, bolted my breakfast down, thanked Mrs. Allegro, ran to my house, grabbed my gear and my javelin, and was waiting at the Allegros' car at 10 minutes before 7:00 a.m. I wasn't exactly wide awake, but I was there. I dozed on the drive to the Academy.

DAY TWO 7:20 A.M.

Sundays normally found us in church trying to learn more about being better human beings. Forgiveness was the current topic. As a congregation of neighbors, we always found countless ways to irritate or wrong our fellow beings, although rarely on purpose. Today was a Sunday service I was glad to miss because I felt a lot of things, but not forgiveness. I suppose one could make the case that Werewolves were also part of God's creatures and merited some consideration, but that argument also begged the question of Satan as a former child of God. Whatever he may once have been, he merited no consideration whatsoever in my book. Today was a day I wanted Old Testament eye-for-an-eye justice. The only prayers I would say this day for any Werewolf would hopefully be over its dead body with a special thanks for good riddance. Our pastor would not have approved of my spirit of loving eradication.

Mr. Allegro dropped us off at the staging area at 7:20 a.m. We used the time to recheck our gear and let the Chief know we were there and ready. Standing around waiting was always hard for me. Casey tolerated down time no better. We were both restless and a little scared. We didn't know what to expect but wanted to be in on the action, whatever that turned out to be. Casey had been deeply affected by Honey's injury. I was still enraged about the Weres' break-in at my house. We were eager to get started. We hoped the Chief had a vital role for us to play.

Turns out he did.

The Chief had set up a search pattern for the fields above the gully. He wanted us out of it. There might be firing from shotguns, rifles, or pistols. His officers were trained how to conduct the search pattern safely and efficiently without shooting one another. We were not trained for that environment. This morning wasn't the time to start. Conversely, his men were not necessarily skilled in conducting woodland searches save for an occasional lost child line of discovery. He noted that some of our more successful previous encounters had taken place in woodland environments. He felt I was at least somewhat proficient in handling danger there.

He asked if I would take Casey and three of his men and run a sweep of the forested area that bordered two sides of the large fields the Chief and his men would search. His area would include the gully and any and all extensions they could find. Each team would be in radio contact with the other. Upon any discovery, the Chief reminded us that the reinforcing team of the Sherriff's deputies would be standing by from 9:00 a.m. for emergencies. They had instructions to join the scheduled search at 10:00 a.m. My team would sweep to the end of the woods. We would then turn around and search back again. That would put a fresh set of eyes on the terrain going back so we would have a solid assurance that we'd missed nothing.

I greeted the three men who were assigned to me, introduced Casey, and noticed immediately that one of the young, single troopers appeared to be giving her a lot more attention than this search warranted. A quick and quiet word to the Chief got me an older, married officer instead. I knew Casey could handle herself, and she was certainly worth a first and second look and then some, but not when Werewolves were around. I wanted guys who were afraid to lose something dear like their life, not someone who hoped to gain something dear like a date with Casey. I took my team back to the edge of the Academy grounds.

As usual, Casey was well aware of the incident. She gave me a quiet "thanks" when we were walking to the Academy's border. She would have handled him in her own way, given some time, but we all might be dead by then because it was an incident that could have been avoided in the first place. When the time came for her to handle it, any lack of focus on our primary mission could cost us dearly should an attack happen at that same time.

That was a principle of leadership Sanchez and Yamata had taught me. Nip problems in the bud, including potential problems, before they build into emergencies. Said another way, real or potential, bad news doesn't improve with age.

I established the search line by putting Casey in the middle. I was on her left, and another officer was on my left flank position. The other two officers took their positions to the right of Casey. I didn't set the lineup to protect Casey. She was in the middle because she had the shortest stride. As we walked along, we would always be looking toward the line's center to keep the line straight. Two of us would always be glancing at Casey as would the other two men on either side of her.

Each of us carried a whistle gripped between our teeth. It was to be blown only in the event of personal danger or to signal a halt. One loud blow and our line would collapse inward along its axis as we ran to the aid of the whistle blower. Three blows and the line halted in place. A weapon fired would have the same effect as one blow. By always staying in our line of axis, the person shooting would know exactly where the safe fire areas were. We needed to kill Werewolves, not each other.

At 7:40 a.m., the Chief started the search. We had three shotguns and the personal weapons carried by the officers in our line, as well as Casey's .357 revolver and my bow and arrows. Dad's Street Sweeper was hung over my shoulder, muzzle down. Both barrels were loaded, and I carried 10 12-gauge buckshot cartridges in my right front pocket. Dad wouldn't be needing his shotgun today, and I might, even though I hadn't asked his permission. I figured that under the circumstances, that would be a mere formality. I wanted to give it to Casey, but its weight and size made it awkward for her to carry. So it ended up hanging from my shoulder.

The going was somewhat difficult. We were in rocky, uneven terrain. Low bushes and entangling vines from some of the trees made the hike tiresome. Visibility was okay.

We could see about 30 to 40 feet ahead or laterally, enough so each flanker could see Casey. After our first 45 minutes of a relatively slow pace, I halted the line and called everyone in. I set everyone in a defensive circle, looking outward. I called an eight-minute water and smoke break. I asked our two smokers to carry out their ashes and paper and any matches. We were in a leave-no-trace mode. Thankfully, they complied.

DAY TWO 8:45 A.M.

We were about 20 minutes into our second march when the terrain suddenly altered. The ground we were walking on was full of dips and rises but reasonably level. None of the shallows or rises we encountered exceeded seven feet, and we were able to maintain a fairly orderly line of march. Almost without warning, we stumbled onto a severe cut running diagonally across the woods at about a 30-degree angle to our line of march. The flanker to Casey's far right was the first to encounter the drop-off, and he immediately sounded his whistle in three short blasts. We all stopped, and I motioned to the flanker on my left to come to me.

Once he reached me, I bade him remain there. I walked down our line to the far right flanker, continuously sweeping my eyes from side to side. As I closed in on him, I could see the cut for myself. There was a 10–12 foot drop-off that formed a 14–20 foot chasm to the far bank. As I walked along it for a short distance, I could see it first widened considerably and then narrowed as I approached a point just ahead of Casey. When I walked a little farther to a point ahead of where I had originally been standing, where the left flanker was now standing in my place, I could see farther to my left. I noticed the gap closed just beyond where our left flanker would be walking had we continued moving forward. Somehow, beneath these trees in an area to which few, if any, came, a small, canyon-like feature was hidden beneath the canopy of trees that formed this part of the woods.

Several rock falls and rock piles dotted the small canyon. It appeared that running water had created a path down the middle of the canyon until the path bent sharply and turned into the far canyon bank. The path then disappeared behind a considerable pile of rocks. All was silent around us. It was like being in the Dead Zone again with no sign of small animal life and no birds in the trees. I'd been listening during our entire walk for some encounter with an animal that might give me a heads-up on what was in the small forest. I had heard nothing and had not sensed anything since our earlier break. That didn't necessarily alarm me, but it did make me extra wary. The feelings stealing over me weren't comfortable ones.

We needed to know where the stream went. Because I was uneasy, I didn't want to send anyone down there alone. Nor did I want to risk us all. A big part of leadership is taking calculated risks, not just risks in general. A big part of staying alive is not being stupid and trying to fight an enemy on their ground, presuming you're in the enemy's territory. That's always a good presumption with Werewolves. I motioned for the left flanker to move to Casey. Walking back along the canyon's lip, I soon came into view of the two police officers on Casey's right. I motioned them to join us at Casey's spot.

Our advance had been silent for the most part. None of us had talked or made any loud noise since the earlier whistle. I didn't want to start now. When we all got to Casey, I whispered that we would walk quietly back to the break site together, an arm's length apart. Now!

The relatively short trek back began and ended in silence. I felt the break site was far enough away from the hidden canyon that we could speak in low undertones. I wanted to apprise the team of my feelings and intentions. When we got to the site, I had two of the police officers kneel facing one way and Casey and another kneel close to them, facing them, slightly staggered. I knelt at the end of their two lines so my words would reach all of them and they could listen while watching the backs of the two team members opposite them rather than looking at me.

I told them we'd stumbled across a geophysical anomaly, just the kind that Werewolves sought out. I had strong feelings that the water bed that disappeared behind the rock pile would probably lead to a cave opening. Caves were the Weres' first choice of habitation. My plan was to walk back and report what we'd found to the Chief. With reinforcements, we'd approach and explore the canyon bottom. This was the sort of activity the Sherriff's SWAT Team had been trained for. I hoped they would be willing to take it on. I explained that there could be nothing there, of course, but better to be safe than sorry.

I was relieved when they agreed with me. Casey quietly gave me a pat on the shoulder. With that, we headed back to where we'd first infiltrated the forest. We reached our starting point without incident. The Sherriff's team had already shown up and was waiting nearby. I told our team to relax for a few minutes while I sought out the Sherriff to make an initial report.

DAY TWO 9:30 A.M.

I'd been speaking with the Sherriff for about 15 minutes when a party of five police officers emerged from the deep gully carrying the dirt-stained body of a Werewolf. A man held each arm or leg, and the fifth man walked behind with his shotgun at the ready. They shouted when they saw us. They brought the Were's carcass over to us and dropped it on the ground. Its throat had been ripped out or, better said, torn away, almost as if something had been clamped on and ripped away, taking flesh and bone with it. However it was killed, it had suffered an ugly and painful death. It was the way a pit bull killed. I smiled. Pit bulls don't go quietly.

Some of the deputies had never seen a Werewolf. They walked over for a closer look. Two threw up. Several turned and walked away faster than they'd walked over. I took a close look and silently said to myself, *Way to go, Bruno! This guy was 10 times your size but couldn't measure up to your fighting spirit. Lockjaw and Honey would be proud.* The police officers had been part of a five-person team sent by the Chief to study the gully for false entrances or anything out of the ordinary. One of them had spotted what appeared to be a cave-in along one side of the bank about a 30-minute walk down the gully, farther than I'd been. While digging around, he saw what appeared to be hairy fingers ending in long claws. He called in his teammates. They'd found the Were but nothing else in the vicinity. They radioed the Chief, who told them to bring the carcass back to the starting point immediately and that he would meet them there.

The Chief showed up with two other armed police officers shortly after. The Chief asked the Sherriff, the county SWAT Team Commander, and me to sit with him for a few minutes while we discussed what we'd found and decided what to do next. Each man gave his report. I explained my supposition that the canyon probably was the site of the Weres' lair, that the discovery of the hidden carcass underscored that. Yes, the Weres had gone to some trouble to hide the carcass, but the burial site would have been generally on the way to their lair. After hiding the carcass, they would simply have had to climb up the gully's bank and head across the fields to the woods. Using the gully as an entry and exit point would also certainly disguise their use of the canyon site, especially if they came and went under darkness.

The Chief bought into my theory. He called the last surface search team back to our mustering point. He suggested that we all take a break in the interim while he, the Sherriff, and the SWAT Commander drew up a plan to storm the canyon. He said he'd like to hit the canyon at midday when the Weres would likely all be at the lair, hopefully sleeping. He then took me aside. Holding my arm gently, he said softly that Casey and I were now excused. She could go home, and I could go see my dad. He reminded me he'd been part of the Quarry Cave offensive as well. He'd learned lessons, too, and now it was time for his men and the Sherriff's deputies to earn their pay. He watched me carefully until I grinned and said I understood, that I would obey him. A big smile creased his face. He patted me on the shoulder and thanked me for bringing his patrol and Casey back safely. Having listened to my debriefing only minutes before, he complimented me on my judgment. He said I'd made the right calls for the right reasons. He then called a police officer over and asked if he would please drive Casey and me wherever we needed to go.

As we turned and started away, I spun about quickly and called back to him that he would need heavy ordinance if there was a cave that had to be shut down. He just looked at me, smiled again, and silently pointed to two white vans parked about 70 yards away at the woods' edge. "Already covered," he said. He was kind enough to keep his grin in place. I smiled back, nodded my head up and down, and then sheepishly turned back to Casey and our escort.

"I'm ready," I said. "Let's go home."

DAY TWO 10:20 A.M.

There were still two police officers in the yard at my house when we arrived. Casey went into her house. I stayed to thank our driver for a safe trip home, explaining that we didn't need his services anymore since I still had my dad's truck if I needed to go somewhere. He waved as he drove off. I stopped briefly to speak with the two police officers in our front yard. All the damaged furniture and other pieces broken by the Were attack had been removed. Several 4' x 8' plywood planks were now nailed over the broken patio windows and sliding doors. Mr. Allegro had done that for us. The police had been waiting to make sure there was no looting in our absence and to make sure I was all right when I returned home. "Chief's orders," they said with a smile.

I thanked them, shook their hands, and sent them on their way. Trudging back to the house, my legs felt heavy, and I started yawning. I called my mom from inside the house, got a progress report on Dad, and decided to take a short nap before I went to the hospital. I was asleep before my head hit my upstairs couch pillow.

DAY TWO 10:00 P.M.

I'd been with my mom in my dad's hospital room for about two hours when the nurse came in and said there was a call for me. It was the Chief. He told me we'd talk in detail in the morning and asked me to be in his office at 8:00 a.m. sharp. There was a cave. Weres were in it, and a fight had ensued. Two SWAT Team members were dead, and three were seriously wounded, one critically. The Chief was about to leave for the hospital with the last ambulance. He wouldn't have time to talk to me once he got there. He would be with the families of the wounded SWAT Team members instead. I said I fully understood and promised I'd be in his office in the morning. He asked me to bring Casey as well. I promised I would, and he hung up. I knew little more than I did this morning but enough now to be grateful I'd trusted my instincts.

My dad was still unconscious from the drugs he had been given for the operation on his arm. The doctor thought the arm could be saved, but it would be a lengthy rehabilitation. Regaining full use again was iffy. More important to the doctor was the possibility of severe gangrene. Mom was just grateful he was alive. She was braver than I was. I cried, and she cried, and we even cried together, then it was time to wipe the tears and move along. I thought Dad's state would make her extra cautious about me, but when we'd cried ourselves out, she took me by both shoulders, looked me straight in the eye, and told me to never let my guard down and to kill each and every Were I found.

She didn't hate them. She simply recognized they were irredeemable. A Were could not change back into a human. That's not how the virus worked. It was a one-way ticket to a special kind of hell. Once in that state, each Were became an advanced, highly mobile killing machine with humans as their number-one target.

I called Casey, apologized for the late call, and delivered the Chief's message. I stayed at the hospital with my dad until midnight. I hoped to have a few conscious minutes with him. I wanted to tell him how much I loved him and thank him for protecting Mom. But he stayed in a drugged state the whole time. All I could do was hold his hand. Mom finally shooed me out and reminded me I had an appointment downtown with the Chief at 8:00 a.m. The hospital was letting Mom stay with Dad overnight. The nurses had a cot they would bring in once I was gone. A hug and kiss good night from Mom, and I was off for home.

To my surprise, there were guards still there when I returned (Chief's orders). I was glad. I wanted to sleep soundly. I knew if I were alone, I'd sleep with one eye open. Just to make sure, though, I stayed in the guest room. I locked the door and put a dresser against it. Even then, it was still a long night.

DAY THREE 8:00 A.M.

The next morning, I picked up Casey, and we drove to City Hall. We were waiting in the Chief's anteroom when he came bustling in right at 8:00 a.m. "Come in, come in," he said and then closed the door behind us as we each took a chair in front of his desk. He sat down with an audible plop. He started right in on his briefing. Twelve Weres had been killed, four of which were adolescents. One female Were had been captured at the cost of two SWAT members' lives. That Were had been sedated and taken to the confinement facility. Dr. Abernathy wanted me out there as soon as my schedule would permit, but two hours ago would be acceptable. I got the message. That was all I got.

The Chief excused me and asked Casey to stay and hear the whole story, which she could tell me later in the day or whenever we saw each other again. The Chief walked me to the door, shook my hand again, and asked me to visit with him when I got back. With that, he shut his door. He left me standing by his secretary's desk with a frown on my face, wondering what he meant—back from where?

The secretary smiled at me as she handed me an envelope. "I think you'll find your tickets and all you need in there, Mr. Dugway. Have a nice trip. Remember, Dr. Abernathy is waiting for you, so do hurry, please."

I still didn't get it. I walked out to my dad's truck, looking at the sealed envelope in my hand, all but scratching my head and wishing someone would kindly tell me what was going on. I climbed into the truck and headed for the Polo Grounds. I was starting to feel just a little bit grumpy and put upon. I was missing class. I thought I might have an excuse because of my dad's injury and hospitalization, but I felt I was on thin ice. I really wanted someone to spell out for me what this morning was really all about. And what was this urgency about Dr. Abernathy needing to see me? Was it about the captured female Were or something in my physical profile and the rehabilitation program in which I was enrolled? Whatever, the drive out to the Polo Grounds was not a long one. I occupied my thoughts with my dad and his situation. I didn't arrive in the best humor.

I parked Dad's truck in my usual place, locked it because of the envelope I left inside, and entered the underground north tunnel through the tack room. It had a shallower gradient than the tunnel did coming down from the main building. It was easier on my knees. I passed several scientists and administrative types as I came into the containment facility. All of them reminded me that Dr. Abernathy was looking for me. By the time the fourth person said that to me, I wanted to shout, "I got it!" But I just smiled, nodded, and asked where Dr. Abernathy was. No one knew the answer to that, so I just headed for her office. She was there, waiting for me. She stood up immediately as I walked in, taking me by the arm and steering me back to the cages where we'd once kept the deputy and the wounded Were. Waiting there, standing back from the cage but studying the recently captured female Were was the unnamed man. When I saw him, everything got more interesting. Things happened when he was around. All sorts of things.

He turned as we walked up. He stepped forward and greeted me with a firm but brief handshake. He then led us both to a nearby office where he asked me to take a seat, and then he closed the door. We spent the next hour or so talking about my dad, my discovery of the hidden canyon, yesterday's fight and capture, and, to my surprise, the examination of the female Were by Dr. Abernathy and her technicians. The female was pregnant.

Studying the female Were could be a major breakthrough in learning about the physiology of Weres, especially whether their hatred of humans was part of the biological process or a learned behavior. The study of the female would take months, to be sure, but the Werewolf problem wasn't suddenly going to get better without using every avenue available to scientists and decision makers to understand the capabilities of this dangerous species. They wanted to start right now; hence my presence.

They wanted to know what the female was thinking generally since being brought to the containment facility. They also had one or two very specific questions. "I know it's hard on you, Cody," said the unnamed man, "but you're the only one we know who can help us out right now, and we are asking for your help."

"Whatever I can do," I answered. "I'm on your payroll, and I actually can follow orders."

"Well, this isn't an order, Cody. We'll save that for later. But it is a request, and we need to know two things. When the female was captured, it sounded like it was using human speech to scream the word *no*. It repeated that word several times. The men who finally subdued it told us what they heard. So *if* the Were can speak, can it understand English? Can it understand what we say in front of it when it's in this cage? Second, does it know if there are any more pockets of Weres around here? And here is the bonus, Cody. Is its group part of the main group we thought we'd killed at the Quarry slaughter?"

I said let's go find out and walked out to the cages. As in the past, I walked up to the floor line painted in front of the cages and stood there looking at the female. It was prowling back and forth. When I walked up, it retreated to the back of the cage instead of rushing forth to challenge and try to attack me. We both stood like that for about five minutes until my legs started to tire, so I knelt down but kept looking at it. The female immediately rushed to the front of the cage, grabbed the bars, and began screaming and growling at me as if it were desperate to reach out and eviscerate me.

After several minutes, the Were tired and leaned against the cage to regain its breath and rest its arms. Like a light switch thrown on, we made a connection. It was bitter, angry, and sad all at once. My headache started immediately, but I kept on with it. After 10 minutes, I could no longer stand it. Dizzy, I came to my feet and backed away from the cage. I held my head while the room spun about me. Dr. Abernathy caught me and led me back to the nearby office where we all sat down. The unnamed man brought me a glass of water, which I gladly accepted.

I explained that apparently all changed females retained some limited ability to speak English or whatever their native language had been, depending, of course, on their ability to shape words with their mouths. They could certainly understand it. Not so males. A female born of a Werewolf did not have that ability, period. Males had no capacity to express themselves except in snarls, growls, howls, and grunts, which actually had meaning by the cadence, tone, and coupling of sounds. It was a primitive form of communication, but they could give basic commands. The hatred of a male Were for humans was exceeded only by the hatred of a female. We humans had no friends and no mercy in either camp. The males would kill for sport or survival, while the females almost always killed for survival, but both would kill gladly.

These last Weres were the survivors of the Quarry Cave slaughter. They had discovered a branching cave while trying to retreat from the flamethrowers. Only a few

Weres made it through before the group was forced to quiet concealment. After the Quarry Cave was sealed, they had no choice but to continue exploring the cave system for a way out. The rock pile cave where Sunday's battle occurred was the only outlet they'd found. They knew who I was. The raid on our house was an attempt to bring attention to my house and the west side of town while they prepared to leave the area. They were headed for the woodlands, several days' travel to the east.

The raid on the terriers had been a mistake. We were glad the Weres who had done that were dead because it jeopardized the small group's survival, but the remaining Weres were nevertheless glad the dogs were dead. Revenge killings were highly prized; hence, another reason for the attack on my home. After yesterday's battle, our female captive now apparently lived only to kill as many of us as it could. Giving birth was a secondary consideration. The Were had invited me into her cage and was furious that I would not come in. At that point, I had to break off the channel because I was starting to lose consciousness. I could barely hear the Were because of the pain in my head.

I told Dr. Abernathy and the unnamed man that there was something the Were had thought or said that I just could not remember. I would tell them as soon as it came back to me. It had to do with the virus, but right now, that was all cloudy to me. I could no longer concentrate. The unnamed man shook my hand again, thanked me, and left the room. Dr. Abernathy, however, stayed with me. She filled me in on what was happening and what lay in my immediate future. In short, she'd visited my teachers and principal and then gone to the head of the school board.

All my teachers had agreed to award me my final grades (all As) a week or two early and credit me with having finished all the requisite courses for my high school and associate's degree. I was released. I graduated from high school effective today. Moreover, I was to be at Cleveland's Burke Lakefront Airport at 3:00 p.m. for a flight to Charlotte, North Carolina. Major Sanchez or one of her sergeants would meet me and drive me to the Major's base of operations north of Hickory. I would be gone from seven to 10 days. I should be back in time for my graduation dance. I could even walk for my diploma if I wanted to.

"Oh," Dr. Abernathy said as I stood up to leave. "Your mother and father are aware of this. You need to stop by the hospital and say your goodbyes before you leave. And thank you again, Cody. You are a remarkable young man whose time has come. You're standing up quite well to the challenge. I just wish you'd chosen Ohio State. You'd make a grand Buckeye!"

She smiled, gave me a brief hug, and ushered me out the door. I wasted no time getting back to Dad's truck. I headed for the hospital, my head still swimming. I wondered how Dad was, what I should pack for North Carolina, and when I would see Casey again.

Yes, indeed, I thought back about the unnamed man. *All sorts of things!*

DAY THREE 3:00 P.M.

I was one of the last passengers to board. I had just settled into my seat when the stewardess closed and locked the door before announcing that we were ready for departure and began her various routines. I couldn't help but notice that she was in her early 20s. I wondered if she really knew what it felt like to be responsible for a number of people in a life-and-death situation. I sure hoped so because I was not all that keen on flying, although Mom and Dad had once flown me to New York and then to Florida.

I'd finally had my chance to visit with my dad. He was groggy. His arm was bandaged from wrist to shoulder, but they'd taken one or two tubes out. He could talk. I hugged him as best I could. I let him know what I was doing and that there had been a fight yesterday that Casey and I had missed. Mom sat with us. She told me what the doctors were saying and doing to treat Dad. She seemed fairly buoyant compared to the night before. We chatted about several things, including the state of the house. I'd told her what Mr. Allegro had done and about the police guard the Chief had mounted. After about half an hour, the nurse came in and told me I'd have to leave so Dad could get some rest. Mom would stay with him until noon, and then she was heading home to start the cleanup and repair work. She would be back at Dad's side around 5:00 p.m. for the remainder of the evening.

A kiss and hug goodbye and I was almost out the door when I turned and told Mom not to worry about her knife. The police had left it behind at my request. I'd cleaned it. It was on the end table by her bed. That brought a grin to both our faces. I blew her another kiss before turning to walk down the hall.

I was anxious to get home, pack, and stop by the Allegros to leave a message for Casey with her mother. That done, I drove to Cleveland and parked Dad's truck at long-term parking and then checked in at the airline's desk. I found a seat in the boarding area. I watched all the other passengers coming and going and the occasional plane taking off or landing. Cleveland was a busy place compared to Chagrin Falls. I liked our slower pace.

The flight to Charlotte was uneventful until we started hitting some turbulence over the Blue Ridge Mountains just before landing. The gentleman beside me didn't miss a snore, but the lady across the aisle practically squeezed her armrest to death. I finally knew what white knuckle meant. She was not a happy passenger. I couldn't tell what she was squeezing tighter, her hands or her eyes. She did help me take my mind off the bumps and tosses we were experiencing, though. I was grateful for that.

I was met in the debarkation lounge by a tall sergeant holding a placard with *Dugway* written on it. I stepped up, introduced myself, and shook his hand. He had big hands and a kind smile. He was the model of efficiency. In no time we retrieved my bag, loaded it into his government car, and were on our way north. He asked me if I'd had a chance to grab lunch before leaving. I said I hadn't but could wait. He smiled and said he was hungry, and we'd stop for a snack at Hickory. We were driving through Hickory to a small village called Blowing Rock near the town of Boone. It was very near the Blue Ridge Parkway. It was quite scenic. He also asked me if I was superstitious. When I said no, he smiled again and said to hold that thought, that things weren't always as they seemed. The Major's headquarters was the old Chapel at the back of one of the town's nearby graveyards, the Woodlawn Cemetery.

We reached our destination without incident except the sergeant expressed some surprise when I polished off two cheeseburgers, a malt, my fries, some of his, and an ice cream cone during our snack stop in Hickory. I guess I was hungrier than I thought. Then I remembered I'd eaten a pretty paltry breakfast that morning at home, and that made me suddenly miss my folks. The sergeant left me at the old Chapel door. He told me I could catch up with my bag at the inn in Blowing Rock later in the afternoon when Major Sanchez let me go. He said I'd find a surprise inside the Chapel. He then tossed me a cheery half salute and drove away.

I stood there all alone, turning around and taking in the scenery, the Blue Ridge Mountains, and the heavy growth of trees that carpeted them. With a deep breath, I turned to knock on the Chapel door. I was in heaven or close to it. There was truly beauty all around me. I just stood there soaking it all in.

But if I thought the land was beautiful, my eyes popped open and a grin plastered itself all over my face when the Chapel door opened. A young woman about my age stood there in green fatigues holding the door open. She was blond and pert, and her eyes twinkled as if they radiated sparks of light. She saw me, grinned, put out her hand, and hauled me inside. For a second or two I couldn't remember my name. I just gawked. I hadn't seen a girl this pretty since I'd last seen Casey, but this soldier (I later learned she was a corporal) was bursting with personality. And I'd never seen fatigues look so good before. I was tongue-tied. I had just met effervescence packaged in as shapely, comely, and energetic a bundle as could be humanly molded. All I could do was gawk.

I suddenly felt a tap on my shoulder and turned to see Major Sanchez standing there with that mischievous grin of hers. "Close your mouth, Cody. I see you've met Dusty. Her real name is Corporal Destine Travis. Her family name includes a hero at the Alamo in Texas. She is a warrior in her own right. She keeps the place organized in my absence and even better when I'm here. If she can't find something on this planet, it doesn't exist. And do not *ever* lie to her. She can spot a fake at three miles and holds a black belt in judo. You do not want her mad at you. Ever."

I looked from Major Sanchez's grin to Dusty's even bigger grin and just nodded. I was a little intimidated. I frankly didn't know what to do except say, "Yes, ma'am." The Major then shook my hand with real enthusiasm and pulled me along to her office.

"We've got work to do, Cody, and these next few days will be very important. Welcome aboard the Rat's Nest. We liked and kept the name. The folks in Blowing Rock and Boone think we're part of a geologic survey funded by the state and federal governments, so let's keep it that way. "You're here on an intern program. This is your orientation visit. I've spread the word that you'll be attending Lees-McCrae. They have a small rivalry with the young men and women attending Appalachian State in Boone, but nothing serious. Appalachian State doesn't have a veterinary preparation program, and there's a latent mutual respect that underlies any rivalry. Just be careful if you ever try to date one of the A-State girls. That might ruffle a few feathers if an A-State boy has his eye on her."

And such was my introduction to the Rat's Nest. It would be my second home for the next few years, and I would come to know almost every blade of grass and tree within 15 miles. But the best of this day was yet to come. I heard a knock on the Major's office door. I turned to see Dusty standing there with two bows and two quivers of arrows, each batch of arrows matching the bow beside it. Both were recurve hunting bows, one a Black Widow identical to mine that I'd left home in Ohio. The second bow was intriguing, however. It was a Grozer laminated bi-composite traditional Turkish recurve bow.

I was stunned and took it eagerly from Dusty. The technology behind the Turkish bow was fairly new, but it was rumored to have the same feel as shooting a horn bow. I'd never seen much less held one, but I'd certainly heard about them. Now I held one in my hands.

"These stay with the Rat's Nest, Cody, but they are yours to use whenever you're here," said the Major. "They're reserved for you alone. You'll find Dusty has had two pretty good firing courses built outside. One is for competition shooting. The other is a hunting course that circles through the woods behind us for about a quarter of a mile. I want you to keep proficient with the Black Widow but also learn how to use the Turkish recurve. It reportedly has an easier draw but fires a heavier arrow. I think we're going to need to upgrade your firepower. I've got a few ideas about loading your arrows with an anti-serum when we go up against the Weres here in North Carolina. The Black Widow arrows can't take the load."

Dusty propped up the two quivers and the Black Widow against the wall behind the Major's door. On her way out, Dusty closed the door. She grinned and winked at me as she brushed by. I just broke into a smile. I actually couldn't help myself. That young lady just exuded sunshine. I would bet she was banned from funerals. I was sold on Casey, but I wasn't dead, and Dusty made a fellow glad he was a fellow. I didn't know it then, but we were slated to become good friends over time. Like Casey, she became another great blessing in my life.

The Major and I spent the remainder of the day catching each other up on what we'd been doing. She was especially interested in our latest Chagrin Falls fracas and what I'd reported to the unnamed man after my visit with the captured Were at the confinement facility. We finished talking at 6:00 p.m. local time. The sergeant who'd met me at the airport took me to the inn in Blowing Rock. He said he'd be back for me in the morning at 7:00 a.m.

The excitement of the day was rapidly wearing off. I found myself much more tired than I thought I would be. After checking in, washing up, and grabbing a quick meal from a small restaurant nearby, I went back to my room and crashed. It had been quite a day. I was truly excited about trying out those two bows on Dusty's courses.

I had no inkling that the next day would hold an even bigger surprise, that I would meet a companion with whom I would spend the next seven years. The Major had only told me that she had someone she wanted me to meet, that she hoped we'd become good friends. She grinned when she told me the someone was a young lady and that she was soft and cuddly, but under no circumstances should I ever upset her. She reportedly had quite a temper and didn't suffer fools gladly. When she was angry, she would make Dusty look like a pushover. Then the Major shooed me out of her office and said she had work to do. We'd start in earnest the next day.

"Get a good night's sleep" were her parting words. I'd intended to do just that—but soft and cuddly? I wondered why she would ever say that. I dropped off to sleep before completing the thought.

DAY FOUR 6:00 A.M.

My wake-up call from the front desk accomplished its mission. By 6:20 a.m., I was showered, shaved, and dressed, and by 7:00 a.m., I was standing outside the inn waiting for the sergeant or his replacement. I'd already grabbed a quick continental breakfast in one of the small rooms near the inn's front desk. I'd commandeered a dirty look from the aging waitress when I generously helped myself to the scrambled eggs and sausage patties she'd so laboriously laid out for apparently all the guests but me.

Well, I was hungry. Besides, I'd presumed my bill would reflect some price for the breakfast. I knew breakfast wasn't free, so I intended to get my money's worth. My car pulled up with a young man in civilian clothes driving. He was a private, but duty with Major Sanchez rarely meant wearing military dress unless you were staying at the Chapel all day. Most of the townspeople knew we were a military detachment and didn't care as long as we were good guests. But the Mayor was a little sensitive because of the tourists who came through. She asked that we downplay our militariness. That was all right with me since I didn't even have a uniform, although I carried the rank of a brevet Second Lieutenant. We chatted amiably on the drive to the Chapel. I was at the door by 7:15 a.m.

I walked in and saw Dusty at her desk, which commanded the entranceway. You had to go by her to get anywhere in the modest-sized building. I grinned, said hello, and was promptly directed to go back outside and around back, that the Major was waiting for me there. I did so. I saw the Major bending over a very large cage when I rounded the corner. She straightened up immediately and turned and beckoned to me to come to her. As I did, I saw that the cage held an animal I'd heard about but had never seen before—a wolverine.

"Meet Gitta," said the Major as she stood aside so I could see in. "I think you'll find her a most unusual young lady." She grinned. "Why don't you introduce yourself?"

I gawked. This was one of the most terrifying and enigmatic creatures of the forest. I thought Gitta was beautiful. She had coal-black legs, a rich auburn chest, and a back with a wide white swath running around her body from one shoulder to the other. A white band ran across her forehead well above her eyes but below her ears. She stood on all fours just looking at me quizzically. She barked once. "Friend or foe?" was what she asked. I answered, "You are beautiful, one of the most beautiful creatures I've ever seen." Then I just stood there looking stupid while my eyes traveled over every inch of her.

She stood still for almost a minute and then broke into what she thought was a smile but what the Major thought was a prelude to her biting my arm off. Gitta's teeth were perfect. They looked about as inviting as a shark's mouth before taking off some surfer's leg. The Major yelped and tried to slam shut Gitta's cage top, but I grabbed her arm and restrained her just before it could close on Gitta's head. Gitta immediately backed up, snarling. I pried the Major away from the cage. I asked her to stand back while I talked to Gitta.

Remembering my mom's teachings, I apologized profusely. I complimented Gitta on her sizable and beautiful teeth and asked if she would care to walk with me. She was a bit huffy, but as I explained further that the Major only had both of our best interests in mind, she accepted the apology and swarmed out of the cage with a quickness that startled both the Major and me. I think that was the only time in the next several years I ever saw what appeared to be a bead of sweat on the Major's brow. The Major stepped away, nodded at Gitta and me, and then, at my suggestion, walked back around the building to her office. Gitta and I were alone. I promptly sat down beside her and began to talk.

The Major came back at lunchtime. She found me asleep against the back of the Chapel, basking in the cool air and warm sunshine. Gitta was curled up beside me, one of her paws resting across my knee with her two-inch claws on full display. The Major discreetly cleared her throat, and I came awake with a start. Gitta opened her left eye. She growled softly, telling me that the Major made a lot of noise. Gitta had heard her when she first stepped outside the Chapel's front door. I stood up immediately. Gitta said she wasn't going to stand on ceremony. Gitta could just continue to bask right where she was, thank you, unless we needed to go.

It is characteristic of wolverines to move either slowly or extremely quickly. They seem to have no middle gear. Gitta was no exception to this rule. I had freed myself from Gitta's paw when I stood up for the Major, who said she'd come to see how we were getting along. The evidence was plain to see. Did I want to go to lunch or just spend some more time with Gitta? I asked if I could take the Black Widow and go hunting with Gitta instead. The Major raised an eyebrow and then grinned. She said to feel free if I felt I'd be able to bring Gitta back. I laughed and said, "Bringing Gitta back would take a darn sight more men than just me if Gitta chose not to come, but I think we're okay."

"Apparently," said the Major with that sly grin of hers. "But while we're on the subject of women with a mind of their own, Cody, I think it best if you be careful around Dusty. She's enlisted, and you carry an honorary but still an officer's rank. The two can't mix. That's just the way it is. Think of her as a close cousin or sister or even aunt, but try to ignore the obvious. Do treat her as an equal team member. She's an extraordinary soldier, and she won't slip up, but you might. If you do, you'll destroy a great career for her. Do you understand what I'm telling you?"

I said I did and then thanked her for not ignoring the elephant in the room. I wasn't very good at courtship anyway. I figured I needed and could use some good friends for the next little while until I really knew what I was doing and where I was going. I told her that between Casey and Dusty, I probably wouldn't find anyone finer in my short lifetime unless I was a whole lot luckier than I thought I was, but I got the message and wouldn't misstep.

"Good," she said. "That's settled. Now your job for the next three to four days is to learn how to work with Gitta before we introduce you both to North Carolina's version of the Weres. You're not going to like what you'll find here."

DAY FOUR 6:00 P.M.

The Major was waiting on the steps in front of the Chapel when Gitta and I came walking back across the cemetery. She watched us from afar. As we got closer, she walked out to meet us. I was feeling pretty chipper, and Gitta was trying politely not to burp. My gosh, that girl can eat! I'd killed a small wild pig and a deer, and Gitta had made short work of both of them. We were learning to work together. She'd spot prey, and I'd try to bring it down from a distance.

She liked that. It was far less tiring for her. I'd even won the equivalent of a bet or two as she tried to spot something in a position that would make for a very difficult shot. Her respect for me and my bowmanship had risen exponentially as a result of the day's outing. We were starting to be a team.

She was also trying to teach me some woodsmanship, constantly asking me to watch her and learn. I was a slow pupil by her standards, but I could kill faster than she could, and she had to respect that. On the other hand, I'd seen her lift a boulder I couldn't move when we thought a rabbit had burrowed under it. Wolverines have been known to bring down a moose, and that fit with her name. Gitta in Hungarian means strong. She was all of that and more.

The Major moved to lock up the office as we approached the building's steps. She offered me a ride back to town. I asked about Gitta. The Major said she'd stay in the cage in back. She asked me what the townspeople's reaction would be if Gitta appeared on the streets of Blowing Rock. I started laughing and told her, "Point made." The Major reached to lock Gitta's cage when Gitta climbed back in, but I asked her why. Gitta would be here the next morning. We'd already decided on a schedule and exercises we were going to do together. If anything other than a Werewolf showed up to bother her, well, Gitta would not be amused but she wouldn't kill or harm a human. At worst, she'd just run away until the person or persons left. Then she'd come on back and go to sleep.

The Major looked at me and then at Gitta. She shook her head, grinned, and said, "I'm so glad you're here, Cody. This is going to be more fun than a Nantucket sleigh ride." Then she dropped the keys to Gitta's cage into my hands. I leaned over into the cage, scratched Gitta behind her ears roughly as she shimmied and shook, and then patted her head. I bid her a safe and good night. She growled contentedly as she curled up. I think she was asleep before we turned the corner of the building. I didn't shut the top of the cage. Why bother? Gitta could tear the cyclone fencing apart in seconds if she really wanted to leave. The cage was just to make humans be careful. To Gitta, it was no more than an annoyance. Gitta told me so.

DAY FOUR 6:30 P.M.

On the way back to the inn, the Major told me that the death of Bruno and Lockjaw had convinced her that animals could definitely help track and kill Werewolves, but the loss of all four terriers also told her that maybe dogs weren't the answer. She'd thought about big cats like a mountain lion or jaguar, but they were barely trainable at best. Moreover, they had a reputation as, well, cats. She didn't want an aristocrat when fighting Weres. She wanted a blue-collar scrapper that had heft, a killer instinct, strength, and a superior sense of smell. By all accounts, that spelled wolverine. She then told me Gitta's story.

A month before, the Major was in a conversation with a friend of hers who was on NATO exercises in Germany. He had come across a Gypsy encampment near the town of Bad Hopfenreich close to the Czechoslovakian border. The Gypsies looked as if they had fallen on hard times. They were talking of selling three animals—a bear, an ape, and a wolverine. The friend recommended the Major get the wolverine if it was still available. It was somewhat used to humans, although as a wild animal it could not be trusted on its own. Nevertheless, it had a fighter's reputation. The big timber wolves of Russia's eastern steppes feared the wolverine more than any other animal. Perhaps it could be taught to go after other types of wolves, too. Two calls and one week later, a plane arrived at Andrews Air Force Base in Washington, DC. It carried a caged wolverine and a very agitated crew chief. It turned out the wolverine had not been consulted about or prepared for pressure changes during landings or takeoffs. She had manifested her displeasure by voiding herself all over her cage and through her cage walls onto the cargo deck of the Air Force C130 Hercules that had brought her to the United States. The two privates from the Major's unit who had gone north to pick up the animal received a tongue lashing that rivaled, if not exceeded, the very best of chewing outs for which the Army's famous drill instructors were normally credited.

It was a humbled crew that eventually drove up to the old Chapel at Blowing Rock with the since-cleaned-out wolverine cage and its frazzled occupant. The Gypsies named her Gitta, the name that appeared on her manifest. The Major thought if she was Gitta there in Europe, she would be Gitta here in the States. Gitta kept her name for the unit roster.

It took almost two weeks for the wolverine to recover from her flight experience. The North Carolina mountain sun and a healthy diet of steaks brought Gitta around. She stayed in the cage only because she was fed so well. She knew she could escape whenever the thought moved her. Still, she grew rather fond of the Major who fed her twice a day and seemed to make a fuss over her. Gitta filled me in earlier on the rest of her story. She was bored and becoming restless until the man who could talk to her—me—showed up.

Gitta had never heard of such a thing. She had immediately bonded with me, who the humans called Cody. She told me all about her homeland, the troubles and sacrifices she'd made to stay alive and try to save her one cub from a wolf pack in the winter that they almost starved to death. The cub was killed, but Gitta survived. She learned all too well to fend for herself. Wolves died eventually as well, but not enough of them for Gitta.

The man, Cody, in turn opened up a whole new world of appreciation and pity for the human race she had been taught to fear. Slowly, that fear was subsiding with Cody. One young human, a female named Dusty, also took an interest in Gitta. She seemed not to fear Gitta as others did. She came by in the day and slipped Gitta a sweet orange sticky log of something called Twinkies. They had become one of Gitta's favorites. She let the woman-human Dusty pat her and stroke her as she chewed and savored each

Twinkie. Gitta, in turn, offered Dusty some of her food by nosing scraps to the fence where Dusty often stood. But apparently, Dusty had a major impairment. She couldn't eat the good food Gitta was served. Gitta pitied Dusty but was too much of a lady to show it. So Gitta kept the growing friendship on an I'll-let-you-feed-me basis for the moment.

But with Cody, life promised to be so much more interesting. Best of all, Gitta thought, they were preparing to go against a large type of predator wolf that was rumored to be particularly vicious, strong, and cruel. In the meantime, there was work to be done as Gitta and Cody figured out how partners from two different worlds might best work together in this plan to kill the Werewolves. Neither found the other dull or reluctant to expand their relationship.

The Major dropped me off at a fast-food joint close to the inn where I was staying. I just wanted a quick bite. The hunting hike Gitta and I took in the afternoon left me ravenous. Two burgers and two additional orders of fries with some slices of pie solved the problem. I was home in my room by 7:45 p.m. I asked the switchboard operator to put a long-distance call through to my home, but she got no answer. I then had her try the hospital and my dad's room. I talked with Dad and my mom for about 20 minutes. It was a good call. I felt somehow connected again.

Dad was steadily improving. Any question about a possible loss of his arm or amputation was off the table. Now it was just a question of healing and exercise. Dad's workplace had given him time off, with pay, to heal. Dad's boss was encouraged in part by a visit from the Mayor and the Police Chief. Mom was settling into the routine of home for the night and errands and hospital during the day. My temporary absence actually helped her concentrate on Dad.

After I finished with them, I had one more call to make—Casey. Her mom answered. When she discovered it was me, she was immediately full of questions. She and the rest of the Allegros were well acquainted with Dad's progress. They'd visited him twice, and my mom had had dinner with the Allegros just last night. But what she wanted to know was what was I doing all the way in North Carolina and if I had a chance to see Casey's school yet. I told her I was on an orientation visit to my future school and was working with a military group doing geologic surveys in the North Carolina mountains. I would be working with them for several years as a way to help earn my tuition.

I also told her that the Lieutenant Colonel at the Chagrin Falls armory had been influential in helping me get this opportunity. And finally, no, I had not seen Casey's school. I reminded her that North Carolina was a big state and that Casey's school was halfway across it, about five or six hours' driving time away. I then asked if I might speak with Casey, who apparently had been asking her mom for the telephone for the past several minutes.

Her mom laughed a bit and seemed slightly embarrassed. She said goodbye and gave the phone to Casey. We chatted for about 10 minutes, but I have no idea what we said. It was just good to hear her voice. I told her about my new bow and all about Gitta. I said I thought I was falling in love with her, and Casey pretended indignation but laughed in spite of herself and said that it was okay to fall in love with any girl whose teeth rivaled those of a shark and whose fingernails needed trimming with a metal file, no matter how soft and cuddly she might be. We chatted a few minutes more and then hung up after talking about the forthcoming graduation dance. It wasn't until after we'd hung up that I realized I'd forgotten to mention Dusty.

DAY FIVE 9:00 A.M.

I was starting to feel the heat of the mid-morning North Carolina sun. Gitta was dozing nearby under the shade of a tree. I had just finished my third round of competition shooting with the Grozer bow. In some ways, it was a dream. In others, it was a nightmare. Getting used to a different draw was proving to be more difficult than I thought. The heavier arrows of the Grozer bow were throwing off all my aim and follow-through. It was as if I had to unlearn the whole feel of the Black Widow and learn anew the feel of the Grozer. I was one frustrated wannabe soldier.

Dusty showed up about that time with some lemonade for me and a Twinkie for Gitta. We both retired to the shade by Gitta. Dusty sat down at Gitta's head, and I tried to find some shade at her tail end. Gitta was sprawled in such a way that despite my gentle nudging, she wouldn't move. It appeared I was going to have to sit in the sun. At last I just reached down and unceremoniously dumped her hindquarters farther back near the tree trunk and sat where she'd already warmed the ground. She didn't even blink so delighted was she to chew on one of Dusty's Twinkies. I told her the Twinkies would make her fat. She opened an eye, turned her head, looked at me, and said, "Really?" Then she grinned her shark's death grin and promptly turned back and ignored me.

I told her I loved her anyway and gave her two of my ice cubes when she finished choking down the last of her Twinkie. All I got was a chuckle before she closed her eyes and fell back to sleep between us.

I talked with Dusty for about half an hour, primarily learning about her background and how she'd tied up with the Major's outfit. Then we talked a bit about Chagrin Falls and Casey and the Werewolves. I was a little surprised she had more questions about the Werewolves than about Casey. Then I realized that the Major had probably given her the same talk I'd received. I decided once again to just make her my newest friend. It was one of my better decisions.

Dusty's Twinkie and lemonade break had truly hit the spot, but she had work to do inside, and I had work to do outside. I wanted to run through her hunting course before lunch, both with and without Gitta. Since Gitta was apparently lost to the world, I decided to go through on my own first. Dusty showed me the control unit that would activate the course timers and photo beams by which the targets would appear and disappear as I made my way through it. She said that hits by my arrows would also register on a test box on Major Sanchez's desk. I got it and told Dusty so. We were continuously being monitored by Major Sanchez for our improvement. She wanted excellence in all things, especially weaponry. Like General Patton in World War II, Sanchez didn't want soldiers who would go out and die for their cause. She wanted soldiers who would go out and help the other fellow die for *his* cause. Dusty was laughing when she went back inside. I laid the Grozer bow and arrows aside and swapped them for my new Black Widow. It was a relief to get its heft and feel back. I set the timer and activated the course. An hour later, I was back. Of 27 possible bull's-eye hits, I made 19, with four hits just outside and four clean misses. I started to shut the course off and take a short break when the Major came out with two of her sergeants. She asked if I would run through the course again.

She saw I was using the Black Widow. She bet Sergeant Saddler $10 that I could outscore him in time and accuracy. He would use an M1 semiautomatic rifle against my arrows. He laughed, said it wasn't right to take an officer's hard-earned money, but for God, country, and his baby, he'd stand up to the challenge. Dusty whispered to me that he was the outfit's crack shot. I was not to have any hurt feelings when he waxed me.

I just played it cool and said it was an honor to learn from a man so well respected. I apologized that I wasn't very proficient with a handgun or rifle, but I said I would try my hardest not to embarrass myself too badly as we went through the course. Oh, and in the interest of showing confidence, however misplaced, would he care to wager against my $10 as well? He laughed again, pulled two $10 bills from his wallet, and gave them to Dusty. The Major and I each put our $10 bills in Dusty's hand as well. The Major walked over to reactivate the course. Sergeant Saddler was to go first. I was to follow 20 minutes later. We would be graded on how fast we went through and how accurate we were. Major Sanchez did make one stipulation. We would both walk the course since I could not run.

"Even better," said Saddler. "I take long strides."

Major Sanchez hit the go button, and the course was activated. Saddler disappeared almost immediately. Shortly after, we heard the first of his many shots. At the 20-minute mark, the Major tapped me on the shoulder, and I started, bow drawn and an arrow nocked. I carried two quivers as I had in my earlier practice round, each quiver with 15 arrows. I had little wiggle room to waste an arrow. One arrow is not a normal margin of safety.

Forty-eight minutes after starting the course, Sergeant Saddler came striding home with a big grin on his face. He'd nailed 26 bull's-eyes, one almost bull's-eye, and two misses. Sixteen minutes later, I came walking up. I'd nailed 26 bull's-eyes and three near bull's-eyes. Every arrow had hit a target, and my time was four minutes faster than his. Dusty and the Major cheered, and Sergeant Saddler just shook his head, walked over, and gave me a bear of a handshake and a slap on the back that almost collapsed my lungs. As Dusty handed both the Major and me two $10 bills, Sergeant Saddler said the Major had bet on me only out of loyalty. She laughed again and said no, she had not, that she had only bet on a sure thing. Everyone wandered back to the Chapel for lunch. The Major took me aside and asked that I not go through the course with my Black Widow again. She wanted me to learn the ins and outs of the Grozer bow and arrows. She asked that I use those for all practices from now until I left for home. The unnamed man was coming back in two days with Lt. Col. Spikes and Captain Yamata. They wanted to see how I was handling the Turkish bow. "Do well, Cody," said the Major. "I think Captain Yamata has something for you. I'll let it be his surprise."

With that, she left. Dusty picked up my Black Widow bow and quivers. She said she would keep them safe for the interim. She asked me to return all arrows to her when I'd policed the course. She then headed back inside, leaving me with a long walk and a sleeping wolverine. "Wake up, Gitta," I turned and shouted. "We're going for a walk." Both of us shambled back to the course head. Sighing, I started to pull all my arrows with Gitta trailing behind me.

DAY FIVE 1:30 P.M.

After turning in all my arrows from Dusty's hunting course, I grabbed a sandwich from the small refrigerator the Major kept for all of us in the Rat's Nest. It wasn't much, but I was excited and didn't really feel hungry. Gitta and I were heading out again with instructions from the Major not to come back until nightfall. We were to explore a two-square-mile wilderness to the Chapel's north side.

Gitta and I spent the remainder of the day wandering back and forth and up and down the mountainside that framed the backdrop for our headquarters. Gitta was as happy as a wolverine could be, I suppose, as we both investigated the flora and fauna of this magnificent location. Gitta was running here and there exploring new sights and scents. She sniffed out a number of tracks in the forest's byways, explaining how this or that animal walked or even felt, depending on the strength of the scent and length of the track. She was trying to school me as best she could. I was trying to learn while still watching where I stepped so I didn't fall or trip and injure myself. I'd not worn my leg braces since coming here but had brought them just in case. If we were to spend much more time in these forests, I would likely strap them back on. Some of the underbrush in this locale was more like tanglewood than a thoroughfare.

It was almost 7:00 p.m., and we were at the base of our small mountain when Gitta came across something strange, a scent she did not recognize but made her react instantly. All her neck and shoulder hair bridled immediately. She let out an involuntary growl. It wasn't a wait-here-while-I-think-this-over growl. It was an I-must-kill-it-before-it-kills-me growl. She raised her head looking this way and that with her teeth fully bared. She scared me. I backed away. We didn't know what it was then, but later we had a chance to verify the scent. We'd stumbled across the spoor and smell of Carolina Werewolves. Apparently, they'd been by this way recently. Traces of their passing left a foul-scented trail behind them.

Gitta soon settled down as we started back up the mountain to the Chapel. I asked her what her thoughts were when she encountered the scent. She couldn't convey them exactly, but the impressions of kill, rend, tear, and maim summed them up. Just remembering the scent raised the hair on her neck and made her ugly. In our short acquaintance, I hadn't seen her so on edge, so disturbed, so intent on destroying something. Whatever it was, I thought, I sure didn't want to be between Gitta and the thing that laid that scent. I could think of much better ways to die, such as standing on a train track in front of an on-rushing locomotive or letting an Army tank rest its cannon on my chest before firing.

We eventually reached the Chapel at about 8:15 p.m. We found Major Sanchez and Sergeant Saddler there. They were buried in a stack of requisition papers and other forms. They were completing a monthly report that apparently both dreaded but was necessary for the powers that be. Knowing they would be working late was why Major Sanchez had taken the time to send Gitta and me out on a prolonged reconnaissance survey. I put Gitta away, fed her, and came into the Chapel. I found a chair to sit on and wait until they were done. I promptly fell asleep. Sergeant Saddler woke me up in an hour or so and dropped me back in Blowing Rock near my now-favorite fast-food chain. There was an order to go, and soon I was back in my room at the inn. A quick shower, a quick bite, and those cool sheets called to me. I was too tired to answer with anything other than the weight of my body as I collapsed deliciously on the bedding. I dreamed of dancing with Casey at the graduation dance and then a really long embrace and kiss good night. It had been a good day.

DAY SIX 11:00 A.M.

I was lost. Gitta sat close by, watching me patiently and sniffing the air for scent traces of small rodents or vegetables or Twinkies or whatever she felt like eating to pass the time. I was well and truly lost and growing more frustrated by the minute.

When I arrived at the Rat's Nest that morning, the Major gave me a terrain map marked with key points I was to tag. She also gave me a compass and a portable flare gun. "Welcome to your first lesson in ranging," she said as she handed me the bundle. "Get back here if you can for a late lunch. We have some briefings to go over this afternoon before Lt. Col. Spikes and Yamata get here tomorrow. They'll be by themselves after all. Try not to get lost, but if you do, try to be back here early tomorrow if you want one of Dusty's homemade donuts. It's generally one to a customer when visitors come, but after Lt. Col. Spikes takes his, there's usually a free-for-all. Trust me, this is not a treat you want to miss."

With that, Sergeant Saddler escorted me out of the Chapel, drove his car around to the back, and let Gitta in. We then spent almost two hours driving on dirt roads, over Jeep trails, and through timber breaks until I was thoroughly disoriented and lost. Gitta rested her paws on the window sill and let her head hang out of the car with the wind rushing over her face. The sergeant stopped when we finally reached a back-country overlook, let me out, and then opened the trunk to hand me the Grozer bow and a quiver of arrows.

"There are Werewolves in this area," he said. "Try not to bother them today, but if you do, try to make it back by tomorrow for Dusty's donuts. They are superb. By the way, it's forty-five miles home by the roads. Better to walk through the hills." He smiled as he climbed back into the car and drove away, leaving Gitta and me standing in the dust. I think he was thinking about those donuts. He sure as heck didn't seem very concerned about us. I spread out the map and tried first to find our location before anything else. I wasn't sure how to use the flare gun, so I placed it in the small backpack Sergeant Saddler had set out for me along with the Grozer bow and its quiver of arrows. After 20 minutes or so of scanning the area, I thought I knew where I was. I then searched the map until I found what I thought was the terrain we'd covered yesterday. I then promptly set a course for home.

I estimated that we were six to eight miles away. At a standard hiking pace of one and a half miles per hour, it looked like we'd miss lunch but could still make an afternoon snack at the Rat's Nest. Rolling up the map and setting my compass, I fastened the quiver to my side, fitted the bow over my shoulder and chest, and set off. Gitta followed along behind, curious as to what I was about.

We had gone no more than a quarter of a mile, most of it uphill, when Gitta spoke to me. She wanted to know if we would be gone all day, and if so, would we have time for her to hunt? I explained we were headed back to the Rat's Nest for lunch and should be able to hunt tomorrow. She shrugged and said waiting for lunch tomorrow didn't seem very appetizing. I asked her what she was talking about. She asked that if we were going to the Rat's Nest, why were we going the wrong way?

I stopped so quickly that she ran into the back of my legs. I fell backward over her. She quickly tossed me off her back. She turned around, sat, and just looked at me.

"What do you mean 'the wrong way'?" I challenged. "I'm pretty sure we're going the right way, and you're my partner so you've got to trust me. Besides, wolverines can't read maps."

"Well, we can't make any sense of that flat piece of paper you are holding, and I don't know what a map is, but wolverines never get lost," she said. "As long as we can see where we're going, we always know where we've been. And if you know where you've been, you can go back whenever you want. And you're not going the right way. The Rat's Nest is behind us over the small mountain back there, not ahead of us." Then she just sat and looked at me with a sort of pity in her eyes, puzzled that humans didn't have this very basic ability.

"Gitta," I finally admitted, "I am lost. I guess I don't have the skill to read this piece of paper like I thought I did. I, for sure, don't have your skills, and I have never had a wolverine as a partner before. You be the lead home. Maybe I can learn how to see where I'm going so I'll know where I've been. I'm sorry I didn't consult you. That's what a real partner would have done."

She came over to me and pushed me with her nose. Then she put her front paws on each of my shoulders and pushed me flat on the ground. Moving to stand over me, her paws now pinning my shoulders, she quickly dropped her head until her nose was practically rubbing mine. Without warning, she gave me a lick from my chin to my forehead.

I didn't know if that was a pre-dinner warning or a wolverine sign of affection, but I stayed still until she let me up. With no further words, I fell in behind her as she waddled down our back trail. Three tough hours later, I was just trying to breathe, but we were over the small mountain and huffing our way back up the hill where I'd killed the deer and wild pig two days earlier. We were almost home.

I stopped Gitta before we broke out into the clearing surrounding the Rat's Nest. I brushed her off and straightened my now-disheveled wardrobe and wiped off my face and hands. I told Gitta when we walked into the clearing that I wanted them to think we were as fresh as if we'd just awakened from a nap and that we were curious if there might be any snacks around. She snorted the wolverine equivalent of a chuckle and, raising her head high, led the way in.

The Major and the rest of the Rat's Nest were all sitting on the front porch chatting. I heard several bets changing hands as we rounded the corner and suddenly came into view. The chatter stopped immediately, and jaws dropped as we strode (and waddled) up. "Sorry we're late," I said cheerfully. "Gitta saw a few things she wanted to eat along the way, but I'm hungry. Anything left?"

Nothing happened for a moment, and then everyone burst out half laughing and half groaning as money switched hands several times with the Major shelling out a considerable amount to eager, outstretched hands. Finally, even she started laughing as Sergeant Saddler stood up, hoisted his bottle of Dr Pepper, and proposed a toast to Gitta and me, the latest survivors of the Lost Trekker Challenge. Not only had we defeated the reigning team of Sergeant Saddler and Private Bucky Moore, but we had beaten Captain Yamata's record by almost two minutes.

It seemed everyone assigned to the Rat's Nest was taken to the overlook on a devious route and forced to try to find their way back. Captain Yamata had the fastest time for three years, with Sergeant Saddler presiding as current champion among those still assigned to the Rat's Nest. Even the Major's time was close to 24 hours, although she always claimed it was her companion's fault. Dusty later told me her own time was 15 hours, best among all the women that had taken the challenge and fourth best of all time until today. Now it was fifth.

It was a challenging but fairly safe course and a way to build *esprit de corps*, Dusty said. The greatest danger was a twisted ankle or broken bone from slipping or falling, especially since there were no known Werewolves near our particular bit of North Carolina. When I stopped her and asked her to repeat what she'd just said, she grew wary and a little defensive. I assured her she was probably right but recalled that Gitta had had an unusual and severe reaction to a certain game trail we'd come across a day earlier at the bottom of the mountain behind the Rat's Nest.

Dusty said a word I didn't think she knew, turned, and quickly left me to find the Major. A hurried conversation between them, and both came back to me on the bounce. The Major asked me where the incident had taken place. I pointed down the hill behind the Rat's Nest. She asked me to take her there immediately after she and Sergeant Saddler had a chance to arm themselves. She also called out to Sergeant Andrew Lighthorse to accompany them. He went by the nickname of Pee Wee, probably because he was 6'3" tall and weighed on the upside of 240 pounds. As a Cherokee Indian, he was the best human tracker in Lt. Col. Spikes's outfit.

I called out to Gitta, who was crouching by the side of the front porch savoring one of Dusty's Twinkies. I told her we needed to lead the Major back to the bad scent trail we'd encountered yesterday. I said to please finish up her snack, now. She gulped down the remainder and came over to stand beside me, snout raised in the air trying to catch the wind. In less than four minutes, we were on the way, Gitta leading. I walked just behind her, and Pee Wee was just behind me.

DAY SIX 3:00 P.M.

It took almost 45 minutes going downhill to get near the place where Gitta had her reaction. I recognized the general area. I asked everyone to stand back and let Gitta cast about on her own without adding our scents as well. In less than eight minutes, we all heard what I came to call Gitta's battle growl. She reacted just as she had when she first encountered the scent yesterday. Pee Wee led the way to her. I called her back to me and sat down, holding my arm across her and stroking her side gently as we watched Pee Wee kneel and study the ground. He would occasionally shift his stance, move laterally, and then gently probe the ground or any bushes nearby looking for some trace of an animal's passing.

It wasn't long before he stood up and walked back to our huddled group. "Werewolves," he said. "Probably three, maybe four, all big adults and moving slowly. They traveled close together, single file. First time I've seen them this close. I'd guess they passed here going north less than two days ago, probably yesterday, early morning."

His news sobered everyone. The Major asked if he would follow the trail for 10 minutes, no more. She asked him to take Gitta and me with him. The Major and Sergeant Saddler would head back. There was obviously much to do to get ready for Lt. Col. Spikes's visit. This news wasn't helping.

Pee Wee beckoned to me as they disappeared back uphill through the underbrush. He asked me to come and see what he had seen. It was my first lesson in tracking. I would have many more with Pee Wee and eventually come to be almost as good, but this day I was all eyes and ears as he began my odyssey in field craft.

The next 10 minutes confirmed what he'd suspected, that four Weres were in the party. Their direction did not change. They moved efficiently through the forest, avoiding all unnecessary obstacles but never varying in their direction or pace. Pee Wee obtained several hair samples, one disturbingly light colored. Gitta remained in a high state of agitation throughout the stalk. It was some time later as we were climbing back uphill to the Rat's Nest before she calmed down and resumed, for a wolverine, her sweet nature.

When we reached the Chapel, we found it full of activity. Some were tidying up (the Major never let it get really messy), and others were finishing various reports or briefing items. I'd been given no assignment until the Major saw me sitting and came over to sit down beside me. She told me Lt. Col. Spikes was going to want to see a run-through of Dusty's hunting course. She asked if I were at top form with the Grozer yet. If not, perhaps I could use the remaining daylight to take a practice round or two while everyone in here continued their preparations.

I took her not-so-subtle hint, grabbed my gear, and was on my way out the front door. Three runs and three hours later as dusk swiftly fell, I gathered up my last arrows. I had finally done well two out of the three times I'd run the course. I felt as ready as I'd ever be. I stopped by Gitta's cage. I fed and watered her and then bid her good night. I told her I'd be back early tomorrow. There were some new folks coming, and they were good friends. They were the reason all of us were here to kill the wolflike creatures whose scent had so disturbed her. They were hunters like she was. She was to learn their scent and movements. Our lives could well depend upon them in a fight, and we were going to have some fights. Gitta could count on it.

DAY SEVEN 8:00 A.M.

We were all standing at attention on and near the front porch when Lt. Col. Spikes and Captain Yamata drove up. Dusty was standing ramrod straight holding a large, flat plate of homemade donuts, trying to keep a straight face and not smile. It was a task at which she was a delightful failure.

Lt. Col. Spikes's grin as he emerged from the car belied his military mien. After returning the Major's snappy salute, he ordered everyone to be at ease. There was a general cheer and a quick rush as everyone jostled to line up behind him and Captain Yamata for one of Dusty's donuts. This was obviously a beloved ritual. I fought unsuccessfully to take my place near the head of the evolving line. I finally managed to secure a spot two from the end and merited a donut all to myself. The last two guys had to split the one remaining donut and complained to Dusty that she'd cooked too few.

She responded that no, she had one for each person, including herself. She counted them twice, once at her quarters and once again when she'd set the plate down on the porch while the Major was lining everyone up. I had a sudden revelation and turned to look at Gitta lying against the wall not far from the porch. As I did, all eyes turned with me.

She sensed immediately that she was the prime suspect. She turned her face into the wall, burying her snout under the fur of her generous coat. I walked over, knelt down, and peered at the ground closely. Sure enough, there were donut crumbs on the ground. I held up my donut and pointed to Gitta. "Behold the thief of Bagdad," I cried out. "A sneaky Special Operations soldier wannabe if ever there was one." That elicited a good-natured cheer from everyone. It grew even louder as I handed my donut over to the two soldiers who'd had to split the last one. "Gitta and I are partners," I explained, "so I'm as guilty as she is, and I'm paying the penalty."

We all mingled about as Lt. Col. Spikes met with and shook everyone's hand. Then all started drifting inside. The Major asked me to join Lt. Col. Spikes and Captain Yamata in her office for a few minutes and then left me to go get her briefing materials. Dusty sidled up beside me and in a low voice told me not to worry, that my generous act would be rewarded with a small gift waiting for me tomorrow, but I was not to let anyone else know. Then she was gone back into the hustle and bustle characteristic of our small quarters. The smile on my face was ear to ear, and my stomach rumbled. Tomorrow couldn't come soon enough for me.

I walked into the Major's office right behind her and softly closed the door at her nod. She'd arranged three chairs in a semicircle on one side of her desk so she could face all three of us as she gave her briefing. I took the chair on the end after Lt. Col. Spikes and Captain Yamata sat down. During the first hour, the Major discussed unit readiness, facilities management, her budget, special weapons, and training. She also briefed Spikes on travel, both projected and the unit's experience to date in the fiscal year. I was asked to step outside for an hour while the three officers discussed personnel, assignments, and deployments, and then they invited me back in for the portion focused on Growler I, the whole reason I had been invited to the party.

Lt. Col. Spikes was well up to speed about developments in Chagrin Falls. He passed along a report that Honey was responding well to treatment but was responding even better to Casey's attention each afternoon when she stopped by after school to visit and pet her. He interrupted the Major when she sought to continue the briefing by asking after my father. I gave him my latest information. His face lit up in a smile at my dad's good progress report. He then asked the Major if she could turn just a few minutes over to Captain Yamata before we got to the meat of the meeting, the plan to raid an outlying encampment of Werewolves that had been under unit observation for some time. They appeared to be getting ready to move elsewhere.

The Major said certainly and nodded to the Captain. At that point, Captain Yamata reached into his briefcase and pulled out a carefully wrapped package about 23 inches long and four inches wide. The package was wrapped in plain black paper, which, when unraveled, left a flat, longish object wrapped in black velvet and tied carefully in knots unfamiliar to me. I knew my Boy Scout knots, but I'd never seen anything like this before. They were wonderful. As Captain Yamata informed me, they were ceremonial knots, intricate and beautiful and simply done to honor the contents of the package.

To my utter surprise, the Captain then turned, stood, bowed, and presented the package to me. The Major whispered that I should stand, bow, and accept the package with both hands. I did and enjoyed the heft of the package. When I had fully received it, the Captain sat down and bid me to do the same. All three officers then watched me closely, and all three encouraged me to open it. I did so with trembling fingers, still not knowing what to expect. When I finally untied the knots, I peeled back one of the satin overlay flaps and gasped. I could hardly believe my eyes. There lay a wakizashi sword whose blade held a gun-black finish with a brass habaki. The scabbard was a clear-lacquered maple burl saya and tuska, with a copper tsuba and black mica tips at either end. It was breathtaking.

"It is yours," said the Captain. "You saved the Major's life at the Quarry Cave and held back the Werewolves long enough for reinforcements to arrive so we could get them between my hammer and Lt. Col. Spikes's anvil. You are a warrior, Cody. You should have a warrior's blade. Keep this with you whenever you go out to hunt. It will seek the blood of your enemies and will defend you with honor until the blade is broken. Do not ever surrender it under threat of force, but give it up willingly to those who would help you accomplish noble deeds. The power of the blade comes from the man who wields it. Remember that men get true power from virtue."

That said, the Captain stood, gave me another swift bow, and resumed his seat. I was close to tears, and my chest was swelling so much that it hurt. I gulped and stammered a thank you and then rose and returned his short bow and sat down, gingerly holding the wakizashi sword. Lt. Col. Spikes reached across to me and shook my hand. The Major walked around her desk and gave me a hug, probably the most awkward moment I'd had since I messed up my first hug with Casey years earlier.

With the ceremony over, all three officers immediately got down to business and began talking about our unit's part in the next Growler I initiative. The Rat's Nest had been carefully selected and positioned because of a number of sightings in the northwest corner of North Carolina over an almost 10-year period. Most people who were reporting large, shaggy creatures moving stealthily in the wilderness believed they were reporting a Bigfoot sighting. Some probably were. But evidence surrendered to state or federal authorities from many sources over time generally established that the creatures were Werewolves, something no federal official in the know was ever allowed to communicate to anyone for fear of mass panic.

Growler I was a three-year operation to seek out and destroy the Weres on a state-by-state basis. The first phase of the program was to discover, disrupt, and destroy Were outposts and communications throughout the selected states. North Carolina was believed to be among the most heavily infested states. Lt. Col. Spikes's unit was dedicated to North Carolina. The unit mission included both active and passive reconnaissance, offensive raids, and intelligence collection against the Weres by overt and covert means.

The mountainous terrain of the state and the solitary nature of the people who sought a wilderness experience made North Carolina a difficult target to exploit. Mountain families were distrustful of any authority, especially federal authority. They were stingy with information and absent whenever help was requested either for fighting or logistics support. Consequently, Lt. Col. Spikes had adopted an offensive strategy that largely depended on small, quick strike raids with 14 or fewer personnel. Such a raid was planned for the next day. I had been invited to the Rat's Nest to have my potential as a regular team member evaluated.

The Major also wanted to introduce animals into the teams that raided suspected Werewolf nests or congregations. Gitta was the second such experiment. The bull terriers at Chagrin Falls had been the first. The Major was convinced that an alliance of soldiers and certain animals would produce in time more effective missions against the Weres as each species contributed talents the other species did not have. The coming raid was more of a trial balloon. Depending on how Gitta and I worked together, raids could begin on a scheduled basis when I was assigned here full time in early June.

At 3:00 p.m., Lt. Col. Spikes broke up our meeting and called in the remaining personnel who would participate in tomorrow's raid. The briefing for the raid began in earnest. It continued for several hours until Spikes was convinced that everyone knew their roles as well as one other role should the unit suffer casualties. He sent everyone home by 6:00 p.m. Our orders were to report back to the Rat's Nest in combat gear at 9:00 a.m. the next day. Weapons would then be drawn from the armory. Each member of the raiding party was encouraged to bring their own personal weapon(s) of choice if they wished.

"Let's have good hunting tomorrow" was Lt. Col. Spikes's last comment before we were dismissed. As we walked out, I asked Sergeant Saddler if he would be kind enough to pick me up at 6:30 a.m. I wanted to shoot one quiver of the Grozer bow before we left. He said he'd be glad to. He added that I needed to remember to bring my leg braces. Where we were going had some pretty steep paths and lots of tanglefoot, his word for the dense underbrush and sprawling ground vines characteristic of the Blue Ridge Mountains.

Lt. Col. Spikes offered me a ride back to the inn and dropped me off with the admonition to get a good night's sleep if I could. He would see me in the morning. He also told me to watch Gitta closely, to help her if she felt under too much stress in any actual fighting, and to stay close to the Major no matter what happened. The Major was fearless in fighting anything in front of her but often ignored her back, so I was to be the eyes in the back of her head. I nodded, said my goodbyes, and went to my room as they drove off.

By 9:00 p.m., back in my room and sitting on my bed after eating a home-cooked meal at the inn's dining room and feeling very tired, I pulled the wakizashi blade from its scabbard one last time. I marveled at its feel and balance. For at least the 50th time, I slashed the throat of an imaginary Were and saved Casey from a fate worse than death. I then bashfully accepted a hug and donut from Dusty and a snort from Gitta as I tottered into the sunset. Resheathing the blade, I remembered that mountain dawns come early. I yawned and lay back. I was asleep in minutes. I held the wakizashi sword in its scabbard tightly across my chest.

DAY EIGHT 10:00 A.M.

The morning went well. I wasn't the only one who came in early. Half the Rat's Nest unit was already there when Sergeant Saddler drove up with me. I headed inside the Chapel to retrieve my Grozer bow and two quivers. I was met by Dusty holding a small sack with two donuts inside, one for me and one for Gitta. She also handed me a Twinkie. "For later," she said. I took that to mean after our fight with the Weres. I stuffed the Twinkie into my breast pocket and went outside to get Gitta. I wanted to run through Dusty's hunting course counterclockwise one time before we "saddled up" and mounted the bus that would drive us to our debarkation site. Rumor was that we were heading about 20 miles to our north-northwest into a particularly isolated corner of the state.

Just before we emerged from the woods at the end of the course, I sat down with Gitta and surprised her with our donuts. They were delicious. The deliberate break gave me a chance to review the upcoming day's activities with her. She didn't seem worried in the least. Still, I stressed that I would be beside her and that the noise and smells aboard the bus would be strange but not really worth bothering about. We emerged from the woods feeling a bit more optimistic than was our due. Dusty's donuts have that effect. They can make a condemned man smile while the noose is tightening around his neck.

I carried the Grozer bow per the Major's request. She didn't expect we would see any direct action since she was providing base camp security for Lt. Col. Spikes while Captain Yamata led the stealth element to the ambush site. I, of course, was assigned to her along with three other men. They would provide perimeter security. Gitta and I would be available for any after-battle tracking with Pee Wee, should some of the Weres escape. We had light plane coverage of the area the day before as well as camera data from three days previous. Indications were that a small number of large bipeds were settled near a stream and clearing in the target area.

Captain Yamata was very comfortable about locating the ambush site and executing the planned ambush. His plan was solid and simple. The best plans always are because when the enemy engages, you can almost always throw a complicated plan out the window. The real problem with overly detailed plans is that no one provides a courtesy copy to the enemy so they know how they are expected to perform.

Twelve of us boarded the bus at 9:45 a.m. We spread out for the expected hour-long drive. Every person checked then rechecked then put away their respective gear. I settled in to an aisle seat across from several team members with whom I was not very familiar. They began to swap stories or experiences to help quell the nauseous feelings common to soldiers before actual battle.

Gitta had boarded with me. The other assault team members gave her a wide berth. There's not a lot of room aboard a bus if a wolverine goes rogue. No one except me was entirely comfortable being in her near proximity. Gitta just ignored everyone and sat on the seat beside me. She looked patiently out the window. Major Sanchez seemed quietly amused. Captain Yamata was more than a little curious. He kept stealing looks at Gitta from time to time as we rolled along going deeper into the Blue Ridge Mountains.

By 1:00 p.m., we were at the designated base camp spot. A lot of the nervousness everyone initially felt was bled off after Captain Yamata's fast, four-mile hike in from our debarkation spot. The bus had stopped at a roadside viewing with no vehicular traffic in sight. It departed immediately after the last person stepped off. It was scheduled to be back by 12:00 p.m. the following day. It would wait there for us for 24 hours if need be and then return with reinforcements and a major rescue and recovery operation if no one showed.

The team was already moving off the road into the woods when Gitta and I stepped off. We fell into formation behind the lead assault team. Lt. Col. Spikes wanted to hit the suspected Were hiding site at 5:00 p.m., just at dusk in these rugged mountains. Captain Yamata wanted us in place with camp sentries out and a silent reconnaissance-at-a-distance team in place at least three hours before the planned strike. Everyone moved with practiced precision. Gitta and I just moved along with them. Nobody spoke. We were in stealth mode. Gitta had no problem keeping the Captain's fast pace. The altitude provided a bit of a respite from the heat that normally came with the midday sun. Nevertheless, we were all glad to hit the base camp site and take a welcome water and bathroom break. Thank goodness the area had plenty of friendly bushes.

On a fast stealth reconnaissance or assault strike, we were advised to eat so we would likely have no bowel movements for 24 hours. A soldier was vulnerable during the elimination process, women especially so. Safety was always more important than appearance. I was told that in enemy territory, it is not uncommon practice to just pee in one's pants when moving fast or hiding from detection. We were also advised to eat bland foods only for as much as 24 hours before a patrol's departure. That would help eliminate the acrid smell of our urine. Even humans have a sense of smell. Some, especially women, have an acute sense. Scent is an important element of consideration for both sides in stealth operations.

Lt. Col. Spikes's team was a practiced unit. The team deployed as he had outlined in the briefing the previous day. Gitta and I were initially relegated to sentry duty in the immediate camp area. I wasn't expecting any action but followed both my instinct and the commands given to me. I found a ledge overlooking the base camp about 40 yards out, giving me a clear view of a game trail that ran nearby. I strung my bow and placed two arrows on the ground in front of me within easy reach. If I had to shoot, I wanted no snags as I reached for an arrow in my kneeling position. I was safely hidden from observation but could see a fairly wide swath of mountains in front of and below me. I'd picked a good position.

I told Gitta to feel free to range and cast about for the foul scent she remembered but not to growl if she smelled any. She was to return to me by the fastest and quietest means possible with the warning. She indicated she well understood what this was all about. She disappeared into the underbrush within seconds. Stealth mode to a hunting wolverine is normal mode. Gitta was very good at being invisible. She was also a seasoned killer.

I'd been in place for almost an hour when I spotted movement down the mountainside from my hiding place. Peering carefully through the foliage, I could see that the creature was upright. I just couldn't see if it was one of our team members. Whatever it was moved slowly and cautiously, taking every advantage of the terrain and trees to stay either fully or partially concealed. Only when the creature came within 20 yards of me could I see that it was Captain Yamata. He moved like a ghost. Watching him was a lesson in grace.

Suddenly, I noticed the flicker of movement behind him. I thought it was a second member of his assault team, that they had both probably been on a reconnaissance probe and were just now returning to base camp. I noted that the second figure was moving faster than the Captain. It would soon overtake him. When the figure briefly emerged into the sunlight, I saw that it was a Werewolf. He was bigger and shaggier than the ones in Ohio. He appeared to be solely focused on the Captain's back.

I quickly drew my bow. I aimed for a killing shot through the neck when the creature simply dropped from sight with a muffled grunt. I heard the sharp snap of what sounded like a bone breaking. I started moving toward the spot where the creature had vanished when Gitta came flying back out of the bushes. She was growling in all her ferocity. The Werewolf suddenly reappeared, a low whine coming from its throat starting to build into a howl, but apparently it was in some real pain.

It was dragging its left leg and trying to hop in the direction it had thrown Gitta. I had a shot and took it. The shaft went in under the Were's chin and ripped out the front part of its throat. Its whining stopped immediately, and it fell to the ground clutching the protruding shaft in a vain attempt to pull it out. The Were was dead as it hit the ground, but Gitta hit it again at that moment. She simply tore its chest apart with her talon-like claws.

I reached the Were about the same time Captain Yamata did. He noted Gitta and me. He asked if I had seen any other Weres following him. I answered no, but he sent Gitta and me back down his trail to stop and wait for a possible ambush. We were to wait there 10 minutes. If nothing moved or came that same way, we were then to report back to base camp on the double.

We scrambled down the trail where both the Were and the Captain had walked and found a likely spot. Hiding ourselves in the tanglefoot and brush, we settled down to wait. I kept an arrow nocked. Gitta kept growling deep in her throat. She was incredibly tense as she waited by my side. She was in killing mode. I could barely restrain her, but she stayed with me as we waited. At the 10-minute mark, I started to rise and move out. Gitta rammed into me and pushed me flat. "Weres," she hissed. "Can't you smell them? They stink like garbage or worse." She kept a paw on my shoulder for several minutes and then told me to get up quietly. The Weres were almost upon us.

I rolled to my feet, pulling back my arrow and firing at the lead Were as soon as I could see it. My arrow took the Were through the right chest and deflated its lung. Gitta had launched herself under the bushes surrounding us as I rolled erect. I watched the second Were suddenly yelp and drop, arms flailing. Gitta had bitten through the Were's leg, crippling it immediately. As the Were hit the ground, Gitta plowed into its neck and started ripping at its throat. Screaming and choking on its own blood, the second Were died in a maelstrom of fury. The first Were was crawling toward Gitta. It had turned its back to me in doing so. I put my second arrow through its right buttock, causing the Were to fall to its left side and howl painfully, a howl that was cut off when my third arrow went into its throat. Choking and gasping, the Were started flailing its forearms and died reaching for Gitta.

Gitta stood over her kill. With her claws, she ripped both carcasses apart before she came waddling back to me. Together, we climbed back up the trail Yamata had taken. We approached base camp and were immediately challenged. I said, "It's me, Cody." I was allowed to approach the camp. Yamata had several of the men haul in the first carcass. I was able to retrieve one unbroken arrow, which I put back into my quiver. I told him we'd killed two more Weres a little farther down the mountain. Gitta had taken one and I, the other. Yamata's widening grin was reward enough. He clapped me on the shoulder and led me over to the Major.

As she debriefed me, I described Gitta's preferred mode of attack and her resiliency. The Major practically glowed at that. She appeared to be in a congratulatory mode. Seeing my quizzical stare, she promptly shook her head as if to clear it and thanked me for just being me. "You have no idea, Cody, how valuable you are. You just have no idea," she said. She then told me to take Gitta and get an hour's nap nearby. Yamata would be taking his team out pretty soon. She wanted the remainder of us rested and ready for anything.

I found a tree close by, settled down, and closed my eyes. My bow lay across my lap. Gitta came and curled up against me, still uneasy but settling down gradually. As she did, I remembered Dusty's surprise. I gave Gitta her Twinkie. A snort and suddenly all was very well indeed.

DAY EIGHT 3:45 P.M.

Captain Yamata finished his last summary briefing right on time. The team members who had been performing our reconnaissance-at-a-distance had been called back in. Everyone had undergone a gear and readiness check. We had carried little in but weapons, ammunition, and water, so we left no campsite to defend. The attack would be initiated from the first group of six called Team 1. Captain Yamata would head that group. Gitta and I would follow Team 1 at a two-minute interval. Our job was simple. Kill any Werewolves that might slip in behind Team 1 as they advanced to the killing ground. Using a bow and arrows, we would not jeopardize Captain Yamata's group ahead of us since we would not be carrying firearms.

Following me would be Team 2 commanded by Major Sanchez. They would follow me at a five-minute interval. Lt. Col. Spikes would be a member of Team 2, primarily as an observer, although he would be armed for self-defense and available for redeployment if the Major so directed. They would provide mop-up should any Weres escape Team 1. They would also be Team 1's reserve if the ambush the Captain had planned turned into a prolonged battle.

Captain Yamata's team would go in using an arrowhead formation. One soldier would be lead, 20 to 25 yards in advance of a column of three, each of which would maintain an interval of five yards between them. Two flankers would advance about five yards behind the lead and about 15 to 20 yards out from the short column. Gitta and I would come along behind them, and the Major would bring her group behind me in a reverse triangle formation. The Major and Lt. Col. Spikes would be in line with me, and a flanker would be out to each side of them at a 15-yard distance. The last person would be behind and in line with the Major at a distance of 15 yards.

The formation would give maximum protection to both teams. Team 2 would be protected against sudden ambush and still be able to come forward immediately to the aid of Team 1. The formation enabled us to wheel and fire to the right or left or both ways, if necessary. It also gave each person some room to fight one-on-one should a Werewolf penetrate our formation. We expected the resistance to be harsh and the band to number about 20 adult Weres.

The Were camp looked to be at the base of a sharp cliff. The stream that ran in front of it was five to six feet wide and about two to three feet deep with a rocky bottom. It rated as a difficult obstacle because of the treacherous footing such stream beds proffered. Crossing a stream that deep in a rapid current with slippery rocks meant that more than one team member would fall in. They would likely lose their weapon or discharge it into a team member as they slipped and tried to regain balance. Consequently, Captain Yamata forbade anyone to cross the stream unless he, Sergeant Saddler, or the Major gave an explicit order to do so.

We expected the Werewolves to be out of their cave on the grassy bank and in the low brush areas in front of the cliffs when we arrived. The point man and outlying scouts would wait in the tree line on this side of the river until Captain Yamata's group closed up the gaps between them. At Captain Yamata's signal, he, the point man, and the three men who had accompanied the Captain would go into action. Each outside flanker would advance clear of the timber line. They would kneel and fire single bullets at specific Werewolf flank targets. Their role would be snipers. The point man, the Captain, and his three remaining team members would charge out of the tree line in a horizontal line, no longer in a columnar formation. Their weapons would be on full automatic. Their combined firepower would be directed at the greatest gathering among the Weres. If the Weres broke and scattered, the four men would fire at will on the best available target. The idea was to put down as many Weres as possible in the least amount of time.

At 4:30 p.m., Captain Yamata tapped the point man on the shoulder and sent him off. Seconds later, the two flankers stepped out and rapidly disappeared into the woods.

A bit later, the Captain and his men stepped forward and made their way into the trees. Gitta and I waited two minutes by my watch and then stepped out behind them.

I was wearing my leg braces and got an immediate boost in confidence as I walked through the tanglefoot. The braces were heavy but sturdy. I could not have worn them and kept pace with the Captain's march to our base camp. Nevertheless, they were perfect for what I was doing now, a methodical march into probable battle on uneven, dangerous ground. I was glad I'd brought them along.

The forest canopy seemed to close over and around us as Gitta and I moved well into the tree line. Some of the ground was spongy, some hard. Leaves and vines were everywhere. There were plenty of trees, so many that I doubted I could shoot an arrow in a straight line for more than 30 yards before it hit a tree trunk. I tried to keep my breathing controlled as I fought down my excitement. I was grateful Gitta was walking in with me.

Her head was up and looking around. Her steps were methodical, yet I could hardly hear her passage. She seemed to miss every twig or vine I stepped on. More than once she quietly snorted. She told me I sounded like a mobile avalanche and to please not embarrass her. I softly scolded her back. I told her she sounded like my mom, not a fighting companion. She snorted back that she was a mom, or had been. I would do well to heed her advice or I might not be around long enough to fight.

I huffed but did try to make a better effort at stealth. My reward was her silence. I could see she approved of my effort. We walked on, occasionally catching a glimpse of the last person in the Captain's element and feeling the silence of the forest close in on us. As the terrain grew steeper, it became more and more difficult for me to walk with both hands on my bow, so I laid my left index finger across the nocked arrow and held my bow to my left. It freed my right arm to help balance me as the grade steepened.

Gitta had no trouble with the footing because of her claws. Walking down the steep hillside was at most a slight bother to her. However, the moist leaves made my rubber boot soles seem like they were skates on ice. The braces helped alleviate a lot of the muscle strain I experienced by keeping myself from falling. I silently prayed the pitch of the mountainside wouldn't get much steeper. Thankfully, it didn't. It gradually began to decrease in its angle of incline. Walking became a little easier. Suddenly, Gitta raised her head.

I heard that involuntary killing growl start from her throat. Weres, I thought. But where are they? I slowed down and edged closer to Gitta. She had so many more working senses compared to mine. I wasn't stupid enough to depend on mine when I was with her. I whispered, "What direction?" She huffed back, "Ahead, to our front left." Slowing down and stepping more carefully, I held my bow in both hands again. I slipped in behind her as she moved forward in her hunting stance.

We'd gone forward about 30 yards when I caught my first glimpse of the Were. It was a cream-colored adult staring forward at what had to be the Captain's element. It was shaggy and ugly in appearance. It made no sound I could detect as it moved forward from bush to tree and tree to bush. It always took advantage of any opportunity for concealment. It was an engine of destruction both terrible and beautiful to watch. I wondered what it would be like when it unleashed itself. Unfortunately, I got my wish.

So intent was I on watching the Were that I stepped on a dead tree limb. It snapped with a loud crack when I put my weight on it. I looked down to see what I had done and then looked up again. The Were had disappeared. In seconds, it seemed as if I had witnessed a true vanishing act. Gitta cringed beside me and gave me a look as if I had belched in the middle of a church service. She started to whisper something to me when she suddenly snapped her head around. She launched herself forward like a modified drag racer. She disappeared around the bole of a large tree just ahead of us. I stepped around to the other side to see if I could find her.

I found the Were instead, about three strides away, moving very fast and heading straight at me. I started to pull the bow up but never got the chance to launch my arrow. I ducked as the beast reached out to capture me. It missed me with its arms, but its body made full contact, and I went heels over head to the forest floor, my bow and arrow heading one way and I another. I was totally disoriented for a moment. I scrambled to get back to my hands or feet, whichever I could unscramble first. I heard a loud howl. When I finally managed to regain my feet, I saw the Were flat on its stomach with Gitta fastened to its back. Her jaws were locked on the beast's shoulder. Her claws were tearing at its back.

The beast screamed and thrashed around. It rolled over and over trying to dislodge Gitta until it managed to reach over its left shoulder and rake Gitta's front left leg with its claws. Gitta grunted. She momentarily lost her grip. The Were managed to bend over and swing around so it could reach Gitta's sides with both arms. At that point, Gitta had sense enough to let go of the Were with her jaws. She pushed herself away from its back as the beast's angular momentum flung Gitta away into the side of a nearby tree. The impact seemed to knock the breath out of her. She fell and rolled slowly back onto her feet. She was hacking and coughing. She was unable to defend herself. I moved toward her and pulled my wakizashi blade. I quickly closed the gap between us.

The Were and I reached Gitta at about the same time. The Were's jaws were fully extended. It intended to rip Gitta apart. I, having cleared the Wakizashi blade, swung down at the Were's head with all the force I could muster. My blade sliced through the Were's neck and shoulder as if I were cutting Jell-O. The Were's head swung out partially to the side as its body hit Gitta and flattened her. I lurched to my feet, my blade poised for a return stroke when I saw the Were wasn't moving. Quickly, I drove the blade into the Were's side. I then jammed the blade back into its scabbard. I knelt to push the Were's body off Gitta. I needn't have bothered. The Were's partially decapitated body was shoved to the side from underneath as Gitta emerged. She favored her left leg, which was bleeding. "A scratch," she said. "Now let's go!"

I quickly knelt beside her. I placed my hands on her shoulders. I was almost crying with relief as I saw the sparkle in her eyes. She was still ready to fight. I wanted to hug her. Both of us knew what the other felt. Another awkward moment in the life of Cody Dugway, for sure, but then we heard the sound of firing up ahead. We both turned to move forward. I told Gitta I had to find my bow. She asked why I didn't just look behind me because it was right there on the forest floor. I started to laugh, saw it, grabbed it, and gave it a quick check. My arrow was gone. I pulled another from my quiver. We moved forward toward the firing as rapidly as we could.

We came to the tree line several minutes later when the firing had almost stopped. The bodies of a number of Weres were strewn about on the grassy area across the stream in front of us. The Captain and two of his men were on the other side of the stream. They were running toward the entrance of a cave-like opening at the bottom of the cliff that towered over the entire area. Our two flankers were still traversing the field of fire. They were shooting at anything not human that moved until it didn't.

The man who was point was standing there waiting for us. His orders were to bring us over as soon as we arrived. We all carefully crossed the stream. I slipped once and recovered before I fell in. Gitta just dived in and seemed to have fun on the way over. She let the stream course down her leg until she felt it had been cleaned of the blood from the Were's slicing tear. Once on the other side, we slow-trotted toward the cave entrance. The Captain and one of his men had gone inside. We could hear shouting, cursing, and yelling issuing forth from the cave's mouth. It didn't sound pleasant in there.

Finally, the Captain emerged, bloody and disheveled. Seeing me, he told me to get in there now as he disappeared back into the cave. I scurried forward, ducked, and entered the cave. A narrow channel ran forward for about 10 feet and then opened up into a fairly big cavern. Three dead Werewolves were heaped against the far wall, and the Captain and his companion were standing over a smaller Were whose legs were missing. Nevertheless, the Were was still alive. It was hissing and growling at the two men. The Were was bleeding badly. It looked to be weakening, but there was still fight in it. It just couldn't move.

"Cody, get over here and link up with this beast. I need to know if this was the whole colony, if there are more, and if so, if they are close by." He tried to catch his breath. "We had to stop the others from killing this one when it was wounded. We barely made it in here in time. Quick, lad! What can this Were tell us?"

I came to the Were's side and knelt just out of arm's length. I mentally reached out for it. A cacophony of jumbled thoughts seemed to explode in my mind. I understood the Were's fright and hatred. It turned and hissed at me when it realized we were somehow connected, but it couldn't stop its thoughts. They seemed to pour into my mind when suddenly, nothing. My headache was substantial up to that moment and suddenly lessened. I looked up with surprise only to see that the Were had died. It had bled out before us. It was a female and an adolescent at that.

The Captain took me by the arm and walked me outside into the air. My headache dissolved as we walked. He suggested that I grab a quick drink from the stream or at least splash water on myself. It was good counsel. I did just that. The Major's group showed up about the same time. The Captain beckoned everyone to come over the stream. When everyone had gathered, he did a quick nose count and made sure everyone had made it through safely.

Lt. Col. Spikes complimented him on the successful action. He asked who had decapitated the blond Were back up the hill. Neither the Captain nor his men seemed to know what Spikes was talking about. I abruptly realized it was me. In the course of fighting, everything can happen so fast that it takes a while sometimes to remember exactly what you did do. Sometimes those memories don't come back until years later, usually with consequence.

I raised my hand and said it was me, as everyone turned and looked. I felt like a bug on a pin. I pulled the wakizashi from my belt and held it up. "With this," I said. "With this. The Were was about to crunch Gitta, and my arm moved faster. But I missed my aim. I was trying for its head and only got part of it and its shoulder. It was my first time to use the blade. Next time I'll try to do better," I said sheepishly.

There was dead quiet all around. Very few people had been able to best a Were-wolf up close and personal as I had. I realized that had the Were been coming for me instead of Gitta, it probably would have been a different story. The unit couldn't hear my thoughts, of course, and just continued to study me. Suddenly, Sergeant Saddler rose to his feet and said, "All hail, Cody-san, the newest member of the Rat's Nest and my kind of hero."

As one, the entire group stood up and cheered. Sergeant Saddler stood beside me with his arm over my shoulder. I stared down at my feet, embarrassed by the attention, when Pee Wee stepped forward and yelled, "Let's baptize him!" He picked me up effort-lessly, walked a few steps to the stream, and unceremoniously threw me in. I came up sputtering and coughing as the group cheered. Pee Wee stood there with his hands on his hips, laughing at me. Suddenly, he yelled and fell forward on his face into the stream.

Gitta stood in his place, smiling that shark's-teeth smile as Pee Wee clambered to his feet. His fists were clenched. He was ready to punch the so-and-so who had pushed him in. That stopped immediately when he saw Gitta. Everyone doubled their laughter but quietly stepped back away from the wolverine. Finally, a grin creased Pee Wee's face, and he held out one of his hands to me. He jerked me to my feet. "I forgot," he laughed. "One doesn't mess with the partner of the Thief of Baghdad without consequence." He then bowed to Gitta and to me. With an arm around my shoulders, he pulled me back onto the grass.

At that moment, Gitta and I both knew we'd found a home. I was an official baptized member of the Rat's Nest, and we had proved we could fight. There were some dead North Carolina Werewolves as evidence of that. I was beaming with pride and gratitude for these folks. I knelt and hugged Gitta. She let me look foolish for a minute or two and then shook me off. She asked if I happened to have another Twinkie. I was glad she was grinning. She really had the most beautiful teeth. They were like bright, shiny, ivory daggers that reeked of death. *Yep*, I thought, *that's my girl!*

DAY EIGHT 6:00 P.M.

The Captain posted sentries on a rotational schedule. The bodies of the Weres were burned in a pile downwind of our campsite. The light from the fire didn't reach back to the area immediately in front of the cave where we were. We'd all brought cold rations for an overnight stay. The thermal emergency blankets we wrapped around ourselves were working fairly efficiently. At least I wasn't uncomfortable yet, but the nights in late spring North Carolina mountains come with a bite, not at all like the Carolina seashores. But even nights there can come with a bite. Only there, it's delivered by mosquitoes and not by Jack Frost's cool breath.

I went over to a small huddle consisting of Lt. Col. Spikes, the Major, Captain Yamata, and Sergeant Saddler. All was quiet. They asked me to describe more of what I'd learned from the small Were. The Captain asked me earlier if this was the whole colony or if we should look for a raid by another equal or larger group. I responded that the adolescent thought this was all her colony. She knew nothing of any other group that might be close or on the way. Satisfied that we could then pass the night here, the Captain posted his first sentries and described the order of evacuation by which we would exit in the early morning.

The huddle was to learn what they could about this colony in particular and the Weres in general. As I took my seat, Lt. Col. Spikes explained to Sergeant Saddler that my talent, if he had not already guessed, was an ability to speak with animals, including Werewolves. This was to be kept highly confidential. Highly! The Sergeant's mouth dropped open for a moment and then he caught himself. He turned and looked at me with a keen glance as if studying me without trying to.

"It's all right, Sergeant," I said. "I don't have two heads, and I didn't ask for this ability, but I prize it and want to serve my country. I'm in this for the same reason you are. I'd personally appreciate your silence on this. Life is easier when no one looks at you like a freak."

He was kind enough to retort, "I'm not looking at you like a freak, Cody. I'm just looking at a brave man with whom I'd deem it an honor to serve and wondering if I can measure up." Before I could respond, the Major interjected and said, "Don't you think we've all shared the same thought, Sergeant? Cody is our secret weapon against the Weres. That's why he has to be protected at all costs, although it looks as if he's usually the one protecting us. Just remember to pass the word quietly. A lot of people need to die before this one is lost."

There was silence for a bit after that until Lt. Col. Spikes cleared his throat and said, "Cody, can you tell us more about the thoughts of the adolescent Were?"

I responded, "Yes, sir." And then I began.

The female had been in shock from the grievous wound. It knew it was dying and that almost all its colony, if not all, had been eradicated. The raid was unexpected. The Weres of this colony thought themselves safe from humans but still tried to be circumspect in all their actions. A patrol of four Weres from a much larger colony to the northeast of here had stopped by two days ago to tell them of their travel and experience on the way to and from a convocation of Weres to the south.

Her colony was asked to prepare to join their larger colony in two full moons. An escort would be sent to them to show them the way. All able-bodied Werewolves, male and female (who weren't pregnant), would be joining together to raid a town south of this place where many human adolescents had gathered. They would be carrying the change serum that only the elder or pale Werewolves could make. They were to maul as many young people as they could and splash them with the serum. That would swell the Weres' ranks almost overnight and give the Weres the numbers they felt they needed to start an open war against the humans.

Abruptly, I stopped. *That's it!* I exclaimed to myself. That was the same thought the female at Chagrin Falls had that wasn't clear to me at the time and that I couldn't tell the unnamed man. I quickly explained myself to the others. Lt. Col. Spikes just sat back and lit his pipe as he pondered what I said. Then he turned to the Major and the Captain and said quietly, "Do you know what this means? It means Werewolves across several states are communicating a plan that can overturn the regional balance of power we now hold over the Weres. It means there's an organization out there heading this plan that we must find and eliminate. It means we have our work cut out for us. It means we have got to capture and interrogate an Elder Were who has this change serum capability, and it means there's a big fight coming in two months more or less since the full moon was last night. I'll bet it's coming to Boone because of Appalachian State and all those college kids."

He then turned to me and said, "Thanks, Cody. You did well, but you may have just done us a bigger service than you or we know. Sounds like we have plenty of work ahead, so let's turn in. I'll be in touch with Clarion tomorrow." As we all stood up and returned to the sleeping areas we'd picked for ourselves, I asked the Major who Clarion was.

She smiled and said, "Why, Cody, he's your unnamed man. Even I don't know his name. He just goes by the code name Clarion. I imagine I'll find out who he really is someday, but I don't really care. He's on our side, and he can move mountains for us when we're in a pinch. I reckon that's all I have to know for now. You, too. Now get some sleep. I'll see you in the morning. And Cody-san, you did good today. I'm very proud of you. So is the Captain. You'd think he was your father the way he's been carrying on to us. Very, very few people impress him. You continue to do so. He wants you on his team, and I told him only when I die."

With that, she turned and walked away to her own site. I just sank down, wrapped myself up in my rubber blanket, and began to chill before I realized that Gitta was sleeping beside me. I conveniently snuggled close to her, laid my head on her rump, sighed contentedly, and drifted off to sleep. What I didn't see was her head as it quietly turned, looked at me, and turned back with a soft snort that sounded all too much like a mom's chuckle. Then both of us were gone to the world.

DAY NINE 4:00 P.M.

The morning hike back to the overview pickup point was made without incident. Sergeant Saddler and Bucky Moore were our demolition experts. They stayed behind to blow up the cave entrance, reducing the opening to nothing more than jagged slabs of rock piled up haphazardly. Before setting out, we policed the area twice to remove any visible signs of our being there. We were a mile or so away when the explosion's boom came faintly rolling up the mountainside. The forest around us squelched the sound enough to make it hard to ascertain its true direction. I saw several in our unit stand a little straighter. A few even grinned. The raid had been a success. We were homeward bound with no casualties. That rarely happened when hunting Weres. Some considered me a good-luck token. Remembering the pale Were's attack, I considered myself just uncommonly lucky and refused to flaunt it.

We waited in the forest until the tour bus showed up. When we saw no cars in either direction, we boarded in groups of three, each group running to the bus with the next group waiting until they were on board. We wanted no witnesses that this had been a military operation. Although the risk of being seen in a daylight pickup at a remote area was really negligible, it was a risk, nonetheless, and one we managed.

Gitta and I were one of the first to board so she could get situated comfortably on the rear seat. She immediately moved to the window and began watching the highway. She remained upright and watched all we passed during the drive home. She was glad to get off at the Chapel. She went immediately to her cage and crawled in. Dusty was there to meet us on the Chapel's front porch. She walked around to the cage with us, presenting Gitta with a Twinkie after she had settled herself. That was one happy wolverine. I told her I'd be back later after some meetings. I walked Dusty back to the office.

We all checked our weapons back into the armory. Dusty asked for both bows, quivers, and all my arrows since I was going home the next morning. I felt a little strange without immediate access to them, but I didn't need them. I asked if she wanted the wakizashi sword as well. She said it was mine, not the unit's, but she would be honored to take care of it for me in the armory vault if I didn't want to travel with it. I didn't. I surrendered it to her. I was glad it would be protected there just as well as it had protected me.

I killed some time writing up my own version of the raid per Lt. Col. Spikes's request. I had some time on my hands when I finished. I asked Dusty if she had a minute until the Major's briefing at 3:00 p.m. She had some free time, so we went to sit on the Chapel's porch steps. There was usually a nice breeze across the porch. On a sunny day in the mountains, my last for a while, I wanted to take advantage of every minute outside.

I gave Dusty a quick synopsis of the raid, including my so-called baptism and Pee Wee's unexpected bath as well. I then recounted what the adolescent Were told me, the intelligence we learned from the raid. She stopped me. With a hand on my arm, she quietly told me that my special abilities were a secret only *outside* the unit. Most had already figured out that I was unusual, especially when they saw Gitta and me working together so closely.

The Major had threatened everyone with a firing squad if not a court martial if my abilities leaked to anyone outside the Rat's Nest. Everyone had sworn that my secret would be safe with them. Dusty made the point that any leak could set me up as a target and that my loss was nothing but the Weres' gain. I felt a little off balance, but as a newly baptized member of the Rat's Nest, I also felt secure. This was a tight unit. We'd grown closer because now we'd fought together. There is a very special bond that grows among people whose lives depend on each other in any profession, especially in the middle of a war.

Dusty asked if I was glad I'd come, if I felt I could work into the unit. I told her it was exciting and challenging, that I felt honored that the folks of the Rat's Nest would even pay attention to me, much less trust me with their lives. I told her as well that Gitta was one of the highlights of my life. She was just an incredible companion. I knew we were going to have some wonderful as well as dangerous times ahead of us, but I was already thinking of her as simply an extension of me. And now that I'd had this brief time at the Rat's Nest, I was beginning to question a number of things I thought I had figured out.

Dusty told me that she'd had some of the same thoughts. She had discovered that high school graduation signaled a fundamental change in her life. The routine and friends we took for granted seemed to change almost overnight. People started looking ahead years instead of weeks. They didn't always like what they saw. Still others were caught up in eager anticipation. They couldn't wait to begin forging their own lives. It was a time of real turmoil.

I told her I agreed with her. She asked what bothered me most. I told her two things. I wanted to go out and make a difference in the world, to do something productive that I could look back on in years to come and say that I mattered. And I wanted a marriage and children of my own, but not yet, and in fact, not for a good while. There was just too much to see and do ahead of me—college, veterinary school, the military, and who knew what else. But there was a conflict in wanting to go out and spread my wings and wanting the security of family and close friends as well.

With me, that confusion was probably because of Casey. Here was a girl I'd grown up with, was close friends with, felt was my soul mate, and had a long running crush on. Yet a big part of me wanted to put the past behind me and venture out into the world on my own. It was scary, it was exciting, it was challenging all at once, and it hurt to think about all that.

Dusty scooted over beside me, put an arm around my shoulder, and then tousled my hair in the back. "You'll figure it out, Cody," she said. "We all do. No one else can live your life but you. We all have faced the same pressures and uncertainties. You're pretty grounded. I wouldn't worry so much. Things will either work out for you or they won't, but they will work themselves out. We're just lucky if we can be on the 'for you' side at least fifty-one percent of the time. Anything else is gravy. As for you and Casey, remember, she has a lot to say as well.

"Maybe she's feeling the same tugs and pulls as you are, maybe not. When you get back, take time out to really have a talk with her. See if she feels as torn as you do, and if she does, why there's your answer. If you and she can't commit one hundred percent to each other right now, then you shouldn't be trying. If it was meant to be, you'll each feel that way without effort. You can't force being in love, and you can't force the future. They both have to play themselves out. From what you're telling me, it sounds like your future has first claim, along with Gitta and the Rat's Nest, of course."

She laughed as she delivered that last line. Standing, she patted me on the head, teasing me. I turned and grinned. She quickly ran back inside. "Briefing starts in 10 minutes," she said.

I really am at a new place in my life, I thought. *I really am, and it's a great place to be.* After the briefing and a visit with Gitta, I caught a ride back to the inn with Sergeant Saddler. I turned in by 9:00 p.m. Tomorrow morning I would be back on a plane heading home. I would be leaving my new home and going back to Ohio. But I would be heading to my real home there. I'd never thought about having two homes before, and I couldn't wait to get back. I had so much to think about, so much to tell my folks and Casey. And I had to get ready for the dance, of course.

DAY TEN 11:00 A.M.

Mom and Casey met me at the airport in Cleveland. I hadn't expected anyone since I'd left Dad's truck in long-term parking, so I was really surprised. Well, maybe more like flabbergasted. It was a wonderful surprise nonetheless. After hugs and kisses from each one, Casey chose to ride back with me while Mom went on into town for some medical aids for Dad's recovery. They were items that Chagrin Falls pharmacies didn't provide. The graduation dance wasn't until 7:30 p.m. Casey told me she had everything ready except her hair. Her mother was standing by for that as soon as she returned home, so I was to drive carefully but not to dawdle, or else.

I didn't.

I spent the hour driving back talking with Casey, first listening to her catch me up on school and her summer schedule. Then she told me about Honey and her progressing recovery. She also told me a little more about my dad now that he was home. Finally, with about 20 minutes left on our drive, she asked me what I'd been up to. I honestly didn't know where to start. I just said that I'd missed her, that we had all day tomorrow to visit before our graduation ceremony. I did tell her that I had a chance to get plenty of exercise in North Carolina and was ready to dance. Casey started laughing at that. Then we both started laughing about other couples coming to the dance who we knew were terrible dancers like me. I promised I'd try to get my dad to show me a few moves before I picked her up for the dance.

She shrieked at that. Laughing, she told me if I did that, it would be at the peril of my life. I told her Gitta would be honored if I added a move or two to my repertoire, that anything would be better than my clumsy, heavy-footed tromp through North Carolina's underbrush. That immediately prompted her to start asking about Gitta. We were well into that conversation when we finally pulled into our shared driveway. She bounced out of the car on the run and called over her shoulder that she had to get inside so she could look beautiful tonight.

I called after her that she needn't bother, that you can't improve perfection, but she was already in the house, and I was left talking to a swinging door. *Oh well*, I thought, *it's time to make the man shine bright, too.* I did a slow (albeit clumsy) dipping waltz down the sidewalk to our den door. Dad was waiting for me when I walked in. He grabbed me in a one-armed hug. That told me he was well on the way to regaining his strength. I smiled as I wrapped my arms carefully around him and hugged him back with equal gusto. North Carolina had been an adventure in every sense, but I was home. Mom and Dad were all right, and I had a date with Casey. For at least today, all was right with the world. I planned to keep it that way.

DAY TEN 10:00 P.M.

I was tired, and my legs hurt from standing around so much. Casey and I had come to the dance in my mom's car. Casey looked radiant, the prettiest girl there by far in my estimation and evidently in the eyes of a number of the fellows there who cast longing glances her way. I wasn't sure their dates approved, but what they thought individually or collectively didn't bother me one whit. I just didn't care. I had far more important things to worry about like trying to keep up with Casey. I thought I knew a goodly number of our classmates, but she must have known them all and their first cousins.

She was here, there, and everywhere saying hello and saying goodbye as our class danced, walked, or stumbled by. But she was happy. That was really what this night was all about. She had worked hard. She had been a school leader since junior high school and was one of the most popular people on our campus. This was her night to shine, and did she ever! I was thrilled that she'd wanted to come with me. There were plenty of other guys who would have invoked mayhem for that privilege. As the dance was winding down, several did.

As the band started their last 45-minute segment, Brad Thorney and a couple of his friends came up to me. They asked where Casey was. It seemed to me that he was slurring his speech. I wondered if he had a cold or a fever. I told them she'd gone with a couple of her friends for a few minutes. She should be right back. He said they'd wait, that he wanted to dance with her once and ask her if she wanted to leave and go to an after-party with some of the team and their friends. I told him I didn't think she'd go for that, that she was here with me, that she wasn't into after-parties and whatever else they'd planned.

He turned to me and told me that was her choice, not mine, that it wouldn't be my best move to stand in his way. I might be Robin Hood in my own backyard, but this wasn't my backyard. His friends then stepped up. Each took me by an arm and quietly steered me off the edge of the dance floor and onto the outside patio adjacent to the Country Club's ballroom. I started to pull my arms away, and their grip tightened so much that it started to hurt, so I just let myself be carried along. I said nothing. When we got outside, they walked me to the patio balcony railing and let me go, standing between me and the ballroom doors.

"I think it best you wait here, Dugbait," said the bigger of the two fellows. "If you want, we'll go find you a wheelchair, and you can ride along home unless Mommy or Daddy is coming for you." I thanked them for their interest in me and their apparent friendship with Brad. I asked them if Brad was feeling under the weather, that his voice was slurred. I was worried about his ability to drive if he were taking some kind of medication. That brought a big laugh. One of them said everyone should try Brad's "medication," and that was what the after-party was all about. I told them politely that I needed to get back to my date. I wanted no trouble. They laughed again and said they were sure I didn't, that they would kick my legs out from under me if I tried to go back in, and I could go right back to being a part-time cripple.

I asked them if they were sure about all this. They said yes. They asked me what part of this confrontation I did not understand. I told them it was all painfully clear to me. That brought another laugh. Then I decked the boy to my right with a left cross and swung around and tried to drive my right fist through the second man's solar plexus. It went in but not through. I really didn't think I could, but the air whooshed out of him like an untied balloon. He dropped like a rock, mouth open and gasping like a fish out of water. I knelt and patted them both on the head. In a low voice, I told them that if I saw them again this night, I would politely and personally break both an arm and a leg on each of them, but only after I fed them their teeth. They started heaving, gasping, and crying, trying to crawl away from me. I stood up and bade them good night. I stepped over the one closest to the ballroom doors and quietly made my way back inside.

I walked up behind Brad Thorney just as Casey was coming back. She saw me and started around him when he grabbed her arm and said he wanted to talk to her. I started to reach for his collar when Casey flicked her eyes at me and barely shook her head "No!" I dropped my arm. I stepped back and gave her some room. She turned to face him. Without a shred of warning, she swung her arm and slapped him as hard as she could. The sound of the slap caused everyone within 15 feet to stop and look at them. She almost spun Brad around. She told him in a dead-even voice to take his hand off her arm or else. Brad—mad, embarrassed, and clearly not thinking—said he'd take his hand away when he got good and ready and not before. She looked up at him and smiled a smile I'd never seen before (and never wanted to see again). She then kicked him down low as hard as she could.

There was a shocked silence as Brad dropped to the floor, writhing on the ground and screaming in a falsetto voice I never knew he had. He made so much noise that all the other guys and gals nearby backed away. They left him spinning on the floor face-down, making unintelligible sounds that weren't normal for a human. I've heard sheep bleat but never a man the size of Brad, but then he really should have known better.

It was Casey's right foot that had done the damage. Her college soccer scholarship was riding on that foot and her ability to kick hard and kick straight.

I suggested to Casey that perhaps we'd like to emulate the others and clear out. Casey brightly agreed. She took my arm and walked slowly away with me with the grace of a true princess. As we passed through the ballroom and into the foyer to find our coats and leave, several chaperones and teachers rushed past us, headed in the direction of Brad's moans, groans, and cries. "What on earth happened in there, Cody?" said Mr. Blanton as he hustled by us. I just shrugged and said, "Beats me." Then we exited the building saying nothing more, arm in arm with big smiles that quickly turned to giggles.

DAY TEN 11:45 P.M.

I brought Casey home by midnight. She asked if I'd like to sit on her side door steps and talk for a while. I said sure and then wrapped my tuxedo jacket around her as we leaned against her door and held hands, both thinking back over the evening. We sat there in silence for about 10 minutes when Casey began recounting the many adventures we'd had growing up here together. I added a few recollections from time to time and corrected some of hers as she corrected some of mine. At 1:00 a.m., Casey's mom opened the door and handed out a plate of cookies and some soda pop. She gave Casey a sweater and then told us to have a good time and for Casey to lock the door when she came in. She was going on to bed. If we were still sitting here at dawn, she'd make breakfast for us both. She then bid us a good night, closed the door, and turned off the light.

When we'd finished the cookies and pop, we leaned back and propped each other up with our shoulders and the door. Then we started telling each other about our plans for college and our fears. Sometime about 2:00 a.m., Casey asked me to tell her in detail about my North Carolina trip and especially about Dusty. "Dusty?" I exclaimed, and almost fell over as I quickly turned toward her. "How in the world do you know about Dusty?" I shouted. She laughed and put her hand over my mouth. She told me to calm down and speak softly or we'd wake up both our folks.

She explained that Dusty had called her to give her a report about me. Dusty told Casey that I appeared to be very fond of Casey and that she, Dusty, would have wanted a progress report on her boyfriend if he'd been off trying to pick a fight with a Werewolf. "Boyfriend?" I murmured. "Dusty has a boyfriend? Why didn't she tell me she had a boyfriend? And how did she even get your number to call you?" I challenged.

Casey told me to take it easy. She laughed. She said Dusty first called my folks with a report. They gave Dusty her phone number. Casey explained that she was so relieved that I'd had such a positive experience and that I'd apparently been accepted by the group I was with. It was a group Dusty referred to as the Rat's Nest. Casey laughed at that name. She said my North Carolina group seemed like a lot of fun, although perhaps a bit quirky.

I sputtered for a second. I said there were a few things about me that Casey didn't know and that I was full of surprises. She asked me sweetly if I meant like the altercation

I had with Brad's friends out on the patio. My jaw must have scraped the top step. I was stunned. I asked her how she could have possibly known about that, that there was too little time from the time I put the guys down until we both met Brad Thorney.

She said it was simple, really. The second-floor ladies' room where she was with her friends had two windows in the anteroom that partially opened. She was looking out the top half of one window when Brad's friends hustled me outside. At first, she wanted to call out and warn everyone so the guys might back off if they knew there were witnesses around. But then I handled the situation nicely with no yelling, little muss, and no fuss. When she hurried down to meet me and Brad intercepted her, she knew immediately what must have happened. She then thanked me for letting her handle her own mess because if I had stepped in, Brad would not have been publicly humiliated nearly enough for her taste.

We both started laughing at the same time. I put my arm around her. She snuggled in closer to me and laid her head back against my shoulder. I then gave her a detailed account of my North Carolina experience. Casey asked a lot of questions at first, but by 4:00 a.m., she was sound asleep in my arms. I was tired, too, so I just closed my eyes. I was totally comfortable in the moment.

Casey's mom found us that way at about 7:00 a.m. when she came out to get the paper. We were fast asleep, Casey wearing her sweater and my tux coat and I with my arm about her, holding her close against me to stay warm, my head bent forward on my chest. Mrs. Allegro called my mom, who came out and took a picture of us. They then woke us up and told us breakfast would be served at the Allegros' in 30 minutes, that we'd best get up, change our wrinkled garb, and report back with an appetite.

It was a dance to remember, but more important, it was the perfect ending to a part of our lives we would always remember but never recover from. Casey groaned as she woke up and started laughing at how she must look. I didn't really see her. My neck hurt so much from the angle I'd slept in that I could hardly stand to straighten up, but an Allegro breakfast was a treat one never missed. Besides, I needed a bathroom break to make room for it.

Yes, indeed, I thought to myself. *It truly was good to be home again.*

DAY ELEVEN 10:50 A.M.

Casey and I were standing outside on the driveway by my mom's car. My folks would be out in about 10 minutes to drive me to the Cleveland airport. I was headed back to the Rat's Nest for my summer assignment and early registration at Lees-McCrae. Our schedules were such that Casey would be gone to her soccer camp when I came home briefly at summer's end. I'd be back in classes at

Lees-McCrae when she came back after her camp before her fall registration. We'd had a good week together sorting out a lot of things between us. We were both looking forward to college. By eventual mutual admission, we were looking forward to its social life as well. But we were reluctant to leave the moment and each other. I, for one, just couldn't understand how to say goodbye to a part of me I'd grown up with. It seemed like a kind of emotional amputation.

I knew that whatever happened, Casey would always have a special place in my heart. But that place was being crowded right now with a wanderlust for new places and new adventures. It truly was a big world out there. I wanted to see, learn, and do as much as I could while I was still young. Casey felt the same way about herself, about me, and about life outside Chagrin Falls. We realized our adventures in life together were not over, that there were still plenty more to come even though we might take different paths for a while. That realization was an anchor. It steadied both of us as we tried to prepare ourselves for life's loops and twists, starting with each other in these, our last few moments together.

I held her gently in my arms as I bid her goodbye. I spoke softly and slowly, taking every opportunity to nuzzle forehead-to-forehead and nose-to-nose as my arms enveloped her and then gently lifted her to her toes. I could smell and feel her tight against me as if we had been tailored. It was like breathing spring while cradling the gentle vapors of my life's best memories against me, intoxicating and ephemeral all at once with the full knowledge that this wonderful woman whose heart beat so fiercely against mine would always be part of me. She would be substantial in mind and memory but destined for a time to be but a wraith whenever she danced into my welcoming arms.

I felt like Humphrey Bogart in the movie *Casablanca* when he and Ingrid Bergman realized they "will always have Paris." It was altogether a sad and bittersweet feeling. I could not speak when the realization of our parting suddenly rushed from my chest to my throat.

So I kissed her, gently at first and then with a hunger I did not understand but eagerly welcomed. She returned my kiss with equal fervor, our bodies almost an afterthought as our minds and passion fused and released and rejoined again and again.

It was a kiss I was never to forget, never to duplicate. Most lives never get a Casey. For those who do, no one ever gets two. The lucky will only get another original.

When my folks came out, I could not speak. They were nice enough to be jovial and quickly climb into the car's front seat as Casey and I stepped apart and then let our fingers trail down each other's arm as I bent and slid into the car's rear seat. Casey was in no better shape. She was silent with eyes that glistened like the sparkle of sunshine on new flowers. Her folks came out to tell us goodbye. Her mother put her arms around Casey. She stood behind Casey, holding her tightly as if to reassure herself that Casey was still there. She was not yet off on her own maiden flight to freedom.

It was kind of our parents to give us a few minutes alone. It was kinder of them to make this parting quick. I turned to look out the back window as my mom drove away down the street. Casey had come to the edge of the driveway. She was by the curb, waving and waving as our car drove off. I put my hand to the window and waved back with tears starting up in my eyes before our car turned the corner and she was lost to my sight. It was clear to me that I wasn't just leaving Casey; I was leaving a special time of my life, and there was no going back.

I didn't know it then, but it would be a long time before I saw Casey again. When I did, it would be in circumstances neither of us could have foreseen that day. But that's another story.

THE END OF EPISODE FOUR, BOOK ONE

EPISODE
FIVE

DAY ONE 10:30 A.M.

My binoculars were centered on a small clearing in the woods—woods that splattered across the ragged mountainside almost a quarter mile ahead of me. The extended forward rims of my military binoculars prevented the steady rain pelting down on our tracking party from running down the outside lenses and blurring my view. Three very dark creatures were huddled in the clearing. They looked to be in serious conversation around a fourth figure lying crumpled at their feet. The three squatting figures seemed to be reaching down in turn to pat the downed figure and then raising their extremities to their mouths as if trying to hide their expressions or what they might be saying, but I knew better.

They were picking at the body they'd killed. They were snacking on its flesh as if they were at a smorgasbord. The figure on the ground was, or had been, human. The three huddled creatures were North Carolina Werewolves. They were shaggy, unkempt, more deadly than their Ohio counterparts, and anything but fine diners. I knew that for a fact. We'd been tracking them for two plus days, relentless in our pursuit.

We pressed them hard for almost 40 hours until the storm hit in the evening of the second day. We lost their trail in the resulting downpour. We picked it up again only by accident a few hours earlier this morning in the steady rain. We were wet, cold, and miserable. Summer thunderstorms with their introductory crushing booms and darting lightning displays in the Blue Ridge Mountains can make a romantic date with an angry electric eel seem like a desirable alternative. Any smart creature at the mercy of a Carolina storm runs for the nearest cover. They get off the bald mountaintops as fast as possible. We'd been smart but late. The Were hostage was now dead and fodder for his captors. We had not found and rescued him in time.

The man they had taken as a hostage was an itinerant worker passing through, a hired hand who was cutting wild timber near the town of Boone when he was taken. He hadn't gone peacefully. He left behind his axe buried in a Were who looked to have a split personality or at least a split head before three other Weres overwhelmed the man and carried him away.

The man's boss and the boss's son cutting wood nearby witnessed the attack and capture from a nearby field. They called the County Sherriff's office as soon as they could get to a phone. They complained that Bigfoot or Sasquatch, as people were beginning to call such creatures, was real. In fact, some were loose in North Carolina. My boss, Major Sanchez, was at the Sheriff's office when the call came in. She was dropping off US military manuals on woodsmanship and survival training as a professional courtesy.

As bedlam started to ensue, the Major quickly volunteered the search services of some of her Rat's Nest engineers. With them, she said, was a new intern (me) who had previously mapped the areas where the worker was taken. She added that he had also mapped the area where his captors might be taking him. The Sheriff accepted her offer. He gave her a small, two-way radio. He told her that this was a law enforcement matter first and foremost. Nevertheless, extra bodies in a search party were always welcome. We were to call him if any contact was made. With her assistance, he assigned several tracts of forest on state land for her teams to search. Hence, Pee Wee, Gitta, and I—Team Bravo—were now thoroughly soaked. We were also thoroughly teed off as we helplessly watched the Weres devour the human they'd killed.

Other Rat's Nest teams were also out in the surrounding mountains. Our team included Pee Wee, a Cherokee and certified tracker; one of my new mentors, Gitta, my wolverine companion; and me, Cody Dugway, Certified Animal Communicator (CAC). Gitta liked Pee Wee. She thought he could move like a big cat in the wild and considered him a worthy adversary if one of them ever went after the other. She told me she thought of me as a big cat, too, as in Caterpillar, a wheezing mechanical monster that moves earth and tears up forests and can be heard miles away when driven by humans hampered by steel braces.

I didn't dignify her cold breakfast comments with a response at the time. I simply turned away, inadvertently catching sight of the Were party crossing a small ridge about a half mile away to the east of us. "Gotcha!" I snapped. I jumped to my feet and pointed the way for Pee Wee and Gitta. Immediately, we were back on the hunt, which eventually led to our current cover, a blown-down oak tree whose root base spanned some 15 to 16 feet across. We were safely hidden behind the uprooted tree base. We studied the Were hunting party on the slope well ahead of us. Now that we could confirm the human was dead, our mission went from search and rescue to search and recover. The difference? On a rescue mission, the use of firearms is permitted. On a recover mission, you just use a stretcher, your shoulder, or in a case such as ours this morning, a double-thick, military-issue gray body bag.

Recovering the body was now our mission. We figured we'd best get to it while there was still enough left to qualify as a body. We wanted to interrupt the Weres' routine but not necessarily scare them our way, so I used an old trick I'd learned years ago from watching early Robin Hood movies. It was a screaming or whistling arrow. It was fairly easily made from scratch. A whittling knife and a wooden arrow shaft were all that was needed to change the arrow from silent to scary. If the shaft was aluminum, one could use some sort of a hole punch. A screaming arrow makes a sound like no other. My bet was that the Weres, knowing they would likely be pursued, were edgy already. They would be very uncomfortable with anything that disturbed the normal routine of the forest.

A few nicks and cuts and the arrow was ready. I was using the horn bow as Major Sanchez had asked. When the rain started the evening before, I restrung it with nylon string. Having nocked the arrow, I turned to an angle perpendicular to our line of sight to the Weres. I fired the arrow high into the sky. The trees around us screened the first high-pitched whine as it rose into the air, somewhat disguising its point of origin. We wanted the Weres to know there was a hunting party in the general area but not exactly where they were. This was a marketing maneuver, not blatant advertising.

It had the desired effect. Pee Wee, watching the Weres through his binoculars, quietly reported that all three jumped to their feet and were rapidly casting about trying to find the source of the sound. With little further ado, the Weres quickly vanished into the woods on the uphill side of their clearing, and all was still again. We settled down to wait, Pee Wee and I taking turns every 10 minutes watching the clearing and the human's remains, waiting to see if the Weres would be back to finish their ghastly meal. After two hours of no movement and nothing apparently unusual, we started forward to retrieve the worker's body, at least what was left of it.

We came to the clearing from three different directions. Gitta came in first, straight from our previous observation post. Pee Wee circled to the right and came in from a two o'clock position. I came in from the ten o'clock position. The entire recovery maneuver took about an hour to execute. When we all finally reached the body, however, we had some degree of assurance that the Weres had truly departed the area. It took a few moments to bag the remains. Pee Wee said a brief prayer at the site, and then we were off, back the way we'd come, alternately carrying the body and hoping to come to a road within the next 12 hours where we could catch a ride back to the Boone Sherriff's office.

We weren't that lucky. We didn't reach Boone until after midnight. We managed to catch a ride for the last few miles from a timber truck driver going our way. Tired, dirty, short-tempered from the rain and blisters that inevitably form in such weather, but hungry enough to eat a small colt, we waited at the Sheriff's office for almost an hour before Dusty showed up in an SUV. She was there to take us home to Blowing Rock.

Major Sanchez, who was nothing if not smart, had sent Dusty. Anyone else but Dusty would have gotten the edge of our disgust and discomfort. However, Dusty's smile and good humor could make an underground cave-in seem like just another opportunity for a picnic or a good country visit. She not only had a gift for lightening another's load, but just being around her made you want to lighten everyone else's load as well. Of course, it didn't hurt that she always looked like a magazine model when everyone else looked like rain-soaked, soiled toupees.

The ride back to Blowing Rock was singularly uneventful. All three of us were asleep as soon as Dusty started the SUV. We had a hard time waking up at the Chapel. The Major saw our condition, let Gitta out so she could amble back to her cage, and asked Sergeant Saddler to take us on home. She would do our mission debrief later at midmorning after we'd had a chance to rest, shower, and change clothes.

I slept all the way back to my room at the inn. I don't even remember climbing into bed.

DAY TWO 7:00 A.M.

I awakened earlier than I planned. I used the time waiting for the bedside clock's alarm to go off to review and savor all that had happened to me since I had returned to the Rat's Nest. Sergeant Saddler had met me at the airport in Charlotte. Once again, we stopped in Hickory for a bite before we headed on up to Blowing Rock. We chatted back and forth along the way. I was surprised at how easy it was to fall back into a routine with him. I told him of my stay in Chagrin Falls, how difficult it was to part with Casey but how excited I still was to be coming back. I also told him a little bit of my apprehension at enrolling in Lees-McRae. High school already seemed so far away. College seemed already almost on top of me.

The Sergeant laughed. He told me that my high school experiences would actually stay with me all the rest of my life, in time even eclipsing some of the college memories I had yet to make for myself. But a good idea at my age, he said, was simply to concentrate now on forging new experiences with a whole new set of friends. That's what he had done for three years until finances had forced him to drop out of college.

He'd entered the Air Force to avoid Vietnam and eventually qualify for the GI Bill. That would fund the remainder of his college degree. By chance, he ended up in the Special Operations arena with a tour of duty in Vietnam after all. He liked it so much that he was now studying in his spare time with Appalachian State so he could finish his bachelor's degree to qualify for a Second Lieutenant's commission. Major Sanchez had been pushing him for the past year to do just that. The end was now in sight. He would qualify for graduation in two more years measured from the end of this month.

Dusty had reserved my previous room at the Blowing Rock Inn for the next two months. She purchased a clean, used, 1954 pale blue Chevrolet Bel Air sedan for me to use during my stay at the Rat's Nest. It was waiting for me when Sergeant Saddler and I arrived at the inn. The keys were left at the desk. My first several days' assignment from the Major was simply to take the car and drive it on every road I could find within a 50-mile radius of Blowing Rock. She wanted me to quickly gain a basic familiarity with the land, the character of the people, and the areas in which we would all live and work for the next while. Other details and learning special cut-offs and cut-throughs would come later. The car was a dream come true. Although somewhat ungainly, it seemed to me to be one of the prettiest sights I'd ever laid eyes on, short of Casey and Dusty, of course. And Gitta.

The Major wanted to know that I was able to go from school to the Chapel and to any of the surrounding communities with some confidence. I was also to take Gitta with me, for once a wolverine sees where it's going, it can never get lost going back. Gitta taught me that. It had helped make me a kind of hero with the Rat's Nest on our first real hike together.

I did exactly what the Major asked. I was stunned at how beautiful this state really was. But I also learned that a great deal of western North Carolina was up and down real estate. There really was a difference between the mountain folk and the flatlanders who lived in the river basins and coastal areas to the east. I found that I preferred the mountain folk.

Each day I went out early to the Rat's Nest to practice with the horn bow. I used both the competition and hunter's courses Dusty had so laboriously created prior to my last visit. Gitta accompanied me everywhere except into stores or towns. If we somehow ended up in the public eye, she stayed with my car while I ran the required errands. She learned to curl up and sleep on the back seat at the drop of a handkerchief. It was a talent I wanted to bring into my own repertoire. We talked every chance we could get, usually me explaining just what we were seeing as we drove along. Gitta was calculatingly curious about the world of humans.

The Major's call to action to help hunt the Werewolves came abruptly at the start of my second week at the Rat's Nest. She assigned teams. I was frankly thrilled to have been asked to work with Pee Wee or, by his formal rank and name, Sergeant Andrew Lighthorse. He was our best tracker. Every day with him was a year's worth of classroom instruction. He held himself to high standards of honor. He would often surprise me with quotes from Shakespeare that seemed dryly appropriate to the situation at hand.

I learned he had a niece attending Lees-McRae who he and his family felt was an extraordinary "healer." It was a gift that did not care if the patient was animal or human.

Pee Wee's many off-hand remarks about her led me to picture her as short, stocky, plain, and belligerent. Her English name was Jennifer. Her last name was Walksabout. Her dad was an accountant. Her mother, Pee Wee's sister, was an elementary school teacher. Jennifer had a younger brother who had been crippled since seven years old when a car backed over him in a supermarket parking lot. Jennifer and her brother were close. He apparently was insanely bright and curious. His English name was Michael. His Indian name was Shadowhawk. His uncle Pee Wee often called him Pain-in-the-Rear because of his incessant questions.

Pee Wee told me Michael wanted to be a veterinarian as well and would be starting his freshman year at Lees-McRae in September. We would be freshmen together. As my experiences in North Carolina grew, in time I would come to love Michael as a brother. He would become my permanent roommate. My favorite expression to him would be "Stuff it, Blackbird!" because of his insatiable appetite for knowledge and penchant for never-ending chatter.

Dusty had been awaiting my return. She was full of questions of her own about Casey and my graduation dance. Dusty was easy to talk to. Since the Major's admonition to me about having no romantic illusions about her and since Casey told me Dusty already had a mysterious boyfriend, I could be myself around her and enjoy her sheer femininity—along with every other man in a 100-mile radius. I also benefited from her competency. Dusty was not happy unless everything was organized and residing where it should. One did not want an unhappy Dusty around.

As I stretched, I was starting to wonder what the day would bring when my alarm finally went off. It startled me. I was quick to shut it down. "Time's a-wasting!" the Major would say, and she was right. I had to be at the Chapel by 9:00 a.m. for a debriefing. There were rumors that Lt. Col. Spikes and Captain Yamata would be coming in this week. Spikes never did anything without a reason. We had much to do to get ready for them. It looked to be an interesting week.

DAY TWO 9:00 A.M.

Major Sanchez was waiting for Pee Wee and me when we showed up at the Chapel. My eyes hurt. I was still a little sleepy, but Pee Wee looked 110 percent go as he always did. Someday I was going to find out how he did that. The Major wasted no time taking us through our mission. She asked a number of questions that would never have occurred to me to ask. It taught me that we often see more than we think we do. We also understand more than we let on *if* the right questions are asked. But Major Sanchez was a skilled interrogator. As I came to learn in time, she was one of the best the military had. And she did it all with her customary luminous smile. She could be as mesmerizing and slick as oil on ice. After our session, I remembered that I'd already resolved never to lie to Dusty, but I made a double resolution to never *ever* lie to the Major. Pee Wee and I and the others who had formed search teams spent the rest of the morning writing down our version of events as we understood them. The Major always wanted a written comparative record. About noontime and hungry, I opted to make a run into Blowing Rock for some lunch. I asked if anyone wanted a ride into town. Since I was the only one there staying in a hotel and had no cooking facilities, eating out was my basis for survival. I was surprised when Dusty asked if she could ride with me. She asked if I would let her run a few small errands after we grabbed a bite. I said sure. The Major had no objections, but she did add to Dusty's errand list. By 12:10 p.m., we were off.

After we stopped for some fast food, Dusty told me it was the Major's wish that we take a short drive out to the Blue Ridge Wildlife Institute (BRWI) at the Lees-McRae campus in nearby Banner Elk, North Carolina. There was someone there she wanted me to meet. Dusty had been there the day before. She knew the way and had already gotten permission that morning for our stopover. In fact, we were expected at 1:00 p.m. by Professor Kimball Warren, a noted veterinarian who had retired and was now head of the BRWI Wildlife Rehabilitation program. It was the most successful institution of its kind in the Southeast United States.

I was excited. I had driven by the campus twice more than a week earlier when my car assignment was to discover the countryside around Blowing Rock and Boone. I had not stopped in. This would be my first visit. I was grinning so much that my face actually hurt when we arrived. Dusty took me to the Professor's office. We chatted for a short while. He was a tall, slightly graying, distinguished-looking man with a shy smile and lanky frame. I trusted him immediately.

He told me the Major had briefed him several weeks earlier that I would be enrolling at Lees-McRae. She told him I had an uncanny knack for communication with animals, sort of an empathetic connection. He said he had at least one other student enrolled at Lees-McRae that seemed to also have an unusual connection. The one in mind was a young woman of Cherokee and Irish descent who went by the name of Sunstar. When she was born, Venus, the Morning Star, was visible in the vicinity of the rising sun, and hence her name.

He asked if we would care to join him on a tour of the rehabilitation facility. Dusty thanked him but said she had errands to run and would not be able to join him at this time. She asked for and took my keys, telling me she'd be back for me at 3:00 p.m. She then grinned, told me to be careful if I started seeing "stars," patted me on the shoulder, and left. I was mentally scratching my head at her cryptic remark as I followed the Professor into the facility's laboratory.

A number of students and several vets were scattered here and there at steel examination tables. Each table featured a different animal. One table was the scene of some loud chatter as five students were circled about a rather old hound dog. "Can anyone tell me what is wrong with this old fellow?" the vet said as the Professor and I walked up. The competing students were trying to guess from appearances. Apparently, none of their answers were satisfactory to the vet. Frustrated, he finally asked what procedures they should follow to ascertain the answer. Jokingly, one tall student with a mop of red hair shouted out, "Just ask the dog!"

That stopped conversation immediately. The vet didn't want jokes or wry attempts at sarcasm. He started to berate the student when I stepped forward, excused myself, and leaned in to pat the dog's head and ask him what was wrong. He immediately perked up, looked at me closely, and told me the answer. He had worms and an infection in his left paw beneath a callous. That transpired almost silently on my part with an answering low growl from the hound. When he was finished, I stood straight, patted him once again, and told the vet what the dog said.

The vet's face went white, and his jaw dropped open. He asked incredulously, "Who are you, and how did you know this dog has worms and a foot infection?" Five curious faces turned to me, and Professor Warren took a step back and to the side of me as he studied my face, waiting for my answer.

"Why," I said, smiling, "I just did as that gentleman said. I asked the hound, although I'm not convinced any animal is really all that good at self-diagnosis."

As I looked around, both the students and the vet seemed to take a step back. They all silently looked at me as if I had two heads. Nobody moved except the dog who, in another low growl, asked why someone wasn't treating him. Realizing that I was a guest and had inadvertently seriously disturbed the class, I apologized for any intrusion. I asked Professor Warren if we might go to the cages outside now where Dusty had asked me to meet some woman who had something for me.

The other tables had stopped their examinations to see what was going on when the students suddenly went silent. All eyes watched the Professor and me as we exited the building. Once we were outside, I heard the uproar start again at twice the volume as the vet tried to quiet his puzzled students. Other students came over to see what all the hullabaloo was about.

Professor Warren escorted me to the area where several types of birds were being temporarily held. There was a hawk, a turkey buzzard, a small owl, and a bird that had placed itself far back in a corner of its cage, one foot heavily bandaged. It was a white gyrfalcon, the largest and most beautiful member of the falcon family. They were not that common in North Carolina, but they were not rare either. They were normally found in Arctic climes. They possessed all the best characteristics of the falcon family—speed, size, strength, fearlessness, and stamina. In Arabia, they were worth a king's ransom.

I could not help myself. I knelt in front of the cage. I introduced myself as a Gatekeeper, a human who could communicate with animals, and asked if I might have the privilege of speaking with it. The falcon bristled at the concept of "it." She informed me that it was a she, thank you very much, and a royal she at that. I told her I should have guessed that from the imperious tilt to her head but that she must forgive me for my manners as I had never seen such a beautiful creature before. I then bowed my head and looked back up into eyes that had softened somewhat. She regarded me askance for a moment, turned full on to the cage's front screen, and briefly flared her wings and bowed slightly back at me. I asked her name. I received the reply that she had none. Everyone at the facility referred to her as the falcon. I asked if I might give her one worthy of her and her noble race. She asked curiously what name I had in mind. "Polaris," I said. "I shall call you Princess Polaris, for Polaris is the night star around which the heavens revolve and to whom all humankind looks for guidance."

The falcon was immobile for a minute and then softly, as gracefully as she could with a damaged foot, bowed slowly to me and regained her bearing. With a shrill shriek that sent every small bird for miles around flying for cover, she asked what I was called.

"Simply the Gatekeeper," I answered and then bowed low to her and again stood erect. "I need your help when you are well," I told her. "I, we humans, face a formidable foe in creatures who are of the bastard wolf family. They are creatures without heart. They seek only destruction and death. We need trusted eyes in the sky to find, follow, and help us destroy them before they destroy the forests, our cities, and all who live in them. It is a task of honor and fearlessness, one no other creature can fill as can you. When the time comes, will you fight with us, with me, not as a trained animal but as an equal partner?"

"I will think on it," she answered after a long pause. "Come and see me again. Soon." And with that, she turned slowly back into her corner and covered herself with her wings.

Professor Warren looked at me critically for a bit. He shrugged and tossed his head as if to clear his mind from a nagging distraction and then turned to walk away. As I turned to follow, still looking back at Polaris, I walked straight into a young woman carrying a bowl of water and feed. She was looking down so as not to misstep. Our impact knocked both of us to the ground. The water bowl drenched me, and the feed bowl seeded me from head to toe. Furious, I looked up and started to yell out my frustration when my words literally choked in my throat. I was looking into the angry eyes of one of the most beautiful and intriguing women I had ever seen, much less flattened.

Her hair was almost blue-black like a raven's wing in the sunlight, her face almost perfectly formed with intense coal-black eyes. Her skin was the color of light tan with a complexion as smooth as melted butter. Her lips, at that moment drawn back in a grimace, were the softest and most inviting lips I had ever seen. I could not make a sound as I studied her. I wondered what heaven had produced *this* angel. She looked like Scarlett O'Hara in the movie *Gone with the Wind* or, at the very least, her better-looking sister.

Coming to my senses, I scrambled awkwardly to my feet. I held my hand out to her as I started to apologize. She took my hand with a grip that told me there was more muscle beneath her slender arms than most men have. She pulled herself erect and, without warning, slammed the side of my head with her empty aluminum water bowl. She knocked me back down to my knees. I literally saw stars. Without a word or further glance, she stomped off back to the rehabilitation facility. I watched as the most athletic, perfect figure I had ever seen disappeared around the row of cages beside me. Despite my intense headache, I had enjoyed the experience all the more because I was literally seeing two of everything.

I sat still until my vision cleared, head down between my legs while I massaged my temples. Finally, able to stand up, I was assisted by Professor Warren who dryly remarked, "I see you have met our healer. Apparently, her talents are not limited. Perhaps she should also be known as the Destroyer." Chuckling at his own joke while amicably brushing me off, the Professor led the way back to his office where we spent the remainder of our time talking about Lees-McRae as a springboard for the veterinary schooling I wanted to have one day.

When Dusty returned to pick me up, I remained quiet all the way back to the Rat's Nest. She noticed but said nothing about the growing lump on the side of my head. I simply could not get that water girl out of my mind. The healer, eh? I wondered if she knew the other healer at Lees-McRae, Pee Wee's niece, Michael's sister, whom I had yet to meet. She would look as plain as paper wrapping against the arresting beauty of the girl who had just clobbered me. My mind wandered as I sat thinking that maybe Michael's sister would be my friend, introduce me to Sunstar, put in a good word for me, and then, well, whatever. I was smiling when we reached the Rat's Nest but had a throbbing headache. As we stepped out of my car and Dusty handed me my keys, she couldn't hold back any longer. "Cody, you must tell me what happened. There's a growing goose egg on the side of your head, and you've been sitting quietly in the car all the way back with the goofiest look on your face. What in heck is the matter with you? What happened back there?"

"I met a gal who seems to have scrambled my brain," I said. "She is a vision of loveliness held together by a steel frame. She literally knocked me off my feet. I also met a real princess with a bad foot," I said dreamily. "I'm sorry, Dusty, but I'm just a little ditsy right now from the incident. I feel a little loose."

"You look like you've got a screw loose," she retorted.

Dusty peered forward to look at me closely for a few seconds and gently touched the sizable lump on my head. She took me by the arm and marched me into the Rat's Nest where she gave me four aspirin and told me to go sleep it off with Gitta, that the Major and she had work to do before Lt. Col. Spikes showed up tomorrow and that I was useless if I was underfoot. I politely responded, "Yes, ma'am," and took her advice. Gitta was sleeping when I walked up, so I sat down, leaned on her cage and the wall behind me, and promptly went to sleep. I guess our two-day scouting foray had worn me out more than I knew.

Dusty came around at 5:00 p.m. and woke me up in time to go back to the inn where I slept soundly until the next morning. But oh, the dreams I had! They were repeated run-ins with the black-haired angel followed by intense scolding from Casey. It wasn't my best night.

DAY THREE 10:00 A.M.

When Lt. Col. Spikes and Captain Yamata showed up at 9:00 a.m., the unit was ready. They were not ready for Lt. Cosic who this time accompanied the Commander and seemed to be right at home. I was carrying the wakizashi blade tucked into my belt, which Captain Yamata noticed immediately. He acknowledged it with a slight lift of the corners of his mouth. Nevertheless, snappy salutes were given all around along with big grins and whoops as Dusty broke out her donuts, this time with one extra. I knew it was intended for Gitta since no one anticipated Lt. Cosic's arrival, so I quietly slipped mine to Gitta when I thought no one was looking. I forgot that Dusty had radar eyes and ears. I was surprised when she later whispered to me that tomorrow there would be a small package for me but not to share it or tell anyone.

As before, the Major asked me to sit in with the officers for their morning briefing. Lt. Col. Spikes informed us that he had two important items to cover before we had a full unit meeting. The first was the impending promotion of Lt. Cosic to Captain, an event that would happen within the week. With that came his pending assignment to replace Major Ludlow who had been killed in the Quarry Cave assault in Ohio. Each of us brightened considerably at the news. All of us then took a moment to shake Cosic's hand and congratulate him before Lt. Col. Spikes addressed the second item.

We were going after a Pale Were, he said. We were going to mount a raid against the second-largest known concentration of Werewolves in the North Carolina–Virginia area so we might capture one of the Were leaders. We were to get the intelligence we needed to stop the supposed mass raid on Appalachian State students timed for July's full moon. He wanted to take two Weres if we could, but we must have one. He said I had to live through it for the follow-on interrogation. "Consequently, Cody," he said as he turned and looked at me, "will have no part in the active hostilities. You will be there," he told me, "but at the rear away from what they expect to be the center of fighting."

I was also to have an escort squad with me at all times, much as the Major had first organized when the full Rat's Nest team had come to Ohio.

This was serious stuff, Spikes reminded everyone. We could expect deaths, probably substantial, but we had no other source of intelligence except a Pale Were and no other plan except a full-scale assault supporting a covert snatch-and-grab operation. Our faces went from eager anticipation to sober reflection. A soldier not only knows that his or her objective is peace but that peace always comes at a cost, usually measured in human life.

We all just sat back a little stunned as Lt. Col. Spikes looked at each one of us in turn to see how we had digested his announcement. When he was satisfied that we'd had a chance to kick it around in our minds a bit, he broke the silence by asking us what we would each need in order to accomplish the objective. We all started in at once, and two hours later, he had the outline of the mission plan. I'd had the least to say but was adamant that Gitta would be part of my guard, a choice Captain Yamata was uneasy about because he wanted her with his unit until he realized he had no control of her without me. And I as a frontline Yamata soldier just wasn't going to happen on this raid per Lt. Col. Spikes.

The target area was Mt. Rogers, almost 50 miles northwest of Boone. It was just across the Virginia border. It was a remote and little-traveled area of the state whether one approached it from the Virginia or North Carolina side. The assault team would come in from the Virginia side. The small snatch-and-grab raiding party would come in from the south, the North Carolina side. Lt. Col. Spikes, Yamata, and Cosic would lead the assault teams. Major Sanchez would lead and I would be with the covert unit coming in from the south.

Light observation aircraft with hand-operated cameras had been filming the area for weeks. The planes and helicopters were marked as geological survey support aircraft. Infrared photography was recently employed at night. The intelligence analysts at the Pentagon pinpointed two nearby areas where bipeds were gathering and from which groups were occasionally dispersed. Estimates of enemy strength went from 75 to 90 fighting males in a total population of 250 Weres or more.

The ground terrain was steep hills with known caves in the area. There were no major water sources close by. The area was heavily forested, accessible only by foot. A five- to eight-mile march from either direction, north or south, would be required. The units would have four days of rations and supplies. We would plan for one day in with reconnaissance, 24 hours fighting, and 36 hours more to egress to the south. An additional 12 hours of leeway time would be allowed for travel in or out or for mop-up fighting as the situation might require.

Werewolf casualties would be burned or destroyed by demolition charges. No recognizable remains were to be found after we left the area. Limited helicopter evacuation for human dead or wounded would be available for a 36-hour window. Three advance reconnaissance teams would be deployed starting a week before. Army Special Forces units from Ft. Benning, Georgia, would comprise these elements as well as the nucleus of the snatch-and-grab covert team augmented by Rat's Nest personnel. The operation would be named Pale Horse after the last of the Four Horsemen of the Apocalypse. Death rode a pale horse in the scriptures, and that's what this raid would bring. Its intent was to capture a Pale Werewolf and permanently cripple the fighting capabilities of this particular pocket of Weres.

We finished our officers meeting at noon. Dusty had sandwiches brought in for the whole unit. I took mine outside and sat with Gitta against the north wall of the Chapel.

It took me about 30 minutes between mouthfuls to explain the general plan to Gitta and to get her buy-in. The prospect of a hunt for Weres always excited her. She did not fear as we did, but she recognized a dangerous threat. Nevertheless, she felt confident in her capabilities to defend herself against the Weres and, when necessary, protect me as well.

What she didn't have was a lot of confidence in my ability to go in with any degree of stealth, given my dependence on my braces. I told her I would practice every day without them in order to strengthen my legs and improve my skills. But I would take the braces in with us anyway should the need arise. That brightened up her countenance considerably, especially when I gave her the Twinkie Dusty had brought for her. We both chewed in silence for a few minutes until I had to go back in for the unit briefing at 1:00 p.m. Lt. Col. Spikes had said that Clarion might attend. I didn't want to miss him. Things happened when Clarion showed up. Interesting things.

DAY THREE 2:00 P.M.

We were 30 minutes into Lt. Col. Spikes's unit briefing when I heard the Chapel door open quietly, and Clarion stepped in. As one of the taller males, I was standing behind everyone else near Dusty's desk. Without any formal ado, Clarion walked over to me and, after a quick handshake, folded his arms and stood beside me as Spikes continued, acknowledging Clarion's presence only by a slight nod of his head. When the briefing and follow-on questions concluded, Lt. Col. Spikes made his way over to us. He shook Clarion's hand and disappeared with him into Major Sanchez's office and closed the door. I was sitting with Major Sanchez when Clarion and Spikes finally came out of the Major's office. Clarion walked over to the Major, shook her hand, and greeted Captain Yamata and Lt. Cosic, congratulating the latter on his pending promotion and new assignment. He then turned to me. He asked how I liked the new horn bow and if I would give him a demonstration if I had time. I said yes, of course. I turned to walk back to my cubicle and gather my weapons when he stopped me. He bent forward and looked closely at the wakizashi blade in my belt. Standing erect again, he said it was beautiful and well won. He shook my hand again. He said he'd wait for me at the front doors and asked if he could meet Gitta before we started the demonstration. I was pleased that he knew of her and wanted to meet her. I said yes, of course. I wasted no time retrieving the horn bow. As we stepped out on the porch, he asked if he might examine it and if I would explain its advantages and disadvantages. I did. When he was satisfied, we went back to meet Gitta.

Gitta was already waiting for us on top of her cage when we walked up. Clarion stood back from me as I approached her. I told her of his importance to both our futures. She peered around me to look at him and then asked if his importance meant she couldn't eat him. I started laughing at that, and she snorted (laughed). It was as close to a laugh as a wolverine can get. Clarion asked what had just transpired. When I told him, he burst out laughing on his own. I then invited him forward to meet her. He walked up boldly, nodded his head, and slowly raised his arm so he might scratch behind her ears. Gitta fell for his overture like a ton of bricks. She waddled closer, sniffed him here and there, and then smiled at him with those beautiful death teeth she possessed.

Clarion didn't even flinch. He leaned forward, raked his fingers up and down her back, and smiled right back at her with his biggest grin. She snorted and pushed her forehead into his stomach. Then she flopped down and rolled over like a satisfied dog. But before he could scratch her stomach and sides, she quickly reversed herself. She bared her teeth and growled her Werewolf growl in a decibel range that even scared me. Clarion leaped back. As soon as he did so, she stopped and, folding her legs in front of her, dropped to the cage top and rested her head on her arms, silently watching him.

"What just happened?" asked Clarion, confused by her conflicting behavior. I spoke with Gitta a moment and started laughing. "She wanted to remind you that while you're the titular boss, hence her rollover, she's still an independent contractor in this endeavor and very much her own woman." Clarion started laughing again and told me I truly had an original here and not to mess her up. He was just sad that she wasn't human so he could put her on his staff, because a woman in that day and age who could think and act for herself, an independent woman, wasn't really appreciated very much. Nevertheless, they usually proved to be more valuable than gold. The best examples he could think of were the Major and Dusty, and Casey who had been at my side throughout the Ohio terrors.

The visit with Gitta concluded. We spent the next hour running through both the competition and hunter's courses. Clarion walked the entire course with me alongside Gitta, occasionally bending over to scratch her as they waited for me to retrieve an arrow. It was a pleasurable hour and time well spent since Clarion had funded Gitta's acquisition and our mutual upkeep. So far, at least, he thought he was making a wise investment. Gitta and I would not prove him wrong.

DAY THREE 5:30 P.M.

Clarion's business with me was over, and Gitta had returned to her cage. I stored my bow and quiver of arrows back in my cubicle and was walking out the door when Pee Wee stopped me. He asked if I might like to come to dinner at the Walksabout home that evening. Michael wanted to meet me, and Pee Wee would introduce me to his niece. Since she was a second-year student at Lees-McRae, perhaps she might be able to answer some of the inevitable questions a prospective student like me might have about registration and start-up campus activities.

I accepted immediately. I left to go back to my room to freshen up and change clothes. I asked if slacks and a shirt were okay. He said that would be fine. I also asked what sort of flowers Mrs. Walksabout liked so I might bring a gift as was customary where I was raised. He thought a minute and then advised me to bring daffodils, a mountain flower liked by all Native Americans. He said he'd pick me up at 7:45 p.m. at the inn. "Just be yourself," he remarked. "You'll do fine."

We arrived at the Walksabout home precisely at 8:00 p.m. I followed Pee Wee to the door. I greeted both Mr. and Mrs. Walksabout there. She accepted my flowers. She remarked that my mother must be very proud of me for my manners. I said no, not particularly, but she would beat me to a nubbin if I forgot what she'd so painfully taught me. I said it with a smile, and everyone laughed. Then Mr. Walksabout ushered me in, and I met Michael. He was walking with a cane and a leg brace, the type I recognized. I, too, had worn that type for several years.

I knelt down and examined the brace when I felt someone behind me. I assumed it was his sister but deliberately pretended I was not aware of her presence. I asked Michael if this brace fit to his satisfaction. He replied not quite, so I showed him how I had taken mine apart and learned the secret of proper adjustment. I pulled out my Swiss pocketknife and spent the next five minutes adjusting his brace until it felt perfect. He grabbed my hand and shook it furiously for a second or two and then asked me to turn around and meet his sister.

I steeled myself to meet what I thought to be a vanilla ice-cream cone and turned only to drop my jaw at what was the whole ice cream soda standing before me. It was the girl who had decked me the day before. She echoed my astonishment. She stood speechless in like amazement, neither of us knowing what to say. Her parents and Pee Wee picked up on the awkwardness immediately. They looked at each of us in a curious fashion. Michael, standing to the side and watching this tableau unfold before him, asked if something was wrong or if we already knew each other. Sunstar and I began to speak simultaneously. Our words tumbled out faster than their meanings. Both of us immediately backed away, each from the other. I stumbled into Michael while she tripped over her dad's foot, and three of us ended up on the floor. Sunstar scrambled to pull her dress down a bit for she was showing far too much leg for her comfort (far too little for mine). I tried to scramble off poor Michael before I smothered him.

Suddenly, both Sunstar and I recognized how ridiculous the situation was. Both of us started to laugh. I managed to roll off Michael. He started laughing with us. Then Pee Wee and Sunstar's parents started laughing as well, although they probably had no idea what was so funny. That would come later over dinner as Sunstar described our first meeting and her first impression of me.

I cannot to this day remember what Mrs. Walksabout served for dinner. I can only remember that she apparently suffered fools gladly as I spent the majority of the evening a bit shy, tongue-tied, and even reticent to answer the normal questions that came my way because I was so enamored with Sunstar. I felt guilty. Even Casey had not affected me this way, and Casey was my touchstone to the wonderful world of women. Casey was the standard by which I measured women, an honor Dusty and one other would also acquire at a later date.

Pee Wee and I said our good nights to the Walksabout family on their front doorstep at around 10:00 p.m. Both of us were full from Mrs. Walksabout's insistence that we eat at least two helpings of whatever she was serving. I shook hands goodbye with everyone. I probably held Sunstar's hand a bit too long, but I noticed she wasn't fighting me to get it back either. I smiled at her and asked if I might call her sometime if I had a question about Lees-McRae, of course. She returned my smile. She said she would like that, especially since she was part of the student welcoming committee and took her duties seriously. I didn't know if she was pulling my leg, but I really didn't care. I would use practically any blatant excuse to spend some more time with her. There was just something about Sunstar that made the world seem right.

Pee Wee watched me with amusement and then grabbed my arm and dragged me away before I could say goodbye all over again. I thanked him in the car on the way back to the inn.

It was a night to remember, and remember I did, for years, usually because Sunstar brought it up again and again. She never failed to find the story immensely amusing, especially the part where she got to tell her family how she had knocked me to my knees with the aluminum water bowl. It hurts even now to remember that part of the episode.

DAY FOUR 7:30 A.M.

I'd been out on the competition range for about 45 minutes when the Major drove up. She parked and, seeing me on the range, walked over to say good morning. "Great! You're here early, Cody," she said. "How are you feeling? Dusty said you had a small accident at Lees-McRae when you were there. I'm glad to see it doesn't affect your aim. Looks like you and the horn bow are becoming well acquainted. Come on back to the Chapel. I've got some arrows we want you to try out. They'll be carrying liquid, only an ounce or two, but the shafts have an opening where a membrane holds back the liquid. We want to see how each arrow's trajectory is affected by both distance and speed."

Curious to see what the Major had put together, I followed her back to the Chapel. Holding the door for her, I followed her into her office. On top lay an elongated box that, when opened, contained five arrows matched for the horn bow. Each arrow had a small, one-inch opening about a quarter inch back from the arrow's barbed head. Inside was a fluid held in check by a thin membrane. It looked like someone had stuffed a very small, partially filled balloon into the opening and then let it expand back to its normal size. Once inside the small opening, the balloon's expanded size made it impossible for it to fall out.

I asked what the arrow was for. I was told the final version, provided these test models proved out, would contain a highly concentrated narcotic designed to render a Werewolf unconscious in literally seconds. The drug had been successfully tested on the captured Were back in the containment facility at the Chagrin Falls Polo Club. What the government didn't have was a tested and true delivery-system-at-a-distance, hence my use of the horn bow. A small, wire-thin plunger ran back from the broadhead tip inside the shaft to the balloon's compartment. On impact the wire was driven backward into the balloon, causing the balloon to burst and the fluid to flow out into the targeted creature. What I was looking at were the initial prototypes. An order of 100 such arrows would be prepared as soon as the final design was approved. That would occur only after a successful test of the delivery system.

I took the arrows, excused myself, and spent the next three hours testing them on both the competition course and the hunter's course. Two of the five arrows performed well, and one of those two performed exceptionally well. I asked Dusty to walk the two courses with me and take measurements at each target hit. We would later average those measurements against arrows I used without the fluid. That would give us a thumbnail sketch of the altered arrow's accuracy and present the best candidate for the final lab tests and configuration changes necessary to produce a manufacturing model. The Major asked me to please hurry. It would take eight days from reaching consensus on a go-ahead design until 100 arrows could be produced and delivered back to the Rat's Nest.

"Why the rush, Major?"

"We launch Pale Horse in 12 days," she replied, "and we barely have enough time to make ready for that." She looked at me with a steady stare. I met her gaze. Then, grinning, I snatched up the two arrows and said, "Follow me."

One and a half hours later, the Major, Clarion, Lt. Col. Spikes, and Lt. Cosic were convinced that we had an arrow design that was a winner. The arrow was hand-couriered out that day to its manufacturer.

At 4:30 p.m., I asked the Major if I might drive over to Lees-McRae and the Wildlife Institute's Rehabilitation Center. I wanted to visit with Polaris again. She asked if my timing might be a little off because they would be feeding the animals about the time I got there. I assured her I would be no bother but wanted to see Polaris's fitness for myself and learn what therapy had been recommended. I wanted to learn as well if they had been diligent about practicing it.

She looked at me for a long 30 seconds. With a hint of a smile at her mouth, she asked who was providing therapy to the falcon. I blushed a moment. I confessed that it might well be Pee Wee's young niece, but I still needed to see if she was as good as they said she was, and who better to tell me than the Princess Falcon herself!

Her smile broke the surface. She told me to go on and get out of there, that she had enough to deal with prior to launching Pale Horse without having to try to cap episodic outbursts of testosterone as well. I heard Dusty laugh behind me as I stepped quickly to the door. Since my back was turned, I was glad she couldn't see my blush as well. It was true. I was hoping Sunstar would be there. She was a healer, and Polaris did need help whether she agreed to help us or not. But this new feeling I had was uncharted territory for me. I had never been interested in anyone but Casey. I wasn't even sure how I felt about Sunstar. I did know that just holding her hand to say goodbye the night before had put a simple touch in a whole new dimension, one that felt a whole lot better than just good. My driving time to Banner Elk and the school's Rehabilitation Center was remarkably fast. After all, I didn't want to get there after they closed. What would be the point of that?

DAY FOUR 5:15 P.M.

Shortly after arriving at the Rehabilitation Center, I managed to find guest parking. I rushed back to the BRWI's open cage area. I think that took more time than the drive over. Polaris was in her cage, but Sunstar was not anywhere around. It was just as well. I really didn't want anyone to know of my talent at this juncture. Sunstar's absence gave me a chance for privacy I'd been almost too afraid to hope for. Consequently, I presented myself once again to Polaris and inquired about her health and recovery. Our conversation went from polite to serious almost immediately. Most animals have little use for small talk, but there are pleasantries to be observed when an animal is royalty.

Those pleasantries aside, we then discussed her recovery (remarkable because of the human woman known as Sunstar), how she obtained her injury (attacking a weasel), and the duration and reason for her flight to North Carolina (long flight, new horizons while young). She remained intrigued with me and the idea that different species could communicate. The gift must be there for a useful purpose, she thought. Otherwise, it was an inelegant breach of nature. In her experience, nature rarely breached anything. Therefore, it must be a good thing. I assured her it was. It could also be made better if two or more species could reach common ground to act on a hidden or long-forbidden common threat such as the Werewolves.

That seemed logical to her. The Princess was nothing if not logical. After a discussion of some length on a wide variety of things, she surprised me by saying she would commit to working with me and my team as soon as she was able. If her progress to date was any indication, that should be within a span of several suns (days). I wanted to shout hooray out loud but decided against it. I started to congratulate her when Polaris's head suddenly snapped up and she made an effort to peer around me.

Quickly she hobbled to the forepart of the large cage and gave a shrill greeting treasured by all falcons but sends chills down the back of every small bird within hearing distance. I spun around to see who the intruder was when Sunstar appeared carrying two bowls, one with food and one with water. As she looked up and saw me, she quickly paused, uncertain as to what to do next. I smiled at her and stepped way back, greeting her and telling her I would honor a 10-foot no-standing-near radius until she got the bowls into Polaris's cage.

She laughed. Stepping forward, she quickly completed her assignment. She asked if I was following her. I told her if I had any sense, I would, but in this case, absolutely not, especially since I had been at the cage first. However, if she felt someone was endangering her, might I be the first to offer my services as a faithful if not always available guard. I then did my best Prince Charming bow. I looked up to see her give a quick curtsy and then start laughing gaily at our exchange.

I took the liberty to approach her. Taking her hand, I shook it softly and then let it go. That corny maneuver allowed me to at least step up beside her. Although I still felt self-conscious, we were off to a much better start than our first meeting. We visited casually for a few minutes while Polaris made quick work of her meal. At first glance, it looked to be comprised of slightly mangled mice. Polaris watched my face as I surveyed the food bowl's contents, but I never flinched. After what I had seen Gitta do to live food, this was a tea party.

Sunstar and I spoke for almost an hour. We retired early on to sit on a rock wall near Polaris's cage that helped define the outside cage area border. Mostly we talked about school, what I could expect at Lees-McRae, some of the good and bad, classes and teachers, what social life was like, and the activities I could sign up for, especially outside or mountain-based activities. Each of us was getting a general sense of who the other person was and some of their particular likes and dislikes. It was an easy, entirely unforced conversation. I decided that Sunstar would be a good friend to have. Certainly I wanted the opportunity to date her, but that was down the line. It seemed we did have one common, pressing interest: getting Polaris well.

She inquired about my interest in falcons. I gave her a general outline of what my summer intern job was (geologic survey), my career desire (veterinary medicine), and my personal interests (archery, backpacking, and falconry). I also explained that I was still recovering from an automobile accident that happened when I was 10 years old. Fortunately, almost all feeling had returned to my legs. While I could move about rather well, I was still awkward in rough terrain and fell down occasionally, to my embarrassment.

She didn't laugh at me or toss off my comments as inconsequential. That really impressed me. Instead, she asked detailed questions about my treatments and exercises and the medicines I had taken to help me. She said she was very good at making age-old potions, unguents, and ointments from plants. She used recipes that had been passed down from generation to generation among her mother's people. The recipes often actually worked better than modern medicines.

She was especially pleased at her brother's progress. He'd responded far better than the doctors had originally told him to expect, only because of her potions, not their Western medicines. What little of that they thought appropriate for him sometimes wasn't. She had been working with the falcon but working in the dark, as it were, because there was no shaman to interpret for her. She didn't know what the falcon thought or how her salves and potions worked with it. It just appeared better. Nevertheless, she knew appearances could be deceiving.

I studied her for a long time and then made a choice. It wasn't one the Major would have approved of, but it was my life, my talent, and my judgment at stake. So I took a chance on Sunstar and on me. I carefully explained to her that I had been given a unique gift, that of being a Gatekeeper, a person who could communicate with animals. For example, the falcon wasn't an *it*; it was a *she*, a princess without a name. I had given her the name Polaris. I named her after a star, the North Star, a royal name such as every princess should have.

The implications weren't lost on Sunstar. She blushed when she heard my explanation. She beamed as bright as Dusty when I went on to ask her solemn promise that she would reveal nothing to anyone except perhaps her uncle Pee Wee. I further explained that he knew generally of my talents and was teaching me woodscraft, tracking, and the wisdom of the forest as part of my assignment. Her eyes grew big at that. Tears started up when she realized the trust Pee Wee must have in me to share his secrets. Her arm suddenly shot out as she grabbed my arm and, in whispered tones, asked if I knew of the Uge-wan-si, the shape-shifter of the forests who were a cross between humans and certain animals, creatures that killed those who traveled into certain forbidden areas of these forests. I saw she was dead serious. I told her I did know of them. I said I had killed several by bow and one by blade. I said the knowledge of these creatures was purposefully being withheld from the country's population at large for fear of riots and slaughter. I also told her I knew they were in these forests because I had Gitta. Gitta was the Hungarian name for my strong wolverine. Gitta was housed at one of the old cemetery Chapels in Blowing Rock. Gitta was my hunting companion and my friend. Our hope was that Polaris would join us to give us the air cover needed to avoid Uge-wan-si ambushes when our surveys took us into these forbidden forest areas of which she had spoken.

She asked if she could meet Gitta sometime, perhaps by coming over at lunchtime when Pee Wee and I might be free. I hemmed and hawed. I tried to slide away from her questions, but that only increased her curiosity. I promised I'd check with my boss and get back to her. With that, I excused myself, said goodbye to Polaris with a bow, got a bow in return, made my way back to my car, and drove on up to Blowing Rock. I felt both elated and apprehensive.

I was elated that Sunstar and I shared such common interests and even a secret among her people and mine. I felt apprehensive because I had come perilously close to blowing my cover by explaining my talent and by my admission to Sunstar that I had killed Uge-wan-si. We both knew they were real, but she had never seen one. I certainly didn't want her to. No one should have to look at those creatures except maybe on a burn pile.

I would find out on the morrow if I had overstepped myself and what, if anything, the Major would have to say to me.

DAY FIVE 9:00 A.M.

It had been a tough hour in the Major's office. I learned I was not especially excited about closed-door, one-on-one meetings with one's superior, especially if that superior had a flat tire on their way to work and was slightly greasy and tired from changing it. I learned not only to pick your battles but to pick the time and terrain as well. It was a lasting lesson, but I was grinning when I emerged.

Dusty was hard at work on something at her desk when I walked out. She never looked up as I walked back to my cubicle. I was grateful for her discretion or her workload, whatever. The Major was very upset with me at first when I related yesterday's happenings to her, taking me to task for what could have been and was perilously close to being a breach of security. Neither her irritation nor her remarks to me were unreasonable, but she was persistent and kept making the same points over and over only with different variations.

I finally had the temerity to respond. I reminded her that I had come to her for advice, that I was aware I was close to the edge, but that there were some very strong mitigating factors at play to which she had given no credence. I pointed out that Sunstar herself was a keeper of secrets, that there was no way I could ignore her given our mutual class interests and her family connections through Pee Wee, that she was directly involved with the falcon we were attempting to employ against a mutually known enemy we called Werewolves and she and her people called Uge-wan-si or shape-shifters, and that her potion talents could be of direct benefit to us or the research going on at the containment facility if we brought her onto our team.

I used several other arguments as well, but the Major got the picture. Eventually, she said she would explore that last possibility but wanted to check with Pee Wee first.

She reminded me that she was aware that I was an adult and could think for myself. In that case, it looked like I did while still keeping the unit's mission and aim foremost in my mind. She said she trusted me. She therefore trusted I would make decisions worthy of that faith, that she didn't like where she thought this would go at first but that my arguments and reasons had changed her mind. So, would I now please get out of her office and go practice so she could talk to Pee Wee?

It was my first real confrontation with authority. I had been passionate but nervous. Still, reason and calm had carried the day. Like Captain Yamata had told me, "Use your anger and fear to work with you, not against you." I rounded up Gitta and went for an exploratory hike on the mountain behind the Chapel, the back nine as Pee Wee called it. I carried my wakizashi in my belt and a javelin in my hand. One never knows what might come calling, and I wanted something deadly if it was Uge-wan-si.

We got back to the Rat's Nest about 12:30 p.m., both of us a little tired and hungry. I left Gitta at her cage and drove into Blowing Rock for some fast food. I only had two choices. Blowing Rock was not a major way station in the commerce of the United States, but it was close to an entrance on the famed Blue Ridge Parkway. A goodly share of tourists and truck drivers usually made their way through the town, enough to support two fast-food eateries at least.

I had just settled into my seat at a table for two when I saw Michael walk in with his cane. He had no sooner taken his place in line when two fellows a bit bigger than him walked in. They were pushing each other and making some noise as good old boys are wont to do in North Carolina. Their antics got a bit more boisterous while they were waiting in line. Finally, one pushed the other into Michael who went sprawling onto the floor. They turned and gave him a casual glance. They saw he was okay enough to try to stand up. They immediately ignored him and went back to their self-absorbed pushing game. I sighed and put my sandwich down. I stepped over to help Michael up, brushed him off, and then pushed the back of the fellow standing next to me. Hard.

He went plowing into his friend, his forehead clipping his friend's chin, and both of them went sprawling. We'd drawn a small crowd by this time. The manager was starting to dial his phone, his eyes about as big as quarters. I motioned him to stop. I bent over to pull first the one and then the second fellow to their feet. I brushed them off and apologized for the accident but that my friend, pointing to Michael, had pushed me like they had and I'd lost my balance. "My bad," I said contritely, and then smiled and held out my hand. "No hard feelings, I hope? Let me buy you a coke or something as a way to apologize."

They were unsure how to respond until the manager caught on and said out loud, "Good choice, guys. What'll it be?" At that, distracted, with a crowd looking on and probably not really ready for a fight, the guys both selected a soda and reluctantly shook my hand. Then they turned away and started talking quietly to themselves.

I stepped up to Michael and mentioned that he sure spent a lot of time on the floor when I was around. I asked if he was tired of that. I said, "How about joining me at my table when you get your order?"

Michael and I spent the better part of the next hour visiting with each other. We had a common bond immediately because of his accident and braces. I didn't ask him one question about his sister. I didn't know what Pee Wee's decision would be about her. I wanted to keep a respectful distance from the Walksabout family until I could see which way the wind blew. But Michael and I really connected. He was adamant about becoming a vet. He had his career path all planned out.

I shared with him that I, too, wanted that same profession but that I planned to get a military commission to help pay for my schooling. He bombarded me with dozens of questions about Ohio. He really wanted to see parts of the United States, and from my descriptions of Chagrin Falls, he wanted to start there. Eventually, I bade him good day and headed back to the Chapel. I had some ideas about a kind of body armor that might work in a Were encounter. I wanted to share them with Sergeant Saddler.

Pee Wee was waiting to see me when I returned. The Major had gone to an appointment. We settled by Gitta's cage where we would have some privacy. I expected a little anger that I'd involved his niece somehow with our doings when he never had. I got an enthusiastic "let's do it" response instead. Pee Wee was particularly caught up in my argument that Sunstar's potions and natural herb remedies could definitely help those who had just been bitten. Especially, he thought, if they had not yet fully turned. He said the Major had given clearance to have Sunstar come over tomorrow so the Major and Lt. Col. Spikes could personally brief her. She was to meet Gitta as well. We—Pee Wee and I—would be part of her briefing.

Pee Wee then reentered the Chapel and told me to get my bow and arrows. We were going out on a deer hunting expedition for Gitta's sake. I would do the tracking under Pee Wee's oversight. He said we had two hours to bag game. If I failed, I would have to wear a pair of Mickey Mouse ears for 24 hours wherever I went. If I were successful, Pee Wee would buy my next tank of gas. I laughed and told him it was a deal.

That night when I went to bed, I caught a glimpse of myself in the mirror. I stopped, looked again, and smiled. I thought the round Mickey Mouse ears looked pretty good on me from just the right angle.

DAY SIX 8:00 A.M.

I'd been at the competition range for a good 45 minutes when Pee Wee arrived for work. He wandered over and complimented me on the ears that adorned my head. I laughed and said they hadn't affected my balance. I promptly put another arrow into the bull's-eye of the target before me. Pee Wee said he appreciated that I'd been a good sport about losing the wager and then asked for the ears back. I reminded him that the 24 hours weren't over yet. He reminded me that his niece would be along at about 10:00 a.m. He wanted me looking my best. Besides, he said, he had an idea he wanted to try out in the woods. The ears would probably be lost or damaged as I bumbled my way around. I surrendered them with a rousing "Hooray!" and went to get Gitta. I felt she was probably getting restless by then anyway.

I met Pee Wee at the entrance to the hunter's course. He appeared with a sack over his shoulder. Laying the sack on the ground, he opened it and produced a crossbow. It was about two and a half feet long. Its bow span was just over two feet. With it he produced seven bolts (arrows) of just more than 10 inches in length. Each was about half as thick as the horn bow's arrows. He wanted me to try to use the crossbow. His reasoning was that stalking in thick woods probably made it difficult for me to fully engage the horn bow whose best kill distance was 40 to 50 yards. The crossbow was designed to kill at 15 to 25 yards. In his opinion, that was the likely effective distance of any shot in thick woods.

I looked at the apparatus for a few minutes and turned my gaze back to Pee Wee. I told him my dad had taught me to be from the if-it-ain't-broke-don't-fix-it school. I had some real reservations about switching to a new weapons system before a major engagement. I suggested instead a test. Both of us would walk through any patch of woods at his choice, and I would fire only on targets he identified. We would shoot twice. He would likely be the first to fire, of course, since he was choosing the target, but we each had to fire twice. We would do this 10 times or until he lost all the bolts.

Pee Wee bridled a bit at that and then accepted my challenge. He loaded the cross bow while I strung my horn bow, and then we set off. Gitta was an interested follower. When I explained what we were doing and that we would need her help to find Pee Wee's lost bolts, she snorted and stepped up to the challenge. She moved to a position right behind Pee Wee, the better to follow the bolt's flight, she told me, hoping she could see what he was aiming at each time he fired. We weren't even out an hour when Pee Wee gave up on his idea. He gathered the three remaining bolts Gitta had found and walked back disconsolately to the Rat's Nest. I tagged along behind. I tried to lift his spirits by thanking him for his idea and concern. I pointed out that even though he usually fired faster than I did when he shouted out a target, I not only hit more often with my first arrow than he did but nailed it with my second arrow while he was still fumbling to load his second bolt.

It was a good exercise since it gave us both a bit more confidence in my ability to use the horn bow in difficult forest situations. My only regret was that I didn't place a staggering bet with him before we started the exercise. I would not have been as merciful as he had been earlier with me. We were needed back at the Rat's Nest by 9:45 a.m. anyway for whatever instructions the Major wanted to give us prior to Sunstar's visit.

Sunstar arrived promptly at 9:55 a.m. just to make sure she was on time. It was a small thing that both the Major and Lt. Col. Spikes noted with approval. It showed her respect for herself and them. It also demonstrated she could plan for traffic, for contingencies, and for anything else unforeseen that might have delayed her. Promptness is a sign of maturity whether in civilian or military environments. Sunstar was all of that and more as her carriage and conduct constantly demonstrated. She carried with her a long, black bag that she placed against the front porch wall of the Chapel as she greeted us.

Following introductions and greetings all around, I went off to find Sergeant Saddler to talk about some ideas I had for lightweight partial body armor against the Weres. Sunstar disappeared into the Rat's Nest with the Major and Lt. Col. Spikes. Pee Wee also disappeared inside, presumably going back to his desk or downstairs to the armory. I would see Sunstar again at 11:00 a.m. when we had scheduled a walkthrough of the hunter's course with Gitta.

I found Sergeant Saddler at our Motor Pool garage. It was a small Quonset hut scavenged from some derelict pile at a former military base. The hut could enclose three vehicles. It sat about 100 yards away from the Chapel but not in plain sight. Instead, the hut was placed in a small cove of trees shielded from sight from both the Chapel and the nearby cemetery. We had two trucks and two station wagon cars assigned to the Rat's Nest, both of which were normally parked and given light maintenance there. Sergeant Saddler was a stickler for performance, often coaxing more out of our vehicles than (I thought) the designers intended. He was a mechanical magician in many ways and was valued for that and much more besides. It was the *besides* part of his talents that prompted me to share my ideas with him.

I told him that in my limited experience, the two most vulnerable human body points in a Werewolf attack were the person's forearms and upper back and neck. It was the forearms because in a frontal attack, humans would raise their arms first to shield themselves from a body blow or swinging claws. Conversely, when the Weres attacked from behind, they would often go for the human's exposed neck or slash at his upper back and shoulder region. The Weres almost always chose to attack this way because of their height and physiology.

My plan was to arm our soldiers in thick leather cylinders that stretched from the wrist to the elbow, either tied or snapped on, a gauntlet as it were such as archers often wore to protect their inner forearm from the powerful slap of the bowstring against their tender flesh. The second armor was a modified canvas pack, perhaps with an internal heavy leather reinforcement sewn in, that could be worn with a slight neck extension that might shield against all but a determined bite or slashing claw when a Were attacked first from the rear. We drew patterns and discussed several off-the-shelf defenses until I had to excuse myself and return to the Chapel for my appointment with Sunstar. Sergeant Saddler had a quirky smile on his face when I left, staring at our drawing and already bending to make erasures and changes as he got into the idea.

DAY SIX 11:00 A.M.

I was waiting impatiently on the Chapel porch when the Major brought Sunstar outside. Dusty trailed along behind. Dusty's smile was big. That meant a good day for whoever entered her orbit. Sunstar was also smiling, albeit a more subdued smile than Dusty's or the Major's. The Major turned Sunstar over to me. She said she'd asked Dusty to accompany us around the course. Both the Major and Dusty smiled mischievously as they noted the look of irritation that quickly flitted across my face, but I bit my lip and muttered, "Great!" I picked up the horn bow and my quiver. Sunstar brought the long, cylindrical black bag she'd previously parked at the porch wall. I was curious to know what was in it, but I held my tongue as we walked around the building to Gitta's cage. Gitta was sitting atop her cage in a sleeping attitude, but one eye opened as we came around the corner of the Chapel. I gently took Sunstar's arm and with her at my side walked up to Gitta. I formally introduced the two. At that point, Gitta stood up on her four feet, dipped her head in a regal bow, and raised it again. She looked squarely at Sunstar and grinned, exposing those deadly white teeth accompanied by a contented hum.

Sunstar curtsied nicely, dipped her head, and stood up again. Then, taking a step closer to Gitta, Sunstar turned to me and said that now she understood what I meant when I said Gitta was among the most beautiful creatures I had ever seen. Gitta looked to me for a translation. When I gave it to her, she walked to the cage's edge and, extending her head, softly placed it against Sunstar's stomach and gently pushed. It was her special, intimate "handshake" given to very, very few.

Sunstar seemed delighted. Without prompting or a heads-up to me, she stepped forward and placed her arms around Gitta and sang a soft Cherokee tune as she rubbed her head against Gitta's powerful neck and shoulders. Gitta slowly sank down and crossed her forelegs under her. She closed her eyes and seemed to sleep as the melody softly dropped out of my hearing range. When she was finished, Sunstar stood back up and said we could go to the range now. Gitta would sleep for a while with pleasant dreams to keep her company.

I was dumbfounded. I had never seen or heard of that being done to any animal, much less one with whom I was familiar. I started to say something out loud, but Sunstar quickly placed her fingers lightly over my mouth and whispered, "No, Cody.

Don't speak." Then she grabbed my hand and led me away. Dusty just stood there, mouth open, and then started to grin the mother of all grins. "Oh boy!" I heard her say to herself. "Cody, my boy, you are in trouble!" And her grin broke into a defiant smile that seemed to grow larger with each step toward the range.

Upon arriving, I found out what was in the black bag. Dusty already knew. When Sunstar unzipped it, out tumbled a bow and a quiver of steel-point arrows, not broadheads I was used to using to kill Weres. I asked Sunstar where the archery set came from. She said it was her own. She had been shooting for a number of years. She was currently on the Lees-McRae mixed team. In fact, she was number two on the team behind a senior, Bob Moore. The team included two other archers, a Russian exchange student named Ivan Thortonsky and Judi Mason, a Texas student interested in animal husbandry and ranching.

"Is the team any good?" I asked. "Have you all won any meets, or do you actually go to meets? What do you have to do to be on the team? Can new students join as well? Could I try out for the team? Did you know I was state champion back in Ohio? You can shoot with me here at the competition course anytime, that is if the Major permits it. Are you going to shoot with me now?" The questions and comments seemed to just tumble out of me as I tried to understand how this good fortune could come to me. Of all her talents, this one made me almost dizzy with expectation. I babbled like a five-year old as I tried to come to grips with the reality of Sunstar's talent.

Dusty was kind enough to come to my aid. She had discovered that Sunstar was a very competent archer when she did some background checking on her prior to this visit. She and the Major thought it would be fun to play a joke on me. They deliberately withheld the information, hoping I would have just the reaction I did. Dusty couldn't wait to tell the Major, but before leaving, she told me to take Sunstar through the course on my own. She had other work to do, and the Major expected her back anytime now. With that, she grinned at both of us and left.

So unnerved was I that I forgot to ask Sunstar what in heck her song to Gitta meant. Sunstar didn't seem to know a joke had been played. I wasn't going to try to explain it to her. I would probably look more foolish than I already did, so I explained the course layout instead, its purpose, and how mastering it had helped me better my efforts on the competition course. I explained that going through the course would be fun. No one would be keeping score. I, for one, wanted to study her technique and equipment if only because I might spot something that would help her improve. I wanted her to do the same for me because, as her briefing had informed her, she might be shooting for trophies, but I was shooting for lives, usually my own.

With bows strung and quivers arranged, we started through the course. She would fire on the first target, and I would have first fire on the second, and so on. We would alternate throughout the course. We would take our time. This was not a competition course but a teaching course. As such, I found myself putting some emotional distance between us in order to more fairly observe and instruct her. I realized I could not truly observe if I was firing as well, so I told Sunstar I had changed my mind and why. I invited her to start when she felt ready.

She finished in one hour and 40 minutes. She lost three arrows but scored hits on 13 of the 15 range targets then active. She scored two bull's-eyes and 11 close hits. I chose at the last minute not to shoot with her, partly so I might observe with full concentration but also in part because I did not know how she dealt with competition. I did not want her mad at me if I could help it. I was foolish to even be concerned.

She asked if she could critique me as I went through. She had plenty of time, and the Major had indicated that I had plenty of time as well. I started to decline, but she walked over, stood in front of me, and placed a hand on my shoulder while holding her bow with the other. Smiling, looking directly into my eyes, she began to sing softly to me in Cherokee. I had no idea what she was singing, but the most curious feeling started to envelop me. It was a feeling of great peace. I felt my apprehensions slipping away. Her eyes seemed to draw me in. Almost as if I were beside myself, I heard myself saying I would love it if she would walk the course with me and critique my efforts. With that, she let her hand fall away from my shoulder. She unstrung her bow, put everything back into her canvas bag, rezipped it, and, stepping to the start of the course, said brightly, "Your turn!"

I scored 15 bull's-eyes in 40 minutes. She said nothing the entire time but watched me closely, as if she were memorizing for a test so she could describe the experience in great detail when and if called upon to do so.

As we walked back up the slight hill to Gitta's cage, she broke the silence with a compliment. "I have never seen such shooting, Cody. You have a gift. There are stories among my people about warriors and even women, although only a few, who have had your gift with a bow and arrows. There are even stories about shamans who could speak with animals, but I have never heard of anyone who could do all that you do, at least not for many, many generations. I think you will be a blessing to my people and to your people, perhaps greater than they or we will ever know. Your name to me now is Awohali. It means the Eagle. You have his eyes. You see what moves below, around, and above you. Your arrows are his talons that fly straight to the target for the kill. The feathers that adorn your arrows keep them on course and help them fly true as do the feathers of the great eagle. Your bow bends like an eagle's wings, propelling the eagle to great heights, speeding its will and talons to their targets so that in them they may carry death. I am called by my father's people Dekanogi'a. The name means the Singer or Chanter. I have the healing gift. With it is the gift of calling forth help from the ancient ones. I use my songs to heal and soothe, to bring peace, to bring help and wisdom. Now that the Major and Lt. Col. Spikes have told me about you and the work you all are doing to eliminate the Uge-wan-si, I want to work with you. We can help each other. I will bring relief from the Uge-wan-si; you will bring death to them. "It is a good match, Cody. We have much to do." She smiled. "One of the first things is to get you on the Lees-McRae archery team. With you, we might just take state this year, something we have never done before."

Gitta was still sleeping as we walked up to her cage. Without pausing to wake her, we detoured around the Chapel to the front porch, Sunstar still carrying her black bag. She stopped on the porch and stood a step above me so our eyes were nearly level. Taking my hand, she thanked me again for trusting her and recommending that she become part of the Rat's Nest, whatever small part she might play. She told me she would do her best. She promised that to me again in order to emphasize her commitment.

I told her I would be at the Blue Ridge Rehabilitation Center around 5:30 p.m. and that I hoped to see her there with Polaris but would understand if her schedule didn't permit it. Her eyes twinkled as she said, "We'll see, Cody," and then she was off into the Chapel to say her goodbyes to Dusty, the Major, and Lt. Col. Spikes. I turned and walked back to the Motor Pool. I wanted to see how Sergeant Saddler had spent the day.

DAY SIX 5:45 P.M.

As I was pulling into the small parking area adjoining the Blue Ridge Rehabilitation Center, I reflected on the course of the day, my challenge to Pee Wee, the visit with Sunstar, and my conversations with Sergeant Saddler. It was the last conversation with Sergeant Saddler that really excited me. He had taken my armor suggestions seriously. He spent the better part of the afternoon designing various items that could easily be carried into a fight with the Weres. We reviewed them together just before I left for the Wildlife Rehabilitation Center. He was going to drive down to Hickory the next day to see if he could get a bootmaker to try to create a few prototypes for us. I urged him to hurry. We had a big fight approaching. I felt that anything that could cut the Weres' one-on-one advantage was important. So of course, he did.

I wandered back hoping to find Sunstar there, but no luck. I was alone for the moment. I thought Sunstar would probably not make it if she wasn't there already, so I wasted no more time. I approached Polaris's cage only to find her missing. I quickly stepped back. I looked in the other cages as well, but all were empty. Had I come to the wrong cage area? Had the birds been transferred, and if so, where? My mind was racing. I started to feel a little sick to my stomach when I heard the distant but unmistakable hunting cry of a falcon. It was Polaris.

She was telling the world she was free, unfettered, and on the hunt. I half hobbled, half ran out of the cage area to a field nearby. Several students were gathered together about 50 yards away holding the various birds. Sunstar was there with a falconer's heavy glove on her arm. All were looking skyward as Polaris wheeled and did figure eights about 800 feet in the air, scanning the field, bushes, and trees for her soon-to-be snack.

Suddenly, Polaris stood on her wing, made an impossibly tight spiral, and dropped from the sky at a 55-degree angle, aiming at a rabbit fleeing across a corner of the field. As fast as the rabbit ran, the falcon was faster. With wings tucked in and legs straight out behind, Polaris fell like a cannonball. Abruptly extending her tightly clasped talons like steel knuckles, the falcon clipped the rabbit from behind and immediately flared to an abrupt and spectacular stop. She settled down to the ground with an ease that belied the physics involved. The rabbit had tumbled end over end when struck, dead before it completed its first somersault. Polaris hopped over and tore the rabbit apart with her beak and talons. When done filling herself, she mounted into the air again, flew a victory lap around the field, and then fluttered down to settle on Sunstar's gloved arm but not before calling out my name.

I hurried to the group. My eyes must have been open in wonder for Sunstar grinned at me and told me that Polaris was almost totally healed. Starting tomorrow, I was to come each day and fly her so we could learn to work together. Nothing could have excited me more save perhaps kissing Casey. We visited together as we walked back to Polaris's cage. I learned something about the care and feeding of falcons. Polaris would soon be released from the Rehab Center into my care. She would then stay with Gitta, but Sunstar would have to come there each day for a while to check on Polaris's physical and mental health.

I spoke with Polaris in some detail after we were back at her cage. I apprised her of the forthcoming events and questioned her closely about her treatment in Sunstar's care. A falcon has a limited vocabulary, but the essence of what Polaris reported was that she would defend Sunstar to the death—Polaris's death, if need be. Polaris felt that no better healer existed and that while it had been good to be healed, Polaris's love for the skies and free air was overwhelming. She simply could not go back to a cage and live. She chaffed even then at being in a cage even though she knew her freedom was coming soon. That almost made her cage bearable.

After securing and feeding Polaris, Sunstar and I sat and just talked for a while. We spoke about no particular thing specifically but a lot of things generally. It was the kind of conversation that begins to fill in the background and perspective of an individual's personal canvas in light of each other's eyes. I liked what I saw. Sunstar was different. It wasn't her implied mysticism and it wasn't her striking beauty. It was the confidence and spiritual faith that emanated from her eyes. If the eyes were the window to the soul, then Sunstar's soul was secure. She was confident within herself. In that respect, she reminded me so much of Casey. And Sunstar was smart and intelligent. Being smart is knowing things; being intelligent is knowing how to apply that knowledge in a moral fashion. Being clever is simply knowing how to violate the expectations of your audience without discovery, but cleverness can be for good or evil and is not a good measure for anyone.

I left that afternoon with a much deeper respect for and keener friendship with Sunstar. I deeply appreciated the time she spent with me. Yet I could not for the life of me figure out just how she made me feel so calm when she placed her hand on my shoulder and sang to me. Oh well, I thought, some mysteries are destined to remain mysteries until they are not. Then I just concentrated on the drive home, watching a gorgeous mountain sunset unfold to my right.

DAY SEVEN 7:15 A.M.

I was sitting on the steps of the Chapel waiting for Sergeant Saddler to show up. Polaris was wheeling lazy circles in the air high above the Rat's Nest. She was looking for breakfast. Gitta was coming slowly awake, lying on top of her cage at the Chapel's rear. She was waiting for Dusty or me to come back and get her, hopefully carrying a cookie or heaven-blessed Twinkie with us. Operation Pale Horse was set to kick off in two days, and everyone and everything seemed to be in motion around me.

I had spent the past four days shuttling between the BRWI Rehabilitation Center working with Polaris and the hunter's course behind the Rat's Nest working with Gitta. I had also been familiarizing myself with some prototype arrows. They were modeled after the one previously selected for production, arrows that could carry the sedative that would hopefully allow us to capture a Pale Were. Dusty and the Major had devised a series of alternative scenarios to prepare me for the one opportunity I might have to take down a Pale Were and then defend my kill if everyone else around me was either missing or busy defending themselves fighting off other Weres.

Sunstar had spent the better part of four hours for each of two days with me. She helped me understand the basics of falconry. I used the time to help her understand the attitude, physics, and appetites of a gyrfalcon. Polaris, Gitta, and I were quickly becoming a team. We had been out on two separate long hikes of 12 miles each to practice communicating with one another in all types of terrain and tree cover. We found that Polaris and I could communicate simple thoughts over several hundred yards and much more complex exchanges over a span of 150 to 250 yards. Gitta and I could exchange impressions at about 100 to 120 yards. We could communicate complex thoughts and exchanges at 85 yards or less. We all felt those distances would improve with trust, time, and practice.

I found myself lying awake at night trying to devise a common vocabulary or a kind of symbolic speak that both Gitta and Polaris could understand. Falcons and wolverines don't commonly speak to one another. I had to deliver my coordinating commands twice every time I addressed both of my team members. It took time and was distracting, but I thought I had an answer. I just needed some practice time to work it out. I also needed a Chanter—Sunstar. Today would be my first chance to test a working hypothesis. Sunstar had promised to be at the Rat's Nest by 7:30 a.m. to help me. She could stay until noon before she had to return to the BRWI. My thought was that we might need all that time. My hope was that we would not.

Promptly at 7:28 a.m., I spotted Sunstar parking her car and starting the long walk over to the Rat's Nest. I wondered if she had a clock in her head or some special sense that kept her aware of each passing minute. I had never seen her wear a watch, yet she was never late. In fact, she wore nothing on her wrists except a series of thin, handwoven, colorful cloth and hand-braided leather bracelets. Today she was also wearing jeans and a heavy T-shirt that was loose enough to be modest but one that clearly clothed a vibrant and healthy young woman. The baseball cap that adorned her head, however, had seen better days. It did not seem destined to see many more. I waved as she looked my way and then just sat and enjoyed the exuberance in her step and the smile on her face as she drew closer.

I stood as she approached the Chapel steps. I asked that she join me in getting Gitta started. Polaris had been circling lower and lower as soon as Sunstar had stepped from her car. Polaris came flying by and snatched the cap from Sunstar's head as we rounded the corner of the Chapel. Sunstar gave a little shriek and started laughing as she stood with her hands on her hips to address the circling falcon. "Well, good morning to you, too, Polaris. Now may I have my hat back?" Sunstar had no animal language skills as did I, so I watched with wonder as Polaris circled swiftly and dropped the cap at Sunstar's feet. Polaris then flew to a nearby tree and perched there. Whatever her skill, Sunstar had an uncanny knack for making her wishes known.

I silently complimented Polaris. I also quietly signaled to Gitta to stand by for we were coming around the corner. As we did, we found there was no wolverine to greet us. I was stunned. We heard a slight rustling sound behind us. Thinking Sunstar had moved closer to me, I wheeled to grab and surprise her but found myself holding empty air. Beneath my self-clasped arms was Gitta, staring up at me with that shark's-teeth grin and snorting with glee.

Wolverines have no word for "Gotcha!" but they do have a sound for "You are dead meat!" It is a kind of rumbling growl that varies in pitch and ends in a short bark. I eventually came to know it well as she practiced her stealth moves on me over and over again until I finally began to exhibit the woodscraft Pee Wee tried so hard to show and teach me.

I certainly heard it this time as Sunstar laughed and laughed at Gitta and me and walked over and sat down beside Gitta for some girl talk that those two had apparently worked out on their own. I was a bit disgusted that Gitta had so easily fooled me. But I was delighted she'd had the thought to run around the Chapel and ambush us from behind while we were slowly making our way to her cage. I loved initiative in anyone, especially wolverines who choose to protect me from the Weres. Polaris, however, just watched silently. In her mind, a Princess should give no acknowledgment to tomfoolery. A Princess should always be above the mundane.

I asked the three of them to wait there for me as I went to find Sergeant Saddler. He'd called me at the inn last night to tell me he was bringing a package of arrows for me to use this morning. He and several of the fellows at our Motor Pool had been tinkering with them for several days. They wanted a demonstration this morning to see if their ideas would actually work. If so, they needed at least 24 hours to make replacements in time for me to use them in the coming assault at Mt. Rogers. I found the sergeant at the Motor Pool. He and several of the mechanics walked back with me, explaining each type of arrow they'd worked on.

The first arrow was a screamer. It was fashioned after an improved model of the arrow I had used with Pee Wee to frighten the Weres away from their feeding. It registered more than thrice the decibels of the original I'd hand-shaped. The second arrow was the sedative arrow, a metal point with an internal plunger that penetrated an embedded capsule of fluid upon impact. It allowed the sedative to flow out into the target. It quickly rendered the target unconscious. The third arrow was a miniature bomb. It carried two highly volatile chemicals that abruptly mixed on impact and simply exploded. It burned with lots of flash and sound. Its purpose was to temporarily distract or disorient. It could also destroy. The last arrow was a fire arrow for use at night. It's front half was coated in resin. A small handkerchief parachute was wrapped around the lower half of the shaft. It was to be used at night as a type of flare or signal.

I was impressed and excited as we walked along. I was eager to show Sunstar, Polaris, and Gitta what we could do. They were waiting behind the Chapel where I expected them to be. We wasted little time explaining to Polaris and Gitta what the arrows' capabilities were. Neither Gitta nor Polaris was overly excited about anything that went boom or made a fire in the sky, but both were game to see just what the arrows would do. We all walked over to the competition range for the show.

DAY SEVEN 9:15 A.M.

Since no one readily volunteered to test the sedative arrow, I laid that one aside and tried the screamer first. Drawing my bow to its full length, I aimed at a 45-degree angle into the sky. I let the arrow fly. I immediately wished I had not. The screeching sound it made was ear-piercing, an eminently annoying noise as if a banshee on steroids had hit her finger with a giant hammer and ripped off the offending fingernail. Sunstar quickly put her hands over her ears as she turned away from the sound. Gitta started wailing, not so much in an attempt at harmony as much as an attempt to drown out the arrow's screech by simply making a louder noise. Gitta was singularly unsuccessful. As for Polaris, she gave an involuntary shriek that sounded like desperate fingernails trying to eviscerate a blackboard. All the remaining humans imitated Sunstar and tried to drive their fists into their ears to dull the sound.

Our consensus was that the screamer arrow could be heard well above the din of battle.

The next arrow I tested was the boom or bomb arrow. I picked up three of them, nocked one, and held the other two in my fingers. Having made sure the range was clear, I fired the first arrow. I shot the following two as rapidly as I could at the 50-yard target. The first arrow hit the target and exploded, demolishing half the target and starting a small fire. The second and third arrows hit within seven seconds of each other and systematically destroyed the remainder of the target. Gitta and Polaris both reacted badly to the sound of the explosive. They quickly recovered when they saw it was only noise to them, offensive to be sure, but only noise.

I tried the last arrow, the fire arrow. It was a wonderful flop. Someone else had to light the arrow once I had drawn my bow. The arrow burst into flames as it was designed to do, but it burned up the parachute that was attached before the chute could unfurl. Still, all bets were that it would be a bright arc in a night sky provided the arrow could fly faster than it burned. Sadly, it could not.

Sergeant Saddler and I agreed that his team would fashion a few of the exploding arrows and some screamers as well as several more sedative arrows. I would carry them with me in the Pale Horse assault. He would barely have time for that and the many other duties he already had getting ready for Pale Horse. Nevertheless, he assured me my armaments were as important as anyone else's. He wasn't going to let me down. I thanked him again and walked back to Gitta's cage with Sunstar. I had some ideas on a vocabulary for both wolverine and falcon. I wanted to try them out with her support. Gitta ambled along behind us. Polaris flew on ahead of us. They, too, were curious about my intended form of communication.

I explained the problem to Sunstar. It was a challenge of time. I had to repeat every command twice since I was talking to two different species that didn't talk to one another. What I wanted was a common language, a third set of sounds that were audible to both species and comprehensible to both as well. I also wanted to use sounds that both species could make, and then we would assign a value or meaning to each of those sounds. That way I could use a single thought or audible sound. Both species would hear and know what I was trying to convey. And vice versa. If Gitta spoke aloud with the vocabulary we intended to devise, Polaris and I would both hear it and follow her lead.

I started with four sounds. I first assigned them a symbol. The first symbol was a circle. It signified water or help. It was a natural element to Gitta but dangerous to Polaris and bothersome to me. When the water sound was uttered, it meant for all to "take care" or "hurt." It also meant water, but the hearer could probably figure out the context. The next symbol was a squiggly line or jagged lightning bolt. It meant "storm" or a weather change. In a storm, one always seeks shelter, so the sound meant "hide" or "lookout," something like a sentry.

The third symbol was a square, a symbol certainly rarely found in nature. Its sound meant a "field" or "safe." It could also mean "food" or "resting place." The fourth symbol was a triangle. The sound for a triangle meant "fire" or "kill." It was a danger sound, not only as in a place of danger but also as the danger from a threat.

With Sunstar's help, we practiced a number of different sounds until we arrived at the first four sounds that would give our symbols life. We all practiced them over and over, standing close together as well as far apart. We listened to the nuances of each other's speech while each tried to voice the sounds and interpret their several meanings. After two hours and uncounted attempts to get it right, it seemed we three all finally spoke on the same page. At that point, I asked Sunstar to do whatever she could to make us remember. Our responses had be second nature, automatic in any situation.

Sunstar was surprised for a moment but bowed slightly as she acquiesced to my request. She went first to Polaris. Softly stroking the falcon's wings, she sang to Polaris in an almost inaudible chant. It seemed to follow the same melodious loop over and over again. Occasionally she uttered one of the four sounds until all had been used and her song was over. Polaris, who I thought had fallen asleep, suddenly lifted her head and gave a great cry, bowed her head, and softly nudged Sunstar's shoulder. Sunstar smiled, gently caressed Polaris's feathers once again, and turned to Gitta.

As Yogi Berra once said, "It's déjà vu all over again." With Gitta, Sunstar followed virtually the same ritual with the same outcome, only Gitta ended her session with a bellowing growl and bark that caused even me to step back. She also nuzzled Sunstar's shoulder, and Sunstar gently rubbed the side of Gitta's iron jaw. With a shy smile, Sunstar turned to me.

I gulped.

She walked over to me, gracefully raised her arms, and placed both hands on my shoulders. Looking into my eyes, she began to sing so softly that I had to strain to hear her. The language, if it was a language, was foreign to me. The sound seemed to first envelop and then embrace me. I was transfixed. Sunstar's eyes were bottomless pools of dark light into which I was forever falling. Her touch was almost lighter than the breeze that played tag with itself as it wound around both of us as we stood there.

With a murmur, Sunstar finally ended her song. I cried out involuntarily. I never wanted it to end. Then Sunstar stepped back just a bit, bent forward at her waist, and gently kissed my cheek. Standing up with a smile, her eyes crinkled as she announced that the three of us would be able to do exactly as I had planned. With a mischievous grin breaking the corners of her mouth, she added that when the time was appropriate, we would be able to do a little more besides.

The grating sound of several trucks rolling up to the Chapel broke our momentary reverie. We all scrambled around to the front of the Chapel to see what was making so much noise. It was our Special Forces team and three companies of combat infantry that had driven up from Ft. Benning, Georgia. The Army troops at Ft. Bragg, North Carolina, had not been invited to participate with us. They were primarily Airborne assault troops. Lt. Col. Spikes wanted grunts whose companions were dirt clods and bushes, not parachutes. Besides, the Special Forces trained at Ft. Benning and Operation Pale Horse combatants would require a lot of close cooperation, something the Infantry and Special Forces troops there practiced all the time.

DAY SEVEN 1:30 P.M.

Our Special Forces team would be under the command of Major Sanchez. They were primarily responsible for my protection and helping with the Pale Weres' extraction. The three Combat Infantry companies would be the assault teams under the respective commands of Lt. Col. Spikes, Captain Yamata, and Captain Cosic. Two Special Forces teams had already deployed earlier in the week. They were providing passive reconnaissance at Mt. Rogers, waiting for our rendezvous in two days. They would be tagged to guide in two of the Infantry companies for the initial assault. The third Infantry company under the command of Captain Cosic would likely be our reserve company. It would be held back to stand ready to come to the aid of either of the other companies as conditions warranted.

The next hour was one of orderly confusion and commotion as the visiting troops dismounted from their carriers and stretched and relieved themselves after a very long drive. Box lunches arranged by Dusty were provided to all. I asked her how she knew how many lunches to get when everyone had eaten and only part of one box lunch was left. She smiled at me and said she'd counted everyone once, added 10 percent to that number for extras, and then doubled it. She reminded me that these were soldiers. Soldiers were always hungry, always complaining, always trying to nap, and ready at the drop of a hat to start a fight with cheerful disdain for personal risk. And they would drop the hat themselves if the enemy wouldn't.

Pee Wee found me talking to Dusty as we were cleaning up the area. We were piling the paper cartons into sacks for later disposal. "On the bounce, Cody!" Pee Wee hollered. "The Major wants us to meet and greet the Special Forces guys. We're to spend some time getting to know them and them us." I reluctantly excused myself. I hustled after Pee Wee, stopping to pick up my kit along the way. I told myself not to act like a star-struck kid when I met these guys, although from the stories I'd heard, they sounded as if they were just short of superheroes.

The Major gathered us all together on the steps of the Chapel and led us back around to the rear of the building to Gitta's cage. Gitta had gone back there when the trucks first drove up. She did not like the buzzing, noisy, clanking, and grating vibrations of mechanical vehicles or machines. Gitta's natural habitat demanded stealth. Silence was her dearest companion. She was standing on top of her cage, poised as if to leap at us when our group rounded the building. The Major immediately called a halt. She asked me to step up and prepare Gitta. While I did that, primarily just soothing and calming her as I explained who these men were, the Major was behind me explaining to the Special Forces team just who Gitta and I were and why they were here with us.

I could feel seven sets of curious eyes on us as I patted and spoke with Gitta, each set burning holes in my back as their owner sized me up and choked back skepticism. The Major told the team that Gitta would be working with them. One man coughed and muttered something to himself. When she looked at him for the interruption, he excused himself. He said he had grown up hunting wolverines, "and they don't cooperate with *anybody*," he proffered. She responded that maybe he didn't know as much as he thought he did, that the first order of business was to meet Gitta. With that, she organized the seven Special Forces soldiers into a single line. She asked me to make the introductions.

I asked Gitta to accompany me. One by one she was to approach and sniff each man so she would know them in the heat of battle or in pitch darkness. She did as I asked, looking up at each soldier when she finished sniffing him and grinning her shark's-teeth grin while rumbling low in her throat. Each soldier stood so still that you would have thought they were statues. When she had finished with her inspection, Gitta returned to my side and suddenly, wheeling about, growled her Werewolf growl and ran a speedy circle around the group.

Each man stepped back when she growled and was stunned at how fast she moved as she circled them. They realized that this was no mascot but an adversary, one that none of them would deliberately take on without the heaviest projectile weapon they could beg, borrow, or steal. When Gitta finished her show, I explained to the men why she acted as she did.

"Before, you thought of her as a mere curiosity. Now you know she can kill and maim with the best of them. She could probably take out three of you before the final four could mount a serious defense. And even then, two more would likely die before she did. Gitta is one of my two best friends here. She is a team member as much as any of you are. She is smarter, meaner, and faster than a dog. She can take down a seven-foot Werewolf. I have seen her do it. She is here by choice, not by coercion, just as you guys are. She is stealth on wheels when she needs to disappear. Give me three Gittas, and we wouldn't need you fellows," I said, and smiled, "but since you're here, let me show you some things we can do."

I called Polaris, asking her to shriek as loudly as she could when she lifted off her branch. All eyes were on me when she chose to make her entrance from behind the Special Forces team. Her hunting cry startled everyone, causing several of the Special Forces guys to roll forward, turn, and come up with their combat knife in their hands ready to disembowel whatever nasty threat had just appeared.

As she alighted on my outstretched arm, I let her preen herself while I introduced her to the group. I explained a bit about falcons, gyrfalcons in particular, and asked each man to come up slowly and meet her. They did so without touching her. Each stood and examined and admired her until each man had a turn. "This is our sentry," I said, "our eye in the sky who will fly our air cover." I explained that falcons literally fear nothing. They could be and had been trained to attack elephants in India. I pointed out that a large gyrfalcon was not the fastest falcon but could come down on a target at more than 150 miles per hour. The fastest falcons had been timed at more than 200 miles per hour.

I told Polaris to go get something to eat while I put on an archery demonstration for the next little while, but to stay in range and come quickly if I needed her. I gave the same option to Gitta, but she chose to tag along behind me. She was interested in this new group. She said there was something about the way they moved that interested her. They seemed to glide over the grass rather than stomp through it. They reminded her of Pee Wee. These were worthy adversaries, she surmised. Gitta liked anyone who was a good hunter.

I led the group up to the competition course. I asked if there were any archers in the Special Forces team and would they join me? There were two. Archery was a hunting skill each team relied on for food and stealth, and as with every Special Forces team, each soldier had a back-up skill; hence, at least two archers per team.

Each of the archers went to get their kits. We sat around while the remaining men introduced themselves to us. They shared their particular skills, giving us some idea of their personal combat experience. All had had at least one duty tour in Southeast Asia. They often operated well beyond the zones of relative safety, crossing borders when necessary, although that remained an open secret only to certain officials with the Military Assistance Command in Vietnam. It was never publicly talked about. Several of the team had been temporarily assigned to Special Operations Groups, each element consisting of a soldier mix from the four services—Army, Navy, Marines, and Air Force. The Army contributed Special Forces (SF) expertise; the Navy gave SEALs; the Marines provided Force Recon troops; and the Air Force had pilots, planes, and Commandos expert in calling in air support and fire support from various Allied and US aircraft in the area.

DAY SEVEN 3:30 P.M.

It didn't take long for the two Special Forces team members to return with their gear. Right behind them came Sergeant Saddler with a double handful of arrows he and his team had worked on the previous evening. I introduced him to the SF team. They were all curious about the modifications he had made, especially to the screamers and boom arrows. The two SF archers were using Bear recurve bows. They were intent on examining my horn bow as we all prepared to string up. I explained the layout of the competition course and its purpose. I invited the two archers—Cpl. Jim Thomyson and 2Lt. Turk Wertzberger, the "Turk"—to have at it starting with the 25-yard target.

Cpl. Thomyson, a gregarious, slim, and wiry man whose easy smile belied a hard-nosed, tough, and resilient personality, had previously been the point man on an Army Long-Range Reconnaissance Patrol (LRRP) team in Vietnam. He was used to danger. He did not shy away from personally taking on tasks a lesser man would have sensibly avoided. I liked him immediately. He was the sort of person one instinctively trusted with one's life. He was a gregarious scoundrel but a daring and decorated soldier. He was more of a loner than a leader, the perfect scout.

His SF team member, 2Lt. Wertzberger, the Turk, was somewhat opposite. He was a stocky man with close-cropped blond hair and a wide smile. One immediately felt his presence without fanfare. He was a born leader and exuded confidence. He spoke with a lazy drawl characteristic of folks from Texas, Oklahoma, and parts of New Mexico. He was bright, articulate, and eager to learn. His smile reminded me of Dusty's. It simply lit up whatever room it was in. People just felt comfortable being in his presence. Both Gitta and Polaris gave him a claws- or talons-up. He couldn't have had a better compliment; they were fighters and recognized and respected a worthy adversary.

Both men took turns on a five-arrow rotation. Thomyson hit his targets with all his arrows. He had two bull's-eyes. Three arrows were within an eight-inch circumference of the center. The Turk hit one bull's-eye but had three within the eight-inch circumference and one miss. After they cleared their arrows and returned to the firing line, I stepped up. With rapid fire, I hit four clean bull's-eyes, one cutting the bull's-eye band. No one said a word for a moment. The Major then spoke up. She told them I was the Ohio State Champion, that they never had a chance.

I interrupted the awkwardness of the moment by handing each one two boom arrows. Keeping two for myself, I invited them to join me in absolutely destroying the 35-yard target that as yet was untouched. They each grabbed their arrows. Thomyson was the first to fire, with the Turk right on his heels. It took five arrows to render the target so much wadding and straw blowing in the wind. The other SF team members were hooting and hollering as each arrow landed and blew up. The noise for a few minutes was fast and furious. "I want some of those," said the Turk. "I gotta have 'em.

I gotta show one to our ordinance guys back at Ft. Benning." Cpl Thomyson was right with him, practically jumping up and down. "These are *way* cool," he yelled. "Way cool!"

The Major brought us all down to earth. She suggested I take Thomyson and the Turk through the hunter's course while she and Sergeant Saddler took the remaining SF team back to the Chapel conference room for an initial planning and strategy session. She wanted to waste no time. She really wanted to get to the conference room before Lt. Col. Spikes, Yamata, or Cosic claimed it with their groups. With that, they were off. Thomyson, the Turk, and I chatted amiably as we walked over to the start of the hunter's course.

With the Major in her briefing, Dusty was free and asked if she might walk the course with us. I said sure. I introduced her to the SF fellows. There was an immediate cessation of their rough ribaldry. The air was thick with "Yes, ma'ams" as they answered her questions. English schoolboys could not have been more solicitous or polite. I had a hard time stifling my laughter. With Dusty standing around, those men shot everywhere but at the target as they tried to divide their attention to cover two things at once.

At the fourth station, after Thomyson lost his fifth arrow, I dryly suggested that things might get a bit more productive if Dusty stood behind the men instead of beside or slightly to the side ahead of them. The Turk blushed. Dusty laughed softly. She excused herself, citing an errand she forgot she had to run. Both SF team members watched her go with rapt attention until she finally turned a corner and disappeared. Both then looked at me kind of sheepishly. I rolled my eyes and invited them to get back to the course. They did. Their accuracy showed an immediate and dramatic improvement. No one said anything. No one had to.

We ended our session about an hour later. I had a chance to give them some tips, and they got serious. They tried to tell me as much as they could about how to handle myself in a combat situation. It was an incredibly valuable experience for me. I thanked the men again and again as we walked back to the Chapel. They were curious to know how I would work with Gitta and Polaris. I explained to them the signaling system I devised and taught each one and then called Gitta and Polaris to me using the sound system. We played out several scenarios for the next little while.

We finally joined the Major's group. We didn't leave the building until after 10:00 p.m. I went to my room at the inn in Blowing Rock, and the SF team bivouaced at the rear of the Chapel. I asked Gitta to keep an eye on them. I told her I'd see her in the morning with a treat. Her eyebrows shot up, and she asked me if a treat was a Twinkie. I smiled enigmatically. I raised and lowered my eyebrows a couple of times like Groucho Marx in an old movie, patted her shoulder, and left. I was tired. It had been a good day. Tomorrow was going to be intense as we faced our final briefings and equipment checks. My last sight of Polaris as I drove away was classic. She was slowly circling high above the Rat's Nest, ever vigilant. She was a majestic sight against the blue-black late afternoon sky. She was our "eye that never slept."

DAY EIGHT 6:30 A.M.

I was up at 5:30 a.m. We stopped by a gas station market on the way over to the Rat's Nest. I picked up two Twinkies, one for Gitta's early wake-up as soon as I reached the Rat's Nest and one for later. Later would be when we left for Mt. Rogers and were aboard whatever truck or bus they put us on. I thought I might even get to the Chapel before the SF guys awakened, but they were way ahead of me. We visited awhile after I gave Gitta her Twinkie and Polaris some raw steak strips the inn had set aside for me the previous night. Once they were settled down, I could turn my attention to the SF team.

They questioned me closely about Werewolves. It was hard for them to imagine a childhood scary fantasy had a basis in fact. I assured them this whole operation was mute testimony that this was not a joking matter. I talked about my experiences with Casey at Chagrin Falls and the containment facility's Director whose stupid mistake in judgment cost him his life and the lives of several others. I talked about how the Weres attacked and what they wanted, which was the utter and complete destruction of humankind.

I also told them about Were speed, their foul breath, and their cunning. And all this evil I pointed out was in a shaggy, angry package that stood seven feet tall or better with razor-sharp claws and teeth that could bend metal. I told them how the old Werewolves, the Pale ones, had the ability to bite with a venom that turned a human into a beast, losing all vestiges of its humanity usually in seven days or less. And that capability was why we needed to capture a Pale or two, hopefully to stop a raid on the Appalachian State College in Boone that could result in hundreds of new Were "recruits."

The Major showed up just as we were finishing. She laid out the operations plan we would follow. We would go in immediately after the initial assault by the three Infantry Companies. The two attacking companies would be known as the Red Teams: Red Team Alpha (A) and Red Team Bravo (B); the White Team or Team Charlie (C), the Infantry Reserve; and the Blue Team or Team Delta (D), us, the capture and extraction team. The plan was simple as all good plans are. The Red Teams would engage the Weres on Mt. Rogers's western and eastern flanks. The Reserve unit, Team Delta, the White Team, would come down to Mt. Rogers from the northeast, down a several-mile-long defile that emptied into the northern part of the forest that surrounded three-fourths of the flanks of Mt. Rogers. The one bare part of Mt. Rogers was its south to southeast quadrant. That was where we expected to drive the Werewolves. Once in open ground as they fled a mile to a mile and a half to the forested shelter of Grayson Highlands State Park, they would be exposed to the arrows of Cpl. Thomyson, the Turk, and me, and to the covering fire of the rest of Team Delta.

We would leave this afternoon so we all would be in place by early evening. We wanted time to rest and prepare for the infiltration that would begin at 3:00 a.m. on the 16th day. Pee Wee, the Major, and Sergeant Saddler would comprise the rest of Team Delta. Our hope was to ambush one or more Weres fleeing south from the battle, knock them out with a sedative arrow to a noncritical part of their body, wait until the remainder of the fleeing Weres had passed, and then retrieve one or more bodies while they were still unconscious. It wasn't complicated, but it was critical we succeed.

The success or failure of the plan didn't lie in its complexity but in its execution. The one glaring weakness would be the availability of nearby caves to which the Weres might run and hide. Lt. Col. Spikes, the Major, Captains Yamata and Cosic, and I knew a great deal about fighting Weres in caves. It wasn't where we ever wanted to be, but if we had to go in, we would. We hoped that suddenly bringing firepower from three sides would encourage or force them into a staged retreat through the one clear avenue that suited our purposes.

The Virginia State Patrol had been alerted by the governor's office that the military would be conducting some live fire exercises at the Mt. Rogers region for several days. They had set up roadblocks the day before and cleared the area of civilians without conducting a campsite-to-campsite search, hoping that word of mouth and visible presence would deter anyone from trying to sneak into the area. They had gone to the Grayson Highlands State Park and personally cleared that area. As a result, they had given us the go signal late the previous evening.

The Major showed up again promptly at 8:30 a.m. We formally began the day with a roll call and personal equipment and arms inspection. It was the first of several. There were briefings and more briefings, communications checks, huddled group exchanges, maps and navigation conferences, and discussion after discussion on the main battle plan and contingency plans should the operation break down or be jeopardized at various events or schedules. By 4:00 p.m., I was glad to board a bus with Gitta. Polaris was perched atop my shoulder. I found a seat and closed my eyes. I couldn't sleep for trying to remember all I had heard and learned.

Sergeant Saddler made good on his promise. I had six sedative arrows, four boom arrows, three screamers, and a compliment of 20 broadhead kill arrows. I was also carrying a .357 Magnum pistol, courtesy of the Major. Everyone on her team carried both an assault rifle of their choosing, at least 300 rounds of ammunition, and a back-up pistol, except me. Even Thomyson and the Turk carried a rifle, although they had traded a substantial portion of their ammunition for their bow and a quiver of arrows.

All our team also carried the M7 bayonet with a carbon steel blade and hardened plastic grip paired with its olive-drab M8A1 scabbard.

Cpl. Thomyson, the Turk, the Major, and I sat close together on the bus. The Major wanted to review with all three of us how we might best position ourselves to assure we would have a shot at one or more Pale Weres. Our assumption was that there would be at least two and probably more given the size of the Were contingent. Gitta was absolutely unconcerned about our subdued murmurings. She sat between me and the bus window silently watching the cavalcade of trees and cliffs pass by. Polaris had migrated from my shoulder to the top of the bus seat when we first entered the vehicle. She seemed firmly lodged there despite the rocking motion of the bus. Her eyes were closed, but I did not think she was asleep. I wasn't sure she ever did.

DAY EIGHT 9:15 P.M.

The convoy of busses and trucks carrying our Strike Force split up at the intersection of three Virginia state roads several miles north of Mt. Rogers, specifically where Konnarock Road changed its name to Laurel Valley Road and was crossed by Whitetop Road. The Red Team Alpha trucks and our Blue Team Delta bus turned south on Whitetop Road at that intersection. The Red Team Bravo and White Team Charlie busses and trucks continued along Laurel Valley Road to their respective designated staging points. Personnel from those two groups were to disembark about five miles from the Whitetop Road–Laurel Valley Road intersection and about four miles away from the eastern and northern slopes of Mt. Rogers. They would infiltrate at the head of a long, sloping defile that would give them cover as they made their way to the slopes of Mt. Rogers. The Red Team Alpha trucks following us stopped at a Whitetop Road switchback about two miles to the west of Mt. Rogers. That point would be their initial staging area. Our bus continued to wind south along Whitetop Road until we turned east on Highlands Parkway. We finally disembarked at a staging point just west of Grayson Highlands State Park. We were about four miles south of Mt. Rogers.

By 10:30 p.m., we were out of our bus and assembled by the roadside. We were met there by two members of the Special Forces team who had been performing part of the passive surveillance on the Mt. Rogers's Weres for the past five days. They would be our guides to our ambush site once the go order was given by Major Sanchez. We were told to take temporary shelter in the woods near the road so we would not be so visible to any onlookers, whether friend or foe. The Major reminded us that we were in hostile territory for our purposes. Talking would be discouraged once we started in. Our estimated go time was 2:00 a.m., about three plus hours away.

I released Polaris after pointing out the general direction of our pathway in. She was free to fly and scout the entire field of operations between us and the far side of Mt. Rogers. She would return when she could. She should be back in time to report in before we actually started forward to our ambush site. I had the same conversation with Gitta. She had not liked being cooped up on the bus. She was anxious to move. She would be back in an hour or two, she said, in plenty of time to act as our advance scout as we moved out. With those two gone, I settled back and tried to catch a few winks. I wasn't very successful. I kept worrying about nailing a Pale Were. I badly wanted to do my part so this whole expedition wouldn't be a waste.

After about an hour of on-and-off dozing, the Major showed up with Thomyson and the Turk in tow. These are your back-ups and bodyguards, she told me. She said that where I went, they would go. Their sole mission was to see that I got back from this alive. They would try to help bag a Were, but if they had to drop their bow to protect me with a Pale Were practically sitting in front of them, they were under orders to drop their bows, pull their other weapons, and kill everything around them that might impinge on my safety. They acknowledged the Major's instructions and sat down with me. If it had to be, there was no one else I wanted in that role. These were two good guys and deadly soldiers. I would probably be safer in a tank, but we didn't have a tank. Thomyson and the Turk were the next best things, so I got them.

We sat around swapping stories about this and that, and they questioned me closely about my previous adventures with the Weres. They found it hard to believe that something so big could move as quickly as I said they could or that they could act intelligently. I reminded them several times to just accept what I told them and be prepared. With Werewolves, there were almost no second chances, *ever.*

DAY NINE 1:45 A.M.

It was almost go time. The butterflies in my stomach were starting to flutter. Thomyson leaned over and told me to go relieve myself behind a friendly tree, that a need to urinate was common before any anticipated major physical exertion. It was part of the body's natural fight-or-flight response to danger and in no way was a sign of weakness. It was common for women, too, and it was always best to listen to your body. The body usually knows what it's doing. So I excused myself and was back in five minutes. The Turk returned about the same time I did.

At 1:55 a.m., Major Sanchez showed up and asked the three of us to take the point position behind our two guides. She asked me to have Gitta at least 30 yards in front of our column and checked one more time to make sure we could communicate at that distance. I assured her we could, that we had practiced a number of times and scenarios and that Polaris would be flying air cover for us as well. Reassured, she punched my arm and grinned. When everyone had fallen in, she checked her watch one more time and gave the go order. From that point on, we would be in stealth mode with hand signals only as the general rule.

Thomyson, the Turk, and I were carrying our bows strung with an arrow nocked. The Turk's arrow was a boom arrow. Thomyson and I were using standard broadhead arrows. We moved slowly, and our two guides were careful to stay close enough to signal dips, obstacles, or anything that might inadvertently cause us to stumble or make an untoward noise. About a mile in, the guides called a halt. I immediately signaled Gitta that we were stopping. She came back with her compliments but asked how we knew from back where we were that a team of two sentinel Weres were just off to our right ahead of us. I almost yelled, "What?" but regained my composure. I asked if she thought it safe to take them out. She gave me a yes and began stalking them. I crept up to the two guides, informed them of what was ahead and to our right. I asked if they needed help taking the Weres out. I could kill them from a distance, silently, with Thomyson or the Turk to help, but if the guides chose hand-to-hand force, they needed to give me or the Major their next-of-kin letters because they would not be coming back. One of them started to protest when the Major crawled over and asked what was going on. I told her. When they started to respond, she shut them up. "Follow him," she told them, "and observe." She added they were not to let me get killed or hurt no matter what the cost to them.

They looked at each other, then at her, and then at me. They shrugged and told me to lead out. In constant contact with Gitta, I was able to generally locate the sentinels after a 10-minute crawl through the bushes. They were silhouetted against the distant Mt. Rogers in plain sight looking east. My first arrow took the farthest Were through the ear. My second took the nearest Were through the neck. Both creatures dropped immediately without a single grunt.

The Major made the entire element pass beside the two carcasses so each of the new soldiers could see what we were going up against. A couple of the soldiers immediately threw up. All of them who had not already gone earlier went searching for a friendly tree before we could start again. It was a very sober crew that moved out minutes later.

Half a mile farther and both Gitta and Polaris mentally shouted out at the same time. Gitta had come across a small cave. To her highly sensitive nose, it smelled like a Werewolf commuter highway. Polaris, covering an area about a quarter of a mile ahead of us, frantically signaled back that four Weres were headed for us on the trot. She guessed it was just a watch change since she could see two more Weres about 200 yards to our left. They were leaving their concealed spot after two new Weres arrived to replace them.

I passed on the messages to the Major. She immediately moved the element to the small cave and urged us inside. Gitta assured us it was currently clear. Reluctantly, all but Thomyson, the Turk, and I bent down and shuttled their way inside. The three of us positioned ourselves on opposite sides of the trail where the four Weres would likely come down. Thomyson and I lay directly opposite one another, and the Turk concealed himself about 20 yards in front of us. He would let the four Weres pass him and take out the last one in line while Thomyson and I took out numbers one and two. The third Were in line was fair game. The first archer free or all three of us would fire at will and try to take it out before an alarm was raised. I figured we had about three seconds once the first Were fell.

I asked Gitta to conceal herself beside the trail in front of Thomyson and me and that she was free to unleash her particular brand of mayhem after the first Weres went down. She scampered to a spot about 15 feet in front of me at the grassy edge of the trail and disappeared. She just vanished. I tried to puzzle out where she might be but could see nothing in the predawn gloom. I knew she was there somewhere because we kept talking to one another, but I learned once again that Gitta in stealth mode is like *The Man Who Wasn't There.*

So we waited.

It wasn't a long wait. We could actually hear the four Weres running toward us as they pushed through some of the heavy brush that dotted the landscape. They were almost past the Turk when all hell broke loose. The last Were must have sniffed or spotted something amiss because it suddenly halted. It barked out a cry as it began to spin around to its right, looking keenly at the foliage beside it. The entire line stopped, as it were, on a dime and jumped off the trail to either side, sniffing and peering down into the underbrush.

Thomyson fired first. His arrow nicked the shoulder of the number two Were who howled a blood-curdling cry that seemed to issue from a giant audio speaker. Any semblance at surprise was now ripped to shreds. I stood up and put an arrow through the lead Were's heart. It dropped like a sandbag. The fourth Were apparently saw something of the Turk's uniform because it dove straight into the underbrush. We heard horrific growls, grunts, and screams from the Were and the Turk as those two combatants wrestled, tore, and stabbed at each other.

I was pulling and fitting my second arrow when Thomyson put an arrow through the left leg of the second Were charging our way. The Third Were in line was hot on its heels coming at us but was momentarily screened from direct sight by the wounded Were in front. The wounded Were suddenly began to tumble as if it were doing a somersault. I had a quick but sure shot at the third Were. I took it without hesitation. My arrow penetrated its high left breast, and it dropped and rolled to its left side.

The second Were completed its roll and, coming to his feet, sprang at me from a distance of 15 feet. I had no defense other than to drop my bow and try to pull my .357 Magnum pistol. I fumbled, and I was slow. I saw a giant black shadow starting to loom over me. I knew I was going to die, but I wasn't going to make it easy. I turned and ducked as quickly as I could. I hoped to take the brunt of the Were's hit on my back when a sudden scream immediately behind me seemed to put our small clearing and my hair on edge.

It was the Werewolf screaming in pain that must have been unbearable. Gitta, her claws dug into its side, rode the air with it trying to literally chew off its head. Gitta had leaped and hit the Werewolf in midair. Her jaws were now fastened on the right side of the Were's neck. Her grip extended to its jawbone. As Gitta closed her own massive jaws, I could hear the Werewolf's jawbone snap and crunch. I watched the Were's neck being shredded. The Werewolf simply went insane, throwing itself all over the clearing trying to dislodge Gitta, but Gitta was intractable. As her claws raked and peeled the Were's outer skin and exposed its rib cage, Gitta's jaws continued to close inexorably. The frantic beast was finally strangled, its head almost severed from its body in the bargain.

When the Were finally lay lifeless, Gitta rose and screamed a growl into the night air unlike any I had ever heard. That single incident probably saved our main attack plan. A series of howls went up immediately from several distant areas nestled at the base of Mt. Rogers. I grabbed Thomyson and had him quickly tie the paws and feet of the wounded third Were that had taken my arrow in its chest. It had been stunned by its tumble and was temporarily tractable, so I bent close to it and, making contact, asked it what the howls meant.

I could feel the Were's mind struggling with mine, but the clear impression I did get was that the Weres believed their sentries had been ambushed by some kind of strange new "bear" and that one or possibly two of the Were party were now dead. The distant Weres had heard the wolverine's grunting cry. Having had no contact with a wolverine before, they assumed it was simply a different species of bear but very unlike the black bears so common in their part of the country.

Meanwhile, we could only hear muffled grunts and wheezing coming from the brush that ensnared the Turk and the number four Werewolf. I leaped to my feet and stumbled over as fast as I could, having finally pulled my handgun and my M7 knife. I saw the shaggy back of the Were as I finally reached the struggling pile. I threw myself on it, closing my left hand that was still holding my handgun around the Were's throat and pulling back with all my might while stabbing into the Were's right side and chest with the M7 in my right hand. I did not want to fire my handgun if at all possible. The sound of a shot would spook the Were colony, and our entire plan of surprise attack would be destroyed, possibly resulting in a bigger bloodbath than we anticipated. I could feel the strength of the Were lessen at every stab I made, but I didn't understand why it was not turning to bite me or why it wasn't sending out a distress howl. I kept stabbing until the Were suddenly went slack. It was as if it had suddenly caved in, but no scream or howl ever escaped its mouth.

279

I climbed off the Were's back. I tried to shove it aside to get to the Turk. I kept urging the Turk to help me. Major Sanchez finally came up and quieted me. Thomyson was right behind her trying to get to the Turk as well. Putting both hands on my arm, the Major turned me away from the Were, looked into my eyes, and told me to stop. The Turk was dead. She led me around the Werewolf. I saw that while the Were had ripped open the Turk's chest with its claws, the Turk had the strength and will to jam his fist and arm down the Were's throat so deep that the Were could hardly breathe. Neither could it scream or close its jaws. It was slowly choking to death even when I started stabbing it. Despite great pain and imminent death, the Turk had the courage and will to probably save us by disabling his attacker.

Thomyson, Sergeant Saddler, and I, acting together, pulled the Were off the Turk and gingerly freed the Turk's arm from the Were's throat. I felt a deep and great sadness come over me. A truly brave and good man had died. His memory and the sound of his easy laughter would stay with me the rest of my life. Some people pass through our orbits of influence only briefly in our life, but their inspiration and influence can be lasting and profound. So it was with the Turk. I had put him in harm's way. His death was my responsibility. I decided at that moment that I would live my life in such a way that his would not be wasted. It was a promise I would never forget.

We all turned back to the wounded Were. It had passed out so I could not question it further. The Major asked one of the Special Forces guys to tie it to a tree and make his way back to our group as quickly and stealthily as he could. We would push ahead to keep to the battle plan schedule. I split the Turk's arrows with Thomyson. We again took our place at the point of our small force. Gitta had gone back into the lead ahead of our two guides. We tried to step along a little faster to make up for lost time. It was a hard introduction to Pale Horse but not the first death our small group would experience in the next 36 hours, not by far.

DAY NINE 4:00 A.M.

We were about three-fourths of a mile south of Mt. Rogers at the edge of a vast triangle-shaped area that converged to a point on the high plateau that formed a boundary with the southern slopes of the mountain. We had a clear field of fire if we chose to stay at the edge of the gravel field. However, Major Sanchez urged us to move to the middle of the cleared area and dig in. She felt we'd have a much better chance of getting a Pale Were if we were literally in their path as the Weres escaped from the firefight Teams Alpha, Bravo, and Charlie were about to bring to Mt. Rogers. I borrowed the Major's shovel and started digging in like everyone else. We dug quickly and carefully. We created a small breastwork around us in the form of a tight circle. Thomyson and I were placed at the northern edge of our small defensive redoubt.

The Major, Pee Wee, and Sergeant Saddler were along the sides of our circular depression. They were interspersed with the remaining Special Forces team members. Gitta took a place behind me. Her job was to attack any Werewolf that breeched our circle and landed in our midst. Her primary job was to protect me. Pee Wee's and Sergeant Saddler's jobs were to protect the Major or kill us each or both if we should become infected by a Pale Were. Polaris continued to circle high above us. Her ever watchful eyes probed the darkness trying to shield us from surprise.

At 4:30 a.m., the far slopes of Mt. Rogers lit up like a Christmas display. Tracers flying in from three sides of Mt. Rogers along with 10 to 12 flares suddenly hanging from the night sky brought a daylight effect to what a few moments before had been dark slopes and sinister trees hovering about its environs. We heard the boom-boom-boom of .50-caliber machine guns on two slopes and the chattering stutters of AR-15s from more than 250 soldiers trying to hit anything that wasn't immediately recognizable as a human. It was like listening to a series of buzz saws alternately starting, stopping, and starting again.

Then the screams and howls started in the distance, gradually growing in volume as they came our way. The surprise was almost perfect. We could hear and faintly detect a growing thudding sound as several hundred paws began to run in our direction. In the early morning gloom, we could see little, but we could feel the ground start to tremble as so many big bodies created the pounding tremors that rolled our way. I felt for a moment like those cowboys of another time must have felt when a full-scale stampede was coming their way and they knew they could not escape to the right or to the left. All they could do was spin their ponies about and ride "hell for leather." All we could do was dig in, brace ourselves, and prepare to unleash our firepower as the first wave roared up.

The two Special Forces soldiers to either side of me were the first to fire. Their rifles were on full automatic, and their bullets acted like a giant scythe. The first group of Weres started falling to their faces at about 50 yards. The soldiers kept up a sustained fire, first one then the other as magazines were swapped out like bandages on a bleeding patient. But as the Weres kept coming, the pile of bodies started creeping closer and closer until, as more of the dawn's early light was exposed, the killing ground was only 20 yards in front of us.

The personnel behind us and to each side of our small circle were also firing by this time, only they were trying to hit individual targets and were firing on semiautomatic. We thought the Pale Weres, if any, would not come directly at us but would use the kamikaze-like charge of their fellow Weres to mask their own retreat. Polaris was watching topside for us and suddenly signaled me that three Pale Weres were coming south on the run and would pass about 30 yards to our left. They were flanked by a small number of dark Weres, some of which were juveniles.

They were moving slower as a group than many of the individual Weres that streamed toward and around us. I called Thomyson over to stand beside me and told him to pull out two boomers. One arrow was to go into the crowd around the Pale Weres, and the second was to go into the ground about 40 yards behind us. If we were lucky, the Pale Weres would think there was another ambush up ahead of them in the direction they were running and would retreat back to Mt. Rogers. That expected retreat would give us a second chance at capturing a Pale Were should our first try fail.

We waited almost no time before the three Pale Weres and their entourage appeared. They were coming at us at a trot rather than an all-out run. Thomyson dropped a boomer just ahead of them as I asked and then immediately turned and loosed one far behind us. Sure enough, the Pale Were group stopped at the first explosion and started forward again. But at the second explosion, they turned like a school of fish and started back against the crowd but at a much slower pace. Now they were fighting the surge of their own crowd.

I pulled a screamer arrow and let it fly in a high arc over the group's head. It was the distraction I had hoped for, but its effect was not what I expected. At its piercing whine, the smaller juveniles began going in slightly different directions. They seemed momentarily to have lost their bearings. They were staggering about, and their movements appeared choppy as if they were suddenly disoriented. That briefly split the crowd barrier that had obscured the Pale Weres since we spotted them. It left one lane open to me. Unfortunately, my disabling arrow hit a few seconds after Thomyson's arrow hit and killed it.

Stunned, I started to turn to him to ask him what he was doing when a series of howls and enraged growls behind us caused all of us in the defensive circle to spin and see a charge of 15 to 20 Weres running our way in pack formation. They had seen the killing of the Pale Were. They seemed to have made a collective decision to risk being martyrs as they ran headlong into the murderous fire of Sergeant Saddler, the Major, and the two Special Forces soldiers on the side that flanked us. The Major and the three others defending our right side flipped their rifles to full automatic fire and waved them slightly left to right like a child plays with a garden hose. They sprayed their bullets into the middle of the running riot at waist-high level.

The carnage was awful.

Bits and pieces of the charging Weres began flying in all directions as the bullets peeled the creatures apart in their suicide rampage, yet still they ran toward us. They were either oblivious to the damage our sustained fire was generating or they were possessed because they were screaming and howling as if they were fiends from Hades. Nevertheless, our firepower finally overcame their faltering momentum. The last of their group fell dead only feet away from the side of our small circle. I turned about. Out of pure reflex and demanding training, I pulled and nocked my arrow as I turned. I was at full draw when I completed my spin. Several Weres had charged us from our rear as we turned to face the first onslaught. Two Weres were practically upon us. I only had time to loose my arrow and put it in the face of the first Were in the Pale Were group. I might as well have kicked a tree for all the good it seemed to do. The Were just bowled me over as it ran me down.

My arrow had lodged in its eye cavity. My bow was knocked from my hand. The claws from the Were's hind leg first ripped my chest open and then my thigh as I tumbled backward. My arms were flailing as I tried to stop my frenetic fall. The Were had no time to recover before Gitta met it full on, her jaws fastening firmly on the Were's neck as both of them fell on top of me. Gitta's claws began tearing out chunks of the Were's flesh as they struggled. But thanks to Gitta, the only danger I was in was being crushed under the weight of the Were. It was far too busy trying to get away from Gitta and save itself than bothering with me, but the favor wasn't returned. I managed to pull my M7 bayonet knife and start stabbing the Were's side while Gitta chewed on its neck. The Were rolled off me in its defense but carried Gitta with it. It stopped fighting and went slack as Pee Wee stepped in, placed the muzzle of his rifle against the Were's head, and pulled the trigger.

The second Were had fared even worse. It had thrown itself at Thomyson who dropped to the ground immediately. That caused the charging Were to almost somersault. It tried to stop its momentum while turning to rake Thomyson. As it did, one of the two Special Forces soldiers beside Thomyson simply turned and, jabbing the muzzle of his rifle against the Were's stomach, fired a burst and disemboweled it. The soldier then stepped back, turned, and began firing again at the advancing Weres running from the Mt. Rogers mayhem. Thomyson immediately stood up and began trying once again to put a sedative arrow through a Pale Were.

I gasped a thanks to Pee Wee. I turned back to find my bow when I suddenly collapsed. I fainted from sudden shock. Gitta broke my fall as I hit and slid off her back to the ground. I was unconscious before my slack body crumpled against the unyielding floor of our small redoubt.

DAY NINE 7:00 A.M.

My eyes didn't seem to want to open. I felt groggy as if I had overslept. I could barely lift my head. There was a sour taste in my mouth. I opened my mouth to ask for a drink of water. Pee Wee's face came slowly into focus as a coarse, rasping sound emerged from my throat. It wasn't my voice. I knew my voice, but as I swam back into full consciousness, I realized that gravelly excuse for a voice was, indeed, mine. *What happened?* I thought. Dizzy and slightly nauseous, I came full awake to find myself still in the defensive circle with several people peering outward around our small perimeter. It was quieter. No Weres could be seen. The sun was out, and there were bodies all around, especially between us and Mt. Rogers, but there were no live Pale Weres.

As I sat up, I glanced down at something that seemed to be restricting my movements. A good six inches of adhesive wrap blanketed my upper chest. A similar bandage was wrapped around my left thigh. I had been wounded, and the realization hit me hard. I thought I was impervious after the many close encounters I had experienced, but the law of averages will eventually catch up to anyone. It had me. The Major heard me stir. Seeing me sit up, she turned and came over to me. Gitta was to be congratulated, she told me. Gitta had saved my life. One of the Special Forces men, a medic, had cleaned, wrapped, and drugged me as a temporary fix. Nevertheless, he cautioned that I needed to see a physician as soon as we returned to the Rat's Nest.

In the meantime, we were in a temporary lull. At full daylight, many of the Weres seemed to melt away before the group's collective eyes. They simply faded back into the forests that bordered the clear escarpment on which we were forted up. Sergeant Saddler and Pee Wee had stepped out of our defensive ring an hour or so before. They completed a field count of the bodies around us. They counted 66 dead Weres. Two Weres were badly wounded and weren't yet dead. Both our men graciously helped them complete their journey. The two Weres made bodies 67 and 68.

We held a small caucus. I was anxious to stand up and move around even though the Major and the medic both advised against it. I pointed out that we had no Pale Weres, one if not *the* reason Operation Pale Horse was conceived in the first place. I called out to Gitta and Polaris, and they came in after several minutes. Gitta had been making sure all the Weres were really dead, and Polaris had been tracking the two surviving Pale Weres. The Weres had disappeared back into the forest. They had run for a cave opening along with several other groups. Polaris had been watching the opening for almost an hour until she received my instructions to come back. I thanked her. I softly stroked her feathers as she preened herself. I told her we weren't finished yet. She would need to direct us to the cave. If falcons could smile, she did, but the glint in her eye told me it wasn't a comforting smile.

I did much the same with Gitta when she wandered in and came over to flop down beside me. We chatted a moment. I told her she had saved my life probably several times over. She snorted. She said she knew that and not to get too mushy. It wasn't about me. It was all about Twinkies. She knew if I got killed, Dusty would never forgive her and Gitta's ration of Twinkies would stop. Forever. I started laughing, and she started snorting. My chest hurt so much I had to choke myself off. That made Gitta snort even more, but she draped one of her protecting paws over my leg as she did. Once a mother, always a mother was my thought, only this one had a streak of sarcasm in her.

Who knew?

We were debating our next move when we saw Lt. Col. Spikes and the rest of the assault force coming out of the trees and walking toward us. They were about the most comforting beings I had seen in a long time. I knew then that all would be well. Lt. Col. Spikes called a short staff meeting when everyone had finished their greetings and started to settle down around us. Before we started, he organized a guard force and a burial detail, only the burial detail wouldn't be for our own forces. Instead, they would be piling up Were bodies to burn. With those activities launched and the wounded brought to an area where the medics could begin a second round of treatments, he motioned us to sit in a tight circle around him and give our respective reports.

As we were talking, a tremendous explosion occurred on the near slopes of Mt. Rogers. A black smoke cloud rose rapidly into the sky. More than 60 Were carcasses had been brought to a single site, and Lt. Col. Spikes had left a demolition team behind to blow up all evidence of them. Apparently, they succeeded. The ground briefly shook where we were seated. I looked up at Spikes. He didn't even raise an eyebrow. He just continued to speak to us. Between the two counts of dead Weres, he figured we'd destroyed about half the population of this particular group, yet we still had no Pale Weres. Our job wasn't done. He had anticipated it might take extra time, hence our original schedule. Fortunately, we still had about 24 hours left on the clock with very few wounded. He asked for our comments and suggestions. He wanted our thoughts exposed before he would tell us of the rest of his plan.

Captains Yamata and Cosic wanted to go after the Weres. They felt that Gitta, Pee Wee, and I could follow them over rock, if necessary. The Major reminded us all of my earlier comment. We didn't have a Pale Were, but Polaris knew where they were and could guide us even if I wasn't up to snuff. They all looked at me. I told them if the medic would redress my leg wound a bit tighter, I'd be as good as I was in Chagrin Falls. As everyone knew, I was the master of the hobble step. That brought a few smiles, and even I chuckled. But I told them I was dead serious. Our job wasn't finished, and good men had died to get us this far. We'd better finish the plan. Lt. Col. Spikes just smiled. He said he'd thought we'd all feel that way. Then he told us his plan.

DAY NINE 9:00 A.M.

The assault force had rested, eaten some of their dinner rations, reloaded, regrouped, and erected a small medic station for the six wounded soldiers we would leave behind with a Special Forces team to guard them. Captain Cosic and Lt. Col. Spikes would take their teams and resweep the side slopes and far slopes of Mt. Rogers. They were to pick up any Weres hiding there and search out and destroy any of their camps or hideouts. Captain Yamata and the Major's team would find the Weres' refuge cave, enter it, and destroy the remainder of the Werewolves while taking a Pale Were captive. I was to stay behind with the wounded.

Thomyson with his bow and arrows would accompany the Major. Pee Wee and Sergeant Saddler would, as usual, be responsible for her safety. I would instruct Polaris to lead the team to the cave and return to me. Gitta would also be instructed to accompany the team into the cave to sniff out any ambushes the Weres might try to set up. In the event of a fight, Gitta would try to not kill a Pale Were, but anything else was fair game. She grinned and bared that shark's-teeth smile when she heard that.

Nevertheless, Gitta was not happy about leaving me behind, but after a few minutes, she understood the necessity of it and agreed to do her part. Polaris simply affirmed Lt. Col. Spikes's instructions. It was the only logical thing to do in light of our overall directive, she told me. I just shook my head. She reminded me of a popular TV show character, a man from another planet with pointed ears, a TV show she would find highly illogical. Such are the ironies of life, I decided.

The respective teams moved out at 9:20 a.m. I sat with the medic and wounded and watched them go. It was a sad feeling. The medic had changed and strengthened my leg dressing and rebandaged my chest. It didn't lessen my desire to get up and follow the Major's team. Being separated from one's group is the hardest part about combat. Men and women who fight together in life-threatening situations bond in ways their civilian counterparts just can't understand. How could they since there are no comparable situations in the civilian world save perhaps police work or firefighting?

Our guard unit was composed of six Special Forces soldiers, three deployed perimeter guards and three resting behind in the medic's tent for shift rotation. Three of the six wounded could not walk. They had been hit by friendly fire or badly ripped by a Were encounter. Three could move about, but two had damaged arms and couldn't hold a weapon. The remaining soldier had debris from a tree gouge his cheek and nick an eye. He was bandaged from his neck to his forehead.

Despite the best plans and field arrangements, casualties happen. Men trip, stumble, discharge their weapons too quickly, and become disoriented. There are a host of other happenstances that seem unlikely or irrational at the moment but are entirely within the context of combat. As with these men, people get hurt when things go boom. But at least these six didn't get dead, the other consequence of combat nobody really addresses up front. I didn't like it that the medic tent was so open in the middle of the gravel field, but it had to be somewhere. At least out in the open, we could see the Weres coming when (and if) they came.

We had been without the working Assault team for about 45 minutes when I could suddenly hear Polaris calling me. She was circling to my west above some piles of tumbled rocks. The chunks looked as if they once wanted to be a small hill that had collapsed on itself. It was now droopy and disappointed. Without warning, Polaris abruptly abandoned her circling pattern and flew straight to me.

She came in very fast and then pulled up in a stall maneuver. She landed practically on my feet. She told me she had seen two Pale Weres and a mixture of several large and smaller Werewolves emerge from a concealed cave in the side of the rocky hill. They had started northward to Mt. Rogers in a stealthy walk. I turned to one of the medics and asked if our radio worked. He said yes and asked why I wanted it. I told him what Polaris told me and that I needed to pass that along to Lt. Col. Spikes immediately. If he and Captain Cosic knew of this, they could lay a trap at the foot of Mt. Rogers. Then I had to tell Captain Yamata and the Major so they could get out of the caves and form an encircling movement behind the Weres. They would be there to capture them if they turned away from Lt. Col. Spikes's ambush and tried to return to their cave.

The light seemed to come on for the young medic, and he turned to grab the radio and hand it to me. He moved too fast. He was neither able to grab it nor hand it to me. What he did do was fumble it in his hands that had moved too quickly. He inadvertently knocked the radio off the wooden table where it rested. Both of us watched in horror as it hit the rocky ground and cracked wide open. Its transistors fell out of the housing like broken teeth out of a prizefighter's jaw that had just absorbed a roundhouse haymaker. We now had no way to communicate with either of the two assault forces that had left here but an hour earlier.

I could not let this opportunity pass us by, so almost without thought, I took my bow and kit, checked to make sure my .357 Magnum pistol was with me and loaded, pulled and resheathed my Japanese blade in its scabbard, and filled my quiver with every boomer, screamer, and broadhead arrow Thomyson had left in the Turk's quiver. I asked if one of the Special Ops fellows would accompany me. I told them there would only be three of us: me, him, and Polaris. I told them one of us if not both *must* bring a Pale Werewolf back to Lt. Col. Spikes.

Staff Sergeant Jamed Abshire immediately volunteered. He was well formed, strong, and shorter than the other soldiers. He made up in dedication and fearlessness what he lacked in height. He was soft spoken as most men from the South were. He seemed to have a perpetual grin. He had merry eyes and coal-black hair and carried himself with confidence and commitment. He was also funny. His manner was firm but unobtrusive.

Of the six Special Forces guys with us, it was Abshire or the other Staff Sergeant D. J. Woody I would have picked to go with me had one of the two not already volunteered. Since Abshire had spoken up first, I chose him as my companion. We left Woody in charge of the guards and the wounded. I told Abshire to pack lightly, just guns, ammo, knives, and any bow and arrows. I was already slightly crippled, but we needed to move fast if we were to intercept and capture a Pale Were. We must get started. He agreed, but made me drink a canteen of water before we started out. He told me that people who had taken the medications I had usually developed a ravenous thirst along the way. This would forestall that experience, one that might compromise us when we least could afford it. And don't worry about having to pee, he told me. We'd move fast enough in the heat that most of the water I took would be lost in perspiration within 30 minutes. It turned out he knew what he was talking about.

We struck a course that would bring us off the bare gravel cap about a quarter mile shy of the first slopes leading up to Mt. Rogers. I figured the Weres would likely maintain a slower, stealthier pace to avoid any of our assault forces. We, however, could afford to move at full speed. And so we did for the first 100 yards or so. After that, it was sweat equity all the way and a steady hobble on my part. My leg wound started bleeding slightly, and the bandage around my chest made deep breathing difficult, but we had lives at stake, and I knew they were counting on us, so we just pushed on. I was in considerable pain and somewhat dehydrated when we arrived at the forest's edge by the southern slope of Mt. Rogers.

I sent Polaris to verify that the Pale Weres were still coming our way. She did, and they were, so we started to look for a good ambush spot. After about five minutes, I found what I wanted.

Abshire would crawl up onto a large stand-alone boulder beside two pine trees. He would be about nine feet off the ground, just high enough so the Weres could not jump up on top with him yet with room for him to move about and create several lanes of fire with his rifle.

I squeezed into a small copse of Aspen trees about 40 feet away from the big boulder. Then we just waited. The Weres would have only one way to get to me, and it would be costly to try. I did have one other trick up my sleeve. I had three screamer arrows, any one of which would alert Lt. Col. Spikes or Captain Cosic that either Thomyson or I was where we shouldn't be and probably needed help. They would come running, I knew. We would just have to hold on by our lonesome until help arrived.

DAY NINE 12:10 P.M.

The first indication we had that the Weres were near was a hunting screech from Polaris wheeling high above us. It was a prearranged signal. It was loud and effective. Polaris repeated it twice, another signal to tell me there were more than nine Werewolves in the traveling group. They came into the clearing between Abshire's boulder and my small copse of trees from an angle that demanded I squeeze forward between the trees to get a clear shot. The risk I faced was one of detection. I had nothing to hide behind. If the Weres turned my way, they would see me, and the fight would be on.

Abshire saved the moment, however. Realizing my dilemma, he lay flat on top of the boulder and threw a large rock in a direction away from both of us. It crashed into the bushes and bounced off some rocks and generally made a mess of the silence we were enjoying. The Weres reacted, as expected. Two large males immediately bounded close to the spot of the noise and stood quietly, peering intensely into the brush for the cause of all the noise. That gave me a moment to line up my sedative arrow on the back of one of the Pale Weres. It dropped with a groan when the arrow took in the right shoulder, above the shoulder blade but beneath the collarbone. Its groans ceased almost immediately, and it lay still. At that point, Abshire fired his rifle on semiautomatic burst and took down a female and a juvenile standing in my sight line to the second Were.

I had already nocked my second arrow and was drawing even as the female fell. The arrow was in flight as soon as my sight line cleared and would have felled the second Pale Were if a male in the group had not turned suddenly and stepped in the arrow's path to better see why the female had fallen. It hit just to the left of its spine. It pitched forward with a cry that shut off as the sedative hit it, but the integrity of the group surrounding the Pale Weres vanished. Werewolves were scrambling in every direction like dandelion heads in a stiff wind. In seconds, most were gone from the site. Only the two wounded Werewolves remained.

I knew we couldn't carry the Pale Were out and that the small pack that had just scattered would be back, probably with help, so I pulled a screamer from my quiver and let it fly almost straight up. The noise was instant, loud, annoying, and welcome. If that didn't bring help, nothing would. But just as I started to step away from my cover, there was a growling, grunting sound to my left over at Abshire's boulder. Instinctively, I fell back between the two Aspen trees that formed the gateway to my hiding place. It was good that I did. The form of a great shaggy Werewolf seemed to materialize out of nowhere in front of me, slashing at me and scoring deep marks on one of the Aspens as I retreated back just out of its reach into the interior of my copse. My eyes must have been as big as saucers, but my reflexes were still top-notch.

In the confines of the small opening, I could not draw and fire my bow without some difficulty. As the Were turned sideways and reached in to tear at me with its claws, I dropped my bow. I pulled out my M7 bayonet and sliced the Were's arm almost to the bone. Howling, it yanked its arm back and dumbly looked with horror at the blood spilling out. Then it renewed its attack with an incredible frenzy. Its bulk and the narrowness of the trees' entranceway was all that saved me. It could only reach in for me, and that alone kept me busy as I tried to counter each of its wild grabs with a stab or slice of my own. In short order, there were red blobs and spots all over me and the inside of the copse as its wild gyrations flung beads of blood in every direction.

The Were's strength rapidly waned as its blood loss mounted. It soon collapsed on its side beside the small opening I guarded. I had no more than taken one small step toward the entrance to finish him off when a female leaped over the male and managed to squeeze its way partially though the gap that formed the doorway to my retreat. It was more hostile and active than the male had been. I found myself bettered on every turn as I tried to fend off its raking arms with my M7. Of all times not to have my wakizashi blade with me! I thought this was probably the worst.

Pushed farther and farther back into my small cubbyhole of a clearing by the frantic attacks of the female, I felt my back hit the small ring of trees that formed the backup to the clearing I was in. I could retreat no farther, and to go forward was death by small cuts. Then I remembered what Casey had so insistently instilled in me, an appreciation for and competence with a .357 Magnum pistol. Without further thought, I pulled mine from its holster and fired several times point-blank into the Were that was accosting me. The impact of the bullets blew it backward. Lifeless, the female Were crumpled against the interior Aspen that framed my doorway of escape. This time, I stepped lively. Peeking my head out to look for possible ambushes, I broke from the copse with my gun in one hand and my bow and quiver in the other.

I ran for Abshire's boulder. He pulled me up after I threw my gear on top. I flopped down to catch my breath and started to tighten the bandage circling my leg when the rest of the Weres showed up. Abshire hissed at me and pointed as the pack ran into the bigger clearing and immediately turned to the copse of trees where I had been forted up. They saw and dragged away the bodies of the big male and the female that had partially blocked the entranceway into my former hideout. They discovered in their efforts that I was no longer in there. Just as well, I thought, as one particularly large Were literally broke several of the more slender Aspens in two with its clubbing paws as it fought to get a better look inside. Enraged at my absence, it threw back its head and gave a long, mournful howl that seemed to embolden and enrage many of the other Weres with it. A chorus of howls ensued, and a number of the Weres started to gather at the bodies of the two Weres I'd sent to sleepytime land.

Abshire and I had not wasted their mourning or false hunt. He had taken one side of the boulder and I another. At my command, he began to fire on semiautomatic, trying to kill or cripple as many Weres as he could before they could get to us. I was more selective. I still wanted that second Pale Were. Failing that, I wanted several of the lighter colored Weres, the ones whose color might indicate middle age or enough age that they were on the brink of becoming a Pale Were. It was the adults that had the power to create the viral serum used for human transformations.

I used two of my last three sedative arrows on two Weres that definitely sported a much lighter hued fur, one a male and the second a female. Then it was just nock, draw, and fire my broadhead arrows in rapid succession while the Weres gathered around the boulder trying to claw us and gain footing to the top. The fight at the boulder gained constant momentum as more and more Weres seemed to materialize out of the forest. Abshire ran through two magazines, and although bodies were piling up, there always seemed to be more coming. Had Dusty been there, she would have recalled the fight at the most famous of all Texas shrines. She would have been hollering, "Remember the Alamo!" as she swung her imaginary flintlock in consonance with those legendary defenders.

Rapidly running out of arrows, I fired first one and then two screamers into the air. The noise was ear-piercing. Even the Weres visibly winced at that particular frequency. Once again, I noted that the younger Weres seemed to lose their balance for a moment when they heard the first sound, almost as if they'd undergone a small stroke. Abshire ran out of ammunition about the same time I ran out of arrows, save one, my last sedative arrow. The clamor paused for a moment and then redoubled as the Weres quickly understood we were now virtually defenseless with only Abshire's rifle and my bow for clubbing.

A big male managed to climb halfway onto the top of our boulder while Abshire and I were defending ourselves with crawlers to our front. A truly bloodcurdling howl split the air, and everything seemed to stop. Just stop. Abshire and I looked at one another and then behind the group of grasping Weres that had been trying to grab or slash at our feet. A large Pale Were stood about 30 feet away, all alone in the clearing. It slowly walked forward, and the crowd parted as he stepped over the living and the dead Weres sprawled before the face of our boulder until it came to a place about 10 feet away.

Before it opened its mouth, I heard a noise behind me. I spun to find the male behind us had finally gained the boulder top. It was standing there, jaws open and arms hanging to its side, eyes burning as it loomed above us. I'd been fighting nausea since the assault on the boulder started. I now felt all the bile and acids of my stomach fighting to erupt. Both of my wounds were bleeding. I could feel myself getting a little light-headed from the exertions I'd just been through and the steady loss of blood. As the adrenaline in me ebbed, my knees started to give way, so I propped myself up using my bow and waited. So did Abshire. We waited for the next act.

To my utter astonishment, the Pale Were began to speak. Its voice sounded like 40 miles of bad road, but it was intelligible. It spoke slowly with a deep resonance to its voice like sandpaper pulled through the lower ranges of a transistor radio. All the Weres turned to watch us as it spoke. I heard our own private, Lurch, behind us take a step closer to us. In its halting voice, the Pale Were spoke to me. It told me it knew me. I was the one who hunted with the small bear the Weres now called Ghost Bear. I was the Archer whose arrows (flying knives) stank of death to its people. The Weres were called Na-ta-heh by the first peoples, the Cherokees. It meant Skin Walker, the bringer of death. Those soldiers with me were called Spat-sheh, the little people afraid to fight who carried small thunderbolts from the sky that the Weres called Grate-soh, the misery of the cowards.

The Pale Were started to tell us that very soon we would lose hundreds of our young ones who would turn and come to be among its kind. It snorted and said we were poison to their pack, the Uge-wan-si, and were to be stalked and killed whenever and wherever found. I heard another step behind me and whispered to Abshire, "Break left when I shout, and I will go to the right. Use your knife, and we'll peel this brute behind us before he eats us." Before the Na-ta-heh could say another word, I shouted the first thing that came to my mind. "Alms for the poor!" I spun to my right, pulling out my M7 as I did so. Abshire did the same to his left. We were frozen for a brief second on the boulder top, both holding our knives out ready to stab the awful creature beside us. Its head swiveled back and forth between us like it was watching a tennis match in double time.

It was in that split second that the wonderful boom-boom-boom sound of a .50-caliber machine gun opened up. The Werewolves that had gathered in front of the boulder were being torn to pieces. Without thinking, I snatched my bow from the rock before me. Drawing the last sedative arrow from my quiver, I shot the Pale Were in the right leg before it could turn and run. I gambled on a 50-50 chance that the brute Were standing on the boulder top behind us would attack Abshire first when I bent and grabbed my bow and made my shot.

I was wrong.

The brute leaped at me and clawed at my back before Abshire could tackle it and plunge his knife into the Were's chest. It opened my shoulder up and peeled a line three ribs down before it died, not from Abshire's knife but from a deft shot by Captain Cosic that literally took off the top of the Were's head. I screamed and fell, sliding off the top of the boulder when Abshire dove and caught my left leg, holding me as I dangled head down over the edge of the rock. The .50-caliber machine gun silenced immediately, and the buzz saw sounds of AR-15s on full automatic were the last things I heard as I passed out.

DAY TWELVE 10:00 A.M.

"Well, well, well. He finally awakes," I heard a woman's voice say to someone. "His color's back, and he'll have a headache and a foggy memory from his medication, but you may stay for a bit. Just don't tire him out. He'll need some time to clear his mind. Oh, and call me if his shoulder starts to bleed again. He moves a lot, almost as if he's reliving something. Try not to get him excited." And with that, the voice faded away.

I opened my eyes after some time had passed with no more voices, and everything seemed to swim before me. There were two hazy faces looking down at me, and I didn't know who they were or where I was. My mouth tasted like I'd been kissing Gitta after one of her meals, and then I thought, *Gitta! Where was she? And Polaris, where was she? And where am I?* I suddenly came awake and tried to sit up in a panic until I could feel four arms pushing me back down and a soft voice telling me to relax, just relax, that everything was all right, that I was in a hospital and Gitta and Polaris were just fine, thank you, and both missed me.

My vision seemed to clear a bit. I saw Dusty and the Major's face looking down at me. Dusty was smiling. That was worth any three days of medicine as I found myself inadvertently smiling back. Then my eyes turned to the Major. The corners of her mouth were turned up as she patted my shoulder. She asked if I'd enjoyed my nap. She followed that up by telling me that I could have the day off but that tomorrow I'd be coming back to the Rat's Nest. There was work to be done. It seemed I'd also made quite a name for myself. The Special Forces guys wanted me to go back with them. Lt. Col. Spikes had to step in and reaffirm to Captain Yamata that yes, I was still assigned to the Major and would be for some time, and that Clarion had called twice to see how I was, and would I please hurry up and get back to Chagrin Falls because they had five Weres to interview at the containment facility. Besides, my folks were asking every three minutes (or thereabouts, it seemed) when I could come home or when they could come to see me. Whew! It's nice to know I'm wanted, but what had just happened at Mt. Rogers? Why was I here in a hospital, and what about Gitta and Polaris? "Lie still," the Major told me while Dusty went to get me a cup of ice water. "I'll fill you in if you *just lie still!*"

So I did.

The Major told me that Sergeant Abshire had managed to retain his hold on my leg. He gradually pulled me back up on top of the rock after the big menacing Were was killed by Captain Cosic's shot. The three Weres into which I'd put sedative arrows were taken alive. They were now at the Chagrin Falls Containment Facility. More than 50 Werewolves were slain in the firefight at the boulder, a few more during the preliminary sweeps that were going on before the groups heard the screaming arrows. Captain Yamata and Captain Cosic both took casualties with eight wounded and seven killed between their two groups.

Gitta had proven to be a better and more deadly fighter than anyone expected, seemingly able to appear from nowhere in the midst of the Weres and then vanish, only to reappear again in the midst of another group, killing or maiming any of the unsuspecting Weres unfortunate to be part of that group. Then she was gone again like a ghost in the night.

But Polaris had been a puzzle. She kept flying in circles about 100 feet above the fighting. She periodically issued several sharp cries to which Gitta seemed to respond.

The end result was that Gitta moved to a new place and suddenly appeared in the midst of a new group of several Weres hiding in the forest or underbrush, and then mayhem ensued. It was almost as if Gitta were flushing them from hiding as a setter would a quail. Just puzzling to watch, the witnesses reported, because falcons and wolverines don't normally communicate. Yet somehow those two seemed to be doing just that.

All the wounded were airlifted out by helicopter to various hospitals. I happened to be sent to the major trauma unit at the hospital in Hickory, North Carolina. Two other soldiers were also there, but their wounds were not as severe as mine. They were being released that same day later in the afternoon. I would be kept one more day and would then go back to the Rat's Nest with Sergeant Saddler. There, I would stay for a day before returning home to Chagrin Falls where Clarion was eager to put me to work. It would be mental work, not physical, because there was a lot to learn from the Weres and little time left to do it.

Operation Pale Horse was declared an unqualified success. The second-largest known concentration of Werewolves operating in the North Carolina area was virtually eliminated, and not one but four Pale Weres were captured alive. My initiative in going after the last Pale Were with Sergeant Abshire was the turning point. Lt. Col. Spikes was of two minds when he finally pieced together all that happened.

At first, Spikes didn't know whether to kill me or praise me for the risk I had taken, but he gradually calmed down and realized I'd done exactly what he would have done under the same circumstances, and I had done it better. So today I was praiseworthy, and my life had not been shortened. "He's quite fond of you, you know, Cody," said the Major, "as we all are. That's why I'm bringing you back to the Rat's Nest for a day to let Sunstar work on you before you two both head out to Chagrin Falls. She's going with you not just to treat you but to start to share her potions and herbs with the biomedical research team there at the facility. We think there is great promise there."

Promise, shomish, I thought to myself. The thought of spending some time with Sunstar in my hometown was thrilling to say the least, and I was perking up already. And then I thought again. Casey! I would have a chance to see Casey, and Sunstar could meet her. Then reality set in, and I remembered Casey was already off with her new soccer squad and wouldn't be back home until the end of August. My enthusiasm dampened immediately, and then I started to feel a kind of curious relief. I wanted Casey to know about Sunstar because I wanted Casey in every part of my life, but I didn't want them to meet at this time after all. It was a difficult feeling, one I'd never felt before. Clearly I was confused and finally blamed the medicine I was taking. That must be it. I was groggy and confused because of the pain medication. Having rationalized my feelings away with a good excuse, I felt better and more peaceful than I had in a while. I started to look forward to the trip home. Boy! Would my folks be surprised!

Who was I kidding? What I meant was this: Boy! Won't Casey's folks be surprised!

DAY TWENTY 11:00 A.M.

It was good to finally arrive back at the Rat's Nest. Sergeant Saddler made it an easy, not fast drive so as not to jostle me too much, but my shoulder was sore, and I keenly felt every bump in the road. I had no appetite for our regular food stop. We came straight back to Blowing Rock where I got a change of clothes and then went on to the Rat's Nest. I was just uncomfortable enough to not be looking forward to the drive to the airport tomorrow or the flight home, except that Sunstar would be with me, primarily to keep an eye on me if I slipped, fell, or succumbed to the medicine's narcotic effects and got a little daffy on the way.

I was greeted by a number of folks in the Major's command when we arrived at the Rat's Nest. Someone went over to the Motor Pool to get some of the leatherware Sergeant Saddler had had made but was unable to distribute before Operation Pale Horse started. The first thing I did was walk around to the back of the Chapel to see Gitta. Pee Wee and Sergeant Saddler walked behind me. Gitta heard my steps and ran around the corner to meet me. She promptly knocked me over backward as she plunged her head into my midsection in greeting. Pee Wee caught me in time and set me down on the ground beside her. I gave her the biggest hug I could with my limited circumstances.

It was a kind of pandemonium for a moment. We all got sorted out eventually. I wasn't ready to let her go, and she wasn't ready to take her paw off my leg, so we just sat and visited a while as we each filled the other in on what had happened since we had last seen one another. The Major was wise enough to let us spend some time together before she sent Dusty around to retrieve me. Almost everyone had drifted away from Gitta and me by that time, so we were surprised and tickled when Dusty produced a Twinkie for all of us, herself included. We three spent another 15 minutes in lip-smacking consumption just visiting in the sun.

Gitta was marginally aware of my injuries. Since I was the only one who could speak with her, it had been a hard time for her with plenty of worry. She was in a much better mood after my visit, although it was probably the Twinkie, if truth be told. Nevertheless, I was able to convey to her how much she was appreciated and how she had saved lives because of her role in the assault. I also explained that she was regarded by everyone at the Rat's Nest as a hero. That seemed to please her. She really grinned that shark's-tooth grin when I told her what the Pale Were had said about her. "The Ghost Bear," it kept mumbling to itself. "The Ghost Bear!"

I told her that seemed like a particularly appropriate name for her during the last part of the assault. She and Polaris had apparently been communicating and disrupting several of the Were groups that were trying to hide from the assault teams. "Her eyes and your stealth and strength made a huge difference," I told her. I told her, too, that I was sorry I had missed her performance but that I was very likely alive because of it.

She said nothing. She just bumped me with her head several times and once again laid her paw across my leg.

I told her I would be gone for a good while, perhaps three to four weeks. I was going back to my home to heal, and Sunstar was going with me. Dusty would be here every day. She (Gitta) would be free to come and go as she wished. Food and the cage would be here for her when she wished and probably an occasional Twinkie. If she wanted to go explore, she needed to flip both her feed and water bowl over so Dusty and the Major would know she was out exploring and wouldn't worry about her. When she returned, she should flip them back over. Dusty would fill them again, twice each day.

I also explained that Polaris would not stay here with her. She would be kept back at the Rehabilitation Center, her home before this became her new home. There were people who could look after her special needs there. With a final, awkward hug, I stood and followed Dusty back into the Rat's Nest. Gitta watched me all the way to the corner of the building and then closed her eyes and napped in the midday sun. She had earned her rest and some time off if anyone had. Like any good soldier, she could fall fast asleep in a New York minute.

My debriefing once I was back inside seemed to go on forever, but we were finished in time for dinner. It was Sergeant Saddler's treat. The Major, Pee Wee, Sergeant Saddler, and I had spent a great deal of time reviewing the good, the bad, and the effective about Pale Horse. We reviewed strategy and tactics and started identifying improvements needed for future such excursions. I couldn't speak for the other two men, but when we were done, I felt as if the Major had found and pulled out every cogent thought I had to include in her report. She did commend me on my initiative in going after the big Pale Were with Sergeant Abshire. She also cautioned me strongly against putting myself in positions where the Alamo became the descriptor for a fight. She told me, too, that the horn bow had been found and brought back. It would be kept at the Rat's Nest during my absence along with my wakizashi blade.

When my shoulder started to act up, the Major noticed immediately and called a halt. She asked me to stop over in the morning before Sergeant Saddler took me to pick up Sunstar and head to the airport. Lt. Col. Spikes would be there. He wanted a word with me. When I asked her if the big Pale Were said anything to anyone when it revived, she looked at me curiously. She asked me what I meant. I repeated to her word for word what the Pale Were said to Abshire and me and told her it had said it *in English*. She recoiled immediately. She said it was the first she'd heard of that. She asked me if I was sure of what I had just reported and queried me again to see if perhaps I was mixing up memories of my encounter. I told her that Sergeant Abshire was a witness. She could call and ask him directly. She immediately reached for the phone and did just that. She was still waiting for him to be located when Sergeant Saddler took me back to the inn for dinner.

I ate little. The folks at the inn were gracious and solicitous when they heard I'd taken a hard fall from a Jeep and seriously injured my shoulder while trying to survey a bad stretch of mountains near Mt. Rogers. I told them I was going home to Ohio to heal before coming back to school. I would probably rent a room with them again when I returned. They mentioned that they had long-term rates. They would sit with me to discuss them when I returned.

DAY TWENTY-ONE 8:30 A.M.

I was gritting my teeth by the time Sergeant Saddler picked me up for a quick breakfast and our trip to the Rat's Nest. I had with me the keys to the Chevrolet. They were for Dusty. She would pick it up and store it for me back at the Motor Pool. With my one good arm, I'd finally managed to dress myself and pack a reasonably decent suitcase. Nevertheless, all the movement and stretching had made my shoulder flare up. I was not in a good mood. Sergeant Saddler told me to take four aspirin and live with it but grinned as he said it. He did check my dressing. He helped me secure it in a much better fashion than I'd been able to do after changing it earlier in the morning. Still, I told him he had a rather desultory bedside manner. He should stick with his goal of Officer's Candidate School. A budding doctor he wasn't.

He just laughed and ignored me.

When we got to the Chapel, the place was already abuzz. The Major and Lt. Col. Spikes were sitting together on a conference call with Clarion. Both motioned me into her office as soon as they saw me. After confirming my story about the Pale Were's English speech to Sergeant Abshire and me, the Major had immediately called Lt. Col. Spikes and Clarion. That set up the conference call.

That a Were, apparently a very important and powerful Were, could still retain the ability to speak English after a change was incredibly important to Clarion. It didn't mean I was expendable. It did mean if I died, they would have some way to try to crack the key to the Werewolves' plans. But they still needed me. Without me, they had no certain way to tell if the Were was lying when it told them something. With me, the Were had no way to know I could read its mind or intentions when in close proximity— not unless it was already communicating with two of the other Weres that had had their chance with me weeks earlier at the containment facility.

We spent the better part of an hour on the phone. We closed when Clarion asked me to swing by the Polo Club when I arrived tomorrow so we could have a chance to talk together. I told him I would be with my parents and Sunstar. He paused for a moment and told me to stop at the house and drop off my mom and Sunstar and have my dad bring me by. My dad was already up-to-date on the facility. Sunstar soon would be, but time was crucial. Clarion wanted me there for his first crack at the big Pale Were. I said I'd see him there. Then he did a nice thing. He said Lt. Col. Spikes had filled him in on my activities during Pale Horse as best he could. Clarion wanted to personally congratulate me on what I'd done. He knew it had come at a cost, almost the cost of my life. He wanted me to know that he and a number of others I would never see or may never know about were also grateful.

His comments touched me. I thought Clarion was one of if not *the* coolest person I'd ever met.

With the conference call wrapped up, Lt. Col. Spikes called a formal assembly outside. All the members of the Rat's Nest were there. This was a uniform day except for me. Everyone looked pretty smart in their Class A buttoned uniforms with cover (caps). He asked me to stand to one side of him. The Major reported everyone present and accounted for. She topped off her report by a snappy salute to Lt. Col. Spikes. He asked her to come and stand by me along with Gitta. Dusty had brought her without telling me.

Gitta was combed and brushed. Dusty had tied a bright red ribbon and bow around her neck, to my utter astonishment and chagrin. I asked Gitta what she was doing. She answered back that she really liked the ribbon. It was such a new concept to the wolverine. She was determined to milk it for all it was worth. I closed my eyes and silently cringed. It was one of those girl things that I just didn't get. But then Gitta had accused me, a human, of guy things that she couldn't fathom either, species notwithstanding.

While this exchange was going on, Lt. Col. Spikes called Sergeant Saddler forth. The Sergeant brought with him three medals with citations. To the Major he awarded the Joint Service Commendation Medal with V device for heroism and meritorious service for her role in planning and helping execute Operation Pale Horse. To Gitta he awarded the National Defense Service Medal, and to me, he awarded a Purple Heart for, as he said, "failing to get out of the way of a bigger, nastier, and apparently faster opponent." That brought a cheer and a laugh from everyone. Then Spikes went on to describe how pivotal my role with Gitta and Polaris had been. He turned and offered his profound congratulations for my efforts with a gripping handshake and a snappy salute. My face was the color of Gitta's ribbon. I was embarrassed, excited, and deeply honored all at the same time. I stood as straight as I could with my heavily bandaged shoulder. He reminded me that the Purple Heart would be worn someday when I received my officer's commission and was a uniformed soldier. It could certainly rest in honor on my dresser or mantle at home until then.

By 11:30 a.m., Sergeant Saddler brought the car around. After a lot of goodbyes and even a peck on my cheek from Dusty, we finally pulled out of the Chapel's parking area and headed for Sunstar's home. It was a bittersweet parting. I didn't want to go because of my new family, the Major's unit. I wanted to go to the Weres' forthcoming interrogation with Clarion. I was starting to learn that the military was an awful lot of bookend hellos and goodbyes. There were also hours of boredom interrupted by moments of stark terror.

Mr. Walksabout was in the front yard waiting for us as we drove up. He waved and disappeared into the house as our car rolled to a stop. In just minutes, Michael, Mrs. Walksabout, Sunstar, and Mr. Walksabout all came out of the house and over to our car. I managed to get my door open. I exited in time to get an awkward hug from Michael and Mrs. Walksabout and a handshake from Mr. Walksabout. They were all interested in my shoulder bandage. They heard through Pee Wee that I'd had a bad accident.

They all knew Sergeant Saddler through Pee Wee. We spent several minutes exchanging pleasantries in their front yard before Sunstar was able to come to my side and stand by me. She held out her hand to me, and I shook it softly and once again forgot to let go as I looked at her and just smiled. I must have seemed like an absolute oaf. I could think of a million things to say to her but couldn't utter a single one. Sergeant Saddler rescued me by saying that the medication I was taking for the pain left me virtually speechless and a little foggy in the brain. That brought a comforting hand and immediate attention from Sunstar and her mother. It left Michael quietly laughing behind their backs. Mr. Walksabout was loading Sunstar's two bags into the trunk as we all chatted. When they were safely stowed, he shook Sergeant Saddler's hand, clapped me on my good shoulder, and bid us goodbye so we'd make the airport on time. It was more than a hint.

We reached the airport without incident and even a bit early. Sergeant Saddler had the soldier's dread of being late and was usually early to all his appointments. It was something most military folks had in common, as I came to learn. It was a good habit to have. The Sergeant helped us check in, get our tickets, and head for the right gate. With a hearty handshake, he bid us adieu. Sunstar simply took my arm and walked me to the correct gate area, found us two seats together, and helped me sit down without wrenching my shoulder. Looking around to make sure we were in a semiprivate situation, she placed her hand on my shoulder and began singing softly. After several minutes, I could have sworn the pain lessened, and I began thinking of quiet places like meadow streams or hillsides covered in flowers. I also found myself dropping into a doze that seemed to be like falling onto a feather duster. I think I actually slept for a few minutes, awakening only when the loudspeaker announced our flight and destination.

For a few moments, I felt terrific and then realized where we were. Taking Sunstar's arm this time, I escorted her out onto the tarmac and up into the plane. I fell asleep as soon as we took off, and Sunstar had to waken me as we landed in Columbus. I could have kicked myself a thousand times, but Sunstar just smiled at me and told me the rest I got was the most important thing I'd done today. Maybe so, I thought to myself, but passing up several hours of one-on-one conversation sitting next to Sunstar seemed pretty lame to me.

My folks were there to meet us. Dad managed to find our bags and, with a porter's help, brought them to our car. Mom made me ride up front with Dad on the way home so she could sit in the back and ask Sunstar about 4,000 questions. The two of them really hit it off and never stopped talking from the time we left the parking lot until we pulled into my driveway. I quietly pouted the whole time until I remembered Clarion's request and quickly asked my dad to take me over to the Polo Club. Dad stayed long enough to carry all three bags into our home and then drove me to the containment facility for my meeting with Clarion. He declined to come in with me saying he had to get back and help my mom, but I really think he just wanted to sit and listen to and stare at Sunstar. She had that effect on all men from five years old to 95.

DAY TWENTY-ONE 5:30 P.M.

I went down to the containment facility through the concealed opening in the main club building. I was a little tired and didn't want to walk down the long ramp, the hidden entrance through the stable tack room. One of the secretaries saw me as I entered the facility and immediately came over, greeted me with a smile, and, gently taking my right arm, escorted me back to Clarion's temporary office near the cages. He was in, and when he looked up and saw me, he leaped from his desk and shouted, "Cody! You're here! My, my, all trussed up and nowhere to go, eh?" Laughing at his poor pun, he strode over and gingerly shook my hand.

"I am so glad you're here," he said. "The large Pale Were you shot that can speak English has been waiting for you. Let's go see him. I need your impressions. Now!" He practically pushed by me in his desire to start questioning the big Pale Were. I walked over to the main cages behind him and stood with him in front of the end cage, just behind the white line. I said nothing. The big Were had been pacing back and forth in its cage while it watched us walk up and take our positions. It unexpectedly let out a tangled howl that was immediately answered by the Weres in the first two cages. It was alerting them to my presence and asking their advice on what to do to resist me. I said nothing and merely looked at the Pale Were, letting my mind empty as I felt its impressions of hatred, loathing, and fear. These are not guys we're going to win over with forgiveness and kindness, I thought to myself.

Clarion stood beside me and addressed the Pale Were in measured tones. "I understand you can still speak," he said. "So speak to me. Why are you hunting and killing our people?" The Pale Were jumped at the cage bars and tried to reach through and slash Clarion, but its claws fell just inches short. I watched in admiration. Clarion neither raised his voice nor flinched. He reminded me of a bookish Stonewall Jackson, immovable in the face of a threat.

"We are not killing *your* people!" came the deep, gravelly voice. "You are killing *our* people!" With that said, the Pale Were began slamming its paws at the cage bars, roaring and howling as if it were demon possessed. I took a quick half step backward. I was sure my eyes were open to the size of quarters. Clarion simply stood still and didn't even blink. If there was ever a king of cool—and I don't mean the clothes or dance or car kind—he was it. I had never met another person who could stand an arm's length away from a frothing, berserk Werewolf and look as unperturbed as if he were ordering a hot dog from a New York street vendor. The man must have had ice for blood.

Clarion let the Pale Were rant on until it began to show visible signs of exhaustion. When the decibel level lowered to that of a passing circus, Clarion spoke again, telling the Were that either there would be a conversation or an execution, it really didn't matter to him. But the Were he selected would find the execution painful beyond words and it, the Pale Were, would be the one administering the punishment. Clarion left it at that and, signaling me, walked back to his office. I followed right behind. I had questions to ask. Plenty of them.

We spoke for about an hour. Clarion informed me that he actually wasn't bluffing. If intelligent life forms could harbor hate, they could also reason to some extent. That meant that the Pale Were, if it thought it had a chance to escape, would will itself to remain alive hoping for that chance. Moreover, it would let one, maybe two of its minions die before it would act to stop it, but then it would probably step in to stop the killing. It was only logical.

A leader needs forces in the face of a determined enemy, and we were certainly determined. Besides, it wouldn't be a loyalty thing to save another Werewolf; it would simply be a logical conservation of forces. Put another way, generals need soldiers if they want to stay generals, and a studied elimination of the Pale Were forces would effectively bust him back to being a private, with no army.

Clarion then questioned me extensively about Sunstar and her capabilities as a healer and potion maker. I explained that she certainly had some powers that were out of the normal and that while I had never tasted her potions, I had seen some truly remarkable healing with respect to Polaris. That seemed to both excite and satisfy him. He told me that the biomed team with whom she would be working was led by a scientist from Utah, a Shoshone Indian who had been trained at Cornell with his doctorate from MIT in Boston. He would often speak of the healing herbs his grandmother used on him when he was a boy and was especially pleased that he would be working with an active practitioner, the Cherokee woman known as Sunstar. The team leader's name was Dr. Clint Walker.

I surmised the last names of Walker and Walksabout derived from a like symbol or idiosyncratic practice common to both Shoshone and Cherokee cultures, that once

Sunstar met Dr. Walker, good things were going to happen. Clarion just smiled. He ventured that he'd take any progress or happy hopes at this stage of the game but that the Weres' assumed deadline for action in North Carolina was fast approaching. He needed tomorrow's promised answers yesterday. I left his office a few minutes later with an increased sense of urgency after calling my dad to come and pick me up. I bid Clarion good night but somehow didn't really think he'd be getting a lot of sleep. I wasn't even sure I'd get much sleep, but I was wrong.

My eyes were drooping heavily by the time my dad picked me up. I fought sleep all the way home and wasn't hungry when I walked in and saw the spread of sandwiches Mom had prepared for me. I didn't see Sunstar and asked quickly if she'd eaten. My mom said yes and that Mrs. Allegro had come over and, after meeting Sunstar, had a great visit and asked her to stay at their house in Casey's old room. She felt that would give each of us young folks a privacy that we might not have enjoyed running around in the same house. My mom thought that was a splendid idea. She helped Sunstar carry her stuff over to the Allegros' house. I listened quietly, said nothing, and inwardly screamed. *What is it about parents? Weren't they ever young once? Can they truly be that dense?*

Didn't they know I wasn't a high school teenager anymore and that being close to Sunstar was my chance to find out about her, not as a recent invocation of Casey but as a separate woman who had her own mannerisms and identity? Every time I looked at Sunstar from now on, I'd probably remember the Allegros and Sunstar as a symbolic substitute for Casey. Of course, there might be problems if Sunstar stayed under our roof, but that was part of the fun of having her here. Besides, I was sure we could handle any problems by ourselves.

You could bet and win that trudging upstairs to bed that night was one of the longest, most disappointing walks I'd taken in years. What hurt the most was that the folks were right, of course. I thought I hated that more than Sunstar's absence. Hmph! Who said growing up was ever easy?

I did call Casey's room phone after I climbed in bed. Sunstar answered tentatively. I stuttered a minute, gathered my wits, and softly told her good night. She giggled and hung up.

DAY TWENTY-TWO 8:30 A.M.

I'd been up since 7:00 a.m. I was killing time at the breakfast table when my dad came in, ate, bid me goodbye, and left again. My mom showed up just after his departure. She fixed a good homecooked breakfast for me with all the things she remembered I liked. It helped me forget completely about Casey and Sunstar. My mom's cooking was wickedly good. In fact, I was polishing off my second helping of eggs when Sunstar knocked on the door and asked if we were up yet. I choked down a mouthful of scrambled eggs while hurrying to the door. I managed to squeak out "Come on in!" before I started coughing. Mom took pity on me and brought a glass of water to me. She also helped pound my back until all my various passageways got straightened out. It was embarrassing to say the least.

Sunstar was grinning ear to ear, and I started to get a bit huffy around the collar, but it quickly wore off when she asked if she could take the place next to me and perhaps have some breakfast as well. Things calmed down after that. We had a fun breakfast, Mom included. Sunstar said she had a chance to look around Casey's room the night before. From the awards, trophies, and medals, Sunstar felt honored that she had been given Casey's room. She opined that if her pictures were to be believed, "Casey must be quite a girl. Beautiful, too!" She even asked me if Casey and I had a thing going because my name certainly appeared on more than one bit of memorabilia in Casey's room.

I stammered at that until my mom came to my rescue. She explained that I was a normally shy boy because of my earlier childhood injuries. Casey and I had literally grown up as best friends. She explained that Casey often accompanied me to various social functions when I was unable or unwilling to call someone else. "Mom!" I yelped. "You make me sound like a pity case. It wasn't like that at all. I just preferred Casey's company because she was so special. If you've got a great steak, why go for a can of beans?"

Sunstar broke out laughing. She reminded me that comparing girls to food wasn't the most flattering thing in the world, although having a brother of her own, she realized that most of the time they were nothing more than an ambulatory stomach looking for a free handout. Then she flat out floored me when she carefully looked at me. She said when I started to get riled up, my brow furrowed and I looked rather dashing, even handsome. "Don't you think so, Mrs. Dugway?" she asked. My mom had the gall to answer, grinning, "Yes, I think you're right. I hadn't noticed, but I do think you're right, my dear." At that, Mom giggled as well.

I stood up with both women smiling at me in a proprietary way and brusquely said we had to go, that we had work to do and should be in the car in five minutes. I told Mom I could drive Dad's truck, and she said forcefully, "No way," that my shoulder wasn't healed and wouldn't be for some time, so I'd better just get used to being chauffeured around. She then turned to Sunstar. Mom told her that this coming Saturday when my dad was home, he would check her out on his truck. Then she'd have some wheels of her own while she was in town. In the meantime, we'd best get ready and freshen up because both of us had to get to the Polo Club very soon.

As I brushed my teeth upstairs in my bathroom, I thought of all the ways mothers could actually do lasting harm to their sons because they meant well and just couldn't keep quiet. I hadn't been home a full 24 hours and already I missed being back at the Rat's Nest. At least Gitta didn't tell little boy stories about me or talk about or treat me like I was 10 years old. Then I put all those feelings aside, remembered that I had the greatest parents in the world, and that they always had my back, even if they sometimes couldn't tell it from my front. I had a good laugh at myself. I had a real crush on Casey. Sunstar was just a current fascination. Yeah. That was it. That's what I told myself, and I was never wrong. Well, almost never.

DAY TWENTY-TWO 10:00 A.M.

As we arrived at the Polo Club, my mom asked me why we were coming here instead of going downtown to meet with the Chief of Police. She had not been briefed on the real workings of the Club and couldn't understand our purpose in coming here. I couldn't breach security, so I told her a part truth. I explained that there were some animals here that Sunstar needed to look at, that she was part of the Blue Ridge Rehabilitation Center (BRRC) and worked in its animal recovery program. The BRRC was connected with Lees-McRae. Sunstar's presence here was part of a research project working with large mammals. As it turned out, several Club officials were aware of the BRRC and were looking to sponsor student research projects, so this was a first for them but a potential win-win for everyone.

As an aspiring vet, I was being allowed to come along and observe since I lived here anyway and was recovering from my accident. My mom thought that was a wonderful opportunity and wished Sunstar well on her project. She asked if we wanted to be picked up for lunch. I thanked her, gave her a quick kiss on the cheek, and declined the noon pickup. I said we'd just catch a ride home when we could. This was an administrative day with schedules to work out, paperwork to fill out, and doctors and trainers to meet. I told her I would call her when I had a better sense of what the day would be like but to expect us home about 7:00 or 8:00 p.m. With a wave as I stepped back, she drove off.

I escorted Sunstar inside and found Clarion waiting for us. He invited us into a small office, closed the door, and after a warm greeting to Sunstar introduced us to a very distinguished-looking man with a long gray-black braid of hair hanging partway down his back. He was Dr. Walker. The next hour and a half was devoted to Sunstar's security briefing and a background briefing about the Weres or Uge-wan-si, as Sunstar knew them. Clarion also covered in summary my history with the Weres and how I got and developed my communication talent.

He explained about Casey and her role as well and gave backgrounds on Lt. Col. Spikes, the Major, and Captains Yamata and Cosic. He finally explained my contract with Lt. Col. Spikes and Clarion and what my future would be if I lived long enough. He made it very clear that admitting to the very existence of Werewolves or the underground containment facility, which she would see later, would be a security breach of the highest order for which there were severe consequences. He was stern and admonished Sunstar not to slip up. He warned me again as well. It was after noon when he finally finished, and Sunstar and I were invited to lunch with Clarion and Dr. Walker in the clubhouse dining room.

Dr. Walker handled Sunstar's introduction to the containment facility and its teams of scientists. Both of us were fascinated as he explained the several directions his own classified research was taking and some of the successes his team had already achieved. The problem of the Weres, however, was as radical and severe a challenge as he and his team had ever faced. They could not seem to isolate or even identify the specific virus that caused a human to become a shape-shifter. Sadly, he said, they could not cure what they could not identify or describe. Dr. Walker thought that Sunstar's talents might lead his team into a new direction that might hold more promise than the ones Dr. Walker's team had already explored. He was a firm believer that whatever nature brought forth as a calamity, nature would also provide a cure for if we humans worked hard enough to find it.

I could see Sunstar's face light up and knew she was already thinking of new ideas and approaches, ways her skills and interests might best fit with Dr. Walker's environment. She really lit up when Dr. Walker asked her what her real name was, her Indian name. She told him, explaining that she was also a singer or chanter and had a gift of healing and soothing. Then it was Dr. Walker's turn to become animated. With a big smile, he explained that his grandmother had been a renowned healer, not just with potions but with ancient, sacred chants or incantations that had been passed down from generation to generation among his people. Then it was Sunstar's turn to get excited as she shared more information with Dr. Walker and he again with her. Smiling, Clarion excused us after an hour or so, pointing out that we had plenty to do and would catch up with the two of them later down below. I don't know if they even noticed our departure, and I was a little miffed, but Clarion reminded me that there was plenty of time in the next several weeks for some time alone with Sunstar, but there was no time for the projected disaster at Appalachian State and the people of Boone, North Carolina, if we didn't get busy.

He was right, of course, and I apologized for letting my attention drift. No need to apologize, he told me. He'd have been worried about me if my attention hadn't drifted. Sunstar could hold her own with anyone, he chuckled, and he was just thankful all the men on Dr. Walker's team were already married with children, even though Dr. Walker wasn't.

He escorted me to his office where he explained the dilemma of Hobson's Choice, an apparently free choice that offers no real alternative. That was what he wanted to extend to the Pale Were. Hobson was once an English liveryman who owned a small stable of horses. People would come to him to rent one of his horses for an errand or task. The choice he gave them was not to pick among his several horses but to either pick the one next in line, the one closest to the barn door, or nothing at all.

He explained that the Pale Were would not voluntarily give up information that would harm its own kind or frustrate their coming initiative against the humans. But we badly needed that information. Therefore, he had to place the Were in an all-or-nothing position of choice while seeming to freely extend an alternative. If the Were made the wrong decision, another Were died, for Clarion had chosen imposed death as the motivating factor for the Were's choice. It would entail the death of a fellow Were, only its death would be imposed by the Pale Were's hand and not by a human hand.

He took me over to the cage area where a large cage of very thick plexiglass was being constructed. It was 10 feet tall and about 10 feet by 10 feet in ground footage. It was a gigantic clear cube. A partially sedated Were would be placed on a steel table in the cage and strapped down. A very heavy weight would be suspended above the Were, inches from its head when the Were's face was turned sideways. The Pale Were would be strapped into a floor-mounted chair close by the table with an activator taped to its paw and the paw placed to press down on the activator. If pressure stopped on the activator, the weight would drop, crushing the first Were. If the downward hand pressure was lessened, the weight would drop only a little, accordingly, but the weight would not be reset. It could only go one way. Down. Sooner or later, the Pale Were's strength would fail, and the Were on the table would be crushed, incrementally or all at once, but a dishonorable death was inevitable.

However, if the Pale Were answered all questions in order (the horse closest to the door), correctly and honestly, both Weres would be spared and kept alive to participate in lab studies to try to find a way to reverse the virus's effect. In short, they would be cooperating to see how a Werewolf might return to being a human. It was an all-or-nothing choice for the Pale Were. It could not let its companion suffer only a little pressure that would be momentarily relieved. Once the weight made contact, the misery of the Werewolf under the weight would only get worse, never better, until an ignoble death finally ensued.

The questions were designed in such a way that to answer the first was not an apparent breach of trust for the Pale Were, but it would yield a piece of important information. It would lead to the next question, one that in and of itself would not be such a breach of trust for the Pale Were. But when answered correctly, it would enlarge the information answered by the first question. And so it would go on until 10 questions were asked in a specific order and hopefully answered. If all were answered correctly, we would know the when and how of the presumed attack, but the Pale Were would not believe it had given so much away.

306

Of course, the Pale Were could simply lift its paw and kill a fellow Were, but we would simply get another prisoner Were and continue. To increase the strain on the Pale Were, we would do the experiment in front of the open cages so all the Weres could see (but not hear) the questioning. If several Weres died, the Pale Were could always plead later that the game had been rigged. But my presence and ability to communicate directly with the Weres meant I would tell them the truth on the spot, and they would decide for themselves what they wanted to do to or with the Pale Were when it was returned to their combined cages. No one had to die, but it was likely that if one died, all would eventually die, and painfully.

DAY TWENTY-TWO 4:00 P.M.

It had taken a while, but the cube was finished and the table and chair placed inside. Both were bolted to the floor. A small forklift was brought in and the weight attached to it by steel cables. An electronic device was wired to the forklift control. Its remote control was taped to the Pale Were's right paw. The sedated Were was brought in and strapped down on the table. The Pale Were was restrained and also brought in and strapped to the chair with its arm extended and the device's remote control button mashed down beneath its paw.

Clarion entered the cube with a folding chair, placed it in front of the Pale Were, and sat down. He explained again to the Pale Were what would happen if it lessened the pressure on the control button. Clarion said he had a list of 10 questions to which he needed answers. The questions were direct, simple, and brief. I was standing outside the cube positioned immediately behind the Pale Were, listening to its mind, which at the moment was full of unbelievable rage. The mind of the Were on the table was full of horror and fear. It was a good match.

Clarion began the questioning promptly at 1630 hours. Clarion asked the first question in a slow, understandable cadence. No answer from the Pale Were. Clarion waited several minutes and reasked the question, dispassionately, without emotion. Again, he waited for several minutes. Then he asked the question again in the same tone, same cadence. Again, no answer. Clarion waited several minutes and once more asked the question in the same tone, one of almost indifference. Again, no answer, but a slight loss of concentration caused the Pale Were to momentarily ease up on its paw, and the weight jerked and slipped slightly.

The Were on the table immediately began howling in a frightened, pleading tone as the great weight swung slowly above its head before its oscillation dampened. The Pale Were reacted by pressing down quite hard on the activator button, but while it immediately arrested the weight's drop, now the Pale Were did not know how much to ease up on the pressure it was putting forth, so its muscles were now under a greater strain. Several beads of sweat popped out on the Pale Were's forehead, and I could sense distress starting to impinge on its anger. What the Pale Were did not realize was that this new physical strain was designed to cloud its perception of the questions even more so it would feel even less inhibited about eventually answering Clarion's questions.

And so it continued.

Several hours passed when Clarion asked the Pale Were the first question in that banal tone of his for the (seemingly) 2,000th time, only this time the Pale Were gave a partial answer. All of us who were watching perked up, but Clarion's imitation of a robot didn't vary. He looked past the Pale Were at me for our prearranged signal—both thumbs up if it was a complete, honest answer; one thumb up if it was an honest, partial answer. Both thumbs down if it was an out-and-out lie; one thumb down if it was an answer designed to mislead, not fully deceive.

I held out my hand with the thumb down, an answer to mislead. Clarion looked at the Pale Were without speaking for several minutes and then spoke. "You are lying to me. I want the complete, honest truth. Let us begin again." And Clarion once more asked his original question in the same unhurried cadence and tone as he had the first 2,001 times. After about 20 minutes of the same-ol', same-ol', the Pale Were finally cracked and answered Clarion's question. Clarion looked at me, and I gave him two thumbs up. He looked at the Pale Were for several minutes in silence, then broke it. In that same aggravating, deliberate, banal tone, he asked the second question.

The Pale Were, out of apparent relief, temporarily lost its concentration and eased up slightly on the activator button. Immediately, the heavy weight fell a few parts of an inch and now rested lightly against the side of the face of the strapped-down Were. The inexorable pressure triggered an immediate screaming bout that lasted several minutes until the affected Were broke into great racking sobs. Once again, the Pale Were pushed the activator button hard into its arm to stop the descent of the great weight. When the tabled Were's sobs lessened and most of its screaming stopped, Clarion again asked question number two. No answer. Several minutes passed, and Clarion repeated his question, flat tone, measured cadence. This went on and on and on for several hours.

At 7:00 p.m., I leaned over and asked one of the administrators to please call my dad and have Sunstar picked up or be given an escort home. I could not leave Clarion, and this was liable to go on all night. I would see Sunstar tomorrow. He agreed, stood up, and left to find Sunstar and get her home. I turned my attention back to the Pale Were and Clarion.

It was almost 5:30 a.m. the next morning before Clarion got the last of his information from the Pale Were. There had been a number of false starts, attempts at deception, and screams, sobs, and tears along the way, but the ending was anticlimactic and inevitable. The Pale Were finally answered Clarion's 10th question, and Clarion just looked at it for several minutes. He said "thank you" in that same unsettling, infuriating, banal tone and rose from his seat. At the flick of his fingers, the weight was lifted from the strapped-down Were's head. The Were and the Pale Were were immediately given a sedative so they could be unstrapped and moved back into their cages.

Clarion came over and thanked me profusely. He knew both the exercise and the drama would be hard on me, but I had played the part that actually made the whole thing work, and we had gotten the information we needed to allow Lt. Col. Spikes and all of us to now thwart the expected Boone attack. Clarion told me to go home and sleep until I woke up and then come back the next day. He still had much to do and wanted my shoulder to heal, not be under any more strain than necessary. As he turned to go, I stopped him and asked if I might ask him a personal question. He turned back to face me and said of course.

I looked at him and asked how he managed to get used to killing something in cold blood as had almost happened several times to the Werewolf on the table. He looked at me intently for a few minutes and then smiled. "Cody, lad, the game was rigged. If the Pale Were had lifted the activator completely off its armrest to let the other Were die, the weight would have fallen only one inch. It could not crush the Were on the table. We anticipated it might try that to see if we were serious, and we would have staged a big acrimonious scene blaming everybody for the system failure. We would have staged a rebuild and started over. If he had done that again, well, we didn't have a Plan C for backup.

With an expression of amazement, I started to smile and then started laughing. "Why didn't you tell me this at the outset?" I asked. "Why leave me swinging on the same gate as the Pale Were?"

"We couldn't tell you, Cody," he replied. "You were in a mental link with the Werewolf, and it might have sensed what you knew if you knew it. You had to be just as outraged and scared as it was in order for this to work. I'm sorry we had to do that to you, but there was no other way. You had no need to know, so you didn't."

I chuckled to myself as he walked away, and I started for the way out and home. I didn't like being tricked, but I had and would continue to trust Clarion. He was one clever cookie, but now I knew he had a weakness. He had no Plan C, something Captain Yamata demanded of us and always had for himself, along with Plans D, E, and probably F. I had made a good decision to join this outfit. I was feeling a little cocky but tired, too. I had played my part. Well.

I wondered what Gitta and Polaris were up to as my driver took me home. I missed them already and thought they would enjoy the story of the Pale Were's capitulation.

DAY TWENTY-THREE 12:20 P.M.

I awoke in my own bed at 0800 hours, at 1030 hours, and again at 1220 hours, the last time for good. I just lay there, perfectly content to wallow in my sheets, dozing. Life was good. About five minutes later, my bladder signaling distress with every move, I hobbled to the bathroom and began my daily ablutions, taking time to cover my shoulder in plastic before I stepped into the shower. I must have stood there for 20 minutes, but it was too soon to leave until I heard my mom faintly calling to me from downstairs. I turned off the shower, poked my head out the bathroom door, and told her I'd be along shortly. Thirty minutes later, I settled down to a breakfast of french toast and sausage. Life at 18 years old seldom got better than that.

But it was about to change. Radically.

My mom sat with me and visited while I ate. She made sure I had plenty to eat and let me know how pleased she and my dad were that I was home again. They both knew I would never be home again for any extended period of time, and the next real home I experienced would probably be my own in seven or eight years, if not sooner, when I graduated from veterinary school. It made me feel older than I was to listen to her, but it also made me eager to be out on my own and start my own new life away from Chagrin Falls. I told her that my life right now was confusing, that I wanted to go and at the same time wanted everything to stay the same, even though I knew that could never happen again.

She bent over, gave me a kiss on my forehead, and stood up. Taking my dishes to the sink, she turned to me, smiled, and said, "I know, honey. Your dad and I felt the same way when we were your age. Just know that we are always here for you and want to help in any way we can, but sometimes our best help is just to let you work things out for yourself, however painful that is."

I stood up, walked over to her, and gave her a two-arm squeezing hug. "Thanks, Mom," I whispered. "I love you more than I can say." I turned and headed upstairs to freshen up before she could see the tears starting up in my eyes. My shoulder was killing me when I entered my room, but great hugs usually come at great cost.

Mom stopped at a drugstore on the way to the Polo Club, and I was perfectly happy to sit in the car quietly while she ran in to pick up a prescription for Dad. I wasn't in a hurry. I just wanted to savor the sights and smells of Chagrin Falls. It would always be my home no matter where I landed, but I was still eager to go find those new landings. While I was waiting outside, I heard several sirens in the distance and saw one city squad car come blasting by the drugstore headed in the same direction as we were about to go. I wondered whose cat was in a tree to cause such a ruckus. Mom asked me about the sirens as she came out of the store and climbed into the car. I shrugged, well, as much as a shrug can be when one's shoulder is bandaged tightly. "I don't know," I said, "but somebody's getting the city's full attention." In saying that, I wondered if one of my classmates had been speeding down Main Street in his or her new graduation car. When we arrived at the Polo Club, there were four city squad cars parked in the gravel driveway that fronted the main building. Both of us got out of the car and stood by the front fender trying to assimilate all that was happening. Although it was broad daylight, two of the cars had not turned off their rotating beacons, and the effect was distracting. My mom walked over to one of the officers standing by his car looking toward the Club and asked what was going on. He turned and, seeing her so close, quickly told her she would have to move back and it would be best if she left. He made a shooing motion with his arms. As she stepped back, she asked him again, and he said he wasn't sure. The Police Chief had asked for backup at the Club, that was all he knew, but rumors were that a large animal had escaped, was somewhere on the premises, and this might end up being a horse chase.

As soon as she got back to the car, I told her I *must* get to the stables, immediately. That's where Sunstar would have gone, I told her, and that's where I needed to be. I asked her to drop me off and go on home. No matter what was happening, no one needed extra cars on the Club grounds or in some driveway. I told her I would find out and call her, but to go finish her shopping. I mean, how much trouble can a horse get into? She giggled and drove me down to the stables. She asked me to be sure to tell Sunstar hello when I saw her and that dinner tonight would be roast beef. "So don't eat too much for lunch, Cody, because we'll be having dessert as well." With that last shout, she disappeared down the driveway.

DAY TWENTY-THREE 4:00 P.M.

I headed immediately for the tack room's hidden entrance and let myself in. The long ramp down and the cross hallways were empty. Everything was very quiet. I let myself very carefully through the door into the containment facility and, closing it softly behind me, stood in silence wondering where everyone was. There was dead silence everywhere. Then I looked to my left and saw that the four Were cages were wide open and a body was lying partially in and partially out of the Pale Were's cage. I walked over as quietly as I could and recognized the body as one of the two sanitation guards who normally managed the parking lot entrance. His face was almost unrecognizable. His face, his front shoulder, and his chest area had been shredded by what looked to be long rips in the flesh and bone. Blood was everywhere, sitting in black pools with red highlights. I suddenly felt very sick to my stomach.

Very carefully, I knelt by the guard's back and removed a revolver he had apparently hidden there in a short holster beneath his shirt. It was now visible as he lay crumpled over. I checked the load. Six chambers, six bullets. It was a .38 Police Special, double action. The trigger could be pulled or the gun cocked and then fired. I held it in my right hand with my arm hanging down by my side and started tiptoeing forward to the main administration offices.

I went about 100 feet when I heard faint murmurings and what seemed to be occasional sobs. As I crept forward, I came to the lunchroom area and saw a number of people huddled there, arms around each other with muffled conversations and some crying. As I started around a cross hallway so I could approach from another direction, I glimpsed two Werewolves crouched down by a body at the edge of the crowd. They were eating one of the younger scientists, yanking his ribs out from a cracked chest cavity and gnawing away with impunity, blood dripping from their paws, claws, and jaws. I said nothing and slowly took off my shoes. I wanted to make no noise until I had a better grasp of the situation.

Turning another corner, I could see into the lunchroom from a second vantage point and spotted a third Werewolf. The Pale Were remained out of my vision. Nor could I see Clarion, Sunstar, or Dr. Walker. The third Were had taken the head off one of the secretaries and was noisily chewing on one of her arms that was hanging from her body by a thread of skin. Shortly, her arm tore away from her socket as a result of the Were's violent movements. No wonder the people in the lunchroom were crying. They were looking at what they believed to be their future.

I had to find the Pale Were before I could do anything because chances were that that's where Clarion and the others were. If I were the Pale Were, Clarion and those with him would be my first priority to hunt. Not only was he an obvious official in charge of things here, he was also the one who personally humiliated the Pale Were by his questioning in the wee hours of that morning. I moved silently away from the lunchroom area and toward the main administration offices and the stairs up to the hidden entrance in the Club. The offices were vacant; there was no sound or evidence that anyone was there, so I started up the stairs.

One foot, one step at a time, I told myself, grateful that the government had originally installed metal steps that didn't creak. When I got to the top, I saw the doorway slightly ajar and tried to gently push it open. It hit something almost immediately and bounced back into my hand. This time I put my right shoulder against the door and leaned in and pushed. I moved something heavy, and I pushed harder. The door opened just enough to let me slip through. Dr. Walker was lying there, dead. His throat had been ripped out, and his head was askew. I didn't need to take his pulse. Most of his blood was soaking into the formerly plush carpeting that was found throughout the Club's environs. That was a benefit to me. In my socks on the carpet, I made no noise.

I found them in the dining room. Clarion was leaning against a wall with a tourniquet around his left arm, his wrist and forearm heavily damaged and the flesh partially ripped away. Some of his bone could be seen. Sunstar was crouched beside him singing softly to him with her left hand on his head. Her right hand was holding

312

her hair, just below the Pale Were's grasp as it stood beside her looking out the window and growling to itself. It was trying to pull it tight and keep her off balance, and she was trying to pull it back so she could administer to Clarion. It was an utterly unselfish and incredibly brave act on her part.

Clarion's eyes were flickering as if he were rotating between being conscious and unconscious. I watched to see if any changes in his countenance were apparent. If that arm wound was inflicted by the Pale Were, I would have to kill Clarion, something I drastically did not want to do. But something would have to be done soon because Sunstar was in grave danger, and that enraged me.

While sitting there crouched down by a doorway, I formulated three plans like Captain Yamata taught us. Plan A: Come in shooting, kill the Were, save the girl and big boss, and get the outside cops to go down and save the scientists and administrators downstairs. Emerge a hero. Plan B: Sneak in, shoot and cripple the Were, save the girl and the big boss, and so on and so on. Plan C: Walk in, offer myself as an exchange hostage for Sunstar, and formulate an escape plan with a wounded and dizzy Clarion while trying to forestall being the Pale Were's exclusive guest at dinner. Emerge a chump. Well chewed.

Without any prompting on my part, Sunstar suddenly looked up, saw me, and with tears in her eyes from the pain she was experiencing, still had the courage to smile at me through those tears while she kept trying to tend to and sing her song to Clarion. *Aw, the heck with it*, I thought to myself. I was going with my John Wayne Plan D, which was to have a general idea of the outcome you wish to achieve and bludgeon your way through it improvisation style. It would probably help if I could walk in slightly knock-kneed as well, swiveling my arms out of sync with my hips and calling the Were "Pilgrim." Dang! It would probably have been best if John Wayne himself pulled this off, but my knees were shaking enough so that at least I didn't have to fake his stagger swagger.

DAY TWENTY-THREE 5:00 P.M.

Taking a breath, I tucked the pistol into my belt at the small of my back so my hands were empty. I stood up and knocked loudly on the door frame. "May I come in?" I asked, and grinning, stepped into the spider's parlor, as it were. The Pale Were spun about so quickly that Sunstar was literally torn away from Clarion and dragged across the Were's feet as if she were a bag of salt. She cried out from the pain of her hair being yanked so badly and reached up with both hands to try to take the strain off. A few more steps forward on my part and I was close enough to make mental contact with the creature.

It wasn't a jovial greeting when we meshed. Clarion now lay slightly behind and to the blind side of the Were, his eyes fully open and watching me. I didn't know if the intelligence I saw there was his or that of an emerging creature, but I felt I couldn't trust him under the circumstances.

Anything I did from this point forward would have to be on my own.

The Were snarled at me and took a menacing step forward. "You're just in time to die, Archer. Where is your bow and that little bear friend of yours? Is he here to die as well?" As calmly as I could, I told him, "I'm not here to die. No one has to die today, least of all you. No, I am here to take the man (I gestured to Clarion) and the woman (I pointed to Sunstar) back to their offices so we can find a way to bring you back."

"Bring me back?" he queried. "Bring me back to what? There is no back for me, you imbecile. There is only death for your kind, and today we will make long strides in seeing to that," he spat out.

"Well then," I said back to him, "you'd best get to it because I have an appointment in a few minutes, and I don't want to be late." And with that said, I stepped forward two steps. Enraged with my temerity, he threw Sunstar to one side and leaped for me, arms and claws outstretched and jaws gaping open. I dropped quickly under the table in front of me, pulling the revolver from my belt as I turned to watch the Were hit the table's edge where I had just stood and pull the table over as it tumbled forward toward the doorway I'd come through.

In seconds, the Were was on its feet. It spun about and was starting to leap at me again when I pulled the trigger on two of my six shots into its head and upper chest. With part of its jawbone and eye socket smashed and blown away, it crumpled slowly to the floor, claws scratching to get me and expiring with a sound like air escaping a torn basketball. I turned and stepped quickly over to Sunstar, gathering her up in my arms and standing with my bad arm around her as she sobbed into my shoulder.

We stood that way for some time. When she finally looked up at me and slightly pushed against my shoulders as if to gain some freedom, I did not return her look but did let her go. I quickly put my arm in front of her and gently pushed her back behind me, my eyes never leaving Clarion. I had been watching him since the Pale Were fell, and he had kept his eyes on mine.

Sunstar looked at the Were, back at me, and then at Clarion again. "Cody, what's wrong?" she pleaded. "What's the matter?" I told her that I would know in a minute but that right now she needed to go outside and stay with the armed police who didn't have a clue what was going on. Clarion lay there silently and watched me. Slowly he stood up, and slowly I brought the pistol up to bear on him. "You're going to get one chance," I said. "The first move may be your last. This bullet is going right into your brain if you so much as breath wrong, so just sit back down while we wait this out." He said nothing but slowly slid back down again, his eyes never leaving mine. Thoroughly puzzled and alarmed, Sunstar pulled on my arm and said, "Cody! What is this nonsense? Clarion's on our side. What's the matter with you?"

"You just might be right," I said, "but we'll wait for a bit and see for ourselves." Sunstar shook her head in frustration as if she were clearing it and asked again, "Cody, what is the matter with you?"

"See his arm?" I nodded. "If that Pale Were did that, our friend Clarion here is about to become a howling Werewolf. Only the Pales can spread the virus, and he's either going to be our newest laboratory sample or a dead Were in the next five minutes, so we'll just wait and see." I half sat on, half rested against the edge of a nearby table, never taking my eyes off Clarion to look at Sunstar.

"Maybe I can help," said a voice behind me, and I jumped at the sound of it. "It's me, Cody, the Police Chief. I was quietly checking all the upstairs rooms and the kitchen area in back. I heard the noise as the Werewolf jumped you. I've been watching you the whole time. You do pretty well without that bow and arrow of yours.

"Now, young lady, please come over here and stand by me. We're going outside and coming up with a story so those police officers will go home, and then you're going to sit in my car while I come back in here so Cody and I can take care of some unfinished business downstairs. Clarion, you just sit tight until I get back. Cody, shoot him in the knee if he tries to get up again. Crippled he can't get far or do much damage, but it would be nice to keep him alive if only to study him when and if he turns."

Sunstar stumbled past me, and the Chief put his big arm around her and escorted her outside where the officers immediately clustered about him, firing questions right and left. I just sat and watched Clarion. His expression was almost bemused, but he just sat and watched me, shaking his head from time to time to stay awake. He was close to going into shock but had the disposition and stamina to hang on. Finally he spoke.

"You're better than I thought you were, Cody. Better than I hoped. This summer's start has really matured you, and I'd take you right now full-time if your education weren't so important. I kept my silence as a test for you. I wanted to see if you really understood what was going on and had the patience to keep control of a bad situation. I see you do." With that, he tried to stand.

"Thanks for the kind words, Clarion, but if you stand up all the way, you'll be missing a kneecap. I'm handy with a bow, but I can also shoot a pistol, and you're all of what, seven feet away? If I miss your knee, it will be because I aimed high, so your femoral artery will likely be blown away. Then you'll bleed out right here on this magnificent rug in seconds. Now, that would be a colossal waste to all, so just sit down, sit still, and talk to me about how this happened. I'm all ears, boss."

Clarion sat back down, looked at me with that quirky smile of his, and promptly passed out. I looked outside and saw several police cars pulling away, and finally the Chief started back into the building. Sunstar went to his vehicle and climbed in. That brought a sigh of relief, but I really started to worry about Clarion at that point. He needed help fast, either a bullet in the head or a doctor and a bed. I gambled and chose the latter, checking Clarion's pulse (weak) before I walked quickly out of the room and to the front door of the Club.

"Better hurry, Chief. He needs a doctor in the worst way, and the closest ones are downstairs. This is going to be a bit tricky."

The Chief called an ambulance from the clubhouse phone before we started downstairs, telling them to come quickly but without sirens. A man was wounded on the main floor of the Club. Pick him up, fix him up, put it on the city's tab for now, and the Chief would get back to them in an hour or so. He smiled at me as he finished and said, "Let's go. Follow my lead. And Cody. Here's a fresh load of bullets for that revolver of yours. These are hollow point bullets. Small hole going in, big hole coming out. Be careful. Some of these scientists are irreplaceable and some aren't worth the ammunition, but I can't always tell which is which, so just be careful." It took us half an hour to secure the downstairs area. The Chief put down the two Weres who had eaten the scientist, and I managed to cripple the beast that had torn off the secretary's head. It was killed by the crowd before I could get close enough, but it did manage to get to me before I could get away from it. It ripped me from my waist down to my knee on my left leg, severing one of the main muscles by my hip. I could neither walk nor stand, and the shock hit before the pain. But when the pain came, it was bad. Real bad. I felt my head spinning in an agony of confusion, and then my world started to dim.

This was getting to be a bad habit, I thought, just before everything went dark.

DAY TWENTY-SIX 11:30 A.M.

I wasn't sure the voice I heard was that of an angel, but whatever language it was using I didn't understand. It made me feel so peaceful, and all my confusion and concerns seemed to recede into some far distance. I lay wherever I was and just enjoyed the moment. If I'm not in heaven, this must be a way stop, I thought to myself. Then I made the mistake of trying to move and open my eyes.

The pain in my left hip hit me immediately, and when I tried to push myself onto my right hip, the pain in my left shoulder was almost as bad. "Ouch!" I cried out. "What in the name of Pete Smith is going on? Can somebody please help me?" I felt a smooth hand gently come to rest on my forehead, and that mysterious song started back up. I immediately felt the pain drop away and wondered what was happening to me as I dropped off to sleep again.

Several hours later, I awakened and tried again, only this time there was no mysterious hand on my brow. There was only my mom dozing in a chair at the foot of my bed. I was surprised she was there and just lay there and watched her for a few minutes and then gradually drifted off again. I felt something pressing on my shoulder and left hip, but it wasn't painful, just pressure. I thought it odd, but it wasn't a concern, and sleep came quickly and easily.

DAY TWENTY-EIGHT 9:30 A.M.

When I awoke again, it was morning. Sunlight streamed into my window, and I looked around and found I was wired for everything but stereo sound. No one was with me, and I struggled to try to sit up straighter but found I could not move. A leather strap held my shoulder to the bed frame, and a cast was fitted around my left hip and upper thigh. Slowly I was able to recall what happened since I lost consciousness at the containment facility. I remembered getting my left leg torn as the Were came at me to escape the crowd pursuing it, but I remembered no pain. Now I was in a cast. *How'd that happen?* I wondered. And what had happened to Clarion and especially Sunstar? At the thought of her, I struggled once again to sit up and made enough commotion that the duty nurse came running into my room and literally pushed me back onto the bed and scolded me as if I were a truculent schoolboy.

"You are *not* to move about like that," she demanded. You are in a hospital, and your parents are outside. Please wait here and I'll get them, but if you try that again, I will have you strapped down by both shoulders and your ankles. Am I clear?" I made no comment. "Am I *clear*?" she growled at me.

"Yes, ma'am," I replied sheepishly. "I understand. I guess I was a little disoriented and didn't fully understand what had happened to me. I'll sit tight, and thank you."

With that, she softened, patted the pillow around my head, and loosened the strap on my shoulder so I could scrunch up to a more comfortable position. "I'll be right back," she said. "Just wait here."

Like I'm going somewhere? I thought.

Mom and Dad were in my room a few minutes later, and both had to fight each other as they tried to hug me at the same time from opposite sides of my hospital bed. I leaned to Mom because she was on my right side, so Dad came around to that side and hugged me just as hard when she was done. I asked about Sunstar when I didn't see her with them, and they smiled and told me not to worry, that she had just stepped away to the women's facility and should be right along. "She spent the last several nights sitting here with you," my mom said, "so she wanted to comb her hair and wash her face in the event you woke up sometime today.

"We've been waiting for you for several days. I sit with you during the day and Sunstar at night. Dad visits when his job lets him." She looked at me tenderly and said, "We've missed you, Cody. Welcome back." Then she started crying and turned her face into Dad's chest. He carefully folded his arms around her and grinned at me over her shoulder. The wink he gave me was priceless.

"I don't even know where to start," said Dad.

"Well, why not let me," said a familiar voice from the doorway. It was Clarion. A great feeling of wellness came over me when I heard that voice. It meant all was well. I would charge hell with a bucket of water to rescue that man, and it was a relief to know I didn't have to. My grin must have belied my condition because he said, "Cody, what is it with you and bandages? Either you're practicing for your First Aid Merit Badge or you've got a thing for pretty girls hanging around your bedside. Hurry up and get out of here. We've got work to do, and the Major says, 'Time's a-wastin'!' Oh, and by the way, Gitta says hello."

Saying that, Clarion stepped into the room. My eyes opened as I saw the cast and peculiar rods that adorned it. "You look like an antenna." I grinned at him.

"And you like a refugee from an insane asylum wrapped up by third graders," he retorted. Then he walked over and shook my hand and gazed down at me fondly.

"So you didn't change after all, eh?" I kidded him.

"Well, not enough to warrant getting my knee blown off by you, but I was afraid you'd actually do it for a while there."

"That's good, Clarion, because I would have. So next time, be afraid. Be very, very afraid." And then both of us started laughing.

He pulled up a chair, settled himself, and gave us all a brief recap of what had happened, abbreviating some of his report because Mom was in the room and didn't have the same clearances that Dad, Sunstar, and I had. But we got the gist of it.

"The Pale Were was smarter and more resourceful than we imagined," Clarion said. "It feigned a stupor when the guard came in to give it another calming shot and killed the guard in seconds. It freed its companions, let them herd the staff into the lunchroom and start feeding while he came after Dr. Walker, Sunstar, and me in the Director's office. Dr. Abernathy was away, and we were using her blackboard. The Were surprised us, grabbed Sunstar, and threatened to disembowel her if we tried anything. Then it made us lead it upstairs and out of the facility.

"It later killed Dr. Walker out of spite. I managed to hit the panic button we installed several weeks ago under the Director's desk after we decided to bring other Weres here for study. It rang the Chief's beeper, and he came running as did several of his officers. He went into the Club's main building to clear the top floors when we were coming up from beneath, and then you showed up. The rest you know. "We'd have been dead without you, Cody, and that's a fact. I tried to jump the Were when we were in the dining room, and this is what I got for my trouble," he said, holding up his cast. "Sunstar saved me by taking off my belt and using it for a tourniquet. I will be weeks trying to get all my hand motions back, if I ever do. The Pale Were ripped out several tendons and sliced some muscles, so rehab is going to be long and hard. But thanks to you, there will be a rehab instead of flowers on some obscure grave at Arlington Cemetery."

He got up to walk out and stopped at the doorway. Turning around, he said, "By the way, happy Fourth of July. And if it's any help, the President of the United States thinks you're a remarkable young man. If you need a college endorsement, he's got paper and pen ready." Clarion smiled and walked on down the hall whistling. I was grinning so hard my eyes ached. My mom and dad just looked at each other, and Mom burst into tears. Dad got to hold her again and gave me another of those don't-come-home-too-early winks I had gotten used to long ago. His grin was bigger than mine.

I couldn't help but burst out laughing.

DAY TWENTY-NINE 11:00 A.M.

Something had been nagging me since my short visit with Clarion yesterday. It was one of those thoughts that roll around your mind, putting you constantly on alert that something is there to which you should pay attention but is too elusive to catch, stop, and study. As they were putting me into the wheelchair that all hospitals now use to protect themselves from liability as they roll you out the door, something the day nurse said in passing suddenly rang my bell, and I sat straight up.

"That's it!" I cried. That's why Clarion didn't turn. He was torn by the Pale Were's claws and *not* bitten. With a great smile on my face, I asked the nurse to please stop and let me make a few calls. She politely declined and rolled me out of my room to the main lobby's loading area where my mom and dad were waiting for me.

"I've got to get a hold of Clarion," I told my dad. "Do you know his number or where I might find him?" My dad laughed. He told me nobody knows just where Clarion ever is except those with him but that he, my dad, had a number in case either of us needed to leave him a message. Well, that settled me down, and since I knew I could call from home, I suffered the day nurse's ministrations and let her cram me into the back seat of my dad's car.

Firmly entangled with a blanket that covered me while I was wearing my hip cast, I asked Dad to please drive carefully and not get in an accident. He looked at me in the rearview mirror, pursed his lips, and said with sarcasm that he would do his best.

Mom said Sunstar had stayed home to arrange a small ceremony for me, and we would see her there. I was excited. Seeing Sunstar would be great and ranked number one, numero uno, on all my lists, but just getting back outside from the confines of the hospital was almost an obsession and ranked ahead of anything else that moment. I took a welcome breath.

I felt a little ambivalent as we turned onto our driveway. I had not counted on being home this summer, but with my injuries, I couldn't really count on being anywhere else. The doctors had given me a good prognosis and said I needed a week or so with little activity. Then I was to enter into a controlled therapy program to regain full use of my shoulder and leg. When asked, they didn't particularly care where, but they did care that it be a medically supervised program because my injuries were relatively severe. Without proper supervision, it was very probable that I would heal but never regain the full flexibility I had enjoyed before my injury.

I managed to choke down a laugh when they said that. I hadn't enjoyed full flexibility in years and years. But I knew they meant well and very much wanted to get me into some program.

Sunstar and the Allegros were waiting in our kitchen when we walked in. Sunstar had made some paper banners and baked a cake herself. Mrs. Allegro had put up some ribbons, and Mr. Allegro had put up some quotes citing Gitta, Polaris, the Major, and Dusty, among others. It seemed that Sunstar had been making calls almost daily back to the Rat's Nest about my progress and whatever goings-on were happening in Chagrin Falls. They, on the other hand, had been feeding her information, and hence the quotes. My favorite was a quote from Polaris. It was written, "SHRIIIIKKK!" ("Go, Cody!").

It was a wonderful return home made extra special when Mrs. Allegro told me about her conversation with Casey. She was up to her ears in soccer and was already making a name for herself as a freshman playing with the varsity team, but she apparently had a hundred questions about me. That made me swell with both pride and confidence until Mrs. Allegro also said Casey had asked about Sunstar, too. Both Sunstar and I perked up at that, and I leaned forward slightly to hear just what she had to say. Mrs. Allegro paused, looked up in the air to her right, briefly touched her lip, and quoted, slowly, "Mom, I know she's pretty. With a name like that and knowing Cody, she has to be, but what's she really like—inside?"

There was a pregnant pause, and all of us sort of inclined forward as Mrs. Allegro thought back before she gave her answer. She looked at each of us and let her gaze come to rest on Sunstar. "I told her Sunstar's the daughter I would have wanted if you, Casey, had not come along first." Mrs. Allegro teared up, and Mr. Allegro put his arm around her. I just sat there glowing.

Sunstar stood up, walked over to the Allegros, and placing a hand on each of their outside shoulders, sang ever so softly a melody I had never heard but was enchanting nonetheless. As she sang, tears came to all our eyes and such a feeling of peace and love came into our hearts that I would remember the moment for years to come. It was a singular and wonderful experience.

When Sunstar stood up with a happy smile, she said it was time for refreshments and went to our kitchen counter to cut cake and dish out some ice cream. I looked around. My mom and dad and the Allegros just sat there blinking at each other, almost too stunned to say or do anything. I understood, but I also understood that ice cream melts quickly and managed to clamber to my feet and walk over to help Sunstar. It was a magic moment, and the chocolate cake with icing and ice cream was delicious. And yes, I had seconds. Even part of thirds, but that was later when no one else was around.

DAY TWENTY-NINE 3:00 P.M.

The nap I took after the cake and ice cream was a lifesaver. I didn't realize how depleted a body's reserves get from injury, surgery, and drugs. I had fallen asleep on the couch and someone, probably my mom, covered me with a throw blanket and tucked a pillow under my head. When I opened my eyes, I just lay there without moving, listening and trying to get my bearings. When I realized I was not in the hospital, I tried to sit up and failed.

My shoulder bandage and hip cast put me off balance. Suddenly there was a pair of hands supporting me from behind that gently helped me sit erect and placed the pillow behind my back to steady me. It was Sunstar. She walked around to the front of the couch and sat down by me. She turned to face me with her legs tucked up underneath her dress and placed her elbow on top of the couch, her fist against her head. She looked at me and grinned, at first a subtle grin and then a much bigger one as she imitated an overbite. Crossing her eyes, she asked me, "Eh, what's up, Doc?"

Bugs Bunny couldn't do it any better. She looked so goofy I couldn't help myself and burst out laughing. I wanted so much to gather her into my arms and just squeeze her, to inhale her scent and drink in the joy and freedom of self she inspired. I reveled in the moment of intimacy she afforded us. If ever a fellow could be head over heels in like with someone, that was me at that moment with my almost inexpressible feelings for her. I felt like $10 million.

Then Dad walked in, and reality dumped me on the proverbial floor. "Did you ever leave that message for Clarion?" he asked.

"Oh, no, Dad. I guess I was overwhelmed by the homecoming and I completely forgot. May I call him now?"

My dad said certainly and brought me the telephone and the number Clarion gave him. I dialed, thinking I would have to leave a message, but Clarion answered. I was so surprised that I couldn't speak for a moment until he asked a second time who was calling, please. I quickly overcame my hesitation, identified myself, and blurted out, "I know why you didn't turn, Clarion. The Were clawed you; it didn't bite you. It used its paws, not its mouth. That confirms the virus must be transferred through saliva."

Clarion's reaction was immediate. He congratulated me for quick thinking and said he would contact Dr. Walker's replacement immediately. His replacement would arrive at the containment facility tomorrow. He was also from Boston. He was a big Irishman named Fitzgerald with a gift for understatement and a wicked sense of humor. He'd been a colleague of Dr. Walker and had participated in some of his research. In fact he'd co-authored several papers with him. Apparently, he held a law degree as well as a PhD but had a penchant for biology.

Clarion asked if I would contact Sunstar and tell her all this. I answered that he could do it himself; she was sitting next to me. I quickly handed her the phone and spent the next half hour listening to a one-sided treatise on homeopathic remedies and the use of mountain herbs, especially one Sunstar called frog shadow, or wa-lo-si tsa-da-yv-la-dv, its Cherokee name.

It was a very rare plant found in the higher Appalachian elevations but only near fresh mountain springs. It was delicious when eaten on the stem but deteriorated quickly when picked. It could not be stored for any length of time. It was dark greenish black with three to four leaves per plant, each of which looked like a stretched shadow of a small frog.

Because all the animals liked its flavor, it was rarely found, but when picked and used as a mash with any fruit, especially strawberries or raspberries, it acted as a major curative. It was sort of like an immune booster on rockets or steroids. It had been known to bring people back from death's door and restore their systems to normal even when they had contracted very serious diseases. It was highly coveted and rarely found; hence, it was worth more than gold. Some of the Cherokee called it life-giver.

When Sunstar finally hung up, the two of us and my mom who had come down in the interim, sat and talked for a long time. I would plan to stay at least a week, maybe 10 days, here at home in Chagrin Falls. I would be on call to the Police Chief and his friends as needed. Sunstar would stay for at least two more weeks, maybe a month, working at the Polo Club, depending on what Dr. Fitzgerald felt was best as they set about actually testing some of Sunstar's legacy medicines.

In turn, I would have the Major set up a personal therapy program for me in North Carolina using some of the Appalachian State facilities in Boone, North Carolina, but would spend the majority of my time there consulting with the Rat's Nest and further developing my team of Gitta and Polaris. The Carolina mountain air and terrain would help me regain most if not all my physical capabilities by the start of Lee-McCrae's fall term, but I would come back to Chagrin Falls at summer's end for a week or so to do my final shopping and any get-readies, and say any overlooked goodbyes before I left for school. I was hoping I might even get in a short visit with Casey, but our schedules looked too out of whack right now for that to likely happen.

With all that said and a call made to Sunstar's family, I went outside to sit on our backyard lawn and just mull over the impact of these last several days. Sunstar soon came out and plopped down beside me when her telephone call to her parents was over. We both shared a companionable silence, nothing forced, nothing needed, just a feeling of great ease and comfort. Without thinking, I lifted up my hand and placed it over hers. Nothing needed to be said. We sat there a long time watching the light from the sunset play over the treetops and the eaves of our garage.

She jumped up and helped me to my feet when Mom called us in for dinner, and I took the opportunity to put my hands on her waist and hold her for a second. She stood still and looked up at me with those deep eyes, saying nothing, but her mouth had the faintest hint of a smile. I felt she would come all the way into my arms if I moved, but I stood still, looking at her and leaning forward as if to nuzzle her with my nose. When our noses were almost touching, the evening twilight holding the world in abeyance, I quickly tickled her sides and croaked in my best Elmer Fudd interpretation, "I'm going to get you, you wascally wabbit!" Then I turned and hobbled toward the house as fast as I could.

I heard a whoop behind me. She started laughing and quickly caught up to me, spun around in front of me, and placing her arms over my shoulders, gently but thoroughly kissed me.

Time and my heart almost stopped together. Then she was gone, dancing back into our house. I was so startled and happy that I sat down with a thump and immediately rolled over crying because I had hurt my hip. Dad came out to rescue me, and Mom kept turning her head between Sunstar and me. One was trying hard to stifle her laughter, and one was trying hard to stifle his tears.

Eventually, Mom shook her head and started setting the table while Sunstar went back outside to the Allegros to freshen up for dinner. She passed by me without so much as a look my way, while Dad tried to help me to my unsteady feet. It was one of the best days of my short life. After dinner, Sunstar and I talked for hours, about what I can't remember. I just remember being filled with a spirit of adventure and happiness.

DAY THIRTY 9:00 A.M.

I awakened in a panic thinking of the Werewolves' planned raid at the town of Boone. So caught up in myself and in my injuries and recovery was I that I had completely forgotten about Lt. Col. Spikes and his proposed defense of the Appalachian State students. Had the raid happened? Were the Weres gathering? Were there any casualties if it had occurred? A host of other questions kept flying through my mind. Without further ado, I walked slowly to my phone, sat down carefully, and called the Rat's Nest telephone number.

Dusty answered, and for a brief moment upon hearing her voice, I was sitting again with her on the Chapel porch, scratching Gitta's ears and watching Polaris fly lazy circles against an azure sky. "Cody!" she screamed. "Cody! How are you, and when are you coming back? Everyone is asking about you. And what is this about a hip cast that Sunstar told us about? Clarion was here two days ago and said you're just loafing so you can spend time with Sunstar, but he said it with a smile. He also said you saved his life and Sunstar's life and that you were not only brave but wise. So what's happening, and when are you coming back here?"

"Dusty, Dusty! Calm down and let me get a word in here, please. First of all, is the Major there? I need to speak with her for a minute, and then we'll visit. But please get the Major on the line or Lt. Col. Spikes if he's around. Okay?" The line went temporarily silent as I heard the receiver hit Dusty's desktop. It wasn't long before the Major was on, and I explained my panic and apologized for not calling sooner. Had the raid happened already, and did I need to be there to interrogate any Weres taken prisoner? And if so, would she forgive me for not being more alert and not trying harder to get well and get to North Carolina?

Laughing, she told me to slow down and take a deep breath. First of all, there had been no raid, yet. Apparently, the capture of the Pale Were left the western Werewolves without key leadership because all sentry sightings indicated that the larger bands had broken into much smaller units and dispersed throughout the western half of the state. They were no longer concentrated in groups any larger than 30 to 40 Werewolves per group. I did need to get well and did need to get back there, but there was no longer a rush or I would have known long before.

"Just because you're physically absent from our meetings, Cody, don't *ever* think you're not on our minds or in our thoughts. Everyone here is waiting for Cody-san's return, especially Gitta and, I imagine, Polaris, too. Just get here as fast as the doctor allows. I've got some new ideas on that protection you and Sergeant Saddler have been kicking around and can't wait to try them out. So get here soon, but keep it safe, okay?"

Dusty was back on before the Major's last syllable faded. We must have chatted for another 20 minutes when I remembered this was a long-distance call. My dad was going to kill me when the bill came. I hung up quickly after promising to call again and just leaned back thinking about and planning my recovery. I was incredibly relieved that there had been no attack on Appalachian State or anywhere else for that matter.

Apparently, I had time and orders to heal and heal properly, the majority of which would likely be done back in North Carolina. I would have my hip cast off in another three or four days and would have greater mobility. Besides, last night Sunstar promised she would accelerate my healing process by an old unguent her grandmother had taught her. It was for healing wounds brought on by battle. It was kept as a tribal secret since it worked so dramatically. I would never find out how it was made, but I would soon find out for myself how it worked. That was exciting, but then if Sunstar said she was going to smear black river mud all over my face, I probably would be just as excited, and more so if she was inclined to sing to me.

Later that morning, I had one more surprise—a letter from Casey. I took it up to my room and slowly sat down again. The letter was long. I suspect it had been written while she was curled up on her dorm bed, probably after a long day of practice. She missed me but was having a blast. The girls were wonderful. She had made a new friend from Texas who was smart, determined, and afraid of nothing. Everyone called her "that Jennings gal." She was also mischievous but very popular with anyone who met and spoke with her. She had that peculiar accent characteristic of Texans. She was occasionally hard to understand. One of the nicest things about her was that you quickly knew exactly where you stood with her. She would also flatten you if you weren't looking when you ran by her.

Casey went on to say that their coach had enrolled all the soccer players in tennis, a sport Casey had never tried. It was to improve their vision and get them used to a ball moving at a very fast pace while they anticipated and planned their next position on the court, the same as they had to anticipate and plan their position on the soccer field. One of the instructors was a man named Paul, a tall fellow with a graceful swing who made everything look easy. She wasn't sure, but he seemed to have taken an interest in her even though most of the other girls were vying for his attention.

At least he had taken some extra time with his arms around her showing her how to properly grip and hold the racket. He made it clear that was a *very* important part of the game. Hold it improperly, and you'd play like you held it. He also made her laugh. He was a sophomore. He had a quiet self-confidence some of the other instructors lacked. She had no idea tennis could be so much fun, and did I know it was a sport she could play the rest of her life when she mastered the basics, unlike soccer? Paul was very encouraging about her ability. He thought she could be very good someday.

She had heard from her mom about my injuries. She chastised me for not waiting until she came back to take on the Weres. She reminded me that nobody was better than she was at protecting my back. She also wanted to know more about Sunstar. Was she really as pretty and gracious as her mom said? And if so, congratulations on making a new friend who was also keen to eliminate the Weres. Casey hoped to meet her either there in Chagrin Falls or in North Carolina. She sounded terrific. Casey's letter ran on and on in that vein with a salutation rather personal and sweet. She did end it on a cryptic note, however. She asked me if I knew the game of tennis was all about "love." Paul told her that. She suggested I try it sometime—tennis, that is.

I had to admit that I liked the letter when I finished it. Still, I was decidedly uncomfortable with that last note and the thought of some testosterone-crazed instructor named Paul being allowed to run loose on the North Carolina campus chasing after and pretending to teach tennis to a tender freshman coed who by happenstance killed

Werewolves in her spare time. But it was a letter from Casey. She did ask me to write her when I had time between slaughtering Werewolves and saving humanity. I carefully put the letter away in my pocket. I pondered what I could say about the changes in my life that had already happened or were looming on the horizon, especially about my new family at the Rat's Nest.

Mom came in later that morning. She found me fast asleep right where I had sat down. She helped me lay over on my right side, stuffed a pillow beneath my head, and threw a blanket over me before she kissed me softly on the head and walked out. I felt wonderful as I snuggled my way deeper into the blanket. I was healing, I was with Sunstar, I had gotten a letter from Casey, Mom was cooking for me, and I would soon be back at the Rat's Nest.

Could it get any better? That was my last thought as I drifted off to sleep.

THE END OF EPISODE FIVE, BOOK ONE

EPISODE
SIX

DAY ONE 8:30 A.M.

I had not been paying attention as I walked the hospital's hallways and suddenly realized I was lost. I stopped at the junction of three corridors, two of which seemed to be unused if the closed doors and partial light down each hallway were any indication. But the third was brightly lit and seemed to have an open door about halfway down on the right side. I walked toward it, thinking I would stop in and ask directions. I heard soft crying before I reached the door. Surprised, I immediately stopped.

I did not want to step into a scene and embarrass whoever was in obvious despair, but I needed directions if I was going to find my way to my appointment with any reasonable sense of timeliness. So I swallowed, coughed loud enough to be heard, and made sure my shoe heels made some noticeable noise on the tiles as I walked the final few paces to the doorway. The crying stopped when I came to the open door. I knocked once and then turned to look in.

The room was empty, lots of furniture, no people using it.

"Anyone home?" I asked loudly. "Excuse me. Is anyone here?"

Silence greeted me. I called out again several times until I realized there was no other door in the room save the one I was standing in. The room was not an anteroom to another as I had first supposed. It was complete in itself. I was calling out into an empty room while standing in the only doorway offering an in or an out.

I shook my head and told myself my ears must be playing tricks on me, that perhaps the crying sound had come from some other office either farther down or across the hall. But when I stepped back outside the room into the hallway and prepared to go to the next door, I realized there was no next door, not on any side of the hallway as far as I could see. Really puzzled, I stepped back into the empty room and let my eyes slowly and methodically look over every inch to see if I had missed a doorway or some sort of a second concealed entrance.

Nothing. There was nothing in the room but furniture, four walls, and the *one* door framing me. I started to feel a little disconcerted, so I turned and headed back down to the hallway junction. I had taken no more than three steps when I heard the crying again. It was coming from behind me, again from inside the room. Rising up on my tiptoes, I snuck back to the doorway and suddenly jumped through it into the empty room. I was ready to pounce on anyone or anything that might be playing this joke on me.

But again, no one, no sound.

A second more thorough search of the room yielded absolutely nothing, especially not a speaker or vent through which I now thought the crying must certainly be coming. I could feel the hairs on the back of my neck begin to rise. I was very uncomfortable. Drawing a deep breath, I stepped out of the room and headed back down the hallway to the junction. Again, I heard crying as I walked away, but this time it was something almost like a faint sobbing. Not so much alarmed now as puzzled, I did not turn back to the room. At the junction, I chose instead a corridor at random and walked quickly down it.

I hoped to come across someone or something like a directory that would show me the way back to my scheduled appointment room at the Veteran's Hospital. Finally, after 10 minutes and several staircases later, I opened a stairwell door that emptied onto the main ground floor corridor that bisected the whole hospital. People were everywhere and moving fast. Somehow, I had made my way downstairs into the hospital's lower basement level. I had gotten lost and then found my way back up and out again.

Relieved to be back in the mainstream, I walked up and down the hall a short way in each direction trying to get my bearings. A passerby, a nurse, I assumed, seeing my furrowed eyebrows and searching eyes stopped to ask me if I needed directions. I explained my predicament, and she told me the floor I wanted was the next floor up, the first floor of the hospital facility after the ground floor. I thanked her, and not wanting to walk far looking for an elevator (for there appeared to be none within sight on the ground floor where I was standing), I turned back to enter the door through which I'd come into the main corridor. I would just take the stairs.

But no door. Plenty of wall from here to there, to be sure, but no door.

Once again I was stymied. What in the name of Gerry's Green Earth was happening to me? What was *wrong* with this place? Why was it so difficult to find my way around and keep a simple appointment? Frustrated, I stopped a passing orderly and asked directions to the nearest elevator. I thanked him, walked to it, entered, and stepped off on the first floor. Asking directions again at the first nurses' aide station I happened across, I soon made my way to my appointed examination room and entered. The receptionist asked me to sign in using my full name—last name first, first name last—and to please take a seat when I was done. The doctor would see me as soon as he finished with the patient who had taken my original appointment.

I found a seat, picked up a well-used magazine on weapons and small arms, and started flipping through it. I had a long wait, but during my lengthy read, I did learn something about sighting in a double action handgun versus a semiautomatic. When the receptionist finally called my name and I put the magazine back on the table beside my chair, I stood up and was glad my first weapon of choice was a bow and arrow. It was much simpler to operate, easier to sight in, and wasn't prone to jam if it was dropped or knocked to the floor. Yep, to this Gatekeeper, a bow and arrow was the proper way to go if given a choice in the matter.

Dr. Roy Gallagher could have cared less. His weapon of choice was an index finger fully extended and locked into position, the better to poke all the sore spots on my hip, back, and shoulder as he cut away my casts and bandages and examined me. His questions were endless and sometimes seemed pointless. I was not in the best of moods despite his cheery candor when he finally pronounced my wounds healed, that I was "ready for rehab."

He cautioned me that while my skin had grown back and presumably my torn muscle, and even though it appeared I wasn't bleeding anywhere, it would still take some time for my body to properly heal. Long walks on the beach at sunset were his recommendation but, failing that, long walks anywhere I could get them, the steeper the terrain rise the better. It sounded like a prescription for North Carolina to me.

As I was putting my shirt back on, I described my difficulty in getting to his office, especially about wandering around in the hospital's lower levels and the crying I'd heard in the empty room. I didn't notice at first just how much attention he was paying me as I tossed off my comments while struggling into my clothes. When I finally looked up after adjusting my T-shirt, I was momentarily taken aback by the intensity of his gaze. "A crying room?" he mused. "And you came up several levels on the staircase before you found your way into the main corridor?" he asked. I replied that yes, I had. While I was sure it was at least two levels, my impressions were that I climbed three stairwells until I found and opened the door to the main corridor.

He sat looking at me pensively for a few moments. I finally asked him if he was all right. I got an affirmative, but I got something more besides. "There are only two levels beneath the ground floor," he stated, "but the second level does not extend under *this* facility and is only found beneath the small engineering complex adjacent to this building. Fact. You can't get here from there. There are no connecting tunnels, but yours is not the first story I've heard about people being lost beneath this building in a maze of quiet corridors. Oddly, almost all the stories have involved a crying room. Very peculiar," he said, and then dismissed it as he told me what sort of a plan I would have to follow to assure my complete recovery. After handing me a prescription for the pain that would come as my body learned to reuse part of itself, he dismissed me cheerfully and asked the nurse to send in the next patient.

I was glad to leave for several reasons, not the least of which was that his finger probes hurt. But I was nagged by the crying room experience. I wondered if it had any connection to my powers as a Gatekeeper, the ability to communicate with animals. I didn't know it then, but I would later learn that Sunstar's healing powers had affected me in ways I would yet learn about, not all of them pleasant and some of them dangerous. Sometimes it is good to be ignorant of things in the unseen world about us. And, I discovered, they really are all about us.

DAY ONE 11:00 A.M.

My trip over to Columbus and the Veteran's Hospital there had been a long day's affair. Dad had driven me over and back. On the drive home, we had an opportunity to visit. It was my chance to bring him up to speed about all that happened in the few weeks I was away in North Carolina. We were both grateful the supposed raid on Appalachian State University students had never happened and that the Pale Were captured there was apparently one of the area leaders. He was important enough to prompt the Weres to postpone or cancel the raid without him. I told my dad about Gitta and Polaris, how we were becoming an effective team. I really missed being away from them. I also confessed my fear that my shoulder injury might permanently affect my archery ability and that I was apprehensive about taking up a bow again lest my fears turn out to be right.

My dad countered by telling me that if I did not start practicing again as soon as possible, my fears would have already won. It was the old bucked-off-the-horse phenomenon. Unless a cowboy steps right back up on the saddle, he'll never be an effective rider again. And unless I rededicated myself to archery and excellence as soon as practical, I would never be as effective an archer as I might have been. His words were encouraging. They were helpful because he tempered everything he said to me with love. That was how my dad worked. The confidence that alone gave me was incalculable.

When you're honest with yourself and your parents about life's pressing issues, there will always be answers and courage enough to pull through any crisis. Sometimes as a teenager, I forgot that, almost always to my disadvantage. Sometimes I would remember too late. But inevitably I learned that the combined strength of my family was always greater than mine alone and, not surprisingly, was always greater than the challenge I faced.

The drive was also a chance to sit and think in companionable silence. That was one of the benefits about being with people you love and respect. No one has to make conversation.

It was late afternoon when we arrived back home. I felt a new freedom without the encumbrance of the casts on my hip and shoulder, even though the stitches remained. But I could stretch and move again and had no weight pressing against my already tender wounds. I wanted to just run and jump like a colt in a field on a bright spring day to try out my body again, but fortunately, I had the good sense not to do that. I could go into a pool, however. The hospital annex in Chagrin Falls had a mobility pool primarily for knee and shoulder repair rehabilitation. It was available for any post-surgery therapy. It would even admit Sunstar as my trainer since someone had to accompany each primary user.

Sunstar and the Allegros were home when we drove up. Sunstar practically flew out of their side doorway when Dad stopped the car and beeped the horn to celebrate. I fumbled at my latch in my hurry to exit. Sunstar was already standing outside my door when I finally got it open. "Look at you!" she exclaimed when I stepped out and stood up. "A new man but the same old smile." And with that she leaned over and gave me a hug and a peck on my cheek. Then she bounced back on her heels with a grin at least as wide as mine, hands clasped tightly behind her back. Mom kidded me that I was blushing, but I quickly corrected her. I told everyone that I'd been on the sunny side of the car driving home, that I was probably a little flushed from that.

"Yeah, right!" said Dad with a grin, and then asked what sun was that since it had been overcast in Ohio since yesterday at noon. Everyone laughed, even Sunstar. I just stood there looking at the pavement and shaking my head. My mom grabbed my arm. She told everyone I needed to get settled, that dinner would be at 6:30. She invited Sunstar to join us and promptly rolled my wheelchair under me and wheeled me away into the house. Dad brought in my first aid kit and extra bandages. I was home again. I was learning to appreciate these in-between visits. I hoped there would be many more of them as I grew and stayed away, first at college and then in my planned military service. In the meantime, all I wanted was a shower and a short nap before mealtime. I only managed the shower. I must have been in there 40 minutes.

DAY TWO 7:30 A.M.

The sunlight streaming into my bedroom just wouldn't go away as I fitfully surrendered to consciousness, gently at first and then more vigorously, stretching every part of my body while twisting into some improbable shapes to work out the kinks in my back and hips. By the time I was done, blood was flowing through every artery and then some. I was fully if a bit painfully awake, and I had managed to plan my day. I was all set to call Sunstar and see if she would accompany me to the therapy pool in the early afternoon. My peaceful reverie was shattered by a phone call from the containment facility. It was Clarion. I just shook my head. That man was everywhere. "Cody! Good 'afternoon,' sleepyhead. It's me, Clarion. Time's a-wastin', as the Major says, and I need you here about 10 minutes ago. Grab a bite to eat and come a-runnin'. I've got some things to share with you. Sunstar says you're practically healed, so get dressed and come on over now. Your mom's already outside warming up the car. I just talked to her."

With that, he hung up. I was left sitting up in bed, my mouth hanging open at the suddenness of it all. Then I grinned to myself and gave a "Whoop!" as I tumbled out of bed. Clarion never made calls without a purpose, and whenever he was around, things happened. I felt like I was back in the saddle again. I was ready to ride. If I'd known why he really called, however, I'd have shot my mythical horse and saved us both some trouble.

My mom was outside and the car was running when I came out. Fifteen minutes later, I said goodbye to her at the Polo Club stable. I waved to her as she drove away. Then it was into the tack room and through the false door to the ramp leading down to the containment facility. I hurried at a fast walk. It felt wonderful to be free of the hip cast. Clarion was waiting for me at the Were cages. So was a new Pale Were. Guess which one was excited to see me?

Clarion walked over, shook my hand, put his arm over my shoulder, and walked me a little ways away from the cage that held the new Pale Were. It was one captured recently and shipped here by Lt. Col. Spikes. Clarion said we needed a sample of the Pale Were's saliva and that every attempt to take it by syringe meant drugging the Were first, which invariably tainted the specimen. It appeared the only way to run a clean test was to make the Pale Were mad enough to literally spit. I had to find a way to get enough sample for some tests to be run by the FBI lab in Washington, DC, and a courier plane would be leaving within the hour.

My job? It was obvious to me. Make the new Were mad and get the sample. Fast. After that, Clarion said I could go on back to sleep or get breakfast. I could go do whatever I wanted to do. My thoughts about the task were pure and simple. Follow Clarion's directions, get the sample, and let the Werewolf kill Clarion.

I was upset. His request could have been a planned chore anytime over the previous 10 days the Were had been here, but as usual, Clarion left some important things until the last minute. Then he usually had to have someone else step in for him, like me, to finish. He was a multitasker before the concept became popular. He left it for others to be multifinishers.

Don't get me wrong. I love the man. He is probably the most enigmatic yet exciting man I will ever meet. Still, he can be a pain in the keister when he has six irons in the fire, realizes they all have to be picked up at once, and hasn't bothered to forewarn anyone earlier because of need-to-know or some other lame excuse. Nevertheless, you can't help but like the guy. He is, after all, my ultimate boss. That's a good thing; otherwise, the Were would have to stand in line to get at Clarion—I would be first.

I pointed out to Clarion that there are several ways to make a Werewolf upset and even more to make him angry. They must be carefully thought out, however, because (1) Werewolves have no sense of humor, (2) Werewolves don't like humans except as table fare, (3) Werewolves are uncommonly strong and can bend things to hurt you with, and (4) Werewolves are hygienically challenged and like debris, human debris. For example, while Werewolf saliva may be toxic, the Weres generally smell bad due to rotten food bits in their mouths or soured blood on their pelts. And they are not happy campers when left in cages, fettered in chains, or frequently drugged.

I asked if that pretty much covered it all, and Clarion laughed, clapping me on the back and saying that fortunately none of those things really applied here. Then he left me to get the sample while he had a conference call with Dr. Abernathy.

The Pale Werewolf and I watched Clarion trot away. I don't know exactly what the Pale Were was thinking, but I was contemplating the arc of an arrow I would need to perfectly position a screaming shaft in Clarion's left buttock, perhaps with a follow-on exploding arrow in his right rear cheek for good measure. Two quick shots, and it would be done. But he turned a corridor corner before I could find a bow. The moment was lost. Just as well, I thought. With my injured shoulder, I'd probably have missed anyway. I hated to waste an arrow.

I turned back to the Were's cage. I walked forward to the white line on the floor in front of it. The Were eyed me warily and slowly crept closer to me as I neared the cage. When it was close enough to make mental contact, the loathing I felt and the bad thoughts it was throwing my way were almost palpable. Ten minutes later, I was on my knees turned away from the cage, holding my head with a splitting headache. Tears were in my eyes. I was short of breath. The exhausted Were had collapsed at the back of the cage. Some of the upper front bars were bent outward from its antics. My shirt back was in ribbons where a lucky swipe had allowed it to catch its claws on my back collar as I hastily turned away from a pending attack.

I mean, who knew a Werewolf could be so sensitive about its pedigree?

I told the custodian and several of the scientists who came running at the Were's ungodly howls and screams and general crashing against the bars that they could find its saliva, thank you very much, all over the upper front bars where its teeth had scoured the metal as it tried to bite through the bars to get me. Having said that, I crept over to the nearest wall and sat there, head down against my knees. I cradled my arms around my legs and took shallow breaths. I hoped my headache would soon go away, but for now, it didn't.

Clarion found me still huddled against the wall when he returned some 20 minutes later. I had pretty much recovered by then. I was watching the Pale Were as it sat against the back of the cage about 40 feet away. It was silently watching me with those unblinking eyes. If death was in a glance, I was a Class A1 zombie and probably worse.

Although my mental contacts with Weres in the past were brief, they were always painful. They usually left me with a fistful of impressions that generally yielded valuable intelligence if someone could help me make sense of them. That was one of the Major's biggest talents. I would be back at the Rat's Nest in two days anyway. I would ask Clarion to give the Major a heads-up about today's experience after I spoke with him. He helped me to my feet. We walked back to his temporary office together. I took a seat as he thanked me profusely. I waited for him to get past the pleasantries and ask me what happened.

We spoke for about half an hour. The Pale Were was an important figure in the Weres' fighting hierarchy. It was even more important than we first thought. Apparently, it was also the senior regional council member over the many scattered Werewolf packs that formed their equivalent of an eastern region. All Werewolves from the Ohio Valley to Canada and east to the Atlantic Ocean reported through this Pale Were. All Weres south of the Carolinas and east of the Mississippi River bounded by the Atlantic Ocean and the Gulf of Mexico were under the control of another Were from a large pack in the north Georgia mountains. It was a pack and concentration we knew little about. Lt. Col. Spikes had hit the jackpot on this one.

Our captured Were was chafing not only at its captivity but because it would miss a planned council meeting in the Georgia highlands. It was scheduled for late August, a warm time of year that made extended nighttime travel easier for Weres moving over the back byways of America. The council was scheduled to last for at least one week. The western and northern delegations would then leave to make it back to their home states before early winter snowfalls made foot travel impractical (easy for people to track them in fresh snow).

Running Werewolves could easily cover 60 to 70 miles per day, more if water and food were abundant. They had a ground-eating stride and were built to run indefinitely. They fed on cattle, dogs, cats, sheep, and small ponies or horses, whatever was handy when they were hungry. They even fed on humans but feared attracting too much attention to eat people when they were traveling in small groups. They went after those humans who were in isolated situations. Joggers were a usual target as were small children playing by themselves in a farmyard, on a country road, or at a deserted schoolyard.

Surprisingly, the Pale Were we captured had been around more than 100 years, yet it considered itself one of the youngest of the Werewolf Confederation's seven supreme council members.

All these thoughts and several others I poured out to Clarion. He was excited and grateful. He again thanked me and complimented me. "You always perform, Cody, and almost always exceed our highest expectations. Someday you will have my job, especially if you don't want it. As long as you stay with SpecOps, you will find yourself challenged and supported. You're already building a solid reputation. You have the respect of some pretty important folks. Just keep that sense of idealism in all aspects of your life, particularly in your social life.

"You're going into an age and experience that can ruin or make you. It's called college. Stay true to what your folks have taught you and what people like Lt. Col. Spikes and the Major teach you, and you'll make it through just fine. And don't forget to listen to what Dusty and Sunstar and Casey teach you. They'll help you be a better man. But listen to me too long and you'll be maimed or dead because, seriously, who wants to live forever, right?" With that, he grinned and shooed me out of his office as he set up his call to Lt. Col. Spikes and the Major.

DAY TWO 1:30 P.M.

After I left Clarion's office, I stopped by the aid station and picked up some aspirin from the intern working there. I sat down in a comfortable chair, waiting for the aspirin to take effect, and promptly dozed off. I awakened just before lunch. I was alone in the dispensary. I wandered out looking for Sunstar's laboratory, hoping to have lunch with her in the Polo Club upstairs. I eventually found her, surrounded by several of the younger staff who were all vying for her attention as they secured their lab before leaving for lunch. Just as they all started to ask her to lunch, she spotted me leaning against a corridor wall. My hands were in my pockets. "Cody!" she called out. "Cody, you're right on time as usual." Then she turned, thanked the fellows for considering her, and without a backward glance ran over to me.

To look at her was to look at beauty and light and all things good and reverent. To look at the faces of the fellows behind her as they looked past the back of her head at me was to stare into the abyss of death. So I couldn't help it. I opened my arms to give her a big welcome hug. As I was doing so, I stuck out my tongue at the crestfallen scientists and crossed my eyes. That sent one young junior Einstein over the top into a frenzy. His companions wisely held him back as Sunstar and I disappeared upstairs to the Polo Club dining room. All of this, of course, was unseen and unsuspected by Sunstar.

A man's gotta do what a man's gotta do, I told myself. I laughed silently all the way upstairs. And to myself, I also thanked my heavenly Father for one of His "tender mercies" (Sunstar) at every step I took.

We had a great lunch. We talked seriously for about an hour. I told her of my experience in the hospital and asked if she might have an explanation for my encounter with corridors that weren't there and a crying room that wanted no one to see it. After the waiter cleared our table, she scooted her chair closer to mine. She lowered her voice and began to explain how the world beside us really was. She said that in her culture, we were children in the Great Spirit's kingdom before we came to this earth. Many of us knew one another in our former spirit home. This earth was created by the Great Spirit as a testing ground for his spirit children to see if we would come into an at-risk situation for a short time, the duration of our lives, however long or short that might be, and, while here, test ourselves against an opposing force to see if we could keep the promises we made before coming here. We would be given bodies of flesh. We would also forget our first home during our lives here so we might live on earth by faith, not memory.

We would prove ourselves or fail. Upon death, we would return to the spirit world that coexists side by side with us on this planet but in a different dimension. There we would be instructed on what we did right and what we did wrong as we review our life with a qualified guide. Having completed our review, we would judge ourselves against a standard, the laws the Great Spirit set for us. To master those laws would entitle us to inherit his legacy. We would have earned his trust, a trust that he then knew we would use to not squander or damage the vast inheritance he had set aside for us.

Our actions here would not interfere with his great love for us nor would he step in to take away his greatest gift of all in whatever kingdom we found ourselves. That was our free agency, the agency to choose good or evil. For those who chose to use this life for evil pursuits, a judgment and lesser reward, even punishment, would await their departure from this mortal life. For those who chose good over evil, a greater reward, even rest and peace awaited.

But just as there was opposition in this mortal life, there must also be opposition in our spiritual life, long before our earthly sojourn started. Spirits, evil spirits, would work against us in our premortal existence and, failing there, would work against us even harder here on our mortal earth. And they would always work hardest against those who possessed uncanny talents or powers such as Sunstar and I had, she with her gift of healing and me with my ability to communicate with species. As we would use our powers to help our brothers or sisters make this passage safely, so we became special targets for the forces of evil who sought to pull us down and wreck our intentions and actions. However, lest we feel we are special and above others, the forces of good will act silently to recommend to our attention that our reward in the next life is commensurate with our willingness to accept this greater capability and responsibility for warring against evil in this life. If we fail, our punishment will be greater than that of our brothers or sisters who had not our abilities.

Sunstar pointed out that two of the best tools of Dus-ta-s'hes in this life are confusion and distraction. Finding myself confused in the subterranean corridors and the trick of the crying room gave the opposition power if it scared me or if it caused me to doubt myself and be afraid to use my special power. However, I was damned anyway if I used my power to serve myself. I was also damned if I denied my power to serve others. Finally, I was damned if I used my powers knowingly to serve evil at the expense of others. I was rewarded only if I used that power freely and wisely for others.

"There will always be unseen powers trying to distract, oppose, and torment us, Cody. It is the nature of this existence. But if we are true and steadfast, if we serve others willingly and well, many of our missteps will be forgiven or forgotten by a loving Great Spirit who wants safe passage home for all his children, both the good and the bad. In my religion, he loves all his children, the errant son Dus-ta-s'hes, the Father of Lies, just as much as he does his other son, Go-da-'mi, the Bringer of Truth and Hope. But he does not trust Dus-ta-s'hes or those that follow him and therefore holds back their rewards. That is the difference. That is why we must expect great opposition and danger in our life. We can always call upon hope and the Ancient Ones to help. The Ancient Ones are those who have gone before, those who are now in the Spirit World all around us. Evil spirits can fight on two levels, but we can only fight in this life on

338

the mortal level. The Ancient Ones have power as well, and they can fight in the Spirit World for us against the evil spirits. Because they have the experience of two lives, they have greater power there than the evil ones. But nobody can fight for us if we do not ask for help. That is what agency is all about. It is humanity's greatest blessing and its greatest curse. It is simple, Cody. In your previous life, you agreed to have special talents in this life. You agreed to use them for good, to serve your brothers and sisters. Because of your promise there, you are granted special powers here. If you use them well and wisely, you may expect a great reward when you return to the Spirit World. If you become selfish and cruel, acting in opposition to the Great Spirit's wishes, you will merit a special hell in the next life, but when your punishment has equaled your crimes, you will be welcomed home. But there you will be given a lesser reward than you could have received. In that manner, the Great Spirit's mercy does not rob his justice. It is fair."

Never had I paid so great attention to any lesson as I did that one. Now I understood my life.

DAY TWO 7:30 P.M.

After lunch with Sunstar, I caught a ride home with the Polo Club courier. I spent part of the afternoon testing myself against my old bow. I couldn't even string it, much less draw it. My shoulder was simply too weak. Nor could I take a settled stance since my left buttock was still sore from its wound. In a fit of pique, I finally laid my bow down and tossed arrows at my target by hand. Not even close. I knew then it was time to head back to North Carolina to fully heal. I spent the remainder of the day packing. I also packed a separate suitcase with a number of items I would need for my fall semester at Lees-McRae and throughout the forthcoming winter. *Might as well take them now*, I thought to myself. *It'll be harder when the airlines are full with returning college students.* Sunstar brought Dad's truck home about 4:00 p.m. After a quick stop at her room at the Allegros, she came on over to see what I was up to. As she came into my room, I told her she was just in time. I asked her to sit on each suitcase as I locked them and wrapped a bright red safety strap around them. I then escorted her back downstairs where we visited with my mom for an hour or so until Mom left for a quick errand before dinner.

I took a minute to thank Sunstar for everything she had done for me, for my folks, and for the Allegros. I thanked her for being generous with her gifts and her time and her patience with me, for embracing my family and Casey's family as she had done. I told her she was truly like a daughter to them. They would support and love her no matter where she went. She was touched at my comments. She covered my hand with hers and slowly leaned forward until her lips were close to my ear. She squawked,

"Eh, what's up, Doc!" I was so startled I jumped back in my chair, and she burst out laughing. She looked so fetching that I had to laugh, too. That's how Dad found us when he came wandering in from work.

After dinner, we all talked about a number of things, especially Lees-McRae. My folks were very curious about this little-known gem of a school tucked away in the North Carolina mountains. Sunstar had much to say, all of it good. Its greatest appeal to me wasn't its claim of the highest campus in the East but rather its focus on wildlife affairs and management.

Sunstar echoed that. She described her first-year experiences at the affiliated Blue Ridge Wildlife Rehabilitation Center and her later experiences with several of the birds brought there, especially Polaris. I listened, fascinated. My folks hung on to every word.

She pointed out that Lees-McRae was a Presbyterian college and that her family, like us, were Methodists. But Sunstar laughed and said they take all kinds. Why, she said as she leaned forward in a conspiratorial manner and whispered aloud, I've heard there are even Mormons there. With that she sat back and giggled as if she had disclosed some daring secret. I could see by the twinkle in her eye that it was a poking-fun kind of statement.

I leaned forward and whispered back to her, "Do they have any atheists?"

"Not many," she replied, "just the teachers and staff."

We all laughed at that nonsense. Our conversation then shifted away to the mundane. What were the dorms like? What services were in the area? What were assignments and homework like at college? Were there more girls than guys, or vice versa? How did the archery program do this past year? And on and on. At 9:00 p.m., we broke up. My folks went on to bed. I walked Sunstar outside. We sat on our backyard lawn and talked for a few minutes before going back to our respective rooms. It was a beautiful, calm late spring night such as Ohio gets once a century or so. No rain and low humidity. As we sat there, Sunstar asked me about Casey. From what she had seen in Casey's room and from the comments the Allegros and my folks had made, she felt Casey must be an exceptional woman. What she hadn't heard was my side of the story. Since I was leaving the next day, this might be Sunstar's last chance to hear all about this marvelous woman while she was still in Chagrin Falls.

It was an immediate and interesting dilemma. As I described Casey and my feelings about her, I found that for every good thing I said about Casey, I could say something equally good about Sunstar. For every one of Casey's exceptional talents, there was an exceptional talent for Sunstar. For every goofy aspect of Casey, there was an equally goofy aspect of Sunstar (as she had revealed them to me), and so it went, on and on. After an hour or so of recounting the many, many stories I had about Casey, I noticed that Sunstar remained enthralled with her. "This is a woman I want to meet," she said. "This is a woman who could be a friend for a lifetime."

I felt humbled and honored when she said that. Casey was so much a part of me that she was woven into my spiritual fabric. Sunstar's admiration meant that whatever happened or didn't happen between us, Sunstar would never ask that that fabric be unraveled. Having friends like Sunstar, Dusty, and Casey meant that love and romance could flow as they would without one cancelling or interrupting the other. These women had given me a freedom, I thought to myself, a freedom to express what Sunstar would say was the Great Spirit's second greatest wish for his earthly children—the gift of unselfish and innocent love.

It was a gift I was to treasure for years. It was a gift I hoped to carry with me to my death. The freedom to love another, male or female, without demands or expectations is truly love because it demands agency and respects its gift.

We ended our evening on that note. I got an unexpected hug. It wasn't one of those nurture hugs either. It was a downright uplifting, rejuvenating, exhilarating hug that made me grin from my toes up, which is a difficult way to reenter one's home when all you really want to do is leap about like a crazed ape and swing from the rafters.

DAY FOUR 7:30 A.M.

I was up and packed, bouncing from chair to divan to stool and back again as I impatiently waited for the morning to unfold. I was too anxious to eat and too hungry not to eat, so I just drank a glass of milk and ate a handful of dry cereal. Somehow, I didn't even miss the sugar. Today was the day I was flying back to the Rat's Nest. My thoughts were all over the place. I really missed the folks in North Carolina. I would miss being around Sunstar, but I really, really missed Gitta and Polaris. I felt my family and friends wanted me around, true, but I also felt Gitta and Polaris needed me around. Big difference. I was anxious to see and make physical contact with those two once more.

About 8:00 a.m., Sunstar joined us. We talked in the kitchen while Mom finished getting ready before she drove me over to the Cleveland airport. Sunstar was not coming along. She had a big day testing some of her potions against several of the virus strains extracted from the Pale Were's saliva. She was worried that she wasn't making a very big contribution to our efforts yet. I thought I put her mind at ease when I explained that things build upon themselves, that success takes time. Sometimes success takes a very different route entirely from what we initially anticipated.

Mom came in about that time. We didn't dawdle but said a quick goodbye. Mom dropped me off at the airport in plenty of time, and my flight back to North Carolina was singularly uneventful. When flying, I like boring. Pee Wee was there to meet me. The Major had Sergeant Saddler out on another mission. We used the time driving back to discuss the escape of the Pale Were back in Chagrin Falls and all the trouble it subsequently caused. Pee Wee told me that Clarion had high praise for the manner in which I dispatched the Pale Were. My recent trip home had not been the rest and recuperation trip everyone had hoped for. Not to worry, though, Pee Wee said. Dusty had baked a special surprise for me. The Major also wanted to get me out in the sunshine with Gitta and Polaris as soon as possible so I might regain my strength. Apparently, I was going to need it. It looked like we might have a special raid planned for mid-August. I needed to be well for that. I knew the Major would fill me in later.

Somewhere along the drive up, I fell asleep while Pee Wee was talking to me. I started to come awake when I felt the car hit some of the gravel ruts on the drive up to the Rat's Nest. I guess my body remembered the sequence of bumps, and my unconscious control started sending wake-up signals to my conscious mind.

I was totally unprepared for the roar that went up when Pee Wee brought the SUV to a halt in front of the Rat's Nest. Everyone was out on the porch or grass shouting a hearty "Hip Hip, Hooray!" as the car came to rest. The noise startled me. I came awake fast as a big grin spread across my face. I recognized where we were and what was happening. The best part was seeing Gitta and Dusty standing in front of everyone else. When I stepped out of the car, I heard far above me the shrill cry of Polaris greeting me as she plummeted from the sky.

It was a race to see who could get to me first, and Gitta won, but barely. She came running when she saw it was me. She hit me midchest and flattened me. Then she stood over me and rubbed her head on my stomach and chest while Polaris banked to a halt beside me and stood in the grass like a sculpture of sun-kissed magnificence screaming ownership of her "kill." I was laughing with what breath I had left. I managed to give Gitta a major behind-the-ears rubdown before she let me up. Polaris flew up to the roof rack of the SUV. She perched there as she calmly watched the many hugs and handshakes I gave out and received. When everyone started to troop back into the Rat's Nest, I turned to Polaris and spoke with her for a few minutes while softly stroking her wings. I told her how much I had missed her. I bowed in acknowledgment of her "Princessness." She, in turn, dipped her head and spread her wings before me as an equal companion. Gitta rolled her eyes at that and headed after Dusty. Gitta knew where the good food came from in my absence. She wasn't a bit shy about going after it. I thought she had a great idea. I followed after.

As I mounted the porch steps, I thought how good it was to be "home" again. I was learning that home was where I was, where someone depended on me, not just some pile of bricks and mortar at an address I occasionally frequented. It was a lesson all soldiers eventually learned. It was one that often hurt.

Once inside, the Major debriefed me for about an hour and a half. As usual, I emerged thinking I knew what a dishrag was like when it was wrung out. If I had a memory left somewhere in my noggin that hadn't been identified and examined, then truly a miracle had occurred. But it wasn't so. The advantage of being subjected to a friendly interrogation by the Major was that I was learning how to think, how to use thought structures to remember, and how to tap into those memories and link apparently disparate things or events together. Every day was a school experience with the Major as my teacher. Not every school day was pleasant.

Dusty had prepared a welcome-back cake. Everyone at the Rat's Nest was chaffing by the time I emerged from the Major's office. Pee Wee led a round of "For He's a Jolly Good Fellow" and then I was ignored as everyone jostled for position to get some of Dusty's cake. She gave me the first and biggest piece, which I immediately took outside to share with Polaris and Gitta. Polaris took incidental bites and only a few, but Gitta ran through the cake like a four-year-old through icing. Dusty came out in time to see Gitta practically standing on her head, twisting her neck to get a last dab of cake that had somehow lodged by her ear. We both sat and laughed at how much fun Gitta was having, yet neither of us wanted to get close to Gitta to reach out to help her capture her last bite. Her jaws were moving so quickly to snatch up each crumb that it would be like putting one's hand into a shredder.

We moved to the edge of the porch as everyone started leaving for the day. We didn't want anyone to trip over us. Dusty asked me question after question about my trip home and all that had transpired. She knew a lot of what had gone on from her almost daily conversations with Sunstar. Nevertheless, I thought she was really trying to get my side of things, especially if I had any feelings for Sunstar. I know I blushed, but I was pretty vague in my responses. That earned me a poke in the arm at one point. I remember shouting, "Ouch!" I wondered what it was about these women in my life that somehow impelled them to become violent just because I refused to answer a trick question.

By 6:30 p.m., I was starting to yawn. Dusty, as usual, was a step ahead of me. She handed me the keys to the old Chevrolet and told me the inn at Blowing Rock had my old room set aside and was expecting me. The Major would want to see me in the morning at about 9:00 a.m. "Wear your hiking boots" was the last thing she called out to me as I headed for the Motor Pool to get the Chevrolet. She headed to the parking lot for her car.

I stopped back by the Chapel and walked around back to make sure Gitta and Polaris were secure for the night. I sat with them for another hour and shared stories and impressions of my trip home. They shared what they had experienced in my absence. Polaris was *not* happy about being kept in a cage during my time away. She made it very clear that if I left again without her, she would stay in the woods near Gitta before she would ever go back to her cage. Either that or she'd leave for points north.

I listened carefully. Polaris was one serious bird. As for Gitta, she had loafed around part of the time and gone on several overnight hunting expeditions the rest of the time.

She had learned the bowl-flip maneuver very quickly. Every time she remembered, a Twinkie showed up in her bowl. Every time she forgot, no Twinkie. Dusty was ruthless. Gitta was attentive.

DAY FIVE 7:30 A.M.

The next morning, I rolled off my bed at the Blowing Rock Inn with carefree abandon until I sat fully upright on the floor. I was immediately dizzy. My shoulder and hip hurt. With considerably less enthusiasm, I moved my shoulder in a slow circular motion until the blood was flowing and my nerves were calmed down a bit. I carefully rose and headed for the bathroom to shower and clean up. By 8:30 a.m., I had finished a light breakfast and was in the old Chevrolet headed for the Chapel. It was a beautiful North Carolina summertime mountain morning. Over the years, I have come to believe that there are no finer mornings on earth than in that season at that place.

I was waiting outside the Major's office at 8:55 a.m. when she opened the door and beckoned me in. Pee Wee and Sergeant Saddler were already sitting in her office. The two of them had been in council with her. Apparently, I was invited to the tail end of the meeting. It was about armament. They wanted to know what might have prevented the injuries that the Turk, me, and others had sustained when in first contact with the Weres. All our wounds were contact wounds. As yet, the Weres had demonstrated no aptitude for weapons of any kind save those they brought with them—their incredible teeth and claws. Therefore, prevention, our defense, began there.

We all agreed that forearm gauntlets and some sort of upper body armor that protected the front and back of the neck as well as the vulnerable upper body torso were needed. It was really just a question of design, materials, and cost. The design must allow for full maneuverability, and the weight must be light enough so the combatant can wear the armor for extended periods. The Major then surprised us by having Dusty bring in some samples of body armor she had some design engineers make from Sergeant Saddler's and my early drawings. She had spent some Research & Development (R&D) money at Duke University so some of their design and engineering master's degree candidates could work up some prototype units for us. The excuse was that the military was interested in protecting its veterinary and military police personnel against large attack and guard dogs that had fallen victim to rabies or distemper or some other such malady.

We were all excited. We tried on several of the units. I thought we looked like 17th-century Samurai warriors, but Pee Wee reminded me that looks had better be the last thing we thought about in a Were fight or else it would be the last thing we thought about. We all chuckled at that because he was dead-on. I toned down my enthusiasm a notch or two. After a half hour or so, the Major asked each of us to take one of the several ensembles, wear them around for two or three days, and then trade for another. She asked me to wear mine while I was doing my daily five- to 10-mile hike around the mountains, an assignment that immediately garnered my closest attention.

"I'm serious, Cody. You've been hurt, and your doctor in Chagrin Falls and I have been speaking daily about a routine to get you back into fighting shape. From now on, we want you out in the fresh air or rain or wind or whatever at least five to eight hours per day, hiking up and down these mountains. Carry your javelin and the Japanese sword for personal protection, and Gitta and Polaris will go with you. Think of it as team building. You start this morning. Dusty will help you put a pack together for first aid, water, and snacks. Stop in here each morning. Pee Wee will have a route designed for you. Expect some surprises along the way each day. Now, take a Twinkie with you when you break the news to Gitta. I think she's gaining a bit of weight, and she'll need an incentive to start working hard again since your recent absence." With that, we were dismissed.

Dusty had a small backpack on her desk and a big smile on her face waiting for me as I left the Major's office. A Twinkie was positioned carefully on top. She told me I looked a little uncomfortable in the set of body armor I was wearing. She encouraged me to stick with the Major's program. "You looked more uncomfortable when the Werewolf clawed you," she said, "so really give this proposed equipment a fair shot, Cody. Please." I nodded that I would.

It was good that I brought the Twinkie with me for Gitta. It bought me a period of silence as she ate while I explained our new daily regimen. It also put her into a receptive mood to agree and come along with me, although I thought her long period of inaction was the real selling point. Gitta was smart and bored easily if she wasn't physically or mentally challenged.

I asked Polaris to lead us on a track to start. She lifted into the air with a squeal of joy at flying. Gitta and I set out behind her, using her cries as our compass. My hip started hurting in the first 15 minutes. For the remainder of the day, it never stopped reminding me that injuries take time to heal. Polaris had two bird kills within the first hour. Gitta also had a kill, a small wild pig we surprised as we fought our way through a thicket to a pond bed we'd glimpsed when coming down a steep hillside almost two hours into our hike.

We stopped at noon by a small stream that was busily cutting its way downhill through some tall grass. I lay back in the grass under the overhang of a stumpy mountain oak tree with just enough shade on my face to inspire a short nap. I told Polaris to go fly for a while and told Gitta that now was her chance to get a short nap with me or go exploring. Gitta had the heart of a Hungarian Christopher Columbus. She was gone in a minute. I knew they wouldn't lose me no matter what direction I walked after I awakened, so I just closed my eyes and drifted off to sleep.

I came awake in a hurry to find my worst nightmare had become my new reality. Not only could I hear Weres nearby, but they were close enough that I could smell their stench just by breathing. I lay as quietly as I could, trying to damp down my breathing while feeling my body start to perspire as the tension mounted. One thing in my favor—if I could smell them, the wind was at their backs and they couldn't smell me. As I lay there, I looked up into the tree above me. It was a scrub oak, not at all the kind of tree that would offer a vertical escape even if my shoulder and hip allowed me to climb into its upper branches. Even the trunk was relatively small with a diameter much smaller than my body profile should I try to hide behind it.

What it did offer was a temporary obstacle should any of the Weres decide to charge me. Its low branches and thin profile would offer a Were about 4.6 seconds of delay if it ran toward me. I thought that was 4.6 seconds better than no tree at all. I reminded myself that not all blessings come in a quantity sufficient for our wants and that a 4.6-second delay was far better than the proverbial poke in the eye with a sharp stick. It then occurred to me that a sharp stick might be handy in the aftermath of my discovery.

The feeling came to me that this was not going to be a nice day after all.

DAY FIVE 1:30 P.M.

After about five minutes of trying to emulate a rock as I lay under the oak tree, the wind stopped being a steady breeze toward me. It began to swirl in gusts. I had thrown down my javelin when I first lay down. I remembered it was several feet away from me, too far to try to reach without revealing my presence to the Weres. But with the wind shifting, my discovery was only a matter of time and no longer a possibility. Sure enough, in a matter of seconds, I heard more than one Were jump to its feet as the sound of sniffing permeated the air. When the first growl started to escalate into a hunting howl, I leaped to my feet. I put the hapless oak between the Weres and me as I scrambled back into heavy grass, mentally screaming for Gitta and Polaris as I half ran, half hobbled my way up the small hill behind the tree.

I could hear the Weres raise a full howl as they discovered and came after me. In my haste, I stumbled across a narrow trail that angled to the left of my headlong flight. I took it for about 10 steps as it curved even farther left. I did a forward leap and somersaulted to my right into a particularly dense bunch of tall grass. I came to rest on my feet, facing away from the chase close behind me. I pulled my wakizashi blade as I spun in place and then crouched and waited for the inevitable rush, my shoulder starting to really hurt after my desperate tumbling attempt.

"Channel your anger," said Captain Yamata when we were first training so long ago. His advice was as sound in the moment as it was when he first delivered it to me. I took a deep breath. I planned how to take the first two attackers that would come for me. The sound of thrashing through the tall grass and the Weres' howls of rage and bloodlust seemed almost on top of me. I suddenly saw two large bodies emerge from a screen of grass to my left and rush by. They were heading on up the narrow, curving trail from which I'd just jumped away. I waited to a quick count of 10 before I stepped back through the great grass clump back onto the trail. I started my run-hobble back the way I had come. I careened back down the hill through the tall grass and back toward the scrub oak tree where my javelin lay unattended.

In my panic and ungainly haste, I stumbled just before the tall grass ended. I was at the opening to a small clearing around the scrub oak tree trunk. Arms flailing to keep my balance, I felt rather than saw something large to my left rush at me. I ducked my head and went into a full somersault. The Were jumping at me from my left barely cleared me as I suddenly dropped away from before it. Its desperate grab for me brought its claws sharply along the shoulder armor I was wearing. To my utter surprise, its claws found no purchase as it sailed over me. Like a carefully choreographed ballet, I came rolling back up to my feet as the Were hit the ground, turned, and sprang back for me, jaws and claws fully extended to rip and tear me apart.

Once again, the wakizashi blade saved me. Off balance and facing in the wrong direction, I nevertheless swung the blade with all my strength behind me in the Were's general direction. The metal easily sliced through the Were's jaws as its body loomed over mine. In less than a second, I had doubled its smile. The lower half of the Were's jaw suddenly broke loose. It hung flapping in the air, held to the head by torn skin and a few sinews. In the Were's momentary shock, I slashed once again, and the blade severed its right arm from its shoulder. Blood poured out of the cut artery in powerful spurts. The Were keeled over in seconds, the victim of massive blood loss and shock. As it fell, I cut off its head as a precaution. I then turned to find my javelin and face the Weres I could hear returning.

They burst into the small grassy area surrounding the scrub oak tree. They immediately ground to a halt. Their jaws were wide open. Their red eyes took in everything before them. Hands raised and claws fully extended, they separated, growling softly to one another. Each crept slowly around me until they were on opposite sides of me. Then they began to close in, snarling and spitting as they crept closer to me. I could either drop the wakizashi blade and use two hands on the javelin or hold the javelin in my left hand, pointing at one Were with the wakizashi blade pointing at the other. I knew I had no power in my injured left shoulder to stab the left Were or turn it if it charged me. I did hope to present at least a formidable picture of defense from the Were's point of view. I chose to point the javelin and wave the wakizashi blade in an ever-tightening circle.

I caught a glimpse of a sudden movement to my right. Turning my head slightly toward it, I took a step backward as well. I pulled my blade back for a wrist slash and thrust. As soon as I did, the Were on my left leaped at me. I saw its shadow on the ground as it closed in on me. Planting my javelin on the ground beside me, I ducked down and extended the point toward the attacking Were. At the same time, I started cutting the air to my right with my blade, hoping to stand off the Were that had moved first.

Two things happened at virtually the same time. I heard a coughing growl from behind me. The Were on my left was violently thrown across the front of me, a fully enraged, golden-shouldered Wolverine fastened to its neck with claws ripping pieces out of the Were's shaggy coat as they fell to the ground together. Gitta had timed her jump perfectly. Her jaws were literally tearing apart the Were's neck and head. The Were's screaming and howling were pitiful to hear but music to my ears as I turned back to my right to confront the second Were.

To my astonishment, the second Were was stumbling around blindly, swinging its limbs and howling in a crazed scream of pain and frustration. Polaris had hit the Were's head at top speed. Her talons had literally torn the Were's eyes from their sockets as her impact drove the Were into the ground. Great gash lines opened the Were's cheeks and forehead. Bloody furrows tore across its visage leaving but ragged holes where the Were's eyes had been torn out by the falcon. I approached the crazed animal and drove my blade through its stomach. Its frenzied howling stopped immediately. It fell to the ground on its knees like a disjointed heap of dirty clothes, hands trying to clasp its abdomen as it slowly bled out.

I knelt by its side and tried to make contact with its mind. Panic and hate engulfed me with flashes of intelligence. These Weres were on a scouting mission, trying to find evidence of a Pale Were that had been captured by an element of humans led by a short man with coal-black hair. The man had confronted and killed two Were scouts that were to protect the Pale Were. He had also wounded a third, leaving it to die as the Pale Were was dropped, netted, and carried away. The third scout had lived long enough to tell the other Weres sent out to find the Pale Were what had happened. A number of secondary patrols were sent out as a result. The Were I stabbed was on one of those secondary patrols. It was grieving, not that it couldn't complete its mission but that it hadn't killed me before it was blinded. It died reaching out to claw me, knowing only my general location. All was quiet save my heaving chest and ragged breath. Gitta stood on top of her kill and deliberately peeled the remaining flesh from its bones as a sign of her contempt. Polaris just hopped on top of her dead Were's skull and started cleaning herself, looking nonchalant, looking as if she was doing nothing more than inspecting possible nesting sites. I sank down to my seat and thanked the gods once again for companions who were as faithful and dangerous as they came, friends who loved me enough not to desert me in my hour of need.

348

Trembling from the unexpected exertion, I slowly stood up and concentrated only on breathing slowly and deeply. It was then that I noticed that the ache in my left shoulder had intensified and that my hip was now hurting as well. I didn't know just how far from the Rat's Nest we'd come. I knew it would be a long walk back. Thank goodness for the javelin, I thought. Without a walking staff, I wasn't sure I could even make it up the hill, much less back to the Chapel.

Three and a half painful hours later, we were back. By that time, each step I took brought tears to my eyes. My stride had deteriorated into a poor imitation of an old man's hobble. I was done for when we reached the Chapel steps. I collapsed in a heap against the wall on the second porch step, unable to stand or move. I quickly fell asleep there in the afternoon sun, too tired to call out, too much in weary pain to climb the last few steps. Gitta sprawled out beside me, and Polaris flew to a perch in the nearby tree, her eyes always returning to me as they constantly swept the sky and forest for any further signs of danger. I could not have been in a better companionship of assassins.

One of the clerks found us that way and told the Major. Pee Wee subsequently came out to help me up and then drove me back to the Blowing Rock Inn with the Major's blessing. Before we drove away, Pee Wee unbuttoned my armor and handed it to the Major. Sergeant Saddler followed us in his car and gave Pee Wee a lift back to the Chapel after I was squared away.

I remembered nothing beyond that point until I was awakened early the next afternoon by a call to my room from Dusty. She asked if I was well enough to come in for a debriefing with the Major before the day was over. I said I was and started to. But I promptly walked back to my room and once again crashed. Too much too soon, but I was up and ready to go at 5:00 a.m. the next morning. There's something to be said for being young and resilient.

Not a lot, mind you, but something.

DAY SEVEN 7:30 A.M.

At last, everyone started to arrive. I'd been at the Rat's Nest for more than an hour waiting for the Major to show up. She eventually did, of course, because she was the Major, punctual to a fault but not an obvious fanatic about it. I had much to tell her, and when she saw me waiting, a big grin creased her face, and she invited me right into her office.

"We've got some things to talk about," she said, "and one of them is learning how to pace yourself. Day before yesterday, you really overdid it, Cody. Too much hiking, too soon, and you won't be getting into shape; you'll be setting your healing back by months. Whatever possessed you to walk so far that you ended up completely exhausted? That really worried us when we found you on the porch."

I told her it wasn't the walk so much as the fight with the Werewolves.

"Werewolves? What Werewolves?" she exclaimed as she almost tipped her chair over trying to stand up with shock all over her face. "What Werewolves, Cody? Were you in a fight? Why didn't you tell us or radio for help? You are *not* to go out hunting Werewolves without an armed escort. You could have been killed. What Werewolves, Cody? Tell me everything, and tell me right now."

She sat back in her chair with several emotions running across her face—shock to anger to concern to a baffled expression—and called Dusty and Sergeant Saddler in to take notes and tape my recounting. I spent the next two hours going over everything in detail several times until she was satisfied she had everything down correctly and in sequence. She dismissed Sergeant Saddler and Dusty and kept me back for a one-on-one talk.

"I'm sorry I overreacted, Cody. I sent you out with Gitta and Polaris and should have realized that they can protect you probably better than we can, save maybe in a pitched battle. I was just in shock and probably a little scared. Lt. Col. Spikes and Clarion would have my hide nailed to a wall if anything happened to you, so please don't be upset if I send Pee Wee with you for the next few times. Knowing that there are Were patrols out there right now is a little disconcerting, but Gitta and Polaris need to be recognized as well. I'd appreciate it if you'd take me out to see them and translate for me right now. I want them to always be by your side when you're away in the hills or mountains."

I did as she asked, and both of them—I think genuinely—appreciated being recognized. But what Gitta really appreciated more was the Twinkie that Dusty slipped to the Major to give to Gitta before the Major went outside. And for Polaris, Dusty sent out the rare steak strips she had planned for her own lunch salad. Some partners are always hungry even if they aren't. Like Marines.

We talked a bit more when we were back inside, and the Major just shook her head at what I'd accomplished with a sore shoulder and bad hip. "Cody," she said resignedly, "I don't know if you're just that good or just that lucky or a combination of both, but you're the best Were fighter we've got, and yet you're the one I can't risk. That's what drives Captain Yamata up the same wall. He thinks you'll be better than him someday and wants nothing more than to train and teach you all he knows. But that's exactly what I want to do, too, and both of us are held in check by Lt. Col. Spikes because Clarion thinks you'll be groomed to take his place someday, and Clarion ranks up there with the *big* boys, so we take a back seat and grind our teeth. Now get out of here while I dream up something to tell Lt. Col. Spikes that won't have him throwing me off a bridge for allowing you to fight unaccompanied, even if you did kill three

Weres—with help, of course." The sardonic grin on her face belied her anxiety, and she gave me a wink as she picked up the telephone and motioned for me to shut the door on my way out.

I stopped before she had a chance to complete her dialing and told her the leather armor I'd worn worked perfectly. "I was fairly active, took a roll or two, was reasonably nimble on my feet, and had a Were try to rip me as it made contact only with the shoulder armor, and here I am with nary a scratch. Tell Lt. Col. Spikes about your latest idea and that I've had a chance to try it out for real. Armored as I was, carrying my wakizashi with Gitta and Polaris accompanying me, do you really think any three Werewolves would have a chance? Four, maybe, but obviously not three." And with that, I shut the door only to see Dusty laughing quietly to herself at her desk. Sometimes I believed she could hear through walls.

DAY SEVEN 10:00 A.M.

I'd been talking with Pee Wee at his desk about the armor when Dusty came looking for me. She said I had a telephone call. "Who'd call me here?" I asked as I picked up the phone. I heard a voice that stopped me cold and brought a smile to my face that really stretched my cheeks. "Casey! Casey, is that really you?" I called out. Heads turned as Dusty made a shushing sound to me and then scolded the others nearby to let a fellow have a little privacy.

I had a million questions. I was all over myself trying to ask them all at the same time. Casey was laughing and trying to ask me about half as many. When we finally paused for a breath, I told her to go ahead and ask her questions first, but before that to tell me where she was and what prompted the call. She was in her future dorm room (to be assigned) with her new roommate (to be assigned) and had just returned from a three-week soccer camp in which she had garnered the Most Promising Rookie award. She was playing striker but had been used a little bit as a center forward as well. Her attack skills were excellent, and she'd made four goals in six games during the three-week period, more than anyone else on the freshman or varsity squads. She was very excited about playing and was so grateful for her scholarship. The school grounds were beautiful, the people nice, her coaches fantastic, and Paul very sweet, showing her some of the sandwich shops and a nonalcoholic club with a really neat band. He was a great dancer, too. She was going to be on campus for a week before her freshman team headed out for a round-robin tournament and skills camp at the University of South Carolina. It would last about two weeks. Would I have a chance to come down and see her? I told her I would have to check on that, but it didn't look good. We had a major assault operation coming up in early August, and I had to be back in shape if

I was to participate. When she asked me what I meant by "in shape," I told her of all our adventures to date and my wounds, my brief hospitalization, and the care both the doctors and Sunstar had given me.

That news changed the nature of our phone call, and I had to spend the better part of the next 30 minutes explaining that I was safe, that I was now an integral part of my unit, that my two companions were outstanding, that I wasn't taking foolish chances, that Sunstar also paid attention to other combatants, that no, we were not dating, that Dusty was off-limits because the Major said so and because she had a boyfriend, that Sunstar really wanted to meet Casey, that her parents had been outstanding in making her feel at home, that no, we weren't dating, that yes, I was sure, and so on and so on for what seemed forever.

When we finally hung up, I looked up to see the Major and Dusty with heads close together, suspiciously close to my desk, and Sergeant Saddler busy filing paperwork in the steel cabinets close behind me, whistling softly to himself. It was a first for him. I was ticked and then started to laugh out loud. These folks cared about me and had taken a maternal and paternal interest in me and were bad actors, but I was glad they cared. I cleared my throat, watched them all suddenly turn to look at me as if I had just teleported in among them, and asked them with a grin if they had managed to hear all they wanted or was there something they had missed that I could fill them in on.

They all started to feign innocence until Dusty started to laugh, and then we all laughed together. I headed out for lunch just shaking my head, smiling all the way. Dusty hollered at me to wait up for a minute, that she had spoken with Sunstar earlier and would grab a bite with me and fill me in over lunch on how my folks and the Allegros were doing. I said okay but that I would get the car while she got whatever it was she needed to get and to meet me at the porch. She was there before I was. Dusty was born ready.

Over lunch, she did fill me in. It turned out that some of Sunstar's natural potions were very promising, and Clarion had added two more chemists to Dr. Fitzgerald's team. Dr. Fitzgerald was a delight to work for, keeping his team in stitches part of the time and in awe the remainder. He pushed them hard, and Sunstar felt for the first time that she had something to contribute. In Dr. Fitzgerald's eyes, that was an apparent understatement. Sunstar actually felt they might have a clue to the key that would thwart the turning process a bitten human would undergo. The promises were almost equal to the pitfalls, but they were persevering anyway.

Then she lowered the boom and asked if I still had feelings for Casey or had they been eclipsed by Sunstar. The question was so direct that it caught me completely off guard. I almost forgot to chew the bite of sandwich I'd just taken. Thankfully, I had the good grace not to let my jaw hang open. That would have totally grossed out Dusty and the other patrons of the restaurant, a social faux pas from which I'd likely never recover.

What I did do was pretend to choke while I tried to get an answer together. But once I started, I didn't have to pretend. I actually did choke. Dusty stood up and grabbed a glass of water. She threw some down my throat while the rest hit me in the face. I managed to swallow the offending piece of crust and get my breath back. I even dried off before the manager could get over to us. Once I settled down, I took it very slow and easy.

I explained I didn't know what my feelings for Sunstar were. Sure, she was smart and inviting and certainly easy on the eyes, and we'd held hands and I probably had a big crush on her. Would I kiss her good night? You bet! But was Casey in her eclipse? That, I wasn't sure of, even though I was starting to think that Casey might be developing other interests whose names were soccer, school, and Paul—in that order. And on that score, part of me was jealous, but part of me was glad, for her and not for me. Casey was my soul mate. If she found someone who could measure up to her standards, then more power to her.

Would I mind? Yeah, and no, because what I wanted most for Casey was for her to be happy. I felt that if the time were ever right and we started dating seriously, she would certainly be the girl for me and I'd propose in a heartbeat. But college is a long time. Many things can play out, so I wasn't rushing anything except to fight against the Weres and enjoy the learning college offered.

I was smart enough to know that each person in a twosome had to be on a matching schedule with the partner. They had to have common goals and interests, common values and expectations, and both had to want to work at the relationship. My feelings for Casey were full of potential but right now were only possible, not even probable. As for Sunstar, well, it looked like Michael and I were probably going to wind up roommates, so I wanted to keep a little distance between Sunstar and me so I would have a chance to develop a relationship with Michael untainted by any big sister influence. It was a hard line to walk, but it would get easier if I kept my eye on the goal of a military commission and my veterinary license. Until then, studies and fighting had to be my primary interests.

Dusty seemed satisfied with that and then filled me in on what Sunstar reported to her about my folks and the Allegros. Apparently, Sunstar felt as if two families had adopted her and were treating her like a princess. She was happy, challenged, and curious in her work and the Chagrin Falls environment, but did miss being home and was looking forward to coming back in a week to 10 days before we launched the raid in North Georgia. She missed her folks and friends and work at the Rehab Center. She was curious about Polaris and thankful the falcon had probably saved my life in the scout ambush, and she was delighted to know that Gitta was still Gitta—half mom, half Twinkie devotee, half explorer, and half assassin—and all steady as she goes in temperament and mission. But Sunstar was mostly relieved to simply know I was okay.

As we got up to go, I noticed that Dusty left most of her french fries on her plate. She saw my hungry glance and asked if I wanted them. They were gone before we walked out the door. If Gitta was hooked on Twinkies, then I was her mirror with french fries. I had to remember to ask Dusty to a hamburger and fries lunch more often.

DAY SEVEN 1:00 P.M.

Gitta, Polaris, and I were waiting outside the Chapel by Gitta's cage for Pee Wee when Dusty came around the corner to tell me I had a phone call from Clarion. Could I take it on the speaker phone in the Major's office? I said sure. I asked the ladies to please wait for me while I answered Clarion and then left them as I trotted back around to the Chapel's entrance. I was curious why Clarion would call me when he normally spoke directly to the Major about anything professional.

I got my answer when I squeezed into the Major's office and sat down on the only empty chair. Pee Wee, Sergeant Saddler, and a new fellow in civilian clothes named Danny Murky were gathered around the Major's desk while she was talking with Clarion. They stopped their chitchat when I came in. I took my seat, and Clarion welcomed me into the teleconference.

Clarion explained that the civilian, Danny, was a GS-11 civil servant who specialized in health care and rehabilitation. He had treated a number of Special Operations personnel for Lt. Col. Spikes, had all the requisite clearances, and was on loan to us for a week or more to make sure I was on a specific program that would bring me back to full capability in the least amount of time. I was to listen to him and do what he said even if it hurt, and because he was a therapist, I was to just accept that it would. The school that taught Danny what he knew was apparently staffed by ex-Nazis who had come to America for political asylum but still harbored secret resentment for any Armed Forces walking wounded. It was believed they took diabolical pleasure in seeing their patients groan and cry. So my orders were simple. Make Danny happy. Groan and cry.

I gulped and looked at the Major. I was somewhat relieved to see they were both smiling, but I did notice that Danny's teeth were showing slightly, and he seemed to be leaning forward with predatory anticipation. Of course, I've been known to have an overactive imagination along the way, so I let it pass. Stupid me.

The Major explained that she had reserved a therapy room at Appalachian State over in Boone available at 10:00 a.m. and again at 4:30 p.m. each day for the next two weeks. We had it for an hour each session. Danny would work on my hip and shoulder on the trainer's table or flex equipment followed by an hour of water therapy and exercise. For that, the Major had arranged for an Appalachian State (A State) coed majoring in sports therapy to be my mentor. Her name was Kathie Doran. She was a junior, and she was quick with a quip, smart, combative, and about as curvy and cute as a speckled pup in a red wagon on a North Carolina mountain spring morning.

She was grinning when she said it, but the Major warned me not to get too friendly with Kathie. She was very popular with some of the A State senior football players, especially the quarterback. They were not disposed to being nice to fellows from Lees-McRae who might be perceived as having more than a passing interest in A State coeds. The Major reminded me that the problem with A State men was that I couldn't use a bow and arrow or a wakizashi blade or a javelin on them. Theirs was a rough and tumble world of physical give and take. Unless I was prepared for that, I shouldn't give them any excuse to give me a hard time.

The Major then closed out the call. She asked me to drive Danny over to the A State campus for a quick look-see so we could start tomorrow and not waste time trying to find the places we needed to be. I went outside to give the news to Gitta and Polaris, telling them that our planned day-long hunts and hikes would now be curtailed to about three hours each day starting at midday tomorrow. The remainder of this day was theirs to do with as they pleased. I did ask Gitta, however, if she might be willing to guide Pee Wee and Sergeant Saddler back to the spot where we killed the Weres the day before. She said she'd be glad to. She would start when they showed up at her cage.

I went back inside and passed the word to Pee Wee. He told me that he and Sergeant Saddler would go after lunch. "Bring Gitta back safely," I told Pee Wee as I walked away chuckling with Danny. It was Gitta's responsibility to bring Pee Wee home safely, not the other way around, and Pee Wee knew it. Still, I knew he would risk a great deal to protect Gitta, so I wasn't worried for any of them. What I was worried about was what Danny planned to do to me. Clarion's crack about ex-Nazis still rang in my head.

DAY SEVEN 4:00 P.M.

We were headed back to Blowing Rock, and Danny was driving the Chevrolet. He wasn't doing a bad job, but every bump we hit jolted my hip and shoulder and brought a suppressed groan from me. I could swear he was looking for bumps to hit as we rolled along. Danny and I had enjoyed each other's company on the drive over to A State earlier in the afternoon, but he seemed to change once we finally found the therapy room and its associated equipment.

He had me do some preliminary exercises on each piece just to familiarize myself with how they operated while he explained their purpose, design, and method of use. I made the mistake of being overzealous as he'd asked and had some pretty sore muscles and kinks to work out, so I just lay on the back seat feeling sorry for myself. Danny told me that was all right, too, since today was just an orientation. Tomorrow would be a day to really feel sorry for myself and likely hate him. Both of us had a chance to meet Kathie Doran. She nearly caused me to fall into the pool. She was in a jumpsuit when we first met her at poolside, and she started climbing out of it when her class of freshman coeds showed up for basic swimming instruction. Danny saved me the trouble of keeping an eye on them and actually had his eyes rolling around and doing things I did not think possible as the coeds crowded in to meet Kathie. I, being a gentleman, kept my eyes strictly on Kathie in a professional manner, of course, since she was going to be my aquatics trainer. I actually felt superior to Danny until she climbed out of her jumpsuit and handed it to me to hang up on the nearest pool wall while she greeted and got her class together. I made the mistake of taking a good look at her two-piece swimsuit, something I had not seen before. Blatantly preoccupied, I almost stepped into the pool until Danny's last-second grab saved me from a watery baptism by enchantment, so to speak.

My cheeks must have been as red as a slice of ripe watermelon because all the girls in the class laughed while Kathie just looked at me and raised a speculative eyebrow. Danny helped me beat a hasty retreat. I hung up Kathie's jumpsuit on the nearest wall peg while we made our exit from the pool area. Danny surmised that perhaps he'd bring his swimsuit along tomorrow so he could expand his curative curriculum and learn more about water therapy, maybe even teach Kathie something about his specialty. I reminded him of the Major's warning. He reminded me that the warning was for my benefit, not his, especially since he was a college graduate with a master's degree in sports medicine.

I told him that quarterbacks have football friends called tackles and that their temperaments usually run somewhere between the Abominable Snowman and Godzilla when fully exercised, especially when their favorite quarterback says, "Sic 'em!" Danny told me he'd been a cheerleader in a past life and was more agile than most, had a terrific winning smile, was able to do a confusing variety of flips and flops all over the place, and had a fast car when a getaway was needed.

Besides, he told me, tackles generally weren't the brightest bulbs on the Christmas tree anyway, so he doubted they'd give him much trouble. I smiled and opined that freight trains weren't known for their intelligence either but would flatten you in a New York second if you happened to be standing on their track when they came rushing along.

We spent an hour or so covering the rest of the campus and had a snack in downtown Boone at one of the famous family eateries across from the stadium. We were just enjoying the day and the hustle and bustle of Boone, a big city compared to sleepy little Blowing Rock. The pain in my muscles finally got my attention as we wandered back to my car and then claimed all of it when I climbed in with no distractions left. That's when I climbed right back out and onto the back seat where I lay down with a muffled groan.

And that's where I was when we arrived back at the Rat's Nest where Danny cheerfully threw open the door and half dragged me to my feet, my protests spilling out as I stood erect. I wasn't as sore as I made out to be, but I had to appear in some pain so tomorrow I wouldn't feel half as bad when coming out of Danny's first real stretch-and-groan session.

If he thought I was really tender now, I thought he'd let up on tomorrow's session so he wouldn't injure me. Wrong. As it turned out, Danny was impervious to any symptom of patient pain as sadists usually are. He wasn't happy until the patient's rage was at kill or better, well beyond a simple maim. But that's what made him effective and what made his patients well, those who didn't attack him.

DAY EIGHT 8:30 A.M.

I was sitting in the Major's office waiting for Lt. Col. Spikes and Clarion to finish their inspection of the Motor Pool and the two additional vehicles they'd requisitioned for us. One was a long-bed Chevrolet Silverado pickup truck with heavy-duty springs. The other was a five-and-a-half-ton truck with a canvas over the frame that could seat 10 people in combat gear, five to a side, with gear and guns secured in the middle between the personnel benches. I was finally getting back to feeling like myself, although Danny Murky had made it a challenge. At least all my parts were working smoothly again.

Danny had been relentless in making sure all my workouts meant something. Kathie Doran had also been an inspiration in her look-but-don't-touch mode, an "older woman" whose curves rivaled the road from Blowing Rock to Boone. She was well aware of my juvenile crush on her and delighted to stand close enough while touching my arm to make me sweat and silently curse the fate that had brought me into the world several years too late. Danny, of course, hung around at my water sessions like a dog waiting for a biscuit filled with gravy, but Kathie ignored him like a doodlebug on a stump.

Still, there wasn't a trip back to the Rat's Nest that didn't have some part of the conversation focused on Miss Doran and her Rapunzel inaccessibility. Even Dusty commented more than once that whatever was going on at A State was sure leaving us each frazzled and jumpy. I told her it was pretty dicey because those A State guys saw that we were swimming each day with one of their hometown favorites, didn't know it was doctor's orders, and boy, could they ever glare at us. Dusty knew I'd killed Werewolves who would eat those fellows for breakfast with half a chance, so she figured our nerves weren't the result of intimidation. She just couldn't figure out that we were smitten by a vision of wonder who could be as snappy as a perturbed turtle when she wanted to be and as alluring as a chocolate frosted milkshake on a hot day when she turned on the charm and smiled at us underlings, especially in that bright red, two-piece swimsuit she favored.

I don't think I would have drowned if she asked me to, but I sure would have swallowed a lot of water before I came to my senses. Sunstar was coming home tomorrow, as Michael, her brother, had told me in a message he left for me at my room in the inn downtown. Pee Wee confirmed it when he showed up earlier this morning. Dusty also mentioned it to me as did Clarion in a conference call yesterday evening that set up this morning's meeting. Pee Wee asked if I wanted to ride down with him to meet Sunstar, but the Major reminded him of my last day at the therapy clinic. It was also my last water torture session tomorrow. I had to choke back my response.

So there I sat, waiting for the briefing we'd all been waiting for these last two weeks, the coming raid in north Georgia at one of the reported Were strongholds. This was to be a stealth snatch-and-grab raid—get in and get out quickly with a Pale Were if we could and leave no Were witnesses if possible. The Special Forces guys from Ft. Benning would be back with us. Both Gitta and Polaris would be coming along. I was not bow strong yet but would have my wakizashi blade and my javelin with me. I would also carry a special lightweight prototype rifle developed for the advisors to the South Vietnamese Army. The South Vietnamese were fighting their North Vietnamese counterparts and South Vietnamese irregulars called Viet Cong. The rifle was called an AR-15.

The rifle was originally designed in 1957, weighed less than six pounds, and shot a .223-caliber bullet that would tumble on impact and tear a hole in anything less than armor. It could fire at a rate of 800 rounds per minute. It was awesome. We would spend the next few days firing it at a makeshift target range that Sergeant Saddler set up about five miles back in the mountains. I wasn't ordinarily partial to rifles. I preferred shotguns and a bow and arrow if at all possible, but I couldn't draw and shoot yet with any accuracy because of my weakened shoulder. This time, I would carry a handgun and the AR-15. *Ought to be an interesting trip*, I thought.

But man oh man, did that ever turn out to be an understatement or, more correctly, an underthought. I would miss Danny when he went home the day after tomorrow. He had been a fun and firm companion. He gave me advice I felt was credible, was a good example, and became a friend. His was the kind of personality that never wilted over the years, that made breathing both fun and interesting. He had a spiritual side that rarely showed in discussion but was apparent from the choices he made and the friends he kept.

About the only thing that constantly bugged me about him was his impassioned interest in golfing. How anyone could ever want to waste time chasing a poor little old ball around a park with a club was beyond me, but apparently it was one of his favorite pastimes. I told him that golf and tennis were carriage trade pursuits, that instead he should take up something that required a working class sweat equity like handball.

That was probably the only time in my life I actually saw a human turn up his nose in disgust. He did it well, but then Danny did everything well except get Kathie Doran's full attention. But heck, only headline guys really captured her attention, even if she was always nice to the little guys. The trail of broken hearts she never knew about followed her like bread crumbs in a fairy tale and lasted about as long. Pining away for pinups like Farrah Fawcett was old hat when you could pine away for a jump-up like Kathie Doran, but you always knew that in the end, neither pastime was very satisfying because imagination is never very fulfilling.

DAY SEVENTEEN 9:30 A.M.

We were almost 45 minutes into Clarion's opening remarks when Dusty interrupted us with an urgent call for Clarion. He left the room and took it at Dusty's desk. We could hear the urgency in his voice from where we sat. All of us craned our heads and ears trying to make out what was being said without being too obvious about it. We needn't have bothered. Clarion ended the call abruptly, walked back in, closed the door, and told us to forget his opening remarks. We had a decision to make. Several of the Special Forces team who had been sent in early to locate and scout the Werewolf concentration had radioed out that the group was on the move. They had trailed them from the Brasstown Bald Mountain Park south to Highway 180. There the Weres had jumped off into the mountain wilderness between Enota Mountain Retreat and Moccasin Creek State Park. It was a little-traveled, heavily forested area of about 100 square miles. Weres needed a lot of room to feed.

The Special Forces team would stay with them for another 24 hours to mark their progress. They would radio back the Weres' new location if they stopped. There were at least 100 Weres in a mixed group of males, females, and adolescents. Three Pale Weres were sighted with a possible fourth in the crowd. They had run at a moderate pace for the first 15 miles. Two of the Special Forces guys had shed all their gear but their rifles, two ammunition clips, and radios and followed after them on the run. The remainder of the team were coming along behind at a forced march. They were bringing the runners gear with them. Best guess was that the colony was on a permanent move to perhaps the southern part of the state. Our chance to capture an important Were was rapidly diminishing unless we moved tonight before the Weres linked up with supposedly larger and stronger groups in south Georgia near the trackless Okefenokee Swamp.

Clarion glanced around the room. He asked each of us if we thought we could do this. We would have little logistics support, our chances for success were between slim and none, and our group would be too small for anything but stealth and, in a firefight, would have odds against us if it lasted more than 12 hours. No more than 10 could go, not counting the seven Special Forces guys already on the Weres' track. We would have to haul in some supplies for them before we launched any combined wilderness raid. We probably had four days of action before us, one to get there, two to go in and get out, and one for insurance and extraction.

Clarion made it clear that this was very important. It would also be dicey all the way due to our hurried-up preparation and lack of intelligence about the wilderness terrain surrounding the Weres. He also made it clear that we were not in the suicide business. Volunteers only for this one, including me.

About the only thing Clarion said that we could count on was a helicopter extraction on our way out. Ft. Bragg would supply the air support. To their thinking, this would be a live fire exercise in the middle of nowhere. It would be a good chance to practice the Army's new doctrine of vertical envelopment and extraction at a tactical level, something being contemplated for the Special Forces advisors intended for Vietnam.

There was silence in the room when he finished his remarks. He surprised us by saying he first would hear from the lowest rank in the room. That was Pee Wee, who had a mouthful to say. It all added up to this: "Why are we still here talking about this when we could be gassing up the new trucks and loading our gear?" Sergeant Saddler, the Major, and Lt. Col. Spikes all had the same answer. Sergeant Saddler's remarks, however, were only a little less colorful than the others. I was the last one he turned to. He cautioned me to think carefully because if I chose to go, someone's life could hang in the balance if I couldn't carry my weight. I told him that thanks to Danny Murky, Kathie Doran, and Sunstar's potions, I was good to go. I would hold up my share of the load and then some, if needed. It was the answer he wanted to hear. He shook hands with all of us with his good hand. We were to be at the intersection of Georgia State Highways 170 and 75 in 24 hours or less, ready to rumble. With that, he left the Chapel to go to Ft. Bragg and arrange our future air extraction.

Lt. Col. Spikes took over. In moments, he designated the actions we needed to take, who would take each one, and where and when to report back to him. It was clear to me that he had done this many times before. We would not have Captain Yamata or Captain Cosic. They and their troops were in South America at the moment. They weren't due back in the States for another week. What we had was us and the Ft. Benning Special Forces team. I understood that Sergeant Abshire was one of the runners. I was absolutely looking forward to seeing him again. That guy was brave enough to take on a shark with a clam shell and would discard the clam shell if the clam needed it back. Not many people could combine chivalry and courage like he could. Or would.

My immediate job was to get Gitta and Polaris ready for this mission. It would be a long and taxing drive down. If Polaris chose to fly, we would paint a large white *X* on top of the canvas covering our two-and-a-half-ton truck. She could spot us from several miles away. We would go probably 150 to 200 miles before refueling. If she got tired, she could land. I would then put her in the cab with Gitta. We would roll along about 50 miles per hour, a strong speed for any bird. Still, a falcon was capable of 55 miles per hour in sustained horizontal flight. The only question was for how long. I would take several strips of raw meat with me so Polaris could refuel along the way should she choose to fly. It would be her breakfast if she chose to ride. Polaris chose to fly. The weather forecast discounted thunderstorms for the next week or more, a relatively uncommon occurrence in the north Georgia mountains in mid-to-late summer. But it was good. We'd take any break we could get.

Dusty was the appointed volunteer to go pick up Sunstar the next day while we were all away. In the interim, she opened up the Rat's Nest armory. We drew the uniforms and weapons we'd used in the last big raid that had landed me in the hospital. The new AR-15s were Clarion's gift. He'd brought 20 with him. Sergeant Saddler and Pee Wee left immediately to sight them in and test fire each one we would use. The fellows who watched over our Motor Pool were busy gassing up the two new trucks. They also filled spare gasoline cans we'd take in the back of the two-and-a-half-ton truck. Some of the folks were calling the truck Moby Duck, the Moby after the great white whale of literature and the Duck after the truck's limited but supposed amphibious capability.

Once started, given the military's penchant for short nicknames for everything that walked, talked, moved, or just lay still, it was affectionately known then and ever after as simply Moby. The pickup truck was a workhorse and Moby's sidekick. It was named after a cartoon character named Little Beaver, a fellow who was always at the side of Red Ryder, a comic book cowboy hero of the 1940s and 1950s. Moby and Little Beaver would be worth their weight in gold as time went on. Who needed mules with those two? By 2:00 p.m., the proverbial dust was beginning to settle. We were outfitted and had our weapons and ammunition clips, first aid kits, area maps, whistles, flare, knives, bug repellant, grease paint, and three days' rations. We would fill our canteens at the point of debarkation. All of us were wearing our dog tags, even me with a special issue. Anyone who wanted to had written a letter home and deposited it with Dusty. Our packs were light on purpose. They would be our pillows or backrests as we traveled through the night to our jump-off point in Georgia. Dusty had ordered take-out sandwiches of every kind, three per person. Two were to be eaten before we boarded and one at the jump-off point. We were going after a target of opportunity, a Pale Were. We were carrying with us two specially made, lightweight, steel mesh nets for what we hoped would be a mere grab, bag, and drag operation.

Lt. Col. Spikes gave us a small pep talk before we headed out. It was short and simple. "You know the mission. You know the folks with you. Everybody comes back or no one comes back. Do I make myself clear?" After a moment of silence, he climbed into Moby's cab and said, "Let's do this!" With a shout, we all climbed up into Moby's rear end. We all tried to get comfortable on one of the two benches, each side placing the bulk of their weapons and supplies on the floor in front of us.

Sergeant Saddler and Pee Wee were in Little Beaver. I was beside the Major in Moby. Two men and one of the Motor Pool squad sat on our bench. They were Sergeants Raymond Pendergast, Randy Cokerun, and Franklin Youngblood, good men all and smart as they come. All of them were hands-on men in the truest sense of the word. They could make things, repair things, design things, and obtain things that no requisition form in triplicate could ever hope to cover. We called them logistic specialists. The military bases around us called them miscreants and thieves. There may have been some truth to those slanderous allegations, but we always remembered that they were *our* miscreants and *our* thieves. We loved those guys.

Gitta climbed in with me. She promptly flopped down on a pile of rations and blankets. No one was afraid of her, but no one wanted to irritate her either, so she was allowed to flop where she dropped. She was curious about Polaris. I assured her that Polaris was going to fly above us for a while but might come inside after one of our rest stops along the way. Lt. Col. Spikes made sure everyone had a shot at the bathroom before we left. I made sure Gitta had that same consideration.

Polaris was on her own in that matter. A Princess of the air made her own rules.

We were rolling by 2:45 p.m. Little Beaver was in the lead. The last communication I had with Polaris for the next four hours was the shriek of jubilation she felt as she launched herself into the mountain air after us. She was going hunting again. It was her life.

DAY EIGHTEEN 1:30 A.M.

The drive was long, noisy, boring, and uncomfortable, but we arrived at the intersection of Georgia State Highways 75 and 180 after midnight. Stopped on the isolated, lonely highway, we dismounted and rocked back and forth or tried to walk, jump, or shake our legs, hoping to restore circulation from our long sit while we waited for our contact to show. It was chilly and slightly damp as nights are in the eastern mountains. Everything is sticky in Georgia, more so if you're facing south.

Gitta bolted for the underbrush as soon as Moby came to a stop. She had the decency to wait until we reached our destination to perform a simple act that would have driven all of us out of the truck. I had managed to plead with her for the last several miles or so. I was about to ask the truck to stop when we came to the designated intersection. A wolverine can move from fair mood to foul on the least of excuses, and when its mood turns foul, you don't even want to be in the same forest.

Wolverines will rend, maim, and kill at the drop of a hat and ask questions later if they even ask them at all. I was lucky Gitta was speaking and listening to me instead of inspecting my heart from the outside in before she chewed it up. All I could think of as I watched her scamper into the underbrush was thank goodness mother wolverines don't eat their young. She had a kind of maternal relationship with me that had saved my life on two occasions. This just may be the third.

Gitta returned as I let Polaris out of the cab where she would now ride with Lt. Col. Spikes. She stayed with us in the air for the first 200 miles to our first refueling stop but recognized that she could probably not make another such leg without resting. We couldn't stop for her when she desired, so I asked her to ride up front where she could look out the windshield. She didn't like to be caged. The back of Moby with its canvas sides pulled down was a mobile cage in her mind.

I fed her some of the rare steak strips from Dusty's salad to help her replenish her strength. Lt. Col. Spikes later asked that I never do that again in his presence. He'd seen a lot of things in his career, but what a hungry falcon could do to a piece of meat was intimidating to say the least. The worst part was when she finished the meat strips and looked him over carefully with those dead killer eyes. I asked her about that. She explained that she wasn't ready to feed on Spikes but was checking to see if he had any other spare tidbits on him. I'm not sure he believed me when I passed that along, but I did notice that he squirreled away some cookies after our quick feed at the debarkation point.

Our contact materialized out of the darkness at 1:45 a.m. It was a difficult climb up to the roadbed where we stopped from where he was maintaining a watch. Nevertheless, he was glad we were there, and it was time to move on. Everyone buckled up again and checked someone else before Lt. Col. Spikes gave the command to move on. He had us do it all over again with someone different, checking each person the second time. Each of us carried our rifles by their handles, leaving one arm free to help control our descent down the mountainside behind our guide. We would switch to live fire mode when we hit bottom. Under no circumstances were we to let go of our weapon. If we tripped and fell or slipped, our weapon went with us until we were dead or unconscious. And if we lost it, Lt. Col. Spikes would make sure we were dead or unconscious. I, for one, believed him. He was not smiling when he said it.

Our order of battle would be a single column behind the guide who would stay in advance of us. I would be directly behind him but no more than three to four yards away. Pee Wee would be the same distance behind me. Gitta would range ahead of us, and we would stay in constant mental communication. Lt. Col. Spikes would lead the rest of the column, following 10 yards behind Pee Wee. Major Sanchez would be in the middle, and Sergeant Saddler would bring up the rear. There would be no outriders on our flanks. We were going into a hostile area and did not want to shoot our own people if shooting started. Rifles would be carried at port arms held in front of us with our fingers beside but not on the triggers. If we encountered scouts, Polaris flying overhead would warn us. Then it was up to Pee Wee, Gitta, and me to kill them as silently as we could while Polaris kept a running lookout for other Weres in the area. Our objective was an early morning rendezvous with Special Forces Team Alpha. We would plan and execute our stealth assault and snatch and grab with them. If we could not link up in 12 hours, we were to return to our debarkation point still in stealth mode. No one wanted that outcome. No one could stand another nine or 10 hours in the back of Moby without some prize in hand.

We did not have a bright moon, and the tree cover hampered what light could filter down. So we employed a trick originated by the British SAS teams. We looked at the trail out of the corners of our eyes, constantly turning our heads from side to side as we walked in. It got us through until our eyes fully adjusted to the dark. Then we could move more quickly.

By 4:30 a.m., we reached the Special Forces camp. It was initially deserted. We first feared everyone had been ambushed by the Weres. Once we were within its natural environs, however, several bodies dropped down out of the surrounding trees. One body rose from a poncho covered with dirt, dust, and leaves that we thought was part of the ground. Several of the remaining soldiers walked in, surrounding us until identification was passed and recognized. Then it was time for a cold camp, an hour's rest and water and sandwich from the Rat's Nest. For a few moments, life was good. I made sure Gitta and Polaris had something to eat as well. We needed them at full strength for what was coming.

We learned that the Weres had settled down for the night in a valley about one mile away. A small stream ran through their sprawling camp. Apparently, they were fed if the animal screams and cries our scouts heard earlier were any indication. Team Alpha had identified seven Were scouts scattered about the camp's periphery, some as much as 200 yards out from the camp. The ravine they were in had a low angle slope on one side and the stream bed and a steep slope up a mountainside on the far side of their encampment.

The three Pale Weres we initially identified back at Brasstown Bald Mountain were camped in the middle of the pack beside the stream. The fourth suspected Pale Were was at the north end, the tail end of the encampment. It looked to be a pregnant female heavy with a pup. A large, dark, male Black Were stayed beside the female. It brought meat scraps for the pregnant Were to feed on. The three male Pale Weres paid it no attention.

After conferring with Team Alpha, Lt. Col. Spikes decided to use a distraction to divert the Weres from our intended objective, the capture of a Pale Were. Team Alpha would provide that. They would move south from the encampment about two miles, well within the Weres' hearing range. They would stage a 10-minute firefight, blowing up some of the mountainside in front of them and generally raising Cain. They would melt back away from their staged fight and double-time back to the encampment. They would remain on a line a quarter mile out from the mountain and be our reserve if we got into more fight than we could handle.

We would send two teams into the encampment after Team Alpha started their fireworks show. One team headed by Lt. Col. Spikes would go in after the three Pale

Weres. A second team with the Major at its head would go after the pregnant Pale Were. Gitta and I would be with Team Two along with Sergeants Youngblood and Pendergast. Pee Wee, Sergeant Saddler, and Randy Cokerun would be with Lt. Col. Spikes forming Team One. The remaining two members of our Rat's Nest squad would provide cover fire if need be for our return.

We would launch our snatch-and-grab sorties after the encampment reacted to Team Alpha's distant fire. We would shoot to kill all dark Weres as needed. When a Pale was taken captive, we would rally at a small hill standing alone on the tilted plain. It was dwarfed by the steep mountain facing it on the other side of the river. Once plans were made, it was time to execute. We gave Team Alpha one hour to get into place. We planted our two snipers on the go-to hill and separated into our two teams.

Pee Wee and I were wearing the new shoulder pad armor cooked up by the Major. I, for one, sincerely hoped it would work if we had any close infighting. We went to the ground near our respective targets and waited. Waiting was the hardest part of any operation because your mind tells you the mission will likely fail. You begin to believe you can't possibly succeed, and you wonder how many things are already going wrong while you do nothing. In the intervening silence, we spotted and marked the locations of three Were scouts. We would kill two by blade on the way in. We would shoot the third on the way out, provided it was still in the area.

DAY EIGHTEEN 5:45 A.M.

When Team Alpha finally opened up, I frankly did not believe that seven men could wreak that much havoc on a lonely mountainside. I thought it was World War III for a minute. I was grateful those guys were on our side. *Thank God for small favors* was my thought, a short prayer well meant. At the first sounds of fire, the entire Were encampment came awake and alert. Most of the Weres just milled around uneasily. After several minutes, one of the Pale Weres howled out some apparent instructions because the bulk of the Weres immediately headed south. They traveled at that deceptive, mile-eating loping run that all Weres exhibit.

It looked for a moment as if Lt. Col. Spikes's plan would work as planned, a rarity in military operations. The hitch came unexpectedly. The three Weres that formed Team One's target started to run after the flood of Black Weres that had just left. That defeated the whole purpose of the distraction, so Lt. Col. Spikes ran toward the Weres. He fired his weapon straight up into the air. He had the good sense not to fire on full automatic. That would have drained his ammunition supply dramatically, and the only good thing you can do with an empty AR-15 is throw it as hard as you can at a worthy target, hoping you can find one. I know. I soon did it.

The three Pale Weres and several Black Weres saw him and immediately turned toward him and then fanned out as they ran toward him. Seeing that small wave of Weres coming his way, Lt. Col. Spikes turned and sprinted back for his former position. He'd picked up his pace considerably. Still, the Pale Weres and a few others were rapidly gaining on him. I couldn't tell whose cries were louder, Spikes or those from the throats of the three Pale Weres. My group started sprinting for the female Pale Were. We did not see the end of Spikes's dash. We had our own story to carve out and little time to do it.

Sergeant Pendergast was the fastest among us. He was within 20 yards of the female Pale Were when he was suddenly cut down from the side by a younger male. The male had been partially hidden by a clumping of bush and rocks that lay in the middle of our intended route to the female. Pendergast had no time to let off a burst from his rifle when the young Were practically bit through his left leg. Pendergast's screaming was nonstop, and then a second Were managed to almost rip off his shoulder from the other side while he struggled to free his leg from the first one. Blood was everywhere in seconds before Pendergast's screams fell silent.

Sergeant Youngblood and I were almost neck and neck as we ran to Pendergast's remains on our dash to the female Pale Were. The second Were sprang for me as I passed Pendergast's body. I skidded to a stop and stitched a line of bullet holes across its body. My rifle was set to full automatic fire. The Were died instantly. With the Major racing up behind us, I turned and sprinted once again toward the Pale Were. I left Pendergast to the Major. Youngblood clearly had the lead. He was unfurling one of the mesh nets even as he ran, throwing it at the female Were at the last minute before the big male tore into him from his right side. It was a brutal takedown, but Youngblood was a fighter. He had pulled his knife as he fell. He was trying to stab the big male even as the male was trying to chew open Youngblood's side. I was there in seconds. I brought my wakizashi blade across the male's neck in a horrific slash as I tried to jump over it and get at the female. The male's head was halfway severed as it fell away from Sergeant Youngblood's body. Its dying gasp barely made it out of its throat.

Youngblood's net entangled the female's legs. She was clawing and biting the mesh as I skidded to a stop beside her. I immediately placed the tip of the wakizashi blade against her abdomen. In such close contact, I relayed that I would kill the pup if she continued to struggle. The female was enraged at me as she struggled in her predicament, but she got the message. Stay still, and you and the pup will live. Move, and both of you will die. I literally felt the female's thoughts as she pictured the pack returning to slay us and free her, the real basis for her decision to stay still while I bound her more tightly in the mesh net. Once that was done I turned to Youngblood to see what I could do about his wounds.

He was a mess. I could see his rib bones and watched in horror as his lung slowly and tentatively inflated and deflated. The big male had literally chewed away about a fourth of the skin and tissue comprising the outside of Youngblood's rib cage. I could not see any broken bones, just the open cavity. We could all hear Youngblood's increasingly labored breathing. I had nothing with me to cover his open wound, so I used the wakizashi to skin away a portion of the pelt on the big Were's side. I slapped the flap against Youngblood's side, binding it in place with duct tape from a roll I'd wound around my rifle stock before we left the Rat's Nest. I wound the tape tightly around his chest. It seemed to stop his bleeding to a major degree. His ability to breath seemed to improve.

Gitta joined me in my haste to try to stem Youngblood's bleeding. The Major also joined us once she killed the young Were that was attacking Pendergast. Polaris continued to provide air cover. She kept a running commentary of the whereabouts of the pack. We could not move Youngblood, so I gathered up Pendergast's remains and brought them over to lie beside Youngblood. The Major and Gitta kept watch. We were stuck until Team Alpha returned. They would help us make our way to the small hill. As we waited, I walked over and managed to pull the female Were close to Pendergast. She was fully entangled in the mesh net now. Her struggles, as surreptitious as she tried to make them, only worsened her situation. Polaris came back about that time with news that the pack had reached the diversion site. Finding no one there, they were on the run back to this encampment as fast as they could travel.

A Werewolf can outrun a quarter horse and run down a Thoroughbred over a mile and a half, so I knew they were coming fast. I positioned myself between Pendergast's body and the female Were. The Major dug in just the other side of Youngblood. Gitta took her place at the head of Youngblood. We formed a kind of defensive triangle. The Major and I put our ammunition clips beside our rifles. She switched hers to full automatic. The Major told me to use short trigger pulls, not sustained fire. That would send out five to seven bullets at a time, plenty enough to do damage to anything I hit. We could not see what was happening or what had already happened to Lt. Col. Spikes's team. That was frustrating. Nor could we raise anyone on our radios. We were temporarily on our own.

I told the Major it didn't matter. When the pack came back, our guys, if any were left, would hear us and "come a-runnin'," as she was wont to say. There were going to be fireworks aplenty for everyone. We waited in silence for about a minute. Polaris suddenly flew close. She told me the Weres were but a minute or two away. I felt a little nostalgic. I asked the Major if we lost our lives here, would she write a note to my mom excusing me from living. She started laughing at that. I smiled with her. "Cody," she said, "if we don't get out of this alive, Lt. Col. Spikes is going to be so mad at me that he'll kill me himself, probably several times over."

"Well, then we'll have to live through it," I said. "But the bright side is that we have the Weres right where we want them. They're about to be all around us, and this time, they can't get away."

The Major turned at that, looked at me, and started laughing. "You are one nutty young man, Cody, and you are dearly, dearly loved. Now shut up and take a deep breath. We're going to need a steady hand in a few seconds. Tell Gitta it's going to get loud. The last thing we need close to us is a fully ticked-off wolverine."

Her grin belied her words. I loved that lady all the more for it. Then it was Ft. Apache all over again as the first wave of Weres came boiling over the shallow slope toward us, fangs fully exposed and claws extended at full stretch. It was so exciting I almost cheered for the Weres in the lead. Then I started cutting them down in short, deadly bursts. Five fell 20-plus yards out and four more at 10 yards. Then it just got nasty, a good old down-and-dirty, mountain-boy fight.

DAY TWENTY 7:30 A.M.

Gitta took two lead Weres down with her as they ran into our small redoubt. The Major was up on one knee firing in repeated bursts that took down or took out any Weres that happened to be in the sights of her AR-15. Bodies started piling up in front of her like stacked cordwood. I had my own fish to fry. Short of an occasional look to see if she was still there, I emptied my rifle several times. I finally threw it at a snarling Were who was determined to scale the body pile in front of my position and shred me. I missed him but did hit the Were behind him. It didn't stop either one.

However, the same body motion that allowed me to throw my rifle at the first Were that challenged me also allowed me to draw my wakizashi blade. With it, I could really start to wreak havoc. That blade would cut through almost anything. I gave it ample opportunity to prove itself. Hair, skin, pelts, muscle, sinew, bones, teeth, whatever, it was the Timex blade of all blades—it "took a licking and kept on ticking." My right arm was growing tired when I remembered my .357 handgun. Why I could never remember it first was beyond me.

I pulled it with my left hand. I would literally place it almost on the chest of a surging Were before pulling the trigger. It made blood spatters everywhere. But it also killed Weres graveyard dead when that slug passed through them and carried away handfuls of their innards with it. A .357 Magnum pistol is a messy but uncannily effective weapon. It's almost as good as a .45 caliber, a slug that will drop a bear in full charge.

We were about to be overrun when the cavalry finally arrived. Three of Team Alpha led by Sergeant Abshire arrived at our position. Their guns were spitting out nothing but .223-caliber bad news to any one of the canine (or distantly related) persuasion. They had full clips even if they were almost out of breath from their run back to us from the diversion site. I've never seen anyone as welcome as they were in our hour of great need.

Abshire's first comment to me in a lull was to ask where I was torn. I asked him what he meant. He told me to look at myself. I was covered in blood. He didn't see how I could still stand. I looked down and started laughing, a perfectly normal reaction to terror on the run. I told him that wasn't my blood. It was from the Weres who'd run afoul of the wakizashi blade. There appeared to be a considerable number of them. The onslaught of the Weres we had endured finally seemed to diminish. The Major quickly ordered two of the relief crew to pull, carry, or roll the female Were to the small hill rally point. Abshire and I were to carry Youngblood as far as we could. We would draw Pendergast's remains as far as we could until someone else came along to help. Gitta brought up the rear. She had left three dead Weres of her own at our battle site. Total count for the Major, Gitta, and me was 37 dead Weres, 11 of which were sliced and diced by my wakizashi blade alone. We hoped Lt. Col. Spikes had been as fortunate.

It would be a while before I felt good about what the Major and I did. At the moment, all I wanted was more ammunition and the presence of good soldiers with a steady aim and fearless conscience, the Special Forces guys to be exact. This was one of those times when wishes were granted in spades. We made the hill. We brought Pendergast's remains out with us. Youngblood was put on a field IV and went through three blood bags before he showed signs of stabilizing. I left Gitta resting beside Youngblood as I joined the Major on the perimeter of our small defensive enclave. I'd left my AR-15 back at the body pile where I'd thrown it at the first Were, so I took Youngblood's from him. I loaded up again on ammunition clips and magazines. I figured we would either hear something soon from Lt. Col. Spikes or we would have to go in and bail him out as Team Alpha had done for us.

We didn't have long to wait.

From out of the morning mist that curled around the stream bed came three men, one obviously being carried by the outside two. I recognized Pee Wee's bulk immediately. He was on my right as I watched the trio stagger forward. As they came closer, Sergeant Abshire and two of his men ran out to meet them. When the man on the outside left raised up, I recognized Sergeant Saddler, but his right arm was hanging useless at his side. The man in the middle was now our concern. I was hoping against hope it was Lt. Col. Spikes. It was not. It was a battered and torn Randy Cokerun. The left side of his chest cavity had been sliced open, and pieces of peeled skin and flesh hung down from his left arm.

As Pee Wee's triumvirate got closer, we could hear his call for "Medic! Medic!" A fourth soldier from Sergeant Abshire's squad came running down our hill to meet the wounded men. Lt. Col. Spikes was nowhere in evidence. I couldn't stand the suspense. I jumped to my feet, hollering at the Major to cover me if anything started up. Nothing did. All was mysteriously quiet. I managed to reach the trio as the medic laid Cokerun on the ground and started bandaging Cokerun's wounds. The trio was obviously exhausted. I grabbed Pee Wee's arm and turned him to me, quickly checking him for wounds. There were none. I patted his cheek and got his eyes to focus on me. "Where's Spikes, Pee Wee? Where's Spikes?"

His answer was dull and almost unresponsive. "They took him," he said. "They took him before he could reach us, and they disappeared down the stream bed. We started after but were hit by wave after wave of Weres. We had no chance to capture him back. No chance at all." And with that, he sank wearily down to his knees and bowed his head, exhausted.

One of the Team Alpha men jogged back up to our group. I heard him mention to Sergeant Abshire, "Twenty-eight dead, two wounded, Sergeant. Want me to put 'em out of their misery?"

"Wait," I cried as I jumped to my feet. "Let me talk to them first."

"Are you kidding?" was his response. "These are Werewolves we're fighting. Not humans who can talk."

"You don't understand, soldier," I said. "Some can. They were all humans once, or didn't you know?" I ran for the two Weres. Both were in pretty bad shape when I came and knelt down beside them. They had taken a bullet or bullets through their spines. Both lay immobile, facing imminent death. One was barely conscious, so I leaned over him. I tried to make mental contact. The wave of revulsion and hate that came back almost staggered me, but I kept searching its mind for some clue of Spikes's whereabouts.

"C'mon, c'mon!" I said. "Tell me where you all were headed and why." Then, faintly at first like an elusive memory that was slowly disappearing, the Were's thoughts came to me. I stayed in contact with the Were until its mind went blank in death. The second Were was already comatose. There was nothing I could gain there. Wearily, I stood up. I walked back to Abshire's group and then on farther back to the Major.

"What gives, Cody?" she asked. "I don't like that slump in your shoulders. Tell me now. Bad news doesn't improve with age."

I steeled myself and said, "They captured Lt. Col. Spikes. They are taking him to a gathering place in the south of Georgia. There he will be interrogated and killed. He is their showpiece just as any Pale Were prisoners are ours. The Were I questioned felt that Spikes would be kept alive until the show trial. The Weres apparently need a victory of some sort if they are to hold the many packs and clans together for their major offensive scheduled for later this year. Spikes is the highest-ranking officer they've captured. They will make a big show of his crimes before they torture him to death. Then he will *be* the feast for the gathering of leading Pale Weres." I took the only chance I could think of to stay in some contact with Lt. Col. Spikes. I sent out my call for Polaris. In five minutes, she dipped to a startling stop in front of the Major and me. I began by thanking her and acknowledging her help. She had taken personal risks and suffered some considerable inconveniences of her own to even get here, and now I was asking for more. I explained what the Weres had done and where they were likely headed.

I asked if she could perform an aerial reconnaissance to keep tabs on the group and Lt. Col. Spikes as they made their way south. It might take several days, and they would likely travel at night, but there would be signs of their passing to one who could look closely and spot them. She was the only one with the strength, talent, and skill to do that. So would she? It would mean several days away from us, and she would be at risk from other raptors such as hawks and eagles, but the need was critical.

Polaris listened patiently to all my arguments and then asked me one question. Would I go to such lengths if she were taken captive? She peered at me with those deadpan killer eyes, unblinking. I looked right back at her and said of course I would. We were a team, and I would go to the same lengths for Gitta. I quoted from scripture that "greater love hath no man than this, that a man lay down his life for his friends."[1] I asked if she understood that, and she silently nodded.

"Then I will go for you," she shrilled, and lifted off through the fading morning mist.

"Godspeed!" I wished her. "I will find you at this Okefenokee Swamp in a couple of days." She was gone into the morning sky, speeding south, eyes sweeping the terrain far below for her first clue of the Weres' whereabouts.

We burned the Weres' bodies in two heaped piles. We doused their bodies with fuel oil or whatever we had that would burn quickly. We stood back and watched the conflagration to make sure it didn't spread. It took several hours. The smoke from the burn piles eventually proved to be an easy beacon for the rescue and pick-up helicopters.

For the rest of the morning, our job was to tend to our wounded and get that promised helicopter support to our killing ground as soon as possible. One of the Team Alpha radios worked, and we managed to make contact with a Forest Service tower. The ranger there relayed our call to Ft. Bragg. Eventually Clarion got our plea for help. To his credit, to expedite our help, he "raised hell and put a brick under it," as the old saying goes. By 2:00 p.m., six choppers arrived. The wounded were flown out first to the military hospital at Ft. Benning. The Veteran's Hospital at Atlanta was closer, but there was no way to maintain security there. That forced us to take the chance on making it to Ft. Benning with wounded still alive. Fortunately, they were.

Since we all exfiltrated to Ft. Benning, we used Clarion's influence to borrow a temporary office for our headquarters, at least until he could fly down. We needed support fast if we were to get to the Okefenokee before the north Georgia Were survivors. We felt only then would we still have a chance to rescue Lt. Col. Spikes. The first thing the Major did was send a radio message to Captain Yamata. She told him to give his command temporarily to Captain Cosic and get himself to Ft. Benning by the fastest means possible, even if it meant chartering a jet. The second thing was to call Dusty and bring her up to speed to handle all the paperwork we would face in reprovisioning at Ft. Benning.

---

1. John 15:13 KJV.

The Army is always a stickler for paperwork, much stricter than the Air Force. Even Army generals have to play the game. A few more calls to the hospital to make sure our wounded were alive and cared for, and we were finally free to relax for the first time in two days. I put Gitta in an unused base kennel area with some food and water so she would be safe. I then returned to the Major per her bidding. I hoped to go to Gitta in the first downtime we had, but Clarion arrived soon after. I never had the chance. Gitta had enough food and water for a day or two. I wasn't particularly worried about her, but I didn't want her to think she'd been abandoned. I needed to stop by her pen as soon as possible. Polaris was fine on her own.

DAY TWENTY-ONE 12:00 A.M.

I was so tired that I almost fell asleep twice sitting at the Major's briefing table. Clarion was there. He was reviewing the sequence of events with each of us who remained ambulatory. He covered in detail the repeated assaults Pee Wee and his team suffered. He finally turned to the Major and me. "Tell me what happened to you folks," he intoned. "Your body count was much higher than Team Two's. Why?"

The Major answered. I listened to her while enjoying my light daze. "Why is simple," she said. "We had the pregnant female. Now we know something we did not before. Turned male Weres cannot reproduce with turned Were females, but maybe they can with Pale Weres, which are exceptions to every rule we think we know. One exception is that they can get pregnant and maybe get someone else pregnant. Somehow that's got to be a key to unlocking this transformation they suffer. Or maybe the Pales don't ever suffer a transformation. Maybe they are an established breed that recruits mules by the venom they spread when they bite. There's so much we don't know, but we do know one thing. Unless we can plan a better snatch and grab for Lt. Col. Spikes, he's going to make either a great dinner or a very dangerous opponent. We don't have an option. It's rescue him or kill him. We cannot afford to have him turned."

Then she began to give her account of the assaults we'd faced from her perspective. When she was through, it was my turn. By midnight, we were done. I fell asleep at the table. Sometime during the night, someone moved me to a cot in the next room, but I was too far gone to know anything about it. I awoke the next morning to the sound of voices.

Sergeant Abshire was talking. He was explaining to Clarion what the uproar in the maintenance shed was this morning and why he called Clarion. When we landed yesterday, Sergeant Abshire had stashed the female Were in an empty maintenance shed. He locked it until someone with greater authority than he had could arrange for the Were's final disposition and transport back to wherever. An impromptu inspection this morning by a gung ho ex-West Point Lieutenant was derailed when the Lieutenant couldn't get into the maintenance shed. He couldn't because Sergeant Abshire had the key.

The Lieutenant demanded that someone come and cut the lock. He figured someone was hiding something in his shed. He would be darned if he was going to put up with any such shenanigans. Sergeant Abshire arrived in time. He tried to explain to the Lieutenant that the shed was temporarily requisitioned for classified reasons. It would be free by the afternoon. The Lieutenant asked by what authority *his* shed had been taken over by some spook outfit working with those renegade Special Forces jockeys. Sergeant Abshire asked if the Lieutenant would wait just a minute so he could get an answer for him. The Lieutenant deigned not to wait. He ordered someone to go get some bolt cutters.

"It was at that moment I called you, sir," Abshire said to Clarion.

"I'm glad you did, Sergeant. You saved us all from a serious security breach. I would have hated to shoot a brand-new Second Lieutenant who had no proper security clearance. It's such a waste of good lead." Clarion grinned. "Seriously, you did the right thing. We all deeply appreciate your quick thinking. Just let me know when you want to get out of this insufferable Georgia heat, and I'll have you transferred to our good guys, but remember, they spend a lot of their time in the hot spots of the world just like you fellows, so maybe you'd be trading the frying pan for the fire."

"Tell you what, sir. I'll stay with my renegades here if you'll not forget to call on us from time to time. Things are always interesting when you and your team show up." And with that, he saluted and left.

That's *my* line, I thought as I chuckled to myself. I figured we're all just learning from one another. Who knows what we stole from Abshire and his renegades?

At least the female Were was safe. That suddenly gave me an idea. Was she tradable? Did the Weres put any value on lineage? Would a mother of one of their babies be worth the life of Lt. Col. Spikes? At the camp, the three Pale Weres had virtually ignored the pregnant Were, true, but had they done so because they were busy in council when we found them, not because of any inferior status the female Were might carry? And was the big Black Were a consort or appointed guardian while the female's mate was in council? I started to get excited. There were some interesting possibilities here that needed to be explored. That meant face time with the captured Were, something I *never* enjoyed. But it had to be done quickly. Clarion was the man to make it happen if it could.

There were no cages here at Ft. Benning that we could adapt, but the net mesh seemed to have held up so far. It would probably get me through a hostile interrogation. It was worth a try, and the sooner the better. After a talk with Clarion, he agreed. The interrogation was set for noon at the maintenance shed.

DAY TWENTY-TWO 10:30 A.M.

Pee Wee went into the shed with me. Team Alpha stood guard outside. If the female Were escaped, their orders were to kill it, hide the body, and burn the carcass as soon as possible without disclosing to anyone just what it was.

The female had not been fed or watered since it was captured yesterday. It was straining against the mesh net when we entered the shed, and its snarls and growls were chilling. I walked up to the cocoon of steel close enough to initiate mind contact and almost crumpled from the hate and loathing spewing out of her mind. This was not going to be easy.

Pee Wee stood by the door with two weapons—a beanbag shotgun that could temporarily stun a rhino and a Colt .45-caliber pistol. He would use the beanbag shotgun if the Were managed to get partially loose. He would use the Colt if it freed itself totally. Under no circumstances was he to give the Were the benefit of any doubt.

I reluctantly stepped up to the mesh covering to start. Some things you just know are going to hurt before you try them. This interrogation was going to be one of those things.

As I tried to make contact with the female, I experienced an extraordinary phenomenon. I could feel two minds linked with mine. One was awkward, innocent, stumbling, and undisciplined. The other was aggressive, disciplined, crafty, and capable of great violence. I was puzzled how this could be until I remembered that the female was pregnant. I was linked with the unborn pup's mind as well as the mother's. It was like experiencing both sides of a personality at the same time, only worse.

I managed to stay linked with the mother for almost a full 15 minutes before I had to break off. The female's mind was a gold mine of information, but I had to mentally wade through so much filth, hate, and fear that it was easier to seek answers elsewhere than cull through the Were's mind any longer than necessary.

Clarion, the Major, and I retired back to our temporary headquarters. I locked the door, and they began at once to debrief me. Thankfully, the Major brought along some aspirin. I took four. My debrief lasted well over two hours. What a mind link can do in a few pictures and impressions can take hundreds of words to describe in a spoken language, especially when the viewer is asked about context. Nevertheless, five key elements came from that brief confrontation.

First, the female Were is far more valuable than we had dared to think. She was the lifelong mate of the Weres' equivalent of the Commander of the US southern region. Her mate was the equal of the Pale Were I killed at the Chagrin Falls confinement facility. Second, while she was important in her own right, her real worth to the Weres (and to us) was the pup she was carrying. Pale Weres have no more than three lineal children in a lifetime, and a lifetime could be 100 years or more. Third, she was being escorted south to take her out of harm's way for the August Conference yet to be held in the north Georgia mountains.

It was considered a gathering of the great Weres; however, fights could and historically did break out if one area chieftain wanted to take over another's territory. In such cases, the chieftain's family was often the first targets of the usurping chieftain. Fourth, the capture of an enemy leader (Lt. Col. Spikes) never included turning him. Leaders were always killed and eaten, not always in that order. Fifth and finally, word was rapidly spreading among the East Coast Were clans that a particular group of humans was hunting them. That meant a complete change of tactics and habitat, if necessary, so the current colonies could survive long enough to start mass attacks and infections in our urban populations to recruit more drones. Drones (Pan Duk) were humans changed into Weres. They could not reproduce, but they could fight and serve the Pale Weres (Pan).

As an interesting aside, I explained that a big part of the determined hatred and loathing the Weres felt for humans apparently ran back well over several thousand years. Sometime in ancient history, the race of humans had gained an ascendancy over animals. It was a freedom from the Were rule that the Pale Weres thought was a right naturally theirs. Hence the basis for the never-ending war and bad blood between the two races. The low propagation rates of the Weres made them very quickly numerically inferior to humans. It eventually led to their withdrawal from an overt world presence to a covert existence, which was yet another reason for their unrelenting hatred of humans.

We talked among ourselves for a short while after the debrief was concluded. Hungry, we broke for a very late lunch. I went to tend to Gitta instead. She had not enjoyed the helicopter ride to Ft. Benning and likely had no food or attention so far today. When I arrived at the kennel, Gitta was nowhere to be seen. I started calling both by voice and by mind while I began expanding my area of search. After 15 minutes or so, I finally got a weak response.

Following the lead, I finally found Gitta inside the shed where the female Were lay trussed up in the steel mesh net. Gitta had missed me. She figured that if she found the Were, she would eventually find me as well. So she started looking. Wolverines are nothing if not resourceful, and Gitta was at the head of her class. I knelt and hugged her. I complimented her on her logic. She was right on the money. But while I was there, I noticed that the female Were was in some obvious distress. I walked up to her as close as I dared. I promised I would soon return with water and food for her. Her response was a rasping, sudden snarl that would curl the hair of a Komodo dragon if the dragon even had hair. My response was, however, quite different. I steeled myself and did not let her see my inward terror. I calmly walked out the shed door, shut it, locked it, and sagged against the wall, breathing hard. There is not one shred of comfort in a Were's presence when you're alone—not one. There's certainly not when the Were is an angry, thirsty, hungry mother-to-be.

Rather than try to stash Gitta somewhere again, I just took her with me. Our temporary headquarters was reasonably close by. I really didn't want her to be discovered by someone and raise a major ruckus. Said another way, I didn't want Gitta to rip apart a soldier who was curious about what kind of a dog she was. Soldiers are known to poke at beehives with a short stick just because they're there. No short stick attitude is worth a wolverine's short temper.

I was a little late when I finally returned to the headquarters room. I still hadn't eaten anything. I told the Major what I'd been up to when she asked. She was kind enough to send out for some sandwiches for me. She then asked me to screw my head on straight because the three of us—Clarion, the Major, and I—were going to have to come up with a plan to rescue or kill Lt. Col. Spikes in less than 36 hours, that was if the wall clock by the door was halfway accurate. She also said that Captain Yamata would be here at 7:30 p.m., give or take a few minutes. He would help us refine our plan.

DAY TWENTY-THREE 9:00 A.M.

It had been a long night. Clarion advised us all to sleep in as late as we could since this would be the last chance for a full rest until Lt. Col. Spikes was either rescued or killed. I could have made it a much longer morning snooze but for two reasons: a scheduled briefing and Gitta. The meeting I probably could have missed without ending up dead. Gitta's needs, however, could not be ignored. Nor would she let me forget that a big part of my job was to attend to the Weres. If having a 60-pound very large female wolverine step on your chest and thrust her nose into your face while she growls to go outside isn't a wake-up call for immediate action, I don't know what is. Gitta always reminded me of that parody of mothers: "If Gitta ain't happy, ain't nobody happy."

One recipe for a long and fruitful life was to keep Gitta happy.

I had to scramble to do it, but Gitta and I were at Clarion's morning briefing on time. As I walked in, I was able to swallow the last bit of breakfast I'd grabbed at the Bachelor Officers' Quarters (BOQ) Mess Hall on the way over. I waved hello instead of my usual vocal greeting. It's hard to talk when you're trying to choke down that last mouthful of buttered muffin without a glass of milk to accompany it. Gitta walked to a corner, curled up, and promptly went to sleep. Sometimes when I watched Gitta, I knew she must have been a soldier in another life, if for no other reason than she could sleep anywhere, anytime and then come awake in a second and rip your throat out. I somehow found that a very enticing aspect of Gitta's mien.

The Major and Captain Yamata were already seated at the table Clarion had commandeered for the meeting. I took a seat by the Major. Pee Wee walked in a few minutes behind me with Sergeant Abshire. They sat across from us beside Captain Yamata. Clarion had the end or command seat. Neither Pee Wee nor Abshire had been with us the night before when we came up with our first draft of Lt. Col. Spikes's rescue plan. We needed their input and buy-in to make it work. We hoped we'd get it, but no one has all the answers in formulating a battle plan. They might very well recommend that we trash our proposal because of fail points they see that we cannot. Then again, they just might endorse and add a few new wrinkles to it. That's what we were hoping for. That's eventually just what we got.

We did not know exactly where the Weres were congregating. After all, the Okefenokee is a *big* swamp. But it is a swamp. Its very name means "shaky ground" or "trembling ground." That referred to the supposed islands that cover so much of its vast surface. They are false islands, easy to step on and easier to step through. They primarily consist of flotsam and jetsam, nature's debris that happens to have an affinity for like detritus. Over the years, it has aggregated into semifirm islands. Werewolves are too heavy for 95 percent of the swamp's false islands. Moreover, the swamp's west side held the Stephen Foster State Park, by reputation well traveled and well policed.

That left several spots on the swamp's east side as their more likely gathering place. Of those, one in particular stood out. It was an area west of the town of Folkston east of the Sometime Hole in the swamp and south of the swamp's House Lake. With a little digging and a few calls to the State Statistics and Index Bureau, we were able to add weight to our suspicions. We noted a greater number of suspected children's kidnappings, missing pets, and missing cattle in the last 10 years that occurred in an area immediately east of the swamp within a 20-mile radius of Folkston. That was more than in any other part of the State of Georgia.

The other two possible Werewolf gathering areas were within an hour's driving distance either north or south of our first target area. We came to call that area the Folkston Bog, or simply the Bog. The close proximity of all three areas gave us confidence that our choice of the Bog was on solid ground, so to speak.

The night before, Captain Yamata took our first plan through a major modification. He demanded that we offer as few opportunities for a major firefight as practical. Smaller numbers going in meant less chance of a quick hostage kill. The Weres had to perceive some advantage if they were to talk and not fight. Therefore, we would go in with the absolute minimum of people to recapture or kill Lt. Col. Spikes. Clarion and Major Sanchez would not be exposed. Captain Yamata, Sergeant Abshire, two of his men who were skilled snipers, Pee Wee, and I would comprise the entire hostage rescue party. Four of us were there to carry Lt. Col. Spikes out, if needed. The two snipers were there to cover us or make sure Lt. Col. Spikes died quickly if we were unsuccessful. I was there to keep the Weres honest. The female Were, fed and watered, would go with us.

We would leave for the Bog at 4:00 p.m. in two Bell Huey helicopters and one Piper Cub. I would fly in the Cub. We would rendezvous with the two helicopters and their passengers at the Suwannee Canal Recreation Area building. The building was about six miles southwest of Folkston. We would meet sometime between nightfall and 2:00 a.m. My pilot would use the Canal Road leading to the Recreation Area as his landing strip. A Piper Cub could fly as slowly as 40 miles per hour before stalling. It only needed a little more than a football field to take off and clear a 50-foot obstacle at the runway's end. It was an ideal spotter plane for our purposes. It also had a special advantage over the helicopters for something I had in mind.

Before we did anything at the Bog, however, I needed to get Polaris's report. Without her input, we didn't know exactly where the Weres were and whether Lt. Col. Spikes was still alive. If he were dead, the whole operation was immediately off. The Bog Weres were not a group worth a retaliatory strike unless they had Lt. Col. Spikes alive. Capturing a male Pale Were remained the overriding mission. Our energies could better be used in planning that engagement. The Bog had simply become a carry-off or kill Lt. Col. Spikes mission. We would need a very different force structure and approach if it were a capture a Pale Were mission.

DAY TWENTY-THREE 8:00 P.M.

My flight from Ft. Benning across Georgia to Jacksonville, Florida, was scenic and boring, the best kind of flight I could have hoped for. Refueling at Jacksonville gave me and my pilot, Kim Smythe, an Air Force Special Operations (Spec Ops) pilot based at Florida's Hurlburt Field, about five hours of actual flight or loiter time over the eastern side of the Okefenokee Swamp. I reckoned that would be time enough to make contact with Polaris and debrief her before our ground mission started.

I got to know a little about my pilot during our flight. Smythe was a big man for a pilot but as fit and gung ho (always ready for action) as one would expect of that strange breed. Spec Ops airmen normally provide air cover, air logistics, air superiority, and fire support for ground missions under the purview of the Army, Marines, or Navy (SEALs). Some men were even assigned to integrated ground units in the role of Forward Air Controllers or Observers (FACs or FAOs).

FACs were Air Force Officers who spoke Air Force language and knew Air Force aircraft capabilities and call frequencies. In a major battle, from the ground, they could better direct incoming aircraft fire against an opposing force. Other Spec Ops officers were assigned to military ground units for covert intelligence purposes as a mission warranted. Their job was to steal secrets or people by guile or by force, bringing them back to US Forces for exploitation. Some Spec Ops personnel did both. The Spec Ops mantra was always stealth where possible. Their unofficial motto was reflective of their training. It was a simple "I wasn't here." My pilot had been a recognized athlete in high school and college. Upon graduation, he chose to enter the Air Force Officer's Candidate program rather than be drafted. He was smart, quick, had a good sense of humor, and most important to me was an expert at whatever he decided to undertake, like flying. He told me that had he not qualified for the Air Force, he might have become a professional cyclist in Europe. But he said that was a passion he felt he could always come back to later in life. I thought if he rode a bicycle like he flew his plane, road traffic had best give him some room. Smythe was apparently passionate (some said intense) about whatever he did. In the press of the moment, it was said that he didn't always share well. But with my life in his hands, he was just the sort of fellow I needed and wanted around.

By 10:40 p.m., it was full dark. We were flying ever-expanding elliptical loops along the swamp's eastern boundary. We were at 1,000 feet above ground level, the altitude Polaris generally favored. I was fully concentrating on communicating with her in hopes that she would be following the Weres in. This was the night they should be arriving, given their average travel time while saddled with a weakened human prisoner. We were betting that their penchant for favoring darkness for their activities and the fact that they would expect to have a celebratory fest and feast with Lt. Col. Spikes as the main course would give us an opportunity to confront them before he was actually sacrificed.

Shortly after midnight, Polaris answered me. We were at the swamp's most northeastern point. We were just turning to fly south once again down the swamp's east side when I heard her response to my query. Excited, I asked if she was all right and if Lt. Col. Spikes was still alive. "Yes" and "yes" responses resulted in a shout and lurch upward in my seat as I raised my right arm in a fisted salute. I seriously interrupted Smythe's quiet reverie. It caused the plane to suddenly dip to the left until Smythe recovered both his and the aircraft's equilibrium. He did so with an interesting commentary that would have earned him a whole bar of soap for his mouth had my mom been with us. In truth, it appeared he had an effective command of abrupt language.

Then came the reason for the Piper Cub. I had rehearsed the next move with Smythe before we left Ft. Benning. We discussed it at length on the flight to Jacksonville. Smythe slowed the aircraft to about 45 miles per hour as I dropped open the window on the small aircraft's right side. I was about to ask Polaris to fly to us. She could fly in under the overhead wing and through my open window. She could land on the Werewolf defense gauntlet covering my right forearm. That would be her interim perch.

Smythe, of course, did not believe that anyone, even the expert falconers at the Air Force Academy in Colorado, could coax a wild falcon into a moving plane, no matter how well they had trained it. But, as I stated earlier, he was game for about anything. This would not likely put *our* lives in danger. It would, however, put Polaris's life in danger.

If Polaris overshot her approach under the wing and missed my window, she would end up shredded lunch meat for any buzzard that happened through the area the next day. The front propeller on a Piper Cub is only about four or five feet in front of the passenger and the pilot. It is entirely unforgiving once it starts spinning. At full throttle, a spinning propeller would shred, dent, crush, crunch, or chew through almost anything nonmetallic before it came to a shuddering halt. I had a small sounding beacon with me that would track her if she were wounded and fell from the sky or was injured while on the ground. I had to place it on her, but the Were pack running far below us would not likely stop while I attended to that convenience. Hence the air-to-air meet-up and landing.

I had already taken major chances with Polaris in previous firefights. Had she been hit by friendly fire, shot by one of our own people accidentally at any time, she likely would be lost for good. She might make it to the ground safely, but a wounded and unconscious falcon from blood loss can't communicate. The Special Forces folks at Ft. Benning had been testing several kinds of retrieval beacons with both dogs and soldiers. It was Sergeant Abshire's idea that we do this for Polaris and Gitta. The devices were in a development stage but actually did work.

When I first told Polaris what we wanted to do for her, she readily agreed. Our visit to Ft. Benning had just made an earlier wish possible. And while Smythe had expressed misgivings about her ability to fly into the Piper Cub window to my arm while we were airborne, I knew Polaris could fly through a 14-inch ring at 150-plus miles per hour. My window was no big deal. Polaris and I both knew exactly what she could do. This wasn't anywhere near her limits.

At just above stall speed, Smythe was having no trouble keeping the aircraft true and stable. Polaris let me know when she was within 15 feet of the plane and could see me and my arm through the open window. She could also see the struts that fastened the upper wing to the fuselage. She felt there was plenty of clearance for her to slip in. After alerting Smythe to hold the plane steady, I gave Polaris the go-ahead. In seconds, so quickly that it surprised me, she was in the window, her talons cutting into the leather brace that encircled my arm. She was steady as a rock, and Smythe was so surprised that he almost put us into a spin. Fortunately, he also had quick reflexes and immediately increased our speed and brought us back to level flight as I folded my window back into place.

I did not tell him I could communicate with animals. He had no need to know that. To him, we had just performed a circus trick that weeks of training would account for. I saw no reason to disabuse him of his notions. Nevertheless, he was a bit unnerved when I fed Polaris some bits of frogs and mice I had put together for her while I was back at Ft. Benning. A falcon has a voracious appetite. The words *table manners* are not in its vocabulary. They never will be.

For the next five minutes, I stroked Polaris gently. As I fastened a small beacon to her leg, we talked rapidly back and forth. I explained the beacon's purpose. She indicated it would not hinder her flight or ability to attack with her talons. She liked the idea that it would help me find her if she were ever hurt and out of my sight. She told me the Weres had covered ground more slowly than she had anticipated with a human in tow. They had finally resorted to carrying Lt. Col. Spikes as they ran. She could see from his increasingly feeble movements when they occasionally rested from their run that he was alive, but barely. She did see him stuff some crumbled cookies into his mouth at one early rest stop the day before. He apparently drew them from his vest since she did not see the Weres feed him anything.

The Were pack was below and slightly behind the aircraft when Polaris came on board. She felt she would have no trouble picking them up again when I released her. I talked her through how she must exit from the aircraft until I was sure she understood both the dive back and away from my window and why it was necessary to avoid the plane's propeller and horizontal stabilizer. I told her where we would be after she left us. She was to come to us as soon as the Weres actually turned into the swamp. It was imperative that we follow them in as soon as possible.

I also told her that whatever happened after that, she was to stay clear of any fighting. And if anything happened to me, she was to fly back to Dusty who would remove the beacon and release Polaris back into the wild. Falcons are not generally demonstrative fowl, but Polaris actually cocked her head to one side and gently rubbed her beak down my cheek and then nipped me hard on my ear as she reminded me not to dwell on such unpleasant subjects. She turned to face out the window I had reopened and, with a haunting shriek, disappeared into the night. Not 30 seconds later, she let me know she had reacquired the Weres. She would see us again at the Suwanee Canal Recreation facility.

Smythe and I were on the ground 45 minutes later. He brought us down on the two-lane road leading to the recreation building. He did it with nary a bump. It was all the more remarkable since our so-called runway was illuminated solely by flashlights held by our other team members. The search lights mounted on the two Huey helicopters didn't hurt either. Once down, we went into an immediate meeting, boarded the helicopters, and lifted off. We waited, hovering several hundred yards apart. We were prepared to immediately move either north or south once Polaris reported in.

She wasn't long in coming. The Weres had turned into the Bog about 500 yards south of what we thought from our maps was a likely path in. Polaris wasted no feathers in coming to us to lead us back to the entrance point. Twenty minutes after that, we were on the ground facing the swamp. The female Were was still in her mesh cocoon but lying on a modified go-kart. Its large wheels and the life jackets wound about the chassis's frame should provide safety if the dry ground give way to water as we went in. The helicopters and pilots were parked several hundred yards behind us.

Captain Yamata wasted no time. He fired off two flares. The swamp and marshland in a 200-meter radius lit up like Times Square at a New Year's Eve midnight celebration. We knew the flares would freeze the Weres until they sent a scout or two back to see who had fired them. We arranged ourselves in a small column, Captain Yamata and I in the lead by 20 yards with no apparent weapons except our respective blades tucked into our belts.

Pee Wee and Sergeant Abshire stood behind us on each side of the female Were. Those two were positively bristling with weapons. The two snipers had disappeared into the underbrush on each side of us within seconds after debarking the helicopters. Each was wearing the latest Army version of night vision goggles (NVG). The NVGs were modern prototypes being developed for Special Forces' use in the jungles of Vietnam. The very first NVG versions were actually developed during World War II.

Then we stood and waited while I slapped mosquitoes by the handful despite the citronella-based repellant I was wearing. Captain Yamata, Abshire, Pee Wee, and the two snipers were apparently unaffected by the swarms that surrounded us. Abshire had shared with them an Army-developed repellant nicknamed DEET before they flew out of Ft. Benning. I had been with the Piper Cub and missed Abshire's generosity. I solved most of my problem by noting which way the wind was blowing and quietly moved to stand downwind of Captain Yamata. There was no question that his DEET vapors saved me from mosquito-generated insanity.

DAY TWENTY-FOUR 1:30 A.M.

Polaris was well above us. She was keeping me informed of the Weres' movements. I could only detect three of the four scouts she said had come racing back to see what was happening at the turn-off point that the Weres had used to access their hidden camp. She told me where the fourth one was hiding. I saw nothing but a bent and gnarled tree. It was outlined against the moonlit night and failing flares. It was a tree without bark but plenty of bite if Polaris saw accurately in the dark. I gave her the benefit of the doubt. I passed her identification on to Captain Yamata. He grunted that he had already seen that Were as well as the three others.

We knew the scouts would see the female Were. We hoped they would report back quickly. Two did and two stayed behind, never letting us out of their sight. Finally, a party of Weres appeared. They almost surrounded us in an open semicircle. They "spoke" with the female from a distance by growls, grunts, and howls, apparently inquiring as to her health and status. They asked whether or not she could free herself. If so, it would set off an all-out attack on us humans.

When they learned she was in good shape but could not defeat the portable mesh cage, some of the Weres withdrew. They were gone for some time. When they reappeared, they were dragging an unconscious Lt. Col. Spikes with them. They dumped him on the ground at their feet. A large Pale Were with a white streak across its chest, a probable former slash wound, emerged from the pack. It hopped and skittered our way. It had three large Black Weres with it. They stopped in front of us about 40 feet away. They hauled Lt. Col. Spikes with them and again dropped him at their feet. The silence was thick with anticipation. We did not trust the Weres. They certainly did not trust us. Each side waited on the other to make a move. Captain Yamata provided it in dramatic fashion.

He called out in English, "I am Yamata-san. I bring with me a claw of steel." At this he drew his blade. "My claw is sharp. It defies its enemies. It brings death with its kiss!" At this point, he bent down, picked up a broken scrub branch about three inches thick, and tossed it into the air. As it fell, he made one unbelievably swift cut with his blade. So swift was the cut that I almost didn't see it. To my fear, it appeared that he missed the branch entirely. The Weres saw it the same way. They began hooting as if they were laughing.

Everything stopped when the Captain stooped down. He brought the branch up holding both ends aloft and quickly pulled them apart to reveal what that awful slash had done. The branch was cleanly severed. He held the two pieces in his hands for a few seconds and threw them to land at the feet of the large Pale Were. Not a sound was heard except the ever-present background insect buzz of the Okefenokee Swamp. The Pale Were knelt and examined the two pieces of the branch. It roughly explored the branch with its claws extended, which did nothing more than barely scrape the wood's surface. When the Pale Were stood back up, Captain Yamata made a dramatic move. He turned, and in six quick steps he was beside the female Were, his blade tip resting on her pregnant belly.

"One push and she and her pup are dead. But you have something I want, and we have something you want. It is time to talk!"

The Pale Were bent down and yanked Lt. Col. Spikes to his feet. As Spikes sagged against the Pale Were, the Were slowly raised Spikes' hand to its mouth and suddenly bit down, taking off Spikes's hand at the wrist. Spikes's sudden screams were pitiful to hear as the Pale Were dropped him in a heap at its feet. We watched silently as a now conscious Lt. Col. Spikes ripped a sleeve from his tattered shirt and fashioned a ragged tourniquet around his forearm. He pulled it tight with his teeth and remaining hand. He whimpered as he did to the delight of the Weres.

Captain Yamata forced a laugh and then used his blade to slice through a portion of the binding mesh around the female Were. He exposed her left arm. With little ceremony, he reached in, pulled her arm out, and sliced through it at the elbow. Sheathing his blade as the female screamed and twisted in her captive pod, the Captain tied off her upper arm at the bicep. He then went one better. With a butane lighter, he seared the exposed flesh of the female Were, cauterizing the wound. He jerked off the tourniquet and draped the burnt and bloody cloth around his neck.

"The last thing you will see is the pup. I will disembowel the female when she has no limbs or head left. We will see how many bites of food a pup can make for the buzzards that will come in the light. Then we will kill you and your pack. We will bring your heads back with us to the mountains. There we will stake them out as a warning to all the Werewolves that death hunts them, that Yamata-san and his killers will not rest until all the Were carcasses are rotting in the summer sunshine."

And with that, he spat on the female's severed arm, picked it up, and threw it to the Pale Were. "But you can stop this if you give us the human," he said. "We will give you the female in return, and we will leave for now. But you will leave this place, too, because we will be back to fight you again. Choose now, or the female's left leg will be at your feet next."

Another slash at the cocoon mesh, and the female's left haunch was freed from its constraint. Her leg fell out, exposed to Yamata's blade.

It was a tense moment. I thought the Weres, by now incensed, would charge at this last provocation. If they did, Lt. Col. Spikes was dead. Both snipers were under strict orders to kill Spikes if the melee started. A rush by the Weres would be just the trigger to start our own Armageddon. I turned and walked slowly back to stand by the Captain, turning around to face the Weres and drawing my wakizashi blade. The message was clear. The female would die by one blade or the other, but she would die.

The Pale Were measured us with its eyes for what seemed to be a short eternity and then spoke. "We will step back. If your human can crawl to you, he will be free. You must cut the female free. If she can come to us, she will be free. Once one of these two comes to their side, our truce is over." The Were kicked Lt. Col. Spikes, knocking him onto his face, and slowly stepped back as its attendants and the remainder of the pack followed its example.

Captain Yamata turned and with a sweep of his blade opened the cocoon mesh all the way. The female rolled free and staggered to her feet. With deliberate steps, she started forward, heading directly for Lt. Col. Spikes. It was clear she meant to do him harm. She was thwarted when Gitta suddenly appeared at Lt. Col. Spikes's side. Gitta had been released as soon as her helicopter landed. She had already scouted much of the area we now occupied. She had gone ahead of the Captain and me when the Were scouts first showed up. She hid in the brush as she moved in her stealth mode. No human or animal was her equal in that. Her sudden appearance by the side of Spikes was a shock to all. But there she was. Gitta and I had been talking during the entire exchange between Yamata and the Pale Were. Gitta knew exactly what to do. With her nose under Spikes's arm, she pushed him into a quasi-sitting position, ran around to his back, and pushed him up to his knees. He was barely able to stand. He did so, visibly shaking. He was in shock, but his disciplined mind and training allowed him a measure of self-control outside the experience of most civilians.

As he started forth, Gitta walked by his side, baring her teeth and claws at the female Were. Gitta made it clear that should the Were try to attack Lt. Col. Spikes, the female's life would immediately be forfeited. Gitta knew that her secret would be passed among all the Weres in short order. She would be marked for death should she ever again be found alone.

The two prisoners—now almost former prisoners—passed within 10 feet of each other, implacable hatred radiating from the female and grim determination framing Lt. Col. Spikes's countenance. He didn't give her so much as a glance as they passed. He remained focused entirely on Captain Yamata.

Yamata stepped forward to embrace Spikes. Yamata laid him on the now vacated go-kart assembly. Likewise, the Weres grouped around the female as they disappeared into the brush. We started immediately for the helicopters, firing off a red flare to tell them it was past time to start up and come get us. In five minutes, we loaded into the two helicopters and lifted off. The lead chopper bearing Lt. Col. Spikes headed immediately for the medical facility in Folkston. Captain Yamata had pulled it off. All of us were grateful to him and to each other. Each person, Polaris and Gitta included, had played a vital role. Best of all, no shots were fired, only three flares.

We would obviously lose the services of Lt. Col. Spikes for a while. Nevertheless, he was at least alive and could not now be used against us. Equally important, as soon as he recovered, he would be even more valuable because of the experiences he had suffered at the hands of the Weres. If you really want to know the enemy, go spend some time with them. If you really want to know your own outfit, go spend some time with them. That was the difference between managers and leaders. Leaders spend time with their people; managers merely spend resources on them.

DAY TWENTY-SIX 9:00 A.M.

It was our first day back at the Rat's Nest. The Major called a general assembly. That meant everyone not on guard duty was to be there. Fortunately, we had no guard duty assignments at the Rat's Nest. Everyone arrived at least 15 minutes early, hunting for a seat and eager to hear what the Major had in store for us. It had been an eventful, long two days coming home. Dusty, as usual, had moved heaven and earth to coordinate our return. She saw to it that Lt. Col. Spikes was airlifted to Walter Reed Hospital in Maryland for treatment and rehabilitation. She even managed to send along one of his favorite pipes, the one that was generally left at the Rat's Nest for his infrequent visits. A welcome home cake awaited us after the briefing (we would have come for one of her cakes without an official summons), and Clarion was to be in attendance. Rumors were that something big was up.

Clarion, the Major, Captain Yamata, Captain Cosic, and two new people, a Col. Jon Kim and Captain John Thyme Maagi (who went by the initials J. T. to his friends and superiors and Cap'n T to all others) were there. He never explained how his last name somehow was dropped in favor of his second initial on all but official correspondence. He also never explained why his parents had saddled him with the name Thyme. It was certainly a better name than Parsley or Sage, but it was still strange. Even stranger, Cap'n T was never late to anything.

Col. Kim was the temporary replacement for Lt. Col. Spikes. He would be in charge of us all for the foreseeable future. We did not know if or when Lt. Col. Spikes could or would return to active duty. We did know his prospects for a disability retirement were somewhere at stratospheric levels. He could certainly stay on active duty, but he would never again be active in a field assignment. That part of his career was over forever.

And as for Col. Kim, it turned out his resume was even more impressive than Lt. Col. Spikes's. Col. Kim was of Korean extraction, slim and tall (about 6'1"). He carried an easy smile and had a wicked sense of humor. He had a memory like a steel trap. He always seemed on the balls of his feet, leaning forward and just ready to burst forth like a coiled spring. He carried a definite sense of energy—high energy—yet he had mastered the art of patience. He never humiliated, never criticized, and never used profanity. But one crossed him at one's peril.

Col. Kim's reputation preceded him. You were part of the team or you were not. If you were not, you were yesterday's headlines. You immediately became part of his problem, especially if your actions ever impaired his team or a member of his team. He was a taskmaster, father confessor, solo artist, and cheerleader to all. He had both guts and brains. He took risks and expected his people to take them, but they were always qualified and never foolish. He would not abide stupidity or prejudice among his troops, and he had no time for selfish and arrogant people. He was on the list for a probable early promotion to Brigadier General, so we did not expect to have him very long, but he made it clear from the first meeting that he intended to make the most of his new command, even if it was a temporary assignment.

But what did we know? In the military, temporary can mean up to 40 years.

As for Cap'n T, he was about as laconic as a man could be and still get the job done. He spoke with a deliberate drawl, seemed about as raw as a fresh oyster, and could level a person with a droll, sardonic comment about as quickly as if he shot them with a gun. Given his wide vocabulary, there were times it seemed a gun was the more merciful of the two.

He was always first to lend a hand, he rarely volunteered for anything, but never refused a mission no matter how inconvenient, dangerous, or ill conceived. He had the mind and approach of an engineer. There was always a solution. He believed good results hardly ever came by luck. You had to work hard, work fast, and work smart. Cap'n T was not one for sitting in a field of lilacs contemplating one's navel. He was the fellow who would plow the field and still come up with seven different ways to retie one's navel. He was an essentially quiet man with an active mind and a biting wit. He was also one of the most courageous men I had the chance to serve with. He led by example.

Although from the South, he did not like nor would he eat okra. Some thought him a very strange man for that alone, indeed. I personally thought it was a brilliant choice.

With our new command structure, preparations for the raid in North Georgia seemed to speed up. I was still assigned to the Major. Cap'n T replaced Captain Cosic who was reassigned as our small group's adjutant. He was the senior administrative assistant to Col. Kim. Cap'n T was responsible for all paperwork. In a nutshell, that meant logistics, finances, legal affairs, administration, personnel records, medical, travel vouchers, and so on. Cosic, however, had a gift for organization and multitasking. Col Kim took advantage of that immediately. He believed we were all gifted in some area.

The trick to a happy and productive outfit was to match people with jobs that played to their talents. He wasn't so much on rank as he was on results. The best man or woman usually got the job. For example, he promoted Captain Yamata to second in command even though the Major outranked Yamata. Yamata was a better fighter and military strategist than the Major. The Major was a better intelligence analyst and planner than Yamata. Since we were primarily a fighting rather than a support outfit, it made sense to have the better fighters in charge. Had our group existed to provide primary support to another group, the Major would have been second in command. She understood processes and protocols and had the patience to put up with one of the largest bureaucracies in the world, the US Military. For every Military front line fighting man or woman, there were at least 10 more behind them providing the total support they needed to pull a trigger more than once.

(And still some people wonder why war is expensive.)

We realized that time was of the essence in trying to take down one of the key Pale Weres. A successful raid on our part would seriously inhibit or degrade the Weres' plan to launch a mass attack this fall on a population center. Their success in an attack meant they would infect and turn people into new Weres by the hundreds, if not thousands. The remainder of our first day back was spent planning, resupplying, reprovisioning, and debriefing all of us who had participated in Lt. Col. Spikes's rescue. Col. Kim and Cap'n T were especially attentive to the debriefs. Each knew vaguely of Lt. Col. Spikes's mission and force. Now they were part of it, the guiding part. They wanted to be sure they had something to contribute, if only how to stay out of the way for a while.

DAY TWENTY-SEVEN 7:00 A.M.

I had returned to my room in the late evening yesterday. I found a phone message from Sunstar asking that I call her at my convenience. I did. We made a dinner date at her house. Her folks wanted to return the favor my family and the Allegros had shown Sunstar during her stay at Chagrin Falls. The dinner was set for this evening at 7:30 p.m. Pee Wee would not be there. Michael, Sunstar's brother, would be.

I was eager to spend some more time with Michael since registration at Lees-McRae was fast approaching. I had a lot of questions for both him and Sunstar. In light of what had just happened with Lt. Col. Spikes, however, my mind and inclination were far from romance. This would be a colleague visit in my mind. I was sure Sunstar probably felt the same way. When you're young, there is magic in a summer encounter that is quickly diluted by the reality of academia about to push out the margins of one's mind.

By 9:00 a.m., Clarion, Col. Kim, and Captain Yamata were well into their new battle plan. We still had not captured a Pale Were from the southern Georgia contingent. They were the ones planning the next town raid. We did know one thing. The Weres would have to be very coordinated since almost every young man or family in the South was well versed in using firearms. In fact, many of the rural population often carried them in their trucks. Georgia, Alabama, Mississippi, and Texas were the standout states for that. Tennessee, Kentucky, and West Virginia were not far behind. If Weres tried anything not well thought out in any of these states, they would likely be shot to doll rags by their supposed prey. The Carolinas were also known for men and women who were dead shots. Nevertheless, they were not necessarily a generally well-armed population. That made them the likely target states, riper than the other southern states.

With that in mind, our thoughts centered on South Carolina as the major target area. We believed Anderson University in Anderson, South Carolina, would be the Weres' likely first strike objective. Anderson University lay midway between Ashville, North Carolina, and Augusta, Georgia. It was located in a relatively rural area. Rugged country and mountains were nearby. A large Were raiding party could sweep in relatively unseen at night and wreak havoc on the isolated student population. Many of them, once turned, would be hidden in canyon countryside less than 20 miles away.

Aikens Technical College and Spartanburg Technical College were also likely targets for many of the same reasons. Nevertheless, terrain and travel stipulations rendered them less desirable than Anderson in our minds. The Weres would want to easily approach, attack, manage, and maintain hundreds of drones as they exited the area and went into hiding. All areas except Anderson were less desirable than Anderson on those last two points alone. Clarion and Col. Kim arranged for continuous aerial surveillance starting immediately to augment what information we could get from ground observers about mysterious sightings.

By 10:00 a.m., my part of the planning exercise was over. I was instructed by the Major to finally start using a bow again, the compound bow, not the hunting bow, since the pull on a compound bow was less stressful than a short recurve bow. I took my bow out to the competition range. I began firing gingerly and slowly at 25 yards from the target. My first few arrows barely hit the target. By lunchtime when I quit, all my arrows were hitting within the second circle. Most were actually hitting in the center ring. My shoulder was starting to hurt by then. It was a good time to pack it in before any real damage happened. I covered my shoulder and arm in so much muscle relaxant and skin-warming product that I could hardly stand to be with myself. My arm and body smelled like a doctor's office. The stuff would wash off when I showered for dinner.

Gitta shied away from me when I came back to her cage behind the Chapel. "You stink!" she said. "What are you eating that you would smell like that?" I explained to her it was not originating from within me but was a topical ointment I had applied externally. It was something to relax my sore muscles and help me heal faster. I don't think she believed me.

Wolverines have no concept of such things unless you count rolling in some other creature's waste products to disguise one's own scent while hunting. I just tucked my feelings back in and let it ride. I did stay outside for the remainder of the day just hiking around the cemetery. I let the smell dissipate while doing a lot of thinking. Occasionally, Polaris used me for target practice.

I needed the exercise, and I used the time to mull over some of the questions I wanted to ask Michael and Sunstar at dinner that night. The prospect of enrolling in college was now on my doorstep. To say I was nervous was an understatement. Although my birthday would be on the last day of August and I would start college as a 19-year-old college junior, I still felt like a freshman. I didn't want to mess up. I was both excited and anxious about this next phase of my life. I envied Casey. She would be nervous, too, but she had teammates to surround her and lean upon. I had only two new school friends, Sunstar and Michael. I felt fortunate to even have those.

At promptly 7:30 p.m., I knocked on the Walksabouts' front door, a small purplish-red Dahlia plant in a green glass-ribbed container under my arm. The gift was for Mrs. Walksabout, of course. It seemed presumptuous to bring something for Sunstar unless there was a romantic connection, but there really wasn't. We were somewhere in that good-friends-slight-crush phase that is the foundation of many solid relationships down the line. That generally occurred when circumstances, egos, and drives finally got themselves sorted out. Right now, she was my colleague, friend, confidante, and occasional but wonderful major distraction.

Mr. Walksabout greeted me at the door with a warm handshake. It let me know he probably crushed cans when no one was looking. The Mrs. gave me a hug that literally took my breath away. Whatever it is they fed these Cherokee Indians, I wanted some. I shook Michael's hand and felt it. That told me Mr. Walksabout's handshake had not totally destroyed all the bones and nerves from my wrist down. Sunstar's hug was a model of decorum. I happily hugged her back. She smelled like a field of fresh flowers. Her grin was as fetching as the twinkle in her eye. She and Dusty had a kind of magic about them that somehow lifted one's spirits. I had missed her. I wanted to hear what she and Dr. Fitzgerald had managed to create. From the excitement in her eyes and the color in her cheeks, I gathered that she was bursting to tell me, too.

We had a wonderful dinner, the first home cooking since I'd come back to the Rat's Nest. Mrs. Walksabout was an excellent cook. She made a cherry pie to die for. She made sure we all had a big piece for dessert and gave me an even bigger piece to take back to my room at the Blowing Rock Inn. In the meantime, Sunstar caught us all up on her adventures at the containment facility lab (she didn't call it that). In turn, I gave them a blow-by-blow account of our Georgia excursion. The Walksabout family was all read in on the Weres and what our respective roles were. Clarion felt that with both Pee Wee and Sunstar intimately involved in the effort to stop and contain the Weres, it would be much easier for all concerned if the family knew what all three of us were doing, especially if Michael and I were to room together. He could cover for me a lot better if he knew what he was covering for.

Being in the Walksabout home was much like being back in my own home. It was a feeling that Sunstar shared with me. Between my mom and dad and the Allegros, Sunstar said she might as well have been at her aunt's or cousin's house. The feeling of love and support was the same. Both Chagrin Falls families had been very respectful of Sunstar's privacy and person. I thanked her for that observation. I asked if I might pass it along to my folks and the Allegros. Sunstar laughed and said to go right ahead. She'd made sure they got that same message when she left. Hearing it again certainly wouldn't hurt anyone.

I was out of the house and on my way home by 10:30 p.m. I knew my next day would be busy. I was sure theirs would be, too. Michael, Sunstar, and I had a chance to spend about an hour together at the evening's end, just the three of us. We asked Sunstar hundreds of questions about college life at Lees-McRae, and she answered most of them to our satisfaction. We would register on September 6. Classes would start soon after.

Michael and I would share a dorm room for the first semester, although we both knew it would be for the full year. The dorms were small. Freshmen and sophomores were the main inhabitants. I wanted a campus experience even if the campus wasn't much more than 10 or 12 buildings. The archery team would also have their first get-together in mid-September. Snow came early to the North Carolina mountains. The fall archery season only lasted six weeks. The spring season and tournaments lasted two months. Shoot-offs for regional and state championships adding a week or 10 days to the tail end of that season. I looked forward to meeting the team to see if I could find a place among them.

DAY TWENTY-EIGHT 8:00 A.M.

Tomorrow was my birthday, the last day of August. I'd told no one. I suspected Dusty knew because she had access to all our personnel records. I reckoned it wasn't a concern to anyone else except me and my folks. If I knew Mom and Dad, there would be a letter or package waiting for me at the inn when I came home tonight. Just the thought of that brought a smile to my face that I wore to work at the Rat's Nest. Both Col. Kim and the Major remarked that I seemed unusually cheerful. They seemed to mark it up to my getting ready to start college.

Even Gitta and Polaris noticed I was in a happy mood that morning. Gitta plied me with questions when I spent the day's first half hour at her cage. She had no concept of a birthday and even less of a celebration because of it. But she was clever enough to ask if that meant she might get an extra Twinkie or two. I told her I thought she was dead-on. I discovered a man hasn't lived until he's had an early morning pre-birthday kiss on the cheek from an excited wolverine.

Polaris, as usual, was a model of decorum. She frowned on Gitta's excessive display. She did fly to the top of Gitta's cage and let me stroke her feathers for 10 or 15 minutes while I fed her raw steak strips. A Princess is always a Princess except when she's hungry. At least that seems to be the rule if you're a gyrfalcon.

Meetings filled in the bulk of the morning. I had a short stint at the competition range with Col. Kim. He'd heard about my prowess from the Major. He wanted a look-see of his own. I was a little stiff when we started but soon found myself getting back into the groove. I kept the majority of my arrows within the bull's ring. The Colonel tried a few shots with the horn bow. We spent a bit of time trying to find and retrieve his arrows.

At least he got the direction correct. Even the Major tried a few. Captain Yamata put everyone to shame, including me. He said he knew he could beat me because I was still recovering and he wouldn't have another chance like that for a long time. So he took it. I was laughing so hard at his personal glee that I couldn't have beaten him if I'd had my best day. Yamata was a man who really hated to lose.

I had the afternoon relatively free. The Major suggested that I take Gitta and Polaris out on a several hour excursion. I was to stay within two miles in case they needed to recall me and get some further information on how Gitta and Polaris could better fit in the Colonel's attack plan.

The Major would have Captain Yamata signal me with a whistling arrow or two. I might not hear or see it, but chances were that Polaris would be aloft and would. I agreed. I went behind the Chapel to see if the ladies were up to an afternoon snoop. I suggested to the Major that I revisit the trail where we'd seen evidence of the Were scouts several weeks back. She agreed but cautioned me to take the wakizashi blade with me. She'd seen what that blade could do in Georgia. She felt a lot better when it was with me. She also asked me to wear my leather armor. The more testing for design and flexibility, the better it would be in the future. I reluctantly agreed. I suited up before we left.

I felt strong enough to take the hunting bow. I packed my quiver with a compliment of broadhead, whistling, and exploding arrows, 12 in all. Out of a growing habit, I also put my .357 pistol in my pack after checking the load and engaging the safety. It felt good to be fully equipped again. The weight of my pack, bow, and quiver of arrows nestled comfortably against my back. I felt a quiet surge of excitement. The three of us were going hunting again, and my birthday was tomorrow. I wondered if it could get any better. I decided yes, it could. All I needed was Casey alongside me to share another adventure. This afternoon's hike I was suited up for looked pretty tame compared to some of the other excursions we'd had together.

By 12:30 p.m., the three of us were off. Gitta led the way. She kept up a running stream of questions about tomorrow and just when she might see a Twinkie. I stifled a laugh or two. I told her I wasn't in charge of Twinkies. Dusty was. When we returned, I'd ask Dusty. That seemed to mollify Gitta. She scampered on ahead of me while Polaris flew circles overhead, her eyes never still. Occasionally, she cried out. She'd seen nothing but was restless.

About 45 minutes into our hike, I began to get an uneasy feeling. We were very near the Were trail. I began to notice the silence. It reminded me of the Dead Zone outside of Chagrin Falls. Even the insects were quiet. I had premonitions before, but they seemed to sharpen since Sunstar started working with me. I wondered if the Elders, the unseen spirits she said were always watching over us, had somehow made a breakthrough to my consciousness because of her influence.

What I did do was call in Gitta. I had her walk much closer to me. Even she sensed something different as we came to the trail. We couldn't shake the feeling that unseen eyes were watching us. It felt like we were bait, not fishers. As we started down the trail, the feelings of unease grew stronger. Gitta remarked several times that she was extremely uncomfortable. Polaris, however, still saw nothing around us. Since no one saw better than Polaris, we continued on. After 15 minutes, I brought us all to a halt at the base of two small but steep hills. The feelings of unease and dread were so strong that I decided to turn back and retrace our steps. That was when they hit us.

DAY TWENTY-EIGHT 3:45 P.M.

We were at the mouth of a short defile that ran about 50 yards. The narrow passage was bounded by fairly steep hills covered with brush, not trees. The hills reached upward for about 50 yards on either side of the defile we had entered. An old stream bed or drainage ditch was beneath our feet. Walking was becoming difficult in the soft earth. A single howl split the quiet as the Weres erupted from the dense foliage lining the top of both sides of the defile.

They came at us from two directions, one group from slightly behind and well above us. The second group came down from the hilltop at the far end of the defile. The far group came down so rapidly that several Weres lost their footing and tumbled into their companions. They knocked the entire group off its feet like pins in a bowling alley. I could have told them that haste makes waste, but I was too busy for polite conversation. I was frantically looking for some kind of cover while I reached without thinking into my quiver and prepared for battle.

The group coming from the far end of the defile had turned into a disorganized horde that rolled and stumbled its way to the bottom of the defile. They spent precious seconds trying to get untangled before scrambling toward us. With a glance over my shoulder at the group descending from above and behind, I drew a screamer arrow from my quiver, called in Polaris, tossed the arrow high in the air, and told her to take it to the Major or Dusty. Polaris was to make as much noise as she could. She was to lead our relief back here on the double. Polaris snatched the arrow in midair. She disappeared almost immediately in furious flight back to the Rat's Nest. That bird could sure cover ground fast when she needed to. Right then she needed to.

I turned to face the Weres coming down from above and behind us. They had seen the calamity of their fellow Weres at the defile's other end. They were coming down at a much slower albeit deliberate pace. I drew a broadhead from my quiver. Without thinking or deliberately aiming, I dropped the first Were at 30 yards and closing. The arrow went through its left chest. As it hit the ground, its sprawl tripped the second Were coming fast behind it. My second broadhead took that one through the throat. The arrow literally ripped out the Were's voice box because its howl stopped immediately. All it could do as it tried to remove the arrow while stumbling downhill was break off the shaft just before it rolled to a dead stop.

Too busy to watch its final throes, I spun and pulled an exploding arrow, letting it fly into the face of the Weres coming at us from the far end of the defile. The resulting explosion crippled the two Weres in the lead. It also momentarily stunned the following three so they pulled up as they tried to clear their heads. Debris from the explosion flew in all directions. It raised a dust cloud that temporarily blocked the far group from my sight.

I wasted little time as I spun back around. Pulling three broadheads, I put two through a Were now only yards away. A third passed through the Were immediately behind him. But there were two more behind the third Were and three more now loping my way from out of the dust cloud. I tried for one more arrow. I had it halfway to my bow when I was knocked flying off my feet. The bow was torn from my hands by a particularly nasty big Were that swung its arm and claws at me like a scythe. Its claws raked my shoulder and traveled down the left side of my back. In my panic, I barely felt the blow. I could not feel any tearing, so I assumed I could still fight. Running through my mind was Yamata's mantra: Channel your anger! I ducked under the big Were's vicious second swipe and rolled to my right to regain my feet. I watched in horror as one of the three Weres coming fast from the far end of the defile threw itself at Gitta and knocked her flat. The Were then tried to smother Gitta in a desperate embrace while biting at her neck. But Gitta was twisting and fighting using her own claws and teeth. The Were had more than it could handle from the screams that arose when Gitta finally bit into the Were's shoulder. A second Were immediately sprang to the aid of the first. It ripped Gitta's back open from her shoulder to her flank. Gitta arched her back and seemed to just deflate. She suddenly went limp. The first Were then raised her up and threw her down near me as the second Were turned its head up to howl its kill song. Gitta's blood was starting to pool. As I looked at Gitta, I suddenly went berserk.

In Viking lore, those warriors who fought without any fear of their enemy would often be so taken by battle lust that they would rip off all their clothes and armor. Naked, without any defense save a sword or battle axe, they would scream at the top of their lungs and charge the enemy. They generally wreaked wholesale slaughter among the enemy's ranks. They fought until they were killed or the enemy routed, ignoring even the most horrendous wounds and seeking nothing but mayhem and death.

Covered in gore and blood-splatter, roaring as if they were animals, leaping into the most frightful situations without regard for life or limb, these Vikings could terrify an opponent and often turned the battle for the Viking raiders. These warriors were called Berserkers. Even the mightiest of their opponents paled when a Viking went berserk and naked, sprinted forward reveling solely in the lust for battle. A Berserker, fueled by momentary insanity, was the tactical nuclear bomb of his age.

I do not remember tearing off my clothes. I think the Weres did most of that for me. I had the claw marks and body wounds to prove it. I do remember pulling my wakizashi blade before my vision went red. Screaming, I charged the largest Were of those surrounding me. I must have been a little insane. Eventually it was Pee Wee who finally tackled me while Captain Yamata pulled the blade from my hands lest I harm one of the rescue parties that finally came for me.

The remains of four of the five Weres that charged Gitta and me were scattered about my feet in chunks. I had somehow overcome my own fear. In defense of Gitta, I had temporarily lost my mind. Four shredded Weres lay about me, and I was ripped in several places. One of my worst wounds was an open slice from my left forehead down to my jaw, just nicking the outside edge of my left eye. I had been a fraction of an inch away from losing that eye. I was left with a face that would probably make children scream. Blood was everywhere, a lot of it mine. I felt weak and nauseous.

The fifth remaining Were was shot at by Col. Kim as it tried to escape down the defile. Just when it seemed it would get away, it was hit by Polaris diving at it at her top speed. The blow of her talons at the side of the Were's head literally knocked the Were senseless. As Polaris pulled up from her crushing dive, the Were flipped end over end until it finally skidded to a rest at the far entrance to the defile. As it tried to stagger to its feet, Pee Wee shot it in the left leg, spinning it around until it once again crumpled to the ground. Two of the rescue force ran down to retrieve it. They were starting to drag it back even as I was coming back to my senses.

They never made it. Apparently the Were regained consciousness from the rough handling it was receiving. With a roar, it tore off the arm of the lead soldier and bit through the shoulder of the second. Their screams brought everyone to attention. Several of the rescue party ran to them even as the wounded Were hobbled away. Neither Col. Kim nor Pee Wee could take a kill shot for fear of hitting one of the rescue party members in the line of fire. The soldier whose arm had been torn off bled out before the party got to him. They were able to save the second man with the ravaged shoulder.

As they were bringing the two men back, Col. Kim and Captain Yamata splashed water on my face from the canteen in my pack. They put a soaked rag around my neck. The disorientation I previously felt quickly slipped away. I surveyed the scene around me. I was fully conscious and in control of myself for the first time since I watched Gitta being ripped apart. I could remember everything except the fight after Gitta was slashed. With that realization, I immediately tried to struggle to my feet. I called out her name and frantically looked for her.

Col. Kim calmed me down. He told me that Captain Yamata had sent Gitta back with two men as soon as they found her. They had closed her wound, were carrying her back in a litter they brought along, and had already radioed ahead for one of the Motor Pool guys to have Little Beaver warmed up and waiting. The pickup truck was to transport her to the vet clinic at Lees-McRae College. There, Professor Warren would operate on her. I sat back down and found myself crying from relief.

Neither Col. Kim nor Captain Yamata said a word. Col. Kim gripped my shoulder for a moment and gently patted me on the back. He then left to regroup the rescue party so we could start back. Captain Yamata dressed some of my more obvious wounds and helped me stand up. The slash down the left side of my face would be a showstopper, he said. Still, if I didn't like being in the service, I could always opt out to be a pirate. His needling helped me face my current situation. When he had my attention, he asked me quietly if Gitta had done some of the slaughter or if it was just me with my bow and blade.

I explained it was pretty much just me, gulping as I tried to get my breath and not start crying in front of the Captain. He told me that my reaction was entirely normal for someone who had experienced great fear and great stress. I needed to understand that my body was trying to dump that stress even as we spoke. Crying did that, but so did shortness of breath and vomiting. I was to think of myself as a man who had reacted to a bad situation in an extraordinary way. Someone I loved had been hurt. The rage I felt was not unlike a mother's rage when her child was threatened.

He told me that he hoped he would never come between me and a loved one. He said it with a smile as he once again helped me steady myself before we started back with the others. I had to grin. The worst was over, I was a little tattered, and the Were that got away would have a story to tell about the Archer. Yamata was betting they'd be giving me another name by now. He laughed and said it wouldn't be pretty.

Col. Kim ordered the bodies of the Weres to be collected. They were burned at the mouth of the defile, specifically in the middle of the Were trail. He wanted to send a clear message. There was nothing like having the charred and burnt remains of your companions dumped onto the middle of one of your chief travel arteries to indicate that you are not wanted. It was hard to get much clearer than that. But in the course of pulling the bodies to the burn pile, several members of the rescue party found that the two Weres I thought had been killed by my explosion arrow were merely stunned.

One reacted violently when the rescue party seized it and started to drag it back. It fought free of the rescuers' grasp. It started to leap onto the back of one man when Pee Wee's shot rang out and the Were's head exploded. The second Were was still insensate. It was brought to the Colonel and me where they dropped it on the grass before us. As the Were struggled with consciousness, I leaned forward to make contact and question it. Its answers were vague, almost as if it were drunk, but once past the bitter hatred, there were a few gems of intelligence I gleaned. First, the ambush was deliberate. The Chapel was being watched. I was a major target, as were Gitta and Polaris.

The patrol that ambushed me was originally coming to replace the watchers that the Weres had already scattered around Blowing Rock. Once replaced, the relieved Weres would form up and run back to Georgia. The timing of my afternoon hike had been unfortunate. Seen by one of the watchers, we were followed for almost 30 minutes. When the Were tracking us decided we were headed to the Were trail, it used a subvocal low frequency call to communicate with the relieving patrol. He told them where I was, what my party consisted of, and what direction we were headed.

It was easy then for the Weres to set up an ambush and wait to spring the trap. They were aware I used birds to spot for me, and that's why Polaris saw nothing. There was nothing to see. The patrol hid themselves before Polaris flew over, so she saw nothing moving. Since I did not have her flying large circles that covered ground we had already passed through, Polaris did not see the watcher trailing behind us feeding information to the Were patrol waiting ahead.

As the Were started to sink back into unconsciousness, I impulsively reached out to shake it. I hoped for just a few more conscious moments. In seconds, the Were turned its head and snapped at my arm. Its jaws crunched down so hard that its teeth must have shattered. Thanks to my extraordinary reaction time, I was able to move just enough so the Were's bite got air and only one or two of the hairs on my forearm.

Col. Kim reacted almost as quickly. He shot the Were through the forehead seconds after its bite closed. We both stood there in silence for a few moments when the Colonel finally looked up. He kicked the Were to make sure it was dead and said, "Burn it!" He helped me to my feet, brushed me off, and with a pat on my shoulder gently pushed me in the direction of the rescue team now forming.

We hadn't taken 15 steps before I passed out. Thank goodness the team had worn their belts. With some shirts and webbed belts, they rigged a litter and brought me back to the Rat's Nest. I remembered nothing more until I awoke in a hospital bed holding Dusty's hand. Her forehead was resting on the edge of the bed atop her arm, and she was sound asleep. The sky outside my window was dark, so I knew it was night. I was warm, comfortable, and groggy from whatever the doctors gave me. I just lay there and quietly slipped back to sleep.

No one was with me when I awoke the next morning. It was my birthday. I was glad to be there, wherever "there" was. If my 20th year was half the year my 19th had been, the adventures ahead were going to be doozies. I smiled and once again slid off to sleep.

DAY THIRTY-TWO 10:00 A.M.

I awakened again when the morning nurse came in to change my dressings. I was still a little groggy. I was able to converse with her for a few minutes before I faded out again. It was so pleasant to sleep. A great deal of that was the morphine they gave me the night before. It enabled me to sleep. The morphine was but a partial cure to the utter exhaustion I felt. Going berserk apparently had a high residual price tag in terms of depleted energy reserves.

I was in the hospital at Hickory. The Major had brought me down with one of the fellows from the Motor Pool. Dusty had stopped by during the late evening for a brief night watch. She'd left an hour or two earlier. Captain Yamata relieved her and left when the nurse in charge signaled the patient's day would soon begin. There were no morning visitors allowed until noon. The Captain indicated that he and possibly some others would be back later. He left only when the supervisor could assure him I was perfectly fine, that I was just sleeping off the sedative the doctor gave me the day before to prep me for the many stitches I had needed.

My first visitors arrived at noon. They were a rowdy bunch. Michael and Sunstar were the first ones in the room, followed by her parents. This time Mr. Walksabout gave me a gentle pat on the shoulder rather than his bone-crushing handshake. Mrs. Walksabout gave me a brief and sweet kiss on my forehead. It was like having my mom in the room. I admit I got a little misty-eyed, but no one seemed to notice. Even if they did, they were all kind enough to not mention it.

Sunstar gave me an interim report on Gitta's condition (serious but stable). She indicated that Polaris was apparently okay. Pee Wee had called Polaris in for a breakfast of raw steak strips. Polaris hungrily devoured them before perching on the Chapel's rooftop weathervane. We visited for almost an hour before I started to get sleepy again. The nurse noticed my half-staff eyelids when she came in to check on me. She gave me my medicine. She promptly but quietly and firmly shooed everyone out "so he can get some rest, people." I drifted easily back into that twilight veil of semiconsciousness.

My second group of visitors arrived at almost 4:00 p.m. The Major, Dusty, and Captain Yamata came together. They brought with them a picture of my birthday gift. Dusty pulled several of her cupcakes out of a bag, two for each of us. Captain Yamata produced a couple of paper roll-up horns that we blew until the floor nurse came running in to confiscate them. She scolded us for making so much noise. We waited until she shut the door of my room before bursting out in laughter. I counted the day a wonderful if all too brief birthday celebration.

My gift was the use of a new IBM typewriter. Col. Kim wanted all the officers and key staff at the Rat's Nest to have them because we produced so many reports. The Major convinced him that as a brevet Second Lieutenant, I needed to be in that distribution as well. She leaned over and told me privately that mine was to be kept in my dorm room. It could be used for my college coursework, too, especially since my future commission was dependent on an eventual graduation. It was a stretch in logic, but anyone who had killed eight Weres on their own could have asked for and gotten pretty much anything they wanted, according to the Major.

On that note, she confided that Captain Yamata had put up his best arguments yet to get me transferred into his command. I had done what no one had ever done. He wanted to train me personally and use me to help train his troops. Col. Kim listened and sympathized but still denied the move, if only because I was the one person they had that could communicate with Weres. That made me virtually untouchable, a vital resource everyone else had to protect.

I was honored again that Captain Yamata would think so highly of me but was inwardly very happy to stay with the Major. She was a teacher by instruction. Yamata was a teacher by example. Both were valuable. I could and was learning from both, but the Major had one thing Captain Yamata did not. She was in charge of the Rat's Nest at Blowing Rock, only a hop, skip, and rock throw from Banner Elk and Lees-McRae College. The Captain's command was down in Florida. It would be a major upheaval for me to transfer to Florida and enter college there. I had no desire to do that. I also did not need the experience. So I stayed part of the Major's command. That was my second best birthday gift.

My best gift came later that evening with a long-distance call from my folks and Casey, who was home getting ready to go back to North Carolina for enrollment the next week. She was upset that I was back in the hospital. My folks started the conversation, but Casey and I finished it. They let me talk for almost 20 minutes with her before coming back on to say goodbye. They told me how much they loved and missed me. The Major told them I'd been in a Were fight and was pretty banged up.

She also told them I would carry a scar on the side of my face for the remainder of my life. Oddly, she said it made me very handsome. It gave me a slightly dangerous look. She fully expected those Lees-McRae ladies to be very excited to meet me, that competition for my time would be fierce. My mom was happy and excited at that news even though I knew Dad was probably rolling his eyes. Mom wanted plenty of little baby Codys one day. To know that her only son was still a babe magnet, as Sunstar had once confided in her, gave her hope for the future. Moms the world over apparently live primarily on a diet of faith and hope with a side order of skepticism.

Casey wasn't impressed, but she was intrigued. I told her I'd have Dusty take a picture of me when my scar healed and send it to her. She promised me a picture as well. She told me that Paul had just gotten a new camera of his own and was teaching her how to use it. She said she'd have him take a picture just for me. It was more information than I wanted, but I remained enthusiastic. I told her I couldn't wait.

I asked her to thank her folks again for all the hospitality they'd shown Sunstar, that we'd gotten a great report over dinner at Sunstar's house just a day or two ago. Casey wanted to know why I was at the Walksabout house in the first place. She seemed somewhat mollified when I told her Michael invited me. We would be roommates this coming year.

Our call ended soon after. She told me I was missed. She said she couldn't wait to see me at Thanksgiving. She reckoned we'd have plenty to share with each other. She was also really excited about the coming soccer season. Freshmen were not allowed to play on the varsity their first year, but by Christmas her advanced honors work would count. She hoped to be on the varsity soccer team the coming spring.

I told her I missed her very much, that my life here was full and exciting but that something always seemed missing. That something was her. There was a moment's pause. Her response was not quite what I expected. She closed by reminding me that there were many adventures ahead for both of us, that we wouldn't always be together. Still, I was always in her thoughts. My folks came on after that. We exchanged goodbyes and hung up.

I lay in my bed for a long time thinking over Casey's delayed response. Maybe I was reading too much into it, but I was betting it was the beginning of a long goodbye. With that troubling thought, I drifted off to sleep thinking about Gitta and how soon I could go to her.

DAY THIRTY-FIVE 11:30 A.M.

I'd been home from the hospital one hour. Home was still my room at the Blowing Rock Inn. The folks there were glad to see me and understood I'd been in a bad accident. I was wearing a number of bandages. Most were under my clothing, but the line of sutures down the left side of my face certainly commanded a second and third look from the folks I passed or spoke with. I thought the doctor had done an excellent job. He told me to tell anyone who asked about the scar that I'd won it dueling with sabers at Heidelberg University at Baden-Württemberg, Germany, during a summer student-exchange program.

"The guys will be in awe of you. The girls, well, the girls will think you're rakish and dangerous, just the person for a date," he told me. He was wrong. The first time I used that line, the guy I was speaking with looked at me again and said I must be pretty clumsy. He shrugged and walked away. I was crushed. Still, I couldn't help but laugh. It was still a better line than blaming a Werewolf.

I had my car again after catching a ride up to Blowing Rock. I wanted to drive to Lees-McRae to see Gitta. It had been four days since I last saw her. I could hardly wait to leave, but the Major asked that I drop by the Rat's Nest first. When I opened the Chapel's main door, everything was quiet. One of the Airmen on phone duty said most folks were over at the Motor Pool building looking at some modifications the mechanics had done for Moby and Little Beaver. He invited me to go there since nothing was happening here. He understood that all the officers were there as well and that's where I'd probably find the Major. With a nod of thanks, I shuffled out the door and gingerly limped my way over.

I could hear a low murmur of talking as I approached the outside of the big Quonset hut that doubled as our Motor Pool garage. Curious as to what modifications had been made, I rolled open the door and walked into one of the better surprise parties of my life. "Happy Late Birthday" posters were pinned up everywhere. A banner was draped over both Moby and Little Beaver. A huge birthday cake prepared by Sergeant Saddler's favorite bakery was on a table in the middle of the room lighted by 20 candles, each in the shape of miniature flamethrowers.

Col. Kim led a round of the "Happy Birthday" song. Several of the fellows brought out a table holding several gallons of ice cream and paper bowls, napkins, forks, and spoons. It was a pig-out party, one I will always remember. I stayed for an hour and then Dusty and Pee Wee asked if they could come along with me to see Gitta. I told them the more the merrier. Off we went after I had a chance to thank the Colonel, the Major, and especially Captain Cosic who'd arranged the get-together for me. I had to admit to myself that I was home. I truly loved being part of the Rat's Nest. I was one of Clarion's Raiders.

The drive to see Gitta was longer than I remembered. The closer we got, the more anxious I became. Pee Wee and Dusty kept telling me all was well, that Gitta had passed her crisis and Dr. (Professor) Warren saw a solid recovery ahead for her. Gitta was being kept at the clinic rather than the outside boarding areas because of her many stitches.

When we got close, I started calling for her mentally and was thrilled when I got back an excited response. It was even better when I finally found her room and stood in front of her. I carefully put my arms around her shoulders and hugged her gently for a long, long time. She licked my face, especially the long row of stitches, and asked what happened. I told her as best I could remember and then told her what others had told me as they reconstructed what had happened. She was impressed that I'd wrought that much horror and destruction on the Weres on her behalf. She gently placed her head against my chest. She held that pose for the longest time.

Dusty and Pee Wee stepped up. They expressed their feelings of concern, which I translated for Gitta. I got back a gracious thanks from her. They walked out of the room to give us some time alone. Gitta felt like me. We had a home together with people who loved and needed us, and we needed them. After a while, we began comparing cuts and new scars. Gitta's long ragged tear certainly beat any of mine, but I stripped down to my boxer skivvies so she could see all the other places I had been ripped and torn by my assailants. Eventually, she had to admit that my cumulative cuts and tears probably equaled her one giant scar, but hers would leave a beautiful white streak down her side while my puny scars would only leave jagged lines on my relatively hairless hide.

I admitted that she was right, that it would be a long time, if ever, before I took my shirt off at the beach again. About that time, Dusty walked back in, took a look at me, and gave a brief shriek. She dropped her hand from her mouth and walked closer. She told me to cool it, that she had brothers and that me in boxer skivvies was no big deal. However, the sheer number of new scars and bandages was. She asked me to shut up, stand still, and let her take a look. I froze and turned a pretty shade of crimson until she nodded to herself after a walk around and called Pee Wee in. Both of them examined a number of the cuts on my stomach, lower back, and legs.

They walked out comparing notes and left me standing there, mouth agape. Gitta suggested that I put on my skins again so I could go and let her sleep. I did. After another soft hug and gentle ear rub, she closed her eyes and was soon snoring. Wolverines are apparently keen on sleep. I emerged from Gitta's room to find Dusty and Pee Wee conversing with Professor Warren. I thanked him profusely as he took a long look at my facial scar.

"What did you two tangle with?" he asked.

I told him we crossed paths with a mother black bear and cub, that Gitta had decided to chase and swat the cub.

His face lit up in comprehension. "Well, you've now learned one of the basic lessons of life, Cody. Don't ever get between a mother and her offspring."

I told him it was a lesson I would never forget. I thanked him again for Gitta's life.

He asked what I was doing with a Wolverine as a semidomesticated pet in the first place. Both Dusty and Pee Wee exchanged warning glances. I was taken by surprise at his question. Thinking quickly, I said that Gitta was the pet of one of the sergeants with the meteorological unit over at Blowing Rock. He had apparently acquired her in

Europe when he was stationed there. I reported through that unit temporarily as part of my pre-ROTC program. I had become friends with Gitta. I thought we were just going out for a stroll, but that's not what happened, and, well, here we were.

He listened and watched me as I talked. Giving his head a quick shake as if to dismiss the image, he smiled at me and said, "Interesting things seem to follow you, Cody. It's going to be interesting to have you here at Lees-McRae. I can't wait to see what's next."

I just grinned, and he left us. The three of us made our way back to my car. The drive back to Blowing Rock was mostly quiet. Each of us was thinking. It's hard to talk when your mind is otherwise engaged. As we all got out of the car in the parking area near the Chapel, Dusty turned to me and grinned. She told me I had great legs.

I must have been beet red when we walked into the Rat's Nest because the Major walked by, took a look, and told me to wear a hat next time I was in the sun. It looked like I was getting far too much, and heat stroke was dangerous. I managed a meek "Yes, ma'am" and headed on back to my cubicle. Dusty was laughing to herself. Pee Wee just grinned and walked on by.

Like I said, it was good to be home.

DAY THIRTY-SIX 7:00 A.M.

I awoke to a radio report that warned of a severe storm off the coast of Georgia that could turn into a hurricane. Areas from Atlanta to Philadelphia were in the storm's probable path. While still a tropical storm, it was gathering strength off Georgia's outer banks. It would probably reach hurricane strength within the next 24 hours. If it came inland, it would most likely swing up the Atlantic Coast. It would plough through Savannah, Augusta, Columbia, Raleigh, and Richmond and probably peter out somewhere near Washington, DC. If the storm became a hurricane as forecast, it would likely build rapidly. It could go to Category 1 or Category 2 strength, severe enough to leave a trail of real damage in its wake.

The good news was that such a storm would probably quash all chances of a Were attack this year in Georgia or the Carolinas due to the damage and post-storm attention that would follow, especially that amount usually given to the upper South's rural areas. Attention and spotlight were not the Weres' modus operandi. Stealth and secrecy were. On hearing the news, half of me wanted a storm. Half didn't because of the projected damage to life and property. But a successful Were raid on humans would do more to wreck national morale and cause widespread panic than any hurricane. My personal prayers would side with the coming storm if it came as scheduled.

In the meantime, I had college registration to prepare for and forms upon forms to complete for the Air Force. They were providing my scholarship. Dusty mentioned that she had put together a package for me that would probably take me the better part of a day, maybe two, to complete. I would also need a current physical (which I had) to show I was upright and ambulatory (which I was), as well as a psychological exam to make sure I was sane (of which there was some question after my Berserker attack on the Werewolves). I would have time to do everything in the next several days if Col. Kim suspended his plans for a preemptory raid against the Weres because of the looming storm. But I wouldn't know that answer until I rolled out of bed and got to the Rat's Nest. So I did just that.

As it turned out, the storm hit when scheduled but with much greater strength than anticipated. Much damage was done along the path the forecasters had described. Volunteers from churches, small towns, colleges, and professional organizations all across the South spent several weeks cleaning everything up. The raid against the Weres was postponed indefinitely. Col. Kim and Captains Yamata and Cosic went back to Florida. Clarion came down for a medals ceremony for those who had participated in Lt. Col. Spikes's rescue. I received a Bronze Star for my fight at the Were trail. I didn't officially get a Purple Heart since that can only be given to full-time soldiers wounded in enemy action. I technically wasn't a soldier yet.

Registration at Lees-McRae interrupted our volunteer efforts. Michael and I moved into a dorm room together. We hit it off immediately, even to our respective choice of bunk beds. I have always favored heights, and his legs discouraged climbing. He dragged me along to several freshman orientation gatherings that were part social and part informational. I met a number of men and women, most of them nice, but with every crowd there is a resident jerk, and he ended up in our dorm. His name was Cecil Derrick. His buddies were in another dorm, but in both disposition and habit, Cecil was a one-man wrecking crew. He soured almost everything he touched. But Cecil had money and a 1964 Pontiac GTO. My old Chevrolet looked pretty lame beside his. I made it a practice not to park near him. That alone brightened my day considerably when all else failed.

Sunstar registered as well, but in those first few weeks of school, I hardly ever saw her. We passed each other often and waved when we could. She was always surrounded by so many guys or gals that I rarely got a clear glimpse of her. That's just as well because I had other things on my mind like books, papers, and remembering the names of my new classmates. One young lady I met had a name I easily remembered—Kathy Niwall. She was cute, sharp, taller than Sunstar, and formed as if she were a manikin model.

When she danced, everyone hung back and gave her some room. Watching her walk down the hall made Michael and I feel glad to be of the opposite sex. She had a brain, liked to use it, and didn't back down from a confrontation. She also rarely lost her head. She was just fun to be around. Her grin was infectious and her optimism unbridled. Both guys and gals liked her. Michael had one of those at-a-distance crushes that freshmen in college are prone to get. I sure couldn't blame him.

Heck, I probably had half a crush on her myself, but I was too busy trying to figure out what Casey meant by some of her questions in our last conversation. So I just concentrated on classes, Gitta, Polaris, meals, and volunteering for every relief effort my schedule would allow. My first impulse was always to help others. I understood compassion and empathy. Maybe that's why I wanted to be a veterinarian. Now I just had to convince a host of teachers and Professor Warren.

I was now a *college man*. My folks were prouder than I was. Me, I was just grateful, really. I was thankful for my new friends, my old friends, and, as Casey had mentioned, the promise of plenty of adventures ahead.

The first came when least expected. It almost cost Michael his life.

THE END OF EPISODE SIX, BOOK ONE

EPISODE
SEVEN

DAY ONE 6:30 A.M.

The vines that held me to the tree trunk weren't giving an inch. I'd been hard at work for the past couple of hours trying to loosen them by twisting this way and that, but nothing worked. My body was covered in sweat, but I still couldn't slip my way into separating from these blasted vines. Besides, my back hurt where they'd beaten me. Most of the blood spilled on the ground was mine.

The Were that tied me to the Spruce tree did so with fiendish glee and some real attention to detail. It knew its life would be forfeited if I managed to escape. The Were appeared to like living. I'd had some circulation problems in the first 20 minutes, so my struggles had not been in vain. But although I enjoyed a greater wiggle factor after my initial efforts, it seemed I was retrogressing. Exhausted, I hung there beneath the tree's bottom limbs. I tried to catch my breath and let my poor abused body recharge.

Face it, Cody, I told myself. *You're going nowhere until the Pale Were who was running tonight's Werewolf council decides your fate. For that Were, it's a no-brainer. You're dead meat.* Disheartened, discouraged, wrapped in my own private maze of vines, dangling from the big Spruce tree propped up at one of the Were caves' many passages, I was the poster boy of despair—until I heard a soft "Cody, where are you?" flitting through my mind. It was Gitta. She had to be near. For the first time in hours, I started to have real hope. If Gitta was near, Pee Wee would be close behind, and the Rat's Nest crew would be hard on their heels. Things were finally looking up.

Now all I had to do was figure out where I was, where Gitta was, and the shortest, safest distance between the two of us. Then I should be home free. It was a tall order for a worn-out, thirsty prisoner, but I'd been through some pretty difficult scrapes before. Things had a way of working themselves out to my benefit. I had confidence in Gitta and in myself, but these vines were pretty discouraging. I had to admit that my confidence had waned a bit. But hearing Gitta's voice in my head had done a lot to restore my confidence as well as hope. At this point, I was game for anything. I called back to Gitta immediately.

It took almost 15 minutes for Gitta to find the particular cave passage I was in. It took another three minutes for her to chew and slash her way through my entangling vines before I could fall to the floor and throw off the last of my bonds. It took another three minutes to find my bow, quiver, wakizashi blade, and javelin, and I was ready to take on the whole Were clan (with Gitta's help, of course). But the chance never came. Pee Wee showed up, stepped over to me, and gave me a silent bear hug. He put his finger to his lips to indicate that there were Weres nearby and practically pushed me back through the side tunnel entrance from which he'd emerged just minutes before. I all but screamed when he touched my back, but sometimes shock is good.

Gitta made it clear to me that Pee Wee wanted out of these caves we were in and back to the surface *post haste*. From his movements and intensity, it appeared he was going to let very few things stop him. I for sure wasn't about to be one of those things, no matter how much it hurt to stumble along. He half carried, half pushed me as we crept up the passageway.

Getting out of the cave wasn't that hard. All we had to do was follow Gitta. Once a wolverine has seen the way to an objective, she never forgets how to go there and back again. Gitta had been awake and alert during the whole rescue mission. We moved swiftly and quietly through several cave levels, always taking the path upward as we came to it. The faint Were yells and screams of frustration started below us just as we felt we were finally nearing the surface level. Shortly after that, we could feel and hear the distant pounding of heavy feet moving in unison. I was a prize the Weres didn't want to surrender. The thought of losing me when I had been in their grasp for hours probably sickened them.

Each moment we could better hear and feel the Were horde moving fast in the lower cave levels coming up our way. Gitta kept telling me we had more cave ahead of us than time, that we needed to find a hideaway before the wave of animated hell rolling up behind us became our final doom. I agreed, called out to Pee Wee as we stumbled along, and saw two things as we rounded a huge boulder that appeared to hold up the cave ceiling. As we came to a stumbling, scrabbling, dusty halt, our eyes opened wide and our jaws dropped.

A Pale Were was standing in front of us, silent and seething, every bit a harbinger of hate, jaws dripping with drool as it eyed our wary threesome. Immediately behind him was Captain John Thyme Maagi, or Cap'n T as we called him. He was holding a shotgun to the Pale Were's head, one hand holding the gun and the fingers of the other hand entwined in the Pale Were's neck pelt.

"Howdy, boys," he said tersely. "Been waiting for you. Why don't you all just get behind me now, and we'll ease on out of here. Me and this old furball will follow along behind you. I reckon he's got some friends coming in a hurry if my ears don't deceive me. I want to make sure he and his pals and I have an understanding when they arrive, if you get my meaning. Pee Wee," he continued, "why don't you and Gitta lead the way while Cody-san and I powwow with these folks when they come busting around that big rock you just passed."

Gitta, Pee Wee, and I squeezed by Cap'n T and the Pale Were. I held my wakizashi blade at the Pale Were's stomach as we did so lest he be tempted to grab us and force Cap'n T to blow his head off. Once past those two, I stood next to Cap'n T. We all started slowly walking backward up the last 50 or 60 yards to the cave's dimly lit entrance. The clamor and howls of the pursuing Weres grew ever louder in our ears. The big Pale Were simply stepped backward in time with Cap'n T whose neck hold never lessened and whose other hand held the shotgun steady against the back of the Were's head.

We hadn't gone 10 yards when about 10 or 11 seriously disturbed Werewolves came scrambling around the big boulder. They all but fell all over themselves trying to stop. They saw and quickly comprehended the Pale Were's predicament. Their yowls and howls suddenly ceased. The quiet suddenly seemed loud. A second Pale Were shuttled out in front of the chasing mob. It stopped and snarled at us, "If you kill him, we will have no reason for restraint. We *will* kill all of you. You have my promise on that. I am called Tenset."

"I will kill him only if you come any closer to us," said Cap'n T. "We want nothing but distance from you. And distance we will have or you and ol' Harvey here will be nothing but a bad memory. So stay back, and don't interfere." With that, we continued our slow pace walking backward up the last slope to the cave's mouth.

The pack of Weres followed us silently. They matched us footstep for footstep. They never took their eyes off us. As quick as they were, we all knew that one misstep was the trigger that would hurl us into a maelstrom of death. We continued our slow-step ballet until time seemed to stretch as the edges of the cave opening grew larger and larger.

When we were within a few feet of the entrance, Pee Wee called out, "Cap'n, we're here." Pee Wee pulled back slightly toward us and drew three grenades from his protective vest. He pulled the pin from two and threw them through the cave entrance, one to each side.

"Duck!" he called out, and dove for the floor. I dropped beside Gitta, turning my back to the entrance. I folded my arms around her and formed a barrier between her and the grenades.

Cap'n T used his foot to kick the legs out from under his Pale Were prisoner. As they both fell to the earth, the grenades exploded. Faint yells were swallowed up in the boom that beat back upon us. Debris and dust went funneling into the cave with a vengeance. It blinded most of and frightened the larger share of the Weres in the group that had been stalking us.

"Quick now, everybody out!" shouted Cap'n T as he rolled back on his feet. Grabbing the back of my belt, he half carried, half lifted me to a stumbling run as we all made for the cave entrance. Gitta was the first out. She gave me an all clear as we burst into the open. Pee Wee then took his third grenade, pulled the pin, and left it on the entranceway floor. He shouted for us to run as fast as we could to the right of the cave entrance. We'd gone about 30 feet when an enormous boom threw all three of us off our feet. Gitta, so close to the ground, was spared that last insult, although I did see her rear end elevate and bounce momentarily as she ran-waddled quickly ahead.

Within seconds, we watched a Huey helicopter drop from the sky. With blades still turning, it leveled off a foot above the ground as its hatch doors were thrown open. Sergeant Saddler and Airman Kenny Cropper were there with AR-15s at full cock, ready and anxious to send streams of .223-caliber tumbling bullets into the first Were that snapped its jaws in our direction. None did. The helicopter rose suddenly as the loadmaster gave the lift command to the pilot once we and Cap'n T finally had scrambled on board.

As we ascended, Cap'n T asked me if I had been sliced or cut in any manner. I said no. I asked if bruises counted. He laughed. He said those never counted in Kim's (now General Kim's) outfit but probably should be looked at and attended to if there was some reasonable damage. I asked him if someone could look at them and treat them if unreasonable damage had been done. His laughter faded off quickly. His response was short as he gave me his full attention. "Show me, Cody. Now!"

I turned my back and carefully peeled away my shirt. My back had big weals and a few open wounds where the Pale Were had lashed me before ordering that I be restrained and temporarily hung from the Spruce tree pending its return. The meeting it had been summarily called to attend was probably what saved my life. I had passed out from its beating. I would probably have been beaten again had not Gitta and Pee Wee finally found and freed me.

With the adrenaline rush of our escape now quickly receding, I found myself starting to shake. I was getting sick to my stomach. Cap'n T gently draped my shirt back over me. He grabbed an in-flight blanket from the small stack wedged behind the pilot and covered me with it. "You're going into shock, Cody. You're going to start to shake and maybe even cry. Let it go. Don't resist. You've got to bleed off some adrenaline. It's the body's way of clearing itself for healing. It can't fight and heal at the same time. Don't fight it."

With that, he laid me on my side. He held my hand as my shaking started to get uncontrollable. He stayed with me the entire time until I finally drifted off to a ragged sleep. I was exhausted and dehydrated both physically and emotionally. The last thing I remembered as I finally lost consciousness was a shot Cap'n T gave me. The thought that my outfit had come back for me sustained me. That's when Gitta curled up beside me and nudged Cap'n T's hand away.

TWO DAYS EARLIER 6:30 P.M.

It had been a good day. I made an A on a biology test earlier that day in class at Lees-McRae. Michael and Sunstar had ridden over to the Rat's Nest with me after their own classes let out. I had some papers to read and sign for an automatic payroll deposit that Dusty, had set aside for me. While I did so, Michael, Dusty, and Sunstar went out on the porch to chat, leaving me alone in my small cubicle.

I didn't particularly feel like reading the documents' fine print after studying for two days for the test taken earlier that morning, but Dusty was a stickler for detail. She wouldn't let me breeze through the documents. So I stayed, read, and actually thought about several things of worth. I eventually signed all the requisite forms. I laid them on Dusty's desk and went back outside. I locked the entrance door behind me. I gave the key to Dusty. We were the last ones at the Rat's Nest. Everyone had gone home earlier since the Major was away on temporary duty with General Kim and Captains Yamata and J. T. (Cap'n T) down in Florida. Today had been one of those rare everything's-actually-caught-up days.

I put on my quiver and wakizashi blade and picked up my javelin and bow before I headed out. I was thinking I might go on an early hunt with Gitta and Polaris in the early morning. The Major wasn't expected back for another day or two. I didn't particularly like wasting time. A hunt before the winter temperatures closed in seemed like a good way to stay loose and limber for all three of us.

Michael and Sunstar invited Dusty and me for a soda pop in Blowing Rock as I locked up. I declined. I wanted to spend a few minutes with Gitta and Polaris before I drove back to Banner Elk and my dorm. They went on without me, chattering away like the fast friends they were becoming. Gitta and I watched them drive away. The sound of their laughter winged its way back to me as they bounced over the gravel road to the cemetery's main drive. I turned and walked Gitta back to her enclosure. I sat by the cage against the wall. Gitta curled up beside me. I idly stroked her neck and head as we talked about one thing and another.

She was curious about my selection of a mate. She wondered whether I would select Dusty or Sunstar as my eventual mate. As a wolverine, she had the final word for who her mate was. She wondered if human females or males made that choice. I laughed. I told her I was at a genuine loss on that one. I suspected it was mutual but that the female probably had the final say. Gitta snorted and said that was as it should be. Males were generally irresponsible, she said, easily turned aside from their duties as preserver and protector of the family for a little more food or an extra wiggle in a young female wol-verine's tail as she waddled by. I started coughing so I wouldn't break out into laughter and insult Gitta. It tickled me that the females of two alien species could be so alike.

Polaris suddenly swooped in from nowhere. She flared to a stop in front of us. Both Gitta and I sat up with a startled cry. "Werewolves are coming, Cody. Get away! Fast!" With that, Polaris threw herself aloft again. She screamed at Gitta to climb into and stay in her cage lest she be killed. I thought that an excellent idea. I pushed Gitta into her cage even as I reached around and swung the cover closed and locked it. I then ran for my car. I had no way to get back into the Rat's Nest. My only hope was to get my car, lock myself inside, and drive back to Blowing Rock at a high speed. It was a footrace for the ages. I was actually winning until just before I flung myself to a stop at the driver's door while fumbling for my keys. Three big shaggy Werewolves suddenly stepped out from hiding behind the car. They threw themselves at me, bearing me down to the ground, the slobber from their distended jaws pooling on my neck and shoulder. These were not Pale Weres. I had nothing to fear from their excess saliva except the basics of bad hygiene, but I figured I had plenty to fear from the Pale Were that stepped out behind those three.

Flattened as I was, held spread-eagled to the ground by the sheer weight of the three Weres, I waited as the Pale Were came to stand over me and give me the once-over, twice. It must have seen what it wanted because it simply asked, "You are the one they call the Archer?" I said nothing. "Of course you are," it murmured as it looked inside my car and saw my jacket and cap. "Take him," the Pale Were demanded, "but first a small gift for him." They stood me up, and the Pale Were hit me so hard that my world suddenly went dark.

I awoke some time later, gagged and tied loosely to a fence board. The Pale Were that had hit me was standing in front of me again. "How do you feel, Archer?" it said as it gently lifted my head up. When I mumbled I'd lived through worse, it eyed me. It raised an eyebrow and said, "Perhaps, but we're not done yet." Then it hit me again in the stomach, and everything I'd eaten since the day before came out. As I raised my head to insult the Were, it hit me with a branch. Once again it was lights out until I awoke sometime after with a splitting headache and blood congealing down the side of my head where my scalp had been split open.

"How do you feel now, Archer?" asked the Pale Were that once again stood in front of me. I was so groggy I could only manage an unintelligible answer, at which point the Were hit me again. This time I remembered little but the fall back into semiconsciousness. I remember my back being beaten not once but multiple times. Sometime later, I came to again only to find myself suspended from a Spruce tree and wrapped tightly in vines. I was dangling inches above the ground by the cave entrance.

I was alone. I immediately started wiggling, trying to force apart the vines that bound me but having no real success at first. I finally managed to loosen my vines to a very small degree, but now I could breathe easier. I had some circulation, but that was looking like a pretty vain victory. I couldn't focus well, and the ground under me was spotted in red. Some splotches were pretty big. Then time had no meaning until Gitta's call interrupted my quasi-delirium.

DAY TWO 7:30 A.M.

I awoke, curled over on my side in a hospital bed. I couldn't hear any helicopter, but I did hear familiar voices around me. I was starting to recognize the nurses and doctors in Hickory's hospital trauma unit. That scared me. There are lots of folks in this world I'd like to know better. Getting to know the ones who put you back together again after a concussion, a beating, casual dismemberment, a poison gas attack, or some other such fate means you might be in the wrong line of work.

In fact, one of the older nurses saw me stir, came over, and looked down at me and said, "You again? Did it ever occur to you that you might be in the wrong line of work?" I peered up at her. I wondered if I had the strength to throw a pillow at her. I didn't, so I dozed off again. Pain medication is a wonderful sleep aid when you're chaperoned in a hospital. It can be deadly otherwise. I decided I liked hospital chaperones—to a point.

Cap'n T and Pee Wee showed up at 1500 hours to check me out. They were there to drive me back up to the Rat's Nest and then on to Banner Elk. The doctor suggested I wait a day or two before driving myself to make sure all my medications had worn off. Cap'n T decided to take no chances. Hence Pee Wee was along to drive my car from the Rat's Nest to Lees-McRae. He would catch a ride back home with Cap'n T.

We talked all the way back to the Rat's Nest. We were trying to understand the Weres' recent focus on me and this last raid. The targeting was so uncharacteristic of the Weres. We suspected but didn't know it then that the Weres had, in fact, adopted a new and deliberate strategy to hold us at bay. Targeting the leaders of the Rat's Nest was only the first step. But now that we felt at least that part of their strategy had changed, we could try to prepare for it.

General Kim would notify the appropriate school and police authorities that I would now be carrying a concealed .357 Magnum pistol at all times as part of a federal task force. They would gripe and bluster, but presidential direction would be given, if necessary. All the other members of the Rat's Nest would also be armed. Taking concealed-carry courses and obtaining proper permits would be our number-one priority starting immediately. Captain Cosic and Dusty would make all the arrangements. General Kim's goal was to have every person in his command armed and dangerous before seven days had passed. We did it in five.

I left the hospital wearing a number of bandages. My back had been wrapped so it was difficult for me to stand fully erect, at least without hurting so much that I wanted another pill. So I adopted a hunch-over that seemed to work. I went with that. The doctor expected the bandages to last about a week. The stitches would fall out on their own when ready. I was to take no baths until they did. I could take quick showers.

I was also to lay off any wild dancing for the foreseeable future. I had to promise to follow the doctor's directions before he would sign my release. It seemed like good counsel, so I agreed. I found myself having great empathy for old men whose bodies were failing them. I hadn't a clue about how old women fared. I suspected better than old men.

Michael was in our dorm room when Pee Wee escorted me in. He immediately dropped his slide rule and math book as he pushed his desk chair back to stand and help me to my bed. He wasn't much help at all since Pee Wee was there. Still, I was grateful for his willingness to lend a hand. He went to some trouble to make the moment easier. Pee Wee stayed only long enough to make sure I was okay. Satisfied, he went out to rejoin Cap'n T. Michael was all over me with questions as Pee Wee disappeared down the hallway.

"You were missing for two days, Cody. What happened to you, and where have you been?" Michael asked. "Everyone's been worried sick. Sunstar and Pee Wee have told me virtually nothing. All I know is that you were called away on a classified weather operation, and Sunstar said you might have had an accident. Now you're back with bandages and an escort. Just what happened to you?"

"I wasn't called away on some weather project, Michael. I was abducted by Werewolves just after you all left to go into Blowing Rock for soft drinks. I remember being knocked out at least three times the first day, literally hung up to dry, and beaten in some cave somewhere until Gitta and Pee Wee came to rescue me. I truly thought I was dead or at least about to be.

"All I know is that my head hurts, my back looks like it was a practice target for charging rhinos, and my ribs and sternum are badly bruised. It hurts to stand up, it hurts to breathe, it hurts to wear a shirt. Other than that, I had a swell time but with whom or where I haven't the foggiest idea. I just need to lie down and sleep a bit. If anyone asks, I was setting an anemometer on a steep ridge, and a wind gust blew me off. This is the result. Next time I'll wear a rope."

I knew Michael was frustrated but not as much as I was. I'd lost two days of my life and almost lost my life. I wanted answers, too, but knew I didn't have them. Someone did. Tomorrow morning I was going to camp on Cap'n T's desk until I had something more than nightmare memories. I told Michael I'd let him know just as soon as I knew anything, and I also thanked him for covering for me. I was starting to make some new friends on our small campus. Our student body was so small that it took very little time before most folks knew someone wasn't there.

Michael had told all our new friends and acquaintances that I was paying for my college on a scholarship from the Air Force. That meant most of my spare time was spent with their small detachment in Blowing Rock. I was earning my keep studying weather patterns over much of the central East Coast highlands. It was a three-year project and involved frequent travel.

At about 8:30 p.m., I drifted off to sleep and slept through the night. Michael awakened me the next morning. After eating a bowl of cereal in the cafeteria, I took my car keys and headed for the Rat's Nest. I had no classes at Lees-McRae until late afternoon. I wanted to make sure I cornered Cap'n T early. As slowly as he talked, it might be 4:00 p.m. before he finished covering all that happened on my first night away. The drive to Blowing Rock was spectacular as usual. Few places on earth are as consistently beautiful as the North Carolina mountains in all their seasons. As I pulled into the Chapel's parking lot, I noticed that the Major's car was already there. That cheered me up immensely. I hurried into the Rat's Nest. If anyone could pull out a story from Cap'n T, the Major could. I wanted to be there to see it. Heck, I wanted to be there if only to learn what happened to two days of my life and how and where they found me.

DAY FOUR 9:00 A.M.

Dusty was sitting at her desk when I hobbled in. A small plate holding two cupcakes sat by her nameplate. An envelope with my name in bold letters was propped up against them. She smiled and stood up to come around and put her hand on my shoulder as she looked closely at me. She then gave me a brief hug and a hearty "welcome back" before returning to her seat. Who needs out-of-this-world cupcakes when you can get any kind of hug from Dusty? My spirits soared immediately. The Major came out of her office to see what the commotion was about.

"Cody!" she exclaimed. "I didn't expect you until later. Bring those cupcakes we've been eyeing for the last half hour and come into my office. Cap'n T, Pee Wee, and Sergeant Saddler were just about to fill in the blanks for me. I imagine you'd like to hear this, too, since it was all about you." She stepped aside, guided me into her office, and closed the door. I acknowledged the others and took the chair farthest from her desk. This wasn't my show; it was hers. I just sat quietly and munched in happiness as Cap'n T brought us all up to speed.

Dusty had been the first one the night of my abduction to notice something had gone wrong. Polaris had landed on the hood of her car at a stop sign, beating her wings against the windshield. Sunstar, Michael, and Dusty took a couple of minutes but quickly figured out I must be in some sort of trouble.

Dusty hastily spun her car around as Polaris led the way back to the Rat's Nest. Polaris flew at about 10 feet off the ground the entire way. She easily outpaced the car but had to slow down several times to wait for Dusty to catch up. They all came back into the parking lot to find my car all alone. Several fairly deep scratches on one side weren't there before. "Weres!" was everyone's first thought. Well, technically not Sunstar's. Hers was Uge-wan-si, which, of course, was the same thing.

Dusty asked everyone to fan out and call my name and then regroup at Gitta's cage. After several minutes of repeated calls, all three came to Gitta's cage. They found it torn open on one side. Gitta was missing. At that point, Dusty unlocked the building and called the Major.

The Major wouldn't say what was occupying her time in Florida but agreed to dispatch Cap'n T immediately back to the Rat's Nest. He would coordinate the search for Cody and Gitta once there. In the interim, Dusty would alert Sergeant Saddler and Pee Wee. They would start an area search of the premises and nearby cemetery that same evening. They would conduct an expanded search the next day. Michael would remain at Lees-McRae in case Cody showed up there. Dusty was to arm herself immediately. Everyone engaged in the search would carry arms with them until further notice. Sunstar and Michael were to be given a ride back to Banner Elk as soon as practical, preferably that same evening.

Nothing much else happened until Cap'n T showed up late the next afternoon. Polaris had flown away the night before as soon as Dusty's car pulled in beside Cody's car. Presumably, Polaris was off to search for Cody and the suspected party that likely took or killed him. As it turned out, Polaris was the key to unlocking the mystery of Cody's disappearance. She had returned twice for only a fleeting stopover. Not finding Pee Wee, Dusty, or Sunstar, she flew off again almost immediately. Pee Wee was gone. He had established the direction in which the party of Weres left the Rat's Nest grounds. He had found Gitta's tracks as well.

Whether she was on her own or a captive of the Weres was somewhat unclear. The path of her prints indicated she was in charge of her actions. The Weres were not necessarily forcing her route. That, at least, was some good news.

Cap'n T arrived by helicopter arranged by Clarion who had been alerted by a call from General Kim. He was standing by to offer whatever other support the Colonel or Captain felt would be necessary once Cap'n T had completed an initial on-site assessment. The Captain dispatched Pee Wee and Sergeant Saddler at once to start following Gitta's trail. They were carrying only water, personal weapons, and a radio for communication with the helicopter.

Cap'n T told them he would wait with one other soldier, Airman Ken Cropper. They would follow in the helicopter as soon as Polaris was sighted on another of her return-to-home visits. The helicopter was loaded with medical supplies as well as several types of weapons and munitions. It then just sat tight, its occupants watching the clock for the time and the skies for Polaris. Dusty and half the Rat's Nest outfit sat on the Chapel steps or in the grassy areas around the Chapel scanning the skies for Polaris.

One of the Airmen from the Motor Pool was the first to spot her. With a yell, he ran to a grassy area between the Chapel and the grounded helicopter. He pointed to the sky and hollered over and over, "Here she comes, guys! Here she comes!" Dusty ran out to join him. She held up her arm wrapped in a towel for Polaris to land.

Polaris easily spotted Dusty and came hurtling down out of the sky only to pull up sharply and gently land on Dusty's forearm. Dusty immediately held up several beef strips for Polaris. When Polaris had torn those apart and gulped them down, Dusty pointed to Cap'n T and the helicopter and made a flying motion with her other arm. She then pointed back in the direction Polaris had come from and said, "Cody! Cody!"

With a sudden leap, Polaris regained the air and swiftly climbed to several hundred feet. She circled slowly until she saw the helicopter lift off and come her way. Then she turned north and began to accelerate as she rapidly disappeared into the distance. The helicopter with Cap'n T and Airman Cropper was in close pursuit. Flying at 300 feet, they were able to contact Pee Wee and Sergeant Saddler. They were already three or so miles from the Rat's Nest. They were following the tracks of Gitta and the Weres.

A quick landing and pickup was arranged. In minutes all four men were strapped in and hanging out the helicopter's open doors, keeping an eye on Polaris as she flew in a north-northeast direction. After 20 minutes, they watched Polaris suddenly begin a series of descending spirals over the Mt. Jefferson State Park area. They dropped altitude with her, eventually landing close by.

Cap'n T and Pee Wee were out of the helicopter, immediately leaving Sergeant Saddler and Airman Cropper as guards. They told them to play it by ear and come running if and when a fight started but otherwise to stay in the area and act as a beacon aircraft to call and guide reinforcements in, if necessary. Cap'n T and Pee Wee ran to Polaris. To their surprise, they were met by Gitta as well.

She had apparently tracked the Weres. She was about to go into a nearby cave in pursuit of Cody when she heard the distant and distinct chop-chop-chop of a helicopter. Knowing what they were from a previous experience, she felt they would be carrying soldiers to help her find and free Cody, and hence her sudden appearance at Polaris's side. The entire group waited the night at a safe distance from the cave opening. At dawn, they came after me.

Gitta led the two men to the cave opening. With a follow-me look over her shoulder, she forged ahead. When I later questioned her about the rescue, this is what she told me:

> The Werewolves could not attack me through my cage and could not tear it apart. I waited until I was sure they were gone and then ripped the fence open and followed after them. Until I heard the helicopter, I thought I was going to have to come and get you by myself. But when

the two soldiers jumped out, I wasn't sure just how to communicate with them until I saw the Tracker (Pee Wee). They are not gifted like you, Cody, but they always seemed fairly bright. I hoped they would follow me to the cave. To my relief and surprise, they did. They were not as clumsy as you but seemed overly cautious. They didn't seem to be able to smell your trace or hear the Werewolves moving about in the many cave passages around us. As I led them, they were going very slow. I don't know how you humans function without good eyes, ears, and sense of smell.

We had gone down one passage when I first smelled then heard a Pale Were at its end. Weres smell like sour pine needles. I tried to signal to the men by turning and snapping my teeth. Finally, the one you call Pee Wee, the Tracker, seemed to get it. He warned the other man with his arm and motioned me to move on. I scooted ahead and ran a little ways past the Pale Were, surprising it and making it jump. I then spun around to growl and confront it. As it reached for me, the one named Pee Wee slammed into the Were from the rear. Pee Wee clobbered its head with the firestick that your kind carries. The Pale Were dropped to its knees. The second human, Cap'n T, stepped forward, put his firestick to the Were's head, grabbed it at the nape of its neck, jerked it to its feet, and began communicating with it. Pee Wee motioned me to go on. I did. I finally found you and freed you. The rest you know.

We all sat and discussed the remarkable intelligence of Gitta and Polaris. They had played out their parts of the rescue perfectly. It had been a rescue of luck, of course. Realizing that, the Captain requested that I start training Pee Wee, Sergeant Saddler, Sunstar, and Dusty on how to work with both Polaris and Gitta so we'd not have this dilemma again. Gitta and Polaris were too valuable to lose as team members if something happened to me.

The Major approved. We started that afternoon before I returned to Lees-McRae for class. Once I explained it to Polaris and Gitta, they were on board immediately. They were excited to learn how to "talk" to other humans. They found that prospect very interesting and a challenge to everyone's intelligence. Eventually, we developed a repertoire of 16 different sounds and gestures that let the four communicate effectively in a hostile or battle situation. From there, we eventually expanded the team's capabilities until, like the early Native Americans of our continent and their pictographic sign language, our team gained an ability to communicate feelings and commands other than just battle-related communication. But that would come *much* later.

DAY FIVE 7:30 A.M.

I was back in my dorm room again, eyes open, lying in bed and wishing the day would start much later. Where was Joshua when a fellow needed him? He was someone who was apparently able to hold back the sun or at least influence someone who could.

I thought about how much needed to be done for two of my classes even before I thought about my duties at the Rat's Nest. I groaned and rolled out of bed. My yelp awakened Michael. It earned a pillow tossed at my head. I ducked and let out a loud yell because it hurt my back to move suddenly. Michael responded with an expression I would bet his mom and dad didn't even think he knew. I told him I was shocked and I wasn't going to stay and subject myself to such insolence. I grabbed his pillow off the floor and pounded him with it in a highly inefficient and awkward manner, hurting myself even more. He started laughing. I just hobbled away to the dorm showers, stepping gingerly as the pain from my back washed over me.

It was good to be at college among friends like Michael. He was fun, he was smart, and he had a knockout sister named Sunstar who was my friend as well. The older male students on campus didn't seem at all impressed by my presence around her, but most of the younger men did. Even the women thought there must be *something* she saw in me. They would at least give me a second look or not ignore me when I smiled and said hello. It was also good to be a junior.

By 1:30 p.m., my classes for the day behind me, I started up my car and drove to Blowing Rock. The Major had called a senior staff meeting for 2:00 p.m. I was expected to be there. She had some information she wanted to pass along to us. Then she wanted us to brainstorm what we thought it meant. General Kim would listen in by teleconference.

Since the storm-induced failure of the Weres' planned college attack many weeks earlier, we were all getting edgy. We were waiting for the other shoe to drop. We knew the Weres wouldn't back down in their attempt to escalate their centuries-old hate for humans into open confrontation. Nevertheless, we were just as determined to keep a lid on the Weres' very existence, to keep them off balance until we could decisively defeat them.

I took a seat between Sergeant Saddler and Dusty a few minutes before the Major's briefing started. I noted that Cap'n T was missing. I asked Sergeant Saddler where he might be. I was told he was already on his way back to Florida. Sergeant Saddler had dropped him at the airport very early this morning. Whatever was going on down there required a full house of fighting soldiers. I knew now from firsthand experience that Cap'n T was exactly that.

We would miss him, but the teleconference might not run as long as I first thought. Cap'n T was many things, but he was not a fast talker. I thought of him as deliberate in both manner and speech. Others at the Rat's Nest thought of him as a conversational speed bump, but they were mostly Yankees anyway, Lord love 'em all. They usually spoke at 60 miles per hour with gusts up to 120. As an Ohioan with Southern leanings, I figured I was somewhere in the middle. Ours was an eclectic group to be sure. The Major called her meeting to order. She began by polishing off a few administrative items to which all bureaucracies are subject, the military being no exception. She then got right into the meat of the meeting. Werewolves in both Georgia and North Carolina were apparently conducting raids on outlying farms on a sporadic basis. More than 12 such attacks or sightings had been reported in the past five weeks. People and livestock were being killed.

Clarion was working with large chain newspapers and small countywide and town newspapers to try to keep a pulse on both the number of instances and eye witness accounts of the savagery employed during each raid. We were conducting a full-scale media blitz blaming feral dogs or black bears as the culprits for the various attacks. Cattle were killed in most instances. Humans were being killed as well and mutilated in four of the 12 attacks; the rest of the victims had escaped by barricading themselves in homes, barns, or cars.

Between three and seven Weres comprised each raiding party. Each attack occurred in the late afternoon or early evening. The Weres would fade into the deepening twilight or adjoining woods as they concluded their attacks. These attacks were hit, rip, and run on a dedicated scale. They were often miles and days apart. The tactic was perfected almost a century earlier by Native Americans from the Apache tribe. It was a tactic geared to be almost impossible to stop while filling isolated survivors and neighbors with quiet terror.

The Weres were conducting seemingly random, brutal, lightning raids on small outlying farms. Such raids required a military response for which the cavalry of olden time was desperately ill-suited. Our group even today was equally unqualified. But everyone in the old Southwest, Apache as well, had to use water from limited sources. Control the water in those days, and you ultimately controlled the fighting capabilities of your enemy. Today, access to natural resources such as water wasn't the limiting factor. Information was that our government had adopted a policy of covert response to a nameless threat that could not be publicized lest the people erupt and riot in the streets in blind panic. Therefore, we could not openly marshal our full forces to fight an enemy, the Werewolves, that no one could publicly declare even existed.

And we couldn't stop the latest Were raids simply by placing unending patrols in all outlying areas of the mid-Atlantic and Southeast United States. Involving thousands of soldiers over a several state area would ensure that the secret of the Weres would be all but shouted from the rooftops. Nevertheless, we thought we might be able to stop them another way using a variant of an old football maxim.

The game of football is all about posing an impossible mathematical axiom. What happens when a highly skilled and prepared offense, an irresistible force, meets an equally highly skilled and prepared defense, an immovable object? Well, for one thing, sparks fly and the game becomes wildly entertaining if only because that specific happenstance never actually occurs.

In real life, either the offense or defense always prevails because of a failure in (1) human performance, (2) the playing conditions themselves, or (3) the formations and tactics employed. And it was in the latter circumstance that we had perhaps the best chance to defeat this latest battle tactic of the Werewolves—the terror raids. We were about to employ the wrong tactical response. Given our current orders (official silence about Weres) and limited forces (the Rat's Nest plus occasional Special Forces augmentees), we could not stop the raids once in progress unless our forces stumbled onto theirs by sheer luck.

But what if we could defer the raids? What if we could do something that dissuaded the Weres from even launching widely dispersed terror raids? What if we could pose an alternative that induced the Weres to stop their raids altogether, to adopt a defensive rather than an offensive strategy? We would then at least regain the old status quo, a tentative peace in the countryside except for occasional, direct hostile confrontations among the Weres, the Rat's Nest, and their allied forces. When a football running back continually breaks through the line of scrimmage and wreaks havoc on the defense, you stop him by ensuring he doesn't break the line of scrimmage. You adopt a stunning defense (trickery) or a swarming defense (mass force) that allows the defensive players to engage the runner before he evens gets to the line of scrimmage, before he reaches full speed, maybe even before he puts his hands on the football.

But while a football defense is usually relegated to waiting for an offensive attack, it can itself attack, thus taking back the initiative of its sham battle with an opponent. But football must always wait until the offense initiates movement or snaps the ball. In the military, however, no battle is a sham battle since military fights employ deadly force. More importantly, defensive military forces are *not* relegated to waiting for the opponent to "snap the ball" or strike first. Unlike football, a *military* defense can strike first. While this is usually an offensive maneuver, in so doing, the defense itself becomes the irresistible force if only for the moment.

To beat the Weres' current terror raid tactics, we had to keep them home, on edge, afraid to venture out because their forces would either be destroyed while on a raid or because their families, leadership, and base of support would be destroyed while they were away. You stop a Were from going out to attack by making it stay home for fear of the damage that will occur when or if it leaves in the first place.

And it was on that consensus that the Major called the meeting to a close. She asked each of us to ponder ways to strike first, strike fast, and strike decisively enough to disrupt or stop the terror raids. But just before she stood up, she looked around to each of us and asked if any of us had anything to say. No one did until she finally came to me. "Cody," she asked, "anything you want to say?"

"Yes, ma'am," I replied, keenly aware that everyone wanted to break off the meeting. "You know we don't have to actually hit the Weres at their support bases. We only have to pose a credible threat. Somehow they have to believe we know where they are, when they will raid, and that we will move heaven and earth to hurt them, with restraint of course. If we can do that, not only will the raids stop but we can influence them to fight us on our terms. I have an idea how to do that, and I'd like to discuss it with you privately at your convenience."

There was silence in the room as everyone looked at me and then at the Major.

"Be back here at 4:00 p.m., Cody. I'm all ears." With that, the meeting was adjourned.

DAY FIVE 8:00 P.M.

The Major and I talked for about two and a half hours. Sometimes it got pretty intense. In the end, we spent some telephone time with Clarion and General Kim but finished with a common accord that we just might pull off the terror raid deterrence scheme with some luck, timing, and cooperation from our Special Forces friends. We were going after the only Pale Were who had ever introduced itself by name. Only a very senior leader would have that effrontery. If we could steal it, the Weres would have to assume we would then know their plans and weaknesses throughout the mid-Atlantic states. It would be a game-changer *if* we grabbed it. It was, of course, the Were we knew as Abba. And we knew just where it was.

But if we could capture it and also ensure the other Werewolves knew it, they would see themselves in danger of ongoing retaliation (for my kidnapping) and preemptive strikes since Abba would know both their broad battle strategy and hideouts. Moreover, they would know many detailed raid plans and dates. They would have to assume that Abba had talked to us. But Abba was last seen in the rabbit warren of caves where I'd been held captive surrounded by many Werewolves.

The next time we dropped in, they would likely be waiting for us if Abba was even still there. I figured we'd used up our dumb luck in rescuing me. Further encounters would be bloody. It was with that sober thought that I drove back to Banner Elk, doors locked and my newly issued loaded .357 Magnum pistol on the seat beside me. After all, the roads in upstate North Carolina are full of blind curves, and the forests are dark and deep at night.

Michael was up when I arrived back at our room. We chatted a bit as I changed into some baggy shorts and an oversized Beach Boys T-shirt. I'd fanatically followed that group in high school and was still a devoted fan. Their songs were about a place and culture in America that I'd always wanted to experience but never had. Hot or cold, Ohio seemed far distant from the carefree life of West Coast surfers the group sang about, especially the surfer girls with their hot cars and bikinis.

Michael wasn't interested in surfing, however. He turned the conversation around to the problem of the Werewolves. It was a new experience for him. Like many, he had a hard time bringing the myth of werewolves into reality. He questioned me long and closely about the adventures Casey and I had had together. Sometime after 10:00 p.m., my eyes started to droop. They closed for the night soon after Michael brought up Kathy Niwall, his current at-a-distance crush. I guess he found my muffled grunts no helpful response to his many questions. By 10:45 p.m., we had lights out.

I was already off in dreamland with Gitta surfing and hanging ten and Polaris perched on my shoulder, wings aloft, helping steer us as we whooshed down a long, endless wave to the cheers of the many California blondes scattered along the beach. I thought I glimpsed Casey in the crowd of worshipful onlookers, a jealous Paul at her side—or was it Dusty or Sunstar waving in my direction? It didn't matter because coming down the wave after me, jaw jutting forward and claws extended as it rapidly closed the distance between us, was a Pale Were. I remember leaning into my board just before a gargantuan curl kicked us both up and out of the wave into the rolling surf following us, and then everything went dark.

DAY SIX 8:00 A.M.

I woke up with a headache and my sheets and blanket twisted around me at the end of my bed. "I'd say the bed won, Cody," piped Michael. He was already up, showered, and dressed. He tossed my pillow back onto the bed from its temporary perch on his desk chair and told me to hustle. It was early October, and we had a class in 40 minutes. The teacher and students seemed to prefer it when everyone who attended was clean, dressed, and washed. Whether class attendees were fed or not was not a concern as long as the gurgling sounds emanating from their stomachs didn't drown out the professor's lecture.

Thanks to Michael, we were actually in our seats when the class started. Nevertheless, I had a last mouthful of a blueberry muffin that Michael had snatched for me while I was yanking on my clothes. I was trying desperately to swallow it as we slid into our seats. It was all I could do to keep from choking. I was quietly uncomfortable until I could finally get to a water fountain.

The day turned out to be one of those catch-up days everyone needs from time to time. It was the kind that never seems to come around on our own preferred schedule.

But it helped ground me and remind me that there was another world out there that wasn't filled with Werewolves. That world's reality was blissfully ignorant of the Weres and their life-or-death challenges to the human existence. It was a day to appreciate an alternate slice of life as Michael's crush-at-a-distance on Kathy Niwall pointedly reminded me. We were eating lunch at the school's small cafeteria when Kathy and a companion walked in. They were looking for someplace to drop their books while they ordered lunch. Most of the four-person tables were filled. Ours was not. Sunstar had a class today and wasn't eating with us. Michael nudged me when he quickly sized up the situation.

He asked me to go ask the ladies if they cared to sit with us. I told him he could go ask them since I was perfectly content with just his company. He reminded me rather forcefully that I wouldn't be if I didn't do this one favor for him. He actually managed to look menacing as he delivered his demand. I started laughing. I got up to go over to the girls. I was cut off on the way by Cecil Derrick, the one-man wrecking crew and my vote for the FBI's most wanted social outcast.

"Watch yourself, Dugway," he exclaimed as I stumbled over the chair he shoved into my path when he suddenly rose from his seat to walk over to the girls. Everyone looked my way as I just managed to miss falling on my face. But I didn't miss his next remark. "You're that Air Force wannabe who falls off perfectly good ledges, aren't you? Small wonder you can't walk through a dining hall without risking someone's life or limb. Why don't you go play with one of your weather balloons?"

With that he walked over to Kathy Niwall and her friend. With a smile, he escorted them to his table. They looked a bit uncertain at first. It was an awkward moment. They must have decided discretion was the better part of valor for they looked at each other and quickly followed Cecil to his table, pointedly ignoring me. Red-faced, I walked back to our table only to find Michael upset with me for messing up his chance to be with Kathy Niwall. Already mad from Cecil's remark, I told Michael he could stuff it. I gathered up my books and tried to make an error-free exit from the dining hall. I noticed that a lot of people made a big show of pulling in their chairs as I walked past them.

The rest of the day played out about the same. Some days you're the windshield. Some days you're the bug. Today I was the bug.

DAY SEVEN 10:00 A.M.

Gitta, Polaris, Pee Wee, Sunstar, and I had been out hunting for almost three hours. It was time for a short break, and we were near a small stream and a copse of woods that offered plentiful shade and protection. The Major had given specific instructions that Sunstar and Pee Wee were to practice their signaling with Gitta and Polaris during this exercise. I was just there as a referee or facilitator. Tomorrow I would be out with Sergeant Saddler and Dusty—same rules.

This was not a normal flop-down, sprawl-out rest stop. Since my kidnapping, every member of the Rat's Nest treated the woods and meadows as enemy territory. We were learning to always keep our guard up, to be armed and ready. I didn't worry too much about an ambush with Gitta and Polaris nearby, but even they weren't infallible. Whenever possible, it was always good to rely on yourself without having to depend upon others.

Sunstar came over to me, knelt down facing me slightly to one side, and asked how she and Pee Wee were doing. I told her that from my vantage point, things were going well, but it was Polaris's observations that really meant something. Polaris had confided in me that she had gained a lot of confidence in Pee Wee and Sunstar in just this one morning. Each had remembered their signals and cues. They were proving to be surprisingly smarter than Gitta or Polaris had expected.

I passed that on with a grin, and Sunstar's face lit up before she started laughing. When Pee Wee, Gitta, and Polaris looked our way, I let Sunstar repeat my remarks to Pee Wee while I told Gitta. Pee Wee laughed heartily, and Gitta started snorting and rolling over. Polaris merely blinked. She barely nodded her imperial head in Sunstar's direction, preening herself while she patiently waited for Gitta to stop snorting. We were becoming a team. Each member was gaining confidence in the others.

I had often heard Clarion say that with confidence comes allegiance, with allegiance comes commitment, and with commitment comes victory. We all had a chance to test that maxim when distant screams abruptly came to our ears. In seconds, Polaris literally leaped into the sky, rapidly gaining altitude as she swiveled her head back and forth trying to locate the source or direction of the screams. When we saw her suddenly veer west and accelerate in that direction, all of us were immediately on our feet and running even before anyone issued a command.

Pee Wee led out as a scout should with Gitta keeping pace beside and slightly ahead of him. Sunstar drew an arrow and clasped it in her left hand against her bow's grip or riser as she broke into the runner's lope we were all trained in. I rolled into the last position as rear guard, an arrow also in my hand against my horn bow's riser. My job was to check behind us from time to time as we ran to make sure nothing untoward was overtaking us. It was difficult to do. Look too long, and you were likely to fall flat on your face by getting entangled in ground cover or tripping over a stump, or any one of a number of other obstacles, including holes in the earth.

We had been running for several minutes when Pee Wee suddenly raised his hand and came to a dead stop, fist clenched. He knelt down immediately to reduce his silhouette. Gitta flattened herself beside him before she disappeared into the underbrush ahead. Sunstar crept up behind him and took a position to his right rear facing back toward the direction we'd come. I took the same position to his left and faced away in that direction. We formed a small triangle. We could talk quietly among ourselves and not be heard a few meters away, but we were also positioned so nothing could sneak up on us without being seen by someone.

I immediately called out to Polaris. I learned that two children were firmly wedged beneath two ragged boulders trying desperately to avoid the reach of two very large Weres. The one Were had a slash of white hair running from the back of its right shoulder across and down its back onto its left leg or haunch. The other had a crippled left arm as if it had suffered a compound fracture that had never been correctly reset. Both were kneeling, trying to reach under a ledge formed by the slightly upended portion of the smaller boulder where the children had retreated. Gitta confirmed what Polaris was seeing from the air when I called out to her. I quickly relayed what was happening to Pee Wee and Sunstar. I invited them to kill the Weres using the signals they had practiced together. I told Pee Wee he was in charge.

Pee Wee's first command was to Polaris. He asked her to verify that the two Weres were the only ones in the fight. Polaris circled in two widening loops and called back that she'd sighted four more Weres about 80 yards away. A man and woman were in a tree surrounded by four Weres that were silently watching them as the couple struggled to hold on to some very slender branches while crying out repeatedly for their children.

Pee Wee called Polaris in. He signaled that she was to watch for reinforcements while he and Sunstar killed the two Weres. He then turned to me and told me to take out the four Weres without being seen, if at all possible. He told me I could take Gitta with me but to go now. He and Sunstar would kill the two Weres trying for the children.

I left silently as he was whispering to Sunstar. I called out to Gitta as I circled the boulder site at some distance lest I be seen or heard by the two Weres taunting the children. Gitta met me in the woods halfway between the two sites. I told her what I wanted her to do. She promptly told me I was nuts but that she would do as I asked. She immediately disappeared into the foliage as she made her way toward the right two of the four Weres.

I gave her 30 seconds and snuck forward on an oblique until I could finally clearly see the left two of the four Weres. I cried out as if I were wounded and dying. The Weres immediately left the tree and ran my way. Upon my silent command, Gitta erupted out of the underbrush. She landed on the back of one of the right two Weres. She dug her talons into its sides and bit into its neck where the shoulder joined it. The Were screeched out its pain. It began thrashing and rolling about trying to dislodge Gitta. But Gitta was fastened on as a permanent fixture. Soon the Were began drowning in its own blood.

My two Weres and the second of the two Weres on the right turned to come to the wounded Were's aid just as soon as the Were's first screams shattered the day's air. I put my first arrow through the neck of the Were on the far left end. My second arrow went through the heart of the other Were that turned when its companion Were fell gagging behind him. Two down. Two kills. I then broke and ran for Gitta as she fought to kill her frantic opponent. I arrived with a clear sight line just as the remaining Were prepared to launch itself at Gitta. My first arrow took it through the shoulder, spinning it around so my second arrow took its throat out.

Gitta rode her dying prey to the ground. She practically decapitated it before scampering back to me as we faded back into the forest. We did not want to be seen by the two adults crying in the treetop. I asked Gitta to please retrieve my arrows before the Weres could gather their wits and come down and find them. I turned and ran for the boulders hiding the children.

I needn't have hurried. Sunstar had put two broadhead hunting arrows through the Were with the crippled arm. Pee Wee had signaled Polaris to dive on the white-slashed Were. Pee Wee hit the Were from the rear about the same time Polaris hit its head from the front. With the Were momentarily stunned, Pee Wee drove his 10-inch SOG (Special Operations Group) knife almost entirely into the last Were's back, slicing into its heart as he pushed the blade through. He watched the Were crumple with a whimper and bleed out before him.

Sunstar and I gathered the children. I asked Pee Wee to cover us as Sunstar and I each took a child's hand and began the walk back to their parents. Polaris, having regained her eyes-in-the-sky sentry position, told me that we were clear insofar as she could see. The children were badly frightened. I told them they had done all the right things and had been very brave. I also told them that this area was not a good area for camping or playing by themselves away from their parents because of many wild bears here who came to steal food. The bears would get angry if they could not find any. Some bears were known to chase and attack smaller animals like children because they smelled like food.

The children were somber. They were acting very brave when we brought them to the tree to which their parents were clinging. Seeing us with the children brought shrieks of joy from their mother. She almost fell out of the tree in her haste to throw her arms around her children. Their father jumped down, slightly twisting his ankle as he hit and rolled in his enthusiasm to join his wife. But no pain could really stop him as he rushed to kneel, sobbing, with his arms around all three of his family members as they snuggled in close.

In their panic and desperation, the parents had not focused on any of the four Weres. It was not hard to convince them that wild black bears enraged by stinging wasps had attacked them. I told them that Sunstar and I were part of the Lees-McRae archery team. We had been out practicing forest shots when we heard the children. We scared off the bears that had cornered them. Sunstar then mentioned that we'd gotten lost and were so happy to find some other humans. She said we would be very grateful if they could give us a ride to or even guide us to the nearest highway.

Within half an hour, we were in their car and on the way to Blowing Rock where they were staying on the first leg of their short vacation. I told Gitta, Polaris, and Pee Wee that we would meet them back at the Rat's Nest and to stay out of sight. My ploy was successful. By the time we reached the Blowing Rock Inn, the couple and their children believed they had been fortunate to escape nothing more than an odd encounter with angry black bears.

Sunstar reminded the parents that this was the bear's last hunting season before winter. The bears had to feed to make sure they would live through their coming hibernation. Therefore, bear tempers were short and appetites deep, two good reasons to enter North Carolina forests only at the state or federal camping sites. They were true believers when Sunstar and I finished with them. Our subsequent parting was convivial but brief.

Dusty met us at the inn after we called her. She gave us a ride back to the Rat's Nest. She was all ears and jealous of Sunstar's hunting experience that day. She expressed her hope that Sunstar and Sergeant Saddler would have an even better experience tomorrow. I just groaned to myself. I silently pleaded with any heavenly being that might be listening on his or her prayer line to please disregard. Dusty knew not what she asked.

DAY EIGHT 7:30 A.M.

Dusty and Sergeant Saddler were waiting for me as I drove up to the Rat's Nest. They were eager to jump into our hunt, especially after attending our debriefing the day before. I was wary of their enthusiasm. I was surprised at Sergeant Saddler. Dusty I could understand. She hadn't done this before. She probably didn't realize just how close to death these encounters really could be. But Sergeant Saddler's enthusiasm bugged me somewhat. Still, I let it pass, checked everyone's gear, and let Gitta set the pace with Polaris flying cover as we moved out.

This time I wanted to explore the area along the old trail where I had fought the Weres alone before being rescued by Captain Yamata. After yesterday's encounter, I had a nagging feeling that the Weres were on the move again. That trail would be the logical Were route to take if they were going to raid anywhere north of us. Dusty wasn't an archer, so she was carrying a .410-gauge pistol-grip shotgun with buckshot. She also carried a .357 holstered Magnum pistol identical to mine. Sergeant Saddler was carrying one of the .223-caliber AR-15 assault rifles Clarion had found for our group. I carried my horn bow, wakizashi blade, and pistol. I left my javelin back in my dorm room in my rush to get to the Rat's Nest so early this morning. I didn't really think I'd need it. I was wrong.

Dusty took the lead as the signal caller for the first three hours out. Sergeant Saddler took over that responsibility for the trek home. The forests had been quiet on our way to the narrow pass between the two steeply sloping hills. Nothing appeared to be out of the ordinary. The birds had not stopped chattering the entire time, and Polaris had seen nothing from altitude. Even Gitta seemed calm. I called a break at 11:30 a.m. I seated myself to take off my shoe and pull out a small rock that had been bothering me for the last several miles. Gitta and Polaris were given sentry duty. Sergeant Saddler came over to speak with me as Dusty hollered that she was going with Gitta to take a bathroom break.

That meant one of us had to go with her and stand guard a proper distance away while she remained out of our direct line of sight. Sergeant Saddler would have merited a guard as well if he had to go. It wasn't about protocol or decency. It was about life or death in now hostile country. Sergeant Saddler agreed to go after her. I took the time to commune with Polaris who was circling overhead about 500 feet above us. Polaris was a gifted bird but still a bird. She had a limited vocabulary and a limited understanding of life beneath her, but she was a quick learner and logical thinker. Her experiences with me and humans in general had exposed her to literally another universe.

She had deep feelings about her sense of right and wrong, yet she was eminently practical. She was also loyal, perhaps her greatest single attribute. I was thrilled every time I was in her presence. She truly was a princess among princesses, as keen and brave a fighter as any soldier would want as a companion. She just wasn't very talkative. Her eyes missed nothing, and her beak rarely let any of it out again, but man, oh man, could she fly! Watching her aerial acrobatics made me wish I was a hawk so I could follow after her as she carved up the sky above us.

It had been a good day. I was thankful we were on the way back. After yesterday, I wanted no part of any more excitement.

DAY EIGHT 11:45 A.M.

The first boom of Dusty's shotgun brought me to my feet. The second found me at a full run toward the echoing sound. I screamed for Polaris to give me a sight reading if she could. As I ran, I heard Sergeant Saddler's AR-15 start chattering. Whatever they were encountering was serious—deadly serious. That was abundantly clear, but no one was shouting yet, and that was good. Shouting meant a lot of things, few of which were good. But people generally called the good kind cheering.

As I ran toward the sound of Saddler's gun, I noticed I was gaining elevation. I entered into a new growth forest. Most of the trees were little more than saplings. There were some 50- or 60-footers scattered in among the new trees. Scrambling up a small rise, I stopped at the top and surveyed the scene below me. It looked for a moment as if Dusty and Sergeant Saddler had stirred up an ant's nest of Werewolves. Twelve or

13 shaggy, dark creatures spilled out of a hidden cave to form some semblance of a semicircle around the two at a distance. That was good. Had a Pale Were been present, the Weres would have already been in a tight circle, probably feasting on one or both of our group. Several Weres were down, some permanently. A couple were moving or crawling away very slowly.

"Dusty, Sergeant, come up here to me now," I called, and then pulled a screamer and an exploding arrow from my quiver. We'd seen what those arrows could do. I wasted no time letting a screamer go almost straight up. The frequency pitch of that arrow made everyone's teeth grate, especially the Weres'. Screamers served to help folks find you (provided they were looking) and to momentarily disrupt or impede thoughtful action by anybody.

In a battle, things happen so fast that there isn't always time or opportunity to think. Your body will take over if you let it, and you'll operate through muscle memory. That's how I was able to nock and fire the exploding arrow at the tightest concentration of Weres below me while most of the others were still cringing at the shriek of the screamer arrow. That last arrow took out four Weres and crippled two more. The remainder scattered like quail. I immediately brightened up, thinking we were already on the way home. Then the wheels came off our so-called wagon.

Two Pale Weres stepped out from a rocky outcropping beyond the milling pack. They stood side by side taking in the scene. One took charge immediately and, with the other, started rounding up the big Shaggy Weres and herding them into some semblance of order. Now I knew we were in trouble. One Pale Were is dangerous. Two or more are danger and destruction multiplied by a bunch. This was not a good turn of events.

I sent Sergeant Saddler and Dusty running back the way I had come. I asked them to find a place to stand off the Weres. We'd passed a broken circle of rocks about a quarter mile back, and that would have to be the place. They left at a good pace that would cover a mile in six minutes. That gave me about two minutes before the race would be on between me and the Shaggy Weres now starting my way. I wanted to make the most of it. I pulled three broadhead arrows from my quiver and held them with my left hand against the horn bow's riser. I checked my quiver and found I had three more broadheads, one screamer, and two exploding arrows left. I also had six shots in my .357 S&W revolver and six cartridges loose in my pocket. Twelve shots in all.

No pressure.

My first thought was to take out the bigger Shaggies first, the ones that looked big enough to rip me apart with one hand behind their backs. But on second glance, that appeared to be all of them. I settled on a different strategy. I would take out the two Pale Weres whose presence had endangered my life exponentially. That might create enough confusion so I could make it to the rocks where Dusty and the Sergeant would soon be holed up. Failing that, I would just turn and run like—well, whatever. It was a

40-yard shot to the Pale Were in charge but well within the horn bow's range. I nocked a broadhead, aimed, and loosed the arrow as I let my breath out. It ran true until a wind gust pushed it slightly sideways. It took the Pale Were in charge through the upper chest rather than its throat. It dropped immediately, but I could see it struggle back to a sitting position, still giving orders. It was time to move on. I turned and fled, nocking one of the two remaining broadheads. I held it against the horn bow's grip with one finger as I ran. I was calling out to Gitta between breaths, hoping she was able to hear me.

I told her where I was going and to leave and try to bring help back if she could. I told her I would also send Polaris and to save herself if going back for all of us risked her life. I did not know if I'd gotten through. It felt like I'd been in contact, but it was like talking to a person who is unconscious. You knew the body hears the voice but don't know if the entity inside the body comprehends. It was a bad and uncomfortable feeling. I loved Gitta and was angry at anything or anyone who brought her grief. I did get through to Polaris. She wheeled immediately midflight at my message and sped for the Rat's Nest.

As fast as I ran, the Weres were faster. I was about halfway to the broken circle of rocks when I heard the first howls coming up quickly behind me. I was in fairly open ground. I had no tall trees for a vertical escape and no breastworks of wood or stone to hide behind. Being caught in the open by any opponent is bad news. One can fight in 180 degrees, maybe even 220 degrees, but virtually no one can fight when you're completely surrounded with no cover. Some part of your back is always vulnerable.

It was a ticklish moment. I had only one option. Since I couldn't outrun the Weres already close to overtaking me, I stopped, spun in a turn, and started running straight at the pursuing group. I fired my two arrows as we closed and then jerked out my revolver as we neared impact. Two Weres went down before they suddenly split apart. I passed right through the middle of their close formation, firing as I ran through. My bullets were hollow points, molded to expand upon impact. At three to six feet away as I fled, the impact was harsh. Screams and grunts punctuated the afternoon air. Three more victims fell on either side of me until I was all the way through the pack.

The turnaround tactic had succeeded beyond my wildest hope. I was alive! I was out of breath, but I was alive—so far. I spun around to start back in my original direction. There before me was the younger Pale Were coming my way fast. I skidded to a stop in front of it. Without delay, I blew its right kneecap away before it could launch itself at me. It screamed terribly. The bullet's impact knocked it off its feet and onto its side. It slid almost to my feet.

The remaining three or four Shaggy Weres suddenly seemed to be moving at a molasses pace. Everything appeared to be in slow motion. My mind was moving faster than the moment. I now had fewer bullets than Weres left, so I threw myself upon the injured Pale Were. I poked the barrel of my gun against its ear. I told it to make its

Shaggies back off or it would never give another command. Two of the big Shaggies were reaching for me when the Pale Were suddenly cried out. It told them to back away. Fortunately, they did just that. For the first time in a number of minutes, I tried to smile again. It came out more like a grimace.

Everything that had been suspended suddenly crashed back into real time. I was gasping for breath. The Pale Were was struggling to move in its pain. The Weres that had caught up to us had arranged themselves in a rough circle. They were but steps away. I had run out of ideas. Kill the Pale Were, and I was instant mincemeat. Hang on to the Pale Were's neck too long while trying to hold my gun against its head, and it would eventually jerk away. Then their feast would begin, and I would be just gnawed bones, blood, and a memory. It wasn't shaping up to be my best day by far.

I heard a rasping voice behind me. A shudder ran through my trembling frame.

"We know you, Archer. This time when we take you, there will be no escape," said the voice behind me. "If you kill him, we will take you. If we wait long enough, you will tire or your attention will waver, and we will take you. Because he is wounded, he cannot stand with you to walk away. If you try to move him you will fail, and we will take you. We have patience you have never seen before.

"We can wait years, even tens of years. We can wait forever. You cannot. You will soon be thirsty or hungry, or you will get tired. Then we will take you. Make yourself comfortable, Archer. You are going nowhere except with us. We will soon take you, and you will last a long time with us, Archer. You will know pain as you have never known it before, and then we will turn what is left of you. So be comfortable." Then he laughed or gave the Were equivalent.

Sadly, the voice behind me was right. Without outside help, I was doomed. I could not use the horn bow. They would be on me before I could fit an arrow and loose it, and I had only a few left. I did have two bullets left in my handgun. The best use of them was to hold the younger Pale Were hostage and save the last bullet for myself, the most unsavory of all options left.

I had nothing left but talk, so I did that.

"You may be right, whoever you are, but touch me or come near me, and this Were is dead. If you value its life, stay back. If you want to talk to me, come around so I can see you."

There was silence for a moment and then a slow step to my back right followed by another and another until the older Pale Were crept into my vision, head drooping and my arrow sticking out of its upper chest, several rivulets of blood snaking down its torso. Its paw was pressing against the impact area, staunching the flow of blood into mere seepage. I could see that the Were was in pain, yet its eyes were as quick and dangerous as a predator's could be. They never stopped sizing me up and looking for an opening.

"Are you the one called Abba?" I asked.

"I am not. I am Abba's cousin. My name is Roddre. These creatures you have slaughtered are of my band. Their deaths are at your feet. Since they are more than you, we will have to kill you several times before I turn you. Then we will kill you for real by setting you against your own kind. You will be unable to resist, but you will know exactly what you are doing. That will make our revenge all the sweeter."

The Were sat down and just looked at me, its eyes never tiring, always seeking an opening as it sat there bleeding, the drool from its jaws ever threatening just by its presence. One bite and my life was over, at least my life as I knew it. And all the while, the wounded young Pale Were I held in my grasp kept shifting and moving and making it difficult for me to relax. Then the thirst and the heat began to play on me.

DAY EIGHT 3:15 P.M.

It had been almost three hours since the older Pale Were had ended its conversation with me. It had taken its place with its band watching me. The sweat on my forehead continually flowed into and burned my eyes. My mouth was as dry as a bone. The young Pale Were had slipped into unconsciousness. It was restless nonetheless. Its jerks and moans were a constant irritation. I was getting distracted and tired. I had heard nothing from Gitta and didn't even know if she was alive. Nor had Dusty or Sergeant Saddler reappeared. I hoped they were still at the broken circle of rocks or had slipped away, but wherever they were, they weren't here with me. My circumstances were deteriorating as I became weaker and tired.

Still the Weres waited, unblinking, eyes glued to me, saying nothing and making no overt movement. They were like predatory statues. From a distance, one would think they were carved from stone. Up close like I was, I could feel their breath and smell their hatred amid their stink. Then I got an idea. Good, bad, indifferent, I didn't care. It was the first potentially useful thought I'd had in three hours. I savored it like a Fudgesicle, not wanting to expose it too fast lest it simply melt away from my consciousness. It was prompted by a silent call from Gitta. She, Dusty, and Sergeant Saddler were on a nearby ridge covering me.

It was my move. I made the most of it.

The senior Pale Were could count as well as I could. He knew the gun I carried could fire six shots and that I had already fired four. But he didn't recognize the exploding arrows for what they were, not at first sight anyway. So with my handgun in my right hand pointed at the younger Pale Were's head, I stood up slowly and reached into my quiver with my left hand. Each of the Weres stood up with me as if pulled by the same puppeteer's string. Their eyes took on a more deadly gleam. They seemed to lean in slightly toward me as they waited for my next move.

I felt like a surfer in a pool of sharks with about as much chance to escape.

I pulled out the two exploding arrows and slowly sank back down on my haunches. The Weres surrounding me did the same, mirroring my every move. Placing the two exploding arrows between my knees, I quickly shifted my .357 Magnum to my left hand and pointed it at the unconscious Pale Were. I then took one exploding arrow in my right hand and jabbed it into the thigh of the unconscious Pale Were. The Weres surrounding me jumped to their feet at that. The unconscious Were stirred and groaned. I tucked the second exploding arrow between my teeth and pulled the wakizashi blade from its scabbard. Carefully, I reached up and took the second exploding arrow from between my teeth. I tossed it out about 10 yards away.

The Weres were puzzled by all this, uneasy. They edged closer to me. It was clear they didn't trust me. Apparently, some were leaning in to make an early attack, come what may. The senior Pale Were was almost as nervous as the rest. He questioned every move I made with his unforgiving eyes.

I spoke out. "The arrow I have jammed into this Were's leg is an exploding arrow. It will blow him and all of us up if I should shoot it or hit it. The arrow I tossed away is also an exploding arrow. They are the same. I will now show you what power is in the arrow and why you all are in jeopardy."

The senior Pale Were snorted at this. It asked me what I was doing. I told it I was just trying to prove a point, that out of consideration for it and its kind, I was going to give them a chance to get away from me. He translated that to the Shaggy Weres to their surprise and angry reaction. The senior Pale Were just smiled a grim smile. It said that this foolishness would end now, that their patience with me had worn thin. I hollered, "Fire on the arrow, Sergeant!" I dropped to the ground using the unconscious Were to shield me from the blast.

Sergeant Saddler immediately triggered off a short burst from his AR-15. The result was a spectacular explosion that killed or crippled three of the Shaggy Weres and blew the senior Pale Were off its feet. The last Shaggy Were behind me had also been blown backward off its feet. I shot it before it could get up. I had one bullet left. I aimed my handgun at the senior Pale Were's head.

"You will not kill me," it said. I replied that it was right, so I shot its knee off. Crippled, screaming, trying to claw or bite me, its frenzied attempts to wound or tear into me were futile and draining. It had calmed down into a heaving, grunting pile of coiled death by the time Sergeant Saddler and Dusty reached me.

Gitta was with them. My first move was to bend and put my arms around her while she, in turn, licked me and repeatedly bumped me with her head. A quick hug from the Sergeant and Dusty was next. I suggested we all rearm ourselves while we had a moment to get ready for the next wave. A few moments later, our weapons reloaded, I directed that we tie up and drag the two Pale Weres with us back to the half-circle rock formation where Dusty and the Sergeant had forted up.

Forty minutes later, fully loaded and ready for battle while firmly ensconced in the rock circle, I took a deep drink of water. I felt a load of tension just melt away. Sooner or later the Rat's Next would show up. We had two Pale Weres the Major could use, thanks in large measure to Dusty, the Sergeant, and happenstance. Things were finally looking up.

DAY NINE 5:00 A.M.

The Rat's Nest crew arrived just before dawn. We had been left alone during the night, and it was reassuring to find our own people here with us at dawn's early light. We had drawn straws for watch duty during the night. Sergeant Saddler drew the first watch. The next choice was mine, so I took the last watch, the pre-dawn hours when all enemies traditionally attack.

Dusty had been assigned the mid-watch. Gitta later confided in me that she had done an almost better job than Sergeant Saddler. Our assignments completed, we fed and watered the two Pale Weres, put them into hobble irons, and alternatively dragged and half carried them along as we started home, two men per Werewolf. They were heavy.

Fortunately, our Jeep called Little Beaver met us shortly after we started. We loaded the two Pale Weres onto the Jeep, tied them down, and sent Dusty back with them. The rest of us just plodded along home, relieved that all of us, Gitta and Polaris included, had made it back safely. That we had managed to send back two Pale Weres was icing on the cake.

We were back at the Rat's Nest by 1:00 p.m. The Major mandated an immediate debriefing. I was out of there and on the way back to my dorm room by 3:15 p.m. After a shower and hearty dinner at the cafeteria, I was snuggled safely back in my bed at just after 10:00 p.m. I dreamed of the demands of this outing and some of the weaknesses it had exposed. Several times after awakening in the night, I made notes on my dreams and then went back to sleep. For me, at least, this was one way my body and brain solved problems.

Classes for the next several days were a welcome respite from the two adventures we'd had. I saw Sunstar once. We had a chance to talk for several minutes while Michael was with us, but not much more was said until I got back to the Rat's Nest at week's end. The Major, Dusty, and I had a late lunch together in her office. She gave me the rest of the story.

It turned out that Dusty was the real hero of our adventure. After she had finished her ablution, she stood up to walk back to where she'd left me. She spotted movement from within the thin woods and underbrush surrounding her. That impelled her to drop to her knee and peer through the foliage to get a clearer look at the creature or creatures causing the brush to move. When she spotted two Weres coming her way, she didn't panic. She simply called out to Sergeant Saddler to cover her because she was coming on the run. When she hollered, the Weres spotted her and started for her immediately. She let them get within 10 to 15 feet and then leveled them both with her shotgun, the two blasts I'd heard. Having clearly located her, Sergeant Saddler was able to lay down covering fire as Dusty scrambled back to him. Then they heard my call.

They ran to the rock circle as I'd instructed, reaching there in about the time I'd thought it would take. Dusty provided cover with her shotgun while Sergeant Saddler started moving stones and shoring up lanes of fire. He feared the pack of Weres would be along, hot on my tail. When I didn't show up, Dusty, the faster of the two, crept back about 50 yards toward my last position. She spotted me as I turned and ran back through the pursuing pack. When she saw me take the younger Were prisoner and the Pale Were sat down in the circle surrounding me, she crept back to Sergeant Saddler and filled him in on everything she'd seen.

Sergeant Saddler knew better than to attempt an immediate rescue with no intelligence on where any more Weres might be, so they simply waited at the rock circle with both on guard alert. After two hours, Gitta showed up, spotted them in the circle, and ambled on in. Dusty gave her a hug and promptly instructed her to perform a perimeter reconnaissance. Dusty used the signal set we'd worked on so diligently. Once Gitta returned, indicating no other Weres were in the area, both Dusty and the Sergeant moved out of the rock circle. Surreptitiously, they made their way to an overlook point where they could support me. Gitta's signal to me was the spark that fanned the ensuing flame. It probably saved me. It certainly was the beacon of hope that lifted my spirits. It also prompted me to effect my escape from the group of Weres that had encircled me.

I told Dusty in front of the Major that she "had sand" that she would do to "ride the river with." Dusty had proved herself as a true warrior, one who could be trusted in combat, one who would not lose her head, and one who would stay the course. But then, no one expected less. When it came to surprises, the Rat's Nest personnel were singularly lacking. They were solid, they were prepared, and they had a wicked sense of gutsy adventure with some unique personalities to match.

I quietly reveled in my good fortune to have ever linked up with an outfit like this one. I think the Major and Dusty each shared that sentiment as well. They just never trumpeted it from the rooftops. Nor did I.

The Weres were taken by Moby to Ft. Bragg where they were flown by Special Operations aviation personnel to Chagrin Falls and the containment facility. Dr. Fitzgerald had already asked that Sunstar be allowed to come back for a few days and that I accompany her. While at the containment facility, I would do the truth-or-lie oversight while Clarion and perhaps some other senior personnel would question the two new Pale Weres.

I would be leaving on Monday. Sunstar was already there. Clarion expected we would both return by the end of the coming week, a four- to five-day stay. Sunstar was staying with Casey's folks again. My folks would meet me at the airport Monday at noon when my flight arrived. Sergeant Saddler would drive me down to Charlotte early Monday morning.

The senior staff at Lees-McRae were read in only in part on the "matter of national security" need for us to be away. They were fully cooperative. I could tell Michael where we were but no one else. This was another of those "Air Force classified balloon retrievals," if anyone asked. I did not want the reputation as Balloon Boy that Cecil Derrick seemed to want to hang on me, but it was a small price to pay for the freedom to engage in our covert fight against the Weres.

I spent the remainder of the afternoon with Gitta and Polaris. I brought them up to speed on where I was going and when I would return. They were getting used to my absence, but since we introduced the signals, they felt very comfortable communicating with Pee Wee or Dusty while I was away. They knew that someone competent was looking out for them. They trusted Pee Wee and now Dusty with their lives. Both had proved themselves as warriors because they had seen them in action. They also knew I trusted them.

Sunstar was a case by herself. She was just, well, different. They trusted her for some very different reasons, but the result was the same. We were all on the same team. The concept of a team to animals whose DNA fairly shouted "individual effort" was very hard to grasp. Nevertheless, they actually liked it, not for its novelty but because of the protection the concept afforded. They were no longer so vulnerable. That was mind-boggling to a falcon and a wolverine, normally the epitome of rugged individualism.

DAY SEVENTEEN 12:20 P.M.

My folks met me at the Columbus airport with all but bells on. Dad was excited to see me. Mom was overjoyed. There's something about moms and young men and women trying to grow up. It seems those are opposing forces, but somehow we all live with and even through it. The drive back to Chagrin Falls was anticlimactic. Between my parents trying to catch me up on what was going on locally and my trying to catch them up on what was happening in my part of the world, I wasn't sure if anyone made any sense of anything said on the trip home.

But we had a lot of fun. Lots of laughter punctuated the conversations no matter how goofy they probably were. I'd missed my folks and let them know it. I couldn't have given them a better gift than that. I also wanted to see Clarion as soon as possible. Dad let me borrow his truck when we got home. The drive to the Polo Club seemed shorter than I remembered. Being in far places alters our sense of distance when we return to familiar haunts.

I went in through the stable tack room entrance. I eventually found Clarion on the way back to his office. I passed the Were cages on my way into the facility. I noted that both Pale Weres from our recent skirmish were there, each heavily bandaged and apparently sedated. Clarion confirmed the sedation. He noted that both Weres were in a withdrawal stage in preparation for the interrogation session scheduled for tomorrow. Clarion wanted them at full alert. He asked me how my mind was doing and about my health in general. I assured him I would be ready.

Reading a Were's mind can lead to an excruciating headache, but not knowing its intentions can also lead to an excruciating death. There are choices, and there are choices. I chose the former. Still, it was not a task that was in any way easy or pleasant. One always had to wade through so much hatred and conflict just to get to the nuggets of thought that made the exercise valuable.

Clarion and I visited for about 30 minutes. I filled him in on our two recent scrapes, praising both Sunstar and Dusty for their courage and initiative. Clarion was especially keen on hearing about how the women performed. His feelings were that women were perfectly capable of participating in the quick-in-quick-out fighting demands of Special Ops but might be overly challenged by historical ground operations where soldiers had to carry heavy packs in all kinds of terrain and weather and still muster the energy to fight, and all that for weeks at a time without a sustained break. I told him he had my vote. Neither of the women, including Casey, wanted for anything in the courage and initiative departments.

I left Clarion to his calls and paperwork. I went to look for Dr. Fitzgerald and Sunstar. Clarion hinted that Dr. Fitzgerald, using some of the herbs recommended by Sunstar, may have made progress in diluting or even partially negating the effects of the Pale Were serum. They weren't at any specific test stage yet, but the research may have found an avenue to pursue that held more than promise. That really cheered me up. Sunstar was so concerned all the time that she would be able to contribute. It now appeared that she had. I was anxious to find her and talk to her. To my disappointment, however, one of the doctor's lab assistants said I had just missed the team, that everyone had already gone home.

I had planned to give Sunstar a ride back but figured I'd just catch her back at the Allegros' house when I got home. Once again, I figured wrong. I didn't see Sunstar again until the next afternoon when the first and second interrogation sessions were over. She'd shown up to comfort me and made sure I drank one of her potions. It turned out she had gone directly from the containment facility to eat out with several from Dr. Fitzgerald's group. Apparently, they all had a grand time. She hadn't made it home yet by 11:30 p.m. when I fell fast asleep. A fellow can only peer out from behind his window curtain for so long before he has to cash it in.

And no, I wasn't jealous. I was just "concerned." Sometimes the bright lights of our small town might seem overly dazzling to a young woman from upstate North Carolina. She might get confused and discount certain behaviors by earnest men who did not share her sense of grace and modesty. As her trusted friend, I felt obligated to protect her, if even from herself. That's what friends do, especially concerned friends. But it was some time before I realized that the only person I really had to worry about wasn't her. It was me.

DAY EIGHTEEN 11:45 A.M.

I rose early and went for a slow jog while Mom fixed breakfast. Running was still new to me even though I had improved almost exponentially over the past few months. I didn't want to overdo anything, but the urge to use my legs again in an exercise long denied me was overwhelming, so I gave in. I did hold my pace back, however. I just enjoyed the yards and flowers of Chagrin Falls. Jogging is a great way to study a place. You get to see the town come alive around you. It actually felt different now that I was in college away from here. This was my town, and yet it really wasn't. Not anymore. It was becoming my hometown.

At 7:30 a.m. and once home, I called over to the Allegros to see if Sunstar needed a ride to the containment facility. Mrs. Allegro answered, spoke an aside to Sunstar, and came back on the phone to tell me no, that Sunstar would be going in later this morning. She would try to catch me during the day. Somehow I was irritated at that exchange but didn't understand why. I finished my breakfast and drove Dad's truck back to the Polo Club grounds.

Clarion was waiting for me in his office when I arrived. Two gentlemen I had never seen before were also waiting there. He introduced me to them but did not introduce them to me. Okay, I thought to myself. I knew this routine. These men were from an unknown US agency that would be left unknown. Their names might as well be Mr. X and Mr. Y. They seemed pleasant enough. They apparently had some history of dealing with the Weres.

We spent about an hour or so going over all the questions that would be asked, anticipating answers and trying to model the right follow-on questions if a wrench or two were thrown our way. I learned that a good interrogation was *always* scripted. There were always answers to be found, and each was ranked in order of importance. The interrogator had to know the objectives cold, yet still be able to shift his or her technique or manner as the circumstances demanded in moving the subject closer and closer to the truth.

A good interrogator did not extract information like a dentist pulls a tooth. No, a good interrogator brings the subject to a point where he or she voluntarily gives up the answer and feels relieved in so doing. Clarion was a good interrogator on humans, but nobody really knew the psychology of Werewolves, especially the Pale Weres.

The two gentlemen spent some appreciable amount of time after we completed the review questioning me about my powers and abilities. Their premise was that if a car accident could expose such a talent in me, then it was probably latent in all humans, certainly more than a few. I was not insulted by their discussion or their appreciation of me as a fortuitous accident. That I could talk with animals (better yet, communicate in various fashions) was what it was. I had a talent I did not seek with responsibilities I did not want, yet my job was to harness and use that talent for my country and the betterment of those around me. I had no ego involved as a Gatekeeper. Instead, I was profoundly humbled.

At just before noon, Clarion said it was time to start. I had refused an earlier request he'd made to see if I wanted a sandwich or something for lunch. The headaches that came from mental contact with a Were could be severe enough to induce vomiting if I had food in my stomach. So I always made sure I didn't, provided I knew a session was coming up. Clarion led us down the hallways to the cages. The two Weres awkwardly crouched as they backed away from the front bars of their cages. Each was hobbled somewhat by the bandages and splints that attended their destroyed knees.Clarion stepped to the line drawn parallel to the front of the cage. His two companions stepped up with him. One stepped slightly over the line. He was too close. In less time than it takes to tell him, the senior Pale Were who had suffered my arrow in its chest was at the bars. It raked its extended claws down the front of the man's suit coat. The man yelped and fell backward, backpedaling as fast as he could but not fast enough to keep his balance or his dignity. He landed squarely on his bottom, the left front of his suit coat in ribbons down his chest. Both Werewolves howled at that, and the senior Pale Were crept back to the back of its cage.

"Very amusing, Roddre," Clarion said. "What's your encore? Scratching the rear end of your partner, or just trying to reach your own? Obviously you're no longer quick enough to meet your own expectations, much less ours. With that knee, you may just be better off here. Bad things happen when a Were starts to lose its touch, right?"

Clarion dropped his clipboard on purpose and deliberately bent over to pick it up. He was well within the senior Were's arm range, but try as it might, the senior Were simply could not reach Clarion's stooped form even though it sprang at Clarion with a great roar. The Were was furious. Clarion never missed a beat, gradually leaning back as he straightened up so his head was just behind the line as he stood up. The claws of the furious Were dangled as close as a Band-Aid to Clarion's head, yet the Were could not bend down enough to reach Clarion.

The Were's heavily bandaged knee did not permit it the full range of motion it sought. Clarion was smart enough to take advantage of that. Taunted by Clarion's close but untouchable presence, the senior Were threw itself into a screaming and howling fit that lasted some minutes. After almost 10 minutes of howls, groans, yips, and yells, the senior Were started to flag. That's when Clarion asked his first question, and I engaged the Pale Were's mind. It was like jumping into a mental cauldron of filth.

DAY EIGHTEEN 2:45 P.M.

On a scale of zero to minus 10, this day was a minus 10. I sat against one of the walls in the hallway with my head cradled in my arms. I tried to breathe slowly and let the pain of my headache lessen. This had been a longer and tougher interrogation than I'd expected. I wanted nothing but to be left alone. There were soft footsteps and then a comforting "Cody? It's me. Sunstar. Please drink this. I think it will help you and remove some of that pain." A small glass was placed in my right hand while her left hand touched and softly caressed the back of my head.

I drank the drink in two gulps and held the glass up so she could take it away. Almost immediately after I heard her soft voice singing words I did not understand, the pain in my head started to rapidly lessen. In minutes, I was almost dizzy. My head felt as if it were bouncing on bubbles and cotton balls in a soft breeze. I felt like living again. I opened my eyes and turned to speak to Sunstar. "Whatever was in that glass or in your words, I want more. Thank you! Your song was so lovely, so peaceful. Now all I want to do is curl up and sleep." Before she could say anything, I felt Clarion's hand take mine and pull me to my feet. "Not so fast there, Cody. Naps come later. We've got work to do," and he bundled me down the hallway to his office where the two unnamed gentlemen were sitting, the one trying to straighten out his torn and shredded suit coat as we walked in.

The younger Pale Were had been of little help. It simply did not know very much pertinent to our needs. We needed to gain intelligence on force placement, the Weres' supply routes, and the decision process within the Were ranks that set targets and allocated groups to conduct raids. The Were didn't lie during the entire interrogation. It didn't have to. It just didn't know much of worth to us. Its main use from this point forward would be as a reluctant participant in Dr. Fitzgerald's research on neutralizing Pale Were venom. We spent less than 20 minutes on him. The senior Pale Were was an entirely different matter.

Roddre, the senior Pale Were, was worth a great deal more. Not only was Roddre a cousin to the Were we had designated Abba, enemy number one, but it was also a senior member of the Weres' southeast area governing coalition. The walk through its mind on which Clarion had sent me was like walking through a booby-trapped cesspool of loathing and hatred. We'd had three 20-minute sessions with it. By the end of the third,

I was almost useless. Not only had my headache intensified, it had lengthened. It had become very difficult to focus on anything.

But while the last 20 minutes had been the most strenuous session I had yet experienced, Clarion felt it was also the most valuable. With the script before me, the four of us reviewed once again the questions Clarion had asked and the answers the Were had given. I would be able to add the things the Were really thought, not just what it had said to Clarion. The scripts would then be vastly different. The two gentlemen were anxious to have Clarion ask more questions in yet another session, but Clarion nixed that even before I could. "Maybe in a day or two, but no more today," Clarion said. "Cody's sanity is more important than this Were's answers. Cody can only stand so much. Nope. No more sessions with the Were today. Let's digest what we have and make the most of it."

The next two hours became a detailed review of each question, the answer the Were gave orally, and what the Were actually thought before or as it gave an answer. My presence had not been explained to the Weres. It would never be explained. We wanted them to think I was there perhaps as a military observer, someone who had a personal interest since I had wounded both of them, but we wanted to give them no indication of what my real presence and purpose was.

The fact that I could walk through their minds didn't raise any flags, either. I could be in their minds without their knowledge. I just had to be in close physical proximity. They had to be in some state that they let their guard down. Anger was one way to remove the natural barrier against my mind probes. We'd not tried drugs yet, and I had no hope that they would voluntarily submit to such a mind probe. So our methodology was set.

About all we needed was me, an interrogator, a strong cage, a ticked-off Werewolf, and a line on the floor that said stand behind this barrier or die. The shredded coat front of the unnamed gent who sat with us was mute testimony to the veracity of that maxim. Clarion released me when we'd had a chance to add or correct any of the answers scrutinized during our review. I shook each gentleman's hand, saluted Clarion, and took my leave. Clarion stood and thanked me again as I turned to go. He asked to see me in the morning at about 9:30 there in his office. I told him I'd be on time. I then left to look for Sunstar.

She wasn't hard to find. All I had to do was walk toward Dr. Fitzgerald's office and look for a gathering of young men like me. Sure enough, I found Sunstar sitting at a lab table with at least four young scientists hovering nearby as she studied several slides through one of the largest microscopes I'd ever seen. She was wearing a lab coat. She somehow made even that shapeless fabric look good. She saw me when she looked up. She immediately exclaimed, "Cody!" and then hopped off her stool, stepped over to me, and threw her arms about me in a close hug. That one act alone raised the collective testosterone level of the room by at least 300 percent.

I was fired up and alert. All the men were also. I wanted to strut and feel important. I was sure they wanted nothing more than to beat me to death with that heavy microscope. Either way, the room was in a testosterone fog. Sunstar was insistent. "How are you feeling, and how's your headache?" she wanted to know. I assured her I was fine, did not want to take her from her work, and would see her later if she needed a ride home.

She smiled. She said that would be great, that she had hoped for that. She asked if I'd had a chance to visit with Dr. Fitzgerald yet, that he'd been waiting to see me. I told her I'd go find him. I would see her later. That got me a peck on the cheek and a death glare from the other four men. *Eat your heart out, guys*, I thought to myself as I floated out of the room. *Eat your little scientific hearts out!* I ambled on down a few doors to the doctor's office. I found him with a piece of worn chalk in his hand, staring at a blackboard festooned in symbols and equations that had no meaning to me. He was deep in thought. He must have heard me for he turned as I stepped in. With a sudden smile on his face, he came around his desk and promptly crushed my hand in his enthusiastic grip. "Cody, it's good to see you. How did the interrogation go? I heard Clarion and his guests were pleased but that it was apparently hard on you. Sunstar said she gave you some palliative care but that recovering from one of those mind trips you're wont to take comes at a dear price. Do you need to sit down? Can I get you something?"

I appreciated his earnestness. I told him a glass of water would be nice. He picked up his phone, mumbled something into the receiver, and hung up as he sat down across from me. We chatted several minutes before one of his lab assistants brought in two glasses of water along with a Coca-Cola bottle and a glass of ice. "Just in case you decide to let it all hang out." He smiled. Then he promptly drank down the contents of his own glass he had filled with Coke.

We visited for almost 30 minutes before we were interrupted by his secretary. She reminded him of a conference call he was scheduled to participate in. I liked the doctor. He was enthusiastic, he was dedicated, and he was funny. He was also very good at what he did if the opinion of Clarion or Dr. Abernathy, the head of the facility, meant anything. Leaving his office I went back to the lab and found Sunstar. I waited until she had made and filed her notes and then walked out with her and drove her home. We had a good visit along the way. We were walking back up the driveway, she to go to the Allegros' house and me to go into mine, when she stopped and asked me if she could ask me a personal question. I must have stuttered because she was quick to correct herself. "Oh, not about you, Cody. It's about me." I looked at her peculiarly and said of course she could ask me anything. That's what friends are for. She looked down and shyly looked up and asked, "Do you think it's improper for a twenty-year-old to go out with a man eight years older?"

I was stunned. I was a little hurt, too, that it wasn't me who was the 28-year-old man in her equation, but having thought that, I also thought of Casey and realized that

Sunstar was somehow different to me. She truly was a dear and trusted friend to be sure. She might not always be that, but that's what she was now. My present duty was to protect and serve her.

"Of course it's all right," I said. "But who's the lucky man?" I was almost on my tiptoes waiting for her response. She softly said, "It's Dr. Fitzgerald. Ediface, or Ed as I call him."

"Ediface? His name is Ediface? What kind of a name is Ediface? No wonder he got his doctorate. I'd kill myself if I had to go around life known as 'Ediface.'"

"Cody, stop it! Just answer my question. Do you think it's all right?" There were almost tears in her eyes. I could see that dear Ediface really meant something to her. I gently held her by her elbows and told her of course it was all right, that she had my blessing. If needed, I would drive them around in my dad's truck so they could hold hands. She threw her arms around me, gave me a huge hug, took my face in her hands, and planted a kiss right smack in the middle of my forehead. She hugged me again and skipped off to the Allegros.

I stood in the driveway by myself for a long time looking at the side stoop and the doorway into the Allegros' home after she'd gone in. I had been on that stoop myself not so very long ago with a girl in my arms who kindled every bit as much if not more excitement in me than the thought of Ediface did for Sunstar.

After a while, I shook my head, smiled to myself, and turned down the back sidewalk to our kitchen door. It had been a long day. Melancholy was a feeling with which I was becoming all too familiar. *I'm too young for this*, I said to myself. I wished Gitta and Polaris were here. At least they were two females who thought I hung the moon, but probably only until I missed a feeding. My shoulders drooped a little. Gatekeepers are seldom alone, but they can always feel lonely.

DAY NINETEEN 9:00 A.M.

I was early for my appointment with Clarion. I decided to stop in and see Dr. Abernathy if she was free. She was. After a brief wait while she finished a call, she invited me into her office. She gave me a solid handshake, a firm hug, and a gentle smile. "Welcome back, Cody! You've been off having some amazing adventures from what I hear. It's good you're still in one piece. I understand you're going to see Clarion in a few minutes, so why not quickly fill me in on what you're up to now."

I gave her a brief recap of the last two months. I dwelt especially on my outing with Sunstar and Sergeant Saddler. When I told her that Sunstar had killed her own Were with a bow and arrow, Dr. Abernathy's face lit up like a Christmas tree. "That's wonderful! We gals have to stick together. Dr. Fitzgerald won't brag on her, but I will. I can't wait for our senior department staff meeting this afternoon. Boy, are some of those stuck-up young fellows going to be surprised. They're just wannabes. Sunstar is the real thing.

"Had I not killed a Were, I'm not sure the men here would respect me and work for me. There is a clear prejudice against women in certain scientific fields, but when a gal can pull her own weight, then everything changes. Her future's virtually assured. And while we're on that point, Cody, what would you think if we offered her a scholarship to get her doctorate at Ohio State? She has an uncanny knack for chemistry, is fully read in on what we're doing here, has been well accepted by our in-house community, and has come up with some potion-based approaches that may solve some of the riddles that have us all stumped.

"I know she's still an undergraduate, but I'm thinking of an accelerated trial program that would give her a doctorate in two, possibly three years. You know a doctorate is given for original research. Well, hers is about as original to us as you can get. What do you think? Would she buy in?"

I sat there speechless for a few moments, absolutely thrilled at Sunstar's prospects if she chose to take advantage of them. It was a matter of taking a few breaths before I could actually speak. "I—I—I can't imagine her *not* accepting such an offer, Dr. Abernathy. Why, that's the most wonderful news I've heard in months. Just to consider her for that is an enormous compliment, one she should gratefully and graciously accept, but she will first probably turn you down."

Before Dr. Abernathy could erupt, I put my hand on her arm, leaned forward, and said, "So don't you let her. Not for a minute. She will be embarrassed at the attention and will feel she probably has to be near her family, but that's not true. It's just that she's never been very far from her home or the woods. We'll find her a family at Ohio State who can watch out for her and look after her. Besides, she's already got two families here. The Allegros and mine."

Dr. Abernathy's smile was once again all across her face.

"Oh," I said. "Tell her this is for her people, too. The Cherokee are very tribal-conscious. They see any benefit to one as a possible benefit to all. This will bring prestige and honor to her home and her lodge, and her parents will be bursting with pride. If you do this, Dr. Abernathy, you will gain a first-class scientist who will use her talents all her life for the benefit of others. She doesn't understand the concept of selfishness as it applies to so many scholars. She does understand service; she is no quitter. She will take all you can give her and more. She will be an inspiration for other women who are contemplating a career in science. You mark my words. This is a wonderful chance for her. Thank you for even thinking of it. And I promise to keep silent until you ask her."

I stood up to go down to Clarion's office, only this time, I initiated the hug for Dr. Abernathy. I'm sure she was used to hugs but probably never one that lifted her off her feet and twirled her around twice before she was set down. The smile on her face when I left was huge, even as she adjusted her hair and straightened her jacket.

The smile on my face was bigger.

I knocked on Clarion's door promptly at 9:30 a.m. I was on a big high, and he spotted that as I walked in. "You look like the cat that ate the canary," he said with a smile. "What's up?"

I told him about my visit with Dr. Abernathy, that she had high regard for Sunstar and her contributions. He agreed. He said that several of the staff had been talking last week and wanted to do something for some of the young folks coming along that would help both them and Clarion's group, especially those in the Growler I Were program. I had already been offered a good deal, he said (I nodded my head yes and smiled), and both Dusty and Sergeant Saddler had been offered deals suitable for their talents and interests. Sunstar was one that everyone agreed needed to be on whatever list they would create. It was his (Clarion's) understanding that Dr. Abernathy had come up with a program tailored for her. He wasn't entirely familiar with the program, but he believed it involved a chance for an early doctorate. Nevertheless, he said, that would all come out in time and I should keep a lid on what he'd just said for the time being. What he wanted to talk about were the findings he and the two gentlemen had come up with as a result of the interrogation. I thanked him for his confidence as I leaned forward. He carefully put down and opened a folder on his desk.

We talked until noon.

He felt my ability and the willingness to use my talent just might be the key that would unlock our quest for victory over the Weres. At the least, we now had learned enough to thwart their tactic of random but ruthless raids. The senior Were, Roddre, was very knowledgeable about tactics and communications in the northern Southern state areas, the Carolinas and Georgia in particular. We would be able to hurt the Weres there to start with.

What Roddre was also sure about was the Weres' belief in the sanctity and secrecy of their mountain cave hideaways and the bases they raided from and in which they kept their colonies. Thanks to my readings and some geologic maps from the three affected states and the federal government, Clarion believed he'd been able to pinpoint at least 70 percent of their larger strongholds. His plan was to attack them in the winter. He would drive the Weres into the cold and follow them to other strongholds, attacking them there and sealing off the caves where they sought refuge along with the homes of those host Weres that took in each group.

He would also leave behind traps and demolitions enough to wound and weary those who came after each raid seeking shelter. He wanted to make them give up real estate they'd known for years for more exposed, less easily defended gathering places— places that put the odds for victory in any attack clearly in our favor. It was not General

Sherman's scorched-earth policy practiced during the American War of Northern Aggression, or the Civil War as it was more popularly known. It was more like General Crook's subsequent campaigns against the Native Americans of the great Southwest. It was a "find them, kill them, drive out the survivors, and keep everyone on the move as our wave of military destruction crept from stronghold to stronghold." With limited resources, we could not hit everywhere at once and win, but we could start somewhere and build upon each victory. We had the firepower, and we had the smarts. What we needed was luck and time.

I liked it. It was a strategy that would wear down and decimate the Weres. It might even eventually render them, in time, just an interesting if not frightening footnote in history. I looked at Clarion for a good minute or so without saying anything. I then asked a question that floored him. "What happens if they decide to join with us, to surrender and become our allies rather than our foes? Could or would we ever trust them? Is there a way for peaceful coexistence? Because if there's not, then all we're doing is pushing this problem further down the line for the next generation to solve. What do we do if the Weres become peaceful and ask to join our society?"

Clarion looked at me twice as long as I'd studied him and then cleared his throat. "You, my good friend, are a pain in the keister, but since you posed the question, you provide the answer."

He politely threw me out of his office, claiming he had much work to do for the senior staff meeting later that afternoon. He shook my hand and walked me to the door. There he turned me to face him directly. "I'm serious, Cody. No one knows as much about these creatures as you do. If anyone can figure out an answer that makes sense, you can, not some politician or scientist in an office or lab. You have dirt under your fingernails and blood on your hands, both figuratively and literally. Go find us an answer, and I'll sell it. In the meantime, gear up because these next months through next spring break will task all of us. We are going to war, and we are going to be relentless. Just keep your grades up and forget about any fairer sex except Gitta and Polaris. You do not know how incredibly important you are to our success and to your country. I hope you never find out. Now go on!"

DAY NINETEEN 12:40 P.M.

I was eating by myself in the lunchroom when Dr. Fitzgerald asked if he could join me. He promptly put his tray down and sat down across from me before I could answer. There were just the two of us. The lunchroom was relatively uncrowded. "What's up, Doc?" I asked as I watched him cringe. "Seriously, Dr. Fitzgerald," I said with a grin, "is everything okay, or are you just seeking an outside shoulder to cry on?

Mine's always here for you, you know, but the price is gab. Now, what's up? A certain young lady friend of mine told me something in confidence, and I'd like your take on her interests. I ask, of course, knowing that I can take you out as easily as a Were, probably easier, and that I will if I think you are any threat to anyone I know or love."

He held my glance for a long count and said, "I know you can and would, so let's talk, if that's all right with you. I'm here as a friend, hopefully one with a future."

We did talk, for well over one hour. When we parted, we parted friends. I knew his interest in Sunstar was serious and above board. I knew he liked her a lot, that he wanted the chance to see if it would develop into a more serious relationship leading to marriage. He felt they had common intellect, common interests, common spirituality, and common goals to serve others through science. He was also totally enamored with her. He thought she was the hottest thing since Marilyn Monroe and felt like he was on cloud nine when she was anywhere near.

I stopped him at the 45-minute point. I told him I was on a sugar-free diet and couldn't take much more of his praise for Sunstar. We both laughed at that. We then spent some time visiting about our own respective ambitions and goals. The Doc was a truly nice guy. His heart was in the right place. I did not know how fast his desired relationship with Sunstar would develop, but I knew he would be honest. I also knew that each of them had deep feelings and respect for the other. I certainly was not going to get in their way. I was serious about bringing down wrath on the Doc if he was ever out of line with Sunstar. As men, we were perfectly clear on that. There would be pain. As a quasi-converted North Carolinian, the idea of mountain blood feuds was starting to make sense to me.

The Doc went on back to his lab. I had the remainder of the afternoon virtually free. I was on call with Clarion, but from his schedule, he would have little time between calls and meetings for me. Nor were there were any emergencies on the horizon. So I went back to the Were cages. I wanted to see if Roddre would talk to me. I wanted to broach the idea of peace between the species just to see what his reaction might be. I wasn't prepared for what he might say, but without a mind link, I knew I couldn't trust him. I'd seen how he lied to Clarion.

Both Roddre and his junior assistant were alert and watchful as I approached their cages. I stood well back of the line in front of Roddre's cage. I addressed the Were in normal tones. "Roddre, I come to speak to you as one warrior to another. I am alone. I am here for me, not those I serve. Will you speak with me?" There was a long pause, and both Weres exchanged glances. Roddre hobbled closer to the bars and, placing his paws on them for support, asked why I had come. His words were curt and terse. I told him I was there for my own interests, that though he was a captive, I honored him and hoped he would honor me as a fellow warrior. I was neither insulting nor dismissive of the Were's response. I asked again if we could speak one-on-one as warriors for our respective species. There was some chatter between Roddre and his companion before he finally turned back to me. He said he would speak to me as an equal for now, but he had questions, too.

"Why am I being held here?" Roddre asked. "Am I some sort of display item your species needs to quell their fears about the People? We are the Elders. You humans are the younger species. Why do you mock the laws of nature and seek to rule us when we were given the right of rule so many millennia past? Have you lost your history? Are you so ignorant that your kind does not understand the setting of things as they once were and are yet to be? You, Archer, have proved to be a worthy opponent. Your friends are also dangerous to us, but your species is weak and selfish. You have no right to rule. You are as children with weapons we cannot understand and cannot make, but you have no wisdom in their use. You often turn on one another like dogs with disease. The People never fight among their own. That is for cowards and those with greedy minds. Such ones we kill would pollute the bloodline of the People. But you are a human, meant by nature to serve us. You are susceptible to the bite. That alone is proof enough of our right to rule and bring order. Yet your kind in fear drives us out from the good places of earth. You condemn us to the shadow-holds. And now you hold me in this cage and ask to speak with me. So, Archer, speak!"

"You do kill among your kind," I replied. The Browns and Grays would agree if there were any left alive. But I am curious why there has been no attempt at peace between our species at least in our recorded history. We are taught to fear your kind from the age of our first understanding. We fear you even more than we fear your lesser cousins, the wolves and dogs. They, at least, can coexist if raised with humans from birth, but that is not so with you. Yet you are an intelligent species. You are our equal in many ways. Perhaps you are even ahead of us in others. But look, you are there and I am here. Tell me, Roddre, has there ever been peace made—or even attempted—between our kinds?"

"You humans are so ignorant," snorted Roddre. "Your history extends to last week. Your future is next week. Do you really not know of the Second Pledge given at the Great Falls of Niagara in the place you now call New York? More than 3,000 years ago, our races met there. You humans pledged peace between our species. Our people would go and stay to the west of the Great River that divides this land. We gave up our rule for this bargain. Your people would stay to the east side. For 2,000 years, this pledge was honored by your people, and then the Years of Trouble came. You humans bred like rabbits. Your people grew faster than the land could support them. You began to encroach on our land. First came the hunters. We tolerated them because there was game enough for all. Then came those who would settle here and there, bothering no one and of occasional help to both peoples. Then, emboldened came the families with their endless children to eat our game and settle on our land. Then came war between our people, and no one stopped it. Finally, the slaughter became so fierce that it was not about land for families—it was about hate.

449

"At that time, there was a great battle. Thousands and thousands of warriors, women, and children on both sides were slaughtered in the land between the two rivers. So many died by weapon or disease or scarcity of food that a council was held. Once again, representatives from the People and you humans met at the Great Falls. Once again, your race pledged to abide by the former rules. That was the Second Pledge. Then again, you betrayed your word and robbed us of our great homes in the West. So now we are a hunted race. Now we live in your shadows. Now we are here in your land because you came and took ours. We have no future with your race. You lie. You are greedy. You despoil the land and war with yourself. Your people are as reeds before a strong wind, easily influenced but hard to root out because you multiply so fast. Our only defense is to turn humans so by sheer numbers we can preserve the root of the People. It is not us who are the aggressors; it is you. And so we fight. We are the Elders. You are chaff in the wind, but so many! So many!"

The senior Were turned and shuffled back to the back of his cage. He lay down facing the wall, turning his back to me. When I turned to look at the junior Were, he did the same. They shut me out after humiliating me, but I felt no anger. I had the glimmerings of understanding with much to think about. I did not see any answers except war between us for now, but my heart hurt nonetheless. I walked away. I headed back to Clarion's office to see if there was anything else he needed from me before I headed home. Thankfully, there wasn't.

DAY NINETEEN 4:00 P.M.

I went home early but left my phone number with the confinement facility dispatcher in the event I needed to be located and called back. Mom and I chatted for a while at the kitchen table. I brought her up to speed on my college life, my classes, my new friends, and anything else she could think to ask about. And she asked plenty. My dad came home around 6:00 p.m. I shared some of the stories about our recent Were adventures, taking care to play down my role and play up everyone else's. Mom listened closely and was mollified, but Dad listened more closely, and I got an occasional thumbs-up or wink and nod that Mom didn't see.

At any rate, we had a wonderful visit. After dinner, I went upstairs to pack. I called next door only to learn to my surprise that Sunstar was out for the evening with Dr. Fitzgerald and two of his laboratory assistants. I guess he wanted to start slow. Smart man. Mrs. Allegro did spend some time on the phone with me, catching me up on what Casey was doing. Turns out she was exemplary in the classroom and even better on the playing field, but it *was* a mom's report after all.

After half an hour, I noticed that she hadn't mentioned Paul, so I casually asked her if Casey was dating and what her social life was like at the big school. I was on tenterhooks for her answer. I did a quiet fist pump when she said Casey wasn't dating anyone in particular that she knew of, that classes and sports just took too much time and commitment. Nevertheless, Casey apparently had a host of would-be suitors standing in the wings if she changed her mind.

"She was always purpose-driven," I added, "and soccer was the way to her education. She plans to get that bachelor's degree and then some. She'll probably start dating seriously after the first semester. I wouldn't worry about it. Casey will never lack for suitors."

"So what's your situation, Cody? Are you dating anyone? Dusty perhaps? Or maybe Sunstar and you just haven't said anything?"

"No, ma'am," I replied. "Between classes and a desire to stay alive, I haven't met anyone worth taking time for. And anyway, just so you know, Dusty is off-limits. It's a rank thing the Major asked me to honor, and I promised. Besides, Dusty has a beau, although oddly I've never met or seen him. I'm sure he's outstanding, though. A fellow would have to be in order to merit her loyalty. And as for Sunstar, well, I think she has some ideas of her own that might bring her back to Ohio more often, and I assure you, it isn't me."

"Well, Cody, since you're not taking the bait and I don't have all night to fiddle-faddle with you on the phone, are you still in love with my daughter? Come clean now. I've known you too long to not know when you're telling me a story."

I gulped and stammered. I honestly didn't know what to say. But I finally managed to squeak out, "About all I can say now, Mrs. Allegro, is that your daughter was the best thing that ever happened to me, and I can see no reason to change that. And as for being in love with her, well, love takes a long time to build, as you and your husband and my folks know, but if push comes to shove, I'm still head over heels for Casey, and that's a fact."

When Mrs. Allegro stopped laughing, I heard her tell her husband to put down the receiver and give us some privacy. After a semisilent click, she kept her response short. "Don't you worry about those North Carolina boys, Cody. And don't sell that young lady of mine short. She's got her dad's brains and my good sense, and you just be here on Thanksgiving. You two will have some catching up to do. My thinking is that you're not going to want to spend a lot of time with us old folks. I think you're going to like the changes in each other. Now you have a good trip back, and be careful. We want you back for Thanksgiving."

We said our goodbyes, and I asked to be remembered to her husband. Then I went downstairs, barely touching the carpet to grab a soda pop. My mom was at the table reading, my dad in the den watching television.

"Have a good conversation?" she asked.

"Yes, I did," I answered. "Those Allegros are cool, really cool."

"Yes, dear, they are. And their daughter isn't half-bad either, I would say."

I caught her grin as she turned back to the paper, so I dropped an ice cube down her back collar as I walked out and ran upstairs. I could hear her shrieking all the way to my room until I shut and locked my door. I laughed for a long time. Things were looking up, and Thanksgiving was only a month away. If Casey doesn't just run off and get married to some Paul or Bob or Worthington Jr., or some such, I'm coming home with a smile.

I was still grinning when sleep overtook me.

DAY TWENTY-ONE 1:00 P.M.

Michael (also called Blackbird) and I stopped for a hamburger in Blowing Rock's best (and only) typical fast-food restaurant. I excused myself for a quick stop in the restroom to wash my hands before we sat down to eat. We were on the way to the Rat's Nest to pick up Sunstar. She'd just flown in, and Sergeant Saddler had taken her to the Rat's Nest for a quick meeting with the Major. I had to be there for other reasons, and Michael wanted to come along to get out of Banner Elk, if only for an afternoon. Besides, he told me, there was always Dusty to visit with.

I told him he needed to bark up another tree, that he might as well chase his own tail for all the good his romancing of Dusty would do. He laughed and told me I had the judgment of a snail, and an ignorant snail at that. He went on in to order. I came out of the restroom to find him almost nose-to-nose with a fellow somewhat older and larger than him man wearing an Appalachian State sweatshirt. The man was flanked by two other men who looked like the man's friends. There was tension in the air. The young lady who wore the assistant manager's badge was nervously watching to see if there were going to be fireworks.

The man was telling Michael to back off and step out of his way, that he was in a hurry and no Indian was going to mess up his schedule whether Michael was next in line or not. Michael deliberately stepped past the man and started giving his order to a very scared young man who kept glancing over at his assistant manager as if he was waiting for some signal that he could take Michael's order. The Appalachian State fellow put his arm out to turn Michael around. At the same time, I stepped up to stand between the two.

"Pardon me, sir, but what car did you come in? There's some kid outside keying one with an Appalachian State sticker on it. I thought it might be yours."

"Hey, that's my car!" said his friend. All three turned to run to the door. I turned and gave the scared young man my order. I then suggested to Michael that we both sit down quickly before the trio came back. We would be called when our order was ready. We did just that. In a minute or two, the trio showed back up at the counter. Everyone else sort of stepped back. They ordered and moved to the side, casting glares at us and nervous glances out the window toward their car.

Nothing more was said as our order was called out. I went to pick it up. Just as I gathered up our two orders, I turned to the fellow who claimed ownership of the car and said, "The guy had on a green T-shirt with a picture of the Grateful Dead band on the front. I hope you guys scared him away. If he'll do it to your car, he'll do it to anyone's, even mine. You guys are heroes."

Then I walked back to our booth. Michael and I promptly chowed down our food, leaving the trio looking at each other with puzzled faces. They shrugged when their order was finally called, looked around once more at us, and then took their meals and left.

"Why did you do that?" Michael asked.

"Easy peasy," I responded. "Didn't want to fight them in here. Ruins the appetite." I chuckled as I bit into my burger. "Now pass that ketchup if you'd be so kind."

Michael was still trying to mop up some stray juice stains on the front of his shirt when I drove up to the Rat's Nest. Sunstar's bag was on the porch. Michael put it in the back seat of my car before we went into the building. Dusty was at her desk. Her eyes lit up when we walked in. It was powered by her smile. Michael promptly plopped himself down on the chair by her desk. I just grinned, nodded, rolled my eyes, and headed back to my cubicle. I could hear the two of them laughing as I sat down at my desk. There in front of me was a small parcel carefully wrapped in black paper. A note was pinned to the side.

The note read "Cowards die a thousand times before their death, the valiant never taste of death but once." It was handwritten in beautiful script. It was a quote I knew well from Shakespeare's play *Julius Caesar*. It was the line Caesar spoke to his wife when she warned him to obey the soothsayer's warning about going out on the Ides of March. There was no address or return address on the package, just my name. I gathered it up. As I walked over to Dusty's desk, I interrupted one of Michael's stories, much to Dusty's apparent relief.

"Pardon me, Michael. This was on my desk, Dusty. Do you know where it came from or who sent it to me?"

She replied that she didn't. It had been in the unit mail bag from Hickory for delivery this morning. She thought I would know what it was. She just put it on my desk thinking nothing much of it. That was the extent of her knowledge. But as she talked, she read the note as did Michael. Both of them pressed me to open the small package.

I shrugged, sat down on the corner of Dusty's desk, and tore off the wrapping. A beautiful, small wooden box was inside. I shook it, and something rattled. When I opened the box and looked inside, I was so startled that I dropped it on Dusty's desk. A shriveled falcon's foot, talons extended, fell out and rolled to a stop on Dusty's desk. The foot had been severed. It wasn't a neat cut. It looked like the author of this surprise had taken two whacks with a dull axe to cut off the foot. Certainly the bird must have suffered. It was a cruel trick. I had no idea who could have done this. I quickly scooped up the bleak foot and its box. I threw the whole mess in the garbage bin by the Chapel's front door. I felt queasy. I immediately ran outside and called for Polaris.

She did not answer. I felt even sicker. Then I saw her coming fast over the tree-tops south of us on a beeline to me. Rarely have I been so moved. She fluttered to a stop on my extended arm. She was careful not to let her sharp talons bite into my flesh while balancing. She then hopped to my shoulder and ruffled her feathers against my cheek. It was a private greeting between the two of us. She had given it one other time to Sunstar when Sunstar had healed her. I rubbed my cheek against Polaris's feathers and told her I had missed her but I was back and we had many hunts ahead of us. It was the right thing to say.

Polaris loved few things more than a good hunt. Even one of Dusty's cookies took second place to a hunt. Polaris made a whirring sound in her throat. She quietly told me she missed me, too. She didn't quite feel like a member of a team unless I was with her. The concept of a team was entrancing to a gyrfalcon. Nevertheless, she was a Princess, and royalty rarely displays feelings in public, so she launched herself at a nearby tree. She settled down there with a regal perch, her sharp, steely eyes missing nothing.

I did not think for a minute that the gruesome surprise had come from anyone associated with the Rat's Nest. But no Were could write that, not even if it tried to on the first day of its change when it still had many human faculties and partial use of its upper limbs. Realizing that, I knew it was either a very poor joke or a rude trick. But if it were the latter, then one or more unturned humans were working with the Weres. *That* was an electrifying thought. I quickly ran back into the building and rooted through the trash until I recovered both the box and the detached falcon foot. Forensics will need these, I thought, but I knew I'd better show this to the Major post haste. I excused myself from the curious crowd that had formed as I rooted through the trash. I walked over to the Major's office. She looked up when I knocked, smiled, and motioned me to come in. Sunstar looked up at me, smiled even bigger, and reached an arm out to pat my arm before she turned back to the papers she was signing.

I placed the box and its contents on the Major's desk. I told her it was on my desk when I walked in. All we knew about the package and its method of delivery, my two suppositions emphasizing the latter, were that some humans and Weres might be allied against us. Certainly no one else knew of Polaris or the role she was playing for us. Most assuredly, the Weres did. With this package, the author(s) of the note knew that a way to get to me was through Gitta or Polaris. My apprehension about someone hurting them made me the coward. Their disregard for death made them the valiant.

The Major's reaction was not what I expected. She held the box and the severed falcon's foot over her desk and mused quietly to herself. "'Curiouser and curiouser,' said Alice."

Curious indeed, I thought to myself. It is all of that. Very curious indeed. The Major carefully wrapped up the package. Dropping both articles into a manila envelope, she sealed it. She asked Dusty to make sure this got out today to the confinement facility. She wanted a full forensic analysis. She then asked me to write down everything I could remember about its original appearance. I was to find the outer wrapping and ship it separately. I was also to write down a chain of events from the time I opened it to the time I brought it to her desk. I said, "Yes, ma'am," and set to work.

I finished by 5:00 p.m. I was one of the last ones out of the building. Airman Cropper locked up behind the last of us stragglers. He asked me when we were going out again. Actually, getting to fight the Weres was the most interesting thing he'd done since signing on a year or so ago. He wanted more of it. I referred him to the Major. I would be perfectly happy never having to go out and fight again. Michael and Sunstar were there waiting for me, and then we left.

DAY TWENTY-TWO 7:30 A.M.

Michael and I were up, breakfasted, and ready for study earlier than we'd ever been. Midterm exams started next week. Lees-McRae had arranged for two days of study review. Students could sign up for study groups in the administration building. Each group would have a teacher or graduate assistant monitoring the class to answer questions and such. The study periods would last for one to one and a half hours each, depending on the topic and number of students signed up. It was the teacher's discretion as to the length of the class.

Michael had two classes with Kathy Niwall. Still, he rarely got to see her, much less have an interchange. He felt if he could get into her study group, he'd have a much better chance of gaining her attention. He was smart. His assignments were up to date. He already had an A going into the midterm examinations. He was actually quite well read in the two subjects the classes covered—organic chemistry and English literature. In truth, Michael was a Renaissance man with eclectic interests and an intellect that would have given Sherlock Holmes a run for his money. He just didn't have good social sense and never acted to hold back his impetuousness. He never had to before college. What he needed was some soft-hearted young lady to sit down and council him repeatedly, and he would emerge a butterfly from his cocoon of awkwardness. I wasn't the person to find that gal for him. I left it to him to find one on his own. I had my hands full as it were, but that's how his crush on Kathy Niwall happened. Somehow, Michael decided she was his long-lost true love, only no one had told her about it yet.

All I could think of was that if Michael got his wish, life was going to get pretty interesting.

The study group lists were posted at 8:00 a.m. We stood and waited, quietly talking to one another for almost 20 minutes until Kathy and her friend Marne showed up. They both went straight to a list and signed their names. Michael was literally right behind Kathy, signing his name after hers and my name after his. I reminded him that I was taking my own classes, thank you, and to please remove me from the list. He whispered that he needed me as a wing man to help him out here, stating quite emphatically that a little review on these important classes wouldn't hurt me, even if I'd aced them in my honors classes back in high school.

I just shook my head. The Walksabout family had not a dull one in the bunch.

The review classes started at 10:00 a.m. We had some time, so I decided to sign up for an after-lunch advanced biology class review. I was a B student in that class. With some work, I could probably move that up to an A, but my Rat's Nest duties and trips just hadn't let me put the time in. I didn't notice at the moment that Cecil Derrick signed up for the same study class several minutes after I did. It wouldn't have meant much at the time, but it sure did later.

Michael and I walked over to the Hannah March Pavilion to wait and visit until it was time for the first study session. The pavilion was a large, temporary structure about the size of a roller rink. It had broad steps leading up to and into the pavilion with a low wooden railing enclosing it. The roof was high, and breezes blew through it constantly. The Alumni Association had originally funded it, but no student currently knew or cared who Hannah March was. We were still grateful. Until we had a student union building, the pavilion would have to do.

It was one of if not *the* main gathering place on our small campus. It was tucked away across the street from the administration building behind the Avery County Farmer's Market. It was not far from the Frog and Monkey. A number of folding chairs had been brought in. Sitting with friends in the shade of its broad roof with a soft breeze blowing across the pavilion floor was a special summer treat.

At 9:45 a.m., Michael alerted me that the ladies were on the move. I struggled back to reality, and we walked along behind them. As we took our seats in the study room, I pushed Michael into one of the two seats flanking Kathy's chair. Her friend Marne took the other side. I took the seat behind Michael and leaned forward far enough to whisper, "You're on your own now." I got a pencil stab in my left knee for my trouble.

I didn't remember much about the class. I was too absorbed in reviewing my past assignment in biology. The first thing the teacher did was ask every person to take a second and meet and greet the persons to their left and right, in front of and behind them. Michael finally got to meet Kathy. During the course of the study hour, he also got to impress her and anyone else with his brain. He was right on as if he had an eidetic memory. He was spot-on so often that after the review session, Kathy and Marne asked him if he would consider tutoring them. I left my poor, besotted, love-struck boy in the care of his new angels. I told him I'd catch him later. If he heard me, it was a miracle. His cocoon was cracking open. It was too loud for him to hear anything from me.

I grabbed a snack for lunch and saw several of the kids from my biology class sitting at a partially filled table. I nodded as if I might eat with them and got a hearty come-on-down wave. One of the women in my class, Jan Witherspoon, was an extremely funny lady but forgetful. She was also an innocent. I thought she still believed unicorns were occasionally spotted here or there and it was just a matter of time before one was captured and proved the whatever-pologists to be liars.

I hadn't the heart to tell her the jackalope on the postcard she'd purchased on a trip to Texas and now used as a wall poster wasn't anatomically correct. Jan also took copious notes with personal observations. They were better than the class notes, so Jan was a favorite study partner. It didn't hurt that she had an IQ somewhere way up there.

I happened to take the chair to Jan's left when we all assembled for the biology study session. Cecil Derrick took the chair behind her. Jan and I were regular classmates, but Cecil was in another class. During the course of the study group, the teacher asked if anyone had a specific position on current stem cell research using embryos. A number did, but Jan and Cecil had opposite views. Both felt strongly about their positions. In the course of explaining their positions, Cecil cited something that some of us vaguely remembered but not as he explained it. Jan immediately went to her notes, found the cite, and countered Cecil, saying his reasoning premise was wrong because he'd either not heard the original quote correctly or did not understand it. The teacher complimented Jan on her notes. She suggested that Cecil would benefit if he compared his notes to hers.

Everyone congratulated Jan and ignored Cecil for the remainder of the study session. As we got up to leave, someone bumped Jan, and she dropped her notes, books, and purse. Several of the kids stooped to help her. I noticed that Cecil managed to collect a handful of her notes just as other kids were gathering them up for her as well. I gave her what I'd picked up and promptly left. So did everyone else. But I got a call later that day from Jan asking if I had turned over all the notes I'd picked up, that by chance had I inadvertently kept a few of hers by mistake. I reviewed my notebook and notes and told her without equivocation that I had nothing of hers. I was the last person of five she'd called after getting back to her dorm room and realizing she was missing some key notes. They included the sheet that contained the cite she'd corrected Cecil with during the study session. Everyone, including Cecil and me, promised her that they did not have the missing notes. She was close to tears and very frustrated.

I told her not to worry about it, that I would study one-on-one with her and that my notes were pretty complete. She thanked me. She told me how important her grades were to her for the scholarship money she would get. I scheduled several hours of study with her over the next few days. I thought no more about the mysterious missing pages.

DAY TWENTY-SEVEN 2:30 P.M.

It had been a difficult but not unexpected last hour and a half. I had just finished my biology midterm, and to my surprise, Mr. Van de Meer, our instructor, had allowed us to use our class notes but no books. I was glad I had taken good notes during the first half of the semester. I was even happier I had a chance to study with Jan Witherspoon. I didn't think I'd aced the test, but I felt I would have one of the higher grades because of the time I put in.

I saw Jan on the porch as a number of us were leaving the building. I caught up to her to thank her once again for her help. We unknowingly formed a small pedestrian bottleneck for other students rushing to vacate the building. There was some jostling going on as some students tried to push through or past us. I took Jan by the elbow and moved out of the main passageway. In doing so, I inadvertently bumped into my new nemesis, Cecil Derrick.

"Hey! Watch out, Balloon Boy," he cried out as he dodged Jan, dropping his biology book as he did so. I instinctively bent to help him as he also bent to pick up his book. We smacked heads hard. That caused him to drop his folder. His notes flew out when it hit the ground. I was holding my head, not even thinking about helping him, when Jan cried out and stood up with several pages in her hand.

She shook them in Cecil's face and said, "You jerk! These are *my* notes! I asked you if you'd taken them by accident, and you lied to me. You used my notes, and that's cheating, Cecil. You're a cheater!" she screamed. She slapped him hard with her notes, turned away crying, and stormed away.

Mr. Van de Meer happened to be exiting the building at that time. He saw most if not all the drama as did a number of students. I never heard anything official, but the grapevine had it that Cecil was given a failing grade. He had to retake the class the following semester. He began avoiding Jan and me from that point on. A number of the students would have nothing to do with him. I was glad for the respite, but I didn't understand Cecil. He was just cheating himself—paying for an education and then negating its value. How could he ever truly measure his progress? Maybe he was satisfied with the status quo, with living a lie.

The biology exam was my last midterm. I headed for my dorm room to meet Michael. I was curious to know if his protégés had done well, if those tutor sessions he'd had with them this past week actually paid off. And did he actually make a date to go out with Kathy Niwall? I heard the whooping and hollering as I walked down the hallway to our room. The door was open. I was sure everyone in the building knew Michael was celebrating, but they probably thought it was for a simple test score. When I saw our cushions thrown all over our room, I knew better. He was jumping on his bed making noise, so I jumped up there with him, and we screamed, jumped, and hollered together. That's part of what good friends are for.

The college charged us $45 for damage to the frame and mattress. After that, we learned to temper our celebrations. But at least Michael had a date with Kathy Niwall.

DAY TWENTY-SEVEN 4:30 P.M.

Everyone at the Rat's Nest Motor Pool was getting ready to call it a day. I was chewing the fat with Airman Cropper and Sergeant Saddler. We were discussing the pros and cons of modifying the leather armor Sergeant Saddler had come up with and that the Major had ordered to be cut and fitted for us. It was a vital part of our fighting uniform now, but troops will always tinker. Everybody has a better way to build a mousetrap. We were no exception. We all agreed the armor had saved lives and prevented some serious injuries. Still, I wanted something that would fit around the lower back to protect the kidneys and adjacent internal organs.

We were interrupted by Michael yelling for me. He had walked over from the Chapel after visiting with Dusty. The truth was she had probably sent him over just to get him out of her hair so she could get some work done. He liked visiting with her and she with him, too, but the military's demands and requests came first with Dusty. Michael didn't quite understand that yet.

I bid goodbye to my companions. I intercepted Michael before he could start discussing the relative merits of a vehicle with four-wheel drive on demand versus one with all-wheel drive constantly engaged. It was a discussion he and Airman Carter, another Motor Pool employee, had had before. Neither would give an inch to the other. I turned Michael around with my left hand and draped my right arm over his shoulders. I started back to the parking lot with him. He'd wanted to come over to the Rat's Nest with me after our ill-fated celebration. I was always happy to be in his company. He was truly a very funny guy. Sadly, most people never saw that side of him.

"Cody, why don't you take me out hunting like you did with Dusty and Sunstar? I mean, if I've got to be a keeper of your secrets, wouldn't it make sense to know what secrets I'm keeping?"

I told him he just wanted to see a Were up close and personal and have the experience of fighting it so his sister wouldn't lord it over him. He hung his head, grinned, and then admitted that was true. But what he was also after was the chance to see Gitta and Polaris in action. I told him we would go out tomorrow morning if he was really serious. I would need to check out a loaded sidearm and shotgun for him before we left tonight as well as get my stuff. Perhaps a quiet outing would be nice after the last two experiences.

I also told him that we would run this time if trouble appeared. I was concerned that he couldn't actually run because he was just like me when I started, the owner of a bad leg. That meant extra caution, that he would have to do exactly as I said because the potential danger we faced as members of the Rat's Nest was deadly. Weres were starting to know us and hunt us, I reminded him. That meant any excursion could end up in a fight. Some fights we weren't going to win.

He was pretty somber when we entered the Chapel. I told the Major what we were going to do while Dusty got our armaments. The Major looked at me for a time and then reminded me that Michael's life was in my hands. I was not to forget that caution is often better than valor. With caution, you can usually crawl home. With valor, someone else usually carries you back—in a bag. I reminded her that she was talking to the world's greatest coward, someone who had no ego in the game but was still anxious to impress on Michael that what we were about wasn't an Olympic sport.

She smiled and dismissed me with a wave of her hand as she bent down once again to a mound of paper on her desk. I thought her a workaholic. Still, she was always there for us, to talk, instruct, counsel, observe, console, or merely listen. And the other officers, including our new boss General Kim, were pretty much the same. They saw rank as a responsibility, not necessarily a privilege. The outfit loved them for it.

I locked our equipment in the trunk of my car, and we headed back to Banner Elk. We stopped in Blowing Rock for a burger on the way. I was a little sad that Dusty wasn't with us. She didn't eat french fries. Michael practically inhaled his and most of mine, the wretch. I guess I didn't mind too much because Michael paid the bill. He was still euphoric about getting a date with Kathy. His smile probably could have been bigger, but we would have had to cut his jaw away to do it. You'd have thought he'd found buried treasure.

DAY TWENTY-EIGHT 6:30 A.M.

Michael and I had prepared our packs the night before. We were on the way to Blowing Rock to pick up Gitta and Polaris. We were heading to Price Lake, a spot five or six miles west of Blowing Rock along the Blue Ridge Parkway. It was a popular recreation spot in the summer, although this late in the fall, very few souls spent any appreciable time there. I planned to scout the small lake and its environs and give Michael a few lessons in tracking. Not that I was that good, but I'd asked Pee Wee if he wanted to join us as a surprise for Michael. Pee Wee jumped at the chance. Michael was family. The Cherokee value family above almost anything.

The Walksabout family considered me family, too, as much as a clumsy paleface with a weird skill can be considered family. Michael said they sometimes thought of me as that uncle no one wanted to talk about, that everyone hoped wouldn't come to visit too often. At least that's what Michael told me before Sunstar chewed him out one day at Lees-McRae. But I knew even then that Michael was just kidding. Mr. and Mrs. Walksabout were never less than swell to me. They appreciated that I always looked after their daughter. As for Michael, the Blackbird, I think they were grateful I just didn't stuff him into a sock and drop him into somebody's laundry bag.

In my conversation with the Major the day before, I told her where I planned to hike and that Pee Wee would be coming along with us. I expected it would be a quiet, eventless day. But I was always worried about the unexpected. It's what you don't know you don't know that comes back to bite you. Nevertheless, Michael was very happy when we pulled up at the Rat's Nest parking lot. Pee Wee was standing there waiting for us.

I left them to chat for a moment. I went around to get Gitta and call in Polaris. Gitta was waiting for me, although she looked asleep. She was sprawled out in the sun when I saw her on top of her cage. Polaris joined us soon after, a small string of intestines dangling from her beak. She was in the middle of a strike when she heard my call and finished in a hurry. Falcons always finish what they start, be it breakfast or an aerial attack.

I loaded both ladies in the rear of my car behind Pee Wee and drove off to Price Lake. It was a beautiful morning. The leaves were crisp and the ground moist, a good day for tracking.

DAY TWENTY-EIGHT 8:00 A.M.

By 8:00 a.m., we were at the lake. I parked my car, gave a spare set of keys to Pee Wee, and with our hunting equipment in tow walked about half a mile from the parked car to an overlook on the east side of the lake. No other cars were in the parking area. From the overlook we could see no other people on or near the shores of the lake. It just lay there in pristine beauty. Virtually no wind disturbed its surface. The reflections of the surrounding hills crowded against its lazy shoreline. The temperature was a crisp 52 degrees. It was too cold for T-shirts and too warm for heavy coats or gloves. It was a perfect day for a hunt.

We checked our weapons and readied ourselves for the exercise as we stood on the overlook. Pee Wee and Gitta were to make separate trails around to the far side of the lake. Pee Wee's trail would be close to the shoreline and Gitta's about a hundred yards or so from Pee Wee's. I asked them to cross every quarter mile so Michael could mark where they crossed. His exercise was to distinguish Gitta's track from that of other animals and tell from Pee Wee's when he had been running, walking, or stalking. We would meet on the far side of the lake in two hours for a snack and review.

Pee Wee carried a cut-down shotgun with 12-gauge buckshot rounds alternating with solid slugs. He also carried a 1911-style Colt .45-caliber handgun. It was a powerful pistol able to drop a charging bear in its tracks if hit right. It worked the same for Weres.

461

I gave Michael the 410-gauge shotgun Dusty had used along with a .357 Magnum pistol like mine. The pistol was not as heavy as Pee Wee's .45-caliber handgun. Still, a slug from a .357 could penetrate an engine block and stop a car. It was a heavy pistol but weighed less and took a smaller grip than a .45-caliber weapon. Besides, to someone not all that familiar with a .357 handgun, the kick wasn't severe enough to split the skin between the base of the thumb and the padded skin at the base of the index finger. I had the horn bow, my usual assortment of arrows, a .357 Smith & Wesson revolver, and my wakizashi blade. I'd left my javelin back in my dorm room on purpose.

Pee Wee and Gitta set out on their separate trails. We gave them a half hour before we stood up and started tracking them. We started after Pee Wee first just to get Michael used to the basics of tracking—how to step, what side of the trail to walk along, and what to notice about the immediate environment and the greater environment that could influence the target's speed and direction. We also looked for disturbances in the trees, bushes, or grass that would indicate that something recently passed that way, among other signs.

Michael was either a natural or had some rudimentary training sometime earlier in his life. He caught on to Pee Wee's gait changes very quickly. He could surmise from the enveloping terrain what Pee Wee was doing and probably why his stride changed. Gitta was more of a challenge, however. After about a 10th of a mile, I directed Michael to move up the hill and try to find and track Gitta. He spent almost 45 minutes casting for her trail before he actually found a possible track and a sign of her passing. Even I had to search hard. When Gitta went into stealth mode, she all but disappeared.

We were moving slowly on a westward track, the rising sun at our backs when I heard a sound I'd never heard before. Michael stopped before I did and, with eyes wide open, turned to me as if to say, "What was *that*?" I gently pushed him down and took a knee with him while we kept listening. It sounded like a howl but none such as I had ever heard. The back of the cry seemed to cut off into a series of diminishing hacks as if a creature were choking. I immediately cast out in my mind to contact Polaris and ask her what was causing that disturbance. She answered me that she could see nothing, but she was way over the middle of the lake watching Pee Wee complete his trek. She could see no sign of Gitta.

The cry suddenly came again, more of a screech this time as if something was being pulled apart. With a sudden start, I realized it could be Gitta in trouble. With a quick command for Michael to stay put, I was up with a bound and running over the hillsides and through scattered trees, continually casting my thoughts for Gitta. I had run almost a quarter mile when I got my first impression from her. She was terribly frightened. She was backed up beneath a tree being challenged by something she described as a giant. I increased my pace. I asked her to describe her stand. I tried to gauge how close I might be from the terrain she described.

As I came loping over the brow of a small hill that folded into a larger hill, I stopped so suddenly that I almost fell over myself. A Pale Were almost one and a half to two times the size of a normal Pale Were, or maybe even larger, was trying to uproot a tree. The sheer power of the creature was hypnotic. It was mauling the tree almost as if it were a sapling. Each push with its huge shoulders tore more of the tree's roots from the ground and shook the upper branches violently. This was a determined creature, but Gitta stubbornly stayed beneath its twisted roots as she scrambled back and forth trying to elude the creature's grasp.

My first reaction was to find and use the nearest bathroom. In a fight-or-flight response to danger, the body's chemistry works to void the contents of the stomach and bladder so the body can act freely. Thank goodness I had made sure everyone had a chance to relieve themselves before we set out this morning. A person worried about wetting themselves in a fight isn't concentrating on the fight. Those people merit the name Defeated or Deceased, take your pick, and I wasn't one of those people.

It takes some self-training, but soldiers in Special Operations are taught to wet themselves as they march or run, as the need arises. A soldier is usually sweating so much that it literally makes no difference in appearance. Several times I had been in an engagement when my entire uniform was wet with sweat and other body fluids at the fight's conclusion. I had no recollection whatsoever of losing a drop of body moisture during the fight.

This creature was bizarre. Its size was intimidating even from a distance. I didn't want to even imagine what it would be like up close, but I felt I was about to find out anyway. I had to do something to pull it away from Gitta and warn Pee Wee. I also wanted to distract the creature from its repeated attempts at local forest renovation. I pulled a screamer arrow from my quiver and let it soar to the west. The sound prompted the creature to immediately halt its attempt to wrest the tree from the ground and expose Gitta. It turned my way as it sought the source of the shrill sound that penetrated all our ears. Spotting me silhouetted on the edge of the small hill, the huge Pale Were dropped to all fours and began running my way. It covered ground much like a bear, deceptively fast with muscles rippling under its light, ochre-colored fur. All I wanted at that point was a flamethrower or claymore mine backed up by several tanks ready and willing to fire at my command.

I turned and scrambled for cover, any cover. At the base of my hill, I saw a bank of rocks that formed a kind of small tower. There was a crevasse at its base big enough to climb into. I made for the rocks with everything I had. Running past the tower, I threw my hat onto the ground near the small entrance and disappeared into a stand of close-growth Aspen on the side of a hill just above and opposite the cairn of rocks. Folding and squeezing between the small trunks and moving deep into the copse, I fought to get my breathing under control as the giant creature crested the small hill and looked down and around the basin that bordered it. It quickly spied my hat and the opening of the rocks beneath the abbreviated rock tower. It sprang for the opening in one sudden jump. It landed just short of the hat and squatted down to peer into the crevasse.

It could see nothing because there was nothing in there to see, just empty space. Enraged, the giant Were started dismantling the rocks with furious sweeps of its muscled arms until very little was left standing. It then used its nose. It started systematically to search all around the rocks until it faced the copse of Aspen in which I was hiding. Somewhat calmer, it trudged up the incline to the edge of the copse and tried to peer in, all the time sniffing the air and trying to pick up my scent.

"I know you are in there, human," its voice rang out. "I am Zikkedd. I will wait here for you until you die from thirst or hunger or surrender to me. No one escapes from Zikkedd. No one ever has. No one ever will. These trees are as reeds of grass before me if I choose to come and get you. My friends will soon come for me. Had I not stopped to kill a strange flat bear, I would have missed you. But now I wait because soon you will tire or try to escape, and I will kill you. My people will rejoice in my victory. Killing humans is better sport than killing small flat bears."

What he said would have provoked Gitta, but fortunately she was out of immediate danger as long as the giant was here with me. I was surprised at the creature's size. I don't know why. Our human race has giants. Most of them play for the National Basketball Association, but many don't. And our race has pygmies, too, so apparently Weres are something like humans since the size of an individual Were can vary considerably, and anomalies do occur. I tried to make contact with Gitta. I succeeded, but Gitta was highly distraught. She was worried about me, not herself. She had seen the giant Were run after me. She knew I was now the one in terrible danger. I assuaged her fears. I told her to run back to where I'd left Michael.

This would all be new to him. He'd get himself killed if he tried to take on a Were or its friends by himself. Gitta needed to lead him back to the parking area. I told her I would also contact Polaris. I asked her to send Pee Wee back to the other side of the lake. Pee Wee had my second set of car keys. He could go for help long before the Were could level this wood copse I was in. I felt okay for now. My primary concern was keeping Michael out of this mess. Gitta was the key to that. Reluctantly, she agreed and broke our contact. I breathed more easily knowing she was off to get him. And then I didn't breathe at all as Michael topped the big rise I had first come running over. Standing in plain sight, he hollered for me, calling out my name over and over. He was at least 80 to 100 yards away and up a hill. The big Were called Zikkedd would make that in a flash if he chose. Michael was as good as dead.

Had I known what Michael was going to do, I would have surrendered right then and let Zikkedd eat both of us. It would have saved a lot of time and trouble, but I was furious. Furious! Why couldn't Michael do as he was told, I asked myself as I fought to get out of the copse. I made enough racket that the Big Were was actually torn between two desires—kill the human on the hilltop or wait and kill the human close by when he emerged from the wood and then go and kill the stupid human on the hill. I started yelling at Zikkedd so he would make the easy choice—me. But he didn't. He dropped and ran for Michael. He left me still entangled in the Aspens as I fought to break free of their stand.

DAY TWENTY-EIGHT 9:00 A.M.

Michael saw the giant Were drop and start its run up the hill. Then Michael did exactly what Pee Wee and I had taught him not to do. He dropped his shotgun and turned and ran behind the crest of the hill as the giant Pale Were hit the lower slopes at a dead run. The Were was traveling so fast in its eagerness that it misstepped and tumbled head over paw pads. That interruption was just enough to give me the moment I desperately needed. I knelt to stabilize myself after lurching through the last of the Aspen cover. I nocked an exploding arrow as I knelt. Drawing it back while taking the Were's measure, I let the first of three arrows fly. I launched my second arrow, a broadhead, before the first reached its zenith. I let the third arrow, my second exploding arrow, fly before the first tore through the giant Were's left leg. The resulting explosion blew part of the Were's leg off. It staggered dramatically to its right and plowed into the turf headfirst.

The broadhead unerringly followed the Were's original path. It embedded itself in the grass about 12 feet ahead and to the left of the big Were's now crippled body. The last arrow hit very close to the second. It blew up with enough force to flip the Were sideways and leave it temporarily unconscious. Gitta arrived at the scene well before I could clamber up the hillside to meet her. While I was crawling up the last few feet, she systematically bit through the Were's right shinbone, bloodying it and breaking its other leg.

I left Gitta there to watch over the Were. She was to kill it or call for help if it tried to damage her. I picked up Michael's shotgun and ran after him. He stopped running about 120 yards away from the crest of the hill. I had repeatedly called out his name, asking him to stop. He was shaking when I came up to him. I was gasping for breath as well, but I placed the shotgun on the ground beside me. I put my arms around him and just held him.

There was no disgrace in panicking when one sees a Were for the first time, especially when it's the King Kong of Weres. I told Michael that we were safe, that the Were was crippled, and that we needed to go back and kill it. He nodded dumbly. He offered no resistance as I turned him and walked back, my arm over his shoulder. I made him carry the shotgun.

When we got back to the Were, it was in a state of partial consciousness. It knew it was badly hurt. It responded to our presence with several fairly uncoordinated, ineffectual swipes of its massive arms and paws. It then tried to boost itself up only to crumple to the ground when its legs could not hold it upright. As we got close to it, we could see it was a male. He was in terrific pain. He would bleed out in time, but the interval between then and now would be excruciating. I turned to Michael, placed my hands on his shoulders, and asked him to look me in the eye. "He needs to be killed, Michael. Not put away, not put down, not terminated. He needs to be killed. Dead. Now. Can you do this? One of us must do this. Can you?"

He nodded that he could, and I handed him the shotgun. With tears in his eyes, Michael walked over to where the Were was lying on the ground like a wet handkerchief. Then, without further adieu, looking the Were straight in the eye, Michael raised the shotgun and blew the creature's head apart. He slowly lowered the gun and sank down beside it. "I never want to hunt or kill anything again," he said. And with that, he promptly threw up.

I pulled my last two screamer arrows and let them fly in rapid succession. Their sound echoed around the lake, and I had no doubt that Pee Wee would soon come to us. We sat down to wait, and I talked with Michael for a minute. I told him that to kill a creature of any merit takes something out of us. It should be an abhorrent task. Killing should never be easy. Some folks simply could not kill. That was okay, too. God did not give us all the same sensibilities. But Michael had volunteered to come and hunt. He had not waited for our invitation. To be honest, I would never have invited him to a hunt. But we were in it, and he had a job to do.

To have not killed the Were would have branded Michael a coward in his own mind, not ours, and that would have haunted him all his life. Now he need never kill again. But in standing up to a chore he so violently hated, he showed his true courage and brought honor to himself.

Polaris flew down to land. She tore some of the meat from the Were's leg and ate it. She then leaped into the air and flew a cover patrol while we waited for Pee Wee. I felt much more comfortable with Polaris on watch close by. Her eyes missed virtually nothing, especially marauding Weres.

We'd been on the ground an hour when Pee Wee joined us. After he saw the dead Were and heard from Michael, he asked me to stand guard while he led Michael through a small Cherokee death ceremony honoring the killing of the giant Were. After that, we cut up and burned the body parts. We finally started back to the car just before noon. Gitta and Pee Wee were in the lead, and Michael was tucked in ahead of me. Polaris was overhead. It was a somber walk back. We caught no glimpse of any other Weres along the way.

DAY TWENTY-EIGHT 2:00 P.M.

We left Polaris and Gitta back at the Rat's Nest, and I drove Michael home. As I pulled into the Walksabouts' driveway, I saw Mrs. Walksabout outside watering her flowers. She saw the serious look on Michael's face and his hollow cheeks. She promptly threw down her hose, turned off the water, and asked us both to step inside. Mr. Walksabout was inside reading. Sunstar came downstairs when she heard the door open and shut. She thought it was her mom. She was surprised to see us. We all gathered in the living room. Sunstar broke the silence by asking Michael straight out what had happened. Why did he look so mournful and serious?

Michael started to say something several times, each time tearing up and unable to form his words correctly. Mr. and Mrs. Walksabout turned to me. In unison they asked me to speak. Michael was in distress, and they demanded an answer.

"Let me tell you the story of a brave young man. He asked for and was granted a favor, but the favor was so much more than he was prepared to receive. Nevertheless, he received it with honor and then vowed he would never again ask for such a favor. The young man was asked to take a life, and when the time came, he took it, realizing only then that his pathway in life was to save and not take life ever again.

"He did not flinch or act in anger when his moment came. He did the job he had first desired and then been asked to do. He will never ask for that again. His courage was greater than his friends'. They held no such reserve about taking an enemy's life. Michael is this young man, a brave and true friend. He brought honor upon himself and upon this house, as did his sister before him and his parents before her."

There was silence in the home for a few minutes as the Walksabout family sat quietly and studied Michael. Then all of them moved at once and threw their arms about him, each also holding the others. I quietly took my exit. I was climbing into my car when Sunstar's hand fell upon my arm and stopped me. I had not heard her come outside. "Thank you, Cody, for helping Michael keep his honor. He is a true warrior, but fighting is not his path. That is yours. His is to heal and help people in other ways, like me. Yours is to defend the weak and remind the strong that they, too, are sometimes weak. You are Awohali, the Eagle, and so it is and so it will be known among our family and people." She gently touched my cheek and ran back into her house.

I kept my .357 handgun on the seat beside me all the way back to Banner Elk and Lees-McRae. I was becoming more aware than ever that the North Carolina mountain roads are dark, twisted, and lonely. I reminded myself that not everything that runs along those roads at night is made of rubber.

DAY THIRTY 10:00 A.M.

It was Monday morning. I'd just left the Major's office. She asked Pee Wee and me to spend some time debriefing regarding our excursion with Michael. She was especially eager that we describe the characteristics and features of the giant Pale

Were. I passed along all Gitta's thoughts as well. That Were had frightened both of us. It wasn't just its sheer size. It had named itself, something most Pale Weres we'd encountered never did. Either naming oneself to the enemy was becoming a fad among the Weres or we'd had an uncommon streak of luck in tackling the upper echelon of Weres that merited a name and were proud to have one.

What really puzzled me, however, was the knowledge that if there were suddenly more and more Weres out crossing our path, why hadn't we heard more about sightings or killings in the general population? North Carolina was filled with folks who spent hours and hours in the woods and on trails. Why did we of the Rat's Nest seem to be getting all the action?

My conclusion, of course, was that our reputation preceded us. We were deliberately being targeted. It had to be that Were patrols were constantly out now, all looking to intercept us. They had not yet made a raid on our small headquarters and likely wouldn't this close to town, but they had tried to raid me and were now trying to close the woods and trails to us in particular. So far we were winning that battle, but only because of Gitta and Polaris.

With these conclusions, I suggested to the Major that she act to reinforce our Chapel and the Motor Pool with welded iron gates on the doors and windows. It wouldn't cost a lot of money, but it could save a lot of lives. She readily agreed. She cleared it with General Kim later that day. Increasing our building security was only a logical next step. I got her to agree to make Gitta's cage out of double cyclone fencing and suggested a trap door into the building that Gitta could use if her shelter came under attack when no one was here. The Major also agreed to that, and a worry lifted from my shoulders. Polaris was a different story. Flight is so much more an advantage than a fortress.

After a short exchange with Pee Wee and Dusty, I drove back to Lees-McRae. I had a class right after lunch in general science. Today's lecture was on 19th-century medical implements and their use. Lectures like that keep me humble. We had made so many advances in medicine since the turn of the century. The last half of the 20th century appeared to offer even greater advances. My goal was to be the best veterinarian I could be. I could not be that if I did not understand the past, for the past is the basis for the future. Some things from the past are not to be carelessly thrown away in the name of progress. I wanted to know everything I could about everything I could. That thirst for knowledge was to carry me into many adventures in the years ahead, but those tales are chronicled in a different book.

A message was tacked to my door when I got back to my room. I was to see the Dean of Students at my earliest convenience, and before 4:00 p.m. would be preferable. I determined to stop over at the Dean's office immediately after my upcoming general science lecture. I could not help but wonder why I'd been asked to see the Dean. I felt my grades were in good order.

Let down by the paucity of information given out during the lecture I'd so eagerly anticipated, I walked slowly over to the Dean's office. My wait in the Dean's anteroom was a short one, less than five minutes. The Dean's secretary came to get me, ushered me into the Dean's office, and closed the door behind me. I had to admit I was apprehensive, but to my surprise, the Dean put me perfectly at ease. He asked that what we were to discuss would be held in strict confidence. Upon my agreement, he asked how I thought I was doing in each of my five classes. When I gave him my answer, he gave me each teacher's opinion as they had reported to him.

We were actually pretty close, but my perception of my progress and standing was substantially more modest than that of each of my teachers. With that in mind, the Dean dropped a bombshell. Provided I could pass an early final given by each of my teachers, I would be given full credit for each course in time for the Thanksgiving holiday. My formal school semester would be over. I would be readmitted into Lees-McRae in May next year in time for a full enrollment in the summer semester. In September of the next year, I would begin my senior year with its full course load. I was to talk this over with my parents and get their go-ahead if I decided to do this. Without their permission, the offer would be immediately withdrawn, and I would return to a normal class schedule. In that case, I would be given no credit for absences unless I was sick and not on military assignment.

I was somewhat taken aback. I asked the Dean what this was all about. Why such an offer and why now? He replied that he had received a telephone call from the President of the United States' Chief of Staff at the White House earlier in the day. Citing a matter of national security, the Chief of Staff mentioned that two students at Lees-McRae were currently critical to a major operation against a hostile force threatening the peace and good order of this country.

Each possessed a unique skill that could be tapped to save both military and civilian lives currently at risk. It was the Chief of Staff's understanding that both students were above average and should be able to measure up to Lees-McRae's academic standards when facing a prolonged absence for field assignments. The military needed their full attention, not their divided attention. They were going to be placed in harm's way. Would the school, the Dean, consider a compromise measure, one that would allow an early demonstration of knowledge for credit?

The Dean had asked to think about what was being asked because there was no precedent for it. The Chief of Staff answered that he understood the Dean's hesitancy, but if it would help, he would ask the President of the United States to verify the urgency and importance of this request. He added that if the Dean felt he needed permission that he, the White House Chief of Staff, would gladly phone the university's superintendent and address the matter with him.

Somewhat shaken at that and not wanting to appear an administrative pawn, the Dean said that would not be necessary, that the authority for the decision rested with him. He would agree provided the parents of the two students agreed. The Chief of Staff accepted that stipulation. He thanked the Dean warmly and asked the Dean to please telephone him back with an answer before the next day was over. That said, the White House operator came on the line and gave the Dean a special number for his callback. She thanked him and terminated the call.

The Dean looked at me expectantly as I mulled over his comments. Finally, after a few minutes of thought, I raised my head and asked if I could call my parents from his phone while the iron was still in the fire, so to speak. He agreed, and I made the call. Thirty minutes later, I left the Dean's office with instructions to meet with each of my teachers by the end of the following day. I was to produce a study, assignment, and test schedule agreeable to everyone.

I knew what had happened. Clarion had stepped in. He forced the issue of divided loyalties. He wanted me full-time for the coming winter campaign against the Weres, but he knew he wouldn't have me physically or intellectually if my school assignments interfered. He had worked it out so they wouldn't. Clarion also knew me well enough to know that I would follow his lead. It was good to know that he had that kind of confidence in me but scary to know that he had the kind of political influence he did. Whoever Clarion really was, he must know where everyone's bones were buried. It would not be advantageous to be on his bad side—ever.

Michael, the Blackbird, would be unhappy about this turn of events. Not so the Major.

DAY THIRTY-ONE 9:00 A.M.

The next day, Tuesday, was a two-class day. Both were in the morning. By lunchtime, I headed back to the Rat's Nest for a meeting with the Major I'd requested during Monday afternoon's telephone call. We'd talked in depth about Clarion's plan and my role in the coming winter offensive. I would participate in a number of raids. I would also spend time back at the confinement facility helping Clarion or General Kim interrogate any Pale Weres we captured.

I would see little of my family or friends from Thanksgiving through late spring. I would be assigned to Cap'n T's strike group when I was not working with the Major or Clarion. Pee Wee and Sergeant Saddler would accompany me on every field operation. One or both would always be assigned to me. Their job was to make sure the Weres did not take me alive.

The Major emphasized that point with me. Just as we had been prepared to kill Lt. Col. Spikes rather than risk his turning, so would Sergeant Saddler or Pee Wee be prepared to kill me if capture was imminent. That order came from well above Clarion's pay grade. It was not revocable. As valuable as I was to our effort, I was an even greater liability should I be captured and turned. In battle, and we were engaged in battle with the nation of Weres, one cut one's liabilities before they could grow into catastrophic disasters. I was like a Navajo Code Talker and had to be protected.

But the Major didn't want some panicky member of Cap'n T's special operations group who didn't know me decide to shoot first and ask questions later if things got hot. So she assigned two of her team to that duty, two people who knew me, had fought Weres with me, and were my good friends. They would wait until the last possible moment to shoot me if the need arose. They would do it regretfully, with love in their hearts, but they would definitely shoot me dead.

I told the Major I was good with that. After all, what are friends for if not to abuse? No, seriously, I said, having been prepared once to take the life of a man I trusted and respected, I was also prepared to surrender my own life for the good of my companions and country.

We talked a bit about the probable schedule of operations and how we might support Gitta and Polaris. I reminded the Major that they were winter creatures. Advantage us! I was then off to Lees-McRae. I had some meetings and a study and test schedule to create.

The few weeks remaining until the Thanksgiving break were filled with study and more study on my part. I supposed it was the same for Sunstar. She was the other student to whom the White House Chief of Staff had referred. Michael had protested loudly that my departure, as well as his sister's, was not what he wanted. He didn't like it. He eventually calmed down when I mentioned that his mission was to get Kathy Niwall through the upcoming finals at Christmas. He responded well to that mission. His protests to our leaving didn't last very long.

I eventually took my early finals. I did well on them all. I credited that to the Major who practically grounded me in my dorm so I could study and complete all school assignments. I was even a little grateful because I would go home at Thanksgiving with no worries about schoolwork left unfinished and waiting for me when I returned after the holiday.

What I did start to worry about was seeing Casey again. A whole range of emotions swept through me when I thought about how I had changed and how she may have changed, her mother's comments notwithstanding. Did she still have any feelings for me other than friendship? Did I really have any for her that were romantic and not based on convenience or friendship? What would I say when I saw her? Would a simple hug be proper, or maybe a hug and a welcome home kiss on the cheek or hair? What if I realized that I might have moved on without knowing it?

These and a hundred other questions kept my emotions and feelings so stirred up in the early weeks of November that I could hardly eat anything. I needed to meet with Casey. I needed to see what had happened to us, if there even was an *us*. I was prepared to settle for a deep friendship, but in my heart of hearts, I was hoping we were still soul mates. I quietly hoped we were somewhat way north of kissing cousins. I had to admit to myself that I desired her. However, I would put a cap on those urges until I saw what she wanted. I felt I loved her too much (despite what I told her mom) to risk losing her as my closest friend.

I flew home on the Wednesday before Thanksgiving. My folks met me and drove me straight back to Chagrin Falls. They told me I had a surprise waiting for me in our living room, someone very special. They would not tell me who. It was the longest ride of my short life.

DAY FIFTY-THREE 5:00 P.M.

When my dad turned down the street that led to our house, I could hardly contain my excitement. I was on tenterhooks and leaned forward from the back seat, putting my hands on the top of the front bench seat where my folks sat and pulling myself forward until my chin rested on the top of the seat. My eyes looked at everything at once. I doubt Polaris could have shared a keener vision of what I saw during those last few yards before Dad turned into our driveway. He coasted down and parked just before the garage entrance where all this started more than a year ago. I paused when I stepped out of the car and looked first at our place and then at Casey's house, trying to remember in a few seconds all that had occurred over so many months.

My mom's hand slipped into mine, and she gave me a gentle kiss on the cheek. "Welcome home, Cody. Welcome home. Now let's go see your visitor." A gentle push and she twined her arm in mine and walked with me (pushed and steered me) to the back door while Dad brought my suitcase, whistling absentmindedly to himself. We paused at the door while Mom rummaged through her purse to find her house key. My patience was wearing thin when she exclaimed, "I've got it!" and then opened the door and pushed me through. I heard a voice from the living room call out, "Cody, is that you?" I didn't recognize it as Casey's. I was a little befuddled when I suddenly realized it was Sunstar. She came into our kitchen just as I realized it. She saw me, ran to me, and threw her arms around me, laughing, smiling and chattering all the while. I was completely taken by surprise.

"Cody, isn't it grand? I'm going to be a houseguest here with all of you for the next few weeks. The Allegros wanted me to stay with them, but Casey's coming home and bringing a friend with her, so her room and the guest room are taken. Your mom and dad said I could stay here instead. We're going to have a great Thanksgiving! Your mom is going to let me help. I've even brought some wonderful recipes from my grandmother that I'm going to make. Your folks also let me invite Dr. Fitzgerald to Thanksgiving dinner. It's going to be a wonderful visit, isn't it, Cody?"

Sunstar took my hand and pulled me over to the kitchen counter where she and my mom had been looking at several cookbooks and Thanksgiving decorating books. I was dumbstruck. I'd been expecting Casey and had a scenario in my mind about how wonderful my welcome home would be, especially with Casey in my arms. I was still trying to get my bearings when suddenly I remembered what Sunstar had just said, that Casey's bringing a *friend* with her. That one sentence sent a chill down my spine. It dampened any enthusiasm I had for seeing Casey again. I felt like an idiot. Of course Casey was bringing home a friend. We'd had little to no contact these past five months, and Casey would have a list of potential or actual suitors a mile long. She was no wallflower. We'd left our relationship completely open-ended when I left. She had no reason to wait for me, and the social activities of a big college like North Carolina far surpassed what our little gem of a school offered. I was suddenly afraid she'd think of me as a bit backwoodsy compared to the fellows she'd probably grown used to there, a homebody and a little too unsophisticated for the tastes she'd most likely acquired, courtesy of her new soccer friends.

I kept all this bottled up inside, however. I tried to make no obvious show of my uncertainties. I laughed with Sunstar and Mom, shared stories with my dad, and generally appeared to have a swell time, but I was dying inside. Mom told me Casey and her friend were driving up and should be in late tonight. Mrs. Allegro said she would call in the morning when everyone was decent. I could come over and say hi to everyone. Oh, and I was to be sure to bring Sunstar with me. Casey and her friend were dying to meet her.

At about 10:00 p.m., I told my folks and Sunstar that I was a little tired. I was going on to bed, if that was all right. Mom came over and kissed me good night. Sunstar was staying in the guest bedroom downstairs across from my folks' new bedroom suite. Our home had been remodeled after the Were attack sometime earlier. I kept my room upstairs. It gave me privacy when I needed it. I went up and closed my bedroom door. I sank down against it about as glum as a fellow could be. I just felt numb. The news about Casey bringing home a friend had deflated every expectation I had. *Some Thanksgiving*, I thought. *Welcome home, Cody. Just remember, you really miss Gitta and Polaris, and at least they love you. Maybe.*

I fell asleep leaning against the door. There was a great heaviness in me.

DAY FIFTY-THREE 11:30 P.M.

The phone ringing in my room woke me up. Shaking the sleep from my eyes, I crawled over to my nightstand and fumbled the receiver off its base, finally getting it up to my ear. If it was a prank call or wrong number, I was going to kill someone. "Hello. This is Cody," I growled. "Who is this and do you realize what time it is?"

There was a pause on the line. I could hear someone breathing and started to hang up, thinking it was some child's prank, when a voice I could never forget, one imprinted on my soul, softly said, "Cody, it's me. It's Casey. Please don't be mad at me. I just couldn't wait until tomorrow to talk to you. I want to see you. Could you come over to my porch steps? Please, Cody? And please don't be mad. I...I'll understand if you don't want to, but I'm out here with my phone, and it's chilly, and I want to see you. I've missed you, Cody. Can you please come and see me?"

I didn't even think to hang up the phone. I left it hanging in the air above the floor as I sprang for the door and half fell, half scrambled down the stairs. I blundered into a kitchen chair in my rush to get to the door. Throwing the door open, I let it slam shut behind me as I started to run to the driveway before I remembered I should exhibit some semblance of restraint in case her friend was with her. I didn't want to appear as a lovesick geek next door if the friend with her was some college stud. But my emotions were well ahead of my feet as I turned the corner of our house and faced Casey standing on her porch steps. She looked vulnerable and beautiful as she waited for me.

Nothing was said for a moment as we both stood and looked at each other. Then both of us broke into a run and practically crashed into one another as arms, legs, lips, and bodies entwined and somehow melded one against the other. I had not realized how deep the ache in my arms and soul had become in the few months without her. I wanted to crush her to me and not hurt her, but the power in my arms threatened to engulf her. Likewise, I could feel the strain of her arms and torso against me as she also pulled me back into her circle of life as fiercely as I struggled with her. We both discovered you just can't put two bodies in one space no matter how hard you try, and believe me, we tried. We were lost in the moment. I picked her up, buried my face in her neck, and twirled her around and around, all the time whispering her name over and over. "Oh, Casey," I said. "I have missed you *so* much. So very, very much. And now that you're in my arms again, I don't *ever* want to let you go. I don't care if this guy you brought home with you is engaged to you. He's not the one. I am! And I'm not going to leave you or let you go until you realize that."

And then I thought to myself, *What are you saying, Cody? Have you gone mad? What if this guy really is engaged to her or she's really in love with him and this was just meant to be a "Hi, old friend" greeting and that she's really not hugging me and she's actually fighting for her life because I'm crushing her?* Suddenly I broke my hold on her and dropped my arms. I stepped back. "Casey!" I exclaimed. "Please forgive me. I did not mean to hurt you or act like some animal. It's just that when I saw you, something came over me, and all I could think of was you in my arms and my lips against yours and, and, well, I'm sorry if I was out of bounds. But I don't care if your friend *is* here. I'll fight him and 10 more if it means I have a chance with you. But please, Casey, give me that chance. I think I'm in love with you!"

I watched Casey step back and try to straighten her mussed-up hair and tuck her shirt back into her jeans. Then she stood as tall as she could. She looked me in the eyes. With a sly grin she couldn't hide, she told me if I didn't get my arms around her post haste and kiss her again with that same enthusiasm I'd just shown that she was going to kick me so hard I'd limp for a week, at which point she'd kick me again harder with her other leg.

"You are very foolish, Cody," she whispered to me after we had kissed for a while. "I will let you know when you're not the right one for me, but it probably won't be in this lifetime, so get used to it." And then we kissed again and again and explored the night, gently turning long-held fantasies into realities. Her mom found us on the stoop early the next morning, Casey curled up in my arms, her head on my shoulder, my head resting gently on hers with a smile on my face. Mrs. Allegro called my mom who came out and took a picture of us. We had talked, giggled, kissed, caressed, and snuggled for three hours before both of us succumbed to sleep's lure. Our passion had crested several times, and I was utterly content to just hold her.

Mom's flash in the morning's gray light awakened me. When I heard the two mothers laughing at us, I softly whispered to Casey that it was time to wake up, that I needed my arm back. It had fallen asleep. When she straightened up, my arm fell back, and I let out a deep groan. It hurt so much as the blood flowed back in that my eyes teared up. Awkwardly, I struggled to my feet and helped her up. Sleepily, she turned back into me. With her head against my chest and her arms around my waist, she started to drift off again. Chuckling to myself, I peeled her off me and steered her into her mother's arms, kissed her cheek, and staggered off to find a bathroom. I didn't look back. I was headed for my room determined to let nothing stop me.

When I came out of my bathroom, I made it to the edge of my bed and simply fell forward. I was asleep before my head hit the pillow. The dreams I had were tender, exotic, and wildly irrational. Casey was the feature around which every plot line was built, and many and often were the secret pleasures we stole in our moments together. Still, no soft kiss or tender caress in my dreams could match what we had shared but a few hours before. We had shared a spiritual and emotional intimacy that no imagination could fathom and no memory could fully reconstruct. Soul mates we had been for a season of our young lives, and soul mates we still were and would be again for seasons yet uncounted.

As I finally awoke in fits and starts, one clear, enticing thought stole over me. It spurred my imagination to frontiers yet unexplored and unclaimed. Casey would be home for another five days. *Five days!* I thought to myself. *Why, it only took the Lord six to make the world.* Five days was almost forever with Casey in my arms, safely cradled in my thoughts, and forever would start in a few minutes when I could roll off the bed, shower, dress, and finally introduce Sunstar to the real girl of my dreams.

Yes, indeed! Chagrin Falls was a great place to be on that Thanksgiving of 1962. I had learned what it meant to love someone, to sacrifice for someone, and to be responsible for someone or, more accurately, someones—Gitta and Polaris. And this fall, I had started to learn what it meant to be truly in love with someone. It was a lesson I would never stop learning. I found that falling in love with someone is a treat beyond measure or description, only compounded when you get to do it again and again with the same person over the years.

Casey taught me many other things that Thanksgiving. We spent time with both families. We even visited the confinement facility but did not visit the Weres. Most of all, we just walked and talked and found every excuse to be together and maintain some kind of physical contact. I did not realize how much fun it was to just hold hands while strolling through a mall or shopping on a street, or just sitting and reading together. And as for the evenings, well, we spent a lot of time on her stoop after sundown. But we didn't stay out the whole night again.

Casey and I took Sunstar and the Doc shooting at the range one day. Casey and the Doc were amazed at how proficient Sunstar was with a bow and arrow. The Doc almost dropped his teeth as well when Casey gave him a lesson in small arms. These were not ladies one would want to mess with.

The days passed quickly. On the last night that all of us would be together, we had dinner at our house. The Doc bragged about Sunstar and what she was contributing to his team's research through her potions and powers. Then he bragged about me and the reputation I had established as the go-to guy everyone wanted to be with if the Weres were out and about. Sunstar filled in Casey and my folks on the adventures she and Dusty had had, as well as several more Pee Wee had told her about in his experiences with me. Both Casey and my mom blanched at several points, but I reminded them both that these were stories, after all, and not meant to be accurate so much as interesting. Sunstar simply smiled knowingly and carried on.

Casey's friend turned out to be one of the girls on her soccer team whose boyfriend happened to be from a nearby town. We saw little of them until she and Casey had to drive back. That was one of the nicest surprises of my life. We had said our farewells the night before when we were alone. And now, we were fairly brief and perfunctory before Casey and her friend drove away. Casey knew our contact would be sporadic because of the upcoming winter campaign, but we both knew that didn't matter. I thought what we had established this trip home would become the basis for our relationship the rest of our lives. There was really only one gal for me, and it was Casey. Some decisions in life are made over and over again. Some just once. This was a just-once decision on my part. Casey Allegro would be part of my life for the remainder of it. I dared not think she might not be of the same mind.

I felt like the luckiest guy in the world as their car disappeared around the corner, each of us frantically waving at each other. No one ever knows what the future holds, but we can always be certain of our past. Often that's more than enough. Sometimes it's much more than many people get.

As I turned to walk back into the house, Sunstar came up to me. She put her arm over my shoulder and walked back with me. There are friends, and then there are friends in life. Sunstar was one of those exceptional people of the first category. She was almost like a sister I never had but still made me appreciate just being a man whenever she was around.

"Come inside and talk to me, Cody. I have barely seen you this past week, and you're shining like a Japanese night lantern. You are lit from the inside out. So come on in and tell me about this fire I see in you, and I will tell you about mine." She grinned as she said that last part to me and spoke barely above a whisper. She put both her arms around one of mine and laid her head on my shoulder as we walked down the driveway. She was humming to herself, and I felt incredibly peaceful.

One always does when the way ahead is clear. That morning, I felt I could see forever!

THE END OF EPISODE SEVEN, BOOK ONE